BLOOD
OF
INNOCENTS

ALSO BY MITCHELL HOGAN

A Crucible of Souls

BLOOD
OF
INNOCENTS

Sorcery Ascendant Sequence

Book Two

MITCHELL HOGAN

HARPER Voyager

An Imprint of HarperCollins*Publishers*

BLOOD OF INNOCENTS. Copyright © 2016 by Mitchell Hogan. All rights reserved. Printed in the United States of America. No part of this book may be used or reproduced in any manner whatsoever without written permission except in the case of brief quotations embodied in critical articles and reviews. For information address HarperCollins Publishers, 195 Broadway, New York, NY 10007.

HarperCollins books may be purchased for educational, business, or sales promotional use. For information please e-mail the Special Markets Department at SPsales@harpercollins.com.

A previous trade paperback edition of this book was published in 2014 by the author.

Designed by Katy Riegel

Maps designed by Maxime Plasse

Library of Congress Cataloging-in-Publication Data has been applied for.

ISBN 978-0-06-240725-2

16 17 18 19 20 OV/RRD 10 9 8 7 6 5 4 3 2 1

MAHRUSE EMPIRE
(AND SURROUNDS)

Desolate Lands

Indryalla

Serdanne

Isnel

Ralkol

Meliror

Attrym

SOTHARLE UNION
OF CITIES

Shikur

N

The Emerald Sea

Eremite

Desolate Lands

The Capital

Riversedge

Anasoma

THE MAHRUSE EMPIRE

The Steppes

Desolate Lands

⊙ The Dareske Ruins

PLASSE
2015

DRAMATIS PERSONAE

CALDAN, an orphan, and an apprentice sorcerer in the Protectors

MIRANDA, an entrepreneur and ex-sailor

AMERDAN LEPHAR, a shopkeeper

VASILE LAURIS, a magistrate, once head investigator for the Chancellor's Guard

ELPIDIA, a physiker

IZAK FOURIE, a noble

LADY FELICIENNE (FELICE) SHYRISE, Third Adjudicator to the emperor

SIR AVIGDOR, Lady Felicienne's assistant

RENNEN, a dealer in information

THE PROTECTORS AND THE SORCERERS' GUILD

SIMMON, a master, Caldan's mentor

JAZINTHA, a master

FIVE OCEANS MERCANTILE CONCERN

GAZIJA, the First Deliverer

LUPHILDERN QUISS, a head trader

MAZOET MIANGLINE, a sorcerer

REBECCI WALRAFFEN, a sorcerer

LADY CAITLYN'S BAND

LADY CAITLYN, a noble crusader

AIDAN, Caitlyn's second-in-command

CHALAYAN, a tribal sorcerer

ANSHUL CEL RAU, a swordsman from the Steppes

INDRYALLANS

KELHAK, God-Emperor of Indryalla

BELLS, a sorcerer

KEYS, a sorcerer

BLOOD
OF
INNOCENTS

CHAPTER 1

Caldan placed Bells on the ground as gently as he could. Her head lolled to the side, and she stirred a fraction before going quiet. They were a few hours from Anasoma, and she'd remained unconscious throughout the journey.

He stretched his back and suppressed a curse. Dark clouds were gathering on the horizon, and he didn't like the thought of walking far in the rain.

Ahead of him, Amerdan was leading Elpidia and Miranda along a dirt track between newly sown fields. Behind them, Rennen was standing still, facing back the way they had come. Amerdan looked back and gave a short wave before jogging toward a farmhouse. Caldan didn't know if they could trust a strange homestead, but they needed supplies, and this was an opportunity to lay their hands on some.

Stifling a groan, Caldan picked Bells up again and resumed trudging along. She wriggled in his grasp, so much so that he could barely hold on to her. She mumbled something unintelligible, and then her eyes opened.

Caldan clamped a hand over her mouth. "Shh," he said. "We're not going to hurt you."

Apparently she made no such promises.

Bells clawed at his eyes, and Caldan jerked his face away. He dropped her and grasped her arm, twisting it behind her back, managing to keep his hand covering her mouth. Bells whimpered and went limp, sinking to her knees. Caldan let himself follow her down as the nails of her free hand dug into his arm. He bared his teeth at the pain but didn't let her go. Instead, he shoved her face into the dirt and forced his knee into the small of her back.

He wanted to throttle her for what she'd done to Miranda. So great was the desire, his hand was on the back of her neck before he realized what he was doing.

Bells breathed heavily, and air whistled through her nostrils. She squirmed, trying to free herself, but Caldan held on tight. Choking back a sob, he released her neck. He couldn't kill her, not yet, not before he'd found out how to cure Miranda. After that, though . . .

"Listen!" Caldan said to Bells. "You're not getting away. We've taken all your craftings. There are five of us and one of you. It will go easier for you if you calm down."

Bells's struggles ceased.

"Good," he said. "Now, you're going to stand up, and we're going to keep walking. Nod if you agree."

For a moment, Caldan thought Bells was going to fight him again, but eventually she nodded.

"I'm going to take my hand from your mouth. There's no one around, so no point in yelling."

Bells nodded once. Caldan slowly removed his hand and twisted her around, grabbing both her arms. She stared at him with pure venom.

"You're a strong one, aren't you?" she said.

"When I have to be," Caldan replied. With any luck, she'd think he knew what he was doing and wouldn't try to escape again.

"It won't matter in the end. I'm going to kill you all."

As Bells spoke, Rennen came running up. "There are seven soldiers following us," he said.

Caldan smiled thinly. "We either make a stand or run." He glanced toward Miranda, then at Bells. "But I don't think we'd make it far before they caught us."

"We also can't fight seven fully armed soldiers."

"By the ancestors!" He knew Rennen was right, but it didn't make the choice any easier. In the end, though, Caldan's crafted wristband wouldn't stand much more strain, and they were exhausted already.

"You're all going to die," Bells said.

Amerdan raised a hand, intending to strike Bells, but Caldan stepped between them.

"No," Caldan said. "She isn't to be harmed."

Amerdan looked at Bells, as if expecting some kind of reaction, but the sorcerer remained silent. "What about sorcery?"

Caldan shook his head. "It doesn't work that way," he said impatiently. "She needs access to craftings, which she doesn't have. As long as her hands are bound and we keep an eye on her, we'll be safe." He made a decision. "Bells is our leverage, and my hope for Miranda. So we run. We have no choice. There are plenty of farms and homesteads around here, by the look of things. They won't want to risk us slipping behind them, so they'll have to search them all. That should give us some time. Come on."

An hour later the skies opened, and a cold rain poured down. It was not pleasant going. At first it had only made them miserable, but it was now heavy enough to drown out the sounds of Caldan's companions close behind him. He was constantly wiping water from his eyes, and the ground was one big puddle. To his left, the placid stream they'd been following had swelled until it raged like a miniature whitewater river. Caldan kept one hand clamped around Bells's wrist and pulled her along to slog through the mud. They'd bound her wrists in front of her, and more rope tied her upper arms to her sides, leaving only her legs free to walk.

"Caldan!"

He turned at Elpidia's shout. Even though she was right behind him, she'd had to yell to be heard over the downpour.

"We've got to get out of this," she said. "Miranda's freezing, and so am I."

"Amerdan's ahead looking for shelter. Rennen said there were abandoned buildings around here," Caldan said. "We have to keep going until we find something."

"It had better be soon."

Caldan nodded. He hadn't realized the rain was so cold. Just as he did, though, he started shivering. He looked around, hoping he'd find some sign of shelter, and as if answering his thoughts, Amerdan appeared out of the downpour.

"Good news," the shopkeeper said. "There's an abandoned building by the stream up ahead. A sizable one, too, with a few smaller buildings around it. Maybe an old mill."

"Thank the ancestors," said Elpidia, and she pushed past Caldan, dragging Miranda by the hand.

Caldan felt a pang as Miranda passed without a flicker of recognition in her eyes.

They followed Elpidia, catching her easily. Amerdan strode ahead, feet splashing, until they reached the old mill. A large barn door was still intact, while a smaller one looked to have been broken open. It lay sprawled to the side, hanging from one hinge. Vines covered half the building, and the inside smelled of mold and animals. A stone stairway led up to another level, but the roof had fallen in long ago. The wooden floor above them kept the rain out, though, apart from a few trickles, and they were in no position to complain. Attached to the living quarters and the mill itself was a storage area, presumably for grain and flour, with the roof partially caved in. Everything seemed rotted through, and it made for a depressing stay, but at least it was shelter.

We'll have one positive thing tonight, Caldan thought, looking over at Miranda.

Elpidia fussed around the young woman, sitting her down in a dry spot and rubbing her hands to try to warm them.

Miranda didn't respond.

Sighing, Caldan climbed halfway up the old staircase, but one look at the state of the next floor, covered in weeds and grasses, was enough to change his mind.

Rennen grabbed his arm as he stepped from the last stair.

"How safe are we here?" Rennen said. "I've led you this far, but soon I'll be heading back. You'll have to look after yourselves."

Caldan removed Rennen's hand. "If you have to go, then go. But if you're going back to Anasoma, then I need you to take a message for me."

Rennen's eyes narrowed in calculation. "What message? To whom?"

Caldan shook his head. "Later, before you leave us. There'll be information you can use. It'll be worth your while."

Rennen nodded and left him to join Elpidia.

"There's not much in here we can burn," Caldan said to Amerdan. "I'll check the other buildings."

"I'll look after the others," said Amerdan.

Caldan cast an anxious glance at Miranda, but there wasn't anything more he could do for her that wasn't already being done by Elpidia. He stood in the doorway, fat droplets cascading in front of him. He squinted through the downpour, spotting three shapes he was pretty sure were the other buildings once part of this mill.

Caldan steeled himself, then ran across the clearing toward the closest one. He ducked inside an open doorway, shook his head, and wiped water from his eyes.

Littering the floor were the remains of a table and chairs, decomposing with damp rot. Streams of water trickled through what survived of the roof—this one seemed to be in better shape than the mill. There was a doorway to the right, and on his left the room opened out into a large clear space with a packed dirt floor. A still intact wooden trough indicated this was where livestock had been kept at night. He searched around and managed to salvage a few relatively sound chair legs. The next room contained a moldering bed and dresser, and Caldan could find only a few more scraps of burnable wood.

He gathered up what he had and tucked it under one arm, then made a dash for the next building. Another dwelling, but this one was empty, without even rotting furniture. Caldan hoped the last building had more he could salvage, or it would be a cold, miserable night. Even with a fire, it wasn't looking good.

A shape moved in the rain, and Caldan frowned. No one should be out there. Metal clinked on metal, and a man's voice reached his ears, followed by another.

By the ancestors!

He ducked behind the wall and held his breath. The soldiers had found them, or stumbled upon their location but hadn't yet realized they were here. He shook his head. *We've had no luck since we escaped Anasoma.*

As quietly as he could, he took a few steps farther into the building. He found a dry spot to put his wood down. The rain pounded the roof above him, drowning out any sound. All his craftings and materials were back at the mill, apart from his almost worthless wristband and Master Simmon's sword. He still had no idea how this trinket worked, so it was virtually useless. Except as a sword.

At least I know how to handle that. Still, against maybe seven men . . .

Caldan crept to the doorway and peeked outside. There was no sign of the soldiers—and then a cry came through the rain. *Elpidia!* A man's harsh laughter followed. Caldan reached back and drew the sword. It glowed with a soft light.

Two soldiers—Indryallans, as he suspected—exited the mill house doorway. One carried a sorcerous globe for light, and their armor and weapons gleamed through the rain. With the limited visibility and the downpour drowning most sound, there might not be a better chance to thin their numbers. The question was, did he have it in him to kill someone?

I don't think I have a choice.

He watched as the Indryallans ran toward the first house he'd entered, hunched over with heads lowered to avoid the rain. They stopped just shy of the doorway and took up positions on either side, swords drawn. One tossed the sorcerous globe inside the building and ducked his head, giving the interior a quick scan. Caldan saw his shoulders relax, and he nodded to his companion. They went inside.

Caldan took a breath and sprinted toward the soldiers. He stopped beside the doorway, exactly where one soldier had moments before. Water streamed down his face, and his hands shook. He was hot, but not with the heat he'd come to expect with his unusual abilities. No, his talents had no place here, and he'd have to rely on his ordinary sword skills. Once more, the thought of killing someone tormented him. But he thought of Miranda, and that was enough to steel him to the task.

For Miranda.

Caldan stepped through the doorway. One Indryallan soldier had his back to him, while the other was nowhere to be seen. *In the bedroom*, thought Caldan. And a fleeting glance confirmed there was a light inside the room.

He took a step toward the soldier and raised his sword. He hesitated at the guilt of killing someone while he was unaware. Unfortunately, the sword's glow caused shadows to move and the soldier, realizing something was amiss, threw himself forward with a wordless cry, away from Caldan.

Caldan rushed him just as an answering cry came from the room to his right. The man in front of him turned and raised his sword in defense. He was young, clean-shaven, and barely past his teens. Caldan batted the man's sword down with his own, driving it to the ground even as he followed through with his left fist, smashing it into the man's face. Blood dribbled out the soldier's nose as he staggered backward and fell to the floor. His sword dropped from his hand.

A scrape came from behind Caldan. He hadn't forgotten the other Indryallan and swiveled—just in time to parry a cut. The second soldier was older, a grizzled veteran with a bushy beard. He shuffled back and circled Caldan to the right. Caldan followed him with the tip of his blade. He lunged, and the soldier leaped back. Caldan ran a few steps toward his prone companion as the young soldier scrabbled for his sword. Caldan kicked it away and stood over him. He reached down and grabbed him by the hair, wrenching his head to the side and exposing his neck. His sword rested against the soldier's delicate skin.

So much life protected by so little, Caldan thought.

The old soldier stopped his advance. Light shone through the fingers of the hand clutching the sorcerous globe.

"Don't take another step," Caldan gasped.

"You ain't killed him yet. Likely you never will."

"Do you want to take that chance?"

The old soldier licked his lips. He muttered a low curse . . . then turned and ran.

Damn!

It wasn't the reaction Caldan had been expecting at all. The soldier's footsteps pounded across the soaked ground. In moments, he would alert the others, and any advantage Caldan had would be lost. He couldn't let that happen.

Caldan threw out a string from his well and reached for the sorcerous globe. It was halfway toward the mill. He felt for the linking rune, found it, then pushed power into the globe from his well and ruptured the anchor.

The globe detonated with a sharp crack, illuminating the clearing for a brief instant. The footsteps ceased, and there was a splash as the old soldier's body fell.

It shouldn't be this easy to destroy, Caldan said to himself. But it was, and nothing he could say would change what he knew. For the moment, he could only hope his use of sorcery—not to mention the explosion—went undetected.

The young Indryallan looked up at him with fear. Crimson leaked down his upper lip. Caldan hit him with the hilt of his sword as hard as he dared. The soldier groaned and tried to wriggle out of his grasp. Caldan hit him again, this time harder. The man lost consciousness.

With any luck he'll be out for a while, and all this will be over before he comes to. Of course, if we're counting on my *luck . . .*

And then his thoughts turned black.

Caldan's hands shook, and his skin burned. The water dripping down felt like ice on his skin. A calm came over him. He'd just killed again with sorcery. And he didn't regret the killing, just the method. What was he becoming?

He crossed the clearing. This time, the rain fell slowly, as if reluctant to land. Everything moved slowly . . . so slowly.

He passed the corpse of the soldier he'd killed. It was a charred mess. Splinters of white bone stuck out in places.

Caldan swallowed. *For Miranda,* he told himself again. He could feel himself sweating, even in the cold air. His blood burned in his veins like molten metal. It thrummed, reminding him of beating wings. His metal trinket ring pricked his finger, as if it had grown thorns. He had no idea how many other soldiers there were, but it didn't matter. He had to kill them, or all was lost.

Inside the mill, Elpidia, Rennen, and Amerdan were close to one wall. Behind them stood Miranda and Bells. Bells was grinning like a madwoman. She knew she'd soon be free. Both Amerdan and Rennen held knives pointed at five Indryallan soldiers. Two faced Caldan, watching for either their companions or whoever had caused the detonation.

Caldan didn't want to look at their faces.

He adopted an upper guard position, sword in both hands, raised above his right shoulder. His senses were sharp. He could smell the earth and the rain, the soldiers' grime and sweat; he could hear their hearts beating.

One of the soldiers sneered at him and stepped forward. "Put that down, boy, or you'll hurt yourself. If we have to take it off you, you'll regret it."

His words came to Caldan slowly, and he moved lethargically, as if hampered.

Caldan ignored him. There wasn't anything to say. Either they died, or he did. A shiver ran through him. His ring grew heavy and felt like it bit into his skin. "I'm sorry," he said.

His sword flashed, a line of glowing sorcery in the night. He leaped forward, blade moving in a blur of shining violence. Cut, from shoulder to hip. Step. Slice upward. Pivot. He attacked with blinding speed, the sword featherlight in his hands. The soldiers barely reacted, as if they moved through honey. Lunge. Spin and cut. A final stroke.

Caldan stood still, scarlet sword raised above his head in the same pose he had started in. Around him lay five bodies, blood soaking into the dirt. A bead of sweat ran from his right temple down his cheek.

Across the room, Amerdan sniggered. "Five," he said softly.

"Shit," exclaimed Rennen.

Caldan turned to find them all looking at him. Bells was watching him thoughtfully, while Elpidia stared in horror at the blood. His strength left in a rush, and the sword became heavy again. He lowered the blade, chest heaving. Bile rose in his throat, and his vision swam alarmingly. He sank to his knees and breathed deeply.

After a few moments, the nausea passed. He felt a hand on his shoulder and looked up at Amerdan.

"You had no choice," the shopkeeper said. "This is for the best."

Caldan lowered his eyes and stared at the blood splattered around the room. The soldiers hadn't had a chance when the fever was upon him, and before that he'd used raw destructive sorcery to kill—once more he was nothing but a killer. His hands shook, and he choked back sobs, overcome by the horror of what he'd done . . . and the guilt and disgust that he'd enjoyed the feeling of power.

Amerdan placed his hand tentatively on Caldan's head. "It's okay. We'll drag them outside and leave at first light. In the morning, we should be far away from here."

Caldan levered himself to his feet, shrugging off Amerdan's hand. He wiped his sword clean on one of the soldiers' cloaks, avoiding looking at the others. Sheathing the blade, he stepped toward the door, then paused.

"There's one still alive in another building. I'll bring him here. Maybe we can learn if there are others coming after us."

When Caldan returned to the house where he'd left the young soldier, there was no sign of him. Obviously he'd come to and run. Caldan sighed and decided not to give chase. There'd been enough death for one day. And all the blood was on his hands. Maybe he'd regret it later, but for now, he'd had his fill of killing.

CHAPTER 2

Caldan tore a loaf of bread into chunks and dipped them into the pot of watery soup simmering over a low fire, careful to keep his distance from the flames. Fire always brought back disturbing memories of his family's death.

That the bread was stale and the soup virtually tasteless didn't bother him as he crouched over the pot, hastily shoveling in a late evening meal. He was bone tired. They all were. They'd spent the last few days putting as much distance as they could between them and Anasoma, only stopping at night for short rests. Caldan only managed an hour or two of sleep each time, his thoughts constantly returning to the soldiers he'd killed.

A stray gust of wind blew smoke into his eyes, and he squeezed them shut. He spooned the thin soup into a wooden bowl and carried it to the hunched figure of Miranda sitting against a tree. He began feeding spoonfuls to her, taking care to blow on each one to make sure it wouldn't burn her mouth. He gently scraped away any dribbles as she chewed and swallowed methodically, her eyes never leaving the fire. When the bowl was half-empty, she closed her mouth and refused to let him feed her another spoonful. Caldan sighed, wiped her lips with a cloth, and walked over to the pot, returning the uneaten food.

Bells sat on the other side of the fire from Miranda. The rope that bound her hands and feet was looped around the trunk of the tree behind her. Caldan glanced briefly in her direction before leaving both bowl and spoon on the ground.

"Don't I get any?" asked Bells with a tinge of amusement. "I haven't had anything to eat since this morning."

Caldan clenched his jaw. "Someone else will feed you later."

Bells chuckled. "But you do it so well, so . . . gently."

Caldan closed his eyes for a few seconds and drew in a deep breath. He still wanted to beat a cure for Miranda out of Bells. But information obtained by force couldn't be trusted.

Still . . .

He realized he hated Bells with an intensity that startled him. She was also responsible for Master Simmon's death, and all the others he'd lost in Anasoma. And it would be sickeningly easy to be done with her. With deliberate steps, he walked to their belongings—barely a few small packs and a couple of sacks. Caldan took the trinket sword from the pile . . . and strode from the camp, looking for Elpidia.

"They'll send more after me," Bells called to his back. "And you won't deal with them so easily next time."

He ignored her.

The physiker sat atop a small rise, watching the sun descend toward the horizon. She didn't stir as he approached. The rash on the side of her neck had worsened, and inflamed red lines ran through it where she had scratched.

He sat beside her, sword across his thighs.

Elpidia shifted her weight, then spoke. "She isn't getting any better, is she? I mean . . ." She waved a hand in the air. "After a few days, I expected some improvement, but . . ."

Caldan shook his head. "I thought the tremors would subside, but they haven't. She still can't feed herself, and her speech hasn't improved, so . . . I guess she needs more time."

"With the medicines I gave her not working," Elpidia said, "I don't know what else to do. If we were in Anasoma or one of the cities, I'd recommend we take her to someone more knowledgeable than me." She eyed Caldan. "Is there a chance we'll make it to somewhere large enough to have a physiker soon?"

"Maybe. If we have to. I don't know the layout of the empire west of Anasoma, but both Amerdan and Rennen say they know where most of the towns and cities are. The farther west we travel, though, the less sure they will be." Caldan watched as Elpidia scratched her neck, then her shoulder before he went on. "It's not a physical sickness; it's her mind. I think they . . . damaged something when they tried to control her. No physiker can fix that. I don't know if anyone can. The best I can think of is waiting to see if she recovers on her own."

Elpidia looked at him. "Don't give up just yet, Caldan. Some physikers study illnesses of the mind, and they'd have a better idea of what to do. I'm not used to waiting to see if someone gets better. I find the more I do for a patient, the better off they usually are. *Usually.* Not everything is curable. If I was trying to heal someone whose mind had been damaged by sorcery, then it stands to reason that someone versed in such sorcery would be a logical place to start."

"No," Caldan said. "I'm not letting her near Miranda to work sorcery on her again."

At his tone, Elpidia held up her hands to placate him. "That's not what I was suggesting. It's just that she has the knowledge, and you have no small skill with sorcery. Perhaps if you questioned her . . ."

"No," Caldan repeated, shaking his head. "We can't trust her, and I wouldn't be able to spot a trap if she tried to set one for me. I just don't know enough, and it would be too easy for her to hurt us."

"You couldn't try anything yourself?"

"I have no idea at the moment how coercive sorcery works, only that it certainly differs a lot from any crafting I know. From what I've seen, it doesn't need a physical object for it to work, which I would have thought impossible."

"How do you know?"

"Pardon?"

"I mean, how do you know it isn't exactly the same as crafting? Both Bells and her partner had many crafted objects on them; maybe one allowed them to use coercive sorcery."

"I . . . I guess I didn't think of that. There's too much I don't know."

She looked at him, softness in her eyes. "You know, you don't have to do everything yourself. And I don't just mean me or Amerdan or Rennen. You have a source of information . . . if you're willing to risk it."

"I'll think about it."

"Good."

"Is there anything you need?" Caldan asked, eyeing her rash. "For your sickness?"

Elpidia turned her face away from him. "You know what I need."

"But what good would it do without a laboratory?"

Elpidia hesitated, and then said, "You don't know as much about alchemy as you think. But what I need most of all is time. Sitting around in the middle of nowhere chafes at me. I can feel time slipping away."

Caldan shifted his shoulders at her words and ran a hand along the sword's scabbard. It was serviceable, unadorned leather, completely unlike the blade it hid.

Choices and priorities ran through his mind, as they had the past few days. The problem was, just like before, he couldn't settle on one. And one of the things that kept his mind going in circles was the woman sitting next to him, and he was no closer to coming to a determination about her. The fact was, Elpidia was desperate, and desperate people did desperate things. He could only trust the physiker to do what was best for herself, and that included any advice she might give.

Moreover, his first priority needed to be getting word to the Protectors outside Anasoma, not worrying about Elpidia's sickness. Did they even know about the invasion and the use of forbidden sorcery by the Indryallans? Did they know Simmon was dead, and that—unworthy as he was—Caldan now carried the master's sword? He felt a stab of grief and closed his eyes at the thought of Simmon. And Jazintha. And Senira. All dead now. Caldan clenched his fists until his knuckles turned white.

He had thought he had found a home with the Sorcerers' Guild, and—more specifically—the Protectors. But his world had been shattered by more than just the Indryallan invasion. No, it was the knowledge that the Protectors used destructive sorcery to combat rogue sorcerers—that they did something they claimed to the rest of the world was impossible. And as much as that threw him, it was where it led him that truly bothered him: Did they also use coercive sorcery? And would he damn himself in their eyes if he dared cross that line, even to save someone else?

He shook his head. There was too much he didn't know. But he couldn't give up on Miranda. He wanted—no, *needed*—to do whatever he could to restore her sanity. No matter the cost.

He glanced at Elpidia waiting patiently at his side, then back to their meager camp. Rennen and the shopkeeper Amerdan were returning from scavenging firewood. Smoke drifted up from the fire as they placed a few branches on the coals and the rest in a pile.

Too many troubles, when only a short time ago all he had to worry about was learning as much crafting as he could and figuring out where to take Miranda for dinner. His hand moved to touch the ring on his finger, his metal trinket, then to the bone trinket around his neck. How things had changed in a few short months.

The sun dipped over the horizon, another day of running and fear over. That's all they had been doing since escaping Anasoma: running, looking over their shoulders, pushing themselves at a punishing pace to get as much distance between them and the city as possible. Caldan reasoned that with Bells missing and Keys dead—along with the six soldiers he'd killed—someone wouldn't be far behind. And he realized *that* was his first priority: surviving.

He scrubbed his fingers over his itchy scalp, then massaged his stiff neck. His head ached again, as it had at the end of every day since they'd started running.

"Stressed? Too much weighing on you?" Elpidia asked. "Now you know how I feel."

Caldan blew out a heavy breath and rubbed his eyes. This wasn't the first time she had tried to make him feel guilty. But her needling was one problem he could at least take care of easily, despite his original misgivings. "Let's get this over with, then."

"What?"

"Get whatever vials and needles you need."

"Oh!" Elpidia's eyes widened, and she stood. "Thank you! I . . ." She wrung her hands, tearing up. "I just need a chance, some hope."

"I still don't see how it can help without a laboratory."

"Oh, hush, will you. You'll see."

He nodded at her. "If it helps, then it's the least I can do." And it would be one less problem weighing on him if he could stop Elpidia skulking around and eyeing him with hunger.

She hurried off and rummaged through her possessions at the camp, returning with two small vials, a scrap of cloth, and a large hollow needle. She squatted and motioned for him to pull up his sleeve, which he did, revealing raw red skin on his left forearm and wrist. His crafted wristband was with his possessions back at the camp. It had been damaged during the fight with Bells and Keys, and he wasn't sure its structure retained enough strength to survive being used. Until they stopped running and he had enough time to conduct some tests, it couldn't be relied on. It was yet another issue plaguing him. And he still hadn't had time to examine the crafted items they'd taken from Bells, either.

Elpidia tutted at the sight of his wrist. "Still not healed yet. It's taking longer than I thought, but it was a bad burn. I've healed crafting injuries before, but most sorcerers know when their craftings are going to fail and take precautions."

"I wasn't exactly in a position to do much about it. I was lucky to survive, as it was."

"How is your other wound, where Miranda . . . where she . . ." Elpidia faltered.

Caldan touched a hand to his side, where a bandage lay underneath his shirt. "It's healing. Better than the burn, for some reason."

"I can take the stitches out later, if you like. That's if . . . I assume I will need to soon."

"Probably. Tomorrow, then, in the morning."

Elpidia wiped the needle with a colorless liquid from one of the vials; the other was empty. "I can give you a little more ointment for it, but I don't have many supplies." She located a vein close to his elbow and placed the tip of the needle against his skin. "Where is the closest city from here?" she asked.

"I don't know. Rennen might—ouch! You could have warned me."

"Don't be a baby."

Caldan grunted and watched as drops of his blood splashed into the empty vial. Soon it was full, and Elpidia drew out her needle. She applied pressure to his puncture wound with her thumb. She filled the remaining space with a clear liquid, then stoppered the vial, clutching it tightly in her other hand.

"I take it that's all you need?" There was something disturbing about Elpidia's eagerness to experiment with his blood.

"Should be, though I might need more. Depends on what I find. Out here . . . I can't do much. We need to get to a big town or a city. There, I can—"

"We need to look after Miranda first. And I'm not going to wait around while you experiment. There are other more important things I need to do."

"Not to me. Perhaps I haven't made myself clear, so listen. This isn't just for me. If I can find a cure for myself, then I can use it for other illnesses—sicknesses that until now would have been fatal, or severely debilitating. Think about it. This is important. It could mean the end of so much suffering."

Caldan sighed. "I know. But after the invasion, it's imperative I warn the Protectors and try to heal Miranda. Hopefully, the Protectors will know what to do."

"Why? Isn't this sorcery no one's seen before?"

Inwardly, Caldan cursed himself for his slip. "Yes," he lied. "But they must have some idea how to heal her."

Elpidia gazed at the glass vial in her hand, red with Caldan's blood. "Well, we should leave early tomorrow. We need tonight to recover. We've been pushing too hard."

"We will. You can go your own way, and I'll worry about the rest."

Elpidia shrugged. "I won't apologize for it—I fear death. But don't forget that if this works, it will save not only me, but possibly many others with similar afflictions. I know it's a small price for you to pay to save others."

"If you haven't noticed, I'm doing all I can to save others," he snapped. He looked down to Miranda, who was staring out into nothingness.

"It's not your responsibility, though," she said softly. "Just get Miranda to a physiker. There isn't much else you can do."

"Maybe there isn't . . . but that doesn't mean I'll stop trying." And he got up and trudged back to the fire. Elpidia followed.

When they arrived back at the camp, Amerdan was sitting cross-legged a few steps from the fire, gazing into the flames, while Rennen stood away from the smoke, hands in pockets. Only Rennen looked up as they approached.

"Ducats," he said.

Amerdan gave a brief smile but said nothing, looking at Rennen like he was a half-wit. Elpidia shook her head and went to busy herself with her gear, no doubt to make sure her precious vial was secured.

"What about them?" asked Caldan.

"I have a business to get back to. We've probably lost any pursuit, and they don't know I was with you. Anyone who could recognize me is dead or . . ." Rennen's eyes shifted to Bells.

"I recognize you." Bells's voice echoed around them. "And I won't forget."

Rennen swallowed and looked away. "I'll head back to Anasoma in the morning and sneak inside. There will be a lot of opportunities because of the invasion. I'm not much good out here, and the city is what I know. I'll head a little way south toward a settlement there, then I'll turn back east. Without . . . er . . . the girl slowing me down," he said, studiously avoiding looking at Miranda, "I can get back pretty quickly."

Caldan nodded slowly. "Makes sense. But as I said, I need you to deliver a message. I want you to find a friend of mine, Izak Fourie, and his friend Sir Avigdor."

Rennen scratched his cheek. "I've heard of them, although I have to admit I'm a bit surprised you have heard of Avigdor."

"You're both in the same business, and trade in something I've had occasion to need."

"Information."

"Exactly."

Rennen shrugged. "I was just curious. Provided he isn't in hiding now, what would you like me to tell him? This'll cost you a couple of ducats, too."

Caldan thought for a few moments. From what Avigdor had said when they'd met, Caldan was sure the man knew more about the Protectors than he let on.

"I don't know how much he knows about the invasion, so what information we have could be worthless to him, but . . . tell him the Protectors in Anasoma are all dead." Caldan hoped he'd know what that meant. "And tell him we'll try to warn the Protectors in the other cities. Also, the Indryallans must be after something in Anasoma. I can't think of any reason why they would seal the city, unless they didn't want someone or something to leave."

"So sure, are you?" interrupted Bells. "Your emperor was sucking the life out of the people. Maybe we came to liberate you all."

"Be quiet," Caldan snapped. He pointed at Miranda, then stopped. He needed to be careful with what he said, lest he give away too much. Which he realized he might have done already.

"I'll be right back."

"Where are you going?" Rennen asked. "Is that the whole message?"

"I said I'll be right back," he hissed, indicating Bells with a tip of his head. "I don't like the idea of discussing our plans with her around, so I'm going to move her away."

"Ah, but he's a smart one," Bells mocked.

"Shut up." He went to the tree and untied Bells, leaving her hands and feet bound. While the others watched, he dragged her out of earshot and tied her to another tree. It was far from the fire, and the nights were cold, but he found he didn't care.

"Now that we're alone, untie me." Bells licked her lips and wriggled against the tree, and Caldan caught a glimpse of bare skin as her shirt tightened across her breasts. "It's getting dark, and they can't see. I'll make it worth your while."

With a frown, Caldan crouched next to her. "I don't see how making me ill is going to be worth my while."

Bells stopped squirming and shook her head. "Your loss. I guess I'm not as alluring as the demure young thing by the fire. So compliant. I'm sure she'd do everything you want."

He made to strike her, and only some small part of him that he still considered decent stopped his hand. She laughed.

"Poor little chit, couldn't handle the backlash. Once she dies, that's one against Keys's death." Her eyes went flat. "Then four more to go."

"We aren't to blame. You brought it on yourselves. If you hadn't chased us, then he wouldn't have died."

"If you hadn't escaped and allowed that master to kill himself, then we wouldn't have chased you."

So Simmon went through with it. Caldan closed his eyes against a surge of grief. He'd been hoping Simmon would have tried to die fighting. Whatever Bells had done to him had left him a broken husk of a man. Another mark against her.

He opened his eyes. "Why *did* you kill the sorcerers and Protectors? The sorcerers wouldn't have been a threat, and the Protectors didn't need to be wiped out so ruthlessly. You could have captured them with sorcery."

"Poor little Caldan, meddling with things he doesn't know anything about."

"Can't you stop playing and give me a straight answer?"

Black eyes pierced his. For long moments, neither spoke, then Bells shook her head. "Why should I?"

"Because maybe if you help me, I can be in a position to help you."

She eyed him warily. Finally, she said, "The funny thing is, I think I can actually trust you when you say that. You really are an innocent."

"So innocent it still hurts that I killed Keys."

She spat in his face.

Wiping it off, he continued to look in her eyes. "I can't say I'm sorry I did it—I had no choice. But I *am* sorry for your loss. And maybe we can find a way to make things right. But it has to start with you. So I'll ask again: Why did you kill all the Protectors?"

Bells's eyes were hard, but he didn't break his own stare. And while her eyes didn't soften, eventually she seemed to sullenly accept the situation. "We were under orders," she said.

"To kill them all? Why? Orders from whom?"

"Because our God-Emperor thought they were a threat."

"And so, what—you just followed his orders blindly?"

Bells shrugged. "No—I had my misgivings. Many of us did. But he is never wrong, and, as the God-Emperor, he must be obeyed."

Caldan stood and paced back and forth in front of her. "I'm guessing you aren't going to tell me why you invaded Anasoma."

"You're guessing correctly. Smart little Protector."

Caldan frowned, though he knew she was only trying to annoy him. "Only an apprentice."

"And look at all you've accomplished! They clearly don't know what real sorcery is, nor your talent."

"And now they never will."

Bells shrugged. "Death comes to all of us. And to you five, it comes soon."

He ignored her prodding. "I thought you said you invaded to liberate the people."

"I did."

"But you just told me you weren't going to tell me the real reason."

Bells laughed, the sound barely audible. "So easy to confuse you. We did come to liberate, though what plans the God-Emperor has, I cannot say. His thinking is as far above mine as yours is above a rat's."

"That far?" Caldan said.

Again, the sorcerer's dark eyes pierced his. "The God-Emperor is . . . the God-Emperor. Nothing escapes his notice; nothing surpasses his sorcery. For more than a hundred years he has been among us. You would do well to fear him."

Caldan scoffed at her words. "A hundred years? Do you take me for a fool? No one lives that long."

"The God-Emperor does. As I said, his sorcery far surpasses any other."

"A hundred years?" repeated Caldan. "You can't be serious."

Bells's eyes bore into his. "But I am. No one knows how he does it, and I believe many have tried to find out. All of them are dead." She shrugged again. "He is what he is. We grow up learning that he is without peer and that he has guided us to greatness, looked after us for generations."

"And you believe this?"

"The proof is indisputable; he has sheltered us all. Our people have prospered under his rule."

"There has to be some trickery here."

"Why? How much have you learned in the last few days that you never understood before? Could this not be the same thing?"

Caldan shook his head. "Maybe he is replaced periodically, by others in power behind the scenes."

"No." She sighed. "He is the same person as when my mother was born, and when my grandmother was born, and her mother. They all spoke of him."

She was exasperated, but the reason for it boggled him. Could she be so deluded as to think an immortal God-Emperor was possible? He could see he wasn't going to get any sense from her. Between the grief she was feeling at the loss of Keys and her desire for revenge, he was surprised he had gotten this much. Granted, she could be feeding him exactly what she wanted as part of her plan, but for some reason, he didn't think so. For now, though, he'd had enough—he would try again in the morning.

"Elpidia will be over soon so you can . . . make yourself comfortable. Though, as usual, we'll ensure you can't escape."

"Lucky me, surrounded by men watching me squat."

Caldan reddened. "We won't be watching, just making sure you don't run." He turned to walk back to the camp.

Her voice followed him. "Watch or not—it makes no difference to me. Because I meant what I said, little Protector . . . I'm going to kill you all."

CALDAN AND ELPIDIA watched Rennen as he slowly disappeared, trudging south toward a small settlement. In the distance, plumes of smoke drifted from morning cook fires, though this far away they couldn't tell how many.

Despite wanting to give the man as much information as he could about the invaders and their use of sorcery, Caldan hadn't been able to think of anything more to say. With luck, Rennen would find Avigdor, who would pass the information to Lady Felicienne, and she'd be able to parse it with all the other intelligence he was sure she had coming in.

Amerdan had spoken to Rennen as well, handing over a few ducats, which Caldan found curious. *Maybe he has family or someone to take care of and wants Rennen to look into it while he's away.*

He didn't dwell on it, though.

When Rennen's receding figure became too small to spot, they headed back to the camp. Off by Bells's tree, Amerdan was sitting in front of her and they were engaged in a low conversation. Miranda sat on his left, staring into the fire. She hadn't moved all night.

Caldan motioned the shopkeeper away from Bells, frowning. Amerdan stood and approached him, smiling as usual.

"She's dangerous. I'd prefer it if you didn't talk to her; she'll probably try to convince you to let her go. And once she's free, she will try to do us harm."

Amerdan gave a shrug. "Kill us?"

"Yes."

Amerdan gestured at Miranda. "She is useless. I would prefer it if we left her."

"What? No. I'm not leaving her."

"Then we will be caught and die anyway. She has no talent. Leave her. Even Elpidia slows us down."

Caldan frowned. *No talent? What does that mean?* "We aren't leaving anyone. Besides, they couldn't know which direction we went."

"A poor assumption." Amerdan pointed his chin at Bells. "This one has teeth. People with teeth will come after her." He paused, as if considering a thought.

Teeth? The shopkeeper had some decidedly strange ways of expressing himself.

Regardless, what he was suggesting was crazy. "I can't abandon them. If you want to go, then go. You probably stand a better chance without us, anyway, but I would prefer it if you stayed."

"No. Of course I would. And you would?"

Scratching his head, Caldan tried to make sense of Amerdan's response. Eventually, he realized Amerdan had answered each of his statements—which means he thinks he *would* be better off without us. *Maybe he would, but right now, he's the only one here who is any use to me.* "Yes—I would. We should keep together. Elpidia is a physiker and can help, and I suspect Bells can aid with Miranda. I need to get the information out of her. And regardless, she's pretty much all the insurance we have at the moment."

"Ah. I see. You need her for something. Well, we had better get packed and start out." Amerdan rubbed his hands together and beamed. Whistling tunelessly, he started to smother their fire with a pot of used washing water.

Shaking the strange conversation from his head, Caldan moved to their pile of gear and buckled on his sword, then gathered up his and Miranda's saddlebags. Elpidia was ready, having swaddled her vial of his blood in cloth before storing it in her pack. Amerdan brushed dirt from his hands and stood next to them.

They all looked toward Bells, still tied to her tree. Caldan knew Elpidia didn't like caring for the woman. Ancestors, no one did. Her demeanor, and the fact she was a sorcerer, left them all uneasy.

"I'll get her," said Caldan. He untied the rope, leaving her wrists bound, and let the sorcerer walk in front of him.

"West again?" asked Elpidia.

Both Caldan and Amerdan nodded.

"Walking is taking too much time. We need to find horses, or at least a wagon for Miranda and Bells," added Amerdan.

"Rennen said there's a town a few days from here," Caldan said, "west of the settlement. I think it's our best option." He pushed Bells, and she started walking.

Amerdan shaded his eyes from the sun and pointed to the south. "I think we may have a problem." On the horizon, black smoke rose from the settlement. "It looks like Rennen may have run into some trouble."

Bells uttered a low chuckle that set Caldan's blood cold.

THE DAY PASSED, and as the sun set, they found themselves by a muddy stream. Amerdan bustled among them, slapping Caldan on the back and heartily telling him how they must have avoided any pursuit—in spite of his earlier protests—all the while setting up a fire and preparing their evening meal of stale bread and cheese. A pot of oats for Miranda steamed over the flames, bubbling away. Semiliquid food was all they could get in her.

After wolfing down his own meal, Caldan sat next to Miranda. The pain he felt when this close to her was almost physical. If she hadn't met him, she wouldn't be like this, and though sorcery might be able to heal her, *he* couldn't do anything about it.

That didn't mean he wouldn't try, though.

He opened his well and stretched himself to examine her mind. And, as on every other night, he couldn't find anything. Nothing to fix himself on. No trace of how coercive sorcery worked, and no idea of how to undo its effects.

Sighing with frustration, he took out his wristband to test the crafting, trying to ascertain whether, after the stresses it had absorbed, it could still function. Around the fire, Elpidia was busy scribbling in a notebook, while Amerdan paced the campsite. *At least he's staying close by this time*, Caldan thought. Some nights, the man couldn't sit still and disappeared for walks, leaving Caldan to watch over the camp and those in it.

Again, he closed his eyes, uncomfortably aware of Bells's penetrating gaze on him. *Just as they watch over me.*

He traced a line from his linking runes, running over the buffers, anchors, and unveilings, knowing all the while they were fine and that the problem would be with the metal itself. Finally, extending his senses, he penetrated the metal, leaking a trickle of his well into the links. His shield surrounded him in a blue haze, steady and strong, at least on the surface.

Internally, it was a different matter. In his hands, the crafting grew warm to the touch as the damaged metal tried to weather the trickling force of his well flowing through it. There was no denying it: after all his effort and time, the wristband was close to useless. Damaged from the strain on it, the metal could hardly contain the small amount of power he was feeding into it, and it wouldn't be enough to protect him. He cut off his well, and the shield winked out.

Making sure to keep his expression calm, he drew closer to Miranda. The night had chilled considerably, and her skin was cold, despite the fire. He hugged her tightly, and her body shook gently.

"How sweet. Can I have a hug, too?" Bells gave a mock shiver. "It's ever so cold and . . . well . . . I don't think she will be offering much for a while. If ever."

Caldan closed his eyes, doing his best to ignore her, though heat came to his face, and he clenched his jaw.

"And how's your shield? All worn out? Poor little Protector."

"It withstood your sorcery."

"Did it? I saw the burns on your arm, and that only means one thing."

He shrugged, but again refused to engage.

"I can help her," said Bells quietly. "All you need to do is let me go. I promise." Teeth flashed white as she smiled.

"For some reason, I don't believe you. After all, you've also promised to kill us."

"Oh," she said, "that was just talk. You've kept me prisoner for several days now. What am I supposed to do? Beg for forgiveness?" She squirmed against her bonds. "I can help her, and you. Just untie me."

He rubbed his tired eyes. With the constant worry and lack of sleep the last few days, he couldn't think clearly. However, he was certain of one thing: the only promise she was definitely going to keep was the one to kill them.

Still, he had to hold out hope. Hope that the shivering girl sitting next to him could ask him for a blanket, rather than just suffer in dumb silence. "How could you help her? If I knew what to do, maybe I could instead."

With a shake of her head, Bells smirked. "She can only be healed with coercive sorcery, which isn't as easy as destructive sorcery. You have to study for years before you know all the intricacies. And then you still need a talent for it. Some people don't, and . . ." She looked up, as if trying to think of something. "Have you ever scrambled an egg? Her mind could end up like that."

"I understand. But I still can't let you go. Is there anything I can do that would get you to help her?"

"Maybe . . . for certain concessions. Although Keys . . ."—she paused and swallowed, voice breaking—"was the one with a talent for it and the craftings. So it could very well be that by killing him, you destroyed her." He started to talk, but she cut him off. "Still, I understand the principles and should be able to heal her. Certainly better than anything you could attempt, even if you had years of study."

Caldan pondered what she said, thoughts sluggish. If the craftings for coercive sorcery were on Keys, then how could she help? They didn't have the materials or resources to craft anything out here. Either she was lying and couldn't, or . . . an idea penetrated his muddled thoughts. He laughed softly.

Releasing Miranda, he stood.

"Where are you going?" asked Bells, her voice strident.

Giving no reply, Caldan strode around the fire and over to their pile of gear. He searched through his until he found what he was looking for: the crafted bells they had taken from her when she was captured. Returning to Bells, he spread them out on the ground in front of her. She looked on in silence.

Eleven bells of different sizes and metals, plus an amulet and a bracelet. He examined the bells, turning a few around with a finger to view the glyphs and runes on their surfaces. A number had smooth insides, while some contained symbols. On closer inspection, one stood out.

A trinket.

Did that mean all the other bells were duplicates? No, the symbols were different, so they weren't replicas. Yet, they didn't have near the strength of the trinket, and he understood they were an affectation, used to disguise the rare and powerful crafting. Without Bells's help, he would never find out what the trinket's function was, provided she actually knew. But the other craftings . . . they were a different matter. Those he could test and try to determine their use. And he was positive one had to be a shield.

"You really shouldn't," said Bells.

"Shouldn't what?"

"Go poking around when you don't know what traps there may be. Do you want to end up like your girlfriend?"

He let that one pass over him. "Which one is the shield?"

"None," replied Bells, too quickly. "Keys shielded me."

"That can't be true, otherwise your shield would have failed at the same time."

Bells raised her eyebrows. "He thinks, finally."

Caldan frowned in annoyance. "I've had a few things on my mind."

"Haven't we all."

"Yes—but there's nothing I can do about your problems. Keys is dead, and for that I'm sorry. I truly am," he said, but it was obvious she didn't believe him. It didn't matter. "But there are those alive who I can help. So either shut up or tell me what I need to know."

Her silence was a definitive no. Her glare was a murderous threat.

So be it.

He doubted any of the craftings would have traps; what would be the point? He glanced at Bells, who now regarded him without expression. He knew far too little. About her, the Indryallans, destructive and coercive sorcery. Wearily, he sat cross-legged in front of Bells, her craftings between them. He shrugged and, taking a deep breath, began examining them.

Picking up each of the bells in turn, he examined them for familiar glyphs and runes, accessing his well and extending his senses in an attempt to determine what they did.

Most were enigmatic, runes and patterns he couldn't recognize; variations of others he did, but he couldn't be certain what the changes meant. For a long time, he sat there immersed in his task while Bells looked on. Periodically, he removed one from the others and set it aside. These were the craftings he couldn't begin to guess the function of, and he was almost certain it was in this pile he would find one related to coercive sorcery, and one to destructive sorcery. He knew Bells had been lying when she'd asserted that Keys was the only one who knew coercive sorcery—she didn't know that he had first heard of this power when Simmon told him in the guild's dungeon. Talking about *her*.

With revelations like this, he felt like the cloud that seemed to hover around his mind cleared just a little bit more. With a wry smile, he separated another bell. This one had glyphs and runes similar to his shield crafting, though with slightly different structures.

"Careful," Bells said. "Scrambled eggs, remember."

Caldan grunted sourly and scratched his jaw.

He cradled the bell in one hand and looked up at the night sky, studying the stars for a few moments, and then glanced in Miranda's direction.

Accessing his well, he probed the bell, careful not to connect to the linking runes. Gently, he followed the flow of the pattern, from the links to anchors, buffers, and bridges, the unveilings and transference runes. A few, very few, he could make no sense of, but the overall pattern and structure was akin to his own shield. Except for the multiple pairs of linking runes.

There isn't much else I can do unless I test it. Choosing the pattern similar to his own wristband, he took a breath, split his well into two strings, and connected to a pair of linking runes.

Nothing happened.

Watching him, Bells gave a small smile. He could sense she had accessed her well to discern what he was doing. That was another thing that worried him. He had no way to stop her accessing her power. And if she got too close to craftings not under his control . . .

Pursing his lips, he frowned. When the apprentices were taught shielding, the trick was to separate your well into two strings and sustain the connection, as wearying as that was. Logically, the better you were at sorcery, and the farther you progressed, the more strings you had to be able to split your well into, and that could serve as a barrier to those with less talent or power.

And it might explain why he couldn't use this crafting: he was coming at it like an apprentice, and Bells was clearly a master.

Bracing himself, Caldan concentrated, splitting his well into four strings. They were slippery to cling to at first, and it was hard to focus his mind on four separate strings—he almost lost his hold on them. He reined them in, however, and paused for a moment before connecting to the other pair of linking runes.

His skin tightened, and his vision blurred as a shield enveloped him. The now familiar scent of lemons and hot metal reached his nostrils. He stood, covered in a multicolored haze that glistened like fish scales. It felt different somehow, more densely packed than his, and drew considerably more from his well. But it was a shield—and *he* had done it.

He turned back to Bells, who watched him with a curious expression.

"Good little Protector," she said. "You may have some use, after all."

Caldan smiled and closed his well, cutting off the flow to the four strings. Then he slipped the bell into a pocket. It seemed the best place for it, considering he couldn't very well tie it into his hair, as Bells had done; his hadn't grown very long since he had left the monastery. Every time he touched it, he remembered what Miranda had said: *Let your hair grow. I think it'll look good on you.*

Maybe now I will.

Ignoring Bells's pleas for him to stay—no doubt she wanted another chance to try to trick him—he stored the remaining bells in his gear and then warmed himself by the fire, shuffling Miranda a little closer. A chill had come into the night air, and he would have to make sure she was warm enough tonight.

Amerdan nodded at him, then went back to pacing. He'd cut a leafy branch from a tree and, after a few passes around, started using it to sweep leaves and twigs from their campsite.

Elpidia pushed more sticks into the fire and stirred the steaming pot.

"Porridge again," she said. "We'll need more supplies if we stay out in the country much longer. It would be best if we found somewhere to resupply—such as a town or a city."

"From what Rennen said, there should be a city a week's travel from here," Caldan said. They had already been over this last night and this morning.

"Yes. Riversedge. I just . . ." She sighed heavily. "I'm eager to begin my experiments."

I know—it's all you talk about. But he also understood her impatience—he would probably feel the same if he were dying. "Soon," he reassured her for the third time that day. "I'm sure you will be able to set yourself up in this city, find work and a place to begin your experiments, whatever they involve."

"I hope so," she said simply.

Amerdan stopped his constant sweeping and approached them. He blinked and scratched his head, then coughed loudly and deliberately into a hand. "Sorry to interrupt your little chat, but someone was out there. Watching us."

Caldan froze.

Elpidia stood abruptly and peered into the night.

"Try not to alert them we know they're there," said Amerdan.

Elpidia backed closer to the fire and frowned. "What are we going to do?" she asked, voice low.

Amerdan shrugged. "Anything but look obvious." He made a discreet gesture at her to resume sitting, which she did, clothes rustling as she smoothed her skirt and hunched over, as if trying to make herself smaller.

"How do you know someone's there?" whispered Caldan, keeping his expression neutral.

"The night noises aren't quite right. It's a talent I have. When I was young, I did some hunting." Amerdan grinned. "I still do occasionally. And there is someone out there; I guarantee it."

Caldan flicked a glance at Bells, who was resting, eyes closed. He was fairly certain she couldn't hear, as they were talking softly and she was a ways off. Still, if she knew someone was out there, she might raise a cry. Or might not. Unless she knew they were her people, it didn't necessarily help her to bring any more attention to their little camp.

She was like the Wayfarer on a Dominion board—he had no idea how she would affect this game.

"You said *was* watching us," Caldan said. "Have they gone?"

"I think so, from what I could tell. They're very good. It took me some time to be sure they actually left."

"What should we do?" Elpidia asked again. "Do you think they'll return?"

"Almost certainly. They were content to watch for a time to gauge our strengths . . . and weaknesses. I believe they'll continue to do so. That they haven't made themselves known to us yet speaks to their wariness and patience. They know what happened when we escaped Anasoma, and for us to have captured one of their sorcerers has to make them cautious. I doubt they will come for us tonight."

It was the longest speech they had heard from the shopkeeper. Caldan and Elpidia exchanged glances.

"But we can't be sure," Caldan said. "Ancestors, we can't even be sure they're with Bells in the first place."

Elpidia looked around at the night. "Should we all stay up and watch?" she asked, trembling.

Amerdan only shrugged, unconcerned. "If we stay, we're exactly where they want us to be in the morning. We don't know how many there are of them, though I think it's likely there's only one or two."

The shopkeeper drew a long strip of ragged cloth from one of his pockets. It looked to have been torn from a piece of clothing. Gesturing, he drew Caldan and Elpidia in close, although Caldan was pretty sure he knew what Amerdan was about to say.

"Gag that bitch sorcerer," the shopkeeper said, confirming Caldan's thoughts—if not the exact words he would have used. "Build the fire up so it lasts for a time, then get out of here." Elpidia began to protest, and he raised a hand to cut her off. "We're heading for the city, correct? But steering clear of the road to avoid any pursuit, which has slowed our progress. And now . . . there's no point, if we've been found. So, as I see it, we need to use the road to move as far ahead as we can. *Tonight.* With luck, and a few hours' head start, whoever has tracked us will be way behind. We could even make it to Riversedge before them and have a better chance of losing them there." He shrugged. "Just my thoughts."

Caldan nodded—as did Elpidia, though reluctantly. To him, the shopkeeper made a lot of sense. Their progress would be slow, though, with both Bells and Miranda limiting their pace. They were weary and in need of more rest, but it was better than waiting here the night, only to be set upon in the morning.

He held his hand out for the cloth strip. "Agreed," he said.

Amerdan smiled. "I'll do it. Just gather your things, and keep quiet about it."

CHAPTER 3

Vasile Lauris sipped his mug of water and studied the hard men around him at the table. He had come to think of them all as inflexible, though the truth was that only one of them was: Aidan. The sorcerer, Chalayan, and the swordsman, Anshul, turned out to be quite adaptable, once he had gotten to know them.

All about, the ship creaked and swayed constantly. The tiny cabin felt cramped and claustrophobic, and the air never seemed to freshen, holding a moist rankness he breathed reluctantly.

He eyed the mugs of ale they drank and licked his lips. His hands had started trembling in the last few days for some reason, and he hid them in his lap under the table. To his left, Mazoet drained another. The sorcerer drank like a fish and, from what Vasile had seen of his appetite, ate enough for three men. And every time Vasile met with Aidan for a talk, either Luphildern Quiss or Mazoet followed him like a shadow.

They had spent days on board since Anasoma had fallen, all the while anchored in the sheltered cove. Gazija, ancestors curse him, told them to be patient. All the while, the old man had been in Vasile's ear, explaining to him the need to persuade Aidan and his men to join with them. Vasile didn't appreciate being used in this way. Gazija and Luphildern may have stumbled upon the truth of his talent, but that didn't give them leave to manipulate him.

He guessed Aidan and his men would be hard to persuade to support anything that was against their code, and even though nothing Gazija's people had done so far was out of the ordinary, the old man's sorcery was almost certainly what kept him from talking directly to Aidan. Possibly Gazija understood that it was a divisive topic for them, for even though Chalayan was clearly in awe of Mazoet, Aidan regarded the sorcerer with an element of wariness, if not outright distrust.

Vasile snorted into his water and coughed, choking as some went down the wrong way.

Around him in the cabin, the four men laughed.

"Water too strong for you?" asked Chalayan with a smirk.

Anshul cel Rau belched and poured himself a refill from a jug, remaining silent, while Aidan smiled. Though they had been stiff and formal when Vasile had appeared, trailed by Mazoet, all four had been drinking for hours, and their manner had become more carefree, as had their banter, and postures relaxed the longer the night went on.

And Vasile thought such suspicion wasn't without merit. That Mazoet was here now meant he was watching on behalf of Gazija. Yet here they all were, drinking and having a good time.

Mazoet crossed his arms and leaned back on his chair, which creaked alarmingly due to his bulk. "So, Vasile," he said loudly and with a jolliness that rang false to Vasile's ears. "How can we trust a man who doesn't drink?"

Vasile smiled weakly. Mazoet should be helping him, shouldn't he? Not making things harder. "I've had more than my fair share of drink, and vowed I'd never touch the stuff again. I don't think that makes me untrustworthy; if anything, it shows a strength most men don't find in themselves."

"Strength?" asked Mazoet skeptically. "Or weakness?"

Vasile scowled. "More strength than you're likely capable of."

"You've no idea what I'm capable of."

"I'm sure you could demolish six roast chickens and a barrel of ale."

Anshul and Chalayan laughed.

"Here," interrupted Aidan. "Enough of that. A man's virtues lie outside his appearance."

"Or inside," added Chalayan.

Anshul chuckled. "Mazoet must be virtuous, then."

"I would have thought that, as someone who saved your lives," said Mazoet with quiet dignity, "I'd be accorded more courtesy."

"A man can drink with anyone," Aidan said, "but it's joking with one that shows true trust. Believe me—this is the greatest courtesy we can bestow. It means we've accepted you as one of us."

Mazoet raised his mug. "To trust, then."

The others raised their ale in a toast, and Vasile followed suit with his water. After drinking, he squirmed in his seat. Aidan's speech had been pretty, but it didn't change the fact that his party's recent appearance raised more questions than it answered. No matter how devoted Gazija's men were to him, it didn't mean that Mazoet couldn't have been fooled into bringing foxes into the henhouse.

I guess it's time to earn my keep.

"You speak of trust, and yet you've given me no reason to believe you're who you say you are."

"That's true," Aidan said. "But then again, we were invited upon this ship, so maybe trust should come from our host, and not from some random man we've just met."

"Oh, it does—he trusts *me*. And that's why he's asked me to speak to you. So, again, I ask: who are you, really?"

Aidan chuckled softly, while Chalayan glared at Vasile with ill-concealed contempt. Cel Rau merely took another swig of his drink. Finally Aidan spoke. "As I said, we have a commission from the emperor himself," he said. "To seek out evil and do our best to destroy it when we find it. He gave Cait— us, a writ. We're beholden only to him." Aidan leaned forward, holding Vasile's gaze with his intensity. "And the things we've seen would likely make you spew."

Chalayan sneered at Vasile, nodding. Vasile rolled his eyes at the man's display. "Save your ill looks for someone who will be intimidated by them."

At that, Mazoet laughed, causing Chalayan to blush. "Go on, Aidan," Vasile said. "Make me . . . spew."

"Foul sorcery," continued Aidan, in a tone that ignored his gibe, "that would make you question your faith in the good of humanity. And jukari, what they and the other leavings from the Shattering get up to . . . you'd better hope you never see. Malevolence and corruption normal soldiers would shy away from. I will not describe it, as I've done everything I can to try to forget. But you want to know who we are? We're part of the empire's defense."

Vasile sensed the truth in Aidan's words, and that gave him pause. Aidan might believe what he was saying—and the man's conviction was strong—but that didn't mean it was the *truth*. It sounded like they were a roving band of mercenaries beholden to no one, with a writ from the emperor condoning whatever they did. No magistrate like Vasile traveled with them, and anyone they considered evil was slaughtered. To his mind, they were no worse than some of the criminal gangs he'd prosecuted.

You're right, young man—the thought of what you are does make me sick.

It put him in a difficult position, though, because no matter what, this little group all had the feel of zealots. That meant that if Vasile got this wrong, Aidan might think they were being manipulated. The soldier was too shrewd to just let that slide and—if what Vasile suspected was true—Aidan wouldn't hesitate to kill them all if he considered Gazija's motives evil. He chewed his bottom lip.

Think, curse you!

With a sigh, Mazoet thumped his mug down on the table. "Such talent, and he doesn't know where to start. A shame, eh, lads?"

Whose side is this fat bastard on?

"What talent's that, then?" asked Aidan. "And what's the problem? Maybe we can help."

"I'm sure you could," murmured Mazoet.

Vasile shot him a dark look. Years hiding his talent, and now they wanted him to reveal it.

He looked at Mazoet. "Do they need to know?"

"About your talent? Of course! It's very amusing."

"Amusing?"

"Yes. Like a conjurer's trick."

Vasile glanced at the jug of ale and licked his lips again. With a start, he wiped his forehead with the back of his hand.

"So what talent's this, city man?" asked Chalayan.

"Not drinking ale, that's for sure," quipped Anshul, and the others laughed.

Vasile shook his head. *I should be asking them what their talents are, since Gazija wants their support so badly.* From what he could tell, it consisted of being drunk and obnoxious. But he had promised he would try to convince them and, more important, had promised himself to finally do something worthwhile with his talent. He had never wanted—no, needed—to expose himself like this before, but perhaps there was a way that wouldn't put them off. He cleared his throat and spoke. "In Anasoma, I worked as a magistrate. I interviewed people who had petitioned us to judge on matters they brought to our attention, and also the people they accused. And sometimes other witnesses. That sort of thing." He clasped his hands together. "A normal magistrate would manage to see maybe twenty to thirty petitions a week. I got through closer to a hundred. Do you know what that means?"

"That you didn't care and weren't very good?" Chalayan remarked.

Both Aidan and Anshul cel Rau laughed.

Vasile shook his head. "No. Far from it. I could see and resolve so many petitions as it's . . . easy for me to tell if someone is lying, or telling the truth, or something in between." He paused to let the information sink in. Mazoet's eyes were fixed on him.

Across the table, Aidan shrugged. "I feel like I'm a good judge of whether a man is lying or not, too. So what?"

"First off, I'm not saying I can read clues to tell if someone is lying or not. I *know*. Without equivocation. If I said someone was lying, there was no doubt behind my words, and therefore no one doubted my words."

"Seems like a neat trick," Chalayan said, echoing Mazoet's sentiment.

"You still don't get it, do you? You see, it means I can work out what's really happening when people are speaking: what they are hiding, or trying to hide, even if I don't want to. Everyone has secrets they don't want known, and they shade the truth when they think it will bring them some advantage." Vasile was trembling now. It unnerved him to speak so openly of what he'd tried to keep hidden for years. "But I *know*. They can't hide from me." He paused and took a sip of water.

Cel Rau looked disbelievingly at his fellows, while Chalayan shrugged.

"I would imagine a great many people wouldn't like that," the sorcerer said finally.

"No, they didn't. But what they did like was using me when it was convenient, when my talents suited them and they needed an advantage over someone else." He looked pointedly at Mazoet when he said this. The large man smirked.

Vasile closed his eyes. *Here's a truth: I do not like that man.*

"Well," Aidan said, sitting back and peering into his mug, "I guess I could use a refill."

"No," replied Vasile, eyes still closed, and Aidan raised his eyebrows. Mazoet smiled.

"Why not?" asked Aidan.

"Because your mug is still full."

"Why, so it is."

Chalayan and cel Rau laughed.

"He probably saw you filling it a while ago and remembered how much you drank!" exclaimed the sorcerer.

With a shake of his head, Vasile opened his eyes and met each of their gazes in turn. "Let's have a wager. One of you state ten things I couldn't possibly know were true or not. I'll tell you if they're true or false. One silver ducat for each answer. But, for every one, the wager doubles. So, if I get two wrong, I owe you two silvers; for three, I owe you four, and so on. Agreed?"

Aidan looked at Chalayan, who was grinning from ear to ear.

The sorcerer rubbed his hands together. "I'll do it. You couldn't possibly know about me, and some spare ducats always come in handy."

Yes—I can certainly use the money.

Mazoet tried to hide a smile behind his hand.

"First, then," continued Chalayan, "does everyone here witness the wager?"

Murmurs of assent greeted his question.

Aidan gave Vasile a penetrating look.

Vasile raised a hand. "They have to be things one of the others knows, else we won't know if you are trying to deceive us or not."

Chalayan looked thoughtfully at the ceiling for a moment. "My mother's name was Spring Blossom." He stared expectantly at Vasile, face devoid of expression.

"FIVE HUNDRED AND twelve silvers?" exclaimed Chalayan. Spit flew with his words.

Aidan rose from his chair and stepped between the sorcerer and Vasile. He resumed laughing, along with cel Rau, who was hunched over in mirth. Mazoet chortled as well, shaking his head.

"You made the wager," said Aidan.

"But . . . he tricked me! That's more than fifty gold ducats! I'm not paying."

"You certainly are," Aidan said. "I expect you to honor the wager." There was a warning in his voice.

To forestall any argument, Vasile broke in. "Never mind. I was only trying to make my point."

"See, he even admits he tricked me."

Aidan shook his head. "No, he admits that he—unlike you—has honor. He knew whether you were lying or telling the truth ten times. That's not a trick."

Chalayan sputtered, then glared and pointed at Vasile. "I'm not paying."

"I said it didn't matter, and it doesn't," Vasile said. "What matters is that now you believe me."

"It could be another trick," Chalayan muttered.

Aidan gave Vasile a thoughtful look. "I don't think so. Anyway, it's best if we end the night there. We can talk about it tomorrow."

Behind them, Mazoet gave Vasile a soundless clap, then stood unsteadily. "Well, I know I've had a bit too much to drink." He squeezed past the table and stood by the door. "Think on what this means," he said to them all. "It's a rare talent, and one that hasn't exactly brought Vasile wealth and prosperity. But it is one that Gazija respects."

So now you help me. Thanks a lot.

Mazoet smiled at Vasile as if reading his thoughts and left the room.

Chalayan shrugged Aidan's hand from his arm and followed.

Anshul rose to his feet, rock steady despite the ale he'd consumed. "Five hundred and twelve," he said, still chuckling, and nodded at Vasile. "Funny man."

Yes. But now the jokes are over. Tomorrow we get down to business.

CHAPTER 4

On the road leading west, Caldan helped Miranda stumble along, her feet dragging occasionally on the stones. Behind him, Amerdan led Bells, while Elpidia trudged at the rear, gaze on the paving in front of her, lost in thought.

Caldan's sword—he had to keep reminding himself it was the Protectors'—had tangled in his legs more than once as he looked after Miranda. He'd adjusted the belt, and now it rested against his back, hilt behind one shoulder, where he could reach it with ease.

For all his experience using practice swords, he'd never been taught how to wear a real one.

They kept walking.

The empire kept its major roads in good repair, for which he was grateful. Once they had found the paved road last night, their pace had quickened considerably. And when the emperor finally sent his soldiers to deal with the invasion, it would allow them to reach Anasoma swiftly.

Caldan frowned. But the Indryallans had to know that, which was why they had sealed the city. The longer it took for the empire to know of the invasion, the better prepared the Indryallans would be when the emperor arrived with his Quivers and sorcerers, and the Protectors. That didn't make sense, though. Why capture a city as important as Anasoma, then wait around until reinforcements arrived and put you under siege? If killing the sorcerers and Protectors had been their only goal, then they were done, and there was no point staying.

No, they had to have another objective. He kept coming back to his conversation with Bells, and how vague she had been about their motives. He couldn't help but feel they hadn't found or finished what they'd come for in Anasoma.

Caldan's thoughts were thrown in a new direction when he felt the sword's hilt press into his back. Simmon had managed to break the hold of coercive sorcery, for a while, and his first action had been to hide the sword. Was the trinket that important, or was hiding it the only thing he could accomplish in the little time he'd had?

And can any of it help Miranda?

Behind him, Caldan could hear that the others had stopped while he'd been deep in thought. Gently, he grasped Miranda's shoulders and halted her shuffling steps.

She blinked a few times, and her head quivered. "Wh— . . ." She swallowed convulsively, and he stroked her hair until she calmed. The others could wait a few moments.

In recent days, her condition had deteriorated. Caldan had thought there was a chance she'd improve, if her mind could adapt to the fracturing, learn how to get around the disruption in some way. But she was slowly regressing.

He patted her on the shoulder. "Wait here," he murmured. "I won't be long." As always, when talking to her, he tried to keep his voice positive, rather than let it reflect the sorrow he felt.

Leaving her standing there, he looked back to see Amerdan, Bells, and Elpidia all staring into the distance, back the way they had come. Gazing past them, he noticed a plume of dark smoke spiraling into the sky from the direction of their abandoned camp. A signal or a warning? He couldn't begin to guess.

As he was looking, Elpidia closed the distance between them. She brushed past Caldan and took Miranda's hand, continuing along the road.

Amerdan turned to him and spoke. A smile played across his mouth. "The smoke's coming from our camp. Whoever was following has only just realized we didn't stay the whole night. They're signaling they know what we've done. They want us scared. Scared and careless. If we continue to keep Miranda and Elpidia with us . . ." He trailed off.

"I will not abandon them," Caldan said firmly.

Amerdan shrugged. "Then we need to find more people to mingle with, as camouflage and confusion. Out here"—he gestured at the countryside—"we're easy to spot and have nowhere to hide."

"Where do you propose we find such a group?"

"Let's hope there is an inn or town just ahead, and we can acquire some horses or join another group traveling west."

Caldan gestured for them to resume walking, leading the gagged Bells onward. "And how can we acquire some horses? We don't have many ducats left, and I can't sell any of Bells's craftings."

She made a sound of protest, clearly not happy about even the possibility of selling her craftings. Caldan ignored her.

Amerdan smiled thinly. "Leave the horses to me."

NOT LONG AFTER, they approached a crossroads with trepidation. Around the intersection, a few buildings crowded close together, and a sizable market had sprung up at the side of the road. Local farmers had set up dilapidated wooden stalls and displayed their produce in baskets and crates: trays of eggs, chickens in cane cages, and vegetables and fruits.

Over the years, the place had obviously become a way station of sorts. No signs adorned the wooden structures, but from the look of them, at least two of the buildings were inns. One was built from stone and had a wooden stable attached to the side.

Caldan could see a number of Quivers patrolling the makeshift market. Two of the soldiers disappeared into the stone building, which he took to be their garrison.

A strong hand gripped his shoulder.

"Make sure you know what you're doing," Amerdan said.

"What do you mean? There are soldiers here. We need to tell them about the invasion in Anasoma." Although perhaps Amerdan had a point. Caldan was wary of losing Bells to the Quivers, but he still needed to get word to them.

"You need their help, and as little as I like it, we don't have much choice with whoever has been trailing us. They want to rescue Bells first and kill us a close second. As we are, we're vulnerable." Amerdan gestured toward Miranda and Elpidia. "Can you convince the Quivers that Bells is too dangerous to leave without you to counter her sorcery? Hopefully, we can persuade them to give us an escort, and that will be safer for all of us."

Caldan hesitated. He couldn't show the Quivers destructive sorcery, but maybe there was a way to convince them not to take Bells into their custody and out of his hands. He nodded.

"Yes, I can probably manage that. They won't know much of sorcery, so they'll have to take my word."

Amerdan waved dismissively. "The how is irrelevant. Lie; do whatever you need to do." He laid a hand on Caldan's shoulder. "The quicker we get to Riversedge, the better. Elpidia can leave us and do whatever she wants. And then we can keep moving on."

"Moving on? No—I need to reach out to the Protectors there, who should be at the Sorcerers' Guild."

"But don't you worry that the authorities there will take Bells from you? Lock her up for questioning, and you won't have access to her?"

Lying to the Protectors didn't sit well with Caldan. They'd been nothing but good to him, but . . . "I'll admit I've been thinking the same thing for a while now. They probably would. She would be too important to them, and I have no rank of consequence. I'm not even a journeyman, so they'd not leave her with me. I might get access to her, but . . . it's doubtful."

"It's not doubtful—it's certain: they won't allow you access to her. You know that. You also know Bells is your best chance to heal Miranda. Seeing how you haven't left either behind in order to find safety quicker, does it really make sense to simply lose them when we get to Riversedge? No, you can't let them take her when we reach the city."

"What, then? I can't pretend to deliver her to them, then run off with her."

Amerdan raised his eyebrows. "Why not?"

"That's . . ." sputtered Caldan. "I couldn't! She has information on the Indryallans and the invasion that could be vital."

"How vital could it be? Regardless, it just means you have to choose what's more important: Miranda, or some scraps of information the Protectors might get out of Bells, *if* they break her, and *if* they can trust what she says. It's up to you."

Caldan's thoughts churned furiously. It was unlikely Bells would give her questioners any details of the invasion. And Amerdan was right: Caldan certainly wouldn't have access to her once they realized he was only an apprentice. Master Simmon had been in the process of raising him to journeyman rank, but even if he'd been officially promoted, they'd still take Bells away from him.

He turned to regard Elpidia, Bells, and Miranda, all of whom returned his stare with blank expressions, but his focus was on Bells. It would take only a few days to reach the city, and he had to find a way to get her to talk by then or . . . he might have to do something he regretted. Not a situation he was comfortable with at all. If Bells didn't respond to threats, did he have the courage to follow through on them? And would he be justified?

"Elpidia can bring word to the Quivers, then," he said finally.

Amerdan nodded, a thin smile on his face. "I'm with you, whatever you want to do." He glanced toward the market. "We need more supplies, and I have a few ducats left. Stay out of sight. I'll buy a few things."

With a grunt of assent, Caldan turned back to the others, while Amerdan headed for the market.

"What's going on here?" said a gruff voice from his right.

He whirled, hand reaching for his sword, and came face-to-face with two Quivers. Elpidia gasped, while Caldan shot them a wary glance. Both were in their twenties, with the clean uniforms and uncalloused hands of men who had a lot of spare time, yet preferred not to keep up with their training. One had a thin mouth and a weak chin he'd grown a beard to hide. The other smiled contemptuously—the grin of someone who thought he was better than everyone else. They didn't have their bows or quivers with them, each of them carrying only a short sword. Both looked at Caldan, Bells, Miranda, and Elpidia with suspicion. They must have come from the nearby building, and he hadn't seen them. Someone bellowed from inside, followed by raucous laughter and the clink of glasses.

Had they been drinking? Nevertheless, he had no option now.

"We were just on our way to see the garrison commander," Caldan said hastily. "Are you two on duty?"

"I'll ask the questions," the bearded Quiver snapped. "Why do you have this woman tied up? And who are you?"

A muffled sound came from Bells, and her mouth worked as if she were trying to push the gag out.

"She's a sorcerer. Anasoma has been invaded by Indryalla, and she's one of them."

The Quivers exchanged a glance.

They know already, Caldan thought. *Or they suspect.* More grunts came from Bells. "She's dangerous. You have to—"

"Be quiet! We don't have to do anything. The commander will want to question you. This could be a trick, for all we know."

"Please," Caldan said. "We don't—"

The bearded Quiver grabbed a whistle hanging around his neck. "I blow this, and more Quivers come running. Not a word out of you. Keep your hands clear of your weapons, and make your way to that building over there. Nice and slow, so we can keep an eye on you."

Caldan hesitated. Should he risk using sorcery and try to get away? He didn't want to injure the Quivers if he didn't have to, but . . .

Elpidia sighed and placed an arm around Miranda. She started moving down the road toward the stone garrison. Caldan suppressed a sigh of his own. He could have sworn Bells was smiling underneath her gag.

He grabbed Bells and pushed her ahead of him.

Inside the garrison, a few Quivers sat around a table behind a wooden counter that split the room in half, playing cards. Only one of them looked experienced, a middle-aged man who sat apart from the rest in a rocking chair—probably their commanding officer. The rest were young, barely needing to shave. Swords and cudgels hung on one wall, along with bows, quivers of arrows, and iron shackles.

Seeing Caldan and the others enter, the Quivers all looked up before going back to their card game and conversation. One of the young soldiers sighed heavily and levered himself up from his chair, approaching his side of the counter. His gaze traveled over them, taking in their unkempt and dirt-stained appearance. His eyebrows raised in interest as he noted Bells's bound hands and mouth. When he saw the two Quivers trailing behind Caldan, however, his eyes narrowed in suspicion.

"What's going on here, Ettmo?"

The bearded Quiver stepped forward. "Well, Barnard, we caught these trying to sneak into town. They were acting all suspicious, probably on account of the woman they have tied up. So we thought we'd bring them in."

The young Quiver, Barnard, paused and gave Ettmo a considered look. "Well done," he said, and then called over his shoulder, "Commander, you'll want to see this."

Caldan lowered his dust-covered satchel to the ground. "If I may, we've come from Anasoma as fast as we could. There's been an invasion."

Barnard scratched his jaw. "An invasion, you say? We'll get to that shortly, but first, answer me this: Why is that woman tied up?" He pointed at Bells. "It's easy to see she's not local."

Caldan turned his attention to the commanding officer, who had risen to his feet and was smoothing his uniform. "Sir," he pleaded, raising his voice. "I beg you to listen to what I'm saying. She's one of the invaders. We—"

"Help me!" screeched Bells, who had somehow worked her gag loose. She backed away from Caldan and Elpidia, eyes wild, a distressed expression on her face. "This man robbed me and took me prisoner! I don't know what he's up to, but please help me!"

"What? No, I didn't—"

"Liar!"

"Wait. She's the one who's lying. Don't believe a word she says." He looked at Barnard and the commander. "She's one of the invaders."

Barnard frowned and held up both hands. Behind him, his fellow soldiers were grinning and watched with amusement while their commanding officer came toward the counter.

"Please, sir, don't leave me with them. He touched me . . ."

Hard eyes turned on Caldan.

"I . . ." he sputtered. "I didn't." He took a step toward Bells.

"Back away," Barnard warned. "Don't go near her. Good. You—" He pointed at Bells. "Move to your right, against the wall."

"Thank you. I will." Bells smiled at him, and the soldier blushed.

Elpidia shook her head disapprovingly at Caldan.

"You have to listen to me," Caldan pleaded.

"Be quiet," Barnard said.

With a curse, Elpidia said, "He's telling the truth—she's dangerous."

"We'll be the judge of that," the commander said. "She doesn't look dangerous to me. Barnard and Ettmo, keep them apart. We'll question them separately."

Bells nodded vigorously at this, and Caldan realized it wouldn't be as simple as coming in and telling the truth. There was a real danger Bells could turn the tables on them, perhaps even have them arrested.

"Why would we enter the town in broad daylight with a bound woman if we'd robbed her?" Caldan asked. "It makes no sense."

"Ettmo said you were sneaking in," the commander said. "I doubt you were going to pay us a visit. Now, you stay quiet as well."

Caldan glared at Bells, who was now whimpering softly and doing her best to look terrified. She was ignoring him and focusing on the Quivers. The situation was rapidly sliding out of his control.

"Should I untie her?" Ettmo asked the commanding officer.

"Please do," Bells implored. "I can't feel my hands."

The commander nodded. "Do it," he said in a gruff voice, then pointed at Caldan. "You'd better have a good reason for doing this. Talk. Now."

"I already told you—there was an invasion in Anasoma," began Caldan, watching as the soldier skirted around the counter and drew a knife. "She's one of the leaders. We escaped after capturing her and made our way here as quickly as we could. Please, you have to keep her tied up—"

The soldier cut through the rope binding Bells's hands, and the rope dropped to the floor.

She rubbed her wrists, a pained expression on her face. "Thank you, good sir," she purred. "The rope was cutting off my circulation. Would you be so kind as to bring me a cup of wine or ale? They didn't treat me well, and I'm parched."

"Of course, my lady." The soldier nodded to Bells, then went to fill a mug from behind the counter, pouring wine from a jug.

Elpidia pointed at Caldan. "He's telling the truth. You have to believe him."

"So," said the commander, "you expect us to believe Anasoma has been occupied by an invading army, and you happened to capture one of their leaders and escape?" He shook his head. "I admit to a certain skepticism, but we'll send someone to find out the truth of the matter."

Bells accepted the mug from the soldier and sipped. "He's lying," she said casually. "He stole my craftings; they're in his bags and pocket."

"They're not yours," Caldan said, a note of desperation in his voice.

The commander's eyes opened wide at the mention of craftings. He waved Caldan silent and regarded Bells. "You're a sorcerer?"

She met the commander's gaze. Approaching the counter, she placed her mug down, leaning on the surface. "I am. A Protector. And I can describe the craftings. The runes and glyphs on each, their size, and what they are made from." She grinned at Caldan. "Can you?"

Damn it.

"This isn't going well," Elpidia whispered. "Do something."

"I . . . can't describe them in the detail she can," said Caldan. "But I can prove I'm a sorcerer."

"So can I," said Bells.

The commander looked at each of them in turn, then sighed. "Well, boys, looks like we won't get much relaxing done this morning. Take them all into custody until we figure this out."

"No!" said Caldan and Bells at the same time. They glared at each other.

The commander cleared his throat. "Until we get to the bottom of this, you'll have to be confined."

This wasn't working out. Desperately, Caldan tried to think of something he could say that would convince them of the truth. He had nothing to identify him as a sorcerer or Protector, which he would have if he had been confirmed as a journeyman. Whatever Bells's plan was, he was sure it would involve him and all the soldiers dead, her reunited with her craftings and swiftly back in Anasoma.

The Quivers moved close, and two latched onto his arms. Out of the corner of his eye, he saw Bells lift a finger and dip it into her mug, then place the tip on the counter's surface. She rapidly sketched two runes in front of the commander and then backed away.

"No!" shouted Caldan, voice booming around the room.

Elpidia flinched at the sudden sound.

Struggling against the soldiers holding him, Caldan thrust his hand into his pocket and opened his well, linking to the shield bell. Across the room, he sensed Bells access her well as the scent of lemons pervaded the room.

A multicolored haze enveloped him. The hands holding him jerked back in shock. He threw himself across the room and onto the counter, attempting to smear the glistening runes Bells had drawn in wine mixed with her saliva.

Too late.

Chaos erupted. A sharp crack of thunder echoed. Caldan felt a twisting in the air, and his heart skipped a beat. Orange sparks spewed from the counter under him. It felt like a horse had kicked him in the chest as he was flung into the air. His shield spewed violet sparkles, straining to contain the vitriolic forces.

Around him, two of the soldiers dropped as if poleaxed, and the others crumpled to the floor, twitching.

Elpidia, who had seen Bells back away before Caldan shouted, reacted quickly and threw herself at Miranda, hugging her tight. As the shock wave hit, they stumbled but remained upright. The commander grunted with pain and tumbled backward. Smoke filled the air.

Caldan slammed into the ceiling, then fell down onto the counter with a thump. Dust and debris from the ceiling rained down on him. He gasped in pain. Turning his head, he saw Bells scrambling across the floor. Sunlight from outside lit the smoke within.

Bells made a lunge for Caldan's satchel. Sliding on her knees, she clutched it greedily, and scrambled for the open door.

Caldan tried to move, but his body refused to respond. "Stop her," he croaked at Elpidia, who looked at him, then quickly shook her head.

Bells took a moment to turn and flashed a feral grin at him. She opened her mouth to speak, but Amerdan's fist connected with the back of her head. She jerked forward, and her eyes glazed over. Body limp, she sprawled across the floor.

Stepping inside, Amerdan waved smoke away from his face and surveyed the scene with calm eyes. Ignoring the immobile bodies around the room, he used the scraps of rope to bind Bells. He then tore strips from his shirt and used them to tie her fingers securely.

"That should do it, I think." He raised a questioning eyebrow.

Caldan nodded, struggling to a sitting position with his legs on the side of the counter. He closed his well, and the haze surrounding him winked out.

"She almost got away," he managed. By the ancestors, he hurt everywhere.

"I could see that. Lucky for us she didn't."

Around them, soldiers stirred. The two least injured helped their comrades to sit up.

Caldan wiped damp hands on his trousers and lowered himself off the counter, standing unsteadily. Miranda hadn't reacted throughout the entire episode, eyes blank. He fought back a surge of emotion and took a deep breath.

All hadn't been lost. Amerdan had saved the situation, and Bells looked like she would be unconscious for a while. Her actions should convince the Quivers of the truth of his words.

A few of the soldiers were helping their commander to his feet. Once he was upright, he turned a furious gaze on Bells.

Before the man did something rash, Caldan decided to intervene.

"Sir, I believe what just happened should convince you I told the truth. She's just tried to kill us all and escape." He attempted to project confidence, but the reality was, he shook inside. Still, he continued. "It is actually I who am a member of the Sorcerers' Guild."

The commander frowned. "Was that sorcery? I've never seen the like. What did she do?"

Caldan thought frantically. He settled on, "Something went wrong. The crafting she used is meant for much stronger materials. It broke down under the strain. I don't know why it reacted that way, though." He coughed into his hand. "But it shows you she is desperate and will try anything to escape. I trust you believe us now?"

The commander's eyes narrowed in thought for a moment. He looked around the room at the lingering smoke. "Maybe. I still have more questions, and I'll need to confirm what's happened in Anasoma. But . . . I'm willing to listen."

HOURS LATER, AS they were preparing to leave, Caldan saw Amerdan in the market—not purchasing supplies, as the commander had seen to it that they were well supplied, but handing out ducats to some of the scruffy-looking children wandering around barefoot.

The noises and smoke from the garrison, combined with their hasty preparations, had drawn attention, though most of the locals kept their distance. They knew better than to stick their noses in the Quivers' business.

A wagon was readied inside the stables attached to the garrison—the commander's idea once they'd told him they were being followed. It was unlikely whoever was following them would know they were in a wagon, and the covering further served to hide them from prying eyes. Two soldiers rode with them at the front, while another two rode behind. The commander, Jarmund, quickly ran through introductions to his soldiers. Corporal Lavas was in charge of their escort, a stocky man with a graying beard. The three soldiers were Breyton, Boyas, and Ettmo. To Caldan's eyes, they all looked young and green. Only Ettmo seemed interested in Caldan and his companions—he was the bearded one who had originally waylaid them; the others looked like this trip was a rare treat for them, away from their regular monotony. According to Jarmund, Riversedge was a week away by wagon.

Caldan and Elpidia helped Miranda inside. Amerdan prodded Bells, who'd come to, until she scrabbled awkwardly up, now hampered by chains.

The wagon lurched forward, and Caldan grabbed ahold of his rough wooden seat to steady himself. The others spread out inside the wagon after securing Bells to an iron ring bolted to a sturdy support. Elpidia sat with Miranda, while Amerdan perched at the back, peeking through a narrow gap in the canvas flaps toward the crossroads receding into the distance.

Caldan fished around in his gear and drew out the crafted bells. He held them for a few moments, pondering whether he had any choice in this since Miranda had been hurt. Underneath the bells, he could feel his ring on his finger. He was still uncomfortable with wearing the trinket, but now he had Bells's shield, he was determined to wear it as much as possible in the hope he found some clue as to its function. Shaking his head, he shuffled over to Bells; the lurching wagon made for unsteady footing.

She regarded him with cold eyes as he approached. A swollen red mark stained her forehead, the result of it hitting the floor after Amerdan had knocked her out. As she shifted her weight, her chains clinked, and she grimaced and stared at the canvas ceiling, ignoring Caldan.

He knelt in front of her for a time, the bells warming in his hands. Then, one by one, he laid them in front of her on the rough wooden floorboards. The tinkling sound they made drew both Bells's and Elpidia's gazes.

To heal Miranda, he needed to know more about coercive sorcery. But was it something he was forbidden to do as a Protector? Would learning about coercive sorcery condemn him in the Protectors' eyes?

He reached up to remove Bells's gag. "Tell me," he whispered to her. "Tell me everything you know about coercive sorcery."

She peered at him intently. "Poor apprentice Protector. There's so much you don't know."

"Teach me."

Bells shook her head. "Why would I? I'm going to kill you when I get the chance."

Caldan clenched his hands into fists until his fingers hurt. He knelt there, trembling. Raising a hand, he slapped Bells across the face, rocking her head to the side.

"Caldan!" Elpidia cried. "What are you doing? Get away from her!"

"She needs to learn I'm serious," Caldan said, keeping his eyes on Bells.

She stared back at him, a red handprint forming on her cheek.

Elpidia grabbed his arm and tugged it from Bells. Caldan resisted for a moment, then let her draw him away.

Bells licked blood from the corner of her mouth and began to laugh until Amerdan returned her gag.

Caldan turned from her and sat next to Elpidia. The physiker was looking at him disapprovingly. He covered his face with his hands.

FROM HIS PERCH on the roof of one of the inns, Mahsonn surveyed the buildings and the market. His position was a good one, and he had been watching for some time.

The empire's soldiers—Quivers, they called them—were scurrying around, moving in and out of their garrison like ants disturbed from their nest. Despite the sun streaming down and warming his back, none would see him with his sorcerous shroud in place.

Shielding his eyes from the light, he watched as a few groups of people gathered in the market, some gesturing toward the garrison and shrugging or shaking their heads.

He knew how they felt, the not knowing, and didn't like the feeling.

While he sat on the roof, three covered wagons entered the garrison stables, then exited a short time later, traveling in three different directions. For a moment he debated rushing down and trying to get a peek inside the wagons, but he discarded the idea immediately. Foolish and stupid. They would know someone was following Bells, and though he believed he could take the soldiers out, you never knew where your luck would fall in combat. One mistake, or a fluke for the other side, and you would be finished. And the fact that someone down there had been strong enough to kill Keys and capture Bells . . . no, that way was for idiots who valued the thrill more than actually getting the job done.

He sat still for a while, thinking. There was nothing for it but to go down and question the people in the market, and maybe get one of the soldiers alone. Using three different wagons was such an obvious ploy it was laughable, but as effective as it was in this situation, he wasn't smiling. He could lose days finding which wagon held Bells, or get lucky and lose no time at all. But games of chance were not in his nature. He liked to be certain.

To the south, oppressive clouds moved closer, and as the wind picked up, it brought the smell of rain. He cursed under his breath. Rain. He hated rain. It made his job that much harder, even with his consummate skill.

A pebble hit the roof next to him. He froze. Below him in the street, a small child looked up at the roof. She bent over and picked up another pebble from the ground. It bounced a good distance below him and fell back into the street. The girl ran to pick it up and threw it again. This time, it went to the left. The girl waited, then shrugged and skipped away toward the market.

Mahsonn clambered over the ridge of the roof and slid down the other side, launching himself off as the edge approached and landing lightly on his feet. Glancing to either side, he checked that he was alone and, satisfied, closed his well. Unlike a normal shield, which made a popping sound when it was cut off, his shroud disappeared silently, and he reappeared.

Striding briskly around the side of the building, he headed toward the market as fast as he could without drawing undue attention. He stopped briefly to pick up the pebble the girl had thrown. He spat in his hands and slicked back his hair, attempting to make himself more presentable. He nodded to a woman walking past with a basket of mushrooms.

There. The girl had joined a group of other grubby-looking children, and they were wandering aimlessly through the market. He shook his head disapprovingly. Where were their parents?

Catching up to the group, he pushed through them from behind and stood in front of the girl. She frowned up at him as he handed her the pebble.

"I believe this is yours?" he said.

She stared at the pebble, then back at him, and her mouth opened. "A real spirit!" she exclaimed.

Mahsonn tilted his head. "Excuse me?"

"The man. He said a spirit was watching. From the roof. Gave me a ducat and told me to throw pebbles at it."

"Ah. Well . . ." He bent over and leaned in close. "Don't tell anyone, will you, my dear?"

Trembling, she shook her head and backed away a step. Around her, the other children watched with terrified awe on their faces.

She hesitated, then held out a hand, palm up.

"What's this for?" he asked.

"The man. He said, if I found you, you had to give me gold."

With a smile, Mahsonn dug into a pocket and drew out a gold ducat. He held it up between two fingers. Six pairs of eyes were stuck to it like glue.

"This man, did he tell you anything else?"

The girl nodded, eyes on the gold coin.

"And what was that?"

Her palm bobbed up and down. "Gold first," she demanded.

Mahsonn wrinkled his nose as he surveyed the children and the market. Too busy. Too many eyes. He placed the coin in the girl's palm.

"The man said, 'Stay with your friends until the spirit comes. It can't hurt you then.'" She nodded, and her friends nodded along with her.

"Anything else?"

"West. The man said west."

With a grunt, Mahsonn turned and strode away quickly, leaving them to squabble over the coin.

CHAPTER 5

Through the wooden hulls of the ships, someone screamed. Raised voices followed the wailing, and boots thumped along decks, some toward the sound, others away.

Lady Felicienne wriggled in her hammock, then twisted to scratch her back. Screams in the night didn't bother her anymore. Neither did the roaches in her room, nor the rats she caught glimpses of through half-lidded eyes when falling asleep.

She was hidden, though, and the discomfort was worth it.

The small number of ships her men had managed to clear in the Cemetery served as her base these days. Having fled her rooms in the keep at the first sign of trouble, she had gathered the few soldiers and functionaries she felt she could trust and organized a tactical retreat. Far from being scared, she had recognized the patterns around her and knew the invasion would succeed early on. She'd sent her man Avigdor to rifle through desks and closets for whatever he could carry to help her once they escaped—mostly purses filled with ducats and lists of informants and important contacts. As always, he was success-ful at the task she assigned him.

The city had been in chaos, although—surprisingly—there was very little fighting. In a strange development, soldiers she was sure were loyal to the emperor had commanded their troops to lay down their weapons. Soon after, the traitors were all found dead, killed by their own hands, which was . . . curious.

The door leading into the hold creaked open, and a man cursed, squeezing between obstacles on his way toward her. She rubbed tired eyes and sat up, swinging her legs over the side of the bed. Her clothes were crumpled and sweat stained, and she reeked like a sailor who had been at sea too long. Over the last few days, she'd had a lot on her mind and hadn't bothered with some necessities. She ran her tongue over furry teeth, vowing to take some time soon to freshen up—once a few things were out of the way. She sighed and ran a hand through her oily hair. Her usual braids had come undone long ago, and she hadn't had a chance to redo them. At least she hadn't lost her ear-rings.

Avigdor appeared from around a pile of crates, looking almost as bad as she felt. He smiled at her, the brief, thin smile of a man with nothing to smile about. Drops of perspiration ran down his face as he stopped in front of her. His smile turned to a frown.

"Out with it," she said.

"I've received news through my friend Izak."

Her eyes narrowed. "I've met him. Continue."

"One of his informants, Rennen, claims to have fled the city after the invasion with a number of people. One of these people we have both met: the apprentice Protector, Caldan. Caldan asked him to deliver some information to us."

Felice shot Avigdor a sharp look, searching for signs he was jok-ing. The young man who'd defeated her at Dominion, and who had declined Avigdor's invitation to join them. And though he had a good reason for the latter, Caldan was still someone she wanted to keep close because of his curious trinket. His fleeing the city might be because of the invasion, or . . . it could be because he had something to hide. But the fact that he was reaching out to her now made her inclined to trust whatever information he was passing along. Something about what Avigdor said, though, had her current attention.

"This Rennen escaped the city, then came back?"

Avigdor nodded.

"Then he must have a way in and out."

"Or access to people who do."

"We can make use of this."

"My thoughts as well."

She waved at him to continue, even as her mind raced at the possibilities.

"Caldan claims the invaders, the Indryallans, are sorcerers of great power, and they used unknown sorcery to destroy the Sorcerers' Guild and the Protectors."

"Unknown?"

"His words. Izak said Rennen was very specific."

Felice scoffed. "Unknown," she repeated. "No ideas, no theories from such a bright young man?"

With a shrug, Avigdor met her eye. "Odd, is it not?"

"More than odd. Decidedly suspicious. The sorcerers who survived have a hundred theories as to how the Indryallans created the flames on the walls, but none of them will state they could replicate them for certain. As for the Protectors, well . . . we haven't found one yet."

"Yes. Caldan's explanation is brief and, dare I say it . . . suspect."

Felice rubbed her pockmarked cheeks, then her eyes. "I agree. He knows about the 'unknown' sorcery but offers no explanation. From what I gauged of the man, if he didn't know, he would have some theories and would make that clear." *So they used destructive sorcery.* She looked at Avigdor. *But he can't know.* Some knowledge was just too dangerous. If the emperor and his warlocks ever found out . . .

In her position as Third Adjudicator she had some idea of what sorcery was capable of, but even she was kept in the dark about a great many things.

"Which means," Avigdor said, "he gained some knowledge he isn't sharing, or he already knew and is hiding it."

"I would say the latter."

"So would I." Avigdor hesitated. "As I told you, he did mention he was an apprentice Protector, which I found strange."

"Indeed. I think we can both see where this is going." She took a breath. "The Protectors knew about this sorcery. I know you must have questions, Avigdor, but believe me when I say you should keep this to yourself."

Avigdor was silent for a few moments, considering her words, then he nodded.

Felice smiled briefly. She hated keeping him in the dark, but it was for his own good. "Perhaps it was only recent knowledge, but I doubt it. The Indryallans targeted the Protectors, knowing they would be the only ones able to offer resistance, then went after the other sorcerers for good measure."

"Just in case they knew something, or the Protectors had contingencies in place."

"It's what I would do. But the invaders' sorcery prevailed, and the Protectors and sorcerers were decimated. Judging from the lack of resistance by the emperor's soldiers, something went wrong there as well."

"We're still working on that," Avigdor said. "Information is scarce, as you know. It still looks like most soldiers' commanders were either misinformed about the attack or surrendered quickly."

"Do you think that is connected to what Caldan is not telling us?"

"I can't say . . . but it seems a stretch."

Felice agreed, yet it still niggled at her. "What else did Rennen have to say?"

"Just that the Protectors were all dead, and we should try to warn Protectors in other cities, if we can, and that the invaders must want something in Anasoma."

"They must want something . . . well, that's obvious," she said dryly. "Perhaps we would have been wrong to recruit him."

"I don't think so, my lady. Part of what made him so intriguing is that there isn't much deception in him—he's an honest sort, and we know they have their uses."

"I suppose. So . . . do we just take this at face value? And, if so, what do we do with it, being trapped here in a city with no Protectors left?"

"Well, he did send Rennen to deliver his message. And Rennen has a way through the blockade."

Felice smiled. "Very true, Avigdor. It seems my time stuck on this ship has dulled my wits a bit. So Caldan thought ahead that far, at least, knowing you would see the possibilities."

"Or you, my lady," he said. He was being gracious, and she was surprised she didn't resent it. He continued, "Using Rennen, we can at least send messages to other cities and any outposts close by. Though anywhere close would already know the city is barricaded, what with traders and farmers and whatnot being turned from the gates."

"But they don't have specific information, which we can provide. So . . . get together twenty of our men and women, split them into pairs, and decide on ten cities and outposts we should warn. They can take it from there, notify whoever they need to. But that's as far as you should go—we have other priorities."

Avigdor frowned. "Other priorities?"

"We need to hit the invaders where we can. I'm not sitting back and doing nothing until help arrives. Let's meet with Izak and see what else he knows from Rennen—though not here; we need to keep this place hidden. If they can take out the sorcerers and Protectors, we wouldn't stand much of a chance. Somewhere in Dockside will be fine. Just make sure he comes alone."

"Of course. And I'll look into finding out more about this 'unknown' sorcery. Perhaps questioning a prisoner would be enlightening?"

"A good idea. We need to know exactly what they're capable of. Be careful, though. Our people are being killed, or just disappearing, at a rapid rate."

Avigdor nodded bleakly.

"Very well. Set up the meeting," Felice said. "And if you can get your hands on a few of the invaders, do what you have to. I dislike torture, but we need to know more about what we are dealing with." She stood, leaving the hammock swaying. "Let's get moving, then."

FELICE SAT ON the sheets, back against the headboard, and closed her eyes. The room screamed opulence and bad taste, as she imagined all the high-end brothels in the city must have done.

Murals of erotic scenes adorned the walls. The furniture was of good quality, though the prevailing deep red color scheme was giving her a headache. It reminded her of blood and the questioning of two of the Indryallans they had captured yesterday after she had put plans in motion. Not pleasant memories, and she hoped they would fade in time. She hadn't learned much from the Indryallans, which was a pity. They were under the delusion they were here to liberate the citizens of the empire, but neither of them knew anything about sorcery. Perhaps she needed to capture one of their sorcerers.

She breathed deeply, trying to relax. Avigdor should be back soon with Izak. He had chosen this place for its discretion—here a clandestine meeting between a woman and two men would be unremarked upon—and she had to admit he had made a good choice, although she hoped no one recognized her. She'd need her reputation after all this was over.

There was a knock at the door, and she drew herself up to sit cross-legged, still leaning against the headboard. A key rattled in the lock, and the door opened to reveal Avigdor, followed by Izak.

Izak was dressed impeccably, as usual: expensive clothes with small silver buttons up the front of his shirt, his graying goatee recently trimmed. In contrast, her own appearance was scruffy and unkempt. She ran a hand over her hair and patted down some loose strands.

Avigdor and Izak were chatting amiably while Avigdor closed and locked the door behind them. With a gesture to Izak, Avigdor ushered him over to a padded chair. Izak turned and stopped in shock when he saw Felice.

"My lady," exclaimed Izak as he bowed from the waist. He strode forward and, before she could react, took her hand in his and touched his lips to the back of it. "As lovely as ever."

Liar. She inclined her head at him. "Please, sit."

Izak did so, boots scuffing the rugs on the floor. Earlier, she had arranged the chairs to face the bed, and Izak avoided her gaze and shifted uncomfortably. The decor of the room, and meeting in a brothel, unnerved him, which was another reason Avigdor had chosen it as a meeting place.

"Forgive the surroundings," Felice said. "But we thought it best to keep this meeting discreet, and the out-of-the-way location made this place ideal, though hard to find."

"Oh, I know it well. No bother." Izak hesitated, then his face went pale as he realized what he'd said.

Avigdor covered his mouth with a hand, hiding a smile.

"What I mean . . ." began Izak, pausing to clear his throat. "My lady, if I may—"

"You may not," Felice interrupted.

Izak stopped, stunned at being cut off so abruptly.

She closed her eyes and sighed deeply. She hadn't meant to start this way, but she was so very tired. Maybe this could work to her advantage. "Forgive my outburst. I'm sure we're all under some stress due to recent events. The fact is, though, time is of the essence. I called this meeting to discuss what we are going to do about the invasion."

"Do?" asked Izak. He looked at Avigdor, who shrugged.

"Yes, *do*. In case you hadn't noticed, we are at war, and we need to do something about it. We know you have connections, and we need to make use of them. So, as of now, I officially draft you into the resistance."

Izak spluttered and rose to his feet. He glanced at Avigdor.

"Sorry," Avigdor said, without much feeling.

Izak turned a glare on Felice. "What resistance? And what could I possibly hope to contribute? I may have condemned myself just by meeting with you."

"Calm down," Felice said. "And sit. Please." She waited while Izak fumed for a few moments, then plunked himself back down. "Good. Now, I'm sure we can all agree the Quivers have been somewhat . . . ineffective."

"Yes," said Izak. "It was hard to miss, what with the lack of any kind of resistance when blue flames suddenly surrounded the city."

Felice smiled thinly. "Which is why we need to bring more people into the cause. Especially those who can help us gather information."

"Not me!" exclaimed Izak. "I'm keeping my head down until this blows over. My plan is to stay out of harm's way until it's all sorted out."

"But I'm afraid that doesn't suit *my* plan, and as someone actually authorized by the emperor, I'm going to have to change yours a bit."

Izak made to protest, but Felice held up a hand.

"Now, the good news is that I'm not going to ask you to do much more than you've been doing. Rather, I want you to take advantage of the position you're in to gather information for us. You're well known to the nobles, and in quite a few of the bureaucrats' circles."

"And the bad news?"

"Obviously, you can't do this by lying low. I need someone on the inside. The Indryallans need the bureaucrats to ensure the system runs smoothly with minimal disruptions. So you must continue to do whatever you normally would . . . and just keep an ear out for us while you're doing it."

Izak frowned and shifted in his chair. "It doesn't sound too bad. I suppose we will need code words, secret places for me to drop letters, that sort of thing?"

She sighed. *They always want codes and safe houses. How come no one ever understands how spying really works?* "No. Just pass any information along to Avigdor."

"Oh. I thought you wanted to . . . Never mind. I'll do it. Only because of what Rennen told me they did to Miranda, Caldan's friend."

Felice sat up straighter and glanced at Avigdor, who looked back equally unsure. "What do you mean?"

"Their sorcery, you know." Izak waved a hand. "They blew apart the tunnel under the walls they used, and somehow they scrambled the poor girl's mind."

"Start from the beginning," Felice said. "What exactly did Rennen say happened?"

"You must know about their sorcery? I mean . . . I assumed you would."

"Pretend we have no idea what you're talking about."

"When Caldan, Elpidia, and the others were escaping, sorcerers came after them."

"Sorcerers?"

"Yes. Two Indryallans."

"Really?" Felice narrowed her eyes at Avigdor.

"I didn't think to question him further," Avigdor said. "Once he told me about Caldan and what he had to say, I brought the information straight to you. Like you said about yourself, all this inaction must have addled my brains."

Felice gave him a withering smile, then turned her gaze back to Izak. "Continue."

"Caldan managed to ward off the sorcerers' attacks. They ripped apart the building covering the entrance to the tunnels, but Caldan delayed them so his group could escape. Apparently, it was quite the sight: lightning flying around, clouds of dust"—he waved his hands in the air—"deafening sounds like thunder. Rennen was in awe of what happened. Caldan made it out safely, more or less, but his girl, Miranda, wasn't so lucky. They did something to her mind. She could barely speak afterward, or walk."

This smacked of forbidden sorcery. Felice kept her expression blank, as Avigdor was watching her like a hawk for any reaction.

"He managed to kill one of the sorcerers and capture the other," continued Izak, "a woman. The one who died was called Keys—that's what Rennen said, anyway. I think they were . . . lovers, or related. The woman was very upset that Keys died."

Felice shot Avigdor a scathing glance. He dropped his gaze to the floor. "It seems you have a lot more information than I was at first led to believe. Could you please elaborate on this fight, and who this sorcerer is, the one who was captured?"

"Rennen said she called herself Bells. I think it was an affectation, as she had a lot of crafted bells woven into her hair. He said she was dangerous. He could tell from how she acted and what she said after she was captured. She had a confidence and arrogance to her. Who wouldn't, if they could throw sorcery around like that?" Izak waggled his fingers. "Thunder and lightning. It gives me the chills. It shouldn't be possible." His brow creased, and he crossed his arms.

Felice waved away Izak's words as if they were irrelevant, though nothing could be further from the truth. They needed Izak, but they also needed to make sure he didn't think this information was too valuable. And so, as pieces fell into place for her, she kept her expression neutral, even as Avigdor's—from behind Izak—showed that he, too, was making the connections.

She knew fragments, things she'd stumbled onto and some information her old master had handed down to her. And she knew a few warlocks, but they were usually tight-lipped. When she'd pressed for more, it hadn't gone well for her. If the emperor or his warlocks tell you to stop digging, that's exactly what you did. It explained much about the invaders, though, and also the Protectors.

Felice unfolded her legs and walked over to Izak. She went down on one knee before him and looked into his eyes. "Thank you. It's an interesting story, and I appreciate you passing it along. But I'll be blunt: We need you. We need your contacts, your network among the population. It complements ours and would go a long way to helping us resist this invasion. Make no mistake, Izak: we are at war, and with a foe we hardly know anything about." Though she now knew a good deal about what they were capable of.

But what are they after?

Izak's face had gone red, whether from pride or her closeness, she wasn't sure—both had been used to get this desired effect. He swallowed hard. "So long as it doesn't get me killed."

"You're definitely no good to me dead," she said, smiling. Felice patted him on the knee and stood. "We need to fight alongside each other. And I mean that in a purely figurative sense when it comes to you, Izak. There is more than one way to resist these invaders, and we have a few men for the physical side. Information is your weapon, and it will be just as valuable. Now, this way out of the city . . ."

Preening at the praise, Izak sat up a bit straighter. "Rennen may have some friends who may have another tunnel. The Indryallans will be all over the one Rennen used before."

"*May?* I assume by that you mean they do, but it may be difficult for us to arrange access?"

"Er, yes. These people . . . they don't make their ducats legally. If someone of your . . . standing were to approach them, I don't think they'd be pleased."

"You can arrange it through Rennen for us. We have twenty people we need to get out."

"Twenty! That'll cost you."

"My lady," Avigdor said. "Ducats are a problem."

"I know. We'll have to come up with a plan." Felice groaned with frustration at their predicament. She had managed to warn most of her department and secure hiding places for them, albeit in the decaying Cemetery ships where she had secreted herself, but they were not soldiers. Extremely competent in their roles, yes, but far from the type she needed to run an effective campaign against the invaders. And, as Avigdor said, their finances were almost nonexistent. What ducats she had managed to salvage before fleeing had mostly been spent. Their resources had started out meager and were getting worse.

She looked up at the ceiling, which was covered in lewd frescoes. "Any suggestions?" she asked.

Avigdor resumed his seat and folded his hands together, taking his time to ponder their position, as was his usual habit.

Beside him, Izak drew out a kerchief and wiped his nose, then held up a hand. "If I may," he said.

Felice waved at him to continue.

"Thank you. Well, we obviously can't go to the nobles for support. At least, ducat-wise. Until they see which way the wind's blowing, we can't rely on them. And the merchants will be the same." He stood and began to pace the room. "Now, they will be holding on to what they have, in case the situation gets worse. Supplies, food, goods, ducats—it would be impossible to get anything out of them, and many would turn you in for the reward. No . . . what we need to do is find someone wealthy and appeal to their innate greed, convince them that this will be over swiftly when the emperor retaliates, and they stand to be repaid tenfold, along with the emperor's thanks. That should be enough of an incentive to reel someone in."

"But, as you correctly stated, no noble or merchant would do such a thing, as the situation stands," Avigdor said.

Felice nodded in agreement. There must be something she could use; she couldn't give up. "What else have you heard?"

"Ah," exclaimed Izak with a smug smile. "There is an interesting rumor from one of my friends. One of the largest merchant companies managed to spend a few days before the invasion transporting as much of their inventory as they could *out* of Anasoma, including their ducat reserves from their banking arm."

"Who exactly are these merchants? They must have known what was coming." What had this company known in advance? And what were they afraid of?

"The Five Oceans Mercantile Concern," said Izak. "A couple of their offices remain open, with a skeleton staff."

Felice ran a hand through her oily hair. It really needed a wash. "Suspicious activity, though. I wonder how they knew . . . and why they didn't pull out completely once they found out."

Felice sat back down on the bed, brow furrowed in thought. Izak opened his mouth to interrupt her but was silenced by a wave of Avigdor's hand.

She examined the situation from every angle she could think of, but it all boiled down to the fact that she needed more information. If these merchants were in league with the Indryallans, they would have stayed. That much was obvious. Unless their leaving was a coincidence—and she didn't believe in such things—they had more information than she did, and that galled her. Izak spoke of dangerous, secret sorcery being used. What if the merchants had known about this, knew what was coming? Was it possible?

She needed to question them, to find out what they knew.

"We need to contact them," she said. "These merchants. And carefully."

"I might point out," continued Izak, "that we don't know why they left, or whether it has anything to do with the invasion."

"It fits the facts," replied Felice.

"As we know them," added Avigdor. "But I agree; the pattern of their behavior doesn't lead to many theories. Izak, you'll have to trust us. These merchants knew about the invasion before it happened, and they didn't want to be here when it did."

"But . . ." stammered Izak. "How could they have known, unless they were allied with the Indryallans? I mean, you didn't know." He stopped, and his face went bright red. "No offense."

Felice sighed. "Chances are, they aren't allied with them. Which could mean they had a better information network than we did, which I doubt. Or they saw a pattern to certain events and deduced the invasion was coming, which again I doubt. That's one thing we excel at, and we didn't see it coming. So they knew some other way."

"How?" muttered Izak.

"Without information, our speculation is useless." Avigdor spoke with nonchalance, meeting her eye and tilting his head toward Izak.

Felice knew he had followed her words closely and would have come to the same conclusions. That Five Oceans had left implied a connection, therefore it might be useful to question them. In any case, they had to be thorough. "We have no choice. Izak, you're going to have to contact them for us." She smiled sweetly.

"Eh? Me? But—"

"Hush. You mingle in similar circles, and no doubt a few of your acquaintances have dealings with the Five Oceans Mercantile Concern. We already know a lot about their business dealings, but we've obviously missed something important. Find out more, and then we can work on a letter of introduction that will pique their interest." But they had to be careful—if Five Oceans was in league with the Indryallans, it could spell disaster for her. It was a dangerous situation.

"I . . . by the ancestors . . ." Izak's face had drained of blood. "What if they're treacherous?"

"Hush. We can arrange to meet at a location where we can keep you safe and eavesdrop on the conversation. You'll be protected. I promise."

"How can you promise? If they think I know something about them they don't want anyone else to know, I'm doomed!"

Felice scoffed. "A well-crafted letter to them, with what we know and a few hints at things we have surmised, and they will be more interested than anything else. Especially if they did flee the Indryallans for some reason."

"*If?* I thought you were certain of it?"

"As certain as I can be."

"But—"

"Enough, Izak, please. It's a simple task. Find out more about this business, then we send them a letter to lure someone of importance to a meeting. Then we question them, and we have loads more information than we had before. See, simple."

Izak swallowed, then nodded slowly.

"Good," continued Felice, rubbing her cheek. "Avigdor will contact you this time tomorrow, and you can pass along what you've learned. By then, I'll have drafted the letter. We need to work quickly."

Izak bowed toward Felice. "Farewell, then. Though I face great danger, I do so willingly, for you, my lady." He held out a hand, which she ignored. Clearing his throat, he made a show of smoothing his goatee. "Ahem. Well, until tomorrow, then."

Avigdor rose and clasped his hand, smiling warmly. A few hushed words were exchanged between them, then Izak left.

Avigdor locked the door after him and approached Felice.

"So," he said, "tomorrow afternoon I have Rennen take charge of smuggling twenty of our people out of the city, then meet with Izak. What about the ducats Rennen will need? The people he will be dealing with will expect payment up front."

"Leave that to me. I'll find something by tomorrow." She'd salvaged a few personal items she could sell. It would keep them afloat for the time being.

With a concerned look, Avigdor raised an eyebrow but remained silent.

Felice glanced around at the tasteless decorations a final time. "Avigdor, can you settle the bill for the room? I've got to get working on making some ducats, and on that letter."

"Of course. I believe it's customary for the man to pay in these situations."

She gave him a tired look. "That's not amusing."

CHAPTER 6

Never before in his life had Amerdan had to endure such restraint. So close they were, Bells and Caldan, and yet something stopped him from acting: a tug, almost physical, when he reached for his knife. He couldn't say what it was, what restrained him. Dotty the rag doll had squirmed like a cat caught inside his shirt when he'd stayed his hand. Two sorcerers, and he couldn't bring himself to kill them . . . yet.

His head buzzed at the thought, and he licked his lips, almost salivating. It was too dangerous, he decided. That was what stopped him. He gave a soft chuckle.

Dangerous. He turned the word over in his mind. He was certain he could take them all. Caldan was the one he needed to most concern himself with, but a quick thrust with his knife would take care of the young man. Then the soldiers, followed by Elpidia. He'd be alone with Bells then.

But that would leave him with only one, and with two such talented vessels for the taking . . . No. That wasn't right. Why take one when two was so much better?

And so he waited. And restrained himself. Night after night. Day after day. The thought of absorbing more talents, though he didn't know what they would be, filled him with warmth and ecstasy. His skin tingled. He still hadn't determined what the young apprentice had passed to him, but he would. In time. Everything he took from the vessels made him stronger.

Amerdan closed his eyes and leaned back against the rough bark of a tree, listening to the night, letting it flow around and through him. Crickets chirped. Small nocturnal animals rustled in the grass and leaves. Voices drifted from the campsite, mostly the crass Quivers, but fragments from Caldan and Elpidia as well. He'd left them some time ago, after they'd stopped for the night. He'd needed to get away.

Now that he was alone, he could start to shed the skin he kept on in their presence. It chafed, a constant weight on his shoulders. At least in his shop he had some time when there were no customers and he could relax. Out here, with them constantly watching, he couldn't let go. Couldn't be himself.

Abruptly, he lurched to his feet and headed even farther from the camp. Long grass brushed his pants and left them damp with evening dew. Animals and insects heard and felt him coming and froze or skittered away. But he saw them all. The night was bright to him and had been for years. One of the vessels he'd absorbed had provided him with some surprising gifts. Or perhaps he'd been on the edge, and the woman's talents had tipped him over it. No matter.

A faint light caught his eye, and he altered his path. It was far away but . . . too steady to be a campfire.

Is this what you are looking for? he asked himself. *Is this what you need?*

He increased his pace, pushing his way through thickets and around trees. A wide stream blocked his path, and he barely paused before wading in, boots held over his head. In the middle, it rose to his waist, and he scooped handfuls of cold water to quench his thirst.

It tasted sweet but did nothing to sate him. He thirsted for something else.

He stopped among the stones on the other side and wrung his pants out, considering the spurts of water as they splashed onto the rocks. The wind picked up, began howling through swaying trees. Dust and leaves blew over him, and he blinked, turning his head from the breeze. He came across a narrow trail. It was well worn, leading to the stream, or from it.

Boots barely making a sound, he followed the dirt line toward the light. To either side of him, wild growth gave way to planted fields. As he closed the distance, the light resolved into two separate sources, both steady. Minutes later, he determined they were square, and he grinned. Windows, then.

Amerdan stayed on the path, not bothering to conceal himself. At this time of night, it was unlikely anyone would see him. They'd be inside their farmhouse, doors barred and windows closed against the wind and darkness.

A gate loomed in front of him, and he halted. It was well made, part of a fence that surrounded an also well-maintained dwelling. There were no missing shingles or weeds growing on the roof. Someone had made a home they . . . loved. A family, perhaps.

A guttural growl alerted him an instant before the guard dog lunged. It yelped as he bore his weight down on its neck and plunged his knife under its armpit, seeking its heart. With one hand, he clamped its jaws shut, reducing its cries to whimpers as it struggled. Soon it lay still. Curiously, there was a red ribbon tied around its leather collar.

Amerdan lay on top of the dog for a minute, motionless and quiet. When he was sure the animal's sounds hadn't been heard over the wind, he stood and brushed off his pants and shirt. It would be rude to come into someone's home dirty and looking disreputable.

Of course, there was nothing to be done about the blood.

To his right, the door of a barn swung open, then slammed against its jamb. The weather must have caught the farmer unaware, and he hadn't made sure everything was locked up tight. Leaving the dog lying in the dirt, Amerdan went up to the barn door and kicked it, slamming it with a crash. It shuddered on its hinges.

Come on, loving farmer. That should bring you running.

One window briefly went dark as someone passed in front of the light source. Amerdan gave the barn door another kick, and again it smashed into the jamb. Taking a few steps to the side, he crouched behind a water barrel.

A vertical line of light split the night as the door to the house cracked open. A head poked out, and Amerdan heard a man curse in a deep voice.

The door swung open, and a tall, brawny man stepped onto the porch, shielding his eyes against the wind. He gave a low whistle and waited. With his enhanced vision, Amerdan saw the man frown when the dog didn't appear. The stupid animal wasn't far away, but he doubted the farmer could see its body, having come from a bright room into the darkness only moments ago.

He rolled his eyes as the farmer gave another whistle. Another curse, then another whistle. Then the farmer shook his head and walked toward the barn. As he was about to latch the door, Amerdan stood and slipped behind him.

Moments later, the farmer was on his back inside the barn, spread-eagled on the floor with Amerdan's hand clamped to his throat. Even in the darkness, the farmer's eyes widened as they took in the knife blade floating in front of his face.

He struggled; they all did. But in the end they knew their time had come. Their usefulness was at an end.

When the man started begging, Amerdan smiled. It was good he hadn't pleaded for his own life but the lives of his wife and children.

He closed his eyes and listened to the thing's mewlings.

MIRANDA SQUEEZED CALDAN'S hand tightly for a moment, then again. She sat where they had placed her hours ago, close enough to their fire for warmth, yet far enough away that she wouldn't stumble into it before someone could stop her. He had been talking to her since their evening meal, inconsequential things about his life at the monastery, the trip by sea to Anasoma when they had met, his trials at the Sorcerers' Guild. All the while he had held her hand, comforting her, making sure she relaxed after their long day's travel in the wagon.

They'd come a short way from the road down a dirt track to a flat grassy area the soldiers knew from other trips.

Standing, he stretched his back and glanced around their makeshift campsite. Bells was still chained inside the wagon, fingers tied with strips of cloth and hands restricted so she couldn't craft. She'd been led out earlier by Elpidia to stretch her legs before being bundled back inside.

Elpidia now had her gear spread out on the ground in front of her—small vials and bottles, along with paper packets and thin wooden boxes. Since they had stopped she'd been fussing over them, preoccupied. At one stage, Caldan saw her pour a few drops from the vial containing his blood onto a scrap of cloth. She then cut the material into four sections and placed each inside a vial of clear liquid, which rapidly turned a pinkish hue. He suspected she'd added a drug to prevent his blood clotting—she was well prepared.

Amerdan had been gone from the camp for some time, saying he needed to stretch his legs. During the day, he had looked ill at ease and was no doubt taking his time, relaxing after being cooped up in the wagon.

The Quivers were talking quietly among themselves while cleaning their gear and examining their weapons. Each carried a sword and a dagger in addition to his bow.

Caldan grabbed his sword and made his way to a fallen log just outside the light from the fire. With their frantic pace over the days since leaving Anasoma, he hadn't had time to wonder about it, and he didn't want to let anyone know he had such a valuable trinket in his possession. So it stayed in the scabbard, and he made sure it never left his sight. With everyone occupied, though, this was the perfect chance to examine it, along with the bone ring, which was another mystery he hadn't had much time to think about. It wasn't formed from the usual unknown alloy all other trinkets were, and that possibly made it the most valuable item he'd ever seen. Far more valuable than ten of his trinket rings. It turned everything sorcerers knew about trinkets on its head. Proof his parents had kept hidden and presumably died for.

He sat and drew out a handspan of the sword's blade, then, unable to resist, another. Such craftsmanship he'd never seen. Even if it weren't a trinket sword, it still would have been a marvel of artistry. As with Caldan's ring, the metal of the blade was an unknown alloy, the formula no doubt lost in the Shattering.

Caldan accessed his well and ran his senses over the sword. Similar to his ring, there were no linking runes to latch on to, nothing that could give the trinket its power—whatever that was. And yet something did—and without the usual well and shaping runes required. Creating such an artifact was a puzzle, one that smarter sorcerers than Caldan hadn't been able to decipher, as far as he knew. He ran a finger over the blade's surface; it was smooth and hard and cold. The silvery metal shone with a muted glow in the night.

Shaking his head, Caldan sheathed the blade and turned his mind from the sword to one of the crafted bells in his pocket. This one was small and silver, no bigger than his thumbnail. He didn't recognize the metal it was smith-crafted from, but he assumed many traces of rare earths would be included in the alloy. The runes and glyphs inscribed on both the inside and outside surfaces were exquisite. They were far too fine to be made from a wax cast, as those on his wristband had been, and it bothered him that he would no longer have the chance to study at the guild to learn more about the bell.

As it was, he knew more about the bell than he had when he had first started examining it days ago. For although he still regretted striking her, his threats to Bells had borne fruit, because after much back-and-forth, she'd pointed out this crafting as the one he needed to heal Miranda. Of course, after that, she'd adamantly refused to give him any ideas about its functions or how to use it, but it was a start. His biggest concern, then, was that he didn't know why she'd given up this information. Perhaps she hoped he'd try to use it and damage himself?

He returned to Miranda's side to check on her, then wandered away from the fire, circling the camp, deep in thought.

"Caldan." A whisper came from the wagon as he passed. "Over here."

He shook his head and continued pacing. Once again, as he passed the wagon, Bells whispered to him.

"Little Protector, come here."

He stopped and fingered her bell-shaped craftings in his pocket but quickly moved on.

We will talk, Bells. But not on your command.

Caldan returned to his gear and fished out three of his small sorcerous globes, the ones they had used in the aqueduct tunnels. He opened his well and linked to two of them, and the glass balls began to glow with a clean white light. Approaching the soldiers, he handed the two globes over with a smile.

"You might find these handy tonight," he said.

They accepted the globes with slightly awed expressions. Sorcerous globes were expensive, and the soldiers had likely never seen them this close before.

"Sir, thank you," blurted one.

Caldan nodded. "I wouldn't presume to tell you your business, but . . . I assume one of you will be on watch throughout the night?"

The three younger soldiers looked toward the eldest of the four, Lavas. Caldan understood the man was a corporal but also had an extra honorific of "broken sword," signified by a badge over his heart. He'd read that the signifier meant someone had seen action in a number of battles.

"That we will, sir. Just split up the watches. Breyton here"—the corporal gestured at one of the soldiers—"gets first watch." His eyes narrowed. "And he better get started."

With a contrite expression, Breyton stood, accepting one of the sorcerous globes, and wandered out into the night.

The older soldier's eyes flicked to the globes. "If you don't mind me asking, are you a journeyman sorcerer?"

"Only an apprentice," replied Caldan with a shake of his head. "Though I was told I'd be raised soon if . . . well, if the invasion hadn't happened."

"Not to worry, sir. Once we get word out, the emperor will be sure to teach these invaders a lesson."

"I'm sure he will. If you'll excuse me." Caldan resumed circling the fire. A tinkle came from the bells as he thrust his hand in his pocket.

Elpidia looked up at the sound, then went back to her work, scratching on a piece of paper with a pen, occasionally dipping the metal nib into a pot of ink. Of Amerdan there was still no sign.

Passing Miranda, Caldan gave her shoulder a reassuring squeeze, then made his way straight to the wagon, hauling himself inside. Against the back wall, he could make out Bells despite the lack of light, but, as when they were in the aqueducts, he wanted to keep this talent hidden.

Once again he opened his well, and once again a clean light emanated from the sorcerous globe in his hand. It illuminated Bells, who sat in the back of the wagon, covered with a blanket one of the soldiers had thrown over her for warmth during the night. She stirred when she heard movement and saw him climb into the wagon, then averted her eyes when the sorcerous globe lit.

As he did whenever he came near her, Caldan split his well into another string and linked to the shield crafting but didn't activate it. Though he knew the crafting had to be on your person to work, he wasn't sure of her capabilities and was wary. If she tried anything, he wanted to be ready.

"Good little Protector," Bells purred.

"I'm not your little Protector."

"Indeed you aren't. Far from it." She eyed him suggestively and squirmed under the blanket, which dropped from one of her shoulders. "I knew you would come, though. We are cut from the same cloth, you and I."

"Far from it," echoed Caldan. "We couldn't be less alike."

"Ahhh," she said, shifting her body so the blanket fell to her lap. "Somehow, I don't think so. People like us . . . talented . . . more so than the others . . . we know we're different."

"I'm not like you," he replied with a hint of irritation. "I don't kill innocent people."

"You killed the soldiers looking for me."

"They would have killed us. Or you would have, once you were free."

"Yes. The thing is, you look at things as black and white. Yet there is no such thing as an innocent person, just as there is no good or evil in this world, Caldan. Just people trying to make the best of what they have."

"So slaughtering the sorcerers and the Protectors was just you making the best of things?" he said. "By the ancestors, spare me your deluded explanation."

Bells shrugged. "We didn't want to kill them. We thought they could be contained, but the God-Emperor thought they were too dangerous. And when he decides on something, you don't argue."

"So you were just following orders, and that washes your hands of the blood?"

"So quick to judge me? There wasn't much else we could do. You don't know the God-Emperor." She shook her head. "Kelhak's been our leader for a long time, and he has absolute power. His sorcery and acumen are second to none. When he orders you to do something . . . well, let's just say if you don't do it, there are plenty of people willing to take your place."

But Caldan had stopped listening. *It couldn't be . . . But the name is the same.* "What did you say? Kelhak?" Caldan frowned and stared at Bells. "That's impossible . . ."

"What do you mean?"

"There was once a Kelhak at the monastery I grew up in, a hundred years ago. He was exiled, traveled to Anasoma, where he won a Dominion competition, then disappeared."

"The God-Emperor has never been beaten at Dominion. Never."

"Coincidence only," Caldan muttered. It couldn't really be Kelhak; that would make him a century old. And yet, didn't Bells say the God-Emperor was over a hundred . . .

No. It's impossible.

Caldan put thoughts of this God-Emperor from his mind. "It's of no matter," he said abruptly. "I came because I need your help."

Bells tilted her head and looked at him curiously. "And here I thought you just wanted to chat, like always. Do you honestly believe

I'll help you? After what you did?" She turned and spat on the floor of the wagon.

"Miranda is innocent. She—"

"There are no innocents," Bells said again. "Everyone's guilty of something."

"Not her. All she wanted was to make a life for herself, without struggling to survive day to day. A comfortable life with no turmoil. That's all she wanted."

"I very much doubt that."

"It's true." Caldan reached into his pocket and withdrew a bell. He held his hand palm up with the bell resting on it. Light from his sorcerous globe glittered on the bright surface.

Bells's eyes flicked to the crafting then away; she appeared uninterested, but he knew it was an act.

"Is there really a way to heal her?" he asked softly.

"You're taking a chance bringing that this close to me." Bells smiled, a feral twisting of her lips that didn't reach her eyes.

"I don't think so. I think that it has to be in contact with a part of you for you to be able to access it, like your shield crafting."

"And if you're wrong?"

"Then we wouldn't be having this conversation." He knelt in front of her. "Teach me how to use it."

His words hung in the air between them. Caldan knew Bells could see how desperate he was. Though she was his prisoner, she had the upper hand, at least when it came to him.

"Why?" replied Bells.

"So I can cure Miranda. She's . . . I can't stand to see her like this."

"No, not why do you want me to teach you; why *should* I? I'm bound for torture and probably a slow death. That's my reward for teaching you?"

"The Quivers wouldn't do that. They'll know how valuable you are."

"Valuable? Once the Protectors extract whatever information from me they can, I'll be worthless, and an embarrassment to them. They have tried to conceal and destroy knowledge of destructive and coercive sorcery for hundreds of years, and here I am, one of their worst nightmares come to life. I'm afraid I won't last long then. So I'll ask again: What do I get out of it?"

Caldan took a deep breath. "Freedom," he said. He clamped down on his uneasiness, not sure this was the right option, but how else could he persuade Bells to heal Miranda? He realized he was wringing his hands together and forced himself to stop. Was his desperation, guilt, and fondness for Miranda overruling his head? Maybe . . . he couldn't be sure.

Bells has to be telling the truth . . . she has to be.

"Before we reach Riversedge," Caldan said, "I'll make it look like you escaped. You can disappear into the city or try to make your way back to Anasoma; I don't care. By the time you get back, the emperor will have sent enough soldiers to retake the city, and most likely the walls will be surrounded. You won't be able to avoid them to get back inside, so whatever happens will probably be over before you find a way in or return to your troops."

Bells regarded him with her dark eyes. "And you give me my craftings back."

"No. I'm not giving them back to you; they're not part of the deal. You'll have to do without them."

Bells sniffed and nodded behind him. "What about your friends? I daresay they wouldn't want to let me go. You'll have to lie to them and come up with a plan where I can escape without them knowing."

"I can worry about that later. Right now, I need you to help Miranda."

"I will. Give me the crafting."

"Do you think I'm stupid? No. You will have to teach me."

"Can't do that, I'm afraid; not enough time. And isn't this something the Protectors forbid? Won't you be damning yourself, if I teach you?"

Yes. But she doesn't need to know that. "I don't think so, and I think it's worth the risk anyway. Besides, it's not like I can ask one of my masters—you killed them all, remember?"

At that she snorted, as if conceding the point. "That doesn't change anything, though, about me teaching you. Coercive sorcery is tricky, much more so than any other kind, and I'm not an expert. The best I'd be able to do—if I were willing—is to pass along some of the things we are all taught early on about how the mind works and repairing damage. But it's rudimentary at best, since it's so dangerous—things can go wrong even when you think you are in control. It's only a very few who are selected to learn more than the basics, those the masters deem to have the mental complexity. Those who survive the initial training."

Caldan nodded, keeping silent. He didn't want to interrupt the flow of words from Bells lest she stop altogether and reconsider her position. She seemed so close . . .

She shifted her weight and stretched her neck, lips pressed into a tight line. "If I show you a few things, then you have to release me, somewhere away from these soldiers, and where I have a few days' head start before any pursuit. Whether I decide to hide in this city ahead of us or go back to Anasoma is for me to decide. You have to promise not to come after me."

Caldan hesitated. He hadn't expected her to take the offer, and now he wondered if she thought she'd get more than freedom from this bargain. "I'll need to think about it."

"Don't think too long, little Protector. Who knows what's happening to your precious Miranda while you wait? I only hope it's not too late already."

Caldan stiffened at her words, while Bells regarded him, unblinking. Knowing she was probably baiting him into making a rash decision didn't help lessen the guilt he felt at Miranda's predicament. He sighed, then relaxed and shook his head.

"And what assurance do I have that you won't carry out your threat to kill us all?"

"Why . . . none. But either you want Miranda back to normal or you don't. As I see it, you really don't have much choice. No one else can help you."

With a grunt, Caldan contemplated the bell still clutched in his palm. She was right. He knew it, and she knew it. He had no choice but to make a deal with her and hope she told the truth. She wouldn't hold Miranda responsible for Keys's death—Miranda was an innocent in all this. And with Bells on her own, with no craftings to use, what could she do that he couldn't shield against?

For long moments he sat, silent, contemplating her words. He analyzed her actions and what she'd said over the last few days, trying to decide if he could trust her in this one thing.

Suddenly, a shrill scream pierced the night—Elpidia, coming from close by the wagon. Caldan jumped to his feet. Outside, shouts from the soldiers escorting them joined the commotion.

"What did you do?" he demanded of Bells.

She grinned, teeth flashing white. "Nothing, but it sounds like I won't need to teach you anything after all."

He backed away, then leaped out of the wagon.

Around the camp, the three soldiers had drawn their swords and were advancing on Amerdan, at whose feet was the body of their comrade, Breyton. The prone soldier's uniform was covered in blood and slashed all over with tiny, precise cuts, as if he'd been struck by hundreds of small knives. Amerdan frowned at the advancing soldiers and raised his hands in a placating gesture. Elpidia looked on with frightened eyes, hands over her mouth to stifle her sobs.

Caldan looked around frantically, searching for Miranda, and spotted her at the edge of the clearing, covered with a blanket. Elpidia must have made her comfortable while he was talking with Bells.

"What did you do?" shouted Ettmo at Amerdan.

The shopkeeper held his hands out, palms up to show he had no weapon. "Nothing," he replied calmly. "I was coming back to the camp after my walk and almost tripped over him in the dark. He was like this when I found him."

Silence reigned for a moment as the Quivers considered his words. Around them, a gust of wind whistled through the trees. It brought a whiff of lemons to Caldan before the scent was whisked away on the breeze.

Breaking the tension, Elpidia hurried to her gear and grabbed her satchel, rushing to the injured soldier and kneeling beside him.

Amerdan glanced down at her.

"Sheathe your swords and help your friend," he said to the soldiers. "I fear he needs all the help he can get."

"You must have done this," said Boyas, and the others nodded.

Amerdan laughed. "We need you, in case you idiots hadn't realized. That's why we came to you in the first place."

Realizing the situation could escalate out of control, Caldan decided to step in. "Listen, everyone! Calm down. There's no reason for him to have done this, none at all. Something else is going on."

Amerdan nodded at his words, while the Quivers muttered among themselves. Over the wounded Breyton, Elpidia sat back on her heels and wiped her brow with bloody hands, leaving a red trail.

"He's . . ." She looked up at the soldiers. "I'm afraid he's dead. Too much blood loss." She shook her head. "There wasn't anything we could have done, even if we had found him earlier. There are too many . . . cuts." She stood and stepped away from the body.

All three soldiers cursed and approached, eyes flicking between the corpse of Breyton and Amerdan, who took a step back to give them room.

"There," said Amerdan. "I couldn't have done this without him making enough noise to alert everyone, could I? And there are hundreds of cuts on his skin; how could I have had time? Surely he would have screamed from one of them?"

"Yeah," Lavas said, "but he didn't, did he? And someone did this to him. Why not you?" Lavas sneered at Amerdan, then directed the other two to get a blanket and cover the body.

"I'm just a shopkeeper," replied Amerdan. He looked toward Caldan. "Was it . . . sorcery?"

All three soldiers followed his gaze and stared at Caldan.

"I think he's right," Caldan said, remembering the lemons.

Still, that didn't seem to satisfy the Quivers. Boyas looked away, disgust on his face, while Ettmo grimaced at Caldan. "Then why are you here? I thought you were our protection against sorcery!"

"I can't protect against sorcery I knew nothing about!"

"So you can't protect us at all, then," Lavas said. He slid his sword into its scabbard. "Leave Breyton," he ordered.

"But we can't just leave him," protested Ettmo.

"For now, Ettmo. You need to patrol the perimeter, both of you, and make sure it's clear. And don't separate. Then get our gear together and prepare the wagon. We're getting out of here."

Nodding, the two soldiers moved out of the light and into the surrounding trees.

"What? Why leave?" Caldan asked.

Elpidia folded her arms across her chest and held herself tight, while Amerdan shrugged and warmed his hands by the fire.

"Because it's not safe here. Whatever happened to Breyton could happen to anyone else on watch." He waved a hand at Caldan. "And you obviously can't protect us. Our safest option is to stay together, and since I assume no one will be sleeping tonight, we may as well put some distance between us and this place. We'll put Breyton in the wagon and get out of here as quick as we can."

"Wait," Caldan said, thinking furiously. "Just wait! What if this is what they want?"

"They?" scoffed Lavas. "How do you know there's more than one? You're guessing and scared, and I get that, but don't tell me you know what's happened or how to do anything about it. We don't have time for this."

Caldan could think of nothing to say in response to that.

Lavas grunted and looked around the camp. His soldiers returned and signaled they had found nothing, then they busied themselves with their gear.

Elpidia watched for a moment, then gathered up her satchel and went to pack up the rest of her belongings.

"We're leaving. No argument." The corporal's words were flat and toneless. "Get your things, and get in the wagon. I want a good bit of distance covered by the time the sun comes up."

Caldan left Lavas standing over the body and joined Elpidia and Amerdan in collecting their gear. Elpidia muttered under her breath and kept glaring at him, though he didn't know how this was his fault.

Amerdan watched them both while they worked; as usual, he didn't have much to pack; every night all he did was take off his belt with pouches and knives before he slept.

Searching through his gear, Caldan drew out one of his few remaining pieces of paper and a pen and ink, using his thigh as a makeshift surface to enable him to draw properly. Soon he had covered the paper with hurriedly drawn symbols. Nothing intricate, but he wasn't aiming for anything complex. After blowing on the ink to ensure it was dry, he folded the paper into quarters, leaving the most prominent symbol visible. He walked over to a tree and selected a thin branch. He used his knife to carve a notch in the bark and slipped the folded paper into it. With any luck, he'd be able to catch a glimpse of their assailant and gain insight into who they were dealing with.

He turned to find Amerdan behind him.

"What will that do?"

"Maybe I should have done something earlier . . . but it's a variation of an attribute I used in my metal automaton. I'll be able to see through it, for a limited time. The paper won't last long."

"Interesting. You'll have to tell me more about sorcery."

Caldan nodded. "One day, when we have more time."

The shopkeeper returned his nod and walked toward the wagon. The soldiers had stowed their gear and were helping Elpidia and Miranda inside. Amerdan lifted himself easily into the wagon, and Caldan joined him.

Again they left their fire blazing and fled into the night. Inside the wagon, Caldan ignored Bells, who sniggered at him as he climbed in.

Opening his well, he split out a string and linked to his paper crafting in the tree, closing his eyes as he prepared to keep watch.

He wriggled his battered wristband onto his left arm and thrust a hand in his pocket, closing his fingers around Bells's shield crafting. He knew his own crafting wouldn't last long if pressed, but any extra shielding might prove the difference if it came down to an all-out fight.

CHAPTER 7

You look worried, Vasile. Anything troubling you?"

"Eh? No, nothing. I mean . . . the invasion, of course, and everything that's happened." Vasile's reply sounded forced to his own ears, but Aidan only smiled before looking away.

Barely past dawn, the morning breeze had strengthened and their ship had turned, the side they were on now facing the shore. Seagulls circled overhead, mistaking the ship for a fishing vessel, and their raucous cries grated on his ears.

Vasile returned to pissing over the side of the ship, a little put off by Aidan's comment and the fact he had chosen to stand right next to Vasile while he too pissed over the side. And that was probably his intent, he realized. He hurriedly tucked his shirt in and did up his trousers before Aidan could finish himself. He turned and almost ran into Chalayan.

"Excuse me," he muttered, moving to push past the sorcerer, who blocked his path.

An expressionless Anshul appeared behind Chalayan, making escape impossible.

Vasile frowned at Chalayan. "What are you playing at?"

The sorcerer gripped his shoulder and regarded him with distaste. "I'm not going to pay you," he said, enunciating each word slowly and deliberately. "Five hundred and twelve silver ducats. I've killed men for less."

Vasile swallowed, acutely aware of Aidan behind him and the two men blocking his path. He doubted Aidan was a bloodthirsty killer, but these two he wasn't so sure of. And Chalayan had spoken the truth about killing someone for less.

"I told you the debt didn't matter. I don't expect payment," he said, hoping to head off any argument.

"This isn't about ducats," Aidan said.

Vasile turned to face him and saw he was leaning against the gunwale, arms crossed over his chest. He looked back to see Chalayan and cel Rau back away before stopping, leaving a few paces between them. He shook his head.

"Then what is it about?" he asked.

Aidan scratched his head. "I thought we should have a talk, without anyone else around to interfere."

"Who's been interfering? Mazoet hasn't been any trouble, has he?"

"No. Not at all. In fact, we've been made welcome—extremely welcome—by these supposed merchants. But I find myself wondering why."

"Why what?" Vasile wiped his sweating brow. Since he'd stopped drinking he'd started to sweat copiously, and his head always seemed to ache.

"Merchants are, by definition, only interested in ducats. Whatever they say, you know all they want is wealth. It's like a . . . a law. There are no exceptions. Except for these merchants."

Vasile swallowed and managed to shrug. "Merchants with a social conscience?" he suggested. "Is that so hard to believe?"

"Quite frankly, yes. Especially when said merchants have sorcerous powers, and obviously know more than they let on. An old man who speaks in circles. And Mazoet, who rescued us from certain death and follows us around as if we need someone to mind us. Then there's you . . ."

"Me!" said Vasile. "I assure you—"

"What?" Aidan said. "What do you assure me of? You are not one of them, that much is obvious. But you're with them, there's no doubt." He looked away, then back again. "What are they up to?"

"What do you mean?"

"They are not merchants, not really. Oh, maybe they go about as if they are, but it's an act. It has to be. The way Gazija talks, orders the others around, he's like a commander, not just the head of a large trading house. There's a difference. They revere him."

He spread his hands. "Really, I wouldn't know. I only just met them myself."

"And yet they want you to convince us of something."

"Yes," Vasile said. "But I'm actually not certain of what myself, other than they want you to join them. In what endeavor, I couldn't say."

"Please," Chayalan snorted.

"Honest! I agree with you, though," he said to Aidan, "that something's not right with Gazija and his people. It's only a feeling, and one I've nothing to back up, except my experience and the way they avoid certain questions and subjects. And yet, all that aside, I *do* trust them. Whatever they are doing, and I don't know what that is, it needs to be done. As I proved last night, they cannot mislead me in any way. So even if you aren't ready to trust them, trust *me*."

Aidan nodded, as if Vasile's speech made a certain kind of sense to him.

Vasile nodded in turn to all three, then pushed his way between Chalayan and cel Rau.

VASILE SAT ALONE. On the floor, with his back against a wooden wall, cross-legged, with a green glass bottle of strong spirits in front of him, just out of reach. The air was cool. A single candle sat on a shelf, causing shadows to flicker around him. It was late. Most of the crew had been asleep for hours.

His cabin was sparse. He hadn't brought any possessions with him. Nothing tied him to his house anymore. That life, one of many he had lived, was dead to him now. He didn't need his talent to know the truth of that. There was no going back. He had a chance to turn his life around and become involved in something useful. But that would mean returning to his old self, and that hadn't worked out well at all. It was a difficult decision.

He rubbed his arms and rocked back and forth. One of his fingers bled where he had chewed the nail down to the quick. He could feel the ship moving, back and forth, back and forth; hear the creaks and groans of wood.

Vasile wiped the blood from his finger on the floor and rubbed at the streaks with his sleeve with an exclamation of disgust, muttering. He looked at the stain on his shirt for long moments and then reached for the full bottle he had stolen from Gazija's cabin earlier in the day, when the old man was on deck. It was good stock, far better than he had seen in years.

In the candlelight, the bottle looked almost mystical, lit by an inner glow. With a twist, he broke the seal and popped the cork out.

"Ahh . . ." The scent of the liquor reached him, pungent, enticing, beckoning.

He tipped the bottle and poured a thin stream of golden liquid onto his chewed and bleeding finger, gritting his teeth as it burned and stung, but he continued to pour the liquor slowly, bearing the pain until the bottle was empty and a puddle spread across the floor in front of him.

His finger ached like it had been slammed in a door, throbbing in time with his heartbeat. He rolled the bottle toward the wall, where it hit and stopped.

"LOOK," VASILE SAID. "I don't pretend to know them or their goals, but I do know that those they're fighting—those who attacked you, let me remind you—are bad people. You've seen for yourself what they are capable of." He was in yet another discussion with Aidan and his men.

"So they saved us," Chalayan said. "It wouldn't be the first time someone's pretended to be on our side to gain our trust before stabbing us in the back." He looked to his companions.

Both cel Rau and Aidan remained quiet.

"They're only interested in the sorcerers, the ones who attacked you. Those are their enemies." Vasile shrugged helplessly.

"And their enemies are ours?" asked Aidan. "Just because they're sorcerers."

"They are because I'm telling you they are. That's why I'm here, so you know I'm telling the truth."

"But we don't, do we?"

"Don't what?"

"Don't know if you're telling the truth." Aidan raised a hand to forestall Vasile's protest. "Oh, you can tell if someone's lying, I'll give you that. But how do we know *you're* not lying?"

He had to admit they had a good point, and all he could say was "What would I have to gain?"

"What indeed? If we knew you better, maybe we could trust you, but trust is in short supply these days."

"Isn't it just," muttered Chalayan.

"So," continued Aidan, shooting the sorcerer a dark look, "I am sure you will understand if we don't take your words on faith." His face creased in distaste. "These are hard times, harder than I'd realized until recently."

Vasile frowned unhappily. "Gazija and his people saved you from certain death—"

"Not certain," interrupted Chalayan. "We don't know what—"

Aidan's upheld hand stopped him. He turned to Vasile. "Agreed. They saved us."

Vasile continued. "Then brought you here, where they have been nothing but kind to you."

"True," conceded Aidan. "But I dislike secrets; they'll kill you in the end." His eyes bore into Vasile's.

Vasile swallowed uneasily, and they stared at each other for a moment. "You know Gazija is against these sorcerers and what they did in the . . . town you stumbled upon," Vasile said slowly, "and his people are bending their not inconsiderable might toward destroying them."

"So they say."

"So they have *demonstrated*."

Aidan conceded the point with a wave of his hand, motioning for Vasile to continue.

"Then why not join them in this task? They will provide whatever supplies you require. If you at any time doubt their intentions, then you are free to leave."

Looking around the room, Aidan hesitated. "Just like that?"

"Just like that. They need your men. And you," he added. "But you aren't prisoners." *I think.*

There was a long silence.

Aidan gazed at Vasile with an incredulous expression on his face. "I hardly think Gazija needs assistance from me."

"I can't say what he needs you for. Just that whatever is happening right now, Gazija believes you can help him stop it."

"I appreciate the honesty," Aidan said quietly. "But surely Gazija has enough resources to accomplish his aims, whatever they are."

"Clearly not. Otherwise, why would I be here? Why would they have me ask you this?"

"To prevent us from leaving," Chalayan said.

"But I just said you aren't prisoners!"

"Then we are free to go." Aidan stood and motioned for the others to join him.

Chalayan and cel Rau came to their feet and headed for the door.

"So that's it? You're leaving?"

Aidan shrugged. "I have not heard anything to persuade me, so we are leaving the first chance we have to get off this ship."

Vasile considered the situation for a moment and came to a decision. "Take me with you."

"Ah . . . now we are getting somewhere."

CHAPTER 8

Caldan, Elpidia, Miranda, and Amerdan sat in the wagon, Breyton's cold corpse between them. The still-shackled Bells was always smiling at one of them, even Miranda.

Unnerving, thought Caldan.

They rocked back and forth as the wagon moved along the road, steadily heading west. At this time of night, the road was empty. Travelers were most likely wrapped up warm by their fires or tucked into beds at inns along the way.

Anywhere but riding with a dead body and a chained psychopath.

Caldan scratched his chin. Coarse stubble had grown since he'd left Anasoma, and it had begun to itch. The monks were clean-shaven, and he had always followed their example. He wasn't used to not shaving for more than a couple of days, and it was starting to irritate him.

He had suspended one of his sorcerous globes from the wooden frame supporting the canvas covering, making sure it filled the space inside with only enough light to chase away most of the shadows, not so much that it might reveal their position. He wanted to give his companions a sense of comfort—though the corpse wrapped in a blanket on the floor did little to chase away their anxiety.

As he had done every few minutes since they fled, Caldan closed his eyes and accessed his well, following his string to the crafting he had left behind in the tree, and again his vision lurched, making him a bit dizzy.

In front of him, their abandoned campsite was lit by the dying fire. A thin trail of smoke rose into the night. He concentrated and held the link in his mind as long as he could, studying the image for anything out of place. Nothing. Again.

Back in the wagon, his head began to ache, and he rubbed his temples. The farther away they were, the harder it was for him to maintain the link, and the more distorted the vision became.

He growled and was preparing to cut his link when a movement caught his attention. There, just outside the glow from the fire. A shadow moved around the campsite, deliberate and constant, unlike the flickering shadows from the firelight.

Caldan watched, willing himself to ignore the building pain in his head as he struggled to hold on to his link. The shadow disappeared among the rest. He held his breath. There was something . . . not quite right . . . His vision wavered and became blurrier than before. No, only a patch did, moving around the campsite. It had to be whoever was following them, concealed with sorcery of their own.

He gasped as tiny white sparks twinkled around the blur, then disappeared, revealing a man wearing faded brown trousers and a creased shirt. Whatever shield the man had been linked to had also effectively camouflaged him until he had revealed himself. Even in full view, and by the light of the fire, he had been hard to see.

The man slowly circled the camp, examining scuffs on the ground where their gear had been and where the soldiers had gathered. Then he went over to where the wagon had stood. Both his wrists bore silver metal wristbands, and around his neck hung a medallion in the shape of a horned beast with emeralds for eyes.

Caldan lowered his head to his hands and pressed hard against his temples. The pain had grown so he could barely contain it. He knew he had to cut his link soon, and then his crafting would be worthless. The man would have moved on by the time he could reestablish contact.

But it was too much.

Taking a deep breath, he ruptured the anchor, and the forces from his well consumed his makeshift crafting. With a sickening wrench, his balance tilted as the pain subsided. He clutched at his seat for support.

Moments passed as he fought to prevent himself from throwing up.

Close by, he heard Bells laugh. "And what did that achieve?" she asked.

He wiped the back of his hand across his mouth, then rubbed his eyes; they ached as well. "I don't know," he answered. With a start, he sensed she was holding her well open, the better to sense what he was doing.

"See something you didn't like?" Bells said.

Caldan looked up, the sudden movement causing his nausea to return. He swallowed and breathed heavily through his nose, quashing the impulse to vomit. Elpidia and Amerdan were watching both him and Bells, Amerdan with his usual disinterest, Elpidia looking frightened. He held up a hand to them.

"Don't worry. I just wanted to catch a glimpse of who's been following us."

"Really?" Bells asked. "Then tell me, my apprentice, who's following us?"

"I'm not your apprentice," Caldan growled.

"Then you don't want to learn how to heal Miranda?"

"Of course I do . . ."

"Then you're my apprentice, technically." Bells smirked. "And you can't unlearn something, which makes you one of us."

"If thinking so helps you pass the time while in chains, so be it," Caldan said. Bells actually laughed at that.

"Who is this man following us?" Elpidia asked.

With a shrug and a tinkling of chains, Bells replied, "How

would I know? My father, come to rescue me?" She laughed. "No such luck, I fear. He's probably too busy at the moment with the invasion."

"Your father is part of the invasion?" Amerdan asked. "What does he do? I mean, is a sorcerer, like you?" Caldan was as surprised by his eagerness as he was by the fact Bells talked at all.

"Of course he is, without peer. It's where I get my talent."

Something clicked into place for Caldan. "Without peer? Are you saying . . . ?"

Bells said nothing, but her smile was a strange one.

"The God-Emperor is your father." It wasn't a question.

"How astute of you. Possibly," she admitted. "Or a few times removed. No one knows for sure. There are many of us, his sons and daughters, grandsons and granddaughters. Which is why he won't personally be coming to rescue me." She made a mock sad face.

"You're lying."

"That he won't come rescue me?"

"That he's your father."

"Believe what you want," she said with an indifferent tone, "but why would I lie? His blood flows strongly in me, and I'm expected to survive without assistance. It's the way it is; the strong survive, while the weak perish."

"So this man has nothing to do with you? That I *don't* believe. I'll ask again: Who is he?"

"Poor little Protector, always fumbling for answers. When I begin your education, you won't lack for answers . . . or power."

He heard a sharp intake of breath from Elpidia and shook his head at her. "Don't listen to her." He turned back to Bells. "Right now I want answers, and I mean to get them. Who is the man following us?"

"What does he look like?"

"I . . . I don't know. He was nondescript, almost deliberately so. But he was a sorcerer, that much I know. His shield concealed him somehow. Everything but . . ."

"What?"

"For a moment, I glimpsed something around his neck. A medallion like a horned beast."

For a long moment Bells was silent. Finally she whistled. "I'm impressed, Caldan. I'm surprised you were able to penetrate his shield at all."

"So you *do* know who it is."

"I had my suspicions, and you confirmed them."

"So," Elpidia asked. "Who is it?"

"My brother—the man who is going to kill you all." She looked at each of them in turn, and even Amerdan seemed to flinch at the intensity of her gaze.

"Does he have a name?" Caldan asked.

Bells shrugged. "Of course he does, but it doesn't matter. All that matters is that he is coming, and that he can kill. That he *will* kill. The God-Emperor would normally not care if I lived or died, so the fact that they sent someone after me means he's taken a personal interest. You do not want the God-Emperor's attention on you."

The threat hung in the air, and though Caldan discerned a touch of melodrama, he couldn't discount the fear in Bells's voice.

But if she's so afraid of the man, then that's exactly why we have to do what we can to oppose him.

"You know," Bells said, "I can help you a lot more if I'm free."

"Nice try. If Miranda's not healed, then I'm not going to let you go. Remember that. You know what I can do, and you must realize there's a good chance whoever they sent won't be able to free you. We will either ward him off or defeat him. He has to act before we reach our destination, which means we know when he is coming, at least to a degree. Now I have your shield crafting, and you know better than I what it can withstand. I'm willing to wager I can use it to delay him until we reach the city and it's too late. Too late for you, since he won't be able to rescue you from hundreds of the emperor's soldiers stationed there."

"Then it's too late for you as well. Because if you're so focused on him, I won't be able to show you how to heal your precious Miranda."

"She has a point," chimed in Amerdan. "Once we reach the city, they will take her out of our hands, and who knows what will happen to her?"

"Exactly," Bells said.

"There you go. Caldan, you need to think of Miranda's welfare."

"That's all I think about," Caldan muttered.

Elpidia stood and glared at Amerdan. "Why are you so interested in letting her go? She said she'd kill us all!"

"Hush, please." Caldan held his hands out and lowered them, indicating to Elpidia to calm down. "This is what she wants: us arguing instead of planning, so please . . . let's discuss this peacefully."

With a glare at Amerdan and Bells, Elpidia sat back down and folded her arms across her chest. "What should we do, then?" she asked.

"First I need to tell the Quivers what I saw. You two stay with Bells."

Caldan left them and moved to the soldier driving the wagon. The others were riding alongside. They didn't look happy when they learned they were being followed by a sorcerer. He advised them to keep extra alert and to fetch him if they saw anything—anything at all—out of the ordinary. Lavas told him to shove his obvious advice into an uncomfortable part of his body.

Back with Elpidia and Amerdan, Caldan felt the responsibility weighing him down. The Quivers would look to him to combat any sorcery; Elpidia and Amerdan were relying on him, and Miranda and Bells were his burdens as well. He needed to free himself from as many distractions as possible, or something would give.

He'd start with one of the more pressing ones.

"At first, I thought we could hand Bells over when we reached the city, but now I'm not so sure."

Amerdan nodded at his words, and Bells smiled. He ignored them both. Elpidia was shaking her head.

"We don't have much time left," Caldan said. "And we need to get rid of the soldiers somehow, preferably in a way that won't have them chasing after us as well."

"If I may?" Amerdan said, and he prodded the corpse between

them with a booted toe. "With what this person following us can do, he might solve our problem for us."

The shopkeeper's words hung in the air. Caldan wasn't sure he had heard correctly, but a glance at Elpidia, who had a look of horror on her face, made him realize he had.

"We can't leave them to be killed or use them as a distraction," he said firmly.

Amerdan gave a quiet laugh. "Oh no, I wasn't suggesting that."

Caldan frowned, sure that was exactly what he had suggested. He and Elpidia locked eyes, and she swallowed and looked away.

"I just want somewhere I can work without all of this," she muttered.

"As I was saying," continued Amerdan, "they are already a distraction. The man following us has to even the odds, does he not? Which was why he killed this poor man here and is likely to go after the others. They're obviously common soldiers, not like us. We're the ones escorting Bells, and if he's been watching, he has to know this. We are the unknowns, and he has to be careful with us. After all, he knows we captured Bells and . . . defeated Keys. Surely he wouldn't go up against us without knowing our capabilities."

The shopkeeper's words made sense to Caldan. "But I'm the only sorcerer," he said.

Amerdan pointed a finger at him. "You are, as is she." He also indicated Bells, then turned his finger on Elpidia. "But how is he to know what our talents are? For all he knows, he faces three sorcerers."

"If he got close enough, he could tell," Caldan said. "He could sense who has a well, if he has that talent."

"There are different talents?" asked Amerdan. "Are all sorcerers different, then?"

"Not exactly. We can all do certain things, but there are distinct talents; some people are more adept at some things than others. I can sense a well in other people, and so can Bells." She inclined her head, acknowledging his words. "But only a few sorcerers can; I would guess one in ten."

"One in thirteen," corrected Bells, to his surprise. "Don't look so astonished. Talents have been extensively studied and cataloged. You would have studied them as a journeyman." She shrugged. "Or so I would assume. Your sorcerers . . . well, let's just say they're not as good as they think."

"Be that as it may, he might find out he's facing only one sorcerer if he can get close enough to sense it and has the talent. And from what I saw, I think he could get close without us knowing."

"One in thirteen," said Amerdan. "I prefer to have greater odds in my favor. I can look after myself, but Elpidia and Miranda here won't stand a chance."

Bells scoffed at the shopkeeper. "Against a sorcerer, you wouldn't last long."

"Maybe," said Amerdan quietly. "Maybe not."

"Knives won't help you."

Amerdan only shrugged.

"We need a plan," Caldan said. He tried to pace, but the lurching wagon and prostrate corpse interfered, and he gave up. He looked at Bells. "What can this man do? How did he kill Breyton here?"

"How should I know? I don't know who he is."

"You just said you did!"

"I said he was my brother. Do you know how many children the God-Emperor has?"

"No, but it's more than that. You recognized him when I told you about the horned beast medallion."

"Maybe so. But I'll ask for the hundredth time: Why should I help you?"

"Because he might kill us, and you want to savor that yourself."

Silence followed Caldan's words. Amerdan nodded, while Elpidia covered her mouth with her hand in shock.

Bells eyed him thoughtfully. "I'll think about it," she said.

"Good. I—"

A strange noise, like a swarm of bees, filled the air, but only for an instant. There was a strangled scream followed by a thump outside the wagon, and shouts of alarm from the soldiers.

Caldan grabbed his sword and leaped over Breyton's corpse,

jumping through the canvas flaps covering the back of the wagon. He half fell, half dropped to the ground, all the while opening his well and linking to Bells's shield crafting. As the haze enveloped him, he flung out his senses in an attempt to pinpoint the Indryallan sorcerer's position. There was something to their left, though it was more of an absence than a presence.

Either way, it shouldn't be here, he thought, focusing his attention in that direction.

He didn't see anything.

Beside him on the side of the road lay Boyas, covered in small cuts like Breyton had been. Blood seeped from the wounds as the man clawed at the ground, writhing in agony. A mewling sound escaped his lips, and he looked desperately at Caldan. Behind them, the wagon continued on for a few moments, then stopped.

Amerdan landed beside Caldan, knives in both hands, scanning the darkness. Caldan could hear Elpidia sobbing inside the wagon. "Please, I don't want to die . . . please."

Light flickered above them for an instant.

Caldan grabbed Amerdan and the wounded Boyas by the arm and extended his shield to cover them.

The light burst, and the shield rippled as it blocked a hundred tiny strikes. Violet sparkles clouded his vision as Bells's crafting hummed, to be swept away in moments, the shield easily dissipating the energy. Caldan frowned, puzzled by the small amount of sorcery involved.

"Get Boyas to Elpidia," he yelled at Amerdan, who was staring at his own multicolored hazy hand in surprise. "And tell the Quivers to keep going. I'll see if I can find this sorcerer."

The shopkeeper nodded, and Caldan drew the shield back into himself, leaving them exposed. "Hurry," he urged, as behind them the other two soldiers dismounted, booted feet thudding as they came to Boyas's aid. When they reached them, their eyes went wide at the sight of their bloody comrade.

Caldan grabbed Corporal Lavas by the arm. "Listen, you have to keep going. Get him into the back with Elpidia; she'll do all she can to save him, then go!"

"No." Lavas shook his head. "Whoever it is, they'll pay for this."

"He's beyond you. I'm sorry, but that's how it is; you'll be going to your death."

Cursing, Lavas glared at Caldan with fury. "Don't tell me what to do. I'll get this sorcerer, and you can't stop me."

You proud fool, Caldan thought, but he didn't have time to convince him he was throwing his life away.

Amerdan and Ettmo were carrying the wounded Boyas toward the wagon. Drops of blood spattered the road, leaving a dark trail in their wake.

"This way," Caldan told Lavas, and he sped off into the night in the direction he had sensed the absence, hoping the corporal would follow.

Once off the road, he focused on his well and crafting, drawing as much power as he could into the sorcerous shield. Lavas didn't look surprised, and Caldan guessed he had seen a lot in his time.

"We don't know where he is, and he's capable of killing swiftly. I have to maintain the shield."

Lavas nodded grimly. "Stay together, then. I assume you can shield me, if you have time?"

"Yes, with enough warning."

"Good, then let's get going." He made as if to move forward, when Caldan pulled him to a stop.

"This way," Caldan said, pointing to his left. If the sorcerer was a hunter intent on picking them off one by one, he would have moved from his previous position already. It seemed a likely bet: there was plenty of cover, and the trees were thicker here.

Together they moved carefully, sidling around rocks and trees, always keeping the trunks between them and the direction Caldan indicated. The wind blew through the dry leaves on the ground, creating a rustling sound that would serve to mask their footfalls. In the distance, the creaking of the retreating wagon reached their ears, hard iron tire on the wooden rim clattering along the paved road.

Caldan focused on his well and concentrated. He stood still, absorbed in his task.

"What are you doing?" asked the corporal.

Caldan took hold of his arm and drew him close, keeping his voice low. "I should be able to sense the sorcerer, his well."

"His what?"

"Never mind. Some of us can sense when other sorcerers are near, and it's one of my talents, but . . . there's nothing." He frowned and shook his head.

"Then let's get going. He could be getting away."

"No, I don't think so. This one will stay close. I hate to say it, but with two of your men out of action and us separated from the others, we may be where he wants us. But we have to find him, or he will whittle us down one by one."

Lavas grunted in agreement. "Fine. Find the damn sorcerer, then," he hissed.

"I can't sense anything, and I should be able to if he's opened his well."

"Then it isn't open, whatever it is."

"That makes no sense. If he wants to protect himself or attack us, then he has to open it. And he's camouflaging himself somehow. That has to use power."

Unless . . .

"By the ancestors!" exclaimed Caldan under his breath. He drew more power from his well to reinforce his shield. "Stay close to me."

Moving a few steps to their left, they crouched behind a tree. Caldan fumbled with his scabbard and drew the trinket sword. In daylight, the blade was white, a ribbon of moonlight; in darkness, however, it was almost invisible, as if drawing the night into itself.

Lavas used one hand to clutch at the bark of the tree and leaned himself around the trunk to peer carefully into the gloom. For a few moments, the only sounds were the wind and their breathing.

"Anything?" asked Caldan.

"No, nothing." Lavas cursed under his breath. "Do some sorcery or something."

Holding back a sigh, Caldan squeezed the hilt of the sword hard in frustration. "I can't see him. I don't know where he is."

"Well, you're the sorcerer."

Caldan glared at him, realizing he was right, and angry at himself for not knowing what to do.

He kept wanting to say *I'm just an apprentice*, but the fact was, that didn't matter at a time like this. Hell, he wasn't sure if mattered at all anymore. What mattered was that he was the only one in their group who could possibly do something about this Indryallan shadow, and it was up to him to figure it out . . .

He sniffed the air.

Then again.

"What are you doing?"

"Shush. Please," he added, giving Lavas's arm a reassuring squeeze.

There was a faint hint of lemons in the air, but Caldan couldn't tell how old or where it had come from. But it was *something*. A plan came to mind.

Reaching into his pocket, he drew out a sorcerous globe; it was dull, since it hadn't been activated. Gathering himself, he focused on the sorcery he wanted to do, the order in which to do it, going over the sequence in his mind until he thought he could execute it swiftly, minimizing the time his well was open.

With a flick of his wrist, he threw the globe about twenty paces away, the noise as it landed hardly noticeable over the background wind.

"We might need that," said Lavas. "And it's valuable."

"Not as valuable as our lives," replied Caldan. "I can always make more."

Once again, the corporal grunted in agreement.

"Close your eyes," Caldan said, "and don't make a sound, no matter what happens."

He closed his own and concentrated. Then he opened his well as fast as he could and linked to the globe.

Light erupted in the night, banishing the darkness. He opened his eyes and as he'd calculated, the long shadow cast by the tree they were crouched behind covered and concealed them. He peered around the tree.

Power surged to their left. Caldan closed his well; as he did, he sensed the power cut off. The sorcerer had closed his own well when he had seen it was only a sorcerous globe and not a true threat. Caldan frowned at what he had sensed. The sorcerer's well had been narrow and jagged, nowhere near the strength he had expected. With a well like that, the sorcerer wouldn't be able to draw much, and certainly couldn't split it into many strings. He surmised two or three at the most, even with the best training and practice. Unless he was concealing his true strength, like Simmon had . . .

By the ancestors, if he is, then we stand no chance.

Once more, Caldan found himself sweating as his skin grew hot. His fear and weariness washed away, leaving him calm and refreshed.

"Stay here," he commanded the corporal, who nodded hesitantly.

Drawing a breath, Caldan spun around the tree and opened his well, sprinting toward the sorcerous globe.

As he reached the crafting, he sensed one more power surge, this time to his right. The sorcerer had moved swiftly to another position while he had hesitated.

He threw himself forward onto the dirt and leaves and split two strings from his well. His hand closed around the sorcerous globe, blocking the light, and he linked to his wristband, shielding himself.

As the haze enveloped him, a sharp crack split the air, and for an instant, a buzzing filled his ears; then his shield exploded in sparkles, hit from a hundred different directions.

Though it was severely damaged, his shield still held, as he'd guessed it would. From what he had sensed of the well, he doubted the sorcerer could gather enough destructive force to penetrate his barrier. It was a risk, but it meant he didn't have to use as much of his own energy keeping Bells's shield up.

Somewhere in the trees, the power faltered, then winked out. He flung the globe in the direction of the sorcerer. Shadows danced in the night as it flew in an arc between the trees.

As it landed, Caldan squeezed his eyes shut and ruptured the anchor. Deafening thunder echoed, the noise slapping down on him. Light flashed through his closed lids.

Two screams sounded in the night. One from Lavas, who obviously hadn't kept his eyes shut, and another from the unknown sorcerer.

Caldan lurched to his feet, well still open. Fires dotted the space around a small crater in the ground, plant life ablaze from the energy unleashed.

A shadow flitted from tree to tree trailing smoke. It flashed briefly, then disappeared. He lifted his sword and rushed toward the location, covering the ground in an instant. Ahead of him stood a man in singed clothing, a look of surprise on his face. The sorcerer's well surged, and he rippled . . .

Then disappeared.

Caldan skidded to a stop, then ducked behind another tree. Sweat dripped from him. By the ancestors, he was burning up! His hands trembled, and with a will, he managed to calm them.

Again, a strange humming filled the air, and his shield strained under the impact of another multitude of strikes. This time it wavered; some sparkles grew bigger before being swept away, and many turned red. On his wrist, which still smarted from the previous burns, the crafting grew hot. He clenched his teeth in pain.

A laugh came from his left. Another hundred impacts sprinkled across him, and he felt his crafting begin to fracture under the immense strain. He broke the link to it and shook it off his wrist, burning the fingers on his right hand as they clawed at it.

Sure the sorcerer couldn't see him in the dark, he linked to Bells's shield crafting, and once again a haze enveloped him. But this time, he throttled back on his well, letting only a trickle through. At such a low intensity, the shield shone blue instead of its usual multicolored haze. Taking a breath, he dropped his spent wristband, hesitated, then stepped out from behind the tree, raising his hands in surrender.

"Oh, that's amusing," the sorcerer said, laughing lightly. "Either your crafting was terrible, or your well is inferior to mine."

Feigning chagrin, Caldan shrugged, still feeding the trickle to the shield but ready to unleash the full force of his well. He couldn't see the sorcerer, who must have been staying hidden until he was sure Caldan was disarmed or dead.

To his surprise, the air in front of him shimmered, and the sorcerer appeared, then his own shield covered his skin. It was blue, too, not multicolored. He looked over Caldan's shoulder to where Lavas approached, sword leveled.

Caldan held his arm out to stop the corporal. "Don't," he said. "You wouldn't get far."

Lavas struggled against Caldan's arm for a few moments, then growled in frustration. "I'll kill him."

"Later," Caldan said, and the sorcerer laughed again.

"Not likely. Your shield's exhausted, and judging by your unfocused attack—destroying a globe, no less—you're no match for me."

Caldan looked down at his right hand holding the sword. His fingers hurt from clutching the hilt hard. "So you say."

"Your shield almost failed a few moments ago, so yes . . . I say." He looked at Lavas. "I'm afraid you'll have to die. It's nothing personal."

Caldan sensed the sorcerer begin drawing more power from his well, and he grabbed the corporal's arm, pushing his shield around him as he flinched. Another flurry of sparkles erupted from the shield and drained away in moments.

With a grin, Caldan shook his head at the sorcerer's puzzled frown and raised his sword, stepping in front of the corporal. "I can sense your well, and it's not very strong. And since you made an effort to open it only when absolutely necessary, I'd say you know it, too. Can you sense mine?"

"No," replied the sorcerer. "And mine should have been enough to get through your shield this time." He hesitated, sensing something amiss. "Ah, well played. You have a second crafting."

Caldan nodded, seeing no reason to keep up his ruse. "Which means you won't be able to get to us."

"But the others won't be so lucky."

Dirt from the ground was flung up into the air as the sorcerer opened his well. Dust surrounded them, clouding Caldan's vision.

"Bloody hedge-pig!" cursed the corporal. "He's getting away!"

Caldan dug into his well and allowed the shield to regain its full intensity. He tugged Lavas toward the road. "This way!" he yelled.

They rushed through the obscuring cloud, stumbling over rocks and hummocks of grass and bouncing off trees.

Luckily, the shield protected them from the dust. They ran on, keen to reach the wagon before the sorcerer did.

As he emerged from the dust cloud, Caldan stumbled forward and lost his grip on Lavas. The now-familiar buzzing erupted from behind him, and the corporal screeched in agony. Caldan heard him drop to the ground and moan. He stopped for a moment and growled in frustration, but the choice before him was no choice at all.

He broke into a run toward the road and the wagon.

And ran full pelt into an invisible force between two trees, which knocked him on his back, dazing him. He felt numb, tried to stand. His sword slipped from deadened fingers, and his vision swam. His chest was aching from the collision, stomach churning. He lay there, stunned, dull witted.

Sparks cascaded around him as his shield absorbed another hundred impacts. He hadn't even felt the sorcery go off, so disoriented was he. He struggled for breath, clutching at the ground. There was a roaring in his ears, and his skin was soaked with sweat.

He was aware of someone screaming in the distance: a woman's voice—Elpidia, perhaps? Shouting reached him over the buzzing in his ears.

"—Don't!" the voice in the distance yelled, followed by a deeper reply, a man's voice.

"—safe . . . have to . . ."

Caldan heard Elpidia scream, a hopeless forlorn wail, then a sharp crack and hum.

"By the ancestors," Caldan heard himself say, and he grabbed the sword, dragging himself to his knees, then to his feet. He started running toward the wagon, thoughts groggy, but managing to retain the link to his shield.

Ahead of him, the wagon was lit by one of his sorcerous globes, held up by Elpidia as she leaned out the back. It was no longer moving along the road, and there was no sign of the soldier who had been driving the horses, or Amerdan.

The sorcerer stood against a tree, wild eyes scanning his surroundings. Blood dribbled from cuts all over his clothes, leaking onto the ground. A trail of dark drops led from him to the wagon and around the vehicle; splashes spread across the canvas covering. One of his hands pressed against his wounds, while the other clutched at a medallion around his neck. Seeing Caldan staggering toward them, a look of panic crossed his face.

He blurred, then disappeared. Caldan cursed and continued his unsteady progress, aware he had no idea where the sorcerer was now.

Reaching the wagon, he grabbed at the side to steady himself. Elpidia looked down at him, gray hair wild, eyes red-rimmed and scared. Tear trails streaked her cheeks.

"He's here!" she screamed at him. "Somewhere! Do something!"

"Where's Miranda?" Caldan shouted. "Is she hurt?"

"No! She's in here with me. Find that sorcerer!"

Scuffling footsteps sounded close to him. He turned . . . and looked into Amerdan's eyes. They were flat, calm, unruffled. A grin flashed across Amerdan's face as he held a finger to Caldan's mouth.

"Shhh," he whispered, moving his eyes to indicate the trees around them. "Listen."

Elpidia disappeared into the wagon. Caldan could hear her sobbing and muttering under her breath.

"Listen," repeated Amerdan. He held one of his knives, blood coating the blade.

Caldan turned his attention away from the wagon and to his surroundings, shaking his head to clear it of the last of the fogginess.

Moans came from where he had first encountered the sorcerer—the corporal, most likely. Amerdan pointed in that direction.

"The old soldier, wounded, dying. Ignore him." He moved his hand to point to their left. Caldan could hear someone scrabbling in the dirt, groaning in pain. "The other soldier, also dying." The hand moved to point inside the wagon. "Elpidia, Miranda, and Bells: ignore them." Again the hand moved to point into the darkness. This time he spread his fingers and moved his hand back and forth. "What's left?"

Caldan strained his ears, which were still ringing. "Wind," he said. "Leaves, grass."

"Good . . . and?"

"Nothing . . . I . . ."

"There is. Listen."

Again, Caldan strained to hear as the ringing subsided, slowing his breathing despite his fears. Over the other sounds, he struggled to discern what Amerdan was trying to reveal to him.

More wind . . . the soft rustle of the grasses and leaves in the trees . . . a drip . . .

"There," Amerdan said softly. "Drip, drip. It's him. His blood."

Another drip, the sound like water hitting a leaf. Caldan could hear the drops clearly and wondered how. Was this part of his special abilities? And how could Amerdan hear them the same as him? It didn't make sense.

Caldan waited. Drip. This time, farther to their right, a drop hitting a patch of dry earth.

He felt Amerdan's hot breath on his ear.

"Can you hear him? I cut him, just like he did the others. Now . . . he drips like they did; can't reveal himself to stop it." Another drop hit a leaf, again to their right. The shopkeeper chuckled under his breath. "I hear you," he whispered to the night.

Swallowing, Caldan opened his well and spread his senses out to the right. It was faint, so faint, but it was there. The sorcerer, close. Very close. What would he do?

Ever so slowly, Caldan lifted his right hand up; the sword came between him and the invisible sorcerer. He didn't know what else to do; he had no sorcerous globes left, nor any basic craftings he could use as weapons by rupturing them with sorcery. The truth was, he was out of ideas and options, and all that was left was a physical fight.

The thing was, though, that it was no longer his fight.

One moment, Amerdan was beside him, then he was gone, a blur. The shopkeeper moved to his left, made a sudden jagged turn to his right toward where Caldan thought the sorcerer was. Never had he seen someone move so fast, except for himself . . . when gripped by his uncontrollable abilities.

Mouth agape, Caldan watched as Amerdan's left hand flashed out. His knife blade disappeared to the hilt. He sprang up and twisted his body, right hand plunging down, and his second knife penetrated flesh.

As a fierce grin stretched across his face, he landed lightly, and the air in front of him blurred.

The sorcerer appeared, eyes wide with shock. He was clutching at the knife in his side with one hand, scrabbling at the blade protruding from his neck with the other.

With a gurgle, he collapsed to the ground, twitched a few times, and then was still. Blood seeped from the two knife wounds, and there were numerous long slashes across his torso, arms, and legs. Dull gray eyes stared at the flickering stars.

Caldan walked unsteadily to the body. Amerdan stood there, unmoving, watching him. Caldan knelt over the sorcerer, who appeared unremarkable, except for the crafted items Caldan could sense through his well. There were a few amulets, two rings, and his metal armbands were dross, ill-crafted and flawed. Nothing else. No weapons at all; no belongings. Nothing, as if the man were moments from home, rather than having spent the last few days hunting them.

"You all right?" he asked Amerdan, voice shaking.

"Of course." He gestured toward the corpse. "He thought he was a hunter, but . . . he wasn't. Not really."

Caldan nodded slowly, then stood, wiping sweaty hands on his trousers.

Amerdan's eyes remained on him.

Caldan cleared his throat. "You move fast," he managed lamely.

With a nod, Amerdan replied. "Sometimes. When I want to. I saw you do it once, right after we left Anasoma, when you killed the soldiers."

Caldan noticed he never said they "fled" or "escaped"; it was always "left" or "departed." He nodded back, not daring to give voice to the realization that hit him. Amerdan said he could move fast when he wanted to. He had a way to control his abilities that Caldan lacked.

It was a shock that Amerdan had similar abilities to his at all.

"I can't control it," Caldan admitted. "I never know when it's going to happen. Usually it brings trouble."

"We are more alike than you realize. I could . . . teach you. In return, you can teach me about sorcery."

It was tempting. But it also raised some serious questions, namely: Why was he hiding as a shopkeeper? Caldan was eager to learn what Amerdan clearly knew, but he still wasn't sure if the man could be trusted.

All the soldiers—dead. Just like he wanted, Caldan thought. *What's that mean?* Amerdan was watching him, offering no answers to Caldan's doubts, so he looked toward the wagon. "Come on," Caldan said, "let's see if everyone's all right."

CHAPTER 9

Mule-headed, dankish pignut, goatf—"

"I take it something's awry?" interrupted Avigdor.

Felice drew a brass telescopic cylinder away from her eye, then squeezed her eyes to adjust her vision. She handed him the lens and brought a perfumed kerchief to her nose.

"He's not cut out for this," she remarked. None of them were.

Avigdor placed one end of the cylinder to his eye and scanned the street below for Izak. "We knew that in the beginning; that's why he doesn't know everything."

She was perched atop the roof of a building that gave them a view of the main street below. Clambering up on dirty, and sometimes loose, tiles had been treacherous, but once there, they had found a position of relative safety where two roofs met. Even with his bulk, Avigdor managed to scramble along behind her, showing a relative spryness, though he always declined to join Felice in her thrice-weekly weapons training sessions and workouts. She believed in being prepared for any circumstance, while he relied on his wits to carry a situation.

Despite the morning sun beating down, their proximity to the docks ensured a cold breeze blew over her, making the heat somewhat tolerable. Though the characteristic stench of Dockside was altogether unpleasant.

Below them, the street bustled with the morning's business and goings-on, which had almost approached normalcy over the last few days. It was strange the way the populace had reacted to the invaders, from the initial fear and anger to resignation, and now to . . . what? Habitual routine? The only change for many of the people was the invaders' patrols in the streets, replacing the Harbor Watch and emperor's Quivers. One master replacing another, with the servants untroubled.

The Indryallans had organized efficient work gangs using the emperor's prisoners and indentured laborers, actually paying them for their effort. The gangs made short work of cleaning up the damage caused during the fighting and burying the corpses of both sides. For days, the road up to the cemetery at Slag Hill had been busy with carts hauling bodies followed by teams spreading sand along the road to soak up any fluids.

Avigdor sniffed his runny nose, then gagged, eyes watering. "Urgh, it's like maggoty fish."

"Stop, you're making me hungry."

With a snort of laughter, Avigdor resumed surveilling the street below, focusing on the frontage of the Five Oceans Mercantile Concern.

"So Izak's inside?" asked Avigdor.

"Yes, though he was followed. Probably all the way from his house, and maybe all night." Felice grunted. "Rebecci Walraffen knows her business."

At her request, Izak had arranged to "accidentally" bump into one of the head traders of the Five Oceans Mercantile Concern at a social gathering. He'd delivered the letter Felice had written, a carefully worded missive to pique their interest—hinting at things they thought no one else would know. Izak was now on his way to pick up their response.

"That's what worries me. Izak took some precautions, and he still had no idea he was being followed. A simple merchant company shouldn't be this adept at subterfuge."

"Of course they should! It's how I would run my business, if I had one."

"If you had one, I'd buy a stake."

She smiled at the compliment.

Avigdor scratched his head. "He's leaving," he said abruptly.

"Keep your eyes on him. Is he still being followed?"

After a few moments, Avigdor nodded. "Yes."

"Is he heading straight to the Cemetery?"

"Seems to be. He's walking north."

Felice cursed. She took a deep breath, fists balled at her sides.

"You shouldn't have told him about it. We have to stop him. We can't let him inadvertently reveal the location of our hideout."

"Agreed, but how?"

Felice turned her back to him and began scrabbling across the roof back the way they had come, thinking furiously.

FELICE LOWERED THE brass telescope and with deft movements collapsed it to a small cylinder and placed it into her belt pouch.

"He ran," she said with exasperation.

Avigdor chuckled. "No doubt he was startled. We were lucky enough to get that urchin to deliver your note, and what it said wasn't exactly subtle. Rebecci's people will probably keep track of him, in spite of his best efforts. Come on, let's get that letter to the brothel owner, and she can obtain the letter from Izak for us. One of our men can deliver it."

"I guess it can't be helped," said Felice, biting her lower lip. She had to give Izak some leeway, though she didn't have to like the way he reacted. This game had much higher stakes than even she was used to, and she found she was enjoying herself, despite the danger.

It was almost noon by the time they reached their headquarters inside the Cemetery. Felice had to keep stopping to give orders to various members of the resistance. Their potential alliance with Rebecci and her company was only one part of their plan, and everything seemed to need constant adjustments and decisions.

They left a group of men on one of the derelict ships after consulting with them and issuing new orders. Then Felice and Avigdor scampered over the hulks and across planks serving as makeshift bridges until they reached the wreck housing their quarters.

Rats and cockroaches scuttled out of their way over graying, worn timbers, an early warning they often joked about. So it was without fear that they unlocked the bright metal latch they had installed and entered Felice's rooms.

Avigdor stood to the side, while Felice fumbled around for a match and lit a lamp. The darkness receded to reveal a figure lounging in one of their armchairs. It was a woman, thin, with white hair in a tangled mess. She was dressed in plain attire—a loose black skirt along with a burgundy tunic—but the cut and fabric were clearly of some quality.

Both of them froze, Avigdor in the process of locking the door, and Felice, hands still on the lamp.

"I was starting to think you wouldn't be coming. This chair isn't the most comfortable, but I still almost fell asleep."

Rebecci, the representative of the Five Oceans Mercantile Concern, stifled a yawn, hand placed delicately over her open mouth. She sat up in the chair and looked at them expectantly.

Felice was the first to move. She put the lamp on a ledge with a faint clank and gave the woman a short bow.

"I see you've made yourself at home. Would you like a glass of wine?"

"That sounds like an excellent idea."

With a brief glance at Avigdor, Felice walked over to the drinks cabinet and drew out three glasses, which she set on the table. She took out a bottle and gazed at the label, then returned it and selected another. After examining the second bottle, she nodded to herself and held it out to Avigdor. "Would you be so kind as to open this?"

"And how am I supposed to do that? With my teeth?"

Felice took a corkscrew from the drawer and handed it to him.

Avigdor took them from her, hands trembling ever so slightly, and started scratching away the wax seal around the cork.

Felice dragged a chair from against the wall and placed it a few feet from Rebecci, along with a second chair for Avigdor, who by now was pouring the wine, a deep, almost black red with flecks of gold.

"Go ahead, please," said Felice, claiming a glass, watching as Rebecci and Avigdor lifted theirs.

She tilted her glass toward Rebecci with a nod and brought it to her lips; the wine's bouquet filled her nose with blackberry and cherries, and a hint of pepper.

"Crafted wine," remarked Rebecci. "Expensive. Even more so, I would imagine, after recent events."

"Something needed to make up for the decor." Felice punctuated her statement by waving a hand at the dilapidated furnishings. The only exception was a shiny brass clock, its mechanical ticking filling the silences.

"Indeed."

Felice studied the woman. Up close, she seemed thinner than Felice had been told. The hand clutching the stem of her glass was gaunt, almost emaciated, the skin nearly translucent. Her presence here after only a brief contact with Izak last night presaged a dangerous level of resources and information. Yet the fact that she was alone—and they weren't being hauled off in chains or dead already—indicated a certain sympathy to their cause. Or at least a willingness to find out more at some personal risk.

Felice took a sip of wine, letting the liquid linger in her mouth for a few moments, then swallowed. She decided to play dumb, though she knew it probably wouldn't work. One couldn't be too careful, though, especially as the make-do leader of the resistance.

"So, it's Miss Rebecci, I believe?"

Rebecci raised an eyebrow and sat back in her chair. She looked at Felice through half-lidded eyes. "Yes," she replied shortly.

"To what do we owe the pleasure?"

"The . . . pleasure?"

"Of your company."

Felice shifted, as if to get comfortable. She crossed one leg over the other, using the movement to drop her left hand close to her boot, where it brushed against the knife she had concealed there. Something about the trader was off. All indications so far pointed to potential support, but if she was able to find their location so quickly, then the invaders might be able to as well. Izak hadn't been caught, so it wasn't him, but someone must have talked. A traitor or carelessness; in the end, the result would be the same. She shoved the disagreeable thought to the back of her mind.

"You mustn't worry so," Rebecci said. "There's no need to fidget and keep your hand close to your knife. You have done well, so far, since the invasion. Assisted, of course, by whoever you had take out two of their leaders. Are they close by? I would like to thank them personally, if I may?"

"No. They are . . . otherwise occupied."

"Ah, a shame. I would so like to meet them. The echoes of that encounter were intriguing to many of us, to say the least."

Felice flicked a glance at Avigdor, who met her gaze and shrugged.

"What have we got to lose?" he asked.

"Everything," Felice replied quietly.

Rebecci tittered at their exchange, a strangely childish sound. "Come now," she said. "We should be associates, at the very least. Collaborators. Accomplices. Friends, even. That would be nice. I don't have many friends."

Felice frowned. "I'm sorry. But you will forgive me if I don't take your words at face value."

"Forgiven. Can I just say, though, that in my perpetually humble opinion, you would be wise to listen to what I have to say?."

"Really," drawled Felice, then stopped herself. "Go on."

"I will speak as plainly as I am able. If I were colluding with the Indryallans, you would be either captured or dead. If any of my people were, you would be captured or dead. If they find you, and they will, soon, you will be captured or dead. And once their God-Emperor arrives, you might wish for a quick death." She paused, wetting her lips with her wine. "My people are divided. Some have thrown their hands in with the Indryallans. Some, like me, think this is a very bad idea. I am here to help you."

Felice remained silent.

"They will find you as easily as I did, and when they do, I do not think you could stand up to them."

Sorcery, thought Felice. No one knew they were here, no one had followed them, and this woman knew far too much about what the Indryallans were capable of. This Rebecci was a sorcerer. There was no other explanation. "Then why haven't they?" she asked.

With a slight shrug, Rebecci replied, "You haven't done anything yet to draw attention to yourself."

"That will change."

"And that's why I'm here: to tell you that's a bad idea," Rebecci said. "You must get out of the city. As should we."

"What good can we do then? I'd rather stay."

"Think about it: right now, the Indryallans are just as trapped as everyone else in the city. But outside, there is freedom to gather the resources necessary to truly fight them. Isn't that why you need ducats? To get people out of the city and warn the emperor somehow?"

"How do you . . . ?" began Felice. "Never mind. So you plan to do what? Sneak us all out?"

"Exactly. As I said, Anasoma is lost. Our plan is to leave the city and regroup down the coast. We have done as much as we can here since the invasion. Outside, I'm certain others of our kind will join us."

"Your kind? I assume you mean from the Five Oceans Mercantile Concern?"

Rebecci smiled. "Of course."

"What can simple traders do?"

"You already know we're not simple traders," countered Rebecci. "Anyway, here is my proposal. Listen and decide."

She stood, revealing two weighty-looking leather sacks on her chair, which had been hidden under her skirt. She lifted one, depositing it on the table with a thump and a distinctly coinlike clink.

"Gold," she said.

The second sack joined the first, with a similar sound.

"Silver."

Rebecci placed her glass gently beside them. "The Indryallan God-Emperor will be here in three days' time. I enjoin you to gather as many loyal men and women as you can and leave the city. I know there are ways, and that is what the ducats are for. Travel down the coast for seven days, then wait. We will find you and explain more then."

She looked at Avigdor, then turned to regard Felice, eyes flinty. "If you do not, you will most likely die."

Felice looked at the heavy sacks filled with ducats, then back at Rebecci. "Death doesn't scare me."

"No? That's smart—you shouldn't be afraid of death. It's what will come before that should worry you."

Felice knew she couldn't face a sorcerer with just her knife. She didn't have much choice but to let her leave. *She keeps talking in circles,* she thought. *I just want one straight answer.*

"Before I agree to anything, I need to know what's going on. You owe us an explanation."

Rebecci shook her head, looking unconcerned at Felice's defiance. "In good time."

"What time is better than now? How am I to trust you if you won't give me more to go on?"

"That's what the ducats are for, Felicienne. What more trust do you need than gold? But I see you remain skeptical. It's an excellent trait—in moderation. Perhaps a demonstration of my ability and seriousness is in order. That I can do. Remember, though: Gather your people and get out. You have three days."

Felice thought Rebecci's eyes flashed, and she reached down to grab her knife. Before she could even brush the hilt, pain as sharp as a needle split her skull, and she cried out. Her glass fell from nerveless fingers, shattering on the floor.

She slumped, muscles turned to water, hearing Avigdor utter a wordless howl.

Pressure in her head threatened to explode. Darkness overwhelmed her.

FELICE WOKE ON the wooden floor, her skull throbbing with remembered pain. She sat up. Rebecci was nowhere to be seen. The door gaped open.

A trickle of blood dripped from her left nostril into her open mouth. With the back of a hand, she wiped at her top lip, then at the drool on her chin.

"Avigdor," she croaked weakly.

She struggled to her feet and lurched over to where he drooped in his chair. He was alive, pulse still strong, but he remained unconscious.

Breathing a sigh of relief, she shuffled to the table and gulped from Rebecci's discarded wineglass. In a few moments, she felt better; the pain in her head receded to a manageable level.

Stumbling, she collapsed into her chair and placed her aching head in her hands.

By the ancestors, what in the world is going on?

CHAPTER 10

They buried the soldiers in shallow graves a fair distance from the road, not wanting to be seen digging by passersby, whose questions would be difficult to answer.

Afterward, they got the wagon rolling, joining the road and heading west. No one spoke for the rest of the morning.

That night Caldan approached Bells again after he'd spent some time trying to get Miranda to eat. Miranda had managed only a few spoonfuls before keeping her lips closed and refusing to eat any more. Caldan could see she'd already shed weight. Her skin had lost its vitality and looked dull, and her face lifeless.

"What should I be looking at?" asked Caldan, moving one of Bells's crafted bells out of his shadow and into the sunlight. Its surface was covered with hair-fine runes, as was the inside. A faint tinkle filled the wagon.

Bells had been surprisingly cooperative since their fight with the sorcerer, oddly so. It was almost as if she were glad the man had been killed.

She rolled her eyes and growled in frustration. "Can't you see it? It's a wonder of modern crafting theory, that's what. And I did it. Me."

Caldan peered inside the bell. "I still don't see it. But then I don't know what half the runes are for."

"Of course you don't. I'm not surprised, with these sorcerers of yours teaching you. I thought the Protectors might have more knowl- , edge, but it looks like they've turned stagnant as well."

"I was only an apprentice, remember."

Bells huffed her displeasure. "I'm teaching you as fast as I can, but I've no knack for it. It would be better if you went to Indryalla to study." She smiled at him.

"That's not going to happen. All I need to know is how to heal Miranda. Anything else can wait."

"Fine. But like I told you, there are people far better at this than me. I know the basics, but intricate coercive sorcery is beyond me."

"Are you saying you don't think you know how to heal her mind?"

"No, I didn't say that. Just that it might take longer than I thought."

"Are you stalling for time?"

"No, you fool-born minnow! You promised to release me when she's healed, so why would I stall for time? It doesn't make sense."

"Not much you have done so far has made sense."

"To me it has."

Caldan had no response to that. His head was starting to ache, as it always did after working so hard with complicated sorcery. He breathed deeply. "Let's go over it again."

Bells shook her head. "Again?"

"Just do it," he said, not adding *And maybe for once, do it without all the commentary.*

Bells rolled her eyes at him. "As you wish. Then tonight, maybe you could untie me. It gets cold at night."

"No," said Caldan firmly.

With a shrug of her shoulders, Bells gave up. "Coercive sorcery isn't about bludgeoning your way into someone's mind—despite what it feels like," she added after a look from Caldan. "It takes a lot of finesse. Juggling multiple threads from your well is hard. Most sorcerers can't manage more than five. A very few can handle seven; even fewer, eight or more. And the more strings you control, the less power they have, depending on your well, of course. Coercive sorcery requires at least seven threads split from a well, and a deft handling of each."

She stopped. "Could I have some water, please?"

Caldan retrieved a waterskin from their provisions and squirted a stream into Bells's open mouth.

"You're a good little Protector."

"Go on."

"Two threads for yourself: one to hold on to your well, another to hold on to your consciousness."

Caldan nodded to himself. She had told him this before. "I called them strings. We were only progressing to them in my training, with generating a shield."

Bells shrugged. "As good a word as any, I suppose. Regardless, that's two threads. Another thread has to carry the remaining four, for insertion. And as I've said, this one is hard to describe; you need a lot of practice on willing subjects before you can master that technique."

Her use of the term "willing subjects" disturbed him, as it had when she'd mentioned it before, but he let her continue.

"It carries the other threads, like a rope of many strands, covering them and allowing them to enter the person's mind undamaged. Then the other threads can do their work, suppressing a person's actions, memories, implanting suggestions, even taking control."

"Go over what you think has happened to Miranda again."

"I don't think. I *know* what's happened. *Backlash. Keys . . .*" Her voice caught in her throat. She stopped and looked at her lap.

Caldan knew he wouldn't get much from her for a while; a number of times she had mentioned Keys and gone quiet. So while he waited, he thought of what she had said, probing it from different angles, examining the information to see if he could make sense of it.

Last time he had questioned her, she had spoken of the backlash, when a coercive sorcery link to someone was severed prematurely. With one swift rush, the threads would be cut at one end, causing them to whip back into the person's mind. Each thread might either thrash around before fading or remain joined with a person's consciousness in some sort of symbiotic relationship. Damage could be either permanent or temporary, fading over a period of time that could drag out to years. She said Miranda's damage was permanent, but then she would say that; it gave him a compelling reason to keep Bells around and not just deliver her to the next Protectors he met.

As far as Bells could describe, Miranda's mind wasn't so much damaged as confused. Her thoughts were scrambled, both conscious and subconscious.

He didn't have much choice but to go along with her assessment, no matter how slight a chance he had to try to heal Miranda. He couldn't bear the thought of her remaining in this state for the rest of her life.

A lump formed in his throat. He realized she had become important to him, more than he had let on to her.

Caldan attempted to change their conversation to a different topic, to distract Bells from her sorrowful thoughts about Keys. "You said the man who attacked us wouldn't be the only one to come. Why would he have tracked us on his own?"

Lifting her head, Bells wiped her eyes with her bound hands, which shook slightly. Constant chafing from the rope left her wrists red and sore, and Caldan could see dried blood in a few places. He didn't like what they were doing to her, but it was necessary, he told himself.

"They shouldn't have sent Mahsonn after me," Bells mused softly. "They should have known, if I'd been captured, he wouldn't be enough to . . ." Her words trailed off.

Wouldn't be enough to rescue you, Caldan finished silently for her. *Which means they made a token effort and didn't care if she returned. Is this part of a power struggle, or something else?*

Bells averted her gaze and continued. "When this is over, I'll have their heads. He was only a Bleeder, but still . . ."

"A Bleeder? What's that?" Though Caldan could guess, judging from the state of the soldiers the sorcerer had killed.

"What and why . . . One question you want answered, and one I do." She looked away, distressed.

"What's a Bleeder?" he repeated.

"A sorcerer." She sighed and shook her head. "One of very few, actually. Not a powerful talent, but rare. Only useful when killing is involved. A sorcerer who is born with a weak well, narrow and rough, is sometimes able to focus power into tiny threads. This talent, combined with a talent to control many of these threads, makes a Bleeder. And I mean a lot of threads. More than most sorcerers can. I say 'most,' but what I mean is almost all." She let out a short, ironic laugh. "A talent any sorcerer would kill to have in someone of almost useless power. Fate can be unkind. Bleeders are usually bitter and twisted, and Mahsonn certainly was."

"That's what caused the buzzing? Many separate threads."

"Good little Protector."

Her insult no longer had venom in it. Caldan fancied she wasn't as angry as when first captured. The sting of losing Keys, though still raw, could be fading. Or she might be acting. He closed his eyes, thoughts running in circles.

Abruptly, he stood, head brushing the canvas covering the wagon.

Bells smiled at him, a grin that seemed both feral and knowing. "You have an aptitude for sorcery, Caldan. I see that. I could teach you more . . ."

"Yes, I'm sure you could. But what would you want in return?"

"To clear your mind of prejudice. We are not the enemy you think us."

Caldan worried that was true.

THE LAST TWO days, farms and homesteads, inns and small villages had become more numerous, until the whole countryside was covered with fields and paddocks, sheds and houses, sure signs they were approaching a large city.

Traffic on the road increased as well, numerous smaller roads joining theirs until there was always someone in sight, either in front or behind them. Dust constantly swirled in the air around them, clogging their nostrils, and the reek of horse and cattle dung baking in the sun made their eyes water. After Elpidia covered her face with a kerchief, Bells requested the same, and both Caldan and Amerdan followed suit. Miranda became agitated when they tried to tie one around her face, though, constantly clawing it away until they gave up and let her be.

Her distress hit Caldan hard. He felt helpless.

His sessions with Bells seemed to progress, but he still felt they were a long way from his being able to fix the damage, and time was running short. When he tried to hurry things along, she only said this was something that was learned in its own time.

It made him want to scream.

Adding to that frustration, Amerdan avoided any questions directed at him about his uncanny speed and skill. The shopkeeper had secrets, that much was obvious, and it made his decision to leave Anasoma and come with them suspect. And the ease with which Amerdan had butchered the sorcerer filled Caldan with disquiet. He vowed to get him alone and press him for answers, though the shop-keeper had kept his distance so far.

Caldan questioned a train of peasants they met on the road and Elpidia, who was driving the wagon, had picked up the pace in the hope they could reach the city before nightfall. He felt relieved when they decided instead to camp one last night and approach the city gates in the morning.

From the top of a hill they looked down on lights too numerous to count, bathing the sky. The stars had become muted compared to their nights in the countryside. A winding ribbon of reflected silver moonlight bordered one side of the lights: a river. He guessed the city was at least as large as Anasoma, though much flatter, situated as it was on a plain.

Caldan glanced at Bells, who stood behind Elpidia, the rope around her neck firmly in Amerdan's grasp.

Shaking himself from his thoughts, he turned back to the others.

"Tomorrow, I'll enter the city," he announced. "There's much the Protectors need to know, and we can't wait any longer. Who knows what's happened while we've been traveling here."

Elpidia lowered her gaze and shook her head, while Amerdan nodded slowly. The shopkeeper took a step forward.

"We'll stay here with Miranda and Bells while you're inside. I imagine you might be gone a few days?"

"Maybe. I . . . yes, probably. They'll question me at length, then want me to remain while they verify my story."

"That could take days, weeks even!" exclaimed Elpidia. "We've been on the road long enough. I can't delay my experiments any longer. I just can't!"

Caldan held up a hand in an effort to placate her. "I won't wait around for days, I promise. I'll leave. The day after tomorrow, at the latest."

"What if they don't let you go?"

"They've no reason to disbelieve what I say. But even if they do try to hold me, I used to sneak out of the monastery to earn ducats on the side, and no one stopped me. And I got away from the invaders at the guild. I'm sure I'll think of something."

Elpidia looked unconvinced. Amerdan's face remained blank.

"Well," chimed in Bells. "Can we stop all this navel-gazing and get started on dinner? I don't know about you lot, but I'm famished."

With a jerk on the rope, Amerdan forced her to stumble to her knees. "Quiet," he hissed.

Elpidia frowned at him, while Caldan stepped over to relieve him of the rope.

"I'll look after her," he said. Amerdan's behavior could be erratic at times, and Caldan didn't like the way he treated Bells. He needed her cooperation.

Amerdan handed him the rope without fuss, a slight shrug of his shoulders showing he didn't care who looked after the sorcerer. Bells's eyes flashed with contempt at him, though she kept silent.

"Tonight, you're teaching me more," Caldan told Bells, his voice hard. He met her eyes. "Any tricks you decided not to tell me, this time you'd better not hold back. Because tomorrow I'm going into the city to see the Protectors, and I haven't decided what to do with you yet. If I think you've been stringing me along and deceiving me, then

I will hand you over to them. Do not doubt I will do this. If you want to stay out of their hands, then tonight is your chance to give me a reason why."

"Caldan," Elpidia said, "maybe you should just give her to them. I mean . . ." She waved a hand, flustered. "Maybe the Protectors can heal Miranda."

"They can't," snarled Bells.

"But you don't know that," Elpidia said. "What is her word worth?"

"If you hand me to them, you'll never see me again. They'll kill me, and Miranda will remain the way she is. Do you want to be spooning her porridge every day? Wiping her drool and cleaning up after her for the rest of her life?"

Caldan's hands gripped the rope tighter; his knuckles went white. "That's one of the things I will ask about when I get there. If they say they can help, then Bells goes to them. If, however, she actually helps me *tonight,* then I will keep my promise."

When no one objected to that, Caldan said, "It's decided. Tomorrow, you can both stay here with Bells and Miranda while I go in. It's dangerous outside the city—I won't pretend it isn't. There could be someone else following, but until we know the situation inside the city, it could still be safer out here."

"As much as I hate to say it, you're probably right. Besides, they wouldn't send others after the first one," Elpidia said. "They'd send them together."

"Maybe, maybe not. The Bleeder could have been just the beginning." Caldan turned his back on the lights below them and began walking down the hill toward the wagon. "Let's make camp."

CALDAN'S STOMACH GROWLED. He gritted his teeth against the gnawing in his gut. He was starving, and had been for the last few days, but their meager provisions hadn't allowed him to eat his fill. Tomorrow he could enjoy a full meal at the Protectors' expense, safe under their roof and among friends. Friends he might be lying to.

A sprinkling of stars shone through the cloudy night sky, and the moon was descending to the west. This far from the road, the air was sweeter, though still redolent of the nearby farms rather than wilderness.

He removed his arm from around Miranda's shoulders and brushed her hair back from her face. Her eyes reflected the orange flames of their campfire. She showed no sign she felt his touch.

Caldan thought for a moment, then kissed her lightly on the cheek. The gesture left him feeling hollow and awkward, because it elicited no response.

He rose, brushed dirt from his trousers, picked up a waterskin, then roamed around their camp. Elpidia had her head buried in her leather kit, muttering to herself, bottles clinking. She looked up at him as he passed, face grim, then returned to whatever she was up to. A strange woman, wrestling with the bleak reality that afflicted her.

Amerdan sat away from the fire, sharpening his knives. The scrape of metal on the whetstone grated on Caldan's nerves, but he wanted to question Amerdan before he disappeared on one of his nightly walks. He had no idea what the man did while away from camp, but he felt safer with him out there.

"We need to talk," Caldan said, approaching him.

Amerdan shook his head and pointed at Bells, then Elpidia. "Not where others can hear. And maybe never."

"What do you mean, maybe never? You've been ducking me for days now!"

"Calm down, and lower your voice."

Caldan realized he'd taken a few steps toward Amerdan, who had stopped honing his knives and pointed one directly at him. Caldan held up his hands and backed away a step.

Would he really use that on me? Caldan wondered, and feared he knew the answer.

"I'm sorry," he said. "It's just . . . I have to find out what we are. It's important."

"In good time."

"But I need to know!"

"And can I trust *you*? When you couldn't get what you wanted from

Bells, you struck her." Amerdan raised his eyebrows. "You're barely in control of yourself. And the secrets I possess . . . they're not for everyone. The knowledge I have came at a great cost to myself, and others. You think I'll just hand it over because you ask?"

Caldan's brow furrowed. "What will it take, then? Wasn't me saving everyone back at the caves enough? Or killing the soldiers at the farm?"

"No," Amerdan said simply.

Caldan fumed for a moment. *He speaks of trust so matter-of-factly, and yet what do I really know about this man? Maybe it should be* me *demanding proof of faithfulness.* But even as he thought that, he knew he didn't want to alienate someone who might help him—who had already helped them flee Anasoma. The man was a merchant, or so he said, so Caldan decided to approach him in a way Amerdan would understand. "What do you want from me?"

"Ah, now you're thinking. Everyone wants something from everyone else. But what do I want . . . ?" Amerdan's voice trailed off, as if he were pondering his own question. He stood and sheathed his knives, then tucked away the whetstone. "I'm going for a walk. Maybe we'll talk again in the morning. But you need to convince me you're trustworthy, and I'll want something in return."

With that, Amerdan turned his back and disappeared into the darkness.

Caldan's frustration was palpable. There was just so much going on that he had no control over. He glanced over at Elpidia, with her sickness and all-consuming need for his blood. Miranda, and her lost anima. And Bells . . .

He moved closer to Bells. She watched him approach through half-lidded eyes.

Caldan smiled. He squatted in front of her, then drew his knife. Crickets chirped around them.

Bells watched the blade as he held it up. In the inadequate light, it was barely visible, an almost insignificant thing. She eyed him warily, pushing further against the tree.

He slid the knife between her hands and began sawing. She whimpered as the rope grated against her chafed wrists, then sighed as her bindings fell to the ground. Her feet were still bound, as they were every night, so he was reassured she couldn't escape.

Caldan put his knife away and held up the waterskin. "Give me your hands," he said.

Bells hesitated, then held them out, fingers still bound with cloth. He poured water over her tender wrists. She hissed at the pain but quieted as the cool water soothed her wounds. As gently as he could, he rubbed away the dried blood.

"I'll ask Elpidia to apply one of her ointments later. I'm sure she has something in that kit of hers."

Bells rotated both her wrists, and then shook her hands. She didn't speak.

Caldan sat cross-legged in front of her. He placed the waterskin next to him, ran a hand through his short hair, and stared off into the darkness. "At this time tomorrow, you'll be either in chains in the Protectors' custody, or here with Amerdan and Elpidia."

Bells licked her lips, eyes flicking this way and that. "She's drinking your blood. Tiny furtive sips," she said with a tight smile. She watched his reaction curiously.

"No, she wouldn't. She . . ." He stopped. His stomach churned at the thought of Elpidia drinking his blood, yet he didn't disbelieve Bells. The sick woman hadn't been able to experiment properly and would try anything she could to cure herself.

"I've watched her. She stares at it, wondering if it could save her. Then . . . she sucks at it greedily, like a child with a sweet." She sniggered, then her expression went solemn. "Just like your emperor is said to do to those who are gifted."

Caldan grimaced with distaste. He had no idea why she was bringing the emperor into this, but if Elpidia was drinking his blood, she must be getting desperate for a cure. He pushed the thought to the back of his mind and hardened his tone. "If you don't teach me something tangible by the morning, I will deliver you to the Protectors and take my chances they can heal Miranda."

Bells remained silent and regarded him coolly, a faint sheen of sweat on her brow the only indication she was worried.

"I'll leave your hands untied and give you some time to think about what I've said."

"Leave the water," Bells said.

Caldan pushed the skin toward her, then rose. He turned and made his way over to Miranda.

"WELL, WELL," CAME a soft voice from above Bells, pitched to carry to her ears. A slight movement revealed Amerdan perched in the foliage. "He's taken his time. Talk about leaving things to the last moment."

Bells didn't react. She reached for the water, dragging it to her side. She used the movement to speak, lips barely moving.

"He's not suited to this game," she replied softly.

Wind whispered through the leaves for a few moments before Amerdan replied, "Not yet. He will be, though. Sooner than you think."

Bells only grunted in reply.

"Don't forget our deal," he reminded her. "He's mine. Do not touch him. You can have the woman, Elpidia, if you want. She's nothing to me."

Bells shook her head slightly.

"Ah, you don't want her. Why would you, I suppose? She's only a burden. A nobody, a nothing." Amerdan paused, moving down a branch, closer to Bells.

Even this close to him, she was hard-pressed to see him move, and he made no sound. Her hands clenched momentarily; they shook. She folded her arms, hiding her weakness from his sight.

A faint rustle alerted her to the fact Amerdan now crouched on the ground close to her, behind the tree, hidden from the camp. She could hear him breathing. His closeness, and the sound, sent shivers up her spine. The hair on her arms stood on end.

"Are you going to teach him anything?" Amerdan asked curiously.

"Maybe," she whispered. "I don't know."

"Come now, you must have some idea."

"I think I might have to."

"To gain his trust? I understand. If he decides to hand you over to the Protectors, it could go badly for both of us." His hand reached around the tree and stroked a lock of her hair. She froze.

"If I were you," Amerdan continued, "I'd show him something tangible. We don't need the Protectors coming into this."

Bells nodded slowly. "I understand. I could deal with the Protectors easily, if I had my craftings, but it would draw attention to me, attention I don't need."

The hand patted her on the shoulder and then withdrew.

"Good. We understand each other. No point adding complications."

She felt rather than heard him back away from the tree.

"I'll leave you to your thoughts, then. Until tomorrow."

Bells waited, listening for signs Amerdan had gone. She couldn't discern anything over the sounds of the night—wind, crickets, the crackle of their fire.

She breathed deeply in an attempt to calm herself. Amerdan was a complex man, and so far he had shown himself to possess many talents. He intrigued her. And if she was honest with herself, even though she feared him, he was a remarkably handsome man.

"WELL," SAID CALDAN, his voice weary from the strain of the last few hours. His fingers pressed into the back of his neck, digging at his muscles in an effort to relieve the pain. "My head's about to burst."

Three silver bells lay in the palms of his hands, cupped in front of him. He sat in front of Bells again, where for the last few hours she had been instructing him on techniques in splitting strings from his well.

"You're getting stronger," Bells remarked.

Caldan frowned. "I don't want to get stronger. I want to be able to heal Miranda."

"That won't happen if you're weak. You have potential, but you need proper training. This isn't simple sorcery. As I've said many times, you have to be proficient in some basics before learning more complex, intricate crafting."

With a sigh, Caldan closed his hands over the crafted bells. "It's not going to happen tonight, is it?"

"Of course not!" exclaimed Bells. She pursed her lips and leaned forward. "You managed to maintain five separate strings; not many full-fledged sorcerers can do that."

"For a moment only," protested Caldan.

"A moment now, a few moments tomorrow, longer the day after. That's how it works. Practice combined with ability. You're getting proficient, more adept. One day soon, it will be second nature to you."

"Just not tonight."

"Of course not. Nobody masters this in an evening."

"I'm not sure I *want* to master it."

Bells snorted. "If you want to heal Miranda, then of course you do. You can't do it any other way."

"I know. It's just . . ." He shook his head. "That's a path I would prefer not to go down."

"Don't worry about your precious Protectors; you don't have to tell them."

"Of course I do."

"No, of course you *don't*. They aren't your friends. They suppress knowledge."

"Dangerous knowledge, for a good reason."

"Do you really think they eschew the use of destructive and coercive sorcery?"

"Yes . . . I mean, I've seen them use destructive sorcery, but only in the cause of good."

"In their eyes. So who determines what's good? And if they use destructive sorcery after telling you it's evil, then how can you be sure they don't use coercive sorcery?"

Caldan found himself nodding at her words and stopped. "Because they wouldn't do that. I'm sure of it . . ." He trailed off, sounding anything but sure.

"Only a fool would abandon a tool he could use. And if, as you say, the stakes are so high, do you take the Protectors for fools?"

"No. Far from it. But I take them as more trustworthy than you."

"You hardly know me."

"I know enough," retorted Caldan.

"Then you know it wasn't my fault Miranda was hurt. That it was an accident when . . ." Bells swallowed a lump in her throat. "An accident. And you can see I am doing all I can in the time we have to help you."

"Perhaps. I can't decide."

"Then let me help you decide." Bells shifted her weight and looked him in the eye. "I can teach you something now, a small sorcery. One I am sure will enable you to come to a decision."

"Show me, then," said Caldan, unimpressed.

"I'll need one of my bells."

Caldan raised his eyebrows.

"For you," responded Bells. "I wouldn't think you'd let me touch one."

Bells described which of her craftings he needed, and within moments Caldan returned with the object. This one was exquisitely crafted with small semiprecious stones embedded inside the bell, a streaky orange form of jasper, if he wasn't mistaken, and more runes he didn't understand.

"Why inside the bell?" he asked.

Bells flashed him a grin. "Nothing to do with the crafting itself, but rather to hide the fact they are there. Really, all those stones are useful for is this basic coercive sorcery." She settled down, her face becoming calm. "What can you sense from the bell?"

Caldan's mind touched his well, not to open it, but to connect with it. He extended his senses toward the bell, slowly, gently.

It vibrated at his contact, and a faint scent of lemons reached him. He sniffed.

In front of him, Bells stiffened for an instant, then relaxed. She blinked. "Do you smell something?"

"No." He wasn't going to let this sorcerer know any more than she had to.

"Tell me, what do you sense?" Her voice became intense. "What can you see, Caldan?"

"Nothing."

"Then you're not trying. Open yourself to the crafting. Go on, it won't hurt you."

As if you'd tell me if it would. Despite that, he opened his well and connected to the bell's anchor.

Around him, the colors of the night drained away. Already muted, their camp now looked as if a veil had been drawn across it, washing away any tint of life.

Except for Miranda.

It was as if her head were a jumble of colors, shifting and conflicting, like iridescent snakes writhing in a pile, or a ball of yarn tangled into an impenetrable mess. The colors roiled incessantly, making his stomach churn.

He hissed, as if in pain, and closed his well. Sweat seeped from every pore. He wiped his brow and exhaled long and slow.

"I see now."

Bells nodded. "If she were under the influence of coercive sorcery, the colors wouldn't be chaotic, they would have form and structure. And when it comes to untangling that mess, one wrong thread cut would mean disaster."

Caldan cursed under his breath. "So that's what I'm up against? Untangling that riotous knot?"

A faint smile played across Bells's mouth. "Yes—without unraveling her mind in the process."

He clenched the crafted bell in one hand and stood, leaving Bells to watch him depart in silence.

CHAPTER 11

Felice watched as the last of her resistance fighters disappeared into a small house two streets from the wall of Anasoma, which still blazed with bright blue fire. With such an imposing barrier, the Indryallans didn't even bother patrolling the walls, apart from a few men keeping watch and guarding siege engines.

Such an unassuming house to be able to sop up a few dozen of her people.

Beside her, Avigdor levered himself up onto a rain barrel—a decidedly peculiar sight, considering his bulk. He scratched a note on a piece of paper resting on his knee.

"That's it," he remarked.

She nodded. It was three hours past midnight, and they had spent the majority of the sunless hours organizing groups and making sure everyone was in position. It had been a struggle to avoid the Indryallan soldiers patrolling the streets, but with her forces split into small groups supported by scouts, there had been no mishaps.

The last few days had started with a flurry of thought, heated discussions with Avigdor, and finally agreement and a plan. Neither of them liked the idea, but their meeting with Rebecci had altered their thoughts on Anasoma and the Indryallans, and more important, what their ultimate goal should be.

Felice would have a few choice words with her when they next met, but she couldn't deny the "merchant" had spoken sense. Since the invasion, Indryallan ships had regularly sailed into the harbor. Laden to the brim, they departed empty after disgorging soldiers and supplies that left already busy streets clogged for hours.

Her people couldn't hope to win a direct confrontation inside a barricaded city, a conclusion which, though painfully obvious, they had debated for many hours. Small groups of skirmishers wouldn't be effective, either, as their resources were stretched too thin.

Joining forces with others remained their only option, though Rebecci's vagueness had given them pause: in the short term, Felice and her people would be on their own, and in the long term, she wasn't sure she could fully trust Rebecci yet. But she knew she wanted to continue resisting, and right now, this seemed like their best chance.

Although, I have added one small change to the plans—something that might make all this unnecessary . . .

"Shall we go?"

Avigdor's question broke her reverie.

"Yes. We had better."

Together, they sidled down an alley, keeping to one wall, both to remain as unnoticed as possible and to avoid the inevitable unsavory muck that accumulated in the back lanes. One never quite became immune to the stench.

"The wagon should be ready," remarked Avigdor.

"It had better be. We don't have much of a window of opportunity."

He drew out a brass watch and squinted at the dials in the faint light.

"There's plenty of time to prepare. We can even have a hot meal and a rest before we need to be in position."

"Sounds good to me." Her words were hollow, though, because she wasn't hungry; she hadn't been eating well since the invasion. She knew, however, that Avigdor hadn't lost his appetite.

An hour later, they entered a warehouse on the south side of the docks. Avigdor, a man of surprising talents, picked the lock on a side door, and they let themselves inside. They were followed by two burly men who had volunteered for their mission, the twins Nilas and Nolar. Another couple of volunteers were scouting their destination for the morning, with a further two making sure their route tonight was free of patrols.

Alchemical smells washed over them, acidic, bitter, and eye-watering. No wonder these warehouses were well ventilated during the day. Felice and her group moved as quickly and quietly as they could through the offices and into the warehouse proper. Barrels, chests, and sacks were piled up in rows, some stacked to twice their height.

Avigdor coughed into a kerchief and produced another piece of paper from a pocket. There was barely enough light to see by, so he moved until he was next to a window.

"Row six, fifteenth stack."

Without a word, Nilas and Nolar made their way to the location, which turned out to be in a corner of the warehouse. A small area was sealed off using a makeshift fence of empty crates. Inside sat square chests, a yard on each side.

"We need ten," said Avigdor, and the twins stepped up to obey, each reaching for a different chest.

"One at a time," hissed Felice, "and don't drop them, if you value your life." Their alchemical contents were volatile, and though transporting them shouldn't pose a problem, if one was dropped . . .

The twins shrugged and lifted a single chest between them, using iron handles on the sides. Soon the last one was deposited in their wagon, and they covered the cargo with a canvas sheet.

So far, all had gone according to plan, though the next part was crucial. Moving their stolen goods through the streets in the middle of the night was fraught with danger. They couldn't risk getting caught. Felice's men were under strict instructions to run at the first indication they were discovered. Each of the three teams of two knew only part of the overall plan, so if one was captured, her scheme wouldn't be revealed.

Their horses required constant and quiet urging on. They eventually stopped behind another house, this one deserted, though available for rent. They would be residents for only one night so hadn't bothered the owner. Ideally suited to their needs, the house had enough room for the eight of them to be comfortable for the rest of the night. After tomorrow, they had no intention of remaining in the city.

The house was located a few hundred yards from the last of the stone piers jutting into the harbor. It was the pier previously designated for the emperor's own ships, now occupied by Indryallan vessels; more specifically, their biggest and best, the berths reserved for their commanders.

Felice and Avigdor made their way through a rear gate into a paved yard, and they assisted the men with unloading the cargo. With their ill-gotten goods stowed in the house, they barred themselves inside.

Felice supervised a spread of food for her men, lavish in its selection and quantity. They consumed the meal quietly. Conversations were carried out in whispers, subdued yet elated. Her men knew she had something cooked up.

Snores from Avigdor brought a smile to her lips. He had lounged across a couch after their meal and soon drifted off. Tomorrow's plan ran through her mind as she examined it in detail for the umpteenth time, tearing it apart, looking for flaws. But the truth was, it wasn't a complicated plan. Her main concern was not getting caught before they could act.

The Indryallan God-Emperor was arriving, and this had the invaders shitting themselves and scrambling over one another with preparations. Further digging by Felice had narrowed the date of arrival to tomorrow, sometime after dawn.

She took a swig from a mostly empty bottle of liquor. Her men had left her some after she gave them the bottle to share. Nilas was finishing cleaning up after their meal; he looked around, apparently satisfied with his work. Catching her staring, he gave her a polite tilt of the head and a brief smile.

Good men, all of them.

THE WALLS OF Anasoma were vast structures peppered with towers and siege engines. It had long been held that any weakness the city had was embodied by the harbor, both its lifeblood of trade and its disadvantage.

Centuries ago, the emperor, in his wisdom, had ordered his appointed rulers of the city to build numerous platforms close to the docks and on the cliffs overlooking the harbor. They were solidly built of raised stone, of a size to accommodate siege engines from ballistae to trebuchets, all positioned to provide defense in case of invasion from the sea. Subsequent rulers had maintained the structures and updated the siege engines with the latest designs. A city of Anasoma's wealth didn't scrimp on its duty to the Mahruse Empire.

During the Indryallan invasion, the weapons had remained suspiciously silent, crews of soldiers absent or drugged into a stupor, while some had been outright slaughtered.

Felice gazed to the east, where the sun peeked over the horizon, squinting against the glare. She couldn't see any ships, but that could change at any moment. They needed to be ready.

From her position on the back of the wagon, she gestured to her men.

At her signal, four drew long knives, and one turned a key, which unlocked the gate into a walled area. They entered, then sprinted up stone steps toward a large trebuchet. Another two men carried buckets behind them.

Two Indryallan soldiers guarding the device fell under multiple blows, blood leaking onto the stones. Both corpses were pitched off the platform into the walled area surrounding the structure.

The men spread sawdust from the buckets to cover the blood. It wouldn't do for them to be slipping around up there.

Felice liked to prepare for any eventualities.

A short time later Felice, Avigdor, and her men sat perched atop the platform surrounded by the ten chests they had pillaged the night before. They moved the wagon inside and relocked the gate, knowing an abandoned wagon with a team of horses might arouse suspicion.

She opened one of the chests. Inside rested two glass globes, each the size of her head, tied together with tough netting. Both contained an alchemical mixture in liquid form, one colorless, the other lurid green.

A hiss of surprise from Nilas made her grin.

"Be careful," she said. "We need all chests opened, ready to be loaded. Avigdor?"

"Yes?"

"Can you instruct the men on where to position the trebuchet?"

"Certainly." He looked around the platform. Chipped into the wall surrounding the platform were numerous markings, lines with symbols. There were corresponding marks on one beam of the siege engine.

"Direction and range," mused Nilas.

"Indeed," responded Avigdor. He tapped one of the marks on the wall, followed by one on the trebuchet itself. "See these two markers? Could you please align the machine to this one here, and it looks like it will require some cranking to reach the required distance."

Nolar pointed at a pile of stones to the side. "Should we load one of these as well?"

Felice smiled. "Why not?"

A short time later, the engine was poised, loaded, and under tension. Avigdor stood in front of it, brass telescopic cylinder raised to an eye, surveying the harbor. The ground sloped steeply down toward the docks here, and the city spread out in front of them.

The device's huge counterweight loomed beside Felice.

"And now we wait," she said.

The sun inched inexorably into the sky.

"THE SHIP'S COMING!" exclaimed Avigdor.

Felice stood. "Stations, please," she said calmly. She raised an arm to shield her eyes from the sun and followed Avigdor's pointing finger out to sea.

Not just one, but at least ten ships approached. She cursed. They would have no way of knowing which one held their target.

Obviously sharing her frustration, Avigdor attempted to reassure her. "We've aimed the trebuchet to hit the closest berth to the city. Most commanders would use this one so they don't have to travel as far."

"Let's hope he's like most commanders."

Felice waited impatiently as the ships neared, becoming clearer the closer they came. Their distinctive size and shape marked them as Indryallan, but she couldn't tell any difference between them. They could only hope the God-Emperor was on the ship they had targeted.

Either way, it will be one less ship full of Indryallans to deal with.

The sling was loaded with one of the stones and four of the glass globes. They'd only have time for a few shots before their position was known and soldiers were dispatched to stop them.

One of the men, Monrad, stepped up to the trebuchet.

"Steady," she said. "Wait until the ship has docked."

Monrad nodded. All eight had drawn straws to see who would fire each of the shots. It was the least she could do for them, though out of boredom this morning they had started a game of dice for ducats that had quickly devolved into using their turns as stakes. She had stopped them before any man lost his straw. She wanted each to take a turn, if they had time.

They waited as the ships approached, far too slowly for her liking.

Close to the docks, a number of ships split off toward the lesser wooden wharves, seven in total. Felice breathed a sigh of relief. That was seven ships that shouldn't hold their target, leaving three possibilities, the ones that approached the exclusive stone wharves.

Avigdor grinned and danced a little jig to the amusement of the men.

The remaining ships closed in on the stone wharf, taking turns to slide into empty berths. Felice was impatient, but they couldn't rush. She knew it would take some time for the ships to secure themselves and for their occupants to make themselves ready to disembark.

Avigdor watched the ships through the telescopic lens, taking his time to examine them. After a while, he shook his head.

"I can't see anyone of note on deck. Most likely, they're still below."

Felice grunted. It was a small hope, but she'd thought there was a chance a leader of note would want to survey the city as it came into view. She shrugged and turned to face her men. "Let's begin."

They stood expectantly by the wheel crank used to raise the counterweight, while the lucky winner of the first shot was poised beside the release mechanism, clutching a wooden mallet.

She stood on the stone wall surrounding the platform. For a moment, she swooned with vertigo looking down at the street below her. She turned toward the harbor; the wind on her face was cold and clean.

"For the emperor!" yelled Felice.

"May he live forever!" her men responded.

At the trebuchet, Monrad paused, taking a breath.

"Surprise," he said calmly, and with a swift blow of the mallet, released the mechanism.

Wood creaked and steel shrieked. The counterweight plummeted down, while the long wooden beam whooshed through the air and released its load. All of them stood frozen, faces toward the sun. Flying out over the city, the boulder and the glass globes grew smaller and smaller. They reached their zenith and began descending toward the harbor, gaining speed as they fell earthward. On the stone pier, soldiers were already leaving the ships and lining up in ordered regiments, unaware their day was about to descend into madness.

Avigdor cackled with delight. Cheers rose from the men around the trebuchet.

"Get cranking," shouted Felice. "We don't have time for celebrations."

The men leaped to obey her, six of them straining with the crank wheel to lift the counterweight while two struggled to load another boulder into the sling.

Felice shaded her eyes against the piercing sun and squinted at their target.

The boulder missed the pier and ships, ejecting a plume of water as it crashed into the harbor a fair distance from the target.

"Pignuts," Felice cursed. "Avigdor—"

"I know, I know," he said, and began issuing orders. Two men left the cranking to adjust the machine's orientation.

She knew they'd need a few ranging shots but had hoped with the markers they'd be more accurate. It couldn't be helped, and they'd planned for this. On the pier, there wasn't much confusion yet. Most people there wouldn't know what caused the water to erupt. And if more experienced soldiers guessed the truth, unless they'd seen the shot being released, they'd have no idea where it had come from.

The second payload was flung into the air with a groan of wood and rope under great stress.

"Come on," Felice muttered.

The second stone struck the pier next to the lead ship with incredible force, shaking the stone to its foundations. It splintered into a thousand jagged shards, along with the glass globes. Alchemical compounds mixed with the air and reacted angrily. A sound like thunder raced out from the impact site, an unstoppable physical wave of force, smashing into soldiers and sailors alike. Skin erupted into flames, and organs turned to jelly. Bones snapped and shattered. From this distance, the destruction of the boulder and the carnage it caused seemed disconnected from reality.

On the pier, soldiers scrambled around like ants whose nest had been trod on.

Felicienne roared a wordless challenge, releasing frustration and rage pent up since the invasion. But it still wasn't what she wanted. They needed to hit the ships.

"Avigdor," she yelled. "The aim was off; fix it, now!"

"Same strength," said Avigdor calmly. "Slightly to the right. Wait! That's enough."

He shooed the men back to the wheel, and moments later the mechanism clicked into place. All was ready for another shot.

"Quickly now," urged Felice. She reached up and gripped her braid tightly until her knuckles went white.

Another man grasped the mallet and, with a nod of permission from Felice, released the next shot.

"Don't wait!" commanded Felice as they watched the boulder disappear. "Crank as if your life depended on it! Which it may well do."

Avigdor backed away from the machine, raised the telescopic lens, and trained it on the lead ship. "Any second now," he whispered.

The second boulder struck the ship dead on, penetrating the deck and continuing down. Splinters of wood erupted, spraying outward. Fire exploded across the deck, searing the men unlucky enough to be there. Canvas sails erupted into flame. A foam of bubbles surrounded the ship.

"I . . . I think it went straight through!"

With a shriek of glee, Felice jumped up and down. "Move it! Move it!" she crowed. "I want to target that next ship! Let's see if we can destroy all three!"

Moving as fast as they could, the men aligned the trebuchet to Avigdor's shouted requirements, then returned to reloading the sling.

"Don't wait for me!" yelled Felice. She left the men to it, confident they were sufficiently well versed in the trebuchet's workings at this point.

"Spyglass, please," she said to Avigdor, holding out a hand. He slapped the instrument into her palm, and she used it to view their targets.

Carnage enveloped the pier and ships. Smoke rose into the sky, and blood covered the stone wharf and wooden deck. She shifted the lens to the second ship. Behind her, the trebuchet groaned as the next boulder shot into the air and arced over the city.

She hissed. Something was off. There, on the second ship. A man stood on the deck gazing toward them, apparently unconcerned he might become the next unwilling victim. He raised his arms.

A violet haze streamed from his hands toward the tallest mast on the vessel. Touching the tip, it then spread out until a sparkling dome covered the ship. And it grew. Felice watched as the base continued outward, spreading across the wharf, enveloping more and more of the pier and ships.

With a sharp crack, their shot hammered into the dome. Huge violet sparkles erupted from the collision and spread across the shield. A flash of light, flame, and smoke covered the area.

The shield remained whole. Globs of flaming stone splashed into the water.

"Bloody goat . . . argh!" Felice screamed at the sorcerer. She had never seen such power, though the flames on the walls surrounding Anasoma should have given her an idea of their capabilities. She knew when she was in over her head.

And then lightning cracked out of the clear sky.

A bright white flash hit the house to their right. Its walls blew outward in a cloud of dust.

Felice looked at the remaining seven chests filled with the alchemical explosive.

"Off, off!" she yelled. "Jump!"

Her men scattered as they realized the extent of their danger, hurdling the low wall surrounding the platform and plummeting to the cobblestones below.

Avigdor ran for the stairs.

"There's no time!" screamed Felice. "Jump!" Without looking back to see if Avigdor obeyed, she threw herself over the edge.

There was an earsplitting crack as lightning struck the wall above her. The smell of burnt metal filled the air and chips of stone showered down on her. She shielded her eyes from the fragments.

Avigdor landed ten yards away in the back of their wagon with a grunt. A sickening crack echoed as his ankle snapped like a twig. He yowled with pain and fell into a heap, clutching at his leg.

Felice lurched to the wagon. "Get that gate open! Now!"

Her men already had it unlocked, and two dragged it open with a screech of metal on stone. They ran for the wagon and piled in. One took hold of the reins, while another gave Felice a hand up.

CRACK! A bolt hit the stones behind them, and the blast knocked her off her feet. She fell to the floor of the wagon.

With a lurch, it moved forward.

"Go! Go!" she yelled. "Stay down!"

The wagon raced out the gate and into the street. Passersby who had taken shelter from the lightning under the eaves of houses stopped to gawk at the chaotic sight.

Felice stood and screamed at them. "Run! Run, or you'll die!"

They scattered to the winds at her words, women screeching, men shouting. A few dragged children along or picked them up to flee.

There was another crack, then the world went white. A wall of what felt like solidified air hit the wagon from behind. The pressure squeezed Felice's skin and made her insides churn.

Nilas, who was driving the wagon, managed to keep control. He slapped the horses with the reins. "Hee-yah!"

Felice glanced behind them.

The trebuchet was gone. Dust and smoke filled the air where it had been, and the stone platform was cracked and chipped. Black stains covered the area, and spots of fire burned out of control. Buildings surrounding the platform were ablaze.

Avigdor cried out with pain as they bumped over the uneven cobblestones, face drained of blood.

She turned to give aid, and as she did, an Indryallan soldier emerged at a run from an alley behind them, skidding to a halt. In moments, five more had joined him. They looked around frantically. One pointed at them when he spotted the wagon racing down the street. A few gave chase, while the rest ran toward the now-defunct trebuchet platform.

Felice turned back to Avigdor's ankle. His trouser leg was soaked with blood. She lifted it to reveal white bone protruding from his flesh. Gently, she covered the ankle.

A strong hand squeezed her shoulder.

"Right-o," said Nolar above the noise of the clattering wagon. "Here's where we scatter." His eyes flicked to Avigdor, a grim look on his face. "There's nothing we can do for him. If we try to carry him, we'll all be caught."

Avigdor gave a weak laugh. "I can't run," he said grimly. "I won't be able to get away."

Felice gritted her teeth, then nodded.

"Good luck, my lady," Nilas said. "We'll see you back at the Cemetery."

Avigdor groaned. His hand clutched at hers. "Get me . . . Let me drive the wagon."

She thought quickly. "Get him up there," she ordered. "Then you can scatter."

In moments, Avigdor had been manhandled to the front seat. He screamed only once. They pressed the reins into his hands.

Teeth clenched with pain, Avigdor waved them away. His face shone with sweat.

"Go," he managed to say. "I'll delay them."

Felice pulled on the reins and directed the wagon to the right, down a main street. For a few moments, the soldiers chasing would have lost sight of them.

One by one, her men leaped off the wagon, scattering in different directions.

She gave Avigdor a last look.

He grinned weakly.

"Go," he said.

"I'll come for you."

"Don't be stupid. Just go."

Without a word, she followed her men into the streets, leaving Avigdor to lead the soldiers on a chase. She wiped her hands on her trousers. Avigdor's blood stained them red.

"COME ON, COME on," gasped Felice to herself. "It's not much farther."

She ducked her head around the corner of the building she was hiding behind. *Pignuts.* Six Indryallan soldiers stood not ten paces from her. With slow, careful steps, she slid away from the corner, back to the wall, until she could breathe easier without fear of being heard.

Her braid was half undone, and her clothes stank of sweat and dirt.

Her legs ached from the constant running, and her chest hurt—even her lungs, used to routine exercise, had been strained to their limits over the last few hours.

The Indryallans were everywhere. Every second street she went down, there they were; every square she wanted to cross held at least a squad. She hoped her men had an easier time of it, but she was doubtful. As for Avigdor . . . She hoped he had given up and not decided to do anything stupid. Next time she saw him, she would slap him if he had.

She wiped at her eyes and sniffed. What were her options? She breathed deeply in an attempt to calm her racing heart.

To her right, around the corner, were the soldiers, while to the left, she would have to eventually cross a crowded square—which wasn't a good idea. Across from her was a narrow alley she would be able to fit down sideways. It was the kind of alley in the kind of neighborhood she wouldn't normally consider as an option. But then, she was pretty much out of options.

She went to cross to the alley and found she couldn't move. Bands of something tightened around her, constricting against her arms and legs. She yelped as she fell to the ground, hitting her head on the cobbles. Wriggling frantically, she struggled against her bonds.

There was a slight hum and a pop. To her right appeared a man where there hadn't been anyone before. He was muscled and handsome, with bright green eyes. She distrusted him instantly.

A rat-loving sorcerer, he had to be. It didn't take much to overcome someone if you didn't have to get close or touch them. Or be seen by them. Her eyes narrowed. That was something she hadn't seen or heard of before.

"Well, well," the man purred, with a voice she could have listened to all night under different circumstances. "What have we here?"

"I was just on my way to the market," Felice protested, feigning outrage. "Release me at once, or I'll see your superiors hear about this."

The man chuckled, one foot tapping the ground. "You'll get to meet my superiors soon enough, Lady Felicienne."

She stopped struggling and sat up, cursing softly under her breath. The game was up. She wouldn't be able to talk her way out of this.

"You've led me a merry chase. I'll bet you're tired."

Felice nodded wearily, not deigning to speak.

"Then let me find you a nice place to recuperate, courtesy of the Indryallans, of course."

She couldn't place his accent. It was nothing like the Indryallans' and sounded almost musical to her ears. And his clothes were so far out of fashion as to be almost laughable. It was as if he had raided his grandparents' wardrobe. A decidedly odd sorcerer. A number of crafted rings adorned his fingers, along with a strange flat torc around his neck.

"Who are you?" she ventured. "You're not one of them, are you?"

He bowed from the waist. "My name is Savine Khedevis, and you surmise correctly. But I am with them and have been tasked with finding the members of the resistance who strangely seemed to have not done much except skulk around and talk. Until today."

Felice gave him a knowing smile. "I'll bet they were surprised."

"Indeed they were. Then angry. Then vengeful."

"I hope they choke on it."

Savine shrugged. "My guess is they will blame me for not finding you soon enough. Still, I will survive. I always do." He stepped closer until he stood over her.

"Now brace yourself," he said cheerfully. "This is going to hurt."

Felice cried out as needles of pain stabbed into her skull. Waves of agony rolled across her body, emanating from her head. Her skin felt as if it were on fire. She crumpled back to the ground and curled into a ball, fingers clawing the cobbles.

Within moments, she was unconscious.

CHAPTER 12

With any luck, I'll be back tonight. I want to get this over with as quickly as possible," said Caldan.

He didn't like the idea of leaving Bells and Miranda with Elpidia and Amerdan, especially since he no longer felt he could fully trust the shopkeeper. But he had to spread news of the invasion, and he'd promised Simmon he'd deliver the sword, and he meant to keep his word. Once he'd discharged that duty, he hoped it would be enough to earn a boon from the Protectors, and they could tell him if there was anyone with the ability to heal Miranda. Then he could decide what to do with Bells.

He buckled on the sword and slung his satchel over his shoulder. One hand brushed the two bells in his pocket, while around his neck, under his shirt, hung his bone ring. In his satchel were the crafted items taken from the sorcerer Bells had called Mahsonn, which he thought might come in handy to study at some point.

Elpidia stood a few steps away the entire time he was getting ready, frowning all the while. Amerdan had disappeared again, saying he was going to scout the area. He'd left just before dawn, without waiting for breakfast.

Caldan glanced at Miranda, then quickly away again. He almost couldn't look at her sometimes.

"Hurry up," said Elpidia, nodding in the direction of the city. She scratched at the rash on her neck, then ran her fingers over a lump on her skin. "The quicker you get this over with, the quicker this whole sorry story can end, and I can get back to my research. Remember, this is bigger than just me. If we can come up with a universal cure—"

"My first priority is Miranda, then what to do with Bells. But yes," he said, cutting off her protest, "I will do as I promised. I know time is crucial, but it *is* my blood. I've gotten us this far, so please just trust me about my pledge, too."

She didn't look happy, but then again, he hadn't seen Elpidia look happy in a long time. Still, at least he had moved her past her only topic of conversation.

Caldan looked toward the city. A pall of smoke and dust hovered perpetually over it.

"Little Protector," called Bells from her tree.

He turned to face her, swallowing a curse. Of course she wanted to rile him just before he left.

"What do you want?" he asked with a sigh.

"Come here."

He strode over, though he stopped a few steps away and half turned toward the road, impatient to be off. "Make it quick."

"I just wanted to tell you something. As a sign of trust."

Caldan remained silent.

"Bells isn't my real name, you know." She uttered a short laugh. "It's the name people called me when I started crafting them. It stuck, like all silly names."

"Why are you telling me this?" He didn't have time for her games.

She looked away, staring at the trees. "Because if I ever get out of this alive—and you do too—you won't be able to find me by using 'Bells.' "

"And why would I want to find you at all?"

"Because I would be honored to continue your instruction. And when you see the truth behind the Protectors, I think you'll seek me out."

"That's not likely to happen."

Bells gave a wry smile. "Strange things happen all the time. Unlikely events. It's what makes living so interesting."

"Fine—what's your real name, then?"

"Sorche. Remember that."

Caldan exhaled long and hard. He turned his back on Bells—or Sorche—and approached Elpidia.

"I'll be back as soon as I can," he told the physiker. "Take this, in case you need to find me." He handed her the crafted compass she'd made. For the first time since he had made his promise to her about his blood, she seemed to genuinely appreciate something he did.

Small miracles, I suppose.

With final glances at Miranda and Bells, he left the camp for the road, puffs of dust springing up with each step.

AMERDAN WATCHED FROM among the trees as Bells smiled brightly and Elpidia scowled back at her.

"Excuse me," said Bells. "These ropes are a bit tight. I don't suppose you could loosen them a little. I can't feel my feet."

Elpidia checked the sorcerer's bindings. "There's nothing wrong with them," she said with some suspicion.

"Ah, that's better," exclaimed Bells anyway, and Elpidia rolled her eyes. It would take a fool not to see Bells was playing with her, but it would take someone far smarter than the healer to know what that play meant.

"You've been so kind to me," Bells continued, and Elpidia frowned at her.

In response, though, Bells smiled. "Which is why I'm going to let you live." That was his cue.

In an instant he was by Elpidia, and before she had half turned, the hilt of his knife was crashing into her skull, and the woman collapsed to the ground.

CALDAN APPROACHED THE gates nervously. He was surrounded by a mass of people trying to enter the city early in the morning, mostly farmers bringing in wagons of produce to sell, livestock traders leading trains of animals, and wagons packed to overloading with cages containing rabbits and chickens. Clouds were rolling in from the south, and an increasing wind was heavy with coming rain.

He slipped in some dung, barely keeping himself upright. A small child sitting atop a pile of goods giggled at him. In return, he smiled and made his way to the side of the queue, then stalked toward the front of the line.

Shouts followed him, jeers and curses for those who jumped the queue. He ignored them, and as he approached the gates, two guards stepped out to meet him. They were dressed similarly to the Harbor Watch in Anasoma, though their leather armor was covered with a brown tabard featuring a yellow key above an owl. They brandished long wooden clubs.

"Halt!" commanded one of them. "What business do you have in Riversedge? You better have a good reason for jumping the line."

He didn't have any kind of identification, but he had thought about that on his way to the gates. Placing a hand in his pocket, he touched Bells's shield crafting; he could tell the bells apart by sense now. With a thought, he opened his well, linked to the anchor, and activated it.

Let's see if this does the trick.

A soft glow enveloped him and the guards took a step back, gasping with astonishment, while a space cleared around him as people edged away in surprise and awe.

"I'm a Protector," Caldan announced. "And I need to talk to them as quickly as possible." He pointed at one of the guards. "You will take me to them. Now."

The guard swallowed and nodded, then spoke to his companion. "I'll get him to the Protectors quick smart."

Caldan cut the link to his well, and the shield winked out of existence.

"Let's go, then," he said simply.

It wasn't long before the guard left Caldan in front of a building inside the city walls. It was a rambling three-story structure, which looked to be surrounded by streets on all sides. Ironbound wooden gates, both propped open, led to a packed-earth courtyard. He couldn't see any guards at the gates.

Taking a breath, he entered and looked around. Leaves littered the courtyard, and weeds grew against the walls. To his surprise, two milk cows were tethered to an iron ring in one corner, both munching happily on a pile of hay. Around them, numerous cowpats littered the ground.

It wasn't what he'd expected. After the discipline and organization of the Sorcerers' Guild and Protectors in Anasoma, he was shocked at the state of the building.

A group of scruffy-looking children playing a chasing game rushed screaming out of a door and across the yard. Caldan winced at the discordant noise. One of the children, a boy who looked to be around twelve years old, stopped when he saw Caldan standing inside the gate. He looked around at his playmates, then wandered over.

Reaching into a pocket, Caldan flipped a copper ducat toward the boy, which he caught with surprising deftness.

"What can I do for you, sir?" the boy asked with deference.

"I need to see whoever's in charge of the Protectors."

"That'll be Master Mold. He's on duty today."

"Mold?"

"As in a cast, not, ah . . . a fungus." The boy's eyes shifted as he made sure no one had heard him.

"Take me to him, then."

"Right you are, sir. Follow me."

The boy gestured to Caldan, but a feeling made him stand where he was. This place wasn't quite right. Something was wrong. These Protectors seemed to be more . . . lax than the ones in Anasoma. There was no one guarding the front gate, and so far, he had walked straight into their headquarters without being challenged. Not at all what he had expected.

Seeing Caldan hesitate, the boy stopped. His eyes flicked toward a number of darkened windows to Caldan's left.

Without thinking, Caldan opened his well. His shield sprang into existence around him, and he reached for the sword over his right shoulder.

"No sudden moves," a voice ordered him from one of the openings—a deep male voice with a no-nonsense tone.

Caldan saw the boy back away. His eyes grew wide when he saw the shield, and after a few steps, he turned and ran. The other children had disappeared without him noticing.

As Caldan turned to face the window, he saw shadows move inside the building. Three crossbows protruded from the opening, all pointed at him. Even this far away, he could sense they were crafted.

Slowly and carefully, he dropped his hand from the sword hilt. He took a deep breath. A bead of sweat trickled down the side of his face. He held his arms out in front of him, palms facing the sky.

"I need to speak to whoever's in charge," Caldan said, keeping his voice steady.

Hushed whispers emanated from behind the crossbows. There was movement, and clothes rustled, then moments later, a door to the right opened and out strode a large man with short, graying hair. He was dressed in well-worn brown leather trousers and a cream shirt. He took a few steps toward Caldan, appraising him with stark gray eyes that peered out from under bushy eyebrows. He looked Caldan up and down, taking in his shabby travel-stained clothes and the dust covering his boots and trousers. His eyes rested on Caldan's ring for an instant before moving on.

"At the moment," the man said—it was the same voice that had ordered him before—"you'll talk to me. I'm Master Mold."

Caldan nodded. He didn't know if the crossbow bolts would penetrate his shield, but he wasn't keen to find out; and he didn't want to start off on the wrong foot with these Protectors . . . if that's what they were.

Mold wore numerous crafted rings and amulets. Carefully, Caldan extended his senses and examined the tear of the master's well. Like Simmon's, it was constricted, his real strength hidden. He would have to learn how they did that.

Caldan lowered his hands slowly. "I've come all the way from Anasoma. The invasion . . . the Protectors there . . . they're all dead."

Exclamations of horrified surprise greeted his words. In front of him, Mold's face grew grim.

"We had hoped things weren't so bad for them," he growled. He ran a hand over his face. "But this is worse than we suspected."

Caldan hesitated. *Best to get the bad news over with.* "The Sorcerers' Guild was destroyed as well. Maybe some survived. I really don't know."

"And just who are you?"

"Master Simmon took me on as an apprentice."

He felt a light touch skitter across his well and realized he'd been examined in return.

Mold looked at Caldan, grim and curious at the same time. "I know Master Simmon well, but we don't take on apprentices. The young ones here are training with the Sorcerers' Guild."

"So I've been told, but it's the truth. I had some training before, and Master Simmon made an exception for me. Unfortunately . . . he didn't make it."

Mold's shoulders slumped, and his face went bleak. "Not Simmon . . ."

"I'm sorry."

Mold said nothing for a few moments. "So Simmon took you in as an apprentice." His tone implied he still thought Caldan was lying.

"Yes," he answered, even though he was pretty sure Mold wasn't asking him a question.

Rubbing his chin, Mold nodded to himself, having come to a decision. "What did he always have on his desk?"

Caldan thought furiously, back to the times he had been in Master Simmon's rooms. He remembered the room, the chests . . . What was on his desk? *Ah, yes . . .*

"Flowers," Caldan answered firmly. "In a vase. From his wife."

The master gave him a thin smile, then spoke. "Lower those crossbows, boys. This one's no threat."

Caldan breathed a sigh of relief as the crossbows trained on him withdrew into the building. He cut his link to the shield.

Mold approached him, holding out a hand. "Quite a strong shield you have there, from what I sensed. Did you smith-craft it?"

Caldan shook his head. "No, mine burned out during the invasion. I picked this one up when I escaped."

"I've a lot of questions for you—starting where you just happened to pick up such a strong shield—and I'm sure the other masters will have as well, but you look like hell. Come, walk with me."

Caldan nodded, and they started moving out of the courtyard.

"We need firm intelligence about what's going on in Anasoma," Mold said. "We know a little . . . a precious little. You're a welcome sight, despite the bad tidings you bring."

"I'll help all I can. But the truth is, I don't know a lot about the invaders." *That I'm willing to tell you just yet*, he thought.

"We'll start with an easy question. What's your name?"

"Caldan."

He fell into step as he was led through the door and inside the building. Doorways opened left and right off a corridor. Sorcerous globes illuminated the interior, each set into a metal cage bolted to the walls, presumably to prevent someone stealing them.

Master Mold touched Caldan's shoulder and guided him up a flight of creaky wooden stairs. Boards nailed to the stringers with sometimes finger-width gaps between them attested to the shoddiness of the workmanship.

Mold noticed him noticing. "Some Protectors, and sorcerers from the guild, are shocked when they first see this place," he explained. "What most of the sorcerers don't realize, especially those who spend most of their time in cities such as Anasoma, is that we don't have time for many niceties here. This building"—he gestured with an arm as they reached the next floor—"is one of the places where most of the Protectors' work is done." He paused and raised his bushy eyebrows. "You know what I mean, don't you?"

Another test, thought Caldan. He nodded. "You search for rogue sorcerers who use destructive sorcery."

"Exactly. As well as dealing with leftovers from the Shattering, of course. There are some nasty things out there."

Curious. Simmon hadn't said anything about this subject. "Like?" he prompted, earning a questioning look.

"Beasts put together with sorcery before and during the Shattering. Vicious, cruel things. Jukari, for one. Then there's the leftover sorcerous laboratories and such. I doubt we'll ever find them all. Dangerous knowledge is still out there."

Caldan frowned, puzzled. "So they're real? Jukari, I mean. I thought they were only tales."

"They are as real as you and I, and much scarier. Most of the Protectors in Anasoma probably hadn't even seen one, let alone had to fight one. They were a bit sheltered. Too much time studying crafting and trinkets, and not enough time in the real world. But I shouldn't speak ill of them. They were all right, mostly. Still, I think you'll find that most of what you know of as 'tales' are in fact the very things we're sworn to fight."

And all things I would have learned if the Indryallans hadn't murdered my guild. Even with that morbid thought, it felt good to actually be getting information once again. After the frustrating journey with the likes of Bells and Amerdan, it seemed like maybe he could finally get some answers.

Mold motioned for Caldan to stop in front of a wooden door. Voices came from the other side.

"The masters have gathered for their regular morning meeting, so you're lucky—we won't have to wait until we can gather a few together. I was dragged out when you showed up. But let me warn you, you'll have a hard time convincing them Simmon named you an apprentice. I can't remember the last time that happened." He gave Caldan a shrewd look. "Though, judging by your well, I can see what he must have been thinking. It's a wonder the Sorcerers let you join us. Although we're considered part of the Guild, there's still some rivalry between sorcerers."

"Ah . . . I think it was my age." Though thinking back, the guild hadn't let him go; Simmon had just used his rank to get him. "They weren't quite sure what to make of me. I only arrived in Anasoma a few months ago."

"And Simmon snapped you up before they could? He always was a crafty one. He'll be missed. Well, are you ready?"

Caldan swallowed, then nodded.

Master Mold opened the door and ushered him inside.

Six pairs of eyes bore into him as he entered in front of the master. He looked back at four men and two women sitting before him, immediately taking in their craftings, including the few trinkets spread out among them. He was about to open his well to sense theirs, but at the last moment thought better of it. *Best not to make them curious about my own abilities.* He was here to provide as much information about Anasoma and the invaders as he could, then leave as fast as possible.

The masters sat in comfortable-looking chairs, while three others remained empty. One wall was taken up with a bookcase filled with leather-bound books and scrolls. A large open window let air and light into the room, under which sat one master, a curl of smoke rising from a wooden pipe in his hand.

"Mold," exclaimed a woman, thin and middle-aged, with long blond hair. "This is a meeting for masters only, as I trust you well know. Unless this is urgent, I recommend you take this young man elsewhere."

"You would think I've never been to one of these meetings, Annelie," Mold said. "Peace—you're going to be glad I interrupted. This lad's traveled all the way from Anasoma to see us. He's an apprentice Protector, so he says, under Master Simmon."

An intake of breath around the table greeted his words, followed by each of the masters laughing and exchanging words.

"Is this a joke?"

"Mold has finally cracked!"

"Really, Master Mold, such unsubstantiated and preposterous claims should be verified before bringing them to us."

"Pignuts and hogwash!"

Mold held up a hand and waited until the room quieted a little. "Hear me out," he said loudly enough to carry over their voices. "You know I wouldn't bother you unless I thought it worthwhile."

Caldan looked around the room. A few masters were studying him critically, and a number of touches brushed across his well. Interestingly, some felt rougher than others, clumsier. One he barely sensed, so featherlight and fleeting was its contact.

Six more masters to convince he knew Simmon and was an apprentice Protector, and he had no idea how many of them had actually met Simmon, let alone would know he kept flowers from his wife on his desk. None, he would wager. They would likely spend hours questioning him and still come to no conclusions, even with Master Mold to vouch for him. Their stupidity would drag on for hours, and he would rather get this over with. The sooner he was done here, the sooner he could get back to Miranda. He could see only one way to convince them of who he was and earn their trust, and to discharge his promise to Master Simmon at the same time.

He stepped into the center of the room and clapped his hands. All voices stopped. Silence settled over the masters.

"My name is Caldan. I was only in the Protectors a short time after Master Simmon took me in. I had no idea you didn't usually take on apprentices, but that is neither here nor there. Whether you believe me about that or not, the important thing is that Anasoma has fallen, the Protectors are broken and most likely all dead, and Master Simmon himself is dead."

The masters began speaking all at once.

Caldan raised his voice over theirs. "I understand you have questions, but let me finish. Before he died, Simmon urged me to escape and seek help. He wanted me to warn you of the destructive sorcery used against them, and of the coercive sorcery."

A few of the masters hissed. One gave a wordless cry of dismay.

"He shouldn't know . . ."

"That knowledge is forbidden . . ."

"Be quiet!" shouted Caldan.

The masters, including Mold, stared at him in shock.

"As I said—let me say what I need to say. I was sent to warn you, but Master Simmon also had another task for me." Caldan gripped the handle of the sword and drew the blade fully from the scabbard. "He asked me to bring you this."

The blade shone, even in the subdued light inside the room. All eyes were drawn to the sword. The masters gasped with astonishment as one, then just as quickly, their expressions went blank.

Caldan felt a hand on his shoulder—Master Mold's heavy grip.

"Thank you, lad," the master said solemnly. "That's . . . Master Simmon's prized possession. One very few people know about. He likely thought bringing it to us would prove your story. If I could just . . ."

Master Mold reached for the sword, and Caldan relinquished his grip. Though the masters were obviously trying to suppress their reactions, Caldan noticed there was a visible lessening of tension in the room when Mold took possession of the trinket.

Feigning indifference, Caldan unbuckled the sword belt and handed it to Mold, who sheathed the blade, leaving only the plain, battered hilt and pommel visible.

Again, Caldan felt as if the tension in the room lessened when the blade was returned to its scabbard. He filed the information away in the back of his mind. Whatever the significance of the sword, whether it was Simmon's or the Protectors', he really didn't care. As far as he was concerned, it validated his story and proved he could be trusted. And that meant he would be done with them and back to Miranda all the swifter.

He braced himself for their questions.

Master Annelie stood and approached. She only reached to his shoulder, and up close, her eyes were a remarkable green. The way the other masters deferred to her indicated she held some power among them.

"Well," she said gently. "I'm sure you have some questions, but they can wait until later. We thank you for bringing us Master Simmon's sword."

"Trinket," corrected Caldan.

Annelie's eyes narrowed. "Yes. Indeed it is. But I'm sure you're in need of rest."

"It's morning, and if it pleases you, I have some questions I'd like answers to now. I'm actually surprised you don't have questions for me."

She shook her head. "Yes, we do. But we can save all of that for later; once you've washed up. We haven't finished our morning's business yet and have much to discuss."

"But . . ."

"Yes," added Master Mold, ignoring his protest. "There are things we need to sort out, the usual business of running things here, nothing to bore you with."

Caldan kept his face expressionless. Whatever it was, he was sure it had to do with either him or the sword, though most likely the trinket. They had certainly been surprised and relieved when he revealed the blade.

Annelie grabbed Caldan's arm and urged him out the door.

He looked at Master Mold.

"Go with her," the master said. "She'll find you somewhere to stay until we need you."

He nodded and let her guide him into the corridor.

"Follow me," she said, and strode briskly away. "We have a few spare rooms. I'm sure you'll be thankful for a decent bed after your time on the road. You'll likely appreciate a bath as well. You do know Riversedge is famous for its hot baths, don't you? Why, I'm sure you do . . ."

Caldan let her constant patter fade into the background as he pondered what to do next. His vow to Simmon was fulfilled, but the Protectors had already shown they would keep secrets from him. He didn't care about all that. Sure, he was curious about their reaction to Simmon's sword, but there was only one secret he cared about now: whether they were practitioners of coercive sorcery and skilled enough to be able to help Miranda. Though how he was going to get that information out of them, he wasn't sure.

Master Annelie led him down a series of steps to the ground floor and continued along another corridor, this one covered with thread-bare and faded rugs.

"Ah, here we are."

The corridor came to an end, terminating in a wall. A small curtain-covered opening led through to another area.

Annelie directed him through, and the floor changed from rugs to stone. Warm stone. Damp air washed over him. Around a corner, the space opened into a large steam-filled room. In the center was a huge bath; it looked like a lake set into the floor. A number of wooden benches sat against the walls, while on one side of the room there were buckets, small stools, and scrubbing brushes.

Annelie opened a cupboard near where they had entered and removed a towel. "Here," she said with a smile.

She pointed to the buckets. "Scrub yourself clean, then have a good long soak. Let the hot water ease your worries away. You're here with us now, and safe."

Caldan thanked her, and she turned to leave, then stopped.

"Oh, I almost forgot. Don't wander around on your own. I'll have someone wait for you outside to take you to your room. We wouldn't want you to get lost."

With that, she left him standing there.

Whatever her motives, and those of the other masters, he did need a good scrubbing. He removed his clothes, making sure to hide all his craftings at the bottom of his satchel, and was soon clean and enjoying the heat of the water soaking into his weary muscles.

After he had washed up, he would worry about the Protectors and how much they knew of coercive sorcery.

Caldan ducked his head under the surface. The hot water felt good. It felt like months rather than days since they had fled Anasoma.

He wondered how Amerdan and Elpidia were coping with Bells while he was gone.

CHAPTER 13

Before dawn, Gazija had them all wakened with orders to prepare themselves for a day trip to shore.

Vasile shook his head and muttered a curse under his breath. *Orders!* As if they were under the old man's command. He'd gone along with it, for now.

They were ferried to shore in rowboats and followed Gazija to the gray, dilapidated, and weed-filled ruins of an old tower. After arriving, Gazija's men started three large fires and began setting up an awning stretching out from one wall of the tower. Vasile warmed himself by one of the fires until they shooed him away and began using them to heat pots of a tasty-smelling stew. Under the awning, they set up a table and filled it with loaves of bread. The whole lot—firewood, pots, bread—had arrived shortly after them, carried on two wagons. Gazija was preparing to feed a lot of people, but Vasile had no idea who they were.

A dismal place for a meeting, Vasile thought. A constant drizzle falling from the depressingly dark sky didn't help, either. Water dripped from his nose and hair, trickling down his neck and inside his shirt. They were clumped in groups around and inside the falling-down structure. He didn't feel like conversation, so wandered around the small hill on which the tower had been built. Aidan, cel Rau, and Chalayan sat on stones that had tumbled loose, barely a word spoken between them. He supposed that men who had spent so much time together on the road would have worn out all conversation long ago.

Clinging to the arm of a woman, Gazija stood patiently, eyes perpetually focused on the north, as if expecting someone to appear any moment. He had been standing like that for the last hour.

Vasile sighed as his pants leg caught on a thorny bush. He disentangled himself and kicked the offending plant. He'd never liked leaving the city; the rest of the world was too chaotic. But at least animals and plants didn't know how to lie to each other. He sniggered at the thought, earning a disapproving glance from Quiss. The thin man stood with Mazoet, and they conversed in hushed tones. Such a contrasting pair.

Over the last few days, Vasile hadn't had a chance to talk with Gazija or Mazoet, as both had been busy doing whatever it was they were up to. That was fine by him; he'd had more time to talk with Aidan and his men, to come up with a plan.

Unfortunately, so far they had decided nothing other than to wait and watch.

Gazija and his ilk might say they were fighting a greater evil, and *believe* it for truth, but that didn't mean they were, only that they held a belief Vasile's talent couldn't verify. Where his talent led him astray, as he often realized, was that just because someone believed something with all their heart and mind didn't make it *the* truth. Just *their* truth. Which was why he preferred to make a judgment based on reason and evidence, with his talent as further confirmation, if possible.

All he had was Gazija and his people's word to go on. *Can I justify helping a lesser evil to overcome a greater? And is that even what I'm doing?*

He shivered in the rain. A sad state of affairs.

A whinny broke his thoughts, and he raised his head—a number of people had drawn near the hill. Five to be exact, with only one horse between them.

Aidan, cel Rau, and Chalayan were now standing, while a few of Gazija's people moved to surround their leader.

In spite of the newcomers' bedraggled and wet appearance, there was an edge to them, a sense of purpose and suppressed readiness. Gazija stepped forward to greet them as they approached, waving an arm in the air. Vasile scurried over to join him as the group approached warily.

"Ho!" shouted Gazija, then broke into a fit of coughing. Hunched over, he gestured to Luphildern, an indication for him to take over.

With long strides of his spindly legs, Quiss strode toward the newcomers. Vasile decided to scamper after him, earning a disapproving stare from Gazija as he passed the old man, which he steadfastly ignored.

The group stopped ten yards from Quiss—three men and two women, all dressed in clothes of different styles, so Vasile assumed they were not soldiers of any kind. Still, there was a ruthlessness to their stares that left him cold. Either they had done cruel things, or witnessed them, or life had been unkind—or possibly all three.

He supposed that description fit a lot of people these days.

The horse carried not a rider but a number of bundles covered with a sturdy cloth and tied with rope.

"Well," remarked Luphildern. "Lovely day for a walk."

Vasile gave him a questioning look and shook his head. Silence greeted Luphildern's words.

The thin man coughed into his hand. "Ah, you must excuse me. My attempts at levity are sometimes . . . unappreciated."

One of the newcomers stepped forward and spoke—a large man, clean-shaven, with black hair neatly trimmed.

"We're just passing through; we don't want any trouble."

"Oh, my, no trouble from us, I assure you." Luphildern looked toward the two women. "Which one of you is Lady Felicienne?"

The clean-shaven man looked back at his companions, who remained expressionless, then back to Luphildern.

"Never heard of her."

Luphildern motioned Vasile forward. "And what do you think, Vasile?" he whispered. "Should we believe this man?"

"Ah, no. They know who she is."

"Excellent!" Luphildern rubbed his hands and raised his voice. "I was told to expect more of you, so I presume they are on their way? No, don't answer; we know of Lady Felicienne, who met with our . . . representative, Rebecci. She arranged for a good number of you to escape Anasoma and explained you would meet friends down the coast. Well"—Luphildern waved a hand to take all of them in—"we are those friends, and we expect Rebecci to join us soon. So I ask again, which one of you is Lady Felicienne?"

The men and women exchanged grim looks. Finally, the first man answered.

"She was meant to join us days ago, the day after we left Anasoma, but she didn't appear at the meeting spot. We waited a few days, but . . . there was no sign of her. We don't think she made it out."

"Either captured, or for some reason unable to escape, then," Quiss said.

Rubbing a weary hand over his face, the man shrugged. "We don't know."

"Well," said Luphildern. "I'm sure she will be joining us soon. From what I've heard, the lady is quite sharp and resourceful. What do you think, Vasile?"

"Of Lady Felicienne? I know of her. A hard reputation. An intelligent and skilled woman, by all accounts."

"There, you see! All will be well. Rebecci might have more up-to-date information when she arrives. Why don't you go back and round up your men; I'm sure they could use a hot meal." He gestured toward the cook fires and the table under the awning.

They moved toward the food, leaving Vasile with more questions than answers.

OVER THE COURSE of the morning, groups of men and women dribbled into the area surrounding the tower. At midday, Vasile ate his fill along with Aidan and his companions. He saw Luphildern turn his nose up at the food, though at Gazija's urging he swallowed a few mouthfuls. No wonder he was so thin. By midafternoon, the flow of refugees had pretty much ended.

Gazija's people kept the fires burning and refilled the pots of stew, though the bread became a little soggy when the wind shifted, driving the drizzle onto the tables. The day moved on.

Vasile's head drooped, and he almost nodded off, despite the cold and rain, when there was movement around the camp.

He grunted as Aidan nudged him in the ribs.

"Another surprise," remarked Chalayan.

Aidan spooned in a mouthful of stew and chewed thoughtfully.

Down the worn path to the tower, a horse approached, this one carrying a rider—a thin, pale woman with long blond hair trailing behind her.

"She's got the look," remarked Aidan, and Chalayan nodded.

Vasile squinted to inspect the woman, looking puzzled. "The look?"

"Thin. Emaciated. As if she hasn't eaten for weeks," said Aidan.

"Like Luphildern," stated Vasile.

"Exactly. We don't know why, but some of them don't like eating."

Chalayan chortled to himself, and they all looked at him.

"Maybe they only drink blood," whispered the sorcerer, eyes rolling around.

"Like jukari," said cel Rau.

Aidan scoffed at the idea. "We know little enough about them without making things up. And jukari don't only drink blood; they eat flesh as well."

As if that makes it better?, Vasile thought.

With a shrug, Chalayan continued to stare at the woman, who had slowed her horse to a trot, then stopped near Luphildern. She dismounted easily and gave the thin man a quick embrace.

"She's loaded with craftings," commented Chalayan. "Maybe some trinkets as well; I can't be sure from here."

Mazoet appeared at Vasile's side. The big man had eaten a loaf of bread by himself, and several bowls of stew. Luphildern had stared at Mazoet with a disgusted expression the whole time he'd been eating.

"Walk with me," said Mazoet, and strode off away from the tower and down the hill, leaving Vasile to shrug at Aidan, then struggle after the sorcerer. For such a big man, Mazoet was surprisingly light on his feet.

"Gazija has a task for us," Mazoet said once Vasile caught up. He had a leather pack on his back, though it looked half-empty.

"What task? And what's my role?"

"You'll find out soon enough, but since it's you, I don't think he wants us to move heavy rocks, do you? The right tool for the job is required." He gave Vasile a dark look. "Are you a tool, Vasile?"

"Eh? What do you mean?"

"Are you a tool? Or are you the craftsman using the tool?"

Vasile felt heat rise to his face. "I don't know what you mean."

"I believe you do. Or are you a craftsman, using his own tools for his—or even the world's—benefit?"

"So far, I would hazard a guess that I've been the tool."

"Then it's time you gave some thought to your predicament."

"Oh, I've thought about it," Vasile said.

Mazoet regarded him evenly. "I doubt you have done much more than wallow in self-pity. You are not the man you once were."

Vasile bristled at his words, and his tone, then his shoulders slumped. He knew Mazoet was right. What was the point of valuing the truth if you couldn't apply it to yourself?

"What do you suggest I do?"

"Do what you are good at. Apply reason and evidence to the problems around you. Reach conclusions, then test them. See if your deductions stand up to testing. Only then will you know real truth."

But what problems? Your problems? Or, rather, Gazija's problems? Vasile found himself unconvinced. The trouble was, Vasile had no idea what he was doing out here, and vague tasks to "find out the truth" meant nothing to him.

And yet, what other options did he have? He wasn't going to learn anything by just sitting on a boat or around the ruins of a tower. Truth. That was what it came down to. He needed to find the truth.

So I will help Mazoet for now, and then maybe more of the truth will actually emerge.

Mazoet remained silent. Their path took them along the road to the south, a little inland so they could no longer see the ocean.

Mazoet paused and looked around. There was no one else in sight. "Come, quickly now."

The big man left the road and made his way toward the tree line marking the edge of a forest. He skirted a lake, with Vasile trailing behind him. They pushed their way through low branches, which thinned out the farther into the trees they went. Soon they reached an area where the trees clumped close to the lakeshore, with only a narrow bar of dark sand between them and the still water.

Finding a relatively unobstructed patch of ground, Mazoet lifted a hand, indicating for Vasile to stop.

"What are we doing?" asked Vasile.

Without a word, Mazoet found a dry stick and scratched a circle a few yards wide in the sand. He then dragged his boot sideways along the line, deepening the circle into the ground.

"One moment," said Mazoet. He turned to face the way they had come. "First, let me check if he's following."

Vasile ducked his head, then realized they were deep in the cover of the trees, and presumably no one had seen them enter.

"The sorcerer," Mazoet said. "The untrained one."

"Chalayan? I wouldn't say he's untrained."

"*You* wouldn't. But then again, how could you? Believe me, his is a mix of tribal and academic sorcerous lore. From what I can tell, he has pieced it together himself. He found he had talent, and his thirst for knowledge has driven him ever since—but he's had no master."

"Like Gazija is for you?"

Mazoet said nothing but was clearly uncomfortable with the line of questioning. *How peculiar*, Vasile thought. *I wonder if he doesn't like any questions about Gazija or has problems with the nature of his relationship to the old man.*

Sometimes he wished he could read minds instead of just the truth. For now, though, he focused on Chalayan. "He's spying on us?"

"Us, you—whoever. He doesn't care. Though I suspect Aidan might have asked him to keep an eye on you."

"On me?" said Vasile, not convinced.

"Yes. Aidan is a canny man, and idealistic. You are a tool to him."

Vasile gave Mazoet a withering look. "I hardly think so."

"Then you might be surprised." He paused. "I can't sense him following, and I would be surprised if he could conceal himself from me. But there is a crafting close by . . ." Mazoet frowned, then turned around the clearing, as if searching for something. His eyes stopped on Vasile.

"Come here," he commanded.

"Why? What's going on?"

With a frustrated sigh, Mazoet approached him. "Empty your pockets."

"I haven't stolen anything."

Mazoet held out a meaty hand; his eyes flashed with anger. "Put the contents of your pockets into my hand. Now."

Shaking his head, Vasile complied. A few copper ducats, some pocket fluff, a piece of string, and a small black stone he'd liked the look of when wandering around the ruined tower that morning.

"Bah," exclaimed Mazoet. "That's not it; put it back. What else do you have on you? Did the sorcerer give you anything?"

"Just my coin purse." Vasile patted a securely tied pouch hanging from his belt. "He gave me a gold ducat as part payment for a wager we had, even though I told him I wouldn't collect."

"Show me."

Vasile rummaged inside the pouch until he produced the gold ducat. Mazoet snatched it from his hand.

"Hey!"

The large man ignored him, holding the coin between two fingers, eyes narrowing. He angled it to a bright patch in the cloud, to better examine it. "Ha! I knew it."

"What is it?"

Mazoet pointed to one side of the coin, and Vasile peered closely. There were scratches on the surface, all the way around the profile of the emperor.

"It looks like . . . writing?"

"Runes, symbols, glyphs—call them what you will. It's sorcery. With this in your possession, he can know where you are at all times. Even listen in. Though it's not active now."

Outraged, blood rushed to his face. "Why would he do that?" Vasile demanded.

"Because you are a tool, an instrument they mean to use. A means to an end."

"And that's not what I am to you?"

Mazoet took a few moments to reply. He smiled wryly, then inclined his head in a gesture of respect, jowls wobbling. "No. You might just be our salvation."

It was not what he was expecting to hear—especially considering the conviction of truth behind Mazoet's words. "I don't understand. What exactly do you mean by that?"

Mazoet didn't answer. Instead, he turned and threw the gold ducat out over the lake. It plopped onto the surface and sank, leaving only a few ripples to mark its passing.

Speechless, Vasile stared at the water where his ducat had disappeared; the ripples slowly vanished. He turned to Mazoet, who shrugged.

"It's only a coin."

No, it's my coin. He disliked being spied on, but he also disliked losing the only gold he had left. Vasile gritted his teeth in frustration.

Watching him closely, Mazoet removed a folded cloth from inside his pack. He opened it to reveal a long thin chain of gold links. Attached to it at intervals were faceted stones the size of pigeon eggs—transparent gems, as well as red and green, along with small flat discs of beaten silver covered with runes.

Vasile stared at the chain, mouth agape.

"That's . . ." he said, and swallowed. "Diamonds?" The chain could have bought a fleet of ships, or a small town. Even a trinket . . . or three.

"Gold and diamonds, and other precious stones," confirmed Mazoet. "A superior sorcerous crafting, if I do say so myself. But it's still just basically rocks. It's still just a *thing*." As he spoke, Mazoet unraveled the chain, pausing a moment to untangle one section. Carefully, he began laying it in the circle he had scraped into the sand. "Your world is on a precipice, though not many people know it. We cannot allow what happened to us to happen here. It is . . . inconceivable. We can't . . . we won't let that happen again. The thought of fleeing is unacceptable to most of us." He stared into Vasile's eyes until Vasile turned away. "We are possibly your world's only hope of salvation, as you are possibly ours. But we must tread carefully, as our intervention may ensure our destruction."

"My world?" asked Vasile.

"Just my way of speaking."

Truth, realized Vasile. And yet, somehow, he thought Mazoet was hiding a greater truth in his words. A chill washed over his skin.

Mazoet stepped inside the circle of gold and gemstones, then he pointed at the chain surrounding him. "All of this . . . gold, precious gems, whatever else you consider has value . . . does not matter if there is another Shattering. We aim to prevent that happening, no matter the cost." He paused to take a breath and held out a hand. "Come, join me inside the circle."

Warily, Vasile stepped over the chain and stood next to the sorcerer.

"Take my hand," ordered Mazoet. "There needs to be contact."

"What's going to happen?" asked Vasile. He grasped the offered hand.

Mazoet closed his eyes. "We are going to speed up part of our plan. The Indryallan invasion came quicker than we thought. Our preparations were not complete."

"You knew the invasion would happen?"

"'Knew' is too strong a word. Suspected, perhaps. We believed something major would happen. Now, please be quiet; I have to concentrate."

Without warning, the chain began to give off heat, and in moments it glowed a bright orange, as if placed into a forge. Under the chain, wet sand sizzled and hissed. Steam rose into the air, swirling in the light breeze.

"What's happening?"

Without opening his eyes, Mazoet said, "We need to be somewhere in a hurry. Horses would take too long, so we have to avail ourselves of other means."

Vasile's stomach sank; he felt ill.

"We are here, then we will be there," explained Mazoet, as if that made any sense.

"What happens to the crafting then?"

"Why, it is destroyed. Take this as evidence of our sincerity, of our commitment, of our intentions. Sacrifices have to be made, and though this is only material wealth, it has to show you how true our intentions are. For words can be molded to seem true when they are not."

Before he could respond to that, Vasile's head and stomach lurched, as if he were being folded in half somehow, physically and mentally. Reality twisted. One of the gems made a cracking sound and exploded. Bright glowing shards sprinkled the sand at their feet.

His vision blurred. Head spinning, he reeled to the ground, only there was nothing there. There was another crack, then two more. Sparks filled his eyes, then faded.

He hit the sand face-first with a thump. Breath squeezed from his lungs. Gasping like a fish out of water, he realized his eyes were still shut. They opened slowly, as if stuck together.

He was sitting on sand, but it was a different color. It was white.

Mazoet sat beside him, regarding him with a nonchalant expression. The trees, lake, and sand were gone. Bright sun shone down from a cloudless sky. Waves crashed against the sandy shore to his left.

A thin stream of smoke rose from Vasile's right boot, and he used his other heel to scrape at the offending spot. His vigorous scuffing dislodged a bright green fragment of emerald, which fell onto the sand and lay smoking. It had almost burned a hole through his boot.

"WELL," SAID AIDAN cautiously, "a few hundred people doesn't make an army."

Gazija cackled and rubbed his withered hands together. The old man was in a good mood today. After all the refugees from Anasoma had gathered among his own people, a grin remained plastered on his face.

"No, indeed not. But small beginnings can lead to greater things. Especially with a little foresight and planning."

"What are you up to, old man?"

"Helping the emperor defend his empire, *young* man. Doing our best in the circumstances, and far more than you've done, I might say."

"It's not my fight."

"Bah! It is. You just don't know it yet."

Aidan sniffed. A droplet of water hung from the end of his nose. He wiped it away. "I'll take some convincing. So far, I haven't heard anything horrific the invaders have done, except for invading, that is. From what I've been able to determine the city isn't that badly off."

He had taken the opportunity to question some of the people after they streamed in. Though they all professed loyalty to the emperor and swore the Indryallans were evil, the only evidence they had was their insistence the invaders had wiped out the Sorcerers' Guild and Protectors.

The fewer sorcerers in the world, the better, Aidan thought. Though they could be useful at times. Such power in the hands of frail-minded humans was a recipe for corruption, but so long as there were people like him and Caitlyn in the world, then evil would not go unpunished. Chalayan would bear watching, though; he had been sniffing around Gazija's people for the last few days, trying to ferret out their secrets. Ever since the battle where Caitlyn had . . . died . . . and the sorcerer had seen the power on display, he had been ill at ease, though he hid it well. Aidan could see he coveted their power. Such need had driven

Chalayan to become a sorcerer in the first place, and now Aidan saw that if he learned more, he could command the very elements themselves. To Chalayan, it would be a sweetness he couldn't ignore.

Yes, I'll be watching him closely.

"So you don't think blue fire that keeps people from entering or leaving the city is a bad thing?" Gazija said, responding to Aidan's comments. He shook his head. "Never mind—it's not worth an argument. I'd rather talk about the men you have out in the forest. More than when Mazoet found you. The remnants of your band."

"You surprise me, old man. You know things you should not."

"I make it my business to know things." Gazija coughed harshly and raised a kerchief to his lips. It came away stained scarlet. He gestured, and one of his servants brought his walking sticks for him to lean his weight on.

Aidan stared at the blood but said nothing.

"You call me old man, and that I am, but never mistake me for a fool, Aidan. As I said, the more you know, the better decisions you can make."

"And the more you know, the more power you have."

"Whoever told you knowledge is power should throw themselves off a cliff. Power comes in many different forms. Knowledge is one, I'll grant you, but so are ducats, and leverage. An emperor has more power than a farmer, does he not? Why? Because of his position. A reward can hold power, as can individual charisma. A fool stops at knowledge."

"So you say."

"I *do* say. I've learned some things in all my years, and that is one of the most important." Gazija coughed again before continuing. "Now, to the business at hand. We will need your assistance, if we're to liberate Anasoma. Some things we're able to do on our own, but we cannot do everything."

"How many of you are there?"

Gazija gave him a penetrating stare. "Enough."

"I don't know if I want to help you yet, old man."

"You will. The fact is, you won't be able to stop yourself."

"And why is that?"

"Because it's in your nature."

"My nature is to find evil and injustice wherever I can and destroy it." Caitlyn's ideals, which he shared. It was what had drawn them together. But unlike her, he wouldn't let it break him.

"Exactly. It is that nature which makes you so useful to us. You and your men. A band well known for what they are and what they do. I'll be honest—I'm glad it's you who leads them, and not Lady Caitlyn. If she were still with you, I fear she would have tried to kill me already."

Aidan scowled. "Do not speak of her."

Gazija bowed his head. "I know her memory pains you. She must have meant a lot to you."

"You know nothing, old man."

"I know enough." Gazija sighed, the deep weary sound of a man straining under many burdens. His shoulders slumped slightly. "I know too much, is the problem. The past is a yoke around everyone's neck, be they young or old." He stirred himself and straightened. "But my mind wanders. We were talking of how you can help us."

"Tell me what you want," Aidan said. His blood ran cold just thinking about working with Gazija and his unknown motives, but he must do what he had to do. Brute force wouldn't win the day here; he needed to be subtle. Only from the inside could he find their weakness. Caitlyn had followed a different path, but hers had led to madness and despair.

"I want you to leave us." Gazija chuckled at the sharp look Aidan gave him. "I know you will be reluctant to depart our company after partaking of our hospitality, but it must be done, I'm afraid. The Indryallans' plans are in motion, our counterplans are in motion, and somewhere out there, the empire's plans are also in motion. And I do so hate not knowing what they are up to."

"Don't you have spies that can tell you?"

"To the world, we are the Five Oceans Mercantile Concern, not spies. Oh, we have sources of information, of course: friendly merchants and traders, people indebted to us who are only too happy to pass along what they know."

Gazija coughed into a liver-spotted hand, a harsh racking sound. A number of his people threw concerned looks his way, shifting nervously on their feet. Aidan looked on without pity. Gazija seemed to notice and sighed again. Although Aidan couldn't be sure, it felt like the sigh wasn't out of self-pity, but sadness on *his* behalf.

Keep your pity, old man. It means nothing to me.

"Obviously we're not really merchants," Gazija said, "but it allows us to operate with a certain amount of freedom. Not that that makes up for the sacrifices." He went on, musing, "It is no life for us. Once such a proud people. Look at us now. We are diminished, a shadow of what we were. We have been running too long. We ran before, and I still believe it was the right decision. But now we face a similar choice, though forewarned in this instance. It is time we stop running, whatever the outcome."

What lies behind this? What "proud people"?

Ancestors, what is this man talking about!

"I ask again," Aidan said flatly, "what do you want?"

"Vasile has two tasks, with gifts uniquely suited to one, and a slight chance he could succeed at the second." Gazija eyed Aidan warily, then looked away. "We want you to help him with the second task."

"And that would be . . . ?"

"By now the news of the invasion is all over the empire. People have seen the flames barricading Anasoma and been turned away. Messengers will have been sent in all directions, as fast as they can travel. Even your sorcerers have ways of communicating. We know the emperor has already been informed and formulated a response. A heavy-handed one, to be sure. His forces will be on their way."

"So we should leave it to them, then. They'll retake the city and mop up the Indryallans, and at the same time send a message to others who might challenge the might of the emperor."

"Maybe . . ."

"What? Out with it, Gazija."

"We suspect something is amiss."

"And what's that?"

"If we knew, I would tell you."

"Would you, really?"

Gazija shrugged. "Probably not."

"Then why should I trust you?"

"Judge us by our actions."

"I can't, if I'm not here."

"True. But you've seen some of our actions so far. Mazoet saving you, for instance. The fact is, whether you are here or not, our actions will be the same." Gazija waved a hand to the north in a gesture Aidan thought was meant to encompass Anasoma and beyond. "This will not be decided by small movements and conversations like this one, though they are part of a grander scheme. Or perhaps it will . . . I cannot see the future. What I mean to say is that the larger events will paint a clearer picture for you."

Aidan had listened to about as much as he could take. He turned his head and spat, the back-and-forth having left a sour taste in his mouth. *Old men and their self-important musings, enamored with the sound of their own voices.* He had joined Lady Caitlyn to escape just such a man—his father.

"Get to the point, old man. Your rambling is getting on my nerves."

Gazija inclined his head. "As you wish. I want you to escort Vasile to the west, away from Anasoma."

"And why is that?"

"Because the emperor will have sent soldiers this way in a response to the invasion. Most likely a great many of them, along with Protectors and his warlocks. Such a challenge to his rule will not be tolerated. And my information is that he will come himself, albeit at the rear of his army, and probably against the advice of his advisors. The chance to see such a victory firsthand is too enticing. To parade into the retaken city at the head of a victorious army, after a true display of power and might . . . He will be coming. I am certain of it."

"What does this have to do with Vasile? And with me?"

"Vasile met the emperor briefly, a long time ago. We believe the emperor might even trust him, to a certain extent. We've tasked Vasile to petition an audience with the emperor and explain what we've done to help. Vasile will then serve as our representative and convince the emperor we can be trusted. I can't reveal everything to you, but it is imperative the emperor sees us as a valuable ally. It is our hope Vasile will be persuasive."

"I don't want to piss on your fire," Aidan said, meaning to do exactly that, "but it seems like a lot resting on a slim hope."

"The world is built on slim hopes, Aidan. Take your mission, for example. You try to eradicate evil, and yet there always seems to be more, no? Does that stop you? Of course not—you keep trying, because it's worthwhile. Yes, we are putting our faith on a lot of *ifs*. But here's something all my *old* knowledge has led me to know is true: empires are complex systems, and emperors are complex beings. You can no more predict what he will do than I can. But the chance is worth it, to be able to explain to the empire the extent of our power— and willingness to help—on *our* terms."

A pretty speech, Aidan thought. And yet, for all its grandiosity, he couldn't help but feel a sliver of trust when hearing it. *I may not think he's telling me everything, but at least his zealotry is tempered with pragmatism.*

Which is more than could be said about Caitlyn . . .

Taking a breath at that thought, Aidan said, "I will consider your request, Gazija, while we wait for Vasile to return. Any idea when he'll be back?"

"Soon, very soon. They have gone to hurry along our army, among other things."

Aidan's mouth opened in shock.

They have an army?

Gazija smiled.

CHAPTER 14

Amerdan's memory of his childhood was jumbled and scattered. Certain scenes were vivid, while others were washed out, faded. He liked to think of the vibrant pockets of memories as the ones that were life changing. It was as if his mind had taken hold of what he saw, smelled, touched, and heard, and etched it into his soul, much like a stain or tattoo. And, contrary to what most people said they experienced, his memories were becoming *clearer*. It was a curiosity he believed to be a by-product of his reinvention, part of his transformation along the way to rebirth.

His clearest memories would often come on him unawares when he was involved with ordinary day-to-day tasks, as if to remind him, to keep him focused.

Perhaps his strongest one was of his family, the faces of his mother and father, his sisters. Of their cozy house, which was a few days' walk from the village. Of his father, who always smelled like dirt and sweat from his day's labor on the farm, though his mother never seemed to mind.

Dust glowed in the sunlight inside their house, streaming through windows wide open to summer. That was the day his father died. And his mother. The day the sorcerer came with his . . . things. Monsters. Looking for children to take for his experiments. Months they spent in the iron cage, judging the passage of time by the light through an iron grate in the stone wall.

Cold, dirty, barely fed enough to keep them alive, Amerdan's sisters begged one of the sorcerer's servants for extra food . . . which they passed to him so he could keep up his strength. After all, he was the eldest. They looked to him to save them.

Amerdan squeezed his eyes shut at the memory—the most painful of all, even more so than that of the deaths of his parents. His failure to protect them. Strength and opportunity to overcome the sorcerer had come on him too late. Even the man's warm blood hadn't been enough to wash away his shame.

Did he hate sorcerers? He often thought on this, and the answer was always yes. Hate was the only emotion he felt. To be fair, he really didn't care about anything. Except what he wanted.

He grasped the silver chain around his neck and drew out his trinket, the second thing of value the sorcerer had given to him. Bringing the spherical pendant to his lips, he kissed it gently then placed it in his mouth, letting his tongue roll around it, moistening the surface. *If only I could absorb you*, he thought. *Subsume you. Become as one.*

Inside his shirt, Dotty moved against his skin. He felt safe with her there, but she couldn't help him if she couldn't see. He didn't know why she'd come alive after all but one of his sisters were killed, but he was glad she had. He liked to think part of his sisters had joined with the doll.

When Caldan had left for the city this morning, Amerdan decided not to wait any longer. Bells wasn't providing Caldan with enough information to make keeping her alive a proposition that would benefit him. And he had waited long enough to determine whether Caldan himself was worth absorbing. Compared to Bells, he was a babe in the woods, despite having bested her in the tunnels under Anasoma, where luck had played a large part in their escape. No, Bells was . . . exquisite. He sucked on his trinket as if it were a boiled sweet, savoring the harsh metallic taste in his mouth. What he wanted—what he needed—was for Bells to take him to meet her God-Emperor. Then she would have fulfilled her function and could go on to serve her last purpose with him.

Caldan had sorted through her craftings and left five of the bells behind, and Amerdan knew it was a sign. When he was returning to the camp carrying the mice Elpidia had wanted, a crow cawed five times, and he was sure the time had come.

He secreted himself outside of the camp and pulled out his rag doll from his shirt. He hadn't minded keeping her there while they were traveling, close to his skin, and to his beating heart.

He asked if she thought he was right about the timing; Dotty agreed, and it was done.

Let Bells think she had persuaded *him* to join her for the ducats. That it was her idea to trick Elpidia. It wouldn't matter. She would find out what was coming and beg for his mercy. In the end, they all did, to no avail.

"Aren't you going to help with the fire?"

Bells's annoyed voice carried to where he sat in the darkness. Through the trees, he could see a faint orange glow. He spat his trinket out and tucked it underneath his shirt. In a few moments, he gathered up the sticks he had left beside him and walked into the light.

Bells had dug a small pit into the soft earth beneath the trees and started a fire, enough for warmth and perhaps a meal. Let her cook what she wanted. After his imprisonment as a boy, Amerdan always preferred his meals raw.

Pits were useful, though. For fires. For burying things.

He stepped close. "Here you go." He gave the sorcerous slit a brief smile. It was what people did.

"Thank you," Bells replied. "Just leave it there."

Amerdan placed the firewood next to the pit. He guessed he had better reinforce her opinion of him.

"Ah . . . when will I get my ducats?"

Bells gave a weary shrug. "When we get back." She eyed him cautiously, as if deciding something. "But that might take longer than you think. We need to go west first."

"Why is that?"

"I was tasked with joining up with the emperor's army anyway. For . . ." The sorcerer hesitated. "For a few reasons. I have to fulfill my mission. You can go back to Anasoma and wait for me, or you can help me succeed."

Amerdan remained still. To the west, the empire would be gathering its forces, and he was sure this sorcerer couldn't take on an army by herself. Which meant . . .

"You're going to meet with the emperor. To kill him, or to negotiate?"

Her eyes narrowed, and he knew he'd struck close to the truth.

Bells looked down, and a brief smile flickered across her face. "To talk with the emperor. Among other things. I can guarantee you'll see your gold; they won't risk killing me."

Lies and more lies. "What about Caldan? Don't forget you promised he was mine. But he killed Keys, and you swore to kill them all. Except for me, of course."

Amerdan chuckled inside every time he threw Keys's death into her face.

"Caldan is yours, but Elpidia will have to wait until I'm finished."

Amerdan gave her a nod. *I don't believe her,* he thought, inwardly smirking. *The slit's trying to deceive me. She is going to keep Caldan for herself. And kill the emperor somehow. Unless I kill him first. What talents might an emperor have that lesser things don't?*

He savored the sweet thought. *One emperor is as good as another. Two is even better.*

"THERE'S A PLACE for you here," the journeyman said, pointing to an open door leading into a bare room. The tall man with lank, greasy hair had interrupted Caldan's bath and hurried him to the journeymen's quarters.

There was an empty wooden bench against one wall, a narrow cot covered with a gray woolen blanket, and the window was shuttered.

Caldan nodded his thanks and dumped his belongings onto the bench with a metallic clink. After scrubbing himself clean, he felt invigorated, and eager to use any spare time he had investigating Bells's craftings.

"If you need anything, call out," added the journeyman, smiling apologetically. "Someone will always be outside. We've been passed word you're to be treated as one of us, but we can't give you the run of the building yet."

"I understand," replied Caldan as the man left and closed the door behind him. And he did. The masters had much to think about and discuss regarding his sudden appearance and the trinket he'd brought with him.

It didn't mean he'd cooperate.

He'd done what he wanted to, and now he needed to get out of here without arousing suspicion. Tricky, considering they would find him leaving so soon a cause for concern, even alarm. But he had to get back to Miranda.

Examining the window, he found the shutters locked. With no exit that way, and a journeyman standing guard outside his room, his options were limited. Breaking through the window with raw destructive sorcery was a fool's choice; it would reveal to the Protectors here far more than he wanted to and wouldn't give him much of a head start. It was likely he'd be caught before he could escape the building. No, he needed to be gone a good few hours before they found out.

He just had to dissociate his mind from the problem and let the solution come to him, as it so often did when he played Dominion.

Caldan looked up as a drop of rain spattered against the window. Then another. Lightning flashed through the cracks of the shutters, and moments later there was a roll of thunder. Drops steadily increased to a constant patter. He hoped Elpidia had moved Miranda into the covered wagon before the rain hit.

He pulled out the craftings they had taken from Mahsonn and sat on the cot. Whatever Mahsonn's abilities, he'd needed craftings to execute sorcery, just like everyone else. The Bleeder had a few tricks, and Caldan wanted to see what they were, in case they might come in handy. Bells's craftings were still far too complex for him to figure out in a short amount of time, but he guessed Mahsonn's would be much easier to decipher.

Two wristbands and a medallion. Not much for a sorcerer who supposedly had a rare talent. And shoddily smith-crafted, too, except for the medallion shaped like a horned beast.

Caldan pushed the other items aside and cradled the medallion in his hand. It had to be the one that enabled Mahsonn to hide from view. The other craftings barely warranted the designation. Though their metals seemed pure, the link between the materials and the runes was patchy at best. Probably Mahsonn's own work, while this medallion was something else: made by a master smith-crafter.

Caldan opened his well and concentrated on it. There were far too many links and anchors for a journeyman, or even a master, to be able to connect strings to. He counted them: thirteen! That was . . . impossible. Yet he remembered what Bells had said: Bleeders were able to focus their power into many tiny threads, and control them.

He threw the medallion onto the cot and sighed with disgust. It was useless to him, specifically designed so only a Bleeder could link to it. Unless he could master splitting his well into so many strings, he couldn't begin to understand how it functioned.

He examined the three other craftings and determined they were practically worthless. One was for shielding, though the quality was so poor it would hardly fulfill its function. A major disadvantage of the Bleeders, Caldan assumed. A practically nonfunctioning well would severely limit what a sorcerer could do.

He pounded on the door, and within moments it opened to reveal the journeyman.

"I need to see Master Annelie," Caldan said firmly. "Or Master Mold. Whoever is free."

"They're closeted in a meeting. I don't think—"

"Knock until someone answers; make a nuisance of yourself. I don't care. Just get one of them to see me. It's important. I . . . forgot to tell them something."

The journeyman looked askance at him but eventually nodded.

MASTER ANNELIE BARELY glanced at him as she entered the room before striding to the window. She poked at the shutters, as if to ensure they were locked, then turned to face him, toying with a lock of her blond hair.

"I'm told there is something else you need to tell me," Annelie said. "Something you . . . forgot. Am I correct?"

Swallowing nervously, Caldan nodded in reply. He wrung his hands to appear anxious, though it was hardly an act. He couldn't predict which way the masters would turn, and he risked Miranda's health by exposing what he knew, but it was the only idea he could think of to reveal how adept these Protectors were with coercive sorcery.

"Before Master Simmon . . . died, he told me he wasn't in control of his actions."

Caldan saw Annelie freeze, green eyes boring into his. Shock flickered across her face before she smoothed her expression.

"How so?"

"He said he did things harmful to the Protectors. That it was like he was a prisoner in his own mind, looking out while someone else controlled his actions."

Annelie broke eye contact. "Go on."

"He believed the Indryallans had used coercive sorcery on him, but he wouldn't tell me more."

Annelie brushed her hair over an ear, revealing an earring, which she touched in an unconscious gesture. Another crafting, set with a small stone. It was a streaky orange form of jasper, if he wasn't mistaken, just like Bells's coercive sorcery crafting.

So they do know how to use coercive sorcery.

"You say Master Simmon was under its influence," she said. "That is disconcerting. That they are able to overcome the defenses a master has in place is not something I want to believe."

"It's the tru—"

"Oh, I *do* believe you. I just don't want to." She shook her head. "Thank you—I'll bring it up with the other masters. Did Simmon say anything else?" Her green eyes regarded him with intensity.

"No. He only directed me to where he hid the sword and told me to warn the Protectors and the emperor, which is one of the reasons I asked to see you. I need to leave, to see the emperor. I promised Master Simmon."

Annelie laughed at his words and placed a hand over her mouth. She shook her head in mock despair. "Oh, my. You're serious. There's no way you'll be granted an audience with the emperor. You're far too low in the hierarchy to even be considered."

"But . . . I promised. Simmon wouldn't have asked if he didn't think it was important."

Annelie waved a hand to dismiss his words. "Simmon probably meant once you informed us of what had happened, we would then tell the emperor."

"Perhaps that's it."

She placed a hand reassuringly on his arm. "I'm sure it is. Don't worry, the emperor is on his way, and we'll have this mess sorted out in no time."

"The emperor is coming here?"

"Yes. He's mobilized a number of armies, and they're scheduled to gather here. The emperor's finest troops will be coming, along with his warlocks. The Indryallans will be no match for them, they will be pushed back into the sea, and Anasoma will be liberated. We'll stand by, as it's not the role of the Protectors to get involved. Then the emperor will look to the Indryallan lands themselves. This will be a show of force that is desperately needed to remind the world of the power of the empire, and the emperor, may he live forever."

Caldan's thoughts churned. Of course a show of force was needed. Of course the emperor would gather an army to march on Anasoma.

Why hadn't the Indryallans foreseen this? Why had they invaded one city and not others? Why had they not continued on to invade the surrounding countryside?

Pieces clicked into place, and Caldan felt the blood drain from his face.

Because they want the emperor to assemble his forces in one place. Anasoma was bait, a lure. The Indryallan destructive sorcery was more powerful than anything anyone had seen since the Shattering. Could they be powerful enough to massacre a whole army?

Caldan feared he knew the truth. His stomach churned at the thought. Weak-kneed, he sat on his cot and shivered.

"Listen. We have to stop him. The emperor. They'll be annihilated."

"What are you talking about?" Annelie said.

"Can't you see?" Caldan all but shouted, surprised the masters hadn't thought of this yet. "This is their design. Think about it. Why invade only Anasoma? Why nowhere else? Why take over the city and do nothing—nothing except wait for the emperor and his soldiers?"

"We don't know that's all they're doing. There must be something in Anasoma they want."

"Maybe, but what? What is worth the risk of annihilation? No. It makes no sense. Invading Anasoma is like kicking an ants' nest and waiting for the ants to come out. But what can they do from there? Surely their destructive sorcery needs a focus, and a powerful sorcerer strong enough to direct where the sorcery should . . ." His voice trailed off.

Bells.

She must have wanted to travel west toward the emperor all along. Which meant he had aided the Indryallans with their plan. And if this was the natural gathering point for the emperor's armies, Bells had come as far west as she needed to.

"By the ancestors' shadows," cursed Caldan. "I've been stupid. I have to go. My friends are in danger."

"What friends? Are you not alone?"

A loud banging on the door interrupted them.

"Master Annelie," shouted a voice. "Come quickly. A crazy woman just drove a wagon into the courtyard. She's screaming for Caldan."

Annelie flashed him an annoyed look, brow furrowed. "Come with me," she commanded.

CHAPTER 15

Felice awoke to cold, dank air. It smelled of human waste and . . . fear.

Her full bladder pressed against her insides, and her head ached. Her jaw hurt, too, as if she'd been grinding her teeth all night. Except, she realized, she hadn't simply been asleep. She groaned and rubbed the skin on her arms, remembering Savine Khedevis.

Half levering herself up from the floor, she found she was lying on rotting straw, some of which stuck to her clothes. She peered around in the dim light. At least she still had her clothes, though everything else of value had been taken.

In return, she had been given a piece of jewelry—an iron shackle clamped around her right ankle, attached to a chain, which in turn was bolted to a wall.

She laughed weakly, throat dry.

Next to Felice was a clay jug, and she fumbled for it. Water. She drank deeply, reasoning they had no need to drug her, at least not yet. In moments, the jug was empty, and she was still thirsty.

The room she was in was large, not a typical cell with a locked door or metal bars. Peering into the gloom, she could barely make out an opening at the far end. She couldn't confirm where she was being held, but the Indryallan headquarters was her best guess. So somewhere inside the keep, which she knew well.

There was no bucket that she could see to relieve herself, so she limped to the closest corner, chain clinking on the stone floor, and did her business there.

Felice had often had occasion to visit prisoners for questioning, but she had never been a detainee. It was a new experience, one she vowed never to repeat. Her men must have escaped, though she doubted Avigdor had managed to get away. He must be here somewhere, a prisoner like she was. Perhaps her men would come for them? No. They were too well trained and knew hopeless odds when they saw them. There was no chance they'd decide to mount a rescue.

Which is how it should be.

Yet she couldn't help but feel frustration. She'd been sure she had evaded pursuit, and yet Savine Khedevis had tracked and captured her. How?

No answers came, but then again, she didn't expect any. It made no difference. She had made a mistake and would have plenty of time to figure out what it was so she wouldn't make it again.

"GET UP. GET up. Get up."

A harsh voice sounded in her head, followed by a sharp pain in her side. Someone had kicked her.

Felice moaned and struggled to roll over. This wasn't how she had imagined her defense of Anasoma proceeding.

A hand grabbed her hair and yanked. Yelping, she struggled to her knees and opened her eyes, blinking rapidly at the light. She held a hand up to block the lantern clutched by an Indryallan soldier. He didn't look too pleased; he seemed uncomfortable, even. She shifted her eyes to see the man who had a handful of her hair: another Indryallan, this one with bad teeth and worse breath.

"Let go, you pignut," Felice said.

A knee crashed into her head, and the room swirled. Her face burned where the knee had made contact, but it hadn't been as jarring as she thought. She guessed the soldier hadn't struck as hard as he could have; maybe he was afraid to injure her. Any thought that she could use this to her advantage fled when she glimpsed a figure in the darkness behind the soldiers.

Savine Khedevis.

He stepped forward when she noticed him.

"Lady Felicienne. It's so nice to see you again." He smiled at her, and she almost smiled back, despite her situation.

He was a remarkably attractive man—almost too attractive. But there was something about Savine that bothered her, which she couldn't quite put her finger on. An attractive and powerful sorcerer who seemed . . . wrong, was the best way she could think to describe him. He made her skin crawl for no reason she could fathom.

She rose to her feet as gracefully as she could, groaning with the effort. Her tongue and mouth were dry, and she looked longingly at the empty water jug. "Could I have some more water, please?"

"Ah. Thirsty, are you? I'm sure you are. Perhaps later. I've a few questions for you. Afterward, provided your answers satisfy me, you can have all the water you need. Is that fair?"

Felice shook her head weakly. "Not really, no."

"Well, you don't have much choice in the matter. So I'll call it fair, and we can progress."

He nodded to the soldiers, and they grabbed her arms. She struggled to no avail. She didn't know what she was supposed to do against two professional soldiers, but she had never been one to go quietly.

A hand gripped her hair, and she choked as her head was yanked back. Her throat erupted in pain, and she could take only short breaths. Her hands clutched at the soldiers holding her. She wondered what would happen if she dug her nails into their arms. Nothing good. She relaxed as best she could and saw Savine nod as she went limp.

"Do you know what's going to happen now?" he asked.

"You . . ." she gasped, "will . . . torture . . . me."

Savine shook his head. "Oh no, nothing as crude as that. You'll tell me everything you know about the resistance you've been running— your men, your locations, what you know of us, and what you know about the Five Oceans Mercantile Concern."

"I won't talk."

"Ah. That's where you're wrong. You won't have a choice."

"Do your worst," she spat.

"You wouldn't like that. My worst is pretty bad. Instead, I'll settle for taking your thoughts straight from your pretty head. Though I have to warn you, it's going to hurt."

The last time he'd said that, she had passed out from the pain, so she braced herself.

It made no difference.

Savine laughed as burning needles stabbed into her mind. She cried out in wordless agony, hands clenched into fists, nails digging into her palms. A fresh wave of pain rolled over her, and a welcome darkness descended.

FELICE WOKE AGAIN. Cold sweat covered her body, and she was shivering. Her pants stuck to her legs, and this time the smell of excrement was her own.

Rolling onto her back with a clinking of chains, she groaned at her pounding head, opened her eyes a slit, then squeezed them tight. Even the dim light in the room was too much for her to bear. Her top lip itched, and when she rubbed under her nose, she felt dried blood.

Someone moved close to her, and she flinched, feeling rather than seeing the movement. Another clink of chains, not her own. A man coughed weakly. Gritting her teeth, she grabbed her chain and pulled the slack to her, doubled it on itself and formed a makeshift weapon. Drawing a breath to prepare herself, she opened one eye, squinting around the room.

Another chain had been attached to the bolt in the wall, leading to a figure.

She blinked. It was Avigdor.

Crawling as fast as she could across the gritty stone floor, she reached his side and cradled his head, which lolled limply. "Avigdor. Are you injured?"

No reply. Then she remembered his ankle. His bones had pierced the flesh, as bad a break as she'd ever seen.

A crude bandage covered the injured ankle, but she saw no sign he had been ministered to by a physiker. The bandage was too loose, and there were no splints. It was an unnerving sight that led her to suspect they didn't have much use for him.

Dried blood also covered Avigdor's top lip, a trail originating from his nose. Hopefully it was a minor side effect, and no permanent damage had been done. She could only speculate; she needed more information. But most of all, she needed to get her hands around Savine's neck and squeeze the life out of him.

The thought warmed her, and she gently laid Avigdor's head back on the cold floor. Shuffling to her bed, she gathered an armful of straw and made a pillow for him. Not much comfort, but the best she could do under the circumstances.

The water jug had been refilled, and she poured a trickle into his mouth, carefully, lest she choke him. After a few moments, he swallowed, and she breathed a sigh of relief. She continued until he drank a few mouthfuls. She took a sip herself, to quench her raging thirst, but left the jug half-full. Best to ration what they had, just in case.

Muffled voices reached her ears, coming from the opening at the end of the room. Boots scuffed on stone. Armor and weapons clanked. Four Indryallan soldiers emerged from the darkness followed by Savine, whose face lit up when he saw her staring at him. One of the soldiers carried a coarse robe.

"Excellent! I wasn't sure you'd be conscious by now. But from what I'd heard of your reputation, I was certain you'd have a resilient mind."

Felice remained silent.

Savine gestured to the soldier holding the robe, and the man flung it at her feet. Another threw a rag at her and slid a bucket of water toward her.

"Clean yourself and get changed. There's someone who wants to meet you: the man you tried to kill at the docks."

She looked at the robe lying on the floor. "You want me to get changed here? In front of you?"

"Yes, please. Now, if you don't mind."

All four soldiers grinned at her discomfort, while Savine shrugged.

"I can always get them to change you, though it might take longer and be quite distressing."

Felice looked at the soldiers, then raised an eyebrow and bent to retrieve the rag and bucket. Keeping her eyes on Savine, she undressed and wiped herself clean as best she could using the rag and bucket of water. She shrugged the robe over her head. It was scratchy on her skin, but at least it was clean. With a foot, she shoved her dirty pants and shirt against the wall.

"There, that wasn't so bad, was it? I have a small demonstration prepared, to show you we mean business. To open your mind."

She trembled, remembering the pain in her head. "Sorcery?"

"Oh no, something simpler."

"Before you do, can I ask you something? Avigdor needs help," she said, pointing to her friend. "A physiker to set his ankle, and something for the pain."

Savine chuckled. "It's as if you read my mind, Lady Felicienne. That's exactly the demonstration I was thinking of." He nodded at the soldiers, and two approached and grasped her arms in viselike grips. The other two went to Avigdor. One removed a hatchet from his belt.

She licked her dry lips. "What are you doing?"

"These people don't like it when someone attacks their God-Emperor. They like to retaliate in a forceful way. To send a message to anyone else with the same idea."

Savine wasn't one of the Indryallans. But who was he, and how did he fit into the scheme of things?

And what was he planning to do with Avigdor . . .

One of the soldiers grasped the foot with the broken ankle and pulled the leg straight. Avigdor moaned but remained unconscious. The axe rose.

"Don't you touch him!" screamed Felice, finally realizing what Savine was going to do.

With a sickening thud, the axe bit into Avigdor's shin. Bone splintered with a crack. Avigdor whimpered and writhed weakly, but remained insensible.

He must be almost gone already, she thought. A small comfort.

The axe rose again, and the soldier gripping the foot jerked back as it came free.

Felice yelled at them, struggling in vain to escape the iron grip of the soldiers holding her. The soldier slung Avigdor's foot across the room and grasped his remaining one. Blood pooled across the stones from the stump of Avigdor's leg.

"No. Please don't," she begged. Bile filled her mouth. She almost choked and then spat.

As the axe rose again, she closed her eyes and turned her head away. Sickening sounds reached her ears. She went limp in the soldiers' grip, sobbing uncontrollably.

Savine's voice came as if from a distance. "It was his own fault. You're lucky Kelhak wants to meet you, or I would have left you in these soldiers' company. But there's still time for that. They'll cut off his hands as well, then they'll hang him outside for everyone to see. For all their talk about liberating the city, they do have a mean streak, I must say. And now you know exactly what they're capable of."

Someone unlocked the chain around her ankle. Feet scraping on the stones, she was dragged away. She didn't dare look back at Avigdor.

SHE DIDN'T KNOW where she was. It wasn't the keep, as she had first surmised. The layout of the place was all wrong, and the color of the stone a shade too light. They had dragged her for what felt like hours but couldn't have been long—up some stairs, down a corridor, a few turns, up more stairs—eventually leaving her in a large room that was vaguely familiar. Perhaps she had heard of it; certainly, she had never been here before.

She squinted in the light of the room, eyes watering and taking time to adjust to the change. A painted ceiling extended two stories above her, and tall, wall-height windows of expensive clear glass allowed sunlight to stream in. Stained glass at the top of each window threw swaths of color across the floor; come sunset, the wall opposite them would be lit, as if by sorcery.

On the ceiling, armies fought over shining objects, blood spilled across battlefields, injured soldiers cried out for help, a pool of inky darkness spread from one man, and sorcerers strode glowing through the carnage. It was a scene from the Shattering, which showed the creation of purified land, where sorcery ceased to function.

In the center of the polished stone floor stood a sizable Dominion board, one of the largest she'd ever seen. Scattered across the boards were knee-high pieces carved from chunks of precious stones and crystals: onyx, turquoise, malachite, amethyst, quartz, lapis lazuli, and even some of gold and silver. Ironwood, blackwood, feathergrain, and burlwood made up the squares of all the tiers. And that's when she recognized it. Songs had been written about this Dominion set, though she realized they didn't do it justice. It was twenty paces to a side, and the upper tiers had to be reached by ladders. Small observation platforms were set up on each side to allow opponents a perspective of the whole board. Around the walls of the room, a viewing balcony ran full length, fed by two iron spiral staircases.

She knew where she was now; there could be no doubting it: the House of Luthais, a former major house reduced to minor status a few hundred years ago. Set overlooking the river Stock in Parkside, this building, along with the famous Dominion board and pieces, was all that remained of the house's former wealth and glory.

She peered again at the mural on the ceiling. *What I would do if I could get Savine in a purified land, where his sorcery would have no effect . . .*

The thought gave her scant comfort, but it was more than she'd had moments ago.

She glanced at the two soldiers guarding the door. They were huge men, and well armored, carrying bared blades almost as tall as they were. Not for show, these guards; they bore signs of knowing hard combat in their poise and watchful eyes. A third, unarmored soldier, slightly bigger than the other two, stood by the middle window, gazing out at the city. Another trained killer, she assumed, all muscle and no brain, though his lack of armor and weapons struck her as odd.

As if sensing her gaze, he turned to regard her with startling blue eyes. Cold eyes.

She swallowed and forced herself to hold his gaze. The effort drained her will rapidly. He smiled and approached her, moving fluidly, like a cat, in spite of his bulk.

A dangerous man. A man to whom killing came naturally, and far, far too easily.

"Lady Felicienne, I presume?" He gestured to a table she hadn't noticed almost overflowing with fruit, nuts, and small pastries. It also bore crystal flagons of water and wine, and two glasses. "Please, help yourself. I'm sure you could use some sustenance."

His smooth voice flowed over her, oddly calming despite her circumstances.

Yes, a dangerous man.

She poured herself a glass of well-watered wine, in order to not dull her senses any more than necessary. Though what she wanted was to drink the whole flagon and be done with whatever games the Indryallans were playing. But she would maintain the strength left to her, and show restraint . . . for now. Taking a sip, she looked up to find the man still staring at her.

She pulled her gaze from his emotionless eyes to the Dominion pieces. "Who are you?"

"They call me Kelhak, God-Emperor of Indryalla."

Felice's mouth went dry, and she fumbled her glass to her lips and gulped at her drink. It tasted of blackberries and spice.

Perhaps she shouldn't have watered the wine. "To Avigdor," she said, raising the glass in a salute.

"Who?"

"A friend. He was a good man."

Kelhak blinked once, then shrugged. "Eat something. From what I've heard, you must be famished. I wouldn't want you fainting in the middle of our game."

"You think this is a game?"

"Well, to be honest, yes. But I was talking about Dominion at the moment."

Felice regarded the set. Not at all what she expected from this man, let alone the circumstance in which she had envisioned herself playing on this board. She took a plum and bit into the fruit, hoping to buy a little more time to think about what was going on.

"I would like to assess your playing, since I've been told you are quite accomplished," continued Kelhak.

"Why should I play you? What's in it for me?"

"Because if you don't, I'll have you killed. But that would be boring, as I have some time to waste before . . . certain plans come to fruition, and I would prefer to judge you based on your play."

He stopped and blinked a few times, as if the light in the room had suddenly brightened. He shook his head and cleared his throat.

Wonderful, Felice thought. *I'm hardly at my best, and I'm playing a deranged killer for unknown stakes.*

A TAPPING OF stone on wood woke Felice. She lay slumped in an armchair next to the table of food and wine. Her empty glass was on the edge of the table, though she didn't remember putting it down. Steam rose from a jug. Someone must have placed it there while she dozed.

She rubbed her eyes and looked around. Kelhak sat perched on the top tier of the Dominion board, legs over the side, regarding her with his cold blue eyes and a self-satisfied grin.

"Your move," he said.

Felice groaned wearily. Her body and mind ached. She struggled to sit up. They had been playing for hours, a long and intricate game. Belying his warriorlike appearance, the God-Emperor was a formidable opponent, and she had struggled from the start.

"I had some tea brought for you—you seem tired."

Seeing as how you just woke me up, that's quite the understatement.

She picked up the jug and allowed the warmth to seep into her cold hands. Sluggishly, she poured herself a cup and sipped at the hot brew for a few moments until she collected her thoughts. Sighing, Felice dragged herself from the comfortable chair and slowly ascended a ladder to the top tier of the board.

Kelhak gave her a short bow and descended, leaving her to contemplate the game in peace.

She didn't know if this man was really the Indryallan God-Emperor or merely a high-ranking soldier. With his muscles and demeanor, he couldn't be just a functionary or some type of administrator, but he had an easy intelligence. He was a well-spoken, thoughtful man.

"So," Felice said, "there was a man named Kelhak who won the Dominion competition at the Autumn Festival quite some time ago. Were your parents Dominion enthusiasts who named you after him?"

Kelhak met her eyes. "No," he said simply. "That was me."

Felice scoffed, then stopped.

Kelhak raised his eyebrows at her.

He is serious.

Seriously mad. "I see."

"Though I have changed from those times. Then I was a larva, while now I'm . . . a butterfly."

Felice kept her face expressionless.

She looked around the board. The play of the pieces was familiar to her, as it should be to Kelhak, if it really was him. All reports placed him at the Autumn Festival so many years ago he should have died of old age long since. It was impossible for someone to live for so long. And yet, she had seen what this man could do, protecting the ship from the trebuchet. Before the Shattering, some sorcerers were said to live longer, but that had not been the case for thousands of years.

So this man was either an impostor, or a sorcerer powerful enough to prolong his life.

Which means he's either mad or able to do things no one has for millennia.

She shuddered at the possibility it was both.

Felice cleared her head and looked back at the board. Her plan for this game had sprung to mind unbidden at the start, born from a desire to cheat this man of his sport and from his familiar name. She would use the same strategy Caldan had used to defeat her, based, as he had said, on a famous game of Kelhak's. Which was what confused her so much. As she thought on it, it was unlikely an impostor would know the strategy, since she herself hadn't until it had been used against her; and if this man really was Kelhak, he would know his own style and approach early on.

Yet so far he had reacted as if he had never seen the strategy before, and moreover, in an intelligent and innovative way. Some of his moves far eclipsed her responses to Caldan's moves in their game. Which left no answers to whether or not he was truly the Kelhak of legend.

Well, she had nothing to lose. She cleared her throat and raised her voice. "You haven't recognized the strategy I'm using."

Kelhak pinned her with his piercing eyes. "Should I have?"

"Yes. It's one of yours. From a long time ago, but still . . . It makes me wonder why."

Kelhak frowned, as if puzzled. Then his eyes lost focus, and his breathing became rapid. For long moments he stared at her, but not *seeing* her, looking through her as if she weren't there.

As if *he* weren't there.

Abruptly he shook himself, and his gaze regained focus. "That's an old design," he said, as if nothing odd had occurred. "It's from a very long time ago. I consider it rather crude these days."

Felice swallowed and nodded. Kelhak had seemed genuinely baffled at first, then gone into some sort of fugue state; then the lights came back on.

There is something very wrong with him.

She turned her attention to their Dominion game, taking it all in. It was as she'd seen before.

There was no way to win.

She was doomed. There was no denying the fact. Doomed in this game; defeat was inevitable. Doomed to remain a prisoner or be killed. And that made her think: Did it really matter if this man was Kelhak or not? Somehow she felt it did but couldn't fathom why. There was a link, an importance to this fact, though she couldn't quite connect the dots.

It was almost funny, really. Now that she knew what he looked like, it would have been no trouble for her to go through the records and sketches of the Autumn Festival at the time. Each festival was well documented, and artists were commissioned to sketch the competitors and the games in the finals.

Except, of course, for the fact that she was trapped here, and very unlikely to ever have a chance to look through those old accounts.

She blinked in the bright light. The sun was setting, and the stained-glass windows spattered colors across the room and the Dominion board.

All I can do is delay the inevitable. And yet, she was determined to do just that.

"I choose to use my remaining five extra turns now."

Her statement was greeted with a flicker of surprise from Kelhak, further confirming he was an impostor. He would have known this was coming, if he were who he claimed to be.

While she roamed the board, moving her pieces, descending a ladder to the second tier to move another two, Felice brought up her recollections of this building's position and location in her mind. She knew with absolute certainty its northern wall was on the river Stock, but how close was it? And how high above the river was this room? About fifty yards, she estimated. She glanced at the windows. There was no way she could get her hands on a rope to descend the wall from here, nor did she think she was up to using her bare hands. Besides, with both Kelhak and his guards so close, she wouldn't get far before they caught her.

She stopped. She had run out of moves.

In more ways than one.

Wiping damp palms on her coarse robe, she moved to the table and picked up another plum. "Your turn," she said to Kelhak, who replied with a frown, then a slight shrug before walking away to examine the board. *He knows the game is won, and whatever I do cannot change that fact. But it's his reaction I'm after.*

"Do you mind if I look around?" She pointed to the mural-covered ceiling. "I've never been here, and the painting is famous. I'd like to get a closer look, if I may, before . . . whatever happens."

"Certainly," replied Kelhak distractedly. His attention was focused on the Dominion board.

Felice took her plum to the closest spiral staircase and ascended to the balcony overlooking the room. A quick glance at Kelhak confirmed he remained focused on the game and not on her. She went over her plan. It was . . . foolhardy.

Kelhak stood on the top tier of the board. Seven steps from the ladder. Forty-one rungs on the ladder. Fifty-seven steps from the ladder to the spiral staircase. Thirty-two steps up the staircase.

Her bare feet scuffed on the carpeted floor of the balcony. She curled her toes in the plush wool and clenched her fists, taking a deep breath, then another. Was it enough? It had to be.

Her unfinished plum dropped to the carpet with a muffled thud. Kelhak didn't look up. She took a step toward the stained-glass window at the end of the balcony. Then another. Her side and head ached where she had been struck. She ignored the pain.

Her steps quickened, sound stifled by the carpet. Gaining speed, she gritted her teeth with effort and willed herself to a sprint. An extra pace or two of distance might make all the difference. Or it might not.

One of the guards cried out in alarm, but it was too late.

Raising her arms in front of her face Felice crashed into the window. Glass splintered, cutting her arms and body as she burst through.

Falling.

Cold evening wind whipped about her body.

She opened her eyes to see the river Stock rise to meet her and curled into a ball, squeezing her eyes shut again.

The water hit her with a force that tore the breath from her lungs. With frantic movements, she kicked her legs to propel her to where she thought the surface lay. She dared not open her eyes in this river.

After what felt like an eternity, her head broke the surface, and she spat out a mouthful of the disgustingly oily water. It tasted like sewage. She coughed and gasped for air, pausing for only a moment to get her bearings. As fast as she was able, she swam for the bank opposite the House of Luthais.

Dragging her sore body up the stone sides of the river and onto the bank, she heard laughter echoing down from a great height.

Kelhak.

She snorted water and phlegm from her nose and fled into an alley, dripping a trail of murky sludge behind her. Stinging cuts from the glass covered her arms and legs, and she knew contamination by the river water could lead to a serious infection.

At least I'm free.

For some reason, though, as laughter followed her as she disappeared into the darkness, Felice couldn't help thinking that maybe she hadn't escaped as cleanly as she hoped.

CHAPTER 16

The room lurched around Amerdan, and he started shivering. Gently at first, then with more violence. Another one of his dizzy spells.

Not now; not in front of her, he thought.

Dotty moved against his flesh, urging him to hide, but he couldn't move. His mind itched again—an itch he couldn't scratch. His face grew hot, and beads of sweat formed on his brow. He staggered.

"Are you ill?"

Bells's voice seemed to come from a distance. He managed to shake his head and lowered himself to sit on the floor. Out of the corner of his eye, he saw her watching him with curiosity and a certain calculation.

"I . . . have occasional spells like this. Nothing to worry about." Even more reason to kill her now, since she'd seen him like this. Yet he couldn't—not before she served her purpose.

Bells moved close and crouched before him. "You're shivering."

Amerdan clenched his teeth. "Yes."

"Does your mind itch?"

He went still, not quite sure he had heard correctly. Did she know something about him? He drew a deep breath and tensed to spring. Against a sorcerer like this woman, he would need surprise on his side. But he had faced worse odds and survived.

"Does it what?"

"In your mind, does it itch? Do you find yourself trying to scratch at something, at a certain spot?"

How can she know this? Is this a type of sorcery?

He nodded slowly. "Yes," he ventured carefully, always reluctant to give out information about himself.

"But you were tested as a child?"

"For what?"

"By sorcerers. To see if you had a well. I thought all children in the empire were tested around a certain age."

He nodded again. He remembered the day the sorcerers had come to their house with clarity. After declaring him and his sisters well-less, they had left, but one had returned a few days later to imprison them. "They found nothing."

"Let me . . ." said Bells.

Amerdan tensed as he saw an aura flicker around her, then dissipate.

Her face went pale, and her eyes opened wide. "That's . . . not possible."

"What do you see? Tell me."

Bells shook her head, then peered into his eyes.

His shivering had stopped, and he stood.

Bells looked up at him from her crouch; curiosity and confusion warred in her expression.

"Tell me," he commanded.

"They were either incompetent or . . ." She shook her head, her recovered bells tinkling with the movement. "I've never seen the like. You have a well, but . . . there is a blockage. As if it's attached to you, but your own mind doesn't recognize it. And that's not all. You have two." Her voice was tinged with wonder. "You have two wells. They're hard to find, blocked as they are, but they're there. It's remarkable."

Amerdan studied her face. She wasn't lying. In moments, the pieces fell into place.

His trinket.

The first person he'd killed and subsumed with it was a sorcerer, the man who had captured them and killed his sisters. And the second sorcerer had been the young apprentice. Two sorcerers' essences absorbed. Two wells. If one well made a sorcerer, then what did two make?

Two made . . . him.

He chuckled for a few moments, then laughed long and hard.

Bells gave him a rueful look. "The God-Emperor will definitely want to meet you."

"You'll have to teach me all you can before then."

"If I can get through your blocks, I will, I promise."

"I have faith you'll do your best." He turned his finest smile on her. "Just make it better than your attempt to heal Miranda."

Bells smirked. "She was easy, if I had wanted. But she and Caldan need to suffer. Until I find them again."

If I let you find them again.

ELPIDIA WAS A sorry sight when Caldan and Master Annelie burst into the courtyard near the Protectors' front entrance. Tears and smudges of dirt streaked her anguished face. At first, she didn't notice him and continued pacing in front of the wagon. Three Protectors armed with swords stood a short distance away, between her and the building. Bells and Amerdan were nowhere to be seen.

Caldan moved toward Elpidia but was stopped by Annelie's hand on his arm.

"You know her?"

He nodded and shrugged himself free of her grasp. "Yes. Let me see to her."

Without waiting for permission, he went to Elpidia. When she noticed him approach, her face became grim. To his surprise, she caught him in a hug.

"I'm sorry," she sobbed.

"Shhh. What happened?" Caldan whispered. He scanned the wagon, and his heart unclenched when he saw that Miranda was safe. "Where is Bells? And Amerdan?"

Elpidia shook her head. "Gone. I don't know where. I was hit from behind." She raised a hand and gingerly touched a patch of dried blood and matted hair. "When I woke, she was gone. Maybe another sorcerer came for her . . ."

"But you don't think so, do you?"

"Well, if she left me alive, I don't see why they would kill Amerdan. But he was gone when I woke, and I didn't see any trace of him anywhere. So either they fled . . . or he was the one who hit me." It was clear from her tone she thought it was the latter.

"By the ancestors," cursed Caldan under his breath. "How do you know Amerdan returned?"

"Mice. I asked him to bring me a few mice for my experiments. There were two in my kit when I regained consciousness. He had to have come back."

Caldan's thoughts churned furiously. Had Bells gotten to him somehow? Had Amerdan thrown his lot in with the sorcerer?

More important, where were they going?

With that in mind, he hugged Elpidia, saying, "I'm so sorry you were hurt." But, pulling her close, he whispered in her ear. "We can't let them know about Bells."

At his words, Elpidia stiffened against him. "Why? We have to. They'll be able to help."

"Because I haven't had a chance to tell them about Miranda yet. I'm still planning to, but if they can't help her, then Bells is our only chance."

"Haven't you played enough games with this woman? She's dangerous, and she's on the loose now."

Caldan grimaced at the truth of Elpidia's accusation. "I know. And again, I'm sorry. But it's the only way I can think of—" From behind, he heard Annelie approach. "Trust me," Caldan urged Elpidia softly. "We'll heal Miranda, and you." He released her and turned to face Annelie.

"Is she well?" the master asked. "What happened? And there's someone else in the wagon."

"She was robbed. Bandits on the road. The woman in the wagon is a friend of ours. She's . . . sick. A disease of the mind, a wasting illness. Elpidia here is searching for a cure."

Annelie gave him a puzzled look. "Bandits? This close to the city?"

"I had them set up camp quite a way from the city. I thought they'd be safer until I knew the situation here. Shows what I know. But I was concerned, because I was leaving them by themselves, and we'd been attacked once before. By Indryallans."

Annelie looked at him sharply. "There's more, isn't there? There always seems to be with you."

"Yes—I'm sorry," he said, using his guilt over Elpidia's injuries and his own lying to aid in looking suitably miserable.

"Out with it, then," Annelie said.

Caldan was about to talk about Bells's attack when he realized that the Protectors might not take too kindly to the fact that Elpidia knew about coercive sorcery. Thinking quickly, he motioned for Annelie to the side with a nod of his head, indicating he wanted their discussion to be private. She moved until he had led them out of earshot of the others.

"Why the secrecy?"

"Because some of what I'm about to say shouldn't be known outside of the Protectors." With a subtle twitch of his head, he drew her attention to Elpidia.

Annelie nodded. "Go on."

"When we were fleeing Anasoma, we were chased by Indryallan sorcerers. They . . . did something to Miranda. I guess sorcery similar to what they used on Simmon. She wasn't herself and attacked us. We managed to restrain her until she came to her senses, but when she did, she was left in this state." He glanced at Elpidia again, hoping he was selling it. *One more lie to those I swore my life to*, he thought with an internal sigh, and pressed on. "It's as if the coercive sorcery addled her mind."

Annelie narrowed her eyes. "Yes—that's definitely something we wouldn't want her to know about. We'll have words about why you didn't tell us this earlier, though. But for now, time is of the essence. We need to examine her and see what we can do."

"Can you heal her?" asked Caldan, unable to contain the hope in his voice.

"Maybe. I won't know until I delve into what's been done to her." Annelie beckoned some Protectors over. "You two, take the woman from the wagon and find a room for her. Stay with her; don't leave her alone. I'll be there soon." She pointed at Caldan. "Go with Elpidia, inside. I'll deal with you later."

"Please," begged Caldan. "I feel what happened to Miranda is partly my responsibility. Can you tell me what happens? I need to know if she'll be all right."

Annelie's expression softened, but only slightly. She nodded. "Stay with Elpidia. I'll send news when I can."

And with that, Annelie bustled off, issuing orders and organizing the Protectors.

Caldan watched as Miranda was lifted from the wagon by two journeymen and carried off. It took all his power not to follow.

He took Elpidia to his room, and they waited for word of Miranda. He didn't know how long it would take, and even after such a short time, the wait seemed interminable.

Elpidia sat on his bed, writing in a notebook. Occasionally, she would pause and stare at the wall, eyes unfocused, deep in reflection.

Caldan paced around the room, but apart from one or two annoying glances, Elpidia seemed inclined to leave him to his own thoughts.

Finally, he found he didn't want to be alone with them.

"I couldn't tell her more," he blurted, when the silence became too much. "If she found out you know about coercive sorcery, there's no telling what her reaction would be."

Elpidia stopped writing and regarded him evenly. "I see that. I don't want them to do anything to harm us, you know that, but you're too fearful of what could happen. You need to think about what the right thing to do is."

"Helping Miranda *is* the right thing to do," Caldan said firmly.

"Yes, but lying to the very people who might be able to help is stupid."

"Is keeping you alive stupid?"

To that she had no answer.

Once more, he paced the room. As much as he warred with himself about lying to the Protectors, he bristled when Elpidia questioned it. She might think he was keeping secrets just for the sake of it, but he didn't think she fully understood the significance of the secret of forbidden sorcery. A secret of that magnitude didn't stay hidden for centuries without deaths to cover it up, and he had no doubt the Protectors took their charge seriously. Good people would go against their morals and beliefs if they thought it was for the greater good—his actions, as benign as the few lies he'd told were, were proof of that. What was it he'd read in *The Letters of Kalistinna*?

For good people to do evil things, that takes a righteous cause.

He had no doubt the Protectors considered their cause to be righteous, just as he'd thought it was when Simmon had first explained it to him.

But for the first time since he'd joined the Protectors, he started to wonder if he believed their cause meshed with his own.

He dragged a chair over to the window and sat, staring outside, hoping Annelie could help Miranda, and trying not to think of what he'd have to do if she failed.

THERE WAS A knock at the door, and before Caldan was halfway to his feet, it opened.

An older journeyman stuck her head in. "Master Annelie wants to see you both. Now. Follow me."

Without staying for a reply, the woman pushed the door all the way open and started walking down the hall.

Caldan glanced at Elpidia, who was calmly packing away her notebook and writing implements.

It had been hours since Annelie had taken Miranda away. Hope warred with fear inside him, and nothing about what was happening now convinced him to lean one way or the other.

They followed the journeyman through the building until she led them into a kitchen. Master Annelie was sitting on a bench with an arm around Miranda's shoulders, a ceramic cup in her other hand. Miranda's head was turned away from the cup. Caldan's stomach sank at the sight. Miranda looked much the same as before.

Annelie looked up as they entered. Her face was haggard and drawn, like she hadn't slept for days. Her face was pale, and the hand holding the cup trembled slightly.

Caldan rushed over to help. "Here, I'll do it. For some reason, it's easier for me."

He took the drink from Annelie, moved to Miranda's other side, and brought it to her lips. She managed a few swallows, water trickling from the corners of her mouth, before clamping her lips shut. He wiped the residue with his sleeve.

Miranda was getting worse. If she continued to drink so little water, she would dehydrate. Caldan cursed inwardly and rubbed his eyes. Although Annelie hadn't said so, it was obvious she'd failed.

The sorrowful look on Elpidia's face confirmed his fears. The physiker stumbled to a table and sat on a bench, putting her face in her hands. She'd also cared for Miranda on their journey, and had come to feel for the woman's plight. His own grief threatened to overwhelm him, but Caldan steeled himself.

He glanced toward Annelie, who had risen and was busy spooning stew into a bowl from a pot on an iron stove. There were also two journeymen in the room, standing by the door. A guard of sorts, he surmised. So Annelie didn't fully trust him yet, despite his information and the trinket he'd carried all the way from Anasoma to deliver into their hands.

She really isn't going to like what I have to say, then.

First, though, he needed confirmation. "I take it you weren't successful?"

Annelie cleared her throat as she approached them. Wearily, she shook her head and sat at a table. She spooned in some of the stew and chewed slowly. When she finished the mouthful, she spoke.

"I'm sorry. Whatever was done to her is beyond us. None of my Protectors have the aptitude. There are books, but even the theory is beyond all but the best sorcerers, the kind the emperor has by his side. We'll keep her with us, for observation, and I'll send word to the capital. Maybe they can help Miranda, if they choose to."

Even as the words hit, he realized he wasn't as disappointed as he had expected, as if he'd always known—deep down—that this was going to be Annelie's answer. It still hurt, but the pain felt like a continuation of his anguish for Miranda, and not a fresh wound to deal with.

Caldan opened his mouth to speak but was interrupted by Elpidia.

"Tell her about Bells!" the physiker blurted, and Caldan briefly closed his eyes.

What has she done? She's just told Annelie she knows something about coercive sorcery.

"Bells," Annelie said. "Who is Bells?"

Caldan threw an angry look at Elpidia before sighing and turning to catch Annelie's eye. "We need to talk in private. Get rid of the journeymen. They can't hear this."

Annelie chewed some stew a few times before swallowing. She waved at the journeymen. "Leave us," she commanded.

Once they were gone, she regarded Caldan with a flinty glare. "Out with it. Now's the time to be truthful. Your story reeks of half-truths and prevarications."

"There were no bandits outside Riversedge," Caldan said. "I mean, Elpidia's research and equipment and some of my craftings and notes were taken, but not by bandits."

Annelie rubbed her eyes and sighed. "Slow down. Take a breath, and start from the beginning. Who stole from you?"

Caldan did as she suggested, taking a few moments to organize his thoughts. He couldn't tell Annelie all he knew about coercive sorcery, so he had to edge around the subject. And the less Elpidia knew about it, the better. He moved a strand of hair from across Miranda's face.

"When we were fleeing Anasoma, two Indryallan sorcerers chased us. They did something to Miranda. The same sorcery they used on Simmon. We managed to kill one of the sorcerers and capture the other. A woman called Bells."

Annelie stood, face red. "You what?" she screeched. "And you're only just telling me now?"

"I'm sorry. I thought I could get the sorcerer to heal Miranda. She taught me a few things and I was able to sense the damage to Miranda myself, using Bells's crafting." He glanced at Elpidia. "We know it was coercive sorcery."

"By the ancestors' shadows! What possessed you? You mean she's escaped and is running loose somewhere? And you tried to learn coercive sorcery from her?"

"Yes. I wanted to tell you—"

"Quiet!" Annelie hissed. She dumped her bowl of stew on the table. "Come with me, now. We don't have time for long explanations and your excuses. But let me make one thing clear: I'm holding you personally responsible for anything she does while she's on the loose."

Caldan looked at the floor as his face grew hot. The almost invisible scar on his cheek itched abominably, and he scratched it. Elpidia regarded him with concern, though when her gaze moved to Miranda, it changed to sympathy.

"I can almost understand why you did it," began Annelie. "Your friend—perhaps she was more—was seriously injured. Possibly changed forever. You'd want to heal her, of course you would. But to offer to start learning coercive sorcery from this Bells? What were you thinking?"

"It wasn't much," protested Caldan. "It was just to see, so I could better understand what was happening."

"And do you think she didn't have an ulterior motive in helping you?"

"She was starting to come around. To see that helping me heal Miranda would benefit her, with . . . whatever was going to happen." He couldn't very well tell Annelie he'd been thinking of releasing Bells.

"And yet she escaped. How did she do that? And was she just biding her time until doing so? There are many questions left unanswered, and I don't think you fully understand the situation. Coercive sorcery is complex and dangerous, apart from being wrong. You can easily lose yourself in the mind of another, if you aren't careful. And I doubt she was careful with you."

"I . . . perhaps."

Annelie made sense, but he'd done what he thought was right in a traumatic situation. *No. Not what was right, but what I wanted to do.* He'd put Miranda's well-being above everything else.

"Naive, bordering on reckless," Annelie said. "If you'd just handed her over with the sword, her escape could have been avoided. Well, you're going to help fix this problem, seeing how it's mostly your creation. And you'll be watched every step of the way."

CALDAN STUDIED THE faces of the two journeymen in front of him. Annelie stood at his side, having just introduced the men. Both of them were old enough to be masters, but he could see that their talents lay in other areas. While one was lean with a hard face, the other was muscled and grim. Both were armed to the teeth with swords and a few daggers in their belts, along with compound bows and quivers of arrows at their sides. They wore hard leather boots and matching clothes, and out from the top of each boot poked a suspicious-looking metallic ball—the pommel of a hidden knife, if he wasn't mistaken. Each wore a number of craftings, but no trinkets, from what he could sense. Though he couldn't always perceive the ancient artifacts; his bone trinket, for example, gave no hint of its nature.

The journeymen were tough men, both. Annelie insisted Caldan accompany them to show them where he'd last seen the sorcerer. He was suspicious their task wasn't just to hunt down Bells, but something more sinister.

"Again, thank you for giving me this chance, Master Annelie," Caldan said. "I'll give Morkel and Keevy all the help I can." He laid a hand on the pommel of the sword at his side. It was simple but well made, a far cry from the trinket he had carried from Anasoma. "And my thanks for the sword as well."

Annelie inclined her head and glanced at the two journeymen. "I want to be clear. If you hadn't completed the task Simmon set you, you'd be locked up right now. Having proven yourself trustworthy, you then undid all the goodwill you'd accumulated, and more. One mis-step from now on and I'll personally see to it you are silenced. I trust that's clear enough for you?"

Caldan swallowed. "Yes, Master Annelie."

Morkel, the lean journeyman, cleared his throat. "Can't have you wandering around unarmed. Any Protector worth his salt knows how to use a blade. Make sure you don't stab yourself with it."

Keevy snorted, and Annelie flashed him a dark look, then turned to Caldan. "Not all Protectors can use a blade; pay no mind to them."

They think of me as an apprentice, Caldan thought. *Good. No doubt Annelie's told them I'm not a journeyman. But she wouldn't be a master unless she was intelligent. She will have told them to watch me for anything untoward.*

"I think it'll be best if we start back at our campsite. It was off the road, and it hasn't been long, so nothing should have been disturbed. With any luck, there will be tracks for us to follow."

"That's what we're going to do," said Morkel. "I'll be able to track anyone, unless they're skilled and take pains to hide their trail. If they were smart, they'd head straight for the road, and we'd lose them there." He shrugged and adjusted his belt. "Let's hope they're not smart."

Keevy snorted again, and Caldan began to think the man never spoke.

"Get it done quickly," said Annelie. "Find the sorcerer, and if you need help, send for it. And get back here as soon as possible. With the emperor and his soldiers on the way, we have to prepare." She gave Morkel and Keevy a stern look, then turned and left them in the courtyard.

"Right," said Morkel. "Let's get us some horses and get moving."

CALDAN NODDED AND squinted, trying to make his expression one of consideration. Morkel's question was a relevant one, but he couldn't tell these men the whole story. He had no idea how much they knew of coercive sorcery, and it wasn't a subject to be bandied about.

They were standing at the edge of the campsite where Bells had escaped and Amerdan, presumably, had gone with her. Both Morkel and Keevy had motioned for him not to enter as they traversed a circle around the area. Caldan shifted his weight from foot to foot until they returned, eager to avoid these delays but unsure of what to do.

"Well?" repeated Morkel. "Why didn't the sorcerer steal your wagon? From the tracks here, two of them left on foot, heading toward the river. Leaving horses and a wagon worth a good deal of coin and an easier way to travel doesn't make much sense. She'd want to take them if she was going to head back to Anasoma."

Caldan agreed with Morkel's assessment. Bells didn't need the wagon. "Because she's not going back to Anasoma."

Morkel flashed a look at Keevy, who grunted.

"What did they take again?"

"Elpidia's kit, her medicines, herbs, alchemical ingredients, equipment. Some of it quite valuable. Plus my craftings, the ones I left here."

"I was going to ask about them. Why would you leave your craftings lying around rather than carry them with you?"

"I left at first light, in a hurry to bring the Protectors the trinket sword from Anasoma. I didn't want to waste any more time. I thought I'd be back soon."

Morkel stared at him, as if weighing his words. Then he nodded to Keevy. "What did you find?"

"The wagon came in, they camped for the night, one man left toward the road—Caldan here, I would guess. The wagon left after him, and two others headed toward the river, though whether together or separately, I cannot tell."

This was the first time Caldan had heard him speak, and the man's voice took him by surprise. It was rough and gravelly, as if it hurt coming out. No wonder he was the quiet type.

"I see the same," said Morkel. "Let's move on."

CHAPTER 17

Dark and silent, the figures remained motionless as Vasile and Mazoet approached them along the beach. Out to sea, five ships lay at anchor, while in the distance, another four approached. Gray seabirds flapped overhead, and fingernail-sized crabs scuttled back to their burrows as the men passed, boots crunching in the coarse white sand. A band of dry seaweed marked the high-tide line.

Vasile shaded his eyes from the sun and regarded Mazoet, whose expression grew grimmer the closer they approached to the group of men. Behind the strangers were five small rowboats, hauled up onto the beach, each with two sailors in attendance. Distinctly odd. Why use five boats to ferry five men to shore?

"You still haven't told me what we're doing here. Wherever *here* is."

"We are negotiating. Well, not really, since the negotiating was done long ago. But we are . . . reaffirming our contract with them."

"And just who are they?"

"Mercenaries. Sellswords. The best we could find. They were expensive, but what use are ducats if you're dead?"

Indeed, thought Vasile. Mazoet had shown a remarkable lack of respect for ducats. Vasile himself didn't care much for coins, as those who did usually had other, deeper issues and wound up defending themselves in front of the magistrates.

He could discern more details of the five men as they drew closer. A hard-looking lot, leather armored and bristling with blades; one even sported a metal-scaled breastplate.

"So that explains why you are here, but why was it necessary to bring *me* here?"

"Ah, now you're asking the right questions. Why do you think?" The sorcerer blew out a breath, cheeks puffing. He'd worked up a sweat on the short walk.

"Because you don't trust them."

Mazoet barked a laugh. "Let's just say we'd hate our hard work to be wasted. Though it's a good sign they're here with so many ships. It was difficult to persuade this many companies to band together. And though we have their assurances—indeed, signed contracts that they'll work for us—some people don't put much stock in their word, spoken or written, as I'm sure you're aware."

"Yes," replied Vasile. "Though if they earned a reputation for reneging on deals, they would never get paid."

"If the coin was sufficient, they might not have to work for some time, and a change of name and appearance is easy enough. Who would know it was the same mercenary band?"

Vasile nodded in agreement. He looked out at the sea, and something niggled at him. "You must have approached these men months ago, in order to have them organized, and to meet here." He waved a hand across the waves toward the ships. "Five different groups, all here on the same day at the same time. From wherever they came from—you haven't said yet."

"Some are from the Sotharle Union of Cities; some from elsewhere. It's of no matter. What *does* matter is that they do the job we're paying them for."

Vasile made no response. If Gazija and his people had organized the mercenaries months ago, then they had known the invasion was coming that far back. And further, they believed the emperor's response, with all the power at his disposal, wouldn't be sufficient to repel the Indryallans. The question was: Why hadn't they warned the empire, then?

The thought sent shivers down his spine. Any answer he came up with was an unhappy one.

"Leave the talking to me," said Mazoet. "I just need you to tell me if they are lying, or skirting around the truth in any way."

"Of course."

"Good."

They remained silent as they traveled the remaining distance to the men across the sand, stopping a few paces in front of them. This close, Vasile could discern a readiness about them, and a discipline he hadn't expected. Their armor and weapons were in good repair and looked well used and cared for. Mazoet watched the mercenaries closely. Vasile felt he was being evaluated by all five and filed away in some section of their minds.

"Greetings," said Mazoet, voice booming above the waves. "I see you all made it here."

The man in the metal-scaled breastplate stepped forward. A huge sword was strapped to his back, and he sported a braided beard.

"Did you think we would break our word? You paid us, so we're here."

"But delays happen, in all things. Some deadlines are never met on time, Selbourne."

"As I said—and as you can see—we are all here." The bearded man, Selbourne, gestured to his companions. "Along with our men, as promised."

"The Black Suns," Selbourne said. The man to the far left, sporting a close-cut goatee, bowed from the waist. "The Broken Blades." The shortest of the men inclined his head. "Diamond Guard." A man with a flat nose that looked like it had been broken many times nodded. "The Red Shields." The fourth man, with two scars running down his cheek, nodded. "And my men, the Forgotten Company."

Mazoet placed a hand inside his tunic and all five mercenary leaders' eyes were drawn to his movements, relaxing only when he withdrew a bundle of papers, folded in half. Broken Nose licked his lips.

"I see they have appointed you spokesman," Mazoet said.

Selbourne shrugged, then nodded.

"You all know," Mazoet said, "the reason for this meeting: for us to ensure you were all on your way, and to hand you the second payments." He brandished the papers. "Writs for payment, redeemable at any of our offices, in any city. As agreed."

A few of the mercenaries glanced at one another.

"Ask him, Selbourne," said the man with the broken nose.

"Shut your hole, Regnar," said Selbourne. "I never liked your notion, but you all want me to ask, so I will." Selbourne met Mazoet's eye. "There's a slight problem. The last writs were honored . . . but what's to say these will be? These are for a much greater amount. And they are, after all, issued by the Five Oceans Mercantile Concern. With a word, you could render them valueless, and then where would we be?"

They might have been mercenaries, but Vasile realized they were far from stupid. Clearly Mazoet never harbored such an underestimation.

"Very well," replied Mazoet. "Though I am aggrieved by your lack of trust, it was thought this situation could occur."

The sorcerer replaced the papers inside his tunic and removed five leather pouches, throwing one to each of the mercenary captains. There were gasps as four of them spilled the contents into their palms. Each had a handful of cut gemstones of all colors. From their shocked looks, Vasile guessed it was more than enough to cover payment. Regnar, the leader of the Diamond Guard, took a few gems and pocketed them before returning the rest to his pouch.

Selbourne remained silent, tucking his pouch into his belt. With a nod to Mazoet, he stepped back to join his fellows.

Mazoet interrupted their gloating. "I have a question. A formality, nothing more."

Steely eyes turned the sorcerer's way, but he remained unflinching under their gazes. "Please answer with a simple yes or no."

Exchanging puzzled looks, the captains murmured their agreement, then Selbourne spoke. "We're under your contract. Ask away."

Mazoet regarded them all for a few moments before speaking. "Do you intend to honor the contract for which you have just received the latest payment?"

Selbourne snorted before turning to face his colleagues. A couple of them shrugged and nodded, while the others voiced consent. He turned back to Mazoet.

"A rather simple question, and one I would have thought had no value. Of course we'll say yes, even if one of us is going to take the payment and run."

"Humor me."

Selbourne turned to the mercenary captains. "Give Mazoet the confirmation he wants, then we can get out of here."

One by one, they answered Mazoet's question in the affirmative. None of them looked nervous to Vasile, but he had seen men and women utter lies as if the truth of their words was as plain as the sun.

Vasile pointed to Regnar, the leader of the Diamond Guard, the man who had taken a few gemstones for himself. "This one," he said tonelessly, fearing what was about to happen. "He's lying."

Regnar's eyes widened with shock, and he spluttered. "Here now. What's this?"

The hands of the other mercenaries moved to grasp their weapons, but other than that they didn't move. Some eyed Regnar, while others glanced from Vasile to Mazoet.

My word won't be enough to convince them, Vasile thought. *It wouldn't convince me if I were in their boots.*

Mazoet paused for a moment, as if deciding what to do. "I just paid you the next installment," he said. "You're mine to do with as I see fit."

Selbourne cleared his throat. "Not quite. But we can't just take this man's word that Regnar is lying."

"I'm with you," Regnar said. "I told the truth!"

"I believe he's lying," Mazoet said. "And that's all that should matter at this point. Are you mine to command now or will you balk at small tasks?" They still hesitated, so he added, "If you take him now, you can split his share."

Two of the mercenaries pinned Regnar's arms to his sides before he could react. Selbourne nodded slowly.

"Kill him," Mazoet said. "Absorb his men into your own bands. Do you think you can do that?"

Selbourne reached over his shoulder and drew his huge sword. "Yes. His men will go where the ducats are. They don't like him much anyway."

At his gesture, Regnar was forced to his knees, arms wrenched behind his back, and a boot tilted his head forward.

"You can't do this," he screamed. "I'll kill you all."

"Shut your hole," said Selbourne. "Die with some dignity, at least."

He raised his blade and brought it down, severing Regnar's head from his body in one blow. Regnar's limbs twitched as his blood and life seeped into the sand.

Selbourne wiped his sword clean on the dead man's clothes. "That's done. Good riddance."

Vasile closed his eyes to the sight.

"A necessary unpleasantness," Mazoet said. "Now, we need you to speed up your preparations. The sooner you arrive at the rally point, the better. The situation in Anasoma has become more complicated, and we fear you'll be needed sooner rather than later. Come, Vasile, our business here is done."

AFTER ANOTHER SHORT walk and a stomach-churning, mind-twisting sorcerous transition, Vasile found himself back where he'd been earlier that day. Scores of miles traveled, and a fortune in gems destroyed, all in less than a day. His mind couldn't quite come to grips with the thought, even though he'd experienced it himself.

Mazoet announced to Vasile his next mission: to find the emperor and use whatever connections and influence he had to gain an audience, and then to explain what Gazija and his people had done and how they could help, all the while using his talent, which the emperor well knew, to persuade him of the truth of their intentions. The emperor would trust Vasile because of the work he'd done for him in the past—and because of the fact that the emperor had a similar talent himself. Vasile had been used before, then sent away because he could discern secrets. And there were plenty of those among the emperor and his counselors.

What his warlocks knew regarding the true nature of sorcery, for one.

Vasile spent the evening and much of the night wandering around the camp, lost in thought. Gazija and his people had done nothing to warn the empire or Anasoma, and now they were offering their "aid" to the emperor? He felt like he was missing something crucial in between those two actions.

When he found his bedroll and turned in, he couldn't sleep. *How am I supposed to advocate for the truth of Gazija when I'm not convinced I know the whole truth myself?*

It was with tired relief that he watched the sun come up.

Vasile rubbed his eyes. He had developed a headache since hearing what they wanted of him, and it hadn't left. By the ancestors' shadows, he could use a strong drink.

Aidan and Vasile stood next to four horses as Chalayan and cel Rau finished readying them for their journey. Gazija had provided the animals and saddles, along with whatever provisions they required. Hard bread and cheese, dried fruit, and nuts were all Aidan had requested. To Vasile, it looked like they wouldn't be stopping anywhere long, and he couldn't say he was unhappy with the thought. Gazija and Mazoet and their people were wearing his nerves thin. They had sought him out and dragged him into their mess, but he knew he wasn't a reluctant participant. That didn't mean he couldn't doubt, right? And because of that doubt, he felt he needed some time away so he could sort things out on his own.

So here he was. Handed over to Aidan and left to his own devices and skittering thoughts. And about to mount a horse to persuade the emperor that the leaders of the Five Oceans Mercantile Concern were here to help, and he should ally with them. All night, he'd had visions of the emperor ordering his head cut off, just as the mercenaries had executed the captain of the Diamond Guard. His stomach churned, and his mouth filled with spit at the thought.

"What's the matter?" asked Aidan. "You look a little queasy. We aren't going by ship, so you needn't worry."

"It's not our method of travel that worries me. It's our mission."

"I have faith in you. No, more than faith, since that would imply I have no evidence of your skills. If anyone can persuade the emperor about the truth of what's happening here, it's you. I can use our connection with him, plus your own familiarity, to gain an audience. The rest is up to you."

"I've only met him a couple of times. I doubt he even remembers."

"Oh, I think he would. He isn't the emperor because of his looks."

"Still . . ."

"Stop worrying so much; you'll make yourself sick."

"That's easy for you to say. You're not the one who has to persuade the emperor." Vasile rubbed his stomach. "Besides, I'm already sick."

Aidan chuckled. "You'll be fine. Use that trick you pulled on Chalayan. If you're lucky, he might even give you the five hundred and twelve silvers."

Despite his mood, Vasile smiled. "It wouldn't work. He already knows what I can do."

"Then you're halfway to persuading him."

"Maybe."

"We can talk more on the road. I want to get out of here. I know you say Gazija has the best intentions, but he makes me nervous."

Now there's something we can agree upon.

Vasile looked at the horse assigned to him and sighed. It was an old brown mare that didn't look pleased to be leaving a comfortable home for a journey into the unknown. At least they had that in common.

CHAPTER 18

Morkel signaled for them to stop and motioned Keevy to his side.

Quickly, Caldan dismounted and joined them. Morkel frowned at two saplings in front of them, slender trunks a couple of paces apart. He looked worried, and as Caldan and Keevy approached, he held a hand up to make sure they didn't pass him.

"I daresay we'll soon have some idea what we're up against," said Morkel.

"The trees?" asked Keevy.

"Yes. She's made the trail a little too obvious. Then there's the curious question as to why someone would veer upslope off the trail, off the easiest path, to pass between two trees."

"You wouldn't," said Caldan. "Unless you had a reason."

"And if you thought you might be chased or tracked, then the only reason would be to lay a trap. Which is what we have here."

Morkel looked around, then retrieved a stick from under another tree. He edged closer to the two saplings, taking short, careful steps.

Gingerly, he squatted and probed the grass clumped around the base of each tree.

"Ah!" With a sudden movement, Morkel thrust the stick between the trees.

Caldan felt Keevy stiffen beside him, but nothing happened. Morkel stood and backed away before turning to face them.

"Well, there are craftings at the base of each tree. Makeshift ones made from sticks tied together with dried grass, but probably no less effective for that. Whatever they're made to do, they wouldn't have to last long."

"When you placed your stick between the trees, nothing happened, though," said Caldan.

"I suspect there's another trigger, or else a wild animal passing through could set it off. And there's not much that distinguishes us from animals, except for metal. Do you have any ducats?" he asked Caldan.

"Which type, gold, silver, or copper?"

"Better make it gold, if you've any."

Caldan handed over a gold ducat, and without ceremony, Morkel tossed it between the trees. Again, nothing happened.

"Hmm," murmured Morkel, wiping his hands on his trousers. "A sophisticated crafting, for one made in a hurry. But we can't leave it where some innocent might accidentally trigger it."

"Maybe it's tuned to sorcerers?" suggested Caldan. "Someone who has their well open?"

Keevy took a step back. "I'm not testing it."

"No one's going to test it that way," said Morkel. "I've an old crafting we can use; it's had its day, anyway."

The Protector pulled a necklace from under his shirt. Suspended from the chain were five crafted medallions. He removed one, then tucked the rest back out of sight under his shirt. "Here we go, then."

Caldan felt him open his well and did the same, stretching his senses to inspect the tear. Quite strong, but . . . jagged somehow.

Morkel's crafting sailed between the trees. A crackling split the air, and a light flashed as bright as the midday sun. All of them flinched and turned away. Caldan winced as his eyes stung and began to water. The scent of lemons and hot metal filled his nose.

Smoke streamed all the way up the trunks of both trees, and from a patch of blackened grass on the other side, presumably where the crafting had landed. Morkel hastily used his stick to drag two objects from the growth under the trees, small shapes composed of twigs tied together with dried grass. The improvised craftings were twisted and blackened almost beyond recognition.

"How did she carve runes in twigs that thin?" asked Caldan. "She doesn't have any ink or pens."

"The twigs themselves form the shapes of the runes. A nasty piece of work. Crude but good. Very good." Morkel squinted at the craftings in his hands, then glanced at Caldan. "I don't think she likes you. It couldn't have been meant for anyone else. And if she can craft functional sorcery out of sticks and grass, we've got ourselves a big problem."

Morkel circled around the saplings, which now had a black line scorched along their trunks, and picked up his crafting. He held up the two pieces of medallion. "Sliced in half. I'll keep this as a memento. Keevy, I think someone's lost a gold ducat in the grass over there. Would you be so kind as to fetch it, and we can use it to buy some drinks when we get back. We could even generously buy a couple for the apprentice here, if that's all right with him."

Caldan nodded his agreement. Anything he could do to get on the good side of these men would help him. A kind word from men Annelie trusted would go a long way.

"Let's get going, then," he said. "Crafting that trap must have taken time, so we're gaining."

Morkel remained where he was, examining the saplings. Keevy went to stand next to him, and they both fingered the black line.

"What is it?" asked Caldan.

"Come here, boy," replied Morkel.

Caldan approached, and Morkel guided him to stand on one side of a sapling while he stood on the other.

Caldan could see Morkel through the sapling's trunk. It wasn't just a scorch mark: the tree was split in two; both were.

Morkel and Keevy exchanged glances.

"I'm not so sure we want to catch up with her now," muttered Morkel, and Keevy nodded.

"I captured her on my own once," Caldan said quietly. "When she had *all* her craftings. There's three of us now."

Morkel grunted. "So you say. Let's see where she goes, then, and determine if that's enough. I've a bad feeling about this."

A SHORT TIME later, they stood atop a hill overlooking Riversedge. Bells's trail skirted in a wide arc around the city before making an abrupt turn where they were now and heading directly for it.

Down below was one of the city's main gates, crowded with people, horses, carts, and wagons at this time of day. It would be easy enough for a stranger to pass through without attracting attention.

With a curse, Morkel mounted his horse. "Looks like our job just got a hundred times harder. But at least we know where she went, and we'll have more support. Come on, let's get back and tell Annelie what we've found."

As they rode down the hill toward the gate, Caldan's chest grew tight, and he drew shallow breaths. *Calm yourself,* he thought. *Breathe.*

But it was hard. So much time wasted, only to end up back in the city they had just left. And Bells—the most powerful sorcerer he'd ever seen—was still on the loose. All because of him. Caldan couldn't help feeling his desire to heal Miranda could cost the Protectors and the empire dearly.

"WE NEED TO find somewhere to hide out," Bells told Amerdan. "A room at an inn, or an apartment, if we can. An out-of-the-way location. The Quivers will be crawling over this city when they find out I've escaped."

Amerdan nodded, though he didn't like the idea of hiding like a criminal on the run. It grated on him. He was used to hiding in plain sight, which lent considerable freedom to his movements. At the moment, though, he'd have to pander to this sorcerer's whims. She was his ticket to greater things and had to be kept . . . viable.

"I have some ducats," he said. "And I'd prefer an apartment. An inn is too . . . busy. People would take note of our comings and goings."

Bells nodded in agreement. "Probably a good idea."

They passed another farmer driving a cart filled almost to over-flowing with vegetables. Ahead, a trader led three pack-loaded mules with a guard in tow. Amerdan wrinkled his nose at the guard's slov-enly appearance and flaccid belly.

Like I couldn't steal whatever I wanted from you, if I were so inclined.

The guard didn't even notice him, which only increased Amer-dan's contempt.

His mood wasn't improved by the line to enter the city. It was get-ting shorter, but still wasn't quick enough for his liking. At least they didn't have to wait behind the farmers and traders with their horses and mules defecating all over the road—people without livestock, wag-ons, or carts formed their own line, which moved at a much faster pace.

As they approached the gate, he felt Bells clutch his arm. He flinched at the touch and frowned at her, barely stopping himself from gutting her on the spot. He chuckled when he imagined the sight. The genteel-looking woman behind them would positively squeal if Bells leaked onto the road at her feet. Then he'd have to silence her, too. Then someone else who saw . . . Where would it end? A fine amusement, but not in keeping with his plan.

"What's so funny?"

Amerdan shrugged but didn't speak.

"If they ask, we're husband and wife."

He nodded. She was up to something again. He'd known that from the moment she'd regained consciousness after they'd captured her. She hadn't squirmed nearly so much as she should have when she'd been trussed up like a pig and in Caldan's hands. When she'd found out they were fleeing Anasoma to the west, she'd become remarkably calm.

Everyone thought she'd resigned herself to her fate, but Amerdan knew her type. You didn't become a powerful sorcerer and a leader of men by quietly giving up. No, Bells was confident she could turn any situation to her advantage. In this, they were similar.

She hadn't confirmed what he suspected her plan was, but she eventually would. A small slipup, something she did; clues would gather, and then he would know.

They passed through the gate after barely a glance from the Quivers guarding the city. The soldiers were haggard, with tired eyes and lethargic movements. A sorry excuse for guards, they were; they looked like they'd been up all night. A quick inspection of all the Quivers revealed a similar tale. They must know about the invasion and have been busy preparing.

The weight and warmth of Bells's arm through his was disturbing. Despite his initial reaction, he found he almost enjoyed it. The sorcerer was beautiful in both a physical and a dangerous way—not to mention how much he desired her essence—and he found he was reluctant to let her go once they were inside Riversedge.

Nestled in his shirt, Dotty moved, brushing his chest, as if to remind him she was still there. *I know,* he said silently to himself. Attachments were hazardous. People were treacherous, as he knew only too well. But . . . she was exquisite.

Much to Bells's chagrin, Amerdan vetoed the first four apartments they inspected, deciding on the fifth, even though it didn't seem to suit her purposes as well as a couple of the others. But he couldn't let her decide. And it was important that she didn't discern any of his patterns.

After paying a toothless crone a few ducats, he took possession of the key. Unlocking the door, he let them in and ran an eye over the place. It would need a good cleaning before it was habitable. The apartment building had a courtyard in the center, and he'd noted a few buckets at a well.

"I'll get some water and a broom, if I can find one," he told Bells.

She shrugged and kicked off her boots.

Amerdan sniffed, catching the stench of himself after so long on the road without a proper bath. "Once we clean the room, we'll find a bathhouse and have our clothes laundered."

At that, Bells finally smiled.

Yes. Exquisite.

CHAPTER 19

At least it isn't raining anymore, thought Felice. Though a brief shower had washed away most of the disgusting river muck from her skin, she was shivering and tired. She'd stopped briefly at a fountain to wash out her mouth and drink, but that seemed like hours ago, and she was parched again.

The narrow street she was on sloped steeply up to the north, and she trudged along the cobbles with weary, shuffling steps.

Why isn't this ancestors-cursed city smaller?

She was in a part of Anasoma called Barrows, on account of the burial mounds that had littered the place back in the early days of the city, now looted and long gone, covered with layers of buildings. It was somewhat ironic that she found herself here, given her plight.

Still, at least if I wind up dead, they won't have to go far to dump my body.

Sweat dripped down her nose, and she shivered violently. By the ancestors, she was cold, but her head felt hot, like it was about to explode. She pressed on regardless. *Time to rest when I arrive at my destination*, she thought, which should be up ahead. Going back to the Cemetery was too risky, and she'd likely be caught tonight. It hadn't taken her too long to come up with another place, somewhere she could hole up until she regained her strength; a place, too, where she could possibly find answers to some questions about Kelhak that had arisen during their game of Dominion.

Ah, there it is. Ahead, the street stopped at a squat building with a heavy iron door: the Records Archives, one of the places Avigdor had searched for clues about Caldan's ring.

Avigdor . . .

Felice stopped and leaned on the wall next to the door, breath coming harshly through clenched teeth.

They'll pay for what they did to him, she vowed. *Kelhak, Savine, all of them.*

Her fist slammed into the brick wall, and she almost howled out loud in sorrow, barely able to stop herself.

Pull yourself together, Felice, you're needed. Wiping her eyes, then sweat from her brow, she clanked the iron door knocker a few times, then a few more for good measure. Inside, she could hear the sound echoing throughout the building.

About to try again, she was lifting the knocker when a peephole opened to her right. A wrinkled face with rheumy eyes peered at her.

"What is it?" the bald old man shouted. "It's not even dawn yet."

Felice drew herself up and brushed her damp hair from her face as best she could. "I'm well aware of that. My name is Felicienne Shyrise, Third Adjudicator to the emperor, and I demand that you open the door."

"Get out of here! Go home and sleep it off."

Felice swallowed the curses that rose to her lips and took a deep breath. "Listen carefully. The fate of the city may very well rest on your decision to let me in. It's of the utmost urgency you do. I need to look through your records for the Autumn Festivals."

"You don't sound drunk."

"I'm *not*."

The old archivist squinted and looked her up and down. "I don't know . . ."

"The Indryallans held me prisoner, and I've escaped. The information I have could be vital, but it needs confirmation. You can help me now and be rewarded, or I can come back with a few men and—"

"Don't threaten me, young lady."

Despite the situation, Felice almost laughed out loud. It had been a while since someone had called her young. Or thought her in a position to threaten them, she realized.

"My apologies. How can I convince you I'm who I say I am? As you can see"—she gestured to her wet coarse-spun robe—"I doubt my appearance helps."

"Pfffft. It's a poor judge of a person that relies on appearance."

Felice smiled. "That's true."

"Let me think . . ." the archivist said. "Answer me this: Who came second in Dominion at the Autumn Festival three years ago?" The old man snickered, as if at his own wit, then yawned.

"Three years ago, that was . . . me. I came second."

"Indeed. Well, I'm not totally convinced, but you've made a start. I'll have a few more questions for you, since I'm not letting you wander around on your own. But for now . . ."

The wrinkled face disappeared, and the peephole slammed shut. Moments later, a number of latches clicked, and the door opened.

Sighing with relief, Felice stepped inside to the familiar scent of musty paper and a faint alchemical tang, the preservative the librarians used on the books and scrolls. In one hand, the old man held a crafted sorcerous globe enclosed in a metal cage on the end of a wooden rod.

"Thank you. You won't regret this, I'll make sure of it."

"Hmmmph. Maybe. First things first. You look like you could use some warmth, a fire, and a hot drink." He sniffed. "And a bath."

Without waiting for a reply, the archivist shuffled toward a corridor to the left. He was right, she did need some warmth and a little time to recover. She shivered again, though her face was flushed and sweating. Her skin itched, and she rubbed at a number of cuts on her arms, a result of the broken glass from the window. They weren't deep and had stopped bleeding, but the river water couldn't have been good for them. She'd have to visit a physiker to treat the cuts—perhaps some ointment. Soon, she promised herself. Once she had some answers.

She followed the archivist until they reached what looked like a common area for them to relax in. An orange glow filled the room from a fireplace, and the librarian threw a couple of logs onto the coals from a pile to the side.

"You," he said, pointing globe at her. "Sit there."

Felice blinked at the bright light thrust at her eyes, then at the chair in front of the fire he'd indicated. Gratefully, she slumped into its warm embrace. "Why do you have someone watching all night?"

"Secrets. There are secrets here, in the information. If you can find them."

"Yes, there are."

"A word here, a sentence there, some numbers . . . Some people can piece it together, and they don't like to visit during the day. So one of us stays awake. There is a side door they usually come to, though; it's more . . . furtive."

He cackled, as if he'd said something funny, gave her a quizzical look, then wandered away, presumably to bring her a hot drink. If he did, she'd probably kiss him.

She held her hands to the heat of the flames and rubbed them vigorously. Bloody hells, she was still sweating. Then why did she feel so cold?

Soon the man returned, cradling a mug in both hands. Steam rose from the top, and Felice smiled gratefully as she accepted the drink. Tea, strong and heavily honeyed. He just might have earned that kiss.

She gulped a few mouthfuls of tea, scalding herself, then cleared her throat. "I really need to see your records. Please."

"In a moment. I want to ask you something else."

"What is it, then?" Felice sipped her tea. She wanted to finish it quickly and then begin her search.

"Tell me what you've been up to since the invasion. As a Third Adjudicator, and a canny Dominion player, you have to have been up to something. And you're on the run, that's clear."

Felice gave him a brief summary of what had happened, skipping over the destructive and coercive sorcery. By the end, the archivist was staring at her in admiration.

"That was you down by the docks? Trying to sink the Indryallan ships?" He gave a low whistle.

"It was," Felice said. "Except that plan failed. Their leader escaped unharmed."

Pausing, as if to think, the archivist scratched his bald head. "What I don't get is why the Indryallans took over Anasoma and just barricaded themselves in."

Felice shrugged. "To make a point? There's something here they want? I don't know." *It's something I've been trying to figure out myself— and I still haven't come close to an answer.*

"Perhaps you'd better think about it more, then. Why stir up a hornets' nest? Especially when you know you can't match the might of the Mahruse Empire."

Why indeed? The man had a point. What reason could the Indryallans have? They'd just painted a target on themselves and were waiting for . . . what? To be defeated and pushed back to Indryalla? The emperor was no fool, and he'd surely have gathered enough soldiers for a strike on Indryalla and to march on Anasoma . . . Pignuts!

Felice stood abruptly, tea sloshing over the side of her cup. "I need to see those records now. From the Autumn Festivals, the old ones from centuries ago. I don't know what year, so you'll have to help me look."

"Come, then. But I don't want to get involved in whatever you're up to. The library is our responsibility, and who rules here doesn't matter to us. We keep the knowledge for everyone."

"Fair enough." *Although I can't promise they won't see your assistance as a violation of your self-imposed neutrality.*

"TRY THESE."

Felice accepted another pile of books, along with loose paper sheets in a number of leather folders. So far, they'd not even found the year she was looking for, and it had been almost an hour. The librarian complained every few minutes about her, the library, his colleagues, the weather, and anything else he thought of; and the way her nerves were fraying, she reckoned the litany of his complaints had passed twenty.

"The lists," she repeated again. "Just look at the winners' list for Dominion, and tell me who placed first."

"I don't think any of these people are alive anymore, if you were planning on taking lessons."

"What would you say if I told you that's exactly what I think?"

"I'd say you were crazy."

"So would I if I were you. Nevertheless, I can't discount the fact without evidence."

Felice opened another book and sneezed. They'd stirred up quite a bit of dust in their search. By the ancestors, she was tired, but at least she'd stopped shivering. The room felt warm, hot almost. The cuts on her skin were getting itchier as well. She'd better see to them as soon as she could. During their search, she'd remained standing, but the empty stool next to the old man looked inviting. Perhaps she could sit for a short time. Later.

Felice leafed through the pages of the book until she found the lists she was after. The Autumn Festival in Anasoma was well documented, with entertainment programs, winners' lists, and detailed games schedules, along with reviews of musical troupes and plays, and sketches commissioned by the nobles.

There. Finally. In the concluding game, a newcomer named Kelhak had defeated the favorite, one Councillor Osmund. She passed a pile of loose paper to the librarian. "Here, I found something. What I need should be in here. Can you search through these pages for sketches of the Dominion games? I'll go through the others." She wiped her damp face with the sleeve of her robe.

"I must say, young Felicienne, you're not looking too well. Perhaps you'd better rest for a while."

"I'm fine. I . . . we just need to do this. We're almost there; then I can rest."

She checked the sketches as quickly as she could, searching for

Dominion games in progress or anything related to the finalist or winners.

And there it was.

The beaming winner of the Dominion competition accepting a token from the emperor's representative, with purses filled with ducats at his feet, thrown by the nobles. The sketch was annotated: *Kelhak, winner of this year's Autumn Festival Dominion Competition. A tall, well-muscled man with radiant blue eyes.*

"Pignuts," whispered Felice.

The room swirled around her, and she lurched for the stool. Hands steadied her, and she managed to sit with their assistance.

"You're burning up. And you've cuts on your arms. What happened?"

Felice closed her eyes. *Just for a moment,* she convinced herself. It was the same Kelhak. But he didn't recognize his own Dominion strategies used against him. Was this a result of the sorcery he had to be using to prolong his life, or something else? This had to mean something, but what? She just wasn't seeing it.

Think, curse you.

"How did you escape? Those cuts are swollen and inflamed; they don't look good."

"I jumped through a window into the river."

The librarian hissed, alarmed. "You need to get to a physiker. River water's not good for anything. Even children know it's bad for cuts."

"There's . . . no time."

"Stupid girl; there's no time if you're dead, either."

"Gaa—" she managed before tumbling sideways off the stool.

CHAPTER 20

Master Annelie was waiting for them before they'd finished washing the road dust from their hands and faces using rainwater collected in a barrel.

"You're back sooner than expected," she shouted across the courtyard, hastening toward them. "I assume you didn't find this sorcerer, Bells?"

Morkel shook his head. "She didn't make straight for Anasoma like we thought she would. She's somewhere in the city."

"Here? In Riversedge?"

"Yes . . . and there's more."

"Keevy," Annelie said, "round up the masters, whoever you can find quickly. Have them wait in the masters' dining room. If they complain, tell them I'll be there shortly with important news."

"Yes, ma'am," replied Keevy and entered the Protectors' building.

Annelie tutted and motioned for Caldan and Morkel to follow her. Inside, she pointed Caldan toward a bench. "Stay here, and don't speak to anyone while I'm gone. I'm sure a few of the apprentices and journeymen will have questions, but ignore them. We'll decide what to do with you later, once we've recaptured Bells. At least we know she's in the city somewhere, and with luck, we'll find her soon. You, though . . ."

The way she left it hanging was far from auspicious. "Master Annelie, is there anything—"

"No. The fact that Simmon trusted you enough to have you bring that . . . sword . . . to us is a mark in your favor. A big one. But don't think you'll get out of this lightly. Now, I have to inform the masters what's happening and organize the hunt for this sorcerer."

Caldan nodded and watched as they strode off, eventually disappearing into a room.

He rubbed aching eyes and lowered himself onto the bench. By the ancestors, he was tired. What the masters would decide about him, he had no control over, but if he was allowed to speak to them, he was sure he'd be able to convince them of his sincerity.

No matter. If they confined him to the headquarters, at least the troubles with the Indryallans and Bells would be off his shoulders. They were a burden he could do without. Still, he was left in a worse position than he'd been in days ago. Miranda was no closer to recovering and seemed to be deteriorating at a growing rate. If the Protectors caught Bells, it surely wouldn't be to help Miranda. Perhaps most urgent, though, was the fact that whatever they did to apprentices who stepped beyond the rules wasn't something he was bound to enjoy.

Which is why he figured it was best not to find out what his punishment was.

Coming to a decision, he stood and made his way farther into the building, stopping the first apprentice he saw.

"Excuse me," he said to the dark-haired girl. "Some friends of mine arrived recently, an older woman who is caring for a younger woman. Do you know where they are?"

"Yes. She's very sick, isn't she? The pretty one, I mean."

"She is," he said, thinking that the girl before him was right on both accounts: Miranda was very sick . . . and very pretty. "Could you tell me where they are?"

"Upstairs, in the sick rooms. I heard she needs a lot of looking after."

Caldan nodded. "She does. Thank you."

Moving as quickly as he could without attracting suspicion, he left the apprentice and climbed the nearest stairs. It wasn't long before he poked his head through a doorway covered by a curtain and found Elpidia. He noted that his gear, and Miranda's, was piled in a corner. The physiker had her back to the doorway and looked preoccupied with various jars and bottles in front of her. She was shaking a clear vial and peering at the faintly pink contents, lost in her own thoughts.

Caldan slipped inside. "Where's Miranda?"

"Oh!" she said with a start. "Don't do that! She's in the next room, and they're taking good care of her. Did you find Bells?"

With a shake of his head, Caldan stepped back toward the doorway. "No. The masters are meeting, and they'll decide what to do."

"So we don't have to worry about her?"

"That's not what I said. I have to try to make this right."

Elpidia's eyes narrowed. "Make sure you know what you're doing."

"I do," replied Caldan, and when Elpidia looked at him dubiously, added, "I'm not going to go haring off on my own trying to hunt down Bells. I have to focus on Miranda."

"Good. See that you do. I didn't know if I should have mentioned this before—probably—but this might help."

Elpidia rummaged through her leather case and produced a folded handkerchief. "Here," she said, presenting it to Caldan.

"What is it?"

"A few of Bells's hairs. I collected them from her clothes after we left Anasoma. Just in case . . . Well, they should come in handy now, shouldn't they?"

Caldan smiled and gave her a brief hug. "They certainly will. Thank you. I didn't think—"

"No, you didn't."

He accepted the rebuke, although he was starting to get tired of her holier-than-thou attitude. But the last thing he needed was an argument, so he inclined his head in acknowledgment. "I'll have to make another compass," he thought aloud. "I just wish I had a bit more time." Caldan took the proffered hairs and rummaged through his belongings. If he could think of something quickly, he might be able to salvage some goodwill from the masters.

With a hasty good-bye, he made his way to the room next door and checked on Miranda. She was sitting in a narrow bed, a blanket covering her legs. Her nose was dripping, and her blank eyes didn't seem to recognize him. He smoothed her hair down and wiped her nose before taking a candle from near the window and settling himself on the floor. He drew out some paper and his inks and pens, lit the candle, and waited for some wax to melt. He envisioned what he needed to do, using the compass Elpidia had made as a guide. Not the perfect crafting, but it didn't need to be.

He had to work quickly. Nothing flashy. As long as it did what it was supposed to, it would suffice.

ANNELIE INTERCEPTED CALDAN on his way back down the stairs. She stood in front of him, hands on hips, a stern, disapproving look on her face.

"I thought I told you to stay put."

"I'm sorry, but I've something to show you."

"It'd better be important, but you'll need to explain later. I was on my way to get you." She inclined her head, indicating for him to follow her. "Come on, the masters have gathered."

Without waiting for a response, she hurried down the corridor, and Caldan followed, clutching his newly crafted paper-and-wax compass in his hand.

She led him into a meeting room, where he abruptly found himself the object of inspection by at least ten masters, including Mold. Returning their frank, appraising stares wasn't easy, but he managed not to look agitated and held his nerve throughout their murmurings.

To his relief, Annelie spoke. "This is Caldan, formerly apprenticed to Master Simmon, and the man who brought us the trinket, preventing it from falling into Indryallan hands."

"And also the person who let the rogue sorcerer escape," added one master, an older man with thinning gray hair. "Why go over his accomplishments without mentioning his shortcomings?"

There was widespread muttering of agreement at his words.

Caldan's face grew hot, but he looked on defiantly.

Annelie held up a hand, silencing the masters' rumblings. "Enough. Whatever his failings, Caldan has proven his worth just by traveling here with the trinket. He knew how much such an object would be worth and didn't hesitate to return it to us, where it rightfully belongs. He's shown he's resourceful and loyal. His judgment in some areas is suspect, though it could be considered understandable."

Nothing like being damned with faint praise.

"Now is as good a time as any," continued Annelie, "to decide who of you will assume the role of his master for the duration of his apprenticeship. Though he'll need to be tested soon, to see if he's talented enough to be a journeyman, that will have to wait until after this rogue sorcerer is apprehended."

Caldan grimaced and took a step forward. They weren't thinking about Bells in the right way, and he needed to warn them.

"If I may interrupt?" he said, and all eyes turned to him.

Annelie looked annoyed at the disruption but with a curt gesture motioned for him to continue.

He took a breath. "A rogue sorcerer she is not. I know that's what you call anyone unlucky enough to stumble onto forbidden sorcery, or who purposely experiments with it, but you have to change what you think about Bells. From what I could get out of her, she's the product of rigorous training, from a young age when she was found to have a well. She's not only proficient in crafting, but she's also accomplished with sorcery I'm not even supposed to know exists. She's been taught for years, by those presumably more skilled than she, overcoming whatever obstacles and tasks they set for her." He looked around the room, meeting the eyes of a few masters. "Make no mistake, she isn't the usual rogue sorcerer you hunt down; she's . . . something more. Her destructive sorcery is focused somehow, far beyond what I've seen . . . saw, Simmon perform. I'm sorry she escaped, but don't treat her lightly—as was my mistake—or people could die."

"But you claim to have defeated her." This from a young woman with red hair and freckles on her nose and cheeks. "Do you expect us to believe that, after what you've just told us?"

Caldan's shrug was resigned. "I'll admit, part of that was luck. But part of it was because I didn't underestimate her . . . at least not at that moment.

"But you don't need to take my word for it. We all know the Indryallans erected an impassable barrier around the entire city of Anasoma. They subverted the nobles and Quivers. That should be a warning to you, if nothing else."

"Thank you, Caldan," said Annelie. "I think we'll continue this discussion among ourselves later. For now, is there anyone willing to take Caldan as an apprentice?"

A few of the masters looked at each other, while others dropped their eyes to the floor. Caldan's gut clenched as he saw their reluctant responses.

"I will," said a man from behind him in a deep, firm voice.

Caldan turned to see who'd spoken as gasps erupted from the masters.

The door swung closed behind a pale-skinned man with close-cropped brown hair. His black trousers and shirt were punctuated with silver buttons shaped like flowers, and he literally vibrated to Caldan's senses, so numerous were the craftings and trinkets he wore. Caldan turned to ask Annelie who this man was and found half the masters with their heads bowed and a few on one knee. He shuffled his feet, not sure how to respond.

Annelie was one of the masters who remained standing, though she gave the man a shallow bow followed by a warm smile. There was respect in her voice when she spoke.

"Joachim. We weren't expecting anyone for days, but it's a pleasure to see one of the emperor's warlocks, as always."

The man, Joachim, grinned briefly at Annelie. "I'm sure it is. I've come in advance, traveling light, as you can see. Though I had other reasons."

"And they would be . . . ?"

"None of your concern. Now, I was just outside and happened to hear mention of a rogue sorcerer?"

Annelie nodded. "We're organizing a search for her now."

"How are you going to find her?"

"We have a description, plus we'll focus on sensing any sorcery and look for anyone with a well."

"I may have something better," interrupted Caldan. "That is, I *do* have something better," he said, holding out his hand, revealing his paper crafting.

"Blood, skin, or hair?" asked Joachim, immediately recognizing the crafting as a makeshift compass.

"Hair. It's all I had."

"It'll do. Annelie, take it and find this sorcerer. And be careful. We'll talk later about Caldan here. Everyone else, out."

Giving Caldan an annoyed look, Annelie took his crafting and left, followed by the other masters. Soon the room was empty, except for Caldan and Joachim.

The emperor's warlock regarded him for a few moments, and Caldan sensed him access his well. Touching Bells's shield crafting in his pocket, just in case, Caldan opened his own well in response.

"Don't fear me, lad. I've traveled a long way in a short time to find you."

Caldan's breath caught in his throat. "What do you mean?"

"Did you think using the trinket would go unnoticed? We've been looking for it, and for the descendants of the person it was given to, for years. When it was activated a few weeks ago, I was sent to find it, and whoever possessed it."

Weeks ago? wondered Caldan. The strange bone trinket had only activated when he'd fought Bells, not weeks before. What had happened weeks ago? The only thing he could think of was when he'd killed the rogue sorcerer by penetrating his shield. Could it have been then? It had to be. But he was sure the bone trinket hadn't been responsible. It hadn't reacted at all, unlike beneath Anasoma . . . That left his silver trinket, the other ring.

"You have something that belongs to the emperor." Joachim pointed to the trinket on Caldan's finger, confirming his deductions. "I doubt you know what it can do, though you may have reasoned something. It takes a certain type of person to activate it, and that usually happens after a period of familiarity. I was sent to track it down and evaluate the situation, so there are certain circumstances in which I have some . . . freedom to make my own decisions."

Heart hammering in his chest, Caldan held up the hand with the trinket. Best to pretend this was his only trinket, until he knew more about this man and what his purpose was. "I was told it was given freely to one of my ancestors, as a reward."

"That is correct; for the term of her life. It remains the emperor's property."

"It's been in my family for generations. It's mine by right. You can't ask me to give it up."

"I can ask you, and I would take it if I wanted to. It is the emperor's, and that trumps any sentimental attachment you may have. But let me ask you a question: Have I asked you for it?"

"Well, no. But you implied I might have to give it up. Which makes me believe you want something from me."

"Ah, you're brighter than you look."

Caldan bristled at the warlock's words but held his tongue. He'd no idea what a warlock actually was, or how much power and influence they wielded, but judging from the masters' and Annelie's reactions, Joachim had the full power of the emperor behind him and wasn't someone to be trifled with. Caldan's skin was still crawling from being close to so many craftings and trinkets. How could the man stand it?

Suppressing that feeling, Caldan asked, "So I'm to be your apprentice? What does that even mean—will I be a warlock? Am I no longer a Protector?" The thoughts were flitting wildly through his mind, and the questions just tumbled out. "What exactly *is* a warlock?"

Joachim laughed, holding up his hands. "I get it—you have questions. Let's start with the last one first, since it's probably the easiest to explain. Some people call us the emperor's shadows, though officially we're known as warlocks. We're the emperor's personal sorcerers, drawn from the Sorcerers' Guild and the Protectors. We do . . . whatever the emperor needs us to.

"But that's enough questions right now—you'll find out more soon. I need to examine you, to see if you're touched by the ancestors."

Caldan blinked. "Touched? What do you mean?"

"I told you no more questions. Stand still. This shouldn't hurt."

Joachim closed his eyes, and Caldan felt him link to something. A chill swept over him, as if a cold wind had blown along his skin from his toes to his head. His arm hair stood on end, and he shivered.

With a noncommittal grunt, Joachim opened his eyes and pursed his lips.

"Well?" asked Caldan.

"Inconclusive. But that's not unusual. No matter. Once we're on our way, I'll have some questions for you, which should straighten things out."

"On our way? I'm sorry, but I can't leave. My friends . . . There's a woman with me who was injured by Bells, one of the Indryallan sorcerers. She used coercive sorcery on her. When it was cut off, her mind . . ." Caldan paused and swallowed, throat tight.

"Was scrambled," finished Joachim.

Caldan nodded. "I'm not leaving her here, especially not without healing her."

"I could just order you to come with me—trust me, I'm more than able to enforce such an order. But I'm not going to drag you anywhere without your consent." The warlock grimaced and looked away, as if evaluating his choices.

"Annelie and the other masters still might be able to help her," Caldan said. "And I'm not leaving until they try again."

Joachim shook his head. "You think the emperor lets the Protectors learn the intricacies of coercive sorcery? They know a little, enough to recognize it, and some basic techniques of defense against it, if they know it'll be used against them, but it's too insidious for them to know more."

"Then who can help? Who should I turn to?"

"Why, me, of course. Though this will delay and drain me more than is convenient. I have no choice, do I?"

Caldan shook his head firmly.

"Very well, then. Come," Joachim said. "Show me where this woman is, and I'll see what I can do. No promises, though. It may be she needs to travel to the capital to be treated. Though, with the emperor and the army on the way here, her salvation might be getting closer as we speak." Joachim left the room, indicating that Caldan was to follow.

Yet again, Caldan felt inklings of hope creep into his heart.

This time, though, he brutally pushed them down.

There will be no more hope until Miranda recognizes me once more.

JOACHIM EXAMINED MIRANDA. She sat in a chair next to the window, a rug covering her legs, an untouched cup of water on a stool by her side. He removed a cloth from his pocket and laid it on the floor next to her. Then he produced a cluster of craftings tied together with a leather thong, separated them, and positioned each carefully on the cloth. Caldan felt him access his well but was reluctant to do the same for fear of disrupting the man's concentration. Long minutes passed while he waited for any sign from either Joachim or Miranda.

"Could I," interjected Caldan cautiously, "open my well and watch?"

Joachim blinked. "Do you think you can?"

"I've learned a little the last few days, enough to be able to see a . . . tangle in her mind."

The warlock waved him permission, so Caldan drew out Bells's coercive crafted bell. Joachim raised his eyebrows when he saw it.

"I assume that's the sorcerer's?"

"Yes. I took it from her."

"Just as well. Did she have any others like it?"

"Not that I could tell. None with similar runes or orange jasper stones."

"There are other stones that could be used; jasper is just the most common. Why don't you show me what she taught you?"

Swallowing his misgivings, Caldan fingered the crafted bell and opened his well, linking to its anchor. For the second time, the colors of his surroundings drained away, all except for Miranda.

"Tell me what you see," said Joachim.

"Her head . . . it's a tangled mess. Threads, are they? A jumbled mass of colors with no sense to them. No structure at all." His stomach roiled, and he felt queasy. He quickly closed his well. Sweat dripped down his face. It was discouraging to see the mess, but he was starting to feel that if he examined the threads for long enough, eventually they would make sense. He'd said they had no order, but now he wondered if there was a pattern. Something about them tickled his awareness, made him think the threads formed a complex arrangement, one he just couldn't see yet. Unfortunately, the longer he looked at the mess, the queasier he became.

Joachim was nodding at him. "Good. That's a start. A better one than many have. It's a wonder you weren't sick on the floor."

"Does that happen often?"

"It did to me the first time, and to others. It'll become easier, if that's where your fate leads you."

The warlock's words stirred something in Caldan—a wariness. Was Joachim saying he might not be forbidden to use coercive sorcery in the future? But how could you unlearn something once you learned it? The answer was, of course, you couldn't. Despite Joachim's apparent willingness to answer questions and examine Miranda, Caldan couldn't help being reminded of what he'd said downstairs: that he had the power to compel Caldan to obey.

Joachim glanced at him. "If you can stand to watch, then link to your crafting again. I can do something for her. A very little, though," he warned.

"Anything. Please."

Without another word, the warlock turned back to Miranda.

Caldan wiped his face and steeled himself for the nausea he knew was coming, then linked to the crafting. He recoiled slightly from the sight of Miranda's damaged mind, but clenching his hands into fists, he pushed himself to face the distressing sight. Moments passed, and nothing happened.

"What are you—?"

"Shh. Don't interrupt."

Caldan shifted his weight, hugged his arms across his chest, and waited. And waited. His mouth filled with saliva from his rising nausea, and he swallowed, forcing the feeling back down.

Which was when he saw something move at the edge of Miranda's mind: a slender white string, not tangled with the rest. The end of it moved back and forth, almost snakelike. It probed forward gently, sliding under a few colored threads and hooking around one before it tugged. The string it moved went rigid, and the others surrounding it wavered slightly, then seemed to settle, as if whatever Joachim had done caused them to become more ordered, though they still remained.

Again, the string probed and tugged. And again.

Caldan watched, fascinated, as slowly, and with a few tugs of great precision, Miranda's mind settled down. And though he still felt sick, the nausea seemed to lessen. Whether that was the effect Joachim was having on Miranda or his getting used to coercive sorcery, he couldn't tell.

The white string finally withdrew, and Caldan closed his well, coming back to the room with disorientating suddenness. His legs wobbled, and he sank to one knee.

A hand touched him on the shoulder.

"Are you well?" asked Joachim.

"Ah, give me a moment." Caldan swallowed to remove the taste of bile in his mouth. It took a few deep breaths before he felt well enough to stand.

"Miranda," he said tentatively, "Is she . . . ?"

"Whole again? No, far from it. As I said, I could do very little. But

I've managed to lessen the confusion in her mind. It might take a few days, but she'll begin to show some signs of recovery."

"How much improvement will she make? When can you try again?"

Joachim sighed and began collecting his craftings, folding them into the cloth. "I can't say for certain. Often it depends on the strength of will of the affected person. And she'll need a lot more treatment, from sorcerers of far greater skill than I."

"Where can I find them?"

"A few are on their way here, with the emperor's retinue. So, in that, you could say you're lucky. I've given Miranda a chance to improve her state; perhaps it'll lessen the fear she's feeling inside. Her deterioration's stalled, but not stopped. She has more time now, and so have you."

Caldan gave Joachim a sharp look. "So that's what this is about. Pushing me in the direction you want."

"No. Despite what you think, I'm not a monster—I would have attempted to heal her anyway. That the act coincides with something else I want is fortuitous."

"Arriving here right now, in my time of need, looks extremely suspicious."

"You can look at it any way you want, but you'd be wrong. The empire is in peril, Caldan, which is one of the reasons I'm here. And yes, I was following your trinket, but I assure you, I couldn't have known you'd need my help. And"—the warlock stressed his words—"would now be in my debt. As I said, fortuitous, but not malicious."

"What exactly do you want?"

Joachim smiled. "Is that any way to treat someone who's just helped you? The Protectors couldn't have done anything except send word to us, anyway. You're lucky I'm here already. And I deserve more respect than you've shown so far. See to it you modify your behavior."

Turning to look at Miranda, Caldan remained silent. Was there more color in her face? Did her eyes show more signs of life? He ran a hand over his head, short hair prickling his palm. "You said before you wanted me to be your apprentice. But that wasn't true, was it?"

"No. That was just to get the Protectors out of the way. I've no time to coddle anyone."

"Are you evaluating me? Pushing and prodding to see which way I'll jump?"

"Always. You may not be my apprentice, but you're still beneath me. I'm not some kindly old mentor who'll guide you every step of the way. Understand that now."

"I didn't think you were."

"*Remember* it. The emperor has given me total discretion when dealing with the likes of you."

"The likes of me? What does that mean?"

"Apart from what you might be, how about trinket thief?"

Caldan sputtered. "What? You know I didn't steal it."

"Do I? Because you told me? You should know that's not a very good argument."

Caldan had no response to that. Finally he asked again, "What *do* you want?"

"Answers. Then I can decide what to do with you."

CHAPTER 21

Aidan returned from pissing against a bush to find Vasile arguing with cel Rau and Chalayan. He rubbed his eyes and cursed under his breath before looking up into the night sky. Thousands of stars winked back at him, and he was sure they were mocking his fate.

Vasile and Chalayan had been at each other for days, ever since leaving Gazija and his company of weird companions. There was something odd in the way those people moved and spoke. He couldn't put his finger on what bothered him about them, but it would take a good while before he trusted anything they said, no matter how much Vasile said he could. He didn't like sorcerers, but cel Rau had a burning hatred for them. If they'd stayed with Gazija much longer, Aidan had been afraid the swordsman would do something rash. And bloody.

He stepped out of the shadows toward their meager fire. "Leave it," he said firmly.

"The magistrate here knows something," said Chalayan, for the tenth time in a few days.

Vasile shook his head in weary denial. "I know no more than you. They're a strange lot and hard to work out. And very careful with their words around me."

"That should tell you something, then. They're hiding information from us. Sorcerous secrets." Chalayan almost hissed the words.

Aidan turned to cel Rau. "You should know better."

The swordsman only shrugged and busied himself laying out his bedding and arranging his pack as a pillow. For a tribesman of the Steppes, he liked his little luxuries. Aidan was sure if cel Rau were back in his homeland among his people, he would be sleeping rough, and likely waking with a sore neck.

Which he would deserve, for not putting a stop to the pain in my neck, which is these two arguing.

Leaving the swordsman be, Aidan stared at Chalayan, who was still eyeing Vasile—with hunger, he realized, and not for the first time. There were sorcerous secrets that Chalayan wanted, no matter if they were immoral or malevolent. He'd seen Mazoet's sorcery at work and found his own wanting—limited and pale in comparison. Aidan would have hated to lose Chalayan, but sometimes life didn't work out as you'd hoped. The sorcerer was worth saving, though, if he could.

Tomorrow, though.

"Let's get some sleep," Aidan said. "And stop arguing."

"Chalayan still owes Vasile fifty gold ducats," remarked cel Rau, unhelpfully.

"By the ancestors," growled Aidan. "Enough. If we turn up in front of the emperor and his retinue like this, they won't take us seriously."

Vasile frowned at Aidan. "I thought you said they know who you are and what you do? That you've a writ from the emperor himself for your . . . activities."

"That we do," replied Aidan. "But Lady Caitlyn was the only one who dealt with the emperor and whoever's around him. I have confidence we'll be all right, though—we've the writ, plus news from Anasoma and our mysterious benefactors."

The magistrate didn't look convinced, but Aidan couldn't care less. With what he'd seen and been through, approaching the emperor with important information he needed was the least of their problems.

The bigger concern was convincing him that the information was true . . . and that was as much Vasile's problem as it was his.

"Sleep," he growled at them, and rolled himself in his blanket.

With any luck, these two would have argued themselves hoarse long before they reached the emperor.

A COLD WIND cut through Vasile's clothes like a sharp-edged knife out of the gray sky. Grasslands populated by sparse bushes and spindly trees gradually gave way to the occasional farmland and small village.

Cel Rau guided them off the tracks and through a stony expanse of undulating land not fit for farming, claiming it would save them some time. Rocky outcrops thrust from the ground at irregular intervals, and dark openings punctured their bases. Cel Rau warned them to be on the lookout for wolves and other predators, but so far they'd seen none, though when they'd sheltered in one of the caves last night, it had reeked of an animal.

Vasile tightened his cloak around himself, wrapping his hands with it before clutching the reins. His horse had been docile enough so far, following behind the others, but he didn't trust the beasts. Born and raised in the city, he was more at home on cobbled streets. But the last time he checked, those cobbled streets had hardly been safe, which was why he found himself plodding along a dirt trail behind three disreputable mercenaries. Not strictly true, though, that label. And yet they did what they wanted: killed, injured, plundered . . . it just happened to be sanctioned.

As if that made a difference.

He'd expected to be sick of these men by now but had found most of the journey so far almost pleasant, apart from the constant jabs from Chalayan. They lied less than most folks, and their leader, Aidan, hadn't spoken a lie yet. Oh, he'd hedged around certain subjects, but Vasile suspected it was more because they were painful than out of a will to deceive.

Ahead of him, Chalayan pulled his mount to the side and stopped, and as Vasile approached, the sorcerer nudged his horse to ride alongside him. Aidan glanced back and, seeing the sorcerer's actions, slowed his own mount to join them.

"Magistrate," Chalayan said. "What do you know of the sorcery these people use?"

There was only one group the man could be referring to. Vasile shook his head. "Not much. I've already told you what I know."

"Go over it again."

Aidan remained silent, obviously interested in what Vasile had to say.

Vasile sighed and shifted in his saddle. "The first sorcery I saw them use—though as I said before, I didn't really see anyone do anything—was when we passed through the barrier the Indryallans had erected around Anasoma."

"So you passed through it? Like"—Chalayan tilted his head forward—"passing through a waterfall?"

"No, they made a hole in it, pushed it aside, like opening a curtain."

Chalayan looked thoughtful, and his hand strayed to touch an amulet around his neck. "They didn't want to disrupt the barrier, then, and have some way of controlling the flames. Did they place a crafting against it first?"

"I told you, I didn't see anyone do anything of note. The boat we were in approached the barrier, a hole opened, and we passed through."

"How did they create the hole without using a crafting in contact with the flames?" mused Chalayan. "It's impossible, unless they know a way of controlling destructive sorcery."

"If that's what it looks like, then that must be it," said Vasile, unsure what he was even talking about, but eager to end this conversation and be rid of the sorcerer.

Chalayan straightened and gave him a piercing look. "Indeed. There is no other possibility, is there? When Mazoet fought the two sorcerers and saved us, I thought they were using trinkets, just ones I'd never heard of before. But the most plausible explanation is that they have found a way around the limitations of crafting and applied it to destructive sorcery."

Vasile knew next to nothing about sorcery, and although much of what Chalayan was saying went over his head—and despite the fact that he really wanted nothing to do with the man—he was curious about something the sorcerer had said. "You'll have to enlighten me. What limitations?"

"That a hard material object is required to control and weather the forces from your well. They can't be directed through you without causing severe injury or death—well, the minutest amount can." Chalayan became quiet, scratching at his head. "Think," he spat under his breath, the word coming out like a curse. "How can it be done?"

Vasile frowned. He was out of his depth here, but an idea was forming. "Have you heard of lodestones?" he said. "Sometimes called course-stones?"

Aidan spoke. "Sailors use them for navigation or some such. They attract iron."

"But that's not all they do. Try to push two together, and they repel each other. There's a force they generate that does this. I remember a colleague talking about them."

"But no one has the slightest idea why they act this way," Chalayan said. "We can use the property for navigation and such but nothing else."

"My point isn't how or why they behave the way they do; it's the simple fact that they do. An invisible force is generated that is strong enough to attract, or push away, a physical object. Couldn't a sorcerer make a crafting to create a similar force and use it to guide the forces rather than the physical crafting? And not only guide, but contain."

Aidan grunted, not convinced, but Chalayan regarded him with a gleam in his eye.

"I must think of this," said the sorcerer, pulling on his reins to halt his horse, leaving Vasile and Aidan plodding along ahead of him.

After they had put some distance between themselves and the sorcerer, Aidan turned to Vasile. "I don't want you discussing sorcery with Chalayan."

"What? Why? He's just asking questions."

"He's going through a difficult time, seeing the sorcery he's endeavored to master his whole life eclipsed."

A half-truth, thought Vasile. It didn't take much thought to figure out why. "He's the type who has to know everything, isn't he? He won't rest until he learns how it's done and can do it himself."

"Yes. And the power of knowing can be addictive."

"As can power itself."

Aidan nodded but remained silent.

"You're concerned he wants the power rather than the knowledge," stated Vasile.

"What I'm concerned about is not for you to wonder."

"And yet you presume to put limits on my actions—whom I speak to or what I speak about?"

"I presume nothing. I'm telling you not to talk to Chalayan about sorcery. It is not a request. We are not your friends, Vasile, just your escorts. Once we reach the emperor and I've helped you gain an audience, you're on your own, and we can get on with our job."

"Searching for evil and snuffing it out?"

"Whatever it takes to keep people safe."

"And an invading army of malevolent sorcerers taking over a city isn't your concern?"

"It's too big for us. Once we return to Gazija, I'll be taking my men and striking out to the south. Perhaps we'll return to the Desolate Lands. I'm sure the emperor is more than capable of dealing with the Indryallans."

"Gazija isn't so sure . . ."

Aidan shot him a searching look. "He said so?"

"No. But he wouldn't be gathering companies of mercenaries if he thought pushing the invaders back would go smoothly."

"That's . . . likely true. Time will tell, though. With the emperor's forces and Gazija's combined, I can't see how they'd fail."

Vasile could think of any number of ways, but didn't feel like saying as much would do anything to add to this already bleak conversation.

"At least we're removed from the fighting. A few more days of uneventful riding and I'll almost feel relaxed."

"JUKARI," HISSED CEL Rau.

He was crouched over what Vasile could only describe as a large rat dropping, dry, with hairs sticking out of it. He cringed when cel Rau rubbed the blob and sniffed his fingers.

"Fresh?" asked Aidan.

The swordsman nodded curtly.

They were crouched behind a low, dry stone wall, which looked to have been erected as a windbreak by frequent travelers in the area. It surrounded a fire pit, and there were scraps of cloth and bits of rusted, broken buckles and other man-made objects strewn around the enclosure. It must have been in use for a long time.

There was a dark patch of dirt close to the jukari leavings, which Aidan scuffed at with his boot. "Blood," he said.

Cel Rau leaped onto the wall and crouched there, eyes scanning the dirt around it. "Four. No . . . five, possibly more. They headed south, after—"

Chalayan sidled up to Vasile. "After eating the hapless person sheltering here. Bones and all, Magistrate. Bones and all."

There was no boast or exaggeration Vasile could detect, and he shivered at the words.

"I don't know how so many have escaped attention so close to civilization," said Aidan. "But we can't leave them roaming around. They're too dangerous."

Both Chalayan and cel Rau nodded their agreement.

Vasile wasn't so sure. "We can't go off on a side quest," he said. "Every day we waste could have serious consequences for Anasoma, for Gazija, and for the emperor's Quivers."

Aidan reached out and clasped cel Rau on the shoulder, but spoke to Vasile. "That may be, but this can't be avoided. This is what we do—what the emperor, not Gazija, ordered us to do. Anasoma isn't going anywhere, but more innocent people might die if we leave this problem unattended."

"Why do you make it sound like this is just a routine problem, easy to fix?"

"Because, Magistrate, it is. As I said: this is what we do."

Aidan gave orders to Chalayan and cel Rau, and soon they were all moving south, though now they led their horses. Vasile had been given strict instructions to gather the reins and control the horses if anything untoward happened.

Cel Rau went first, leading them at a swift pace, presumably following jukari tracks, but any time Vasile tried to see them, they'd been overlaid with the footsteps of the three men in front of him and their own mounts.

Chalayan muttered to himself, while Aidan was silent. Cel Rau kept touching the hilts of his swords. Each of the men prepared for whatever might happen in his own way. Vasile's bladder felt full. He followed behind the others, eating their dust, until cel Rau called a halt at the bottom of a rise. To their left was another of the upthrust rocky outcroppings.

Cel Rau beckoned to them, and they gathered to hear what he had to say. Vasile looked around for a place to relieve himself, made his excuse, and left them to deliberate. He wouldn't be of any use, he was sure, and they could just tell him their plan when he got back.

Another cave bore into the rocks, and he avoided getting too close, shuffling to the side and opening his trousers with relief.

Behind him, he could hear the others arguing, as they always did. He glanced over his shoulder to see them tying the horses together and sidling toward the top of the rise, crouched low, as if they were trying to avoid attention. Something must have spooked cel Rau, else they wouldn't be so cautious.

A clatter of rocks drew Vasile's attention to the cave. He peered into the blackness. Was that movement? There was a muted snuffling, then two yellow eyes gazed back at him. Something growled.

He turned and ran, managing a few steps before his trousers fell down around his ankles, tripping him into the dirt. Rocks clattered behind him, and he twisted to see a bulky form move toward him out of the dark of the cave.

Sunlight hit the creature, and it flinched, turning its head away from the glare, blinking. It was a full yard taller than a grown man. Its skin was a mottled gray, head covered with short, thick black hair, almost furlike. Two slanted yellow eyes peered out above a protruding beak of a nose.

A jukari. The first he'd seen.

Vasile remained frozen, hoping if he kept still it wouldn't notice him, and that Aidan, cel Rau, and Chalayan had seen the beast and were rushing toward him.

The creature wore thick leather trousers stitched together with crude seams, and from its neck dangled a chain of finger bones, along with a crude medallion. In one hand, it carried a sword spotted with rust, the biggest Vasile had ever seen.

He risked a glance toward the rise and bit down on a curse. Aidan and the others were lying low at the top and hadn't seen his predicament. He inched his way backward. Sweat dripped into his eyes, stinging them, and he blinked furiously. His foot scraped against a rock.

The jukari stopped moving. It sniffed the air, moving its head back and forth. It knew something had disturbed its rest, but coming from the darkness of the cave into the daylight, its eyes hadn't adjusted yet.

It's only a matter of time, realized Vasile. He leaped to his feet and dragged his trousers to his waist, making a dash toward the horses. With luck, it would focus on the animals . . . if he made it that far.

Loud hoots came from behind him, followed by a harsh barking.

To his horror the call was answered by others beyond the rise.

Vasile lurched for the horses. He expected that huge sword to split him in two at any moment.

Stumbling around his mount, he risked a look behind. The jukari was heading straight at him, but slowly, as if it knew he couldn't escape. Aidan, cel Rau, and Chalayan rushed down the rise toward him. They weren't shouting to distract the jukari, which he found distressing, but cel Rau had drawn both his swords and raced ahead of the others. Chalayan stopped and was doing something sorcerous.

He hoped.

Vasile prayed the jukari would burst into flames before remembering sorcery didn't work like that.

What's the point of sorcery if you can't shoot fire at your enemies?

He was pretty sure Chalayan would agree with that.

He watched as cel Rau sped toward the beast, and it noticed his approach.

He isn't going to . . . He is. Madness, thought Vasile, yet he was still relieved he wasn't the jukari's target anymore.

The huge sword rose above the jukari's head, ready to strike at the swordsman. Cel Rau aimed himself at a waist-high rock, then used it to launch through the air, straight at the nightmare beast.

Grunting in surprise, the jukari swung its sword. Too late.

Cel Rau's initial thrust penetrated its left eye, while his second blade punctured its neck. The jukari bellowed in pain. Cel Rau's feet struck it in the chest, and he used his grip on his swords to twist his body out of the way of the beast's blade, which flashed past him, a finger's width from his shoulder.

Wobbling, the jukari stumbled to its knees, cel Rau riding the beast down, staring into its good eye. He shouted something, but Vasile couldn't make out the words.

The swordsman stepped from the jukari onto the ground, pulling his blades from the dying creature, then thrusting one into its chest. Placing one foot beside his sword, cel Rau ripped it free, and the jukari thumped to the dirt, lifeless.

Vasile stared. By the ancestors, if things had been different, he might be dead. Nausea rose in his throat.

Aidan strode up beside him. "Quite the showman, eh? We're lucky there was just one in that cave." At his words, more hoots and barking came from beyond the rise, and Aidan's expression turned grim. "But clearly not elsewhere. Come on, we have to get out of here. They have our scent now."

Aidan pushed Vasile toward his horse as both cel Rau and Chalayan approached at a run. The sorcerer's eyes were fear filled and wild, while cel Rau looked nervous. After his display, Vasile felt that if the normally taciturn swordsman looked nervous, they were in trouble.

Vasile dragged himself into his saddle and urged his horse in the direction of Aidan, who waved him past. In moments, Chalayan caught up and began to overtake him.

"Hurry, Magistrate," hissed the sorcerer. "Fall behind, and you'll be for the cook pot—except they won't cook you." With a humorless laugh, Chalayan cast a frantic look over his shoulder, then rushed ahead.

Aidan came up behind and slapped Vasile's mount hard across the hindquarters, spurring it to greater speed. "Keep up, Vasile. You don't want to be left behind."

"So Chalayan said," he shouted. "Cel Rau killed one, and he said there were only a few. Four or five."

Aidan shook his head. "There's more than that now. The ones we were tracking must have been a splinter group or scouts, detached from their main force."

"Main force?" repeated Vasile. Jukari hadn't been seen together in large numbers since the Shattering.

"Look behind us," said Aidan. "Then you'll stop asking questions until we're well away from here."

Shifting in his saddle, Vasile twisted and peered back the way they'd come. Dust from their horses swirled around, but there, close to the upthrust rocks the jukari had come from, several large figures milled around. *Not several*, Vasile thought with dread, as more joined them, and still more. They poured like ants over the top of the rise where Aidan, cel Rau, and Chalayan had been only a short time before. Among them were other smaller, darker, humanoid shapes, though fewer in number. This far away, Vasile couldn't see them in detail, but sunlight glinted from shiny metal objects they wore.

"Enough gawking," shouted Aidan. "We've horses and they don't, but there might be more ahead of us. For now, we ride like our lives depend on it!"

Which they do, thought Vasile.

VASILE WATCHED AS Aidan slid from his horse and led the beast by the reins. Both cel Rau and Chalayan followed suit, and Vasile reluctantly did the same.

To their left, the orange sun was cut in half by the horizon, and light was fading fast. It was best they lead the horses now, but Vasile couldn't help wanting to keep riding, knowing what they'd left behind. All three of his companions had remained tight-lipped for the last few hours, speaking only when absolutely necessary.

He was tired. And thirsty. And hungry. He'd drained his last waterskin some time ago, and they hadn't passed a stream where he could refill them. Clearing his throat, he wiped dust from his face, regretting using water to wash it earlier. Riding last wasn't pleasant, but it was better than no horse at all.

"Aidan," he croaked, throat dry. "I need more water."

Aidan shook his head but took a full skin of his own, waited for Vasile, then handed it to him.

"You need to be sparing with your water," said Aidan. "And refill every time you can, since there's no telling when you'll get the next chance."

Vasile nodded gratefully, rinsed the dust from his mouth, and spat. After a few swallows of water, he coughed and spoke. "We're going to keep walking through the night, aren't we?"

"Yes. There's no helping it. We've some distance on the jukari, but we need more, and we need to get to Riversedge as fast as possible."

"To inform the Quivers, so they can send out a patrol and kill these monsters?"

Aidan looked at him, eyes hard. "It'll take more than a patrol to deal with this. We need to warn the city what's coming so they can prepare."

Vasile swallowed. "How many were there? I didn't see."

"Too many. More than I thought existed. Along with a few vormag. And those . . . no one's seen or heard of them for decades." Aidan cast a worried glance behind them and wiped his hands on his shirt.

"Vormag? Surely you jest? They're from children's fairy tales."

Except he knew Aidan told the truth.

Aidan laughed mirthlessly in reply. "So most people believe. And that's the way the Quivers like it. The less people know, and the safer they feel, the better. We didn't only hunt jukari, you know; there's all manner of foul creatures from the Shattering out there, some much worse."

Vasile thought more about the tales he had heard as a child. Vormag had been created after the jukari, a supposed improvement on the intelligent yet clumsy beasts. Stories had them leading the jukari during the Shattering, one step below the sorcerers who'd created them. A thought rose to the surface.

"They're sorcerers, aren't they? That's one of the tales."

With a grim smile, Aidan nodded. "Some are. The Protectors wiped out as many as they could, and they still look for them. But vormag are cunning, and far more intelligent than jukari."

"Why have they gathered?"

"Your guess is as good as mine, but ultimately it doesn't matter. Their thoughts and motives are unfathomable, they are too numerous, and . . ." he said, looking over his shoulder once more.

"And they are coming."

CHAPTER 22

Caldan entered the room, immediately looking to Miranda and stepping to her side. The floor creaked under his weight.

"How is she?" he asked Elpidia.

"Better," replied Elpidia, rinsing a cloth in a bowl. "Whatever you did, it's working. Will she be whole again soon?"

"No. Joachim did his best, but she needs someone better than him at coercive sorcery to heal her. He's given Miranda more time, stopped her mind degrading, but—"

"Let me guess; there's a hook? It was convenient, him turning up now."

Caldan nodded. "It was now or later. If Anasoma hadn't been invaded, then he'd have found me anyway. Perhaps it's for the best it was earlier. It certainly is for Miranda."

Elpidia sniffed. "Some of your troubles have been lifted, then, or at least lessened. Which brings me to my troubles."

Caldan brushed Miranda's hair away from her face. "What do you need? Alchemical supplies? The Protectors should be able to help, though they're busy right now."

"I'll ask them for what I need; you don't need to worry about that. But . . . I need more from you. More blood."

"Do you know how ghoulish that sounds?"

"You've done it before, and it's helped me, it really has. But now my supply has run low."

Caldan bristled at her tone. It sounded as if he were just a commodity to her. But once again, he thought, if he were dying and he believed a cure was within reach, perhaps he'd act the same. "Prepare your needle and vial, then," he replied, to Elpidia's obvious surprise. "I made a promise, and I'm keeping it. I truly hope this helps."

"It *has* to."

The fervor in her voice had been growing throughout the journey, and Caldan almost hesitated in offering up his arm. In the end, though, he couldn't start to fathom what Elpidia had gone—and was going—through, and he knew he couldn't put it off anymore. Still, he had to be sure *she* was sure.

"Have you thought of verifying your theory somehow, before relying on it?"

"I don't know anyone I could approach to discuss this with. Perhaps there's someone in the capital, but . . . not anyone I'm familiar with. They must have master alchemists and physikers, though. But I'm certain it will work."

Caldan sighed. She was single-minded, yet he found he could respect that—wasn't he the same way in terms of Miranda? Delaying no more, he approached her and rolled up his sleeve. "Like I said, I hope so. Because, after this, I don't know how much more I'll be able to do for you. With Anasoma and the Indryallans, with Miranda and Bells, and now with this warlock Joachim appearing . . . things have become complicated."

Elpidia prepared her instruments. "You look after Miranda and yourself. I don't require any supervision."

"And yet you always insist that I do."

She said nothing, and then there was a sharp pain in his arm. He watched as blood filled her vials, and yet that sight didn't disturb him as much as the almost hungry look on Elpidia's face.

THEY'D LEFT MIRANDA asleep an hour ago, the warlock having dragged Caldan with him after the young man hastily ate and washed up. They now sat in a corner of the Protectors' courtyard, watching the commotion as Masters Annelie and Mold organized groups to search for Bells. Caldan had been told his compass, though it should be working perfectly, couldn't pinpoint her location, only her general whereabouts. Obviously, one of the craftings she'd recovered was masking where she was, something Caldan hadn't thought possible, but Joachim had shrugged, saying he had a similar crafting as well. Now she'd had time to make other craftings—and ancestors only knew what she was capable of.

The warlock leaned against the wall, resting his eyes. He seemed to be settling in.

"Aren't we going to join one of the groups looking for Bells?"

Joachim waved a hand in the negative. "They won't find her. At best, they'll keep her occupied with evading them, and out of mischief. They're competent enough, so she won't risk attacking them; there's no gain in it for her. So she'll wait. After I've rested, we can lend a hand. I'd rather not face her while I'm weak, and I doubt you'll get the better of her again."

Blood rushed to Caldan's face, but he knew the warlock spoke the truth. He looked away, thankful no one else could hear Joachim's frank appraisal of his abilities.

Instead he asked, "How long until you recover?"

"A few hours, perhaps longer. The process took a lot out of me. That type of sorcery is one I haven't used for a while, and unless you're practicing often, you can get rusty."

"And how do you practice?"

Joachim flashed him a furtive look. "Best you don't know some things for the moment, though that might change. As I said, what happens next depends on your honesty and your behavior."

Rubbing his spiky hair, Caldan nodded. *So you keep reminding me.*

"So let's get started. What do you know about your trinket?" asked Joachim.

"Not much," admitted Caldan. "Though now I suspect it was what enabled my sword to penetrate a sorcerer's shield, which was what led to you finding me."

He continued, "I only found out about the trinket a few months ago. My parents died when I was young, and I was raised by monks on Eremite. It was only when I was leaving they told me about my parents and gave me the ring."

Joachim grunted, though his face gave no hints as to his thoughts. "So you've no idea who they really were, or why they hid themselves away on an island?"

"No. They're a mystery to me. As for the trinket, I took to wearing it after smith-crafting a shielding wristband. One of the masters in the Protectors—Simmon—took me along when they went to apprehend a rogue sorcerer. I attacked the sorcerer and my sword was somehow able to penetrate his shield. Though I've no idea how or why it activated then. I didn't even know it was the trinket. Nothing seemed to change about it. It gave no indication."

"No, the trinkets attuned to the Touched aren't flashy."

"Trinkets? So there's more than one type of them?"

"That there is," Joachim said, but didn't elaborate. Instead he asked, "Have you been hungrier than usual sometimes? Has anything out of the ordinary happened to you?"

He knows, realized Caldan. *He knows exactly what's happening to me, and it has something to do with my trinket.* And yet, when he'd injured Marlon, he hadn't been wearing it. The masters had insisted he keep it concealed, for good reason. *Which means whatever's been happening is still related to me, and the trinket is something additional. If Joachim knows, there's no point dissembling.*

"Yes, I eat a lot. More than anyone I know. And sometimes I get hot, like my blood is heating up, and I start sweating." Caldan looked at Joachim, who nodded at him to continue. "Everything slows down, as if the world is moving through honey. But . . . it doesn't affect me, and to others it looks as if I'm moving faster than normal. It happened when I was sparring with Simmon. I beat him, though my sword work isn't that skilled. It was because I was moving faster, wasn't it? It comes and goes, though; I can't control it."

"That's normal. Control comes with time, and with some craftings and trinkets."

"But what is it? What's happening to me? And what does it have to do with my parents?"

Joachim stretched his arms above his head and yawned. "The eating is usually the first sign we look for. Your body starts using more energy and needs food, as well as building your bones and muscles to deal with the added strain. I'm sure you've noticed you've filled out more the last year or so?"

"Yes. But I thought that was the exercises the monks prescribed."

"They would have helped, but part of what you are drives your body to change. You won't become a hulking monster"—Joachim gave a brief smile—"but you will grow more solid, denser. Then there's the extra burst of speed, which usually only happens when you're in danger. In the state you are in now it's almost uncontrollable, and you can't rely on it."

"I know that already. So far it's mostly been troublesome, or not happened when I needed it to."

"You are what we call Touched. It's been studied for centuries, and yet no one really knows what it fully means. We do know it's passed down through families, however, which means it's a hereditary trait. Sometimes it skips a generation, or disappears entirely. Regardless, we keep track of those who are Touched. The emperor values them . . . you . . . highly. Your ancestor Karrin Wraythe was Touched, and in the emperor's service. The trinket was given to her as a symbol of her office. It has certain functions that helped her in her . . . role. To be clear, though, it was never meant as a reward, but as a tool to help her do the emperor's . . . work."

Caldan could think of many tasks suited to someone who was Touched, remembering with sick dread the soldiers he'd killed so easily. Joachim's reluctance to clarify what she did led him to the obvious conclusion.

"She was an assassin?" he ventured.

Joachim pursed his lips. "She made certain problems go away, yes."

"I'm not like that," Caldan said firmly.

"It's not up to me to decide what's to be done with you—and it may not be up to you, either."

And that was the crux of the situation: Joachim hadn't locked Caldan up, but he felt imprisoned all the same. No wonder people would keep this ability hidden, he mused, thinking of Amerdan.

"There was a man who escaped Anasoma with us. Called himself Amerdan, a shopkeeper I knew by chance. He . . . moved like I can sometimes. Then he told me he could control it. Are you searching for him as well?"

Joachim shook his head, looking thoughtful. "I've never heard of him, and we keep a close watch on those that have potential. What does he look like?"

"A handsome man of average height and build, short hair." Caldan found himself trying to think of any features of the man that stood out, but nothing came to mind, though Elpidia thought he was attractive. "He moves with grace, and so far, with all we've been through, nothing has rattled him."

"You say he has the same abilities as you? How do you know?"

"One of the Indryallans came after us. Bells called him a Bleeder. He killed the soldiers with us before Amerdan overcame him. I saw it myself. Amerdan moved fast—too fast. After, he told me that we were the same, and he could teach me."

At his words, Joachim stiffened, frowning. "That's . . . odd. It's possible that we've missed some of you, but highly unlikely. Something doesn't sound right about this Amerdan. Does he wear any trinket rings like yours?"

"No, none that I could see."

"And he was of average build, you say?"

"Yes. I thought he was just a strange shopkeeper until a few days ago."

"Where is he now? I'd like to talk to him."

Caldan spread his hands. "I don't know. He was with Bells and

Elpidia when I left. No, that's not right. He wasn't in the camp; he was out hunting or something. He liked to disappear for lengths of time."

"Would he have joined with Bells?"

"I think so . . . But I don't know why."

"Why indeed," said Joachim softly. "We have to consider all possibilities. If he is Touched and doesn't have any trinkets, then he can't control what's happening to him. And that's not good. If you see him, or he contacts you, come straight to me."

"So that's what the trinket ring does? Allows greater control?"

"You'll find out in time, if you're allowed to keep it. Let's just say that, without it, you'll likely do yourself a permanent injury, and without our help, you'll likely die."

Caldan was skeptical but held his tongue. Whatever Joachim's motives, he was obviously trying to make sure Caldan thought he was tied to him, and that only Joachim could help him. "Then I'd better stay close," he replied with a false smile. "What's next?"

"I'm not sure what to do with you. I didn't expect you to be a sorcerer. I don't think that's happened before—someone both Touched and with a well. It may be the emperor and his advisors will have to rethink their plans for you."

"So they've plans for me?"

"Everyone is useful to the emperor, in one way or another. You'll find out soon enough. You can keep the trinket for now. Remember, we can find you when it activates, and it'll be doing that more often now."

"And if I sell it?"

Joachim gave a short laugh. "After what I've told you, I'm sure you wouldn't want to do that." He yawned again and rubbed his eyes. "That's enough for now. I need to rest. We'll talk again when I wake."

The warlock wriggled until he was comfortable and folded his arms across his chest. His eyes closed, and within moments he was breathing deeply, apparently fast asleep.

Caldan cast an eye over Joachim. Even asleep and not accessing his well, the man literally tugged at his awareness, much like the boxes in Simmon's office. It made his skin tingle, and he shivered, rubbing his arms.

He needed to do something. His wristband and automaton had both been destroyed, and though he had Bells's shield crafting to replace his, he felt the need to work on a project to keep himself busy. Waiting for Joachim to wake was already intolerable, and who knew how long he would be resting?

He didn't ask about the bone ring, thought Caldan. Perhaps he doesn't know about it? But that made no sense—he had to. From what Felicienne had said, the bone ring was linked to his trinket. Which made it curious that Joachim hadn't talked about it.

Shaking his head to clear his thoughts, Caldan left the warlock and went to find the Protectors' workshop.

And for the first time in days, he felt like he was about to do something useful.

CHAPTER 23

Felice groaned and sucked in a deep, relieved breath. Her head ached fiercely, and she was tired, so tired. Finding she couldn't move, she tried opening her eyes, but they resisted her efforts. Moving them felt as hard as lifting a horse.

She coughed weakly, which set her head to pounding.

Cold. *Why am I so cold?* Her clothes stuck to her skin, soaked with sweat, as if someone had thrown a bucket of water over her, which would explain why she was freezing.

Avigdor?

She whimpered in pain as she remembered what had happened to him. *Savine, curse him.*

And Kelhak, or whoever he really is.

"Ah, I see you're finally awake."

She twisted at the voice, which took all her effort. The archivist.

With a groan of effort, she finally pried her eyes open. He stood a few paces away, wringing his hands and shifting his weight from foot to foot.

She noticed she was covered with at least two thick woolen blankets, which didn't feel like they were doing their job.

"Here," said the archivist. He came over and held a cup under her chin, pushing a reed straw between her lips.

She sucked greedily at the lukewarm water until the cup ran dry. The librarian transferred the straw to another cup, and again she drank. This time, it was an herbal tea of some sort, its bitterness masked with honey. Again, she drained the cup, settling her head back down when she was done.

"I . . . take it . . . I passed out?" she croaked, words tearing like knives at her throat.

"Yes. The river water did its work. I've heard of people becoming ill like that, mostly children or the infirm, but never so quickly. Most likely it was the number of cuts that caused the illness to spread rapidly. Lucky for you, the physikers knew what to do and had alchemical and herbal remedies readily available."

"Yes. Lucky."

"They had to er . . . force you to drink them, though, as well as flush out your wounds."

"Is that why my throat . . . ?"

The archivist nodded. "They had to use a tube. If they hadn't been able to get you to drink and keep it down, I'm afraid you wouldn't have lasted long. How do you feel?"

"Cold. Thirsty. Sore."

"Good," he said to her with a smile. "That means you're feeling something. Sometimes, when a disease from the river spreads, people lose feeling in their extremities, and then . . . well, they have to be amputated."

Felice closed her eyes. Though there was only a small lamp lighting the room, the flame was far too bright.

"How long?" she asked.

"Well, amputations are permanent—"

"How long . . . unconscious."

"Ah. That would be . . . let me see . . . almost two days."

Felice groaned. She couldn't afford to waste so much time. She should get up, but she was so tired. Perhaps a short rest, then she'd decide what to do.

She closed her eyes.

A CLATTERING WOKE her from blissful darkness. She yawned and stretched as best she could, which wasn't much. Her muscles felt stiff and sore, and now that she was aware of them, the blankets seemed to weigh her down. A rich, spicy scent reached her nostrils, and she opened her eyes. The archivist was sitting on a stool by her side, stirring a thick broth in a chipped bowl. He must have noticed her eyes were open, because he stopped stirring and held out his hands for her to grab.

"I'll pull you up," he said. "There, just let me stuff another pillow behind you. Ah, much better."

Felice's head swam, and she placed her hands on the bed to steady herself. Moments later, the sensation passed, but sweat trickled down her face. Her clothes reeked, and she gave a weak laugh. The old man would have been too embarrassed to change them, but if she'd been out for days, then someone must have looked after her, else the bed would be filthy.

She gazed at the bowl and licked her lips. "Who else knows I'm here?"

"No one. Just me."

Felice sighed. And the physikers the old man said had seen to her, and whoever else he'd told about her. "Can you . . ." She gestured to the broth. "I'm too weak to do it myself."

"Yes, I was just . . ."

The librarian paused to blow on a spoonful of broth to cool it before feeding it to her. She sucked at the liquid hungrily. Chunks of soft meat and vegetables floated in the salty broth.

After a few spoonfuls, she spoke. "Thank you for taking care of me."

"Oh, you're welcome. I couldn't leave you there to die."

"I appreciate it," she said dryly. "But now I need you to be honest."

"What do you mean?"

"We both know someone else has been looking after me. I need to know who."

"It . . . was my daughter, Lisbet. She won't tell anyone, I promise. I didn't tell her who you were, just a stranger off the street."

"And what about your colleagues? Do they know who I am, and where?"

The archivist shook his head. "I had a boy help me drag . . . er, I mean, carry you here, and afterward I sent him for a physiker. As I said, no one knows who you are, which I assume is the way you want it."

Yes. But what I really want right now, she thought, looking down at the empty bowl, *is more food.* "More, please."

"Of course. I'll just go and refill the bowl. Excuse me." He shuffled off, closing the door behind him.

Before it closed, she could see a narrow corridor outside, dark and ill lit.

Lying back, Felice considered her options. At the moment, though, none of them mattered until she recovered—enough to walk, at least. There wasn't time to be lying around in bed while Kelhak and his people were still in Anasoma.

The sketches, where are they?

Frantically, she scanned the room until her eyes caught a book beside her bed. *There.* She sighed with relief. The old man had had the foresight to keep the books and papers, and with any luck the information on Kelhak was inside. With a groan, she reached for the book, but her outstretched fingers were a few inches short. She collapsed back on the bed, growling in frustration.

No matter, they'll keep. She'd already found what she was after and ran through the facts in her mind.

Kelhak had come from the same monastery as the young man Caldan, entered the lists for Dominion at the Autumn Festival, and, to the surprise of many, won. That was around a hundred years ago. Now Kelhak, who she no longer doubted was the same man she'd seen in the sketch, had returned to Anasoma at the head of an invading army, calling himself the God-Emperor of Indryalla.

The question was: Why?

Why was Kelhak alive after all these years? Why did he not seem to recognize his own Dominion strategy at first? Was it such an old strategy, as he claimed, as to be irrelevant to him now? And did that have anything to do with the invasion?

There was something . . . a pattern she couldn't quite see, along with a sinking feeling that when it became clear she wouldn't like her conclusions.

One thing she knew for sure: she wouldn't find answers by lying around sick.

Clenching her teeth with effort, she sat up, threw off the blankets, and placed both feet on the cold floor. She'd broken out in a sweat and shivered. On a table by the wall was a pitcher she assumed contained water. Sweet, cool water.

"Come on, you can do it," she said to herself . . . and didn't move. "Stand, you lazy f—"

She broke off as the door opened, and the archivist entered with another steaming bowl. When he saw her sitting on the edge of the bed, his face broke out in alarm.

"My lady, you mustn't—"

"There's no time. Leave the broth with me and bring your daughter here. I'll need new clothes, and water to wash with."

"Are you certain you want to get up? You could use a few more days in bed."

Felice shook her head, lank hair sticking to her face and neck. "Believe me, I'd love to go back to sleep. But you and I, old man, we've a city to save."

AMERDAN LOOKED DOWN from his perch atop the building into the Protectors' courtyard. He'd easily clambered across the rooftops, jumping two alleys, to find the best vantage point. Sitting in the shade against a chimney, he was sure he'd remain unnoticed, and by the looks of the excitement and activity among the Protectors, that would continue to be the case. Still, he tugged his recently obtained wide-brimmed hat down over his face, just in case. Caldan and that useless woman Elpidia could recognize him. It was unlikely, at this distance, but only a fool took chances when they could be avoided.

And he was no fool.

As if to demonstrate that, he glanced back around the chimney, making sure he hadn't been followed and there wasn't someone sneaking up on him.

All clear, as it should be, but the one time you don't check is the time you get your throat cut. Amerdan chuckled. If someone was fast enough to do that to him now, he'd be surprised.

Bells was preoccupied with whatever sorcerous things she was making, and she'd become quite focused now. Apparently, whatever she was smith-crafting was difficult, and judging from her haste, she needed it finished in a hurry. She'd waved away his questions about wells and sorcery, and the few attempts she'd made at unblocking his wells hadn't been successful.

Maybe she doesn't want to succeed, came a whisper from inside his shirt.

He slipped a hand inside his shirt and stroked Dotty. It had been a hard journey so far for her, kept stuffed inside his shirt, but soon things would change. Very soon.

Maybe. What Bells had been able to tell him was that she'd never seen anything like his wells before, but that really didn't do much to help him.

Below, he spied Caldan deep in conversation with another man dressed in black with silver buttons, probably a Protector. After a time, the man sat back and Caldan left him. No threat there. Watching Caldan as he disappeared inside one of the buildings, Amerdan moved his hand toward his knife.

Should have taken him while you had the chance, came another whisper.

Amerdan rocked back and forth on his perch. "No," he said. "There wasn't an opportunity on the way here. And they have secrets I need to know."

Caldan could wait. And Elpidia was nothing, a diseased woman waiting to die. She'd find the mice he left for her and realize he could have killed her. *What will she make of that?* he wondered. To know that, despite all her futile efforts to stave off her inevitable death, she could have died at someone's hand. A reminder she was insignificant. Unlike Caldan.

And Bells.

Bells was his key, and he was the lock. One she should be able to open soon, unblocking his wells. Then she would die, and he would absorb her.

And he would see if her well also transferred to him.

He smiled at the thought of Bells under his knife.

SAVINE STOOD BEFORE Kelhak, who was lounging, one leg hanging over the arm of his chair. Four of Kelhak's personal guard were stationed around the room, large, violent men sworn to take vengeance if anything befell their leader, then to kill themselves afterward.

Inwardly, Savine sneered at their idiocy. If your leader died, then you positioned yourself as best you could to be the one to replace him, or to be indispensable to the man who did.

Kelhak held a glass of wine, almost empty. The same glass that had been coated with half of the poison; the only glass in the room. The God-Emperor used only clay or wooden cups to offer guests wine, and Savine thought it a petty show of power, as if saying, *See, I drink from glass while I offer you clay.* But Kelhak rarely did things for such obvious reasons, and his methods were usually beyond Savine's understanding. One of the reasons he had to die.

The God-Emperor knew where Gazija's blind followers were hiding in the city and yet had done nothing, despite Savine's repeated pleas for them to be wiped out. The knowledge that Rebecci and the others had secreted themselves and were most likely plotting to kill Savine gnawed at his gut. He'd broken from his people, abandoning that fool Gazija and his unworthy plans for them, aware he was risking everything. But he dared not go against Kelhak's wishes. Not yet.

Kelhak waved at him to take a seat and leaned forward.

"Your friend escaped."

Savine frowned. "Friend?"

"Lady Felicienne. Threw herself out a window into the river, and in the middle of an interesting Dominion game, too. Rude of her."

Savine had all but forgotten the woman. When he'd seen the machine's load arcing through the sky straight toward Kelhak on his ship, he'd thought the man was doomed. Until he weathered the destruction as if it were nothing.

Another reason he had to die.

"You wanted her . . . my lord," he replied. "And I delivered her to you."

"And what happened to her comrades? She couldn't have wound and loaded the shot by herself. I heard a rumor someone died in the cell with her. A fat man." Kelhak made a hacking motion with his free hand. "Had his feet removed. Chop, chop."

Savine had learned very quickly that Kelhak sometimes hid his intelligence behind simplistic speech. "He was nobody."

"A fat nobody . . . like the one who defeated your two pets? What are their names? Two against one, and they ran like rats."

Savine swallowed. *How could he know?* It was impossible. "I . . . didn't think it was worth mentioning."

"Ah. Didn't think. You should have stopped there."

For one fleeting moment, Savine thought about accessing his well before ruthlessly quashing the idea. He doubted he could defeat Kelhak, and he wouldn't give him an excuse to attack him. Before he could muster words to respond, Kelhak spoke again.

"There isn't much I don't know. And this incident with your pets almost escaped my notice. But never mind; it's of no interest to me."

If he didn't care, then why bring it up? "My people have split, as you know. And . . ." Savine's voice trailed off as he watched Kelhak swallow a mouthful of wine. He calculated that the quantity of poison in that amount of wine alone should be enough to kill ten men. He blinked and continued. "There are still occasional fights among the two factions, small skirmishes, tests of strength, probing for weaknesses."

"If I remember rightly, you told me the split was over leadership.

This . . . Gazija held undue influence over people, and some of you rebelled, under your guidance."

"Yes," lied Savine. A half-truth. He had no intention of telling Kelhak the reality of their situation. That they subsisted on others, relied upon them for their own existence. About one thing, Gazija was right: the backlash if the truth was known could very well lead to their destruction. "The young ones like Aslaug and Vibesse are occasionally led astray by their . . . youthfulness, and their exuberance leads them to rash action."

"Ah, to be young again," mused Kelhak. "Everything looked simpler then; it's when we mature that we really see. Do you see?"

Savine hesitated. Was Kelhak telling him he knew he was lying? Then why not come out and say it? "I believe I . . . see."

"Good." Kelhak waved his wineglass at the guards around the room. "These men, they see, but only a small portion of reality: only what they need to see; the rest is unimportant to them."

Though he wasn't making much sense, Savine nodded in agreement. Kelhak's behavior was often odd, sometimes unfathomable, but so far he hadn't made an error of judgment that Savine knew of.

"Those two young ones of yours, they're quite intelligent for their age, aren't they?"

Kelhak's question caught him by surprise, and he floundered for a moment. "Their parents were both gifted, and they must take after them," he managed.

"What happened to their parents?"

"They died some time ago," replied Savine, warming to his cover story. "A wasting disease. We've looked after the children since."

Kelhak grunted. "They far surpass other children their age. I should know; I've a few of my own. It's almost like they're adults."

Savine froze, then self-consciously made his expression thoughtful and shifted in his chair, thoughts churning furiously. He coughed and cleared his throat. "Indeed, they act far older than their years, but, what with their parents dying, they've been through trials that . . . developed them. They lost their youth a long time ago."

"So did we all." Kelhak turned and refilled his glass.

Savine pulled his gaze from it, lest he look suspicious.

"Now, this Felicienne woman," continued Kelhak. "I want you to find her again, after she's run around the city for a few days. The men with her were killed, so she'll need to gather other allies to help her. She knows better than we who she could turn to, and she will lead us to them."

Savine nodded. "Yes, my lord."

"Maybe we can finish our game then; she had me in quite a bind."

"I'm sure you would have won in the end."

Kelhak looked thoughtful. "Perhaps. Anyway, back to your . . . people, as you call them. They need to limit the sorcery they use for a week—unless their lives are in danger, then they can protect themselves."

"Surely you jest?"

"Surely I don't. It's not a request."

"But . . . why?" A ban on sorcery would severely hinder Savine's plans. There was much they still had to do, and preparing to remove Gazija from power couldn't wait much longer. If only he could push Kelhak in the old man's direction, make him think he was a threat. If the Indryallans sent some of their sorcerers and soldiers after Gazija, Savine's plans would become easier. Even when Kelhak died, it wouldn't be a problem, as long as the wheels had been set to turning.

"Because I commanded it," snapped Kelhak.

"Of course. I mean, is there a reason for this? It seems drastic."

Almost instantly, Kelhak's expression changed from one of irritation to thoughtfulness.

"There are two reasons. My daughter Bells is on a task, one I set her before she led the invasion of this squalid city."

Savine smoothed a frown, considering Kelhak's incongruous choice of words. From what he understood, Anasoma was one of the most progressive cities in the empire, and far more illustrious than anywhere in Indryalla. Why would Kelhak describe it as squalid? It paled in comparison with the cities of Savine's homeland, but Kelhak couldn't possibly know about them, could he? It was impossible.

Kelhak hadn't noticed his preoccupation and continued. "She is to send me two signals, of a unique sorcerous nature. And as she's so far away, any local sorcerous emanations could disrupt my ability to detect them."

"You can detect sorcery from such a distance? You must have a trinket."

Kelhak laughed at his assumption. "Do I look like I need crutches? No, this is but one of my talents, among many others. And the other reason is closer to home. But first, let me tell you something."

"Yes?" replied Savine warily, still stunned by Kelhak's admission. To be able to detect sorcery from such a distance without a crafting or trinket was . . . not unheard of, but . . . there was only one creature he knew could do such a thing: Ik'zvime, the ancient sorcerer whose knowledge and power were able to defeat death itself. And whose perverted madness had destroyed their world, and almost them along with it. But its horror was far in their past, and best forgotten. Kelhak's ability was another oddity of this world, he decided.

"I know you want Gazija dead, not just captured and imprisoned. And I know your pets, Aslaug and Vibesse, are older than they look. Now you know it's impossible to keep secrets from me."

Savine wrung his hands and lowered his eyes. "My lord, forgive me. I—"

"Enough," interrupted Kelhak. "So long as you know. Now, look at me."

With dread, Savine raised his head.

The God-Emperor Kelhak looked him in the eye. "The other reason is . . . someone's trying to kill me."

Savine forced himself to hold Kelhak's gaze and not look away.

Not so impossible, he thought.

CHAPTER 24

Knowing he needed to start his craftings somewhere, Caldan had found a couple of journeymen idling in the halls. Taking a chance, he asked if they had any spare craftings he could purchase. Just as with the Protectors in Anasoma, there was an illicit trade in craftings, and these two were hard up enough to need the coins Caldan offered. He took only those he thought were of good quality and deflected the journeymen's questions about what he needed them for with noncommittal answers and brief smiles. They didn't press, but rather pocketed the ducats and went on their way, even as he went on his.

He left the Protectors' headquarters, following directions he had obtained from a different group of journeymen to avoid anyone putting two and two together. He moved down the streets eagerly, ready to get started. His time on the run had left him itching to continue the work he had begun in Anasoma, especially after his automaton and wristband had been destroyed. They had both saved his life and he felt their loss deeply.

This is it, thought Caldan, standing before a shop. It had taken only a few minutes' walk from the Protectors' to a traders' square, and in front of him was a nondescript door. Above it hung a sign displaying two gears.

When he pushed the door open, a metal chime rang out, and he entered a room not unlike the clockmaker's shop in Anasoma in that it had clockwork pieces in it. Other than that, he was disappointed. The devices were obviously of lesser quality, and they didn't shine as the ones in the other shop had—probably due to the thin layer of dust that covered everything. On one, he even noted a spot of rust. There were no sorcerous globes, only a couple of lamps in addition to windows letting in light.

He closed the door behind him, and a young woman appeared as if out of nowhere. Caldan realized she must have been bending over behind the counter where he couldn't see her. She had on a pair of spectacles similar to the clockmaker's in Anasoma—designed with magnifying lenses to aid in working on the tiny mechanisms. She looked over the top of them to see him properly.

"Hello, young sir," she said, eyes flicking to his sword and the trinket on his finger. "I don't see many Protectors in here; I usually deal with the Sorcerers' Guild. But I'm open to everyone," she added hastily. "Perhaps it's help with a crafting you're after? Or was it something else—a gift, maybe?" Her eyes lit up.

Business wasn't doing so well, surmised Caldan. The woman's obvious interest in selling him something and the state of the shop were clear indications. That—coupled with the fact that she had deduced he was a Protector from his appearance—made him hopeful they could come to an agreement beneficial to both of them.

Caldan cleared his throat. "I'm sorry, I'm not after a gift—perhaps another time." The woman's gaze fell to the floor, and Caldan took pity on her, deciding to get to the point of his visit. "I have some craftings you may be interested in," he said, and he shook a cloth sack he held, which jingled.

"Oh," she said, disappointed. "Unfortunately, I can't purchase any except from a guild master."

Not that you could afford to purchase anything, he thought.

"I understand, but I was hoping we could help each other out. Especially since I'm not after ducats in exchange."

The clockmaker regarded him with interest.

"I need you to work on something for me in return, a few odds and ends that I don't have the time or expertise to craft myself."

He waited while she squinted at him, obviously deciding whether to take up his offer.

"Here," he said, holding out the sack. "Look them over. I know from another clockmaker they'll suit your needs. Meanwhile, I can sketch what I want in return. If I can use your counter?"

Waving him permission, the woman opened the sack and deposited the contents on the counter, while Caldan drew some paper, pen, and ink from his pocket and began scribing what he wanted.

"These are . . ." she said, "quite the little collection. And worth a number of ducats. I'm not sure I can afford them."

"As I said, I don't want ducats; I need your expertise."

Caldan watched as the woman nervously fingered the craftings, then nodded. He felt slightly ashamed he was taking advantage of her unfortunate situation, but if she hadn't been desperate, he'd still have tried to enlist her help, and at least now she'd be better off for the exchange.

"I . . . don't have a lot of materials to spare," she admitted. "But tell me what you need."

Caldan spent the next few minutes explaining his ideas and going over what he required: pieces for another automaton similar to his previous experiment, along with a few other smaller objects. When he was satisfied that the clockmaker understood what he needed, he continued sketching his designs while she watched, eliciting the occasional comment from her when she thought his schematics needed adjustment.

Behind him, the chime tinkled as another customer entered. He turned to see the tall figure of a cloaked and hooded woman closing the door. He went back to sketching, while the clockmaker smiled and bent to retrieve a wooden box. She grunted with effort as she lifted it and took small steps around the counter.

"Here you are," she said. "Everything you asked for."

The clink of coins marked the exchange as the woman left the shop without a word. There was another chime as the door closed behind her.

Caldan froze, pen in hand, a splotch of ink growing larger as it leached into the paper. When he'd entered, a metallic chime had sounded, completely unlike the tinkling of a bell. Slowly, he laid down his pen and turned to examine the door. He was right. But . . . surely not . . .

The clockmaker walked back behind the counter, giving him a curious look.

"Who was just in here?" he demanded.

"What? Another patron. She placed a custom order."

"What did she look like? Was she tall? With long dark hair?"

"Well, yes. But why would—?"

"Did she have any bells on her, small ones made from metal? In her hair?"

"Yes, she did. One or two. I thought it odd, but . . ."

She broke off as Caldan left his schematics and lunged for the door. He grabbed the handle and pulled.

It didn't budge. He could smell lemons.

Ancestors! Bells had recognized him and somehow crafted the door shut.

Heart pounding, he ran for the rear exit. "Stay here. I'll be back soon."

"Hey, you can't go in there!"

Leaving the startled woman in his wake, he forgot about the crafting and his designs; all that mattered was finding Bells. The wooden container she'd picked up had been heavy, so she couldn't be moving very fast.

Through the back door was a weed-strewn yard with a chicken coop. Stone walls surrounded him, and an iron gate opened onto a back lane, but it was barred and secured with a heavy padlock.

Cursing, he used the crossbars of the gate as a makeshift ladder and scrambled to the top, throwing himself over and landing awkwardly.

His sword tangled his legs, and he almost fell. Gripping the hilt firmly to keep the blade under control, he understood why some swordsmen preferred a scabbard across the back for their shorter blades.

Caldan dashed down the narrow lane and took the first turn he could toward the main road, emerging among a crowd of people in the street.

Frantically, he peered over their heads, searching for signs of Bells. *Why do hooded cloaks have to be in fashion?* There were too many, none of which were hurrying away. She had to be one of them, didn't she? Or maybe she had crossed the street and disappeared down an alley?

"By the ancestors," he muttered. He'd lost her. The delay caused by the door had been enough for Bells to slip away. There was no chance he'd find her now, unless he was lucky. And if he went haring off down an alley, she might have left another surprise for him, like the one between the trees that Morkel had spotted before it killed one of them.

Bells had been so close; she'd been right behind him. She could have stuck him in the back with a knife and he wouldn't have known until it was too late.

Which brought up another question: she'd obviously recognized him, hence the locked door. So why didn't she just kill him?

He had to tell Joachim and the Protectors. But he also needed to conclude his business with the clockmaker. And all of it warred with the urge to continue searching for Bells. Struggling with the options, he headed back to the shop.

Long term, the craftings are more important than anything else.

From the outside, there was no obvious crafting on the lock, except . . . there. A tiny round metal circle near the base of the door. Caldan accessed his well and probed the object. It was similar to the paper craftings he'd used to lock his door when he first arrived in Anasoma. Not sensing anything dangerous, he took out his knife and pried it loose.

A crafted metal tack, ideal for attaching to wood or anything you could push it into. Careful not to prick himself, he pushed the door, and it opened smoothly. Inside, the clockmaker stood there glaring at him, arms folded across her chest.

"I'm sorry," he apologized. "The woman was someone I'm looking for."

"Did you catch up with her? And what was wrong with my door?"

"Er . . . it was stuck a little. You shouldn't have a problem with it from now on." At the woman's frown, he continued. "What did she have you make? Anything like my designs?"

"No. Mostly she needed materials."

"Metals?"

The clockmaker nodded.

"What types? Gold? Silver?"

"No, mostly copper and some rare earths. She asked me to acquire them for her; said she didn't have the time or the patience to do it herself. Paid well, too."

Copper? wondered Caldan. He chewed a thumbnail. It didn't make sense. Why use a metal that couldn't withstand the forces flowing through it for long? Copper was what most apprentices practiced with. It was soft and easy to work with, and to melt down and reuse, but not something he'd expect a master crafter to use.

Shaking his head, Caldan returned to the counter, under the now watchful gaze of the clockmaker. She probably didn't know what to make of his behavior.

"Sorry—never mind about that. Can you make these?" Caldan tapped his schematics.

She nodded. "I looked them over after you ran out. I knew you'd be back; no one would leave these craftings here without wanting something in return. I can make them, but it'll take a few days, possibly a week."

"A few days," he said firmly. "And these craftings are enough to cover payment, right?"

"More than enough, if I'm truthful." She placed a couple on the counter, small squares of metal covered in etched runes. "Here, take these."

With a smile, Caldan shook his head and pushed them back toward her. "Keep them. They're for your silence about what happened. The woman is very dangerous, and the Protectors are looking for her."

"I had no idea. She was so nice, though."

"I guess she could be, if she wanted."

He'd never seen that side of Bells. It was hard to think of her as a normal person.

"I'll come back in a few days. In the meantime, some Protectors may come and question you. They probably will. I'd appreciate it if you let on as little as you could about why I was here."

"I can be discreet."

For the amount of ducats those craftings were worth, he didn't doubt she felt she at least owed him that. Caldan nodded and bade her farewell, leaving the shop, one thought on his mind.

What is Bells up to?

Caldan was sure she'd be lying low, but it looked like she was in the process of crafting something. Now that she had materials, she needed somewhere to work unnoticed, and there weren't many places suitable for working with metals. Any blacksmith's would do in a pinch, but for finer work, jewelers and silversmiths had the necessary equipment.

With racing thoughts, he hurried back to Joachim.

AS JOACHIM BEGAN another tirade, Caldan listened, his ears ringing from the warlock's scathing words. Apparently, he'd expected Caldan to sit around doing nothing while he slept, and he wasn't pleased his new charge had wandered off. The fact that Caldan had inadvertently stumbled into Bells and found out she was planning something didn't mitigate his "carelessness."

Master Annelie rushed into the room, flanked by two heavily armed Protectors. Joachim raised his eyebrows at her bodyguards but said nothing.

"Caldan here just had an encounter with our rogue sorcerer," Joachim said without ado. "It seems she's determined to make a nuisance of herself and has been acquiring crafting materials from a clockmaker."

Annelie's eyes narrowed, and she turned to Caldan. "What were *you* doing at a clockmaker's?" She held up a hand. "No, tell me later. What happened with Bells?"

Caldan ran through the encounter, emphasizing the fact he hadn't realized it was Bells until after she'd left and barred the door with her crafting.

"She's up to something," he finished.

"Well, that much is obvious," said Annelie. "But what? She's in a foreign city, on the run, and presumably hiding from our searchers, though that doesn't seem to have stopped her wandering around in daylight. And she has to know the emperor's forces are on their way; everyone in the streets knows it by now. What has she to gain by staying?"

"An excellent question," said Joachim. "And one we probably won't be able to answer until we capture her. We can, however, make an assumption."

Annelie frowned. "Which is?"

"She's hardly going to be hiding in a hostile city without good reason, when she could easily be on her way to Anasoma. It's highly unlikely she's in Riversedge for personal reasons, which only leaves the Quivers here in the city and the emperor's forces on the way. If either one suffered a major setback, it would advantage the Indryallans."

"But we're on guard now against coercive sorcery," exclaimed Annelie. "We have masters on the lookout, and since we're keeping our sorcery to a minimum, it's unlikely we'll miss any activity. The Quivers have been alerted and have doubled their guards; I can't see how she'd be able to do anything to disrupt them, especially since she's alone."

"Then that leaves the emperor's forces," said Caldan. "Which makes sense."

Both Joachim and Annelie regarded him.

"After Bells escaped," he continued, "I wondered if she hadn't been biding her time, as we were taking her in the direction she wanted to go anyway. It was only a feeling, but . . . if you have a plan that could severely hamper the opposition forces, then wouldn't you wait until you could cause the most disruption?"

Joachim grunted. "And by disrupt, you're thinking of an attack on the emperor himself?"

Caldan nodded.

"But that's madness," Annelie said.

"Yes—to *us*," Caldan said. "But that's because we might not think she can do anything if we're on our guard. But *Bells* thinks she can. And who knows more about what she's capable of than she does?"

"Good point," muttered Joachim. "We need to get word to the emperor. Annelie, could you organize a messenger, a fast one?"

She nodded. "Morkel will do it."

"Good. And gather the other masters. We'll be stretched thin for a while and want everyone's attention focused on this until the emperor and the warlocks are informed and can send help and look to guarding themselves. Here." Joachim drew a coin from a pouch. It was black, as if burned in a fire. "Bring Morkel to me."

At Caldan's and Annelie's confused looks, he explained. "It's a crafting that I'll attune specifically to him. Any warlock will recognize it's from me, and the messenger will be granted safe and speedy passage to the emperor's closed council. Without it, he wouldn't get anywhere near."

"I'll go find him," said Annelie, and she bustled out of the room, bodyguards following close behind.

Caldan watched her retreating back and then turned to Joachim. "Bells might not be able to use coercive sorcery if we're on guard against it, but her destructive sorcery was more than enough to overwhelm my shield. Her sorcery is far in advance of what we can do, and her craftings were mostly a mystery to me."

"That's one of the things I'm afraid of," said Joachim, a grim look on his face. "Any normal rogue sorcerer wouldn't be a match for the Protectors, let alone us warlocks. But the Indryallans have shown their capabilities are beyond ours. How? Well, that's a question we'll find the answer to eventually, I'm sure. As long as we can prevent them from doing too much damage in the meantime."

"But how do we prevent it? They've some way of focusing their sorcery. If I hadn't seen it myself, I wouldn't believe it's possible, but . . . the flames on the walls of Anasoma . . . Bells's destructive sorcery, aimed at me . . ."

"Keep those thoughts to yourself," warned Joachim. "If they've discovered a way to create order out of their wells in a destructive way . . . We haven't seen the like since before the Shattering. And I don't need to tell you what happened then. Luckily, not all knowledge was lost from those times."

"The Protectors."

Joachim looked at him, face expressionless. "That's right."

But something's not right here, thought Caldan. *Because if they had the knowledge, they'd be more adept at it, right?* Which led him to another, darker thought: Did the emperor and his warlocks claim the sorcery for themselves, with the Protectors used only as tools for keeping the knowledge suppressed? It made a sick kind of sense to him, and he wondered if destructive sorcery wasn't as forgotten as everyone thought—and Joachim maintained.

Could he trust anything this man said?

Joachim was regarding him, and Caldan realized he was frowning, betraying the direction of his thoughts. He quickly made his face neutral and looked back at the warlock. They stared at each other for a while, and Caldan was surprised when Joachim broke the silence.

"There's one other thing," Joachim said casually. "It almost slipped my mind. Did your parents have another ring, one carved from bone?"

Caldan resisted the urge to touch the ring around his neck, hidden under his shirt, and pretended to look puzzled. "No."

"Are you sure? Do you remember seeing a bone ring? Perhaps they kept it hidden?"

"I was only a child when they were . . . they died, and never even saw this trinket," he said, holding up his hand, "until my last days at the monastery. If it's hidden, it's still hidden . . . or burned in the fire that destroyed our house."

Joachim shrugged, apparently unconcerned, and Caldan suddenly wanted to punch the warlock in the face. *It's like you're shrugging off my parents' death,* he thought. He seethed inside as Joachim said, "No matter. It was another crafting the emperor loaned to them. I was tasked with returning it as well."

Then why not mention it with the other ring? And Caldan knew it was a trinket, not a crafting. He composed himself.

"I can't help you," replied Caldan. "I don't know anything about a bone ring."

The door opened, and there was a rustle as Annelie entered, trailed by Morkel and her two guards.

Joachim beckoned Morkel over and held up the black coin. "Don't worry," he said, smiling. "This won't hurt."

"THERE," BELLS SAID softly from behind him. "That man."

Amerdan looked down from his spot on the roof and scanned the front gates of the Protectors' building. Riding through on a brown horse was a Protector, lean and hard-faced, carrying more weapons than any competent man needed, including a bow. Amerdan sneered and touched one of his knives, the only weapon he'd ever used or required. Close work was far more satisfying.

"He was one of the Protectors who followed our trail. After Caldan spotted me, I knew they'd send someone."

"*Your* trail," corrected Amerdan, and Bells frowned at him. His hand itched to open her up then and there, but no, not yet . . . *Patience.* The time wasn't right; nothing was right, and there'd been no sign. He felt Dotty shift inside his shirt, reminding him. Bells confused him, and he didn't like the change from his usual isolated life. Depending on others made you weak. She was unreliable; the other one, Caldan, would make a much better teacher. And he was an orphan like Pieter and Annie, and Amerdan. He banished the thought before he could remember more.

Bells shut her eyes, and Amerdan watched her closely. He felt a tingle, which Bells had assured him was her accessing her well. Part of his mind began to itch, and he mentally scratched at it. This time, it felt as if his thoughts caught on something, a rough patch. He grinned. There was much to smile about these days.

"Yes," whispered Bells. "He has one."

The itching disappeared, and she opened her eyes. They watched as the man rode down the street and out of sight around a corner.

"A crafting of some sort, you say?" asked Amerdan.

"Yes. An amulet or medallion, something small. He'll be carrying it on him, somewhere safe."

"And this will admit him to the emperor's inner council?"

"Most likely. Into the warlocks, at least."

"Close enough, then," murmured Amerdan.

"I can't go after him myself, or I won't finish my craftings in time. You'll have to do it."

"As I said I would." Amerdan turned and slid a few paces down the roof. "And you promise you'll spend more time with me, fixing the problem with my well?"

"Yes, yes. Just bring the crafting back to me. It's useless unless it's attuned to someone, and there are safeguards in place in case it's tampered with."

Amerdan nodded, then slid down the roof to the gutter on the other side. He dropped over the edge, hanging on for a few moments, dangling above the alley, then let go, leaving Bells to keep a watch on the Protectors.

AMERDAN YAWNED. SIGHING, he shifted his weight and scratched his leg. The rough bark of the tree was digging into his calf, making his position uncomfortable. In front of him, his knife jutted from the branch where he'd stuck it, waiting.

He craned his neck and looked back down the trail and across the stream.

The Protector was taking his time watering his horse and filling his waterskins, even stopping to piss in the long grass.

Fool. Wasn't he on an urgent mission to warn the emperor or some such? That was what Bells had told him they'd do. Shouldn't he be in a hurry? He wasn't sure why it bothered him so much, considering he was planning on killing the man, but he found such incompetence upsetting.

Amerdan scanned the brush around his perch, searching for a convenient location. There was a fallen tree some distance from the road, an old thick one. Behind it, he should be concealed well enough. Not ideal, but the best he could do in the circumstances. He wanted more time to prepare, but . . . he was adaptable. That was one thing that separated him from everyone else.

The horse's snorting shook him from his musing. The soft clop of hooves striking the path. The sound became louder as the man approached, now mounted.

He gripped his knife. *Soon. Wait.*

The horse snorted directly under him, and Amerdan pulled his blade from the tree and swung from the branch, dropping like a stone.

He landed just behind the rider, legs astraddle, then used them to wrap around the man's waist. His arm clamped around the thing's neck, and with short quick thrusts, he stabbed it five times.

The man made a gurgling sound as its horse skittered sideways, alarmed at the sudden extra weight on its back. As the thing went limp, Amerdan grabbed the reins, guiding the horse forward. On the other side of the fallen tree, he slipped off the horse, dragging the thing to the ground, where it coughed weakly, hands scrabbling in the dirt.

Perfect. As usual.

He straddled the thing, knife in one hand. With the other, he drew out his spherical trinket and clenched it in his fist, a soft glow shining through his hand.

Amerdan shivered. Goose bumps rose on his skin; hairs stood on end.

Inside his shirt, his rag doll wriggled against him, eager to watch.

"Shh," he said to her. "I know. It has been too long."

Amerdan began his work, and the scent of blood filled the air, metallic and pungent.

Birds took flight in alarm as the vessel screamed from loss and despair.

ABOUT TWICE A day, Bells took out one of her craftings and spent a few minutes with her eyes closed. When Amerdan had questioned her, she'd said she was merely resting, recovering from the rigors of sorcery. He knew she was tired; he could tell from her drawn face, and from the fact she hadn't been getting much sleep, preferring to work on her craftings throughout the nights, drinking coffee and tea to keep awake.

He also knew she was lying to him; he could smell it on her. Deceit and wickedness were deep in any sorcerer's bones. He knew this for a fact.

She was resting again when he entered their apartment, which consisted of a few rooms in an unremarkable district in this unremarkable city. It reeked like a brothel, and no matter how many times he wiped the furniture and swept the floor, the stench wouldn't go away. He needed to mop, or the place would soon be unbearable. He'd paid the landlord for a week, but Bells thought they might have to stay longer. Such uncertainty. He didn't like to rely on other people at all; they couldn't be trusted and always let you down.

Waiting for Bells to open her eyes, Amerdan perused their meager store of food: the remains of a loaf of bread, along with some nuts and dried fruits. His stomach rumbled, and he almost left her there to find himself a good meal. After absorbing a vessel, he was always hungry and liked to splurge on a fine meal and wine, a reminder of how far he'd come from when he was an impoverished child on the streets.

No matter. It wouldn't be long until she stirred, so he'd sate himself after handing over the coin. He took out the crafting and examined it.

Such a small thing it was, and if you had one, it admitted you to the inner circles of the empire's power. Though, as Bells had told him, once the vessel was killed, the crafting was no longer attuned, and any sorcerer close to the emperor would know the coin had been stolen.

Clothes rustled as Bells shifted in her chair. Her lips moved, forming words he couldn't make out. She hadn't done that before. Was she talking to someone? Was that possible?

Moments later, she opened her eyes and looked straight at him. She scrubbed her face with her hands and stifled a yawn. "Do you have it?" she asked.

"Here."

Amerdan flipped her the black coin, and it sailed across the room. Bells caught it easily, and Amerdan's mind itched as she accessed her well.

She frowned, rubbing the coin between her thumb and fingers.

"A coin. That's interesting. It's . . ." She broke off and peered at him, puzzled. "You did kill him, didn't you?"

"Yes."

"But it's still attuned. You mustn't have."

"I did," he said flatly. He wasn't used to being doubted like this, and from a sorcerer.

"Let me check. Something's not right here."

Bells continued frowning at the coin, then her eyes flicked to Amerdan. "What did you do?" she demanded. "How did you kill the Protector?"

He patted the knife at his hip. "With this. He didn't see me in time."

"That's . . ." She broke off, biting her lip. "It's still attuned, only now it's linked to you. How is this possible?"

It must have been my trinket, realized Amerdan. When he'd absorbed the vessel, whatever crafted link there was between it and the coin had transferred to him. Did that mean the coin was useless to Bells? Could he use this turn of events to his advantage?

Amerdan only shrugged. "I don't know. Lucky, I guess. Can you still use it?"

With a shake of her head, Bells cursed. "To get some way into the emperor's forces, it'll serve its purpose."

She cursed again, and her foul language made him flinch. He imagined his knife cutting out her tongue.

"But you got what you asked for, and now it's your turn to repay me."

"I'll need to adjust my plans now, but once I've finished my craftings, I'll have more time to help you. Believe me, I want to find out what's wrong with you as much as you do, and why you've more than one well."

Annoyance at his impatience tinged her words, and Amerdan clenched his fists. It was all he could do to stop himself squeezing the bitch by the throat. Instead, he smiled.

"I understand, but you can also appreciate why I'm eager to see what you can do to help me. I'd never thought I'd be a sorcerer."

Bells snorted. "You'd be a long way from being a sorcerer even if I could unblock one of your wells. It takes a great deal of training and discipline."

"Which you can provide." *Or any other sorcerer.*

"Yes. We'll have plenty of time once this is over and we're on the way back to Anasoma. And once there, other sorcerers more suited to teaching can take over your training. That's if I can unblock one of your wells."

"Thank you," said Amerdan. "Now, are you hungry? It's been a busy day, and I'm famished."

CHAPTER 25

Vasile staggered to the side of the road and threw up the remains of his breakfast. Weak-kneed, his legs wobbled like jelly, and he sank to the ground, wiping his mouth on the back of his sleeve.

"Come on, Magistrate," sneered Chalayan. "Keep moving or get eaten. That's all you need to think about."

Vasile cast him a glance with as much venom as he could muster. Which wasn't nearly enough. His horse started to wander away, and he scrambled in the dirt for the reins dragging on the ground. If it got away, he doubted he'd have the strength to chase it after days of fleeing ahead of the jukari and vormag. Run, ride, walk, ride . . . The hours blurred into one jumble of day and night.

Clutching the reins as tightly as he could, he lay on the ground, eyes watering.

"Get up," said Aidan, standing over him.

"Just a few moments, that's all I need," Vasile croaked.

"The moments add up, and before you know it, you've lost half a day."

"A short rest . . . please." Vasile squeezed his eyes shut, and tears leaked from the sides. *Cursed dust on this trail . . .* He blinked repeatedly to clear them.

Aidan didn't look pleased but whistled ahead at Chalayan and cel Rau, who hadn't stopped to see what the holdup was. Vasile breathed a sigh of relief as their footsteps approached. He'd heard tales of jukari and what they did to the people they caught, and the thought terrified him. Among these hardened veterans, he felt emasculated, sure they'd leave him in their dust, given half a chance.

No, that was unkind of him. So far, they'd shown themselves to be humane, though hard.

Strong hands gripped his arms, and he was hauled upright, sitting in the dirt.

"Thank you, thank you," he whispered, then softly, "Don't leave me here."

Laughter met his words of weakness.

"If you're alive, we won't leave you," said Aidan. "But better your heart give out under the strain than you slow us down and we all die."

"Get him on his horse," Chalayan said. For once, he didn't sound harsh.

Cel Rau grimaced. "The nag's almost done in."

"So's the horse," Chalayan joked.

"We can't do anything about that," said Aidan. "I suspect we'll leave them all behind before this is over. Doesn't matter which one goes first."

There's the hardness I was expecting.

They lifted Vasile to his feet and, with grunts of exertion, manhandled him into his saddle. Vasile looked around wearily at them and nodded his thanks. Without a word, they continued ahead with tired steps, pushing themselves for the moment in order to save their mounts. He knew a time might come when a burst of speed from their horses would save them, and that's when he would likely be left behind.

He sat there, gathering his thoughts and strength, and noticed his horse was covered in dried sweat. It had been days since the animals had been cared for properly.

Clenching his teeth, he slid out of the saddle, groaning in pain as his knees buckled. Wrapping the reins around his hand, he took a step forward, dragging his foot through the dust.

Suppressing agonized moans, he trailed after his three companions.

"WE'RE FAR ENOUGH ahead to risk a few hours' rest."

Vasile wasn't sure he'd heard correctly and shuffled along, head down, staring at the next spot to place his feet.

"Vasile," snapped Aidan, shaking him from his reverie.

"I didn't ride," he croaked.

"I know. Good man. Wait here while we check the cave out."

Aidan wandered off, and Vasile lifted his head, gazing around. A stream bubbled nearby, and Chalayan led three horses toward the sound, while over to his left, Aidan and cel Rau drew their swords and stood to either side of a dark opening gashed into a cliff face. Vasile glanced behind him and could see only forest. They must have left the rocky plains long ago, and he hadn't noticed.

He shivered as a cold breeze brushed over him, rapidly cooling his sweat-slick skin. Daylight was fading, and the shady forest was a blessing after the last few days. His body felt hot, despite the breeze, and he was ready to collapse. His feet throbbed like they'd been hit repeatedly with hammers, and his legs were on fire. He coughed a few times, then spat out brownish saliva, no doubt dust he'd breathed in.

Aidan and cel Rau disappeared into the mouth of the cave, and he waited a few moments. Chalayan appeared unconcerned, so hearing nothing, Vasile tugged on his reins and followed the sorcerer.

A short distance away, he found the sorcerer watering the horses at the stream, boots off and feet soaking in the water.

Vasile's horse moved ahead of him, eager to drink its fill, and he dropped the reins, allowing it to drink with the others.

Slumping down next to Chalayan, he tugged his boots off to reveal swollen red feet covered in blisters. Sighing with relief, he lowered them into the cool water.

"Before we leave, wrap your feet with cloth, if you've a spare shirt or the like. Else you won't be getting your boots back on, not with those blisters."

Vasile nodded, not daring to speak. Those were the first temperate words the sorcerer had spoken to him for days. Could it be his attitude toward Vasile was softening?

"Once they've cleared the cave, we'll hole up and get some rest," continued Chalayan. "Not long, though; can't let up too much just yet. Mostly for the horses: they're no good if we can't use them when we need to. I'll set up some craftings to warn us if anything approaches."

Vasile remained silent, content to let the sorcerer ramble on. It looked like he was in need of a good talk to let out some tension.

Someone shoved his shoulder.

"Eh? What?" he mumbled, rubbing gritty eyes.

"You nodded off. Come on, you need to help them set up in the cave while I . . ." Chalayan waved a hand in a vague gesture. " . . . do what I do."

Groaning, Vasile struggled to his feet, which ached abominably. Watching Chalayan's retreating back, followed by the horses, he limped along after him, wincing at every step. The water had helped relieve the pain somewhat, but now each step was agony, even on the soft earth.

At the cave, he ignored his discomfort and joined Aidan and cel Rau, who were dragging thick branches to cover the entrance and weaving sticks between them. After helping cel Rau move a particularly heavy log to the cave, Vasile stopped for a few moments, breathing heavily.

"I take it we're making the barricade because we're expecting trouble?" he asked.

Cel Rau shook his head. "Being cautious."

"If anything does happen, it's best to be prepared," said Aidan. "Expect the best, prepare for the worst. Caitlyn always used to . . ." He broke off and looked away.

Cel Rau flicked Aidan a glance, then busied himself wedging more sticks into the barrier.

A colleague? wondered Vasile, then out loud, "Caitlyn?"

"Yes," Aidan replied curtly, then paused. "She was a great woman, who ventured too close to evil herself. She had been our leader."

"But no longer?"

"She . . . died."

There was more to this story than Aidan let on. Vasile remembered when they'd first met and Aidan had told Gazija circumstances had led to him taking over the leadership.

"How did she die?"

Aidan glared at Vasile, nostrils flaring. While they stared at each other, cel Rau continued working.

"Curse you and your talent," hissed Aidan. "I killed her."

Vasile held up a hand to placate him. "I'm sorry. It must have been terrible. But I'm sure you had reason."

"Reasons don't make things easier."

"Sometimes they do."

"Not this time."

Something in his tone made Vasile sure that Aidan hadn't just killed a woman he respected. He took another step back. "I . . . didn't mean to pry."

"Of course you did. It's what you do, isn't it, Magistrate?"

Vasile hesitated, then nodded slowly. "I guess it is. Part of my curse, I think. The need to know the truth, to push past the veneer people present, though it may hurt them." He looked away, eyes watering. "It's what drove her away in the end."

"Who?"

"Never mind. You can't change the past." If only he hadn't pushed her to reveal her secrets. But knowing each time she lied, he hadn't been able to let it go. Some stones were better left unturned. Vasile looked around for more sticks, but the ground around the cave had already been stripped. "I'll get some firewood."

"No," said Aidan. "No fire tonight."

Vasile sighed. "Of course."

"Start unsaddling the horses while I help cel Rau finish this. Then you can rest."

Wearily, Vasile nodded, knowing the horses were as tired as he was, if not more. And without them, they were likely doomed. Beyond that, he was starting to enjoy the animals.

At least they couldn't lie.

"OOF," VASILE EXCLAIMED, struggling to wakefulness as a hand clamped over his mouth and something jabbed his ribs. He blinked, and a shadowy Aidan materialized above him, a finger in front of his lips.

"Quiet," he said in barely a whisper.

About to reply, Vasile heard the horses outside moving and whinnying. A cold dread crept into him. He met Aidan's eye and nodded, and Aidan removed his hand and crept toward the cave entrance. Cel Rau and Chalayan were peering out through the entrance hole in their makeshift barricade.

Vasile rolled out of his blanket onto the dirt and felt around for the sword they'd given him. It had been so long since he'd used a blade, it felt awkward in his hands. He stood and followed Aidan's lead, moving as quietly as he could to join them.

Chalayan cast him a withering glance before whispering to Aidan.

"Something passed the crafting I placed down the trail."

"You're sure?"

"I'm sure."

"Could it have been an animal?" asked Aidan.

Chalayan shook his head. "Not unless it's a big one." The sorcerer was sweating, despite the cool night air in the cave, and he stopped to wipe his hands on his trousers before continuing. "We can't lose the horses."

"Can you tell how many there are?"

"No. But where there's one, there's more."

A frightened whinny penetrated the night, and the horses snorted, clomping around.

Cursing under his breath, Aidan drew his sword.

Chalayan grabbed his arm. "We don't know how many there are, and . . . there could be vormag."

So filled with dread were his words, Vasile began to regret not asking more about the vormag, but he'd had other things to worry about on their way here.

Aidan shook off Chalayan's hand. "As you said: if we lose the horses, we're dead anyway."

Somehow during all this, cel Rau had drawn both his swords without Vasile noticing and pushed them into the hole in the barricade, wriggling his way through.

"Me next," Aidan said. "Then Chalayan, then you, Vasile."

As cel Rau's feet disappeared through the hole, Aidan followed.

"Why did we make the barricade, then?" Vasile hissed to Chalayan, who had one hand frantically searching through his pockets and the other clenching an amulet around his neck.

"It's a last resort," explained Chalayan. "In case we're surrounded."

"But if there are enough to pen us in here, we won't stand a chance. We'd just be prolonging the inevitable."

Chalayan knelt beside the hole as Aidan's feet disappeared. "No. It's not so we can hold out if we're surrounded. It's to give us enough time to kill ourselves." With that, the sorcerer shoved himself into the hole and wriggled through.

Vasile squeezed his eyes shut and groaned. Drawing a few deep breaths, he clenched shaking hands. Swallowing, he threw his sword through the hole and went to join his companions. As he emerged, he saw cel Rau fade into the night to his left, and Aidan crouched low, scuttling behind some bushes to the right. Chalayan was hunched over what looked like a few small rocks covered in runes, muttering to himself.

Vasile half stood and brandished his sword, peering into the darkness.

Without warning, the horses shied, straining against their tethers. Wild-eyed and snorting in fear, they moved to the right, making him think whatever danger there was came from the left.

By the ancestors, he needed to piss. Where were cel Rau and Aidan?

Thrashing noises came from the night, followed by a howl, which trailed into silence.

Vasile gripped his sword tighter.

"What do I do?" he said softly to himself.

"Nothing," answered Chalayan unexpectedly. "Wait a few moments."

The sorcerer ran around the clearing, dropping his rocks in what seemed like random places, finally rolling one under the horses before scurrying back to Vasile.

"Now!" Aidan's command pierced the air.

Chalayan stood, lifting his arms.

Flashes of light as bright as the sun sliced away the darkness, and Vasile shielded his eyes, blinking furiously as spots swam in front of him.

Growling erupted from around them, and though he was scared, he forced himself to look.

Sorcerous globes hung from trees around their cave, illuminating the forest. Chalayan must have used some trick to cause them to shine brighter than normal . . . and if they blinded Vasile, they must have done the same to whatever was out there.

Cel Rau didn't seem to be affected, though, and Vasile watched as he ran back into the clearing, leaping a fallen tree that'd been too heavy for them to move. He looked around and positioned himself above one of Chalayan's strange rocks. Twigs snapped, and leaves rustled from the direction he came from, then a large shape leaped over the same tree.

A jukari.

The monster bellowed, dripping saliva onto the dirt. It held a rusty blade, the sword looking like a dagger in its huge hand. Blinking in the light, it took a step back.

Cel Rau hissed at the creature, but it didn't attack, waiting for something. It scanned the clearing, taking in the horses, then Chalayan and Vasile. There was something in its eyes, an intelligence Vasile hadn't expected.

Another jukari pushed through bushes into the open. Seeing cel Rau, it moved to join the other beast. This close, Vasile could see their gray skin was scarred with lines and symbols, like crude tattoos.

Cel Rau remained still as one took a few steps to its left, and the other jukari moved to its right, attempting to get on either side of the swordsman.

"You will not escape," grated one of the jukari in a guttural snarl.

It sounded strangely human, though deeper and menacing.

Cel Rau spat at the monster. "You will die first."

Both jukari snorted and laughed, a chuffing noise full of menace. Vasile hoped he'd never hear the sound again.

"Our master is coming, and he'll suck the marrow from your bones."

"Vormag," cursed Chalayan beside him, fear in his voice.

Cel Rau turned his head and gave a quick nod to the sorcerer. "Now," he said, and he placed his foot on top of the rune-covered rock.

The jukari both leaped at cel Rau, only to be met by a hazy blue shield that sprang up around him. Echoing howls of pain erupted as they thudded into the glowing shield, which slammed into them with crushing force as it pulsed outward from the rock.

Both jukari flew backward, landing in the dirt. One beast lost its grip on its sword, which clattered to the ground. The shield winked out, and cel Rau struck.

The swordsman darted forward faster than Vasile had seen anyone move, blade piercing the side of the still-armed jukari. It howled and gurgled, coughing black blood. Answering howls came from the forest.

Cel Rau ran to its companion, which was scrabbling in the dirt for its sword.

Too late. Cel Rau stuck it twice in the back, then again. It twitched feebly, gray hand a yard from its lost blade, then went still.

Beside him, Vasile heard Chalayan snicker.

"Two down," the sorcerer crowed. "Who knows how many more, eh, Magistrate? Better start swinging that sword soon."

Vasile's mouth went dry.

Aidan entered the glow of one of the globes to the right, sword dripping black blood. He took in the scene and grunted. "That's only three, then."

"Four," said cel Rau, indicating one he must have killed earlier, before Vasile had even gotten out of the cave.

Chalayan cursed. "Four means a band, so maybe ten, plus a vormag."

"You'll have to counter it," Aidan said. "I know you can do it; you've done it before."

Chalayan wrung his hands, licking his lips and shaking his head. "That time, there were a lot more of us, and Caitlyn—"

"She's not here, and never will be again," said Aidan. "Didn't you learn anything from Mazoet that could help us?"

"Hints only, nothing substantial. But I've been working on something . . ." Chalayan broke off and shook his head. "Too dangerous."

"Vasile," commanded Aidan. "Find one of Chalayan's shield rocks and stand over it, but keep one foot on it. Chalayan has to know who's in contact with them to direct his sorcery, otherwise you'll go flying like the jukari did."

Vasile nodded and searched for a rock, then did as he was told, placing a foot on the crafting. The hilt of his sword was slippery in his grasp, and he had to constantly wipe his hands on his shirt.

Around him, both cel Rau and Aidan did the same, while Chalayan hunkered down, making himself as small as possible next to their barricaded cave.

Vasile swallowed. Scanning into the darkness past the light from the globes, he thought he could see shapes moving. A twig snapped behind him, and he whirled, but it was only Aidan shifting his position above his crafted rock.

Sighing with relief, he turned back to see a monstrous jukari lumber out of the night, heading straight for him. A full head taller than the other two, its chest was covered with crude medallions. It closed the distance to him in a heartbeat, raising a steel hammer big enough to crush boulders.

As the hammer came down, Vasile closed his eyes. *I'm going to die . . .* Heat flared under his foot, and his skin tingled. Flashes of light penetrated his eyelids, and there was a thud.

He opened one eye to see himself surrounded by a dissipating blue haze, and the jukari on its back about ten paces away, still clutching its weapon. Black blood dribbled from its nose, where it must have hit the shield, and it groaned, shaking its head, as if to clear it.

"Kill it," Aidan hissed at him. "Quickly. And try keeping your eyes open when you do!"

Gathering his courage, Vasile approached and struck at the jukari, but at the last instant, it raised an arm, and his sword bit into its hand, splitting between two of its fingers.

It gave a cry of pain, then its yellow eyes met his. Vasile trembled as it rolled onto its side.

"Do it!" yelled Aidan. "Kill it before it recovers!"

Vasile stabbed the jukari, only to feel the point of his sword stop and slide away, catching on one of the beast's medallions. Snarling, it jerked up and swung at him. A massive clawed hand clipped his head and sent him reeling.

Scrabbling on the ground, he whimpered as the jukari came after him. Groggily, he turned and lunged for Chalayan's rock. As his hand closed around the crafting, he looked for the sorcerer, praying it wasn't a once-only sorcery.

Again, his skin tightened, tingling as the shield ran over him.

Vasile broke contact with the rock to see the jukari being pushed back once more. It stumbled to its knees.

This time, he didn't hesitate and ran at the creature with a wordless scream, driving his blade deep into its chest. Hot, dark blood covered his hands. The jukari bellowed and clawed at him. He danced backward to avoid its talons.

And the beast fell, slumping to the ground.

Vasile swallowed his rising gorge and kicked the jukari. It remained still. As fast as he could, he pulled his sword from the body. Backing away, he again stood above his crafted rock.

Chalayan's laughter rang out. "Bloody ancestors, Magistrate, haven't you killed anything before?"

Vasile looked at his hands covered in black blood from the dying monster. "No," he said. "You may be surprised, but killing isn't what most people are used to." He closed his eyes for a moment, but more growls from the forest shook him alert.

Another jukari came into the light, sharp teeth bared and wielding a two-handed sword, one Vasile thought he wouldn't be able to lift.

A second emerged to stand beside it, then a third.

Vasile jumped as a hand touched his shoulder. Cel Rau.

The swordsman jerked his head toward his abandoned crafted rock in the dirt. "These are mine, Magistrate."

Slightly ashamed, without knowing why, Vasile nodded and edged toward the rock, keeping his eyes on the three jukari.

What are they waiting for?

Then another growl came from behind Aidan, and two more jukari appeared from the forest. Like the others, these two also stopped, as if waiting.

Aidan looked frantically toward Chalayan, who clutched his amulet and was muttering to himself. Another, smaller jukari stepped into the light, a runt compared to the others. No, it was darker skinned, and it grinned with a mouth full of fangs. Matted dreadlocks of wiry hair fell past its shoulders. Weaponless except for a knife at its hip, it wore a number of rings and medallions, all covered with what looked like sorcerous runes.

A vormag.

Chalayan stood and took a step toward the mythical creature made real. It barked a harsh command, and the jukari sprang at them.

Vasile stomped his foot down on his crafted rock as hazy blue domes sprang up around cel Rau and Aidan. Too early. The jukari weren't knocked back but merely pushed off balance.

Chalayan's eyes were locked on the vormag, distracted. Preoccupied as the sorcerer was, it wasn't likely he'd be able to time the shields well enough to be truly effective, as they'd been before.

Sweating like he'd only stopped drinking yesterday, Vasile glanced from cel Rau to Aidan, trying to decide who needed help the most.

Cel Rau fought three jukari, but he was dancing around their lumbering forms as if they couldn't touch him. One jukari clutched at an arm sliced to the bone, while another backed away, wiping at a wound on its cheek, a cut from cel Rau that had barely missed taking the creature's eye out. Without thinking, Vasile rushed toward him, and watched horrified as the shield crafting pulsed just as Aidan's foot slipped off the rock. The shield slammed into Aidan, throwing him to the dirt like a rag doll. He landed next to one jukari, while the other creature stumbled near Vasile.

Vasile screamed and slashed at it with all his might, sword biting into its arms, which were raised in self-defense. It batted aside his next slash, and he stumbled, off balance. The jukari lurched to its feet and overshadowed him, snarling through fangs. Inhuman eyes filled with hate bore into his, and Vasile's legs quivered. From the corner of his eye, he saw Aidan crumble under an onslaught of heavy blows, sword flying from nerveless fingers.

What was Chalayan doing?

A rock rolled across the ground, coming to rest near Aidan, and Vasile saw him reach for it.

Vasile turned and ran toward Aidan, diving for the rock. Their hands clutched it together as Aidan's jukari raised its sword, and Vasile's stomped behind him, growling with menace.

"Chalayan!" shouted Aidan when nothing happened. He flung himself to the side as the jukari's blade swung down, and it was all Vasile could do to hold on to the rock as they both twisted in the dirt.

Vasile's skin tingled as the shield erupted again. The jukari yelped and flew backward as it thudded into the barrier, which then winked out. The jukari writhed on the ground half dazed, while Aidan scrambled in the dirt toward his sword.

Vasile rushed at the jukari with the injured arm. Baring fangs at his approach, it snarled, shaking its head to clear it. He jumped, both feet landing on its stomach, knocking the wind out of it with a whoosh. It coughed, gasping for air. Vasile slashed his sword across its throat. Black blood sprayed from the gash, drenching his face. The stench made him gag. As the jukari thrashed, he hacked frantically at its head, two hands on his sword hilt. Eventually, the thing uttered a whimpering moan, and its body went still. Vasile stood over it, breath coming in harsh gasps, sweat and blood dripping down his face.

Looking around, he saw Aidan cradling his arm, injured from the heavy blows. Still the man struggled to his feet, face filled with pain.

"Magistrate. Cel Rau." Aidan jutted his chin at their comrade.

Vasile had forgotten about the swordsman. He blinked sweat from his eyes and stumbled away from Aidan, who fumbled for his sword with his good hand.

He turned around to see a scene from a nightmare.

Chalayan was screaming, cords standing out from his neck. The vormag snarled and snapped its fangs as it inched toward him. Chalayan was shielded, but the vormag held two craftings against the barrier, and it crackled and buckled like a thin piece of metal under a blacksmith's hammer. Rivulets of sweat streamed down Chalayan's face, then he howled as his legs crumpled beneath him. He knelt in the dirt, bending to the vormag's sorcery.

Yet the shield still held.

It had been but a moment since he'd left Aidan, and yet the enormity of what he was seeing seemed to drag time on and on. For even as Chalayan battled the vormag, cel Rau was dancing between two jukari, swords flicking at them with astonishing speed. Shallow cuts covered his arms, and blood trickled down his neck from a deep gash on his head.

A third jukari was on its knees; a slash had hamstrung the creature. Bellowing and snarling, it snapped fangs whenever cel Rau came near. Almost ineffectual, it still remained an impediment to cel Rau as the other two kept him boxed in. The jukari were using their fallen companion as a barrier cel Rau couldn't pass, keeping him from Chalayan's crafted stone.

Vasile stopped, hesitant to join the fray for fear he'd put Chalayan or cel Rau off balance. As he paused, wondering what he could possibly do to help in a sorcerous battle, the swordsman stumbled.

Deflecting one sword and sliding to his left, cel Rau stepped back to avoid a blade and moved too close to the kneeling jukari. Claws dug into his calf as the monster latched onto his leg. Hooting with delight, the other two jukari watched as cel Rau turned to slash at the hands clamping his leg.

Vasile blinked away tears. He sucked in air, afraid for cel Rau, afraid for them all. He could feel the truth of their hopelessness, the reality of their death at the claws of these creatures from the Shattering. He would never know who Gazija was or of his plans, never know why the Indryallans invaded. They would never make it to the emperor.

I will never redeem myself.

"No." It was nothing more than a whisper, but it seemed to roar in his ears.

He lurched into motion, skirting the gloating jukari. His fingers closed around the crafted stone. He needed to get close to the vormag and hope Chalayan noticed. Vasile took a few quick strides toward the creature.

Blue light erupted from his hand. Pain flooded his mind as his arm bones cracked and twisted, and he was flung across the clearing.

Darkness descended on him, but he willed it away with strength he never knew he had, groaning and drooling as he rolled in the dirt. Shouts and curses echoed around him. *I've failed. I finally found my courage, and it was too late.*

Vasile looked up to see cel Rau still struggling with the jukari, and the thought of the swordsman falling crushed his spirit more than he would have thought.

I'm sorry . . .

But a movement caught his eye, and he glanced to the entrance of the cave, amazed to see Chalayan was now on his feet. The shield that had sprung up around the stone Vasile held had also distracted the vormag. The sorcerer's and the beast's positions were now reversed: the vormag was on its knees and its expression turned to fear tinged with shock as a thin tendril of violet extended from Chalayan's shield.

The sorcerous filament penetrated the vormag's shield, which popped out of existence. There was a sound like a thousand bees humming. The vormag's scream was cut off—as Chalayan's sorcery cleaved it in two. The sorcerer turned toward the jukari, and his cord whipped at them, slicing through flesh and bone as easily as a stick through water. Their howling cries died abruptly. Cel Rau ducked his head as blood sprayed across the clearing.

Vasile looked around frantically. Were there more jukari? He tried to get up, but a burning agony in his arm stopped him.

Ancestors!

A hand touched his shoulder. He didn't have the strength to scream.

"Magistrate?" cel Rau said. "Don't move. You shouldn't have picked it up without Chalayan knowing. But you might have saved our lives by doing it."

"Are they all . . . dead?" Vasile managed, his eyes closed.

But cel Rau had gone.

Vasile opened his eyes and saw the clearing painted red. Pieces of jukari lay scattered around. Mostly identifiable. His arm felt soft, as if his bones had turned to jelly. Vasile cradled it to his chest and closed his eyes again, lying back on the ground.

Behind him, Chalayan howled with glee. The sorcerer's laughter echoed around the carnage. It was tinged with a madness that scared Vasile more than the vormag had.

"It worked!" the sorcerer crowed. "Magistrate, you're a genius!"

Footsteps approached. Water splashed onto his face, into his dry mouth. He gulped a few swallows, then turned away.

"I won't lie to you, Magistrate," Aidan said. "You acted when it mattered, but . . . you may lose the arm."

Aidan's blunt assessment of his situation didn't surprise Vasile. He nodded. "The others? Cel Rau?" He groaned. Even talking caused him pain.

"A badly gashed-up leg, but he'll mend. My arm's better than yours, but it's still broken. You did well, Vasile. Chalayan killed the vormag when you distracted it, then the jukari." There was consternation in Aidan's voice, and Vasile wondered why, if the sorcerer had saved them.

He could still hear Chalayan's laughter, and it was the last thing he heard as he lost consciousness.

WHEN VASILE CAME to, he was still lying in the same spot. His thoughts felt fuzzy, as if he were still in the days when he drank. *Oh, how I wish that were the case.* Thoughtfully, someone had placed his coat under his head and propped him up against a saddle. His mouth was dry.

"Water," he croaked, trying to pry his eyes open.

A shadow approached, and blissfully cool water splashed into his mouth.

"Not too much," Aidan said. "Here, I've some medicine for you to take. It's the best we can do to dull the pain at the moment."

A soft pellet was pushed between his teeth, and he chewed slowly, tasting herbs and bitter medicinal compounds. More water washed it down.

There was a strange buzzing noise and a flash of light from the edge of the clearing, and Aidan gave an irritated sigh.

"What?" said Vasile. Despite his agony, he could sense something was wrong.

"Nothing," lied Aidan. "Just rest."

"You . . . can't lie . . ."

"To you? Right. This is starting to get annoying."

Vasile managed a ghost of a smile before twitching with pain.

"It's Chalayan," continued Aidan. "Just . . . keep an eye on him. It seems he's gained a new trick—one that would have been better off left alone. And he got the idea from you."

"I don't . . ."

"—Know anything about sorcery?"

Vasile nodded.

"You didn't need to. It was the idea, the concept. He's been experimenting for a few days, apparently. But when the jukari and vormag attacked, he took a chance, one that could have seen him killed, but it worked. And that's what worries me: that Chalayan risked his own life for the knowledge—and possibly ours. Down that path lies . . . well, nothing good."

Vasile swallowed as he was given more water, then darkness descended again.

CHAPTER 26

The day dawned warm and grew hotter. It was unseasonal weather that had most of the Protectors in good cheer. Caldan looked for Joachim after working on his craftings, but he had no luck. The warlock had disappeared. He questioned several journeymen and apprentices, but they couldn't, or wouldn't, reveal where the man was. It made Caldan uneasy. Joachim was still an unknown, and despite his apparent helpfulness, it was hard to view his appearance as anything but too sudden and convenient.

It was almost midday when Caldan spotted the warlock entering the Protectors' compound. Joachim took Caldan to a corner of the courtyard, sitting in his usual spot, and started asking questions about his family, the monastery where he'd grown up, Simmon, Anasoma, and Bells.

It all sounded false to Caldan's ears.

For some reason, Joachim still hadn't given up about the bone trinket, and this roundabout way was a rather bald attempt to draw it out of Caldan, as if he would slip up. Whether he was doing it because the warlock believed Caldan was lying or because he was desperate wasn't clear, but it was annoying to have to be on guard—especially when he wanted to know about the trinket himself.

Caldan's thoughts turned to whatever reward the emperor would heap on the person who retrieved the bone trinket for him. For that's what it was, there was no mistaking it now: a trinket that wasn't a trinket, or at least not of a type anyone knew. How could it withstand the forces flowing through its structure when it was made out of bone? It shouldn't be possible, and yet it was unscathed after weathering the sorcery thrown at him by Bells when his own crafting had failed.

The thought niggled at him as he searched for connections, going over and over what had happened in the caves beneath Anasoma. He came up empty, but he could feel there was a link. He was missing something, and it had to do with the Indryallans and their ability to focus destructive sorcery. Patterns were emerging, swirling around him, but as yet, he couldn't get them to solidify into a concept.

"Did your family have a close relationship with the monastery?"

This was the second time he'd asked the question, and Caldan feared what would happen to the monks if he gave Joachim cause to think they had possession of the bone trinket.

"No. From what I remember, my parents kept mostly to themselves and didn't visit the monastery."

"Strange indeed. A place of learning so close, and with your mother a sorcerer, I'd have thought she'd have jumped at the chance to go there and converse with the monks, peruse their books."

"She'd given that life up. I didn't see her use any sorcery."

"No one just gives up sorcery, young man. Who could give up such knowledge? And the ability to craft items of power? No, it's not easily relinquished. I don't know anyone who would do so willingly."

Then they must have been unwilling, thought Caldan. *And now I know what kind of man Joachim is: one who wouldn't give up his sorcery for anything.*

Caldan wasn't sure how long he could continue dissembling, and besides, he had to find out what reason his parents had for keeping the ring hidden from the empire.

It was time to take a chance.

"Joachim, I'm not stupid. I know you're asking these questions because of the trinket," he said, being deliberately vague about which ring he meant. "What's so important about it?"

Joachim paused, staring at Caldan for a moment before looking away.

Caldan could almost hear the warlock's thoughts grinding as he deliberated over whether to tell him anything—the truth, lies, or something in between. All Caldan had to do was figure out which was which.

"Your grandparents," growled Joachim, "were thieves. Wait, perhaps that's too harsh. They served the emperor, may he live forever, faithfully for many years. Your whole family did. The trinket presented by the emperor to Karrin Wraythe was allowed to be kept in her family's possession, so long as they served."

"But," interrupted Caldan, "it's only useful to someone who's Touched, correct?"

"Yes, and your family had a string of Touched descendants. In most cases, the abilities skip a generation. But some families remain pure, their blood . . ." Joachim hesitated and licked his lips. "They are the most prized by the emperor, and he rewards them well. So not only did they have that," he said, pointing at the ring on Caldan's finger, "but also the bone ring."

He's hiding something. Or at the very least leaving the truth out.

"Why would my grandparents steal a bone ring? If they were valued and rewarded, why risk so much for a ring?"

Joachim sniffed and waved a hand dismissively. "As I said, they were thieves. The ring is an heirloom, passed down from emperor to emperor from the time of the Shattering. It has no power in and of itself."

That's definitely a lie.

"I guess I don't get it, then. They had to know the emperor would come after them, and for something so personal, I don't know how they escaped his notice for so long."

"Bah! Who knows why some people do what they do. Nine times

out of ten, ducats are involved. Plenty of nobles would pay a fortune to have the ring in their possession. Its worth isn't material, it's in its provenance. It's part of the emperor's regalia, and some ignorant nobles would believe, if they possessed the ring, it would give them legitimacy."

"But why . . . wait—to overthrow the emperor?"

"Of course. Some people have high ambitions."

"But . . . no one would follow them. The emperor's family has held the empire together for centuries."

"Reality hasn't stopped many people from taking stupid actions." Irritation tinged Joachim's voice. "Enough of this subject. If you recall anything, let me know. Now leave me. I've work to do. Make yourself useful by helping the Protectors, and find out what progress they've made locating Bells. You'd think a crafted compass attuned to her would be enough, but no . . . Some people are useless."

Caldan nodded and left the warlock to his thoughts. He didn't particularly like being ordered around by someone he knew was lying to him, but what else could he do? Joachim had answers, and alienating or irritating the warlock wasn't going help Caldan figure them out.

He yawned and stumbled, still tired from staying up most of the night crafting and sitting by Miranda's side. He'd been using what skills he'd learned from Bells, and her crafting, to see if there was any way he could speed up Miranda's recovery. Unfortunately, he still couldn't do anything to help her. Joachim had neatly tied Caldan to him by stalling Miranda's deterioration and claiming he couldn't actually heal her. Who knew what the truth was?

He passed the meeting room, where he knew Master Annelie held council and was directing the Protectors in their search for Bells. Let Joachim find out for himself, if he was interested in capturing or killing the sorcerer. It wasn't exactly like he'd shown much concern so far. And that in itself was curious.

Caldan found himself with a few hours to spare. He could have used some sleep, but there was much to do. In the few days since they'd been at the Protectors', he'd managed to make progress on his newest automaton. The clockmaker had been true to her word, and her metal parts were of excellent quality. All he'd been left to manufacture were a few smith-crafted metal pieces, and then he'd etched runes over the whole thing. It lacked only a few gems to make it whole.

He hurried to the smith-crafting forge, eager to finish his piece and assemble a smaller one he'd also designed, which was far more intricate than any before it.

"IT WON'T BE long until this is over and Joachim can have the other warlocks heal you," said Caldan to Miranda, staring at her face, looking for any sign that she'd heard him.

Miranda blinked and tilted her head toward the light streaming through the window, but then returned to her customary stillness.

Caldan sighed. He took her hand in his and gave it a reassuring squeeze. "Soon. I promise. If I have to find Bells and capture her again myself, or if I have to give up my trinkets to save you, I will."

Elpidia burst into the room, door banging against the wall. Her eyes were big and round, and she'd dressed in a hurry, her tunic half off her shoulder.

"Caldan," she gasped, holding out another empty vial, presumably for him to fill. "It's gone. I need more. Please."

Caldan felt ill as he realized why his blood had been used up so fast. She had drunk most of it herself. "Not now," he said curtly. "Tomorrow. Maybe."

Elpidia uttered a short laugh. She looked . . . relieved?

"It worked. My experiments . . . They were taking too long. So I . . . drank it."

Caldan kept quiet, not trusting himself to speak.

"It was only a drop at first," Elpidia continued. "Once a day, then a few more. I had to try something." She was babbling and didn't look like she'd be stopping. "These things take time, and I didn't have long. I knew it. I was going to die. I had to try something. So I took some, and it worked! See." She pulled down her shirt, revealing scabbed, patchy red skin. "Look!"

Caldan averted his eyes. "It looks the same to me."

"No, it isn't. It's getting better. Look at me!" she screeched, grabbing his head and forcing him to look into her face. "My hair, it's growing out darker. Can't you see?"

Caldan peered at her hair and saw she was right. Though the strands were gray, the roots were dark, as if she had dyed her hair gray and her natural color was growing out.

He sat up. "Miranda. Would she be cured?"

Elpidia shook her head. "No, I don't think so. Hers is an injury to the mind, while mine is a physical disease. I couldn't say for sure, but it's unlikely she would benefit."

"But we can try."

She nodded slowly. "We can, of course. But you might be disappointed. Wait here. Let me get my equipment, and we can extract more."

Without waiting for him to reply, she hurried out of the room with a spring in her step, one hand tugging her shirt up over her shoulder.

My *blood*, wondered Caldan. It must be because he was Touched. Elpidia told him his unnatural healing was linked to his blood. He thought back to what Joachim had said only a few hours earlier, when Caldan had thought he'd been hiding something.

Those families remain pure, their blood . . .

A secret as big as this would become known, and those who could profit from it would do their best to ensure no one else knew about it—or had access to it. Which explained why the emperor wanted all the Touched under his control, and which was possibly another reason Caldan's family had been hunted and his parents killed.

Caldan seethed and clenched his fists, nails digging into his palms. Did Joachim know? Or did he suspect? Maybe they all did, those close to the emperor.

If Elpidia's disease could be cured and her hair grow back a different color, as if she'd become younger . . . what greater lure for those in power than staying young and disease free? And what better way to reward those around you and keep them in check?

Again he wondered, How much did Joachim know? Surely only a select few knew the real secret. It would be easy to disguise blood as an alchemical potion of some sort. Some herbs, maybe a strong spirit added, and no one would be the wiser. The real source of the miracle would remain hidden.

How much would a wealthy noble or merchant pay to heal an ailing wife or child? More ducats than Caldan would know what to do with, of that he was certain.

As Elpidia bustled back in with her blood-drawing paraphernalia, he came to a decision.

"Close the door," he said firmly.

"What? Yes, of course. People would ask questions if they saw, but—"

"Stop and listen, Elpidia. You cannot tell anyone of this."

Elpidia gave a timid nod. "I thought as much. You wouldn't want everyone clamoring after you. Some would want to drain you dry."

At her words, Caldan felt a chill up his spine. *Drain you dry.* Was the emperor capable of such a thing?

As soon as the thought crossed his mind, Caldan knew he would be. No one that powerful, and with the resources he had, would be ignorant of such things happening. Which meant he was an accomplice to them, at the least. To some immoral people, letting the Touched go or die would be a waste.

They'd be of far more value if their blood was retained.

His mouth went dry. "Exactly. No one else can know."

"Don't worry," Elpidia said cheerfully. "We'll keep it between us. We can start making alchemical potions for the sick. We'll give it to the poor for free, while charging the nobles a fortune."

Caldan grabbed her arm, and she squealed.

"Ouch! You're hurting me."

"Elpidia, listen. The emperor must know already. I think Joachim may as well, which is why he's here. They've kept this hidden for centuries, perhaps longer. Who knows? There is great danger in this knowledge. I fear . . . they'll kill you, if they think you know this secret."

"Don't be silly. This could be a great benefit to everyone! We can use the ducats from the nobles to help the sick and the poor—"

"Stop! You're not listening. If we start curing all these sick people—if people start getting younger, like you—they'll put the pattern together . . . and people will get hurt. I don't think Joachim would hesitate to kill you to keep this knowledge secret."

At his words, Elpidia went quiet. She looked around the room, frowning, then nodded. "I can see how some people would try to keep this to themselves . . ." She trailed off.

"What do you know about the warlocks? Or even the nobles and councillors in the emperor's inner circle?"

"I don't . . . What do you mean? Do you want to know what their roles are, what they do?"

Caldan shook his head. "No. Do any of them ever die from disease? The wasting sickness? Do they live longer than normal?"

"I . . . I've never heard of one of them dying, other than of natural causes, or violence. But that doesn't mean . . . and the emperor wouldn't . . . he just wouldn't . . ."

"Why not? What makes him so special that he would resist such a powerful gift? We always say 'may he live forever,' but have you ever thought what that means?

"I always assumed it was sorcery. Trinkets and craftings that help prolong his life."

"No sorcery I know of can extend life. If there was a way before the Shattering, it's been lost . . . or perhaps that's another secret. Regardless, it means they are willing to keep hidden something that would benefit everyone, and what kind of people would do such a thing?"

Elpidia's face had lost all color. "What . . . what should we do?"

Caldan rolled his sleeve up and held out his arm. "For now, take more blood, just to make sure all's well with you. Then we can worry about what to do. But we speak to no one about this. No one here knows you were sick, so it shouldn't be too hard to keep it secret. We must prepare for the worst, and hope for the best."

AMERDAN MADE SURE he wasn't seen, even avoiding entering the mouth of the alley when a drunken man spilled out of a nearby tavern and wandered past him. He continued on and made a few left turns, completing a circuit of the surrounding streets before once again approaching the alley.

With the streets clear in the dark night, he slipped into the even darker opening, then through a locked door. Up the flight of steps, he paused at their door, knocking softly before letting himself in.

Bells barely glanced at him as he entered their apartment, focused as she was on her craftings. He could sense them itching at his mind. There were a few places where he couldn't scratch the feeling away. The sorcerer had been sparse with her explanations of what she was up to, but he had a feeling it wouldn't be good for the empire or the Protectors. Whatever she was doing, she'd barely paused in her work, except when she needed more supplies or to snatch some sleep. She hadn't been sleeping well when she took breaks from her work, tossing in her sleep and murmuring to herself. A few times, he'd heard her moan Keys's name, and at those times, Amerdan smiled to himself.

Adding to her frustration was the fact that a number of her craftings had cracked or warped, and she'd discarded them with curses.

No sleep, and time wasted. Not a great combination for someone hiding in the midst of the enemy. Not that he minded the wasted time—it was actually part of his plan. He felt certain she'd dispose of him as soon as he outlived his usefulness. That's what sorcerers did. She'd given him some time when he'd freed her, but she was going to kill him soon.

Or so she thought.

Amerdan gave her a smile, though she wasn't looking anymore, and deposited a cloth-wrapped parcel on the table next to her.

"They're all there?" asked Bells.

"Yes. The merchant wasn't too happy about parting with his merchandise to a nonsorcerer, but I managed to persuade him."

"Good." Bells opened the cloth to reveal a small pile of rare earth crystals. She used a finger to search through them, separating out a few blue stones, then turned to Amerdan with a frown.

"There's only three here. I told you I needed at least five."

Five, thought Amerdan. He remembered very well what she'd said, which had led him to keep the other two crystals for himself.

He shrugged.

Bells cursed. "I can't go into the streets anymore, not during the day. You're going to have to do better than this. There isn't much time."

Amerdan stopped his hand as it moved toward his knife. *Not yet. She is needed.*

"It was all he had. I'll try again tomorrow."

Bells ran her fingers through her dark hair, newly crafted bells tinkling. "Another night lost," she muttered. "Close. It's getting close."

Until the emperor and his army arrive was left unsaid. It was plain she was planning to assassinate the emperor, except now she couldn't use the sorcerous coin Amerdan had taken from the Protector to get close. Her plans had been altered, and he wasn't privy to them.

Time to push her, he decided. The longer she put it off, the longer his wells would remain unblocked. As soon as she was able to accomplish her mission, his usefulness ended. If it was going to happen, it had to happen now . . . before he had to kill her before she killed him.

Despite the urgency, his skin crawled at the thought of her inside him, and he almost did her then and there. Better her than a stranger, he reminded himself. With an effort, he restrained himself after taking a step toward her. Inside his shirt, Dotty squirmed.

Bells noticed his proximity and regarded him with a curious stare. "Is there something you wanted?" she said.

Amerdan swallowed, forcing himself to calm. "As a matter of fact, there is. You've yet to fulfill your part of our bargain."

Bells waved his words away with a hand. "Soon. I've still much to do here before everything is ready. You'll have to wait."

She was lying. She would try to capture him to study, or worse. He'd seen it himself. Soon he'd have to find someone else to teach him.

"You won't be able to do much tonight without the crystals."

Bells paused. "What makes you say that?"

"You said it yourself a moment ago. And I've watched your progress. Places for the stones are ready, but you're two short."

She eyed him shrewdly. "An astute observation. I suppose I could use the time to rest."

"Or perhaps this is an opportunity to take another look at my problem?"

They stared at each other, silence stretching. Eventually Bells shrugged.

"Very well. Make yourself comfortable. But I'm tired, so I won't be able to do much this session."

"Thank you, thank you," he gushed, sure that was how he should react—a grateful, simple shopkeeper who could see himself joining the elite ranks of the sorcerers.

He sat in a chair, and she approached, taking his head in her hands. Again, he had to stop himself from sticking her for her presumption. He had a vision of Bells lying naked on the table, with him on top of her, trinket in one hand and bloody knife in the other.

He smiled widely, breathing her scent in as her hair caressed him, and trembled with anticipation.

"It's all right," Bells said, looking him in the eye and trying to reassure him. "This shouldn't hurt."

Strangely, the kind words and the smell of her made him forget killing her. In the dim lamplight, Bells was an attractive woman . . .

No. *That way leads to pain.*

Forget her, whispered Dotty.

I'm trying.

Amerdan settled back and closed his eyes, concentrating on what the sorcerer was doing. The last time they'd had a session, he thought he'd been able to see flashes of light, tendrils of . . . something coming from her.

His fists clenched as he felt her scratching inside his head. He thought back to her lying naked under his blade until calmness returned.

Dark. That was all he could see. Darkness of a sort, but with a graininess he couldn't describe. A patch of light wove into his mind.

He could feel her invading him. The last and only sorcerer to invade him physically and mentally hadn't been prepared for what he'd created, and Amerdan had gained his trinket as a result.

Scratch. Scratch. Bells scrabbled around inside his head, focusing on a patch of something. What was it? One of his wells, that much he knew, but why was it different from a sorcerer's well? Any other talents he'd gained from his trinket had eventually revealed themselves. But this one, he wouldn't have known if it wasn't for Bells. And it was blocked to him. That was frustrating, knowing such power was close, so close, yet not being able to access it.

A spike of pain stabbed into his skull. "Argh," he murmured, opening one eye to look at Bells.

"Sorry. But there's something to one of these blocked wells. It feels older somehow, and the barrier is rougher, more brittle."

"What did you do?"

"I've managed to wiggle a thread through a chink, which was what caused the pain." Bells paused to wipe sweat from her brow. "But . . ."

"Out with it."

"That was the smallest intrusion I could manage, and it obviously hurt. I'm at a loss for what to do . . . If I expand the thread or try to force the chink open farther, the pain will be excruciating. It's unlikely you'll be able to bear it for long, and I'll need a great deal of time to work it wider."

Amerdan snorted. For this, he could tolerate anything the woman could do to him. The older, more brittle blockage must be from his childhood, when he'd killed the sorcerer who'd kept him captive and mutilated his sisters, all but one . . .

The breath left his lungs. Even after all this time, the memories pained him. Would he never be rid of them?

Maybe the pain would do exactly that.

He tensed and nodded to Bells. "Do whatever you have to. I'm ready."

She looked at him and shrugged. "I'd probably say the same if I were you, but you'll feel differently soon."

He could sense her as she scrabbled inside his mind. Pressure grew in his head, until it felt like it was about to burst. Needles dug into him, stabbing and stabbing, over and over again. He swallowed bile as tears leaked from his eyes.

Agony tore at his head, traveling down his neck, through his bones, under his ribs, and into his legs. He clutched at the chair, but his hands had gone numb. He thought he cried out but couldn't be sure. His back spasmed as the pain went on and on.

It ebbed a little, and he gasped for breath. Colors swam on the insides of his eyelids. The pain was excruciating . . . but cleansing. It was fitting, in a way.

As the agony returned, his body convulsed. A surge tore at his mind, and he struggled to hold on.

Then everything ended.

AMERDAN CAME TO with his head cradled in Bells's lap. She was stroking his hair and crooning softly. He was surprised he wasn't flinching at her touch.

It was oddly . . . soothing.

She'd managed to drag him to the bed, and he lay sprawled on damp sheets, wet with his sweat. He blinked at the too-bright light from the lamp, then closed his eyes. As she stroked his hair and sang, his thoughts drifted back to the only happy time in his life, before the sorcerer had come. He was playing in the fields with his sisters, a game of hide-and-seek, which no one ever won. A child's game. Their mother called for them as the sun sank behind the hills, and they rushed to her, hungry for dinner. And then . . .

That night, everything had changed. He must not forget it was the sorcerer's doing. And Bells was one of them. He shuddered and turned, looking up at her.

She smiled at him, reminding him of his sisters. "You did well. I don't know how you stood it for so long. Would you like some water?"

"Please," he croaked.

She took a cup from the table beside the bed and poured small sips into his mouth, which he swallowed greedily.

"You've been a great help to me," she said. "And with your . . . uniqueness, you could be a great asset for the God-Emperor."

Amerdan nodded, not sure what she was getting at. *Perhaps she wants me to pledge my allegiance to him, someone I've never seen or met.*

"Without you, I'd be either locked up or dead already. And when Keys . . . my brother . . . was lost, my only thought was revenge, even if it meant I'd die as well. But the last few days, I've been thinking, and I've come to a realization. I don't want to die. And revenge won't fill the space he left."

Amerdan remained silent, watching her. She was getting to something, hopefully soon. But she was wrong: revenge was the only thing that assuaged the hurt others did to you. That was life: pay back others, and make yourself stronger, less liable to be hurt.

"I guess what I'm trying to say is . . . I don't want Keys's death to leave me twisted and bitter, to have a hold over me for the rest of my life. I need something to hold on to. Do you understand?"

She bent over, soft hair brushing his face, and brought her lips to his.

CHAPTER 27

F elice stumbled in the dark street, almost toppling over. She coughed into her hand to muffle the sound—a harsh hacking cough torn from her lungs and throat. She swallowed, wincing at the pain it caused, and leaned against a building to steady herself.

By the ancestors. She was trying to be quiet. If she stopped every fifty paces to have a coughing fit, she wouldn't get very far before waking everyone around her.

She doubled over as another wave of coughing overcame her will, claws tearing at her throat. After a few moments, she straightened, wiping tears from her eyes.

Water. I need water. Or hot tea.

What she really needed was a physiker who knew her business, and a week of rest, but there was no time for such luxuries.

Felice laughed quietly to herself.

She wiped her sweaty hands on her trousers. The pants were a present from the librarian, along with undergarments, a serviceable shirt and boots, and a sheathed knife tucked into the small of her back. She'd borrowed them from his daughter, with assurances she'd repay them.

Most of the city slept. She'd waited until the early hours of the morning to make her move, when the only people who'd be about were shift workers, drunks, prostitutes, and the unwary—and the people who made their living from them.

Ahead of her, buildings opened out into an apparent clear space, and from the stench that had been growing stronger for the last few minutes, she knew the river was close. *Good.* That meant she wasn't feverish enough to have lost her sense of direction, though she certainly felt like she could have wandered in circles and not noticed.

She stopped at the corner of the last building before the river Stock. If they could see it now, whoever had come up with the amusing name centuries ago, they'd laugh themselves silly. The stock was more like a stew. Not her, though. The thought of coming close to the disgusting water made her retch. She'd felt and tasted enough of it to last her a lifetime. A few lifetimes.

Felice racked her memory for directions. She knew the house she was looking for was in Parkside, which meant she needed to cross the river. *Where is the closest bridge?*

A scuff of boot on stone from behind warned her in time.

She leaped forward and spun, hand reaching for the knife at her back.

"Whoa there, missy," said a short man dressed in dark clothes, carrying a wooden club. "It's not safe out at night."

"For you it's not if you don't move along." Felice bared her teeth and her knife, waving it in front of her. "Be on your way."

The man held up a hand, eyes flicking left and right to see if they'd been noticed. The street was empty. Licking his lips, he paused, then, after eyeing her knife, took a step back. "Good evening, then, missy."

Felice kept her knife level in front of her, pointed at the would-be robber . . . or rapist, or slaver, or murderer. She ground her teeth. "Wait," she said reluctantly.

"Oh ho, up for a good time, are we?"

"No. Where's the nearest bridge across?"

"That'd be toward Dockside. I can escort you, if you'd like."

"No, thank you. Be on your way. Don't make me stick you." She nodded toward the street they'd both emerged from.

With a smirk, the man tilted his head and turned, strolling away as if nothing had happened.

Bloody city is turning into a shambles, she thought. *This wouldn't have happened in this district before the invasion—maybe in the poorer sections, though.* Without the Quivers to keep order, and with the Indryallans leaving everyone alone, people were reverting to their baser natures. It would take some time to restore order once the invaders were pushed out.

Felice shook her head to clear it. Those were thoughts for later, once the emperor came and killed the lot of them for their presumption. It was odd, though, that someone as intelligent as Kelhak, with sorcery beyond what most in the empire knew, would have boxed himself and his forces inside Anasoma. Why wait? It didn't make any sense to her. Unless . . . She weighed the pieces of the puzzle, and what she came up with made her grimace. Anasoma was bait in a trap, the city itself the lure. She should have seen it sooner. She cursed, blaming her infection and sickness for her lack of insight.

Glancing toward the dark street, she made sure the man had gone and wasn't waiting for her to turn her back. Seeing he had disappeared, she went to sheathe her knife but stopped. Best to keep it in hand for a while, in case she ran into more trouble, at least until she made it safely to Izak's.

She flipped the knife so the blade rested against her forearm to hide it from casual passersby and trudged east along the river until she came to the bridge crossing into Five Flowers. After her encounter, she cast anxious glances about her, eager to avoid any more incidents.

Her problem was that, after crossing the bridge, she had no idea where to go. She wasn't exactly friendly with Izak, and although she knew he lived in Parkside, she wasn't exactly sure *where*.

Another coughing fit racked her frame, and she trembled, staggering to the side of the road. Weakness crept into her body, and she sat in a heap, breathing heavily.

By the ancestors, where is Izak's house?

With an effort, Felice gathered her thoughts. She couldn't wander around the district the rest of the night hoping she'd run into him.

What was I thinking?

She looked around, seeing a brightly lit area down the street. A *tavern* . . . This late, it was one of the few types of legitimate businesses still open, and she could trust—to an extent—the people there more than someone she ran into on the street. And one of the patrons—or the bartender—might be able to give her directions to Izak's place.

Groaning with effort, she stood and lurched toward the lights and was soon standing in front of two noisy taverns, as well as a brothel marked by a sign that featured a gold and a silver ducat along with a man and woman holding hands.

The effort of walking the last hundred yards left her with a sheen of sweat, and she stood for a few moments, gathering her strength.

Which tavern first? One was obviously better off. The other had cracked and peeling paint and dirty windows. Or perhaps that was an affectation? People did strange things for business, and it wasn't a stretch to believe well-off nobles and merchants would get a thrill out of visiting a disreputable establishment. In safety, of course.

She scratched her head. Where would Izak be better known?

She turned and walked into the brothel.

A huge black-skinned man looked her over as she entered, no doubt a bouncer of some kind. He was dressed in dark clothes, as if they wanted him to blend into the dim interior so customers forgot he was there. His meaty hand clamped onto her arm, and he shook his head.

Felice realized she still carried her knife. "Oh. Sorry."

"Hand it over. You'll get it back when you leave."

"Of course. Sorry." She handed him the blade, which looked as small as a fruit knife in his hand.

She gave him a nod, which he returned before going back to gazing around the room, a luxurious affair with numerous couches and curtained alcoves to the sides. What happened in there? Surely they didn't . . . out in the open like that—

Before she had a chance to finish her thought, she was interrupted by a woman.

"Welcome, my good lady. I'm Madame Jensette. May I take that satchel for you?"

Felice stared at her. She was . . . breathtaking. Huge round eyes under tightly curled platinum hair, flawless tanned skin, and pouty red lips. It had to be the dim light and makeup . . . surely . . .

"Er . . . No, thank you. I'm looking for someone."

Madame Jensette laughed, a musical sound that wasn't counterfeit. Felice thought she must be very good at her job.

"Aren't we all. What type do you prefer?"

"An older man; he's about so tall . . ." Felice raised a hand to indicate Izak's height, then stopped, realizing she wasn't thinking clearly. She took a breath. "I'm sorry—I should be clear. I'm not looking for someone here, but someone I think might frequent . . ." She took another breath. "Sir Izak Fourie," she said slowly and carefully. "Where does he live?"

"My, my, does Izak have an admirer?"

"Please. Just . . . I need to know where he lives, that's all."

Jensette tapped her cheek with a finger. "And why would you need to know that?" Her expression grew concerned; she took in Felice's sweating face and trembling appearance. "Are you well?"

"I'm fine, just a little under the weather." *Perhaps she'll be more forthcoming if she thinks I'm really ill. Or maybe . . .* Felice made her legs wobble and held a hand to her brow. "I think I'm coming down with something. I'm sure it's nothing, though."

Jensette took a step back, face hard. "If you're sick, you need to leave. I won't have you infecting my girls."

Felice nodded wearily. "Perhaps it's the baby." She touched her stomach. "Could I have a glass of water, please?"

Jensette's expression softened. She issued an order, and a woman approached bearing a cup.

Felice took it, trying to make herself look relieved and grateful at the same time. She sipped at the water.

"Thank you," she murmured, lowering her eyes. "If you could tell me where Izak is . . . He needs to know. Please."

"That scoundrel," muttered Jensette. "He's on Winterpetal Street, a few streets over toward Gallows, in an apartment above the grocer's; he doesn't live in his house anymore."

"Oh. Thank you."

"If he doesn't do right by you, come back and let me know. I'll make sure some sense is knocked into him. Now, if you'll just . . ." Jensette ushered her toward the exit, and Felice hurried out, making sure to retrieve her knife.

"Come back again," rumbled the bouncer tonelessly, and she frowned before realizing he probably said that as a matter of rote to everyone who left.

Felice skirted three drunken men that spilled from one of the taverns, and it wasn't long before she stood in front of the grocer's. A rickety wooden staircase led up the side of the building to the second floor. She struggled up each step, legs as heavy as lead, and hammered on the door at the top.

No reply. She pounded again. "Izak, you pignut, wake up!"

There was an exclamation inside, and some clanks as the door was unbarred and unlocked. It swung open to reveal Izak, clad only in a nightshirt, thin legs protruding underneath. She pushed her way inside as he spluttered.

"Lady Felicienne, you're alive!"

"Yes, yes. Can you put some clothes on, man! And do you have any tea?"

"Tea?"

"Yes. The drink."

Izak rubbed sleep from his eyes, looking around blearily, as if some tea would magically materialize. "Ah . . . no. No tea."

"What do you have, then?"

"Wine?"

"That'll do."

She watched as he bustled around the apartment. It was only one room with a bed in the corner, which Izak was surreptitiously shoving dirty clothes under with his foot. After much ado and apparent tidying up—which made very little difference she could see—he poured wine into a glass he'd just wiped clean with a rag.

"It's, er, a clean rag," he said as he handed her the wine.

"Thank you. Do you have any water as well?"

"Ah, no. No water."

That figured. The apartment wasn't at all what she expected from Izak. She'd thought he was fairly wealthy and wouldn't be caught dead in a place like this, living above a shop.

"What happened to your house? Lose it at cards or Dominion?"

Izak shook his head. "I couldn't go back there after what happened. What if they came for me?"

"Who? The Indryallans?"

"Yes! I heard you'd been captured. What if I was next?"

Felice chuckled. "It didn't take me long to find you. If they were after you, you'd be in their custody by now."

"How *did* you find me?"

"Madam Jensette told me where you were. If you go into hiding, it's best to leave old habits behind."

Izak had the good grace to turn red and look away.

"Well," he said. "I'll know for next time."

"Can I sit down? Is there a chair or . . ."

"Ah, no. Only the bed. It's . . . clean."

Felice took a mouthful of wine on the way to the bed and shrugged the satchel off her shoulder. Sighing, she rubbed her neck and sat. Izak retreated across the room and looked at her like a mouse would a cat that had it cornered.

"I need your help," she began as firmly as she could. "And a safe place to stay."

"Here is—"

"Is known to everyone around here who knows you. And now Jensette knows I've come here. It's not safe anymore."

Izak looked around, eyes darting this way and that. Clearly afraid, almost comically. Felice would have laughed, if she hadn't been so tired.

She took a sip of wine, then put the glass aside regretfully. She couldn't drink too much, and the way she was feeling, one glass might do her in.

"Izak, listen carefully. We have to get out of here. Tonight."

Izak stroked his goatee and bobbed his head. "Yes. Not safe, as you say. But where?"

She had been thinking about this. "Rebecci. We can ask her for refuge."

"She's disappeared. Hasn't been seen in social circles since my last meeting with her. I don't know where she'd be. Is there somewhere else?"

She couldn't think of anywhere else, but it was probably wise not to let on to Izak. "Pack some things. Whatever's important to you." She looked around the apartment at empty tables and chairs; even the dresser was devoid of anything personal. Chests and wooden crates filled with Izak's belongings were stacked against a wall. He'd not bothered to unpack yet, or he hadn't had time.

She sat still while Izak shoved clothes and personal effects into a sack, along with a small jewelry box and a few coin purses. Which reminded her.

"I'll need some ducats. Not a great deal, mind you. Whatever you can spare for now, just in case I require them."

Izak hesitated but nodded and handed her a few silver ducats, which she pocketed. He stood in the middle of the room and turned a full circle, as if deciding what else to take. Eventually, he shrugged. "I'm ready."

"Good. I'm sorry, Izak."

Izak hefted his bulging sack and slung it over his shoulder. "Where to now?"

This time Felice did laugh. It felt like years since she had. "Perhaps you'd better get dressed first."

AFTER LEAVING THE apartment, Izak had started walking toward the docks, but Felice insisted they head back to West Barrows, where the Sorcerers' Guild and Protectors used to be located, and where the Indryallan forces were headquartered.

She dragged Izak by the arm, and he followed, though his eyes were a little wild. To the east, the horizon was beginning to brighten, and Felice guessed the streets would soon be filled with people on their way to work. Already they'd passed some early risers, mostly apprentices and laborers, and women on their way to the communal ovens to bake their bread.

"We shouldn't have come this way," hissed Izak.

"I've an idea, and no time to explain."

"No time? We've been walking for an hour."

"I know things you don't, so you'll just have to trust me. Do you have a gold ducat?"

"Yes, but . . ." Izak sighed, fishing in a purse and handing her the coin.

"You'll get it back."

If Rebecci had felt she needed to go into hiding, Felice thought, then why hadn't she left with the rest of the Five Oceans Mercantile Concern? No, she was still here, continuing to look after their interests. It was only a matter of following the trail of ducats back to her. And there was one business in Anasoma no one knew was associated with the Five Oceans Mercantile Concern, except for a select few—one of which was Felice.

Outside the offices of Empirical Commerce, a queue of people stretched down one side of the building and around the corner. With the Five Oceans Mercantile Concern closed indefinitely, people rushed to do business with the second-largest bank in the empire, which seemed to have more custom than it could handle. Not yet dawn, and already people jostled in the line. A few hours of waiting, and it would be chaos.

Four unhappy-looking guards were stationed outside the copper-clad double doors, which were closed and wouldn't likely open for some time yet. Bankers did like their sleep-ins.

"Come on," said Felice, and strode up to the nearest guard.

He took in her plain appearance with disdain. "Queue starts around the corner."

"I'm aware of that." She held up Izak's gold ducat between her index finger and thumb and smiled at the guard. "We need to see whoever's in charge today, as soon as possible." She extended the coin toward the guard. "It's urgent."

He blinked and shuffled his feet. "Urgent, is it?"

"Yes."

"A matter of life and death?"

"Certainly."

The guard took the coin and motioned to his fellow, who pushed one of the copper doors slightly ajar. "Inside, please, before this rabble starts to think we've opened for the day."

"Thank you. Come, Izak."

She slipped into the gap, and they found themselves in a marble-tiled entryway. Ahead was another set of open copper doors. As they passed through into a room filled with polished wooden counters, their footsteps echoed off the floor. A smartly dressed woman hurried from the other side of the room to meet them.

"Excuse me," she said imperiously. "How did you get in here?"

"Bribed the guards," Felice said, and the woman's mouth dropped open. "We need to see whoever's in charge."

The woman frowned. "That's me today, but I don't see how I can help . . ."

Felice shook her head and leaned in close to the woman. In barely a whisper, she spoke. "No, no, no. Rebecci. We need to see her. Tell her it's Lady Felicienne Shyrise and Sir Izak Fourie. She'll see us. If she's out, we'll wait."

The woman's eyes narrowed, then she nodded curtly, turning heel and disappearing through a doorway behind one of the counters.

It didn't take long before she returned, waving them over. She ushered them through the doorway and down a corridor, then up a short flight of stairs and into a sparse-looking office.

"Wait here," she commanded.

Felice sat in one of two hard wooden chairs in front of a desk, leather satchel in her lap, and waited as Izak paced in front of her.

"I don't understand," he muttered to her. "Why would Rebecci be here? Empirical Commerce is the Five Oceans Mercantile Concern's main rival."

"Stop pacing and sit down. It's simple: they're not rivals. The Five Oceans Mercantile Concern owns half of Empirical Commerce. Well, not quite half—the empire has a controlling interest—but close enough."

Izak stopped pacing and stared at her. She could see him taking a few moments to organize his thoughts around the information.

"So it's all fake? The greatest business rivalry in the empire is a sham?"

"Yes. And Rebecci wouldn't go into hiding somewhere she wouldn't be able to keep an eye on what's going on, to assess any developments. So she's here."

Izak slumped into the chair beside her. "This is insane. Why own two banks?"

"Why not? They can afford to 'compete' with each other because all the profits go back to them, but since they don't technically control all of Empirical Commerce, the emperor gets to at least seem like he's doing something to curb the monopoly."

As she finished, Rebecci entered the room, looking as emaciated as usual, her white hair in tangles.

"I warned you to get out of Anasoma," she began without preamble. "I even gave you ducats. Bags filled with them. And yet . . . here you are. And you—" She pointed at Felice. "You have a taint."

"It's the river. I had cuts on my arms, and they became infected."

Rebecci sniffed. "No. A *taint*," she stressed. "You've been close to him."

"Kelhak?" ventured Felice.

Without warning, Rebecci grabbed Felice's head with thin hands. It felt like she was being squeezed in a vise. Felice gasped for breath, trying to scream, but all that came out was a whimper. She could hear Izak shouting, but it sounded like he was underwater.

Suddenly the pressure eased, and she could breathe again. Izak was kneeling beside her, wiping drool from her chin.

"Lucky. Lucky," said Rebecci. "You must have escaped before he'd had a chance to take you."

Felice pushed Izak away. "Thank you," she said, embarrassed. She turned to Rebecci. "What did you just do? And what do you mean, take me? Not . . . sexually?"

"Probably that as well, from what I've heard." Rebecci sat behind the desk and frowned at Izak, who brushed at his knees before sitting next to Felice.

Felice touched the leather satchel in her lap, thoughts coalescing. The Five Oceans Mercantile Concern had known the Indryallans were coming, they must have. Yet they hadn't warned the empire. She should tread carefully until she knew their angle. But Rebecci had also given them aid when she didn't have to.

"He's the same Kelhak, but he's a century old," she blurted. "You know what's going on, don't you? But there's also something else . . . there's something wrong with him. What is it?"

Rebecci froze for a moment, so quickly Felice would have missed it if she hadn't been watching.

"Perhaps it's not who he is," continued Felice, "but *what* he is?"

"He is Kelhak, but . . . it's complicated, and not my place to tell you."

"Of course it is. Anasoma's in peril, possibly the empire. They wouldn't take over the city and just wait unless they have a plan. You need to be truthful with me."

"As I said, it's not my place."

"Whose is it, then?" demanded Felice.

"You were supposed to leave Anasoma."

"Well, we didn't. Who were we supposed to meet? You said we'd join you, but you're still here as well."

Rebecci tapped her fingers on the desk, staring at her. After a few moments, she spoke. "Our leader, Gazija. You were to meet him, and he would have explained some things to you."

How cryptic, thought Felice. She guessed this Gazija wouldn't tell her the whole truth, either.

She leaned forward. "Who is Kelhak?"

For the first time since Felice had met her, Rebecci looked unsettled. She dropped her eyes to the desk. "He is beyond you."

"Beyond me. Maybe. But the Indryallans are stuck here like rats in a trap. The emperor will kill most of them and push the rest out to sea and back to Indryalla. Then—"

But Rebecci was shaking her head, though she remained tight-lipped.

With rising dread, Felice met Izak's eyes.

Rebecci didn't think the emperor would be able to defeat the Indryallans.

CHAPTER 28

What is she doing here? Amerdan thought as Elpidia placed fresh herbs into her basket. The physiker thanked the trader before strolling to the next stall along. Another herbalist, but this one's herbs were not as fresh. Elpidia sniffed and wandered past. Even from his vantage point across the street Amerdan could see wilted leaves, saggy and lifeless. She was smiling, which puzzled him. He didn't recall her smiling at all the entire time they were together. Her step seemed livelier, too, as if she were somehow ecstatic and barely restraining herself.

He realized his mouth was stretched into a grin, and he schooled his expression into one of vague amusement. What were the chances they'd run into each other in such a large city? Was this something that had to happen?

Dotty moved inside his shirt, and he reached up to soothe her.

Amerdan glanced around to make sure he didn't bump into any of the passersby, then he joined the slow mass of people wandering through the market. He kept his arms by his side so he didn't inadvertently touch anyone.

They were all filthy. Riversedge was even worse than Anasoma. At least by the ocean, the sea breeze went some way toward clearing the stench.

Amerdan felt he was breathing air that had passed through a multitude of lungs. It sickened him. But here he was, out shopping for Bells. They both required food, and she also needed a few items for her crafting.

Or so she said. Sometimes, he thought she might be getting rid of him for a time.

Men and women bustled around him, oblivious to one another. Unaware. He snorted, drawing a curious glance from a woman next to him. Amerdan ignored her and cast his gaze around for Elpidia again.

She'd halted in front of a communal oven with a baker's stall to the side. She took her time perusing the bread and cakes, then chose a crusty round loaf, along with a small cake sprinkled with sesame seeds. She paid the baker and tucked them into her basket, then turned to look straight at him.

He averted his eyes, bending his head and turning to the stall next to him. But he knew it was already too late.

When he looked back up, Elpidia had her back to him, walking along the street, apparently unconcerned. But Amerdan knew better. She was nothing to him—he wouldn't even try to absorb her. But their chance encounter could only end one way.

He moved to a nearby stall selling metal implements, making sure he could keep an eye on Elpidia in the reflections of the windows of the building behind the vendor. He selected a hammer and a tempered chisel designed for metalwork—two of the items Bells wanted.

In one window, he could see Elpidia glance hastily behind her, notice Amerdan's back was to her, and dart toward a side alley. A moment later, her head popped out as she tried to furtively keep an eye on him.

Despite her apparent fixation on Caldan, she wasn't stupid. She must have worked out that Amerdan had thrown his lot in with Bells.

The mice he'd left for her should have given it away. *Squeak, squeak!* Amerdan thought, sniggering to himself.

She was going to follow him, perhaps even see Bells, then tell Caldan and his Protector friends where they were. Well, let her think he was the mouse and she was the cat.

He paid for his items and walked along the market street in the same direction he'd been going before, passing Elpidia, who'd slunk into the shadows of the alleyway. Not bothering to look behind him to check if she followed, he continued through the market a ways, not hurrying, but not slow enough to give the impression he was looking for something else to buy.

He came to the fifth side street from where Elpidia had seen him, then turned and passed between a stall selling bolts of cloth and another displaying various hats. He made sure he kept his pace to a stroll. None the wiser, Elpidia followed. As he made his way back toward the apartment he shared with Bells, the buildings to the sides started to look the worse for wear, and a number of beggars and dirty street urchins watched him pass. He turned down a shadowy alley, saw there was no one ahead of him, then turned back to face the way he'd come.

Waiting.

Leather footwear scuffed on cobblestones, then Elpidia turned the corner. Her head was down, and she looked lost in thought—and she almost bumped into him.

"Sorry," she muttered. "Excuse me."

"Hello, Elpidia," Amerdan said, smiling.

He covered her mouth with a hand, while his other gripped her throat. Frantically, she clawed at his arms and hands, trying to pull them off her, scrabbling for purchase. But his arms were as hard as steel, his grip far stronger than hers.

Amerdan pushed her back against a wall, hand still clamped around her throat. He uncovered her mouth, and she sucked in a breath. He brought the hand up again. This time it held his gleaming knife.

"Puhl . . ." she managed to squeeze out.

"Please what?" Amerdan hissed. "You are not worth taking."

His knife flashed, and again. Amerdan released his grip, and she slid down the wall, slumping to the cold ground.

Elpidia moaned, her eyelids fluttering. She tried to inhale but couldn't. There was a wet sucking sound.

Amerdan wiped his blade on her skirt, and then left her in the gutter.

A SQUAD OF Protectors filed inside as Caldan emerged into the fading light. This was the third time he'd visited the courtyard searching for Elpidia. He half hoped she'd walk through the gates at that very moment, but he'd had the same thought the last two times someone had appeared, only to be disappointed.

He watched as Master Annelie exited the building with Master Mold, and they approached the weary Protectors. One of them shook his head and handed Annelie something: the compass, surmised Caldan, which he judged would burn out very soon. So still no sign of Bells, and the compass was useless.

Where was Elpidia? She'd left in the morning to go shopping, saying something about needing more herbs and wanting to get out of the Protectors' confines. Almost overnight, she'd become a changed person, smiling more and decidedly less grouchy. He supposed being cured of a universally painful and fatal illness would change anyone's outlook.

But now she'd been gone the whole day, and he was worried. Riversedge was under the control of the Quivers, and there wasn't much violence or crime, but it still happened. The emperor's harsh penalties for criminals were enough to deter all but the stupidest, or smartest, lawbreakers. He couldn't envision someone risking their life to waylay Elpidia, which meant it was far more likely she'd been delayed for another reason.

And the one he kept circling back to was Bells.

"By the ancestors," he cursed under his breath.

He couldn't wait around for Elpidia to turn up anymore. Hastening back to their rooms, he searched her belongings. From her hairbrush, he plucked a few of her hairs, then made his way to his own room and took out a sheet of paper.

As fast as he could, he made another compass, beginning with scribing runes on the paper. Without using metal and semiprecious gems, it was hard, but it would last a few days due to the relatively low amounts of sorcery flowing through it. It was the shape that was troubling. For a while, he stared at his sheet of paper as the runes dried. In the end, he decided on a bird. If he placed it on the palm of his hand, it could balance on a point, and its beak could lead the way.

A short time later, it was finished, Elpidia's hairs folded carefully inside.

Glancing out the window, he took a few of his sorcerous globes and shoved them in his pockets. What else? Fearing the worst, he buckled on his sword. It might mean being delayed by the Quivers when they questioned him, but if he could persuade a master to come with him . . . perhaps Master Mold.

Rushing down the stairs, he ignored the startled looks from apprentices and journeymen alike. Mold wasn't in the courtyard anymore, and Caldan didn't want to spend time searching for him.

Over in the corner, Joachim was in his usual spot. Though he was sipping from a mug and apparently oblivious, Caldan could feel his attention. Joachim didn't miss much, was Caldan's guess. You wouldn't rise to become a warlock in the emperor's inner circle without being intelligent. Joachim couldn't be trusted, but that didn't mean he couldn't be used.

Caldan walked over to him. "I need your help," he stated bluntly.

"More than you know," replied Joachim. "With what specifically, though? I told you I can't do more for Miranda."

"It's Elpidia. She left this morning and hasn't been seen since."

"And you think . . ." Joachim's voice trailed off.

"I think she may have run into Bells. She's no match for the sorcerer, and it wouldn't have gone well for her. She could be captured or . . . worse."

"Your compass hasn't been able to find Bells yet. But I presume you need me, as you're not confident of facing her again?"

Caldan nodded. A bead of sweat trickled down his brow. Time was wasting. "She couldn't face us both together. I've made another compass using hairs from Elpidia's brush." He held out the paper bird and placed it on an open palm. As if blown by a light breeze, it jerked minutely, then swiveled to point in a northwesterly direction.

Joachim smiled. "This could be the break we've been waiting for."

"Not if it means Elpidia gets hurt."

The warlock waved away his concerns. "Yes, yes, of course." He drained his mug and stood, adjusting his belt. "What are we waiting for?"

Together, they exited the Protectors' headquarters, following Caldan's makeshift compass to the northwest.

Joachim walked a pace behind. It made Caldan nervous, but he realized he was projecting his unease about the man onto the current situation. Shaking his head, he focused on Elpidia. Whatever Joachim's motives were in terms of Caldan and the trinkets, right now he felt he could trust the man was just here to help with his missing friend and a potential encounter with Bells.

At least he hoped so.

"Is something wrong?" asked Joachim.

"No, I was just . . . hoping Elpidia is safe. My mind can get carried away sometimes."

"If you're right, and she's been captured, she'll lead us straight to Bells. But I'm sure she's well. It's a big city; she may have just gotten lost."

But Caldan could tell he hoped Elpidia had been captured, and for what seemed like the hundredth time, he reminded himself that Joachim was not exactly a good man.

His bird led them steadily northwest. The streets became dark as the light faded. While the main thoroughfares were still crowded, side streets became almost deserted as people partook of their evening meals. A few curious onlookers stared at Caldan as they passed—a young man striding through the streets with a crafted paper bird balanced in his hand.

Soon the bird led them down a market street, stalls mostly deserted for the day as the vendors had packed up. Only a few remained open for the evening, most selling foodstuffs, from bread to ready-to-eat meals.

The bird swiveled in his hand, pointing to the left. For such a marked movement, Elpidia had to be close by. Caldan stopped, and Joachim came to his side.

"It just moved to the left," Caldan explained, pointing down a side street. "That way."

He didn't wait for Joachim to respond, and he broke into a jog, careful not to drop his bird. As he ducked around corners, the compass swiveled.

Close. She must be close.

He sped up, Joachim's footsteps echoing his in the early night. Another corner.

Three Quivers stood around a pile of clothes on the ground.

Ancestors, no . . .

A clothed body, unmoving. A pool of blood spread from underneath the corpse.

"Elpidia," moaned Caldan, and rushed ahead.

As he approached, two of the Quivers moved to restrain him. "Back away, young man. This isn't something you want to see."

"Let me past," Caldan said. "I have to know."

"Let him go." Joachim's command rang out around the street.

One of the Quivers, an older man, hissed in surprise. "This one's a warlock, boys. Look at his clothes. Better do as he says."

The two Quivers holding Caldan reluctantly released him.

Immediately, he rushed forward, sliding to a halt beside the body. It was Elpidia. Blood covered her chest in two dark patches.

"No, no, no," he whispered. Tears rolled down his cheeks, and he cradled her head in his lap. Behind him, he could hear Joachim and the Quivers talking, but none of their words registered.

It wasn't fair. She had lived for so long looking for a cure, and when she'd finally found it, she'd been killed. The last few days she'd been so full of newfound life, and now here she was, cold and lifeless in his arms.

"She was . . ." he began, and stopped himself.

"She was what?" asked Joachim.

Healed, he'd been about to say.

Choking back sobs, Caldan gently rested Elpidia's head on the cobblestones. He stood and turned to the Quivers. "She shouldn't be lying here."

One of the Quivers spoke up, a bearded man. "We're waiting for a wagon. It'll arrive soon, and we can take her to the closest physiker."

"A physiker? What good would that do?"

"The body will be kept in a cold room for a few days until we identify the woman. Then we'll decide what to do from there."

Caldan wanted to tell the Quiver more, but the words couldn't move past the tightness in his throat.

Joachim stepped in. "No need. She's a physiker from Anasoma, traveling with this man. He's with the Protectors and enlisted my help to search for her when she didn't return. We know who she is, and that should be enough for you."

The Quiver made a few notes in a small notebook. "Ah. We'll still need to question the young man, then." He turned to Caldan. "Do you know if she had any enemies? People who would wish her ill? We don't have many violent deaths around here, and we'd like to catch the culprit."

Before Caldan could speak, Joachim replied. "None that we know of. It may be she wasn't careful flashing her ducats around at the market and drew the attention of some unsavory types. It looks to me like she tussled with them when they tried to rob her, and they panicked."

For a moment, the Quiver hesitated, glancing toward Elpidia's body, then back to the warlock. Caldan saw Joachim raise his eyebrows, and the Quiver swallowed nervously.

"Right you are, sir. That's what it looks like to me, and that's what'll go into my report."

"Good. See that it does." Joachim turned to Caldan and took him by the arm. "Come. These men have a job to do, and we're in their way."

Caldan wrenched his arm from Joachim's grip. "I don't want to leave her lying in the street."

"They'll take care of her. There's nothing else we can do to help."

Caldan turned to the Quiver. "When will she be buried? And where?"

The man glanced at Joachim before replying, as if expecting directions on how to reply. "As the body was found here, the northern cemetery. It's outside the city gates a ways. We can . . . schedule her in for tomorrow, if you'd like. On account of, well . . ." He nodded at Joachim. "She can move to the front of the queue."

Joachim patted Caldan on the back. "Excellent. We'll attend, won't we, Caldan? To make sure everything's done properly and with . . . respect."

Numbly, Caldan nodded, and as Joachim and the Quiver exchanged farewells, he turned his back on Elpidia and wandered down the street. Barely perceiving anything around him, he shuffled along, concentrating on placing one foot in front of the other.

For the first time, he noticed blood was smeared on his hands and shirt. Elpidia's. He looked blankly at his red hands, then wiped them together in a vain attempt to clean them.

The streets and people went by in a daze, and it wasn't until he was in front of the Protectors' that he realized Joachim had been walking beside him the whole way. For the first time his grief was replaced by something else: anger. And confusion.

"Bells wouldn't have used a knife," he said. "She wouldn't need to. This was someone else's work."

"I agree. And that someone was good with a knife. Able to . . . do the deed in daylight without being seen. I doubt it would have gone unnoticed if she'd been dragged down the side street. Which means she ran into someone she knew or recognized."

Caldan's chest tightened. If it wasn't Bells, there was only one other person he knew Elpidia would recognize who could be in the city: Amerdan. He remembered the knives the shopkeeper carried, and what he'd done to Mahsonn.

The question was, why would he kill Elpidia? It didn't make sense. Unless . . . he was in league with Bells.

"Amerdan."

Joachim guided him through the gates into the Protectors' courtyard. "That's what I'm thinking. Elpidia," he said. "Had she known Amerdan for some time?"

"No, not as far as I'm aware. The first time they met was after Ana-soma was invaded. Just before we left."

Joachim grunted. "Well, I'm not sure why he killed her, but if I had to guess, she recognized him . . . and maybe Bells, too, and he needed to ensure that news didn't come back to us. Although we clearly got the message anyway. No matter the reason, he's a danger." He gazed at Caldan, taking in his bloody hands and shirt. "Go inside and wash up, and put on some clean clothes. Have something to eat and a drink or two. Then get some rest."

He heard the words, but they didn't quite coalesce. "Miranda," Caldan was saying. "I'll need to take care of her now Elpidia's gone."

"I'll have the Protectors appoint someone to help."

"Thank you. I'll stay with her anyway. She needs someone around her that she knows."

With a nod, Joachim assented and clasped his shoulder. "We'll find this Amerdan and determine if he did it."

There was an eagerness to Joachim that Caldan once again found distasteful. This had nothing to do with Elpidia, he was sure. He suspected finding Amerdan had become one of Joachim's priorities ever since he'd mentioned his abilities. If someone Touched was out there whom the warlocks didn't know about, they'd want to bring him under their control. And if they couldn't . . . it wouldn't go well for the Touched they were after. He had a vision of himself strapped to a table with needles sticking out of his arms, filling vials with his blood, a grinning Joachim looking on.

And right now, he couldn't think of a way to keep that from happening.

CALDAN DRAGGED HIMSELF out of bed before sunrise, unable to sleep at all. Bleary-eyed, he washed and dressed, leaving Miranda's needs to the girls who had been assigned to help her.

Joachim joined him as he exited the Protectors' headquarters, apparently attuned to the fact Caldan would want to head to the cemetery early in the morning, or because he'd been told by whoever he had keeping an eye on Caldan. Either way, it didn't matter; Caldan knew Joachim was watching him for any slipup or sign he would be rebellious, and so he was at pains to act normal, and ignorant.

He passed through the streets of Riversedge in a daze. Before he knew it, they'd arrived. Just outside the cemetery, a woman sold flowers, and Caldan purchased a bunch, holding them gently, as if he feared the slightest pressure would crush their petals.

The cemetery was a bleak affair, as expected. Hard-packed earth paths wove between graves, and a cold wind stirred up dust, blowing around weeds and tombstones. Caldan noticed shards of bone mixed into the dirt at his feet and grimaced. In the main cities, space was at a premium, and he suspected parts of the cemetery were reused after many years.

As he waited, Joachim disappeared to have words with the cemetery workers, and he returned followed by two men, one wheeling a wooden barrow in front of him. Inside the barrow was a body tightly wrapped with cloth.

They followed the men past tombstones of various sizes and materials, from marble edifices to short wooden planks hammered into the ground, until they came to a stop before a large pit containing other cloth-wrapped corpses.

"Wait," said Caldan. They were going to dump her in a mass grave? "I've ducats for a private burial."

"That'll be a silver."

Caldan handed over the coin without looking up. The two men pushed the barrow to another section of the cemetery, where there was a row of individual grave sites.

They stopped before one and tipped Elpidia into the hole, where she hit the bottom with a thud. Without waiting, the men scurried off, taking their barrow with them. Two shovels stuck out of a pile of loose dirt to the side, but it looked like the men were in no hurry to do their work.

Caldan stared at Elpidia's body, not knowing what to say or do. Behind him, he heard Joachim pacing impatiently.

Eventually, he tossed the flowers onto her body, picked up a shovel, and began to fill the grave.

CHAPTER 29

Struggling with weariness and their wounds in the aftermath, Aidan decided to risk using sorcerous globes to provide enough light to see by. He was confident they'd encountered the only pack of jukari in the area—likely advance scouts for a larger group, though.

Taking the time to physik their injuries as best they could, they rested for a bit, but no one was able to sleep. The clearing had taken on an eerie look as the night began to fade.

After stitching and bandaging their wounds, Aidan directed them to gather whatever they could. "Maybe there's something here that'll provide a clue as to why the jukari and vormag have returned," said Aidan. He used a boot to prod the pile of the creatures' belongings they'd gathered after the fight. He ignored Chalayan's and Vasile's protests, because they wasted valuable time that could be used to get far away from here.

Part of him felt there were answers here, ones they couldn't afford to ignore. Not if the jukari and their masters were returning. But time lost brought their pursuers ever closer. They'd need to be about this quickly.

Cel Rau nodded, poking at the objects with a finger from where he squatted to the side.

Aidan winced as he moved too hastily and jarred his arm. He didn't complain, though—he'd come out the other side of their encounter relatively unscathed, compared to Vasile anyway.

He glanced at the magistrate, who sat with his back against a tree, face pale and sweating with the immense pain he must be feeling. They'd splinted and bandaged his arm as best they could, but Aidan feared he could lose it if a competent physiker didn't minister to him soon. His own arm had been tended to as well, but as his was a clean break, he wasn't in as much pain as Vasile. A cold comfort.

Chalayan was brewing some herbs in water for Vasile over a fire he'd started remarkably quickly. And smiling, always smiling since the fight. Aidan knew why, too. He'd thought the sorcerer's quest for knowledge would become a problem, and he was clearly very close to going over the edge to where he'd be the target of what Aidan's men were pledged to destroy. Chalayan had started on a dangerous path few returned from. Aidan needed to talk with him about it, lest the sorcerer go the way of so many before him. It might even be too late. Chalayan was a problem for another day, though. Right now, Aidan needed to concentrate on the jukari's and vormag's belongings.

Cel Rau put the creatures' weapons to the side. They were well made and worth some ducats to collectors, but too heavy for humans to wield properly. They'd have to leave them here with the bodies.

The vormag's craftings, on the other hand, could be quite useful, and Aidan knelt to help cel Rau sort them into a small pile. There weren't many, but more than usual for a single vormag. It could be nothing, but still . . . Thoughts niggled in Aidan's mind about the vormag. This one plus the few they'd seen days ago when they first came across the jukari gathering added up to far more than he'd ever heard of appearing together, let alone seen for himself. A virtual population explosion of vormag, gathered in one corner of the empire. His guts twisted at the thought of the evil they would do. Lady Caitlyn had insisted that the beasts from the Shattering needed to be killed, that their unnaturalness couldn't be tolerated, and on this point he remained in firm agreement with her.

Cel Rau pointed at a thin leather-bound book, and Aidan nodded. He'd been avoiding it, didn't want to touch it, but it had to be done. The only other vormag he'd seen—killed when he'd just joined Caitlyn's company—had carried one as well. He hadn't been able to examine that book, as Caitlyn had burned it immediately. The thought that these creatures had their own written language made him sick, and their foul use of sorcery was even worse. They had no right to have survived the Shattering. They should have died along with their creators.

But this book might explain more about them. He dreaded this path. Caitlyn had learned too much about the enemy—become like them—and that had ultimately led to him having to kill her. Yet he couldn't think of another way to find out why the vormag and jukari were gathering in such large numbers.

Taking a breath, Aidan reached for the book, skin cringing as he touched the leather. It was probably only cow or goat, but still . . . he wouldn't put it past them to use human skin.

He flipped the book open to reveal pages of indecipherable angular letters, along with the occasional cryptic diagram. He sighed. As he suspected, it wouldn't be of any use at the moment, so he tucked it into his shirt.

"Gather up the craftings, and we'll dump them in the first pond or lake we come across. No point leaving them out here for anyone to find, or to be returned to the jukari."

Cel Rau nodded. "Best we be going, anyway."

"Yes. Once Vasile's had some of Chalayan's brew. Me too, probably." He looked over at cel Rau's bandaged calf. "You should drink some as well."

Cel Rau laughed gruffly. "I'd rather drink fermented horse piss."

But Aidan saw his eyes flick to the fire. He was in pain; they all were. The only one to come out completely untouched had been Chalayan, and Aidan feared the sorcerer was now marked in other— worse—ways.

He watched as Chalayan stirred his herbal potion. Though Aidan was more concerned about Mazoet and the other sorcerers around Gazija, Chalayan couldn't be allowed to go his own way. Aidan wouldn't take pleasure in the deed, but it wouldn't be the first time they'd killed one of their own. Chalayan wasn't the only sorcerer who'd dreamed of the powers from before the Shattering, and he wouldn't be the last.

Aidan narrowed his eyes and allowed himself a tight smile. Chalayan's newfound knowledge presented its own problems, but in the meantime, they'd be able to use it to their advantage, depending on how much control the sorcerer had.

Leaving cel Rau gathering up the jukari's craftings, he approached Chalayan.

"Won't be long," said the sorcerer. "Just a few more minutes to steep."

Aidan remained standing for a moment and sighed inwardly. If he pushed Chalayan, would that hasten him down the path of destruction? There was no way of knowing, but they needed all the help they could get. He squatted next to the fire, upwind and away from the smoke.

"Chalayan," he said, hoping to put the sorcerer at ease, "what you did tonight—it was amazing. But how is it possible?"

Chalayan flicked him a glance, then returned to stirring his mixture. "I'm not sure . . . I was experimenting, and when the vormag appeared, I became desperate . . . tried a few things. I lost control, and it almost ended me." He gave half a laugh. "But I managed to close my well for an instant before everything went awry. It'll take years to work things out, and Mazoet . . . I've no idea how he did most of his sorcery. Likely he has access to lifetimes' worth of knowledge, and probably training. What I know is, my craftings are useless for this." Chalayan shook his head. "It's a whole different way of looking at sorcery and the wells. Almost obvious, when you think of it, but who would?"

Aidan wasn't sure he liked the idea that Mazoet, and likely Luphildern Quiss and Gazija, were sorcerers who were adept at destructive sorcery Chalayan thought would take lifetimes to master. It spoke of an organization of sorcerers hoarding knowledge since the Shattering, and hiding in plain sight for centuries. He needed to be wary of them, but right now Chalayan was his main concern.

"I don't like the way this is going." It was best to be blunt with Chalayan.

"You're still seeing this as black and white," protested Chalayan. "Just like Caitlyn."

At the mention of her name Aidan's chest tightened.

"How much harm," continued Chalayan, "can I do, compared with the enemy?"

Justifications, thought Aidan. This was what he was afraid of, Chalayan following this path. And yet, there was something in what he said. Caitlyn's rigidity had eventually driven her mad.

"You're suggesting becoming proficient with this sorcery," Aidan said. "For it to be another weapon in our arsenal."

Chalayan nodded eagerly. "How much good could we do . . . if this sorcery enables us to survive? What would we be capable of if we could use this against evil?"

You, you mean. The power would be all yours. But he did have a point. Without it, they might all die. But . . . would Chalayan be seduced by his growing power? How far might this go?

"I'll give you this concession," Aidan said. "Can you craft anything that might delay our pursuers?"

"Maybe . . . probably. Whatever I craft wouldn't last long, but it might be enough."

"Good. I'll take over here, and you can get started. But first, we need to know what this new type of sorcery entails. Explain it in terms I can understand. One day soon, our lives may depend on it."

Chalayan scratched his ear, taking a few moments to think. "It's as Vasile said a while ago, when we were talking about it. I thought nothing of it at the time, but the idea wouldn't leave me alone. I found myself thinking about it constantly when we traveled, and at night. You see, craftings are only as good as the materials used and the sorcerer making them—"

"I know. Everyone knows—"

"Let me finish. It's not the only factor, though. The skill and talent of the sorcerer making the crafting also plays a part, so two craftings made of exactly the same materials could have different strengths. Destructive sorcery goes against all I've been taught. Against everything any sorcerer's been told. The easiest way to explain it is as a trick to bypass the crafting, but the crafting is still essential."

Aidan held up a hand. "Wait. That doesn't make much sense."

Chalayan licked his lips, began to speak, then paused. "How do you control a force that's too strong to flow through a normal metal crafting?"

"I don't know," replied Aidan, glaring at him.

"The short answer is, you don't. At least, not through the crafting in the usual way. You create a crafting that itself creates a force to control the power. Do you see?"

Aidan nodded slowly. He did see. "Like the shield craftings?"

"Yes. Well, no. Not exactly. But similar. The destructive sorcery doesn't flow through the material but through channels created by the crafting. That way, the material's strength isn't withstanding the forces, as they're not flowing through it."

"So a wooden crafting could create as much destructive sorcery as the best metal crafting the Sorcerers' Guild could make?"

"Yes."

"In other words, any sorcerer could use it, and be as powerful as the sorcerers who caused the Shattering."

"Well . . . with a lot of training, and they'd have to know how to make the craftings, but . . ." Chalayan's gaze flicked to him, then away. "I guess . . ."

"How were you able to create your craftings to test your ideas, if you had no idea how destructive sorcery worked before Vasile inadvertently put you on the right track?"

Chalayan shrugged. "It's a simple reversal of the shield, though I doubt many would know the runes. The shields are designed to keep things out, whereas destructive sorcery needs to keep things in."

Though it didn't make much sense to him—wouldn't they be the same?—Aidan nodded. He pointed at Chalayan's tea. "This looks like it's ready. I'll pour some for Vasile and cel Rau, and for myself. You get to work on those craftings. I want a few nasty surprises waiting for the jukari chasing us."

Though he looked doubtful, Chalayan nodded. "I'll do what I can, but I can't promise anything. As I said, I need to experiment to get the sorcery right."

"Time we don't have. Do your best." Aidan glanced to the east and judged it wouldn't be long before full daylight. All things considered, they were fortunate to lose only half a day, but they were pretty beat up. It was Vasile he was worried for; another spell of traveling at the hard pace they'd kept up for the last few days wouldn't be good for his arm.

"We'll leave in an hour," Aidan continued. "You'd better get to work."

Chalayan cursed and grimaced, but he knew better than to complain. Whatever the sorcerer came up with would be better than nothing, and they all needed the extra rest.

Aidan found three cups among their belongings and poured equal quantities of the concoction, before adding an extra measure to Vasile's. He rummaged through his gear until he found a cloth-covered green vial filled with a powerful painkiller, a mixture of concentrated poppyseed oil and other extracts. There was no point saving it; if there was ever a time it was needed, this was it.

With care, he dosed Vasile's cup with five drops, paused, then added two more. The magistrate would need all the help he could get in the next few days, if he was to make it to Riversedge alive.

LUPHILDERN QUISS FOLLOWED Gazija a short distance away from the encampment toward the sea. The First Deliverer refused his assistance, though the walk obviously pained him. Often his walking sticks would drag across the ground rather than be lifted up, as if even the weight of such small objects was too much for him. It distressed Quiss greatly to see Gazija in such a state, though he understood the need for him to show the others the way.

The easiest paths are often the ones leading to evil, thought Quiss. They all knew that, but some forgot. He shook his head in disgust. How they could forget, after what had befallen them all, he would never understand, but the trauma of their existence affected every single one of them differently.

He trailed behind Gazija slowly, close enough to catch him if he fell. To his great relief, that didn't happen, and they ended up at the top of a cliff overlooking the bay where their ship was moored.

A cold wind from the south whipped at their clothes, chilling Quiss to the bone. He still wasn't used to this place and its alien land-scape. Bright orange clouds obscured the setting sun and gave the sea's surface a warming glow, despite the biting wind. Dark clouds gathered to the south.

"Good," said Gazija, voice cracking. The old man cleared his throat before speaking again. "This wind will speed our friends' arrival."

"They're not our friends. Far from it. They are mercenaries."

Gazija harrumphed. "Anyone who does what you want is a friend."

Quiss remained silent. This place had changed all of them, Gazija no exception. Though all remembered him as their savior, he'd become harder during their time here. Hope was almost lost for them, and the strain of their predicament was showing.

"We'll come through this," he said. "Savine and the others will see reason, eventually. We'll survive, as we always have."

"I don't want us to just survive," snapped Gazija. He remained still, clutching his walking sticks, peering out over the ocean.

For a long time, they stood there, unmoving in the wind as it gained strength. Southward, the dark clouds roiled toward them, now covering half the sky. Flashes of lightning illuminated them from within. A distant rumble reached their ears.

Gazija turned and began the walk to their camp. "Let's return. There's a storm coming."

CHAPTER 30

As Amerdan slipped through the door into their apartment, Bells stopped fiddling with her craftings and glanced at him. She brushed dark hair over one ear before returning to her work. It was an alluring move, and the fact that he recognized it as such bothered him.

He knew she was using him physically, as a release, and he'd better keep in mind that he was nothing but a tool to her. She probably thought she had him fooled into thinking it was something more, but all sorcerers were alike. He went to her and murmured sweet words of endearment. It wouldn't do for her to suspect, not at all. She was useful now, and this development could be used to accelerate his progress. On the other side of the room, at the bottom of a leather pack he'd purchased and filled with spare clothes and gear, he could sense Dotty squirm with irritation and impatience.

Bells briefly touched his hand. "Did you get the tools I asked for?"

"Yes." He dug into the basket he carried and handed her the hammer and chisel.

"Thank you." Bells returned to the table and set them down. "Did anyone see you?"

"No. I also bought some bread and a cake, if you're hungry." He felt a stab of amusement at feeding Bells the food he'd taken from Elpidia's corpse.

"I am hungry, but . . ." She glanced reluctantly toward her craftings, then back to him. "I can finish this later, once we've eaten. I'm afraid we've only cheese left to go with it."

"Cheese would be fine. I thought after eating, you could try to unblock my wells again."

"Of course. Although I'm loath to hurt you further. I don't know how you can stand it."

Amerdan placed the basket on the table and removed the loaf. Taking his knife out, he examined it to ensure he hadn't missed any of Elpidia's blood. Satisfied it was clean, he began slicing the bread. The disorderly state of the table and the mess irritated him, but he swallowed his displeasure and tried to remain as calm as he could.

He thought of something appropriate to say. "If it means I'll become a sorcerer, then I'll bear it."

"I'm sure I'm close to breaking through one of the blocks; it won't be long now. And you'll see. The God-Emperor will value your uniqueness highly. You'll be greatly rewarded for your loyalty."

No one will put a leash on me.

His hand holding the knife twitched. It was all he could do not to slit her open right there. *Calm,* he told himself. *Not yet. She's needed.*

But when should he? He'd pondered this since she'd claimed she could unblock his wells. If she succeeded with one, would she have outlived her usefulness, or should he allow her to continue with the other? If it wasn't her, he'd need another. Or would he? Was it possible he'd be able to do it himself, once he was a sorcerer? It was doubtful; not without training. And that was another thing she could offer. Knowledge and expertise, given willingly and without reservation.

Her scrabbling inside his mind, and in bed, was a torture he'd have to endure for the time being.

He cut slices of cheese and placed them on the bread, and together they ate. He tuned out most of her chatter as she talked about Indryalla and its splendor, but he found himself intrigued when she spoke of the greatness of the God-Emperor, whom she was apparently related to, as were most of the sorcerers there—the last part, especially.

"Excuse me, what was that? How could one man have so many children and grandchildren?"

Bells laughed, a tinkling, irritating sound. "He's a god. He's ageless and has blessed us with his offspring. We're called his daughters, us women, just as the men are called his sons, but I'm actually a great-great-granddaughter."

Interesting. "How has he lived so long?"

"Because he's divine. He can even heal the sick and diseased. We owe everything to him. Without the God-Emperor, our sorcery wouldn't be so far in advance of the empire's. He freely shares his knowledge, and his compassion."

There was fervent worship in her voice, and Amerdan chose his next words carefully. He didn't want to jeopardize their newfound arrangement yet.

"I can't wait to . . . serve him," he uttered with a false tone of pride.

"It's because of his kindness we invaded Anasoma. The empire is evil. You've seen the way it treats its citizens. All it wants is to have everyone under its control and squeeze ducats from them. Taxes and more taxes, ducats wasted on building monuments and edifices to its own imagined greatness. It has to be stopped. The God-Emperor wants everyone to be free."

Amerdan nodded, even while he thought that one empire was as bad as another, no matter who was in charge. Replacing the emperor with a God-Emperor didn't seem like a beneficial change to him. In fact, it looked like a change for the worse, for more control and oppression under an apparently immortal tyrant.

"Well," he said. "Then we'd better work on my blocks. The quicker they're broken, the better I can serve you . . . and the God-Emperor."

Bells stood and took his hand, leading him to the bed. "It'll be years of training before you'll become a master sorcerer. But I'm confident you will. Now, lie down; you'll likely pass out, as you did before."

Amerdan complied and looked up into her face. She was pretty, but that wasn't a talent he wanted; it was her talent for sorcery and her well he had his eyes on.

"Close your eyes, my love. I wish this didn't hurt, but . . ."

"It's all right," he reassured her. "I trust you."

Closing his eyes, he squeezed his mind into a tight ball, preparing for the onslaught of pain. Whatever he had to bear to become a sorcerer was worth it. He'd be the first sorcerer with multiple wells, more powerful than any of them.

Perhaps greater than even the God-Emperor.

AMERDAN CAME TO still lying on the bed. Bells wiped a damp cloth under his nose and crooned softly to herself. He felt himself relax as she continued to wipe away the blood that had come from his nose, periodically rinsing the cloth in a bowl of warm water. Her ministrations were soothing, and this made him uncomfortable, for reasons he couldn't fathom.

"How are you feeling?" she asked softly.

His head felt heavy and sore, and he turned to face Bells, wincing as the movement brought a fresh wave of pain.

"It's . . . tolerable," he replied.

She rinsed the cloth again, and this time wiped his brow and the rest of his face. "You were sweating a lot. You'll need to bathe, once you're able to get up."

Amerdan refrained from nodding.

Bells folded the cloth and placed it on the bed next to him. Gently, she took his head in both hands.

"Ah . . ." he gasped.

"I'm sorry. It'll fade soon. Can you feel anything?"

He met her eyes. "Did you . . . ?"

She nodded, biting her lip.

Ignoring the throbbing pain, Amerdan closed his eyes and extended his senses into his mind, feeling for . . . what? He had hardly been able to feel the wells himself before. Yet there was something . . .

an absence where she'd spent hours scratching and probing. A thin veil. Beyond was a roiling, chaotic force, and he pulled back.

"Did you feel it?" asked Bells intently.

"Yes."

"It is done. That's one well mostly unblocked. It'll take some time to get used to it, and for me to teach you how to use craftings. Making your own will have to come later, but it will come. And once you've recovered, I can work on your other well, though it'll be harder. It's blockage is stronger, smoother. It feels more recent . . . if that makes any sense."

"No. But I'll take your word for it." Except it did make sense to him. Inwardly, he was grinning, his satisfaction at becoming a sorcerer eclipsed only by his hatred for them. Now he was one of them. What did that mean? He couldn't hate himself. No, there must be a reason this had happened to him.

He looked at the pommel of his knife, sheathed at his belt, then at Bells.

Not yet. She had more work to do. And until he could ensure Caldan would take over from her, she could continue to live.

"JOACHIM AND HIS lies," cursed Caldan softly.

Elpidia was dead, and the pattern of logic led him, and Joachim, to believe it might have been Amerdan who'd killed her. Another liar. And Bells had lied to him, too.

Caldan paced back and forth in front of Miranda. Her color had improved, but again, he doubted whether what Joachim had told him about her recovery was the whole truth.

Lies and more lies, heaped one upon the other.

Everyone out for their own interests with no thought to the consequences, except for themselves. And he was guilty of the same. For when he'd decided not to deliver Bells straight to the Protectors and tried to use her to heal Miranda, he'd allowed her to escape. And if he was right, she was planning a strike when the emperor arrived. Whether at his forces, or a direct attempt on his life, Caldan couldn't be sure, but there was no other reason for her to have remained in Riversedge.

And now, because of choices he had made, Elpidia was dead. Miranda was no closer to becoming whole, despite the suspension of her deterioration, and he was tied to Joachim, a man whose motives were questionable, in order to have some hope of healing her. Caldan suspected all Joachim wanted was the bone trinket, and to deliver him into the emperor's hands, where he would be exploited until he was no longer useful.

With the emperor and his armies approaching, Caldan didn't have much time. Once they arrived, along with his warlocks, his choices would be stark. And as yet, he couldn't see a way out of the situation. Now that the warlocks had found him, they would never let up, never cease looking for him, unless he was dead. Or they thought he was dead.

Caldan turned the idea over in his mind, not liking the conclusions he drew. Fooling Joachim would be nigh impossible. Then there was his trinket, which had led Joachim to him in the first place. He would never again be able to wear it. He pushed the idea to the back of his mind. Maybe a plan would bubble to the surface, but for the moment, it was too hard and too risky.

He needed to take matters into his own hands. Joachim asserted the Protectors knew hardly anything about coercive sorcery, but they had to know something, else they would be woefully prepared to counter it. Caldan suspected Joachim had played down their knowledge as another way of binding him. What better way to keep Caldan in line than to make him think Joachim was Miranda's only hope?

He needed to find out what the Protectors knew about coercive sorcery. The books Annelie had mentioned would be his best start— knowledge of coercive sorcery they didn't understand, secreted away. If possible, he also had to find some way of teaching himself how to counter it, and how to heal Miranda. If he was successful, there would be nothing binding him to Joachim. Except he had a feeling the warlock wouldn't let him go so easily.

First things first. Any books on sorcery would be in the masters' library, with coercive sorcery books kept well hidden and secure. He didn't like the idea—it was against everything he'd been taught—but he was desperate.

Tonight, then, when everyone was asleep. He'd spend the rest of the day working on crafting his new automaton, then see what he could find. It was risky but, in his mind, well worth it.

CALDAN MET NO one in the corridors—not surprising considering the hour of the night. Cricket chirps came through the window on his right, which looked out from the second floor onto a garden, and the air felt humid from an approaching storm.

A wooden floorboard creaked, and he muffled a curse, moving slightly to the side, where a row of nails extending out along the corridor indicated the wooden support beam underneath. Walking the dotted line should limit any more protests from the floor.

Clothed in a tight-fitting black shirt and pants he'd gone out and purchased in the evening, he would have some explaining to do if anyone stumbled upon him, crouched as he was in the shadows next to a painting of a past master. The stern-faced man gazed down on him in disapproval. Caldan shrugged. Some things you have to do, no matter the consequences.

Moving stealthily through the dark halls, he felt a quiet exhilaration. Slipping a paper lion out of his pocket, he accessed his well and linked to his creation. Runes covered its surface, and its single-clawed feet would be enough for it to grip onto any rough surface, for he needed it to act as a lookout. Such a meager use of sorcery within the Protectors' building should go unnoticed, or appear unremarkable. The symbols on its surface flashed in the darkness before fading to a muted glow—his tether was in place. It wasn't inconspicuous, but it was the best he could come up with in such a short time.

He crept along until he came to a locked door, across from which was another painting of a past master. He placed his paper crafting on top of the painting's frame, pointing its head toward the door opposite. With the lion in place, he would have advance warning of someone passing or approaching the door.

Caldan slipped across the hallway as silently as he could. The door looked ordinary. He couldn't feel anything different about it, no vibration, no power emanating from the wood. The lock must have been subtle, which stood to reason if it was crafted by one of the masters. He rubbed his hands in the chill air to warm them, then placed his right hand against the wood. He crouched motionless for a few moments, expanding his senses, searching for any hint of an active crafting. Still nothing.

Taking a stick of chalk from his pocket, he quickly drew on the lock—shifting runes and a linking rune, the same as he'd used to enter the Sorcerers' Guild with Miranda.

Once he focused his well, it was the work of a moment before the lock clicked open. It was becoming easier for him. He stood, quickly entering and closing the door behind him.

Even with his sight having adjusted to the meager light in the corridor outside, Caldan could barely see his hand in front of his face. He stood motionless, the only sound to reach his ears his own breathing. A pinprick of light caught his eye, ahead of him and off to his left— moonlight peeking through a crack in the window shutters. He dared not open them, as someone might see, or the hinges could squeak and draw attention, but he knew he didn't have to. The room appeared brighter already; his eyes adjusted quickly to the lack of light, as they'd done in the tunnels underneath Anasoma. But he still wouldn't be able to read in this light.

There should be . . . ah, there. From the table next to the door, he took a small glass ball. Rolling the smooth surface in his palms, he opened his well and linked to the anchor on the sorcerous globe. It sparked into light, faintly at first, then with increasing intensity. He restricted the flow from his well and dimmed the glow.

Sweat dripped from his brow. Sneaking around the Protectors' headquarters, breaking into the masters' library to steal books, wasn't how he imagined things would end up.

Now he could make out blurry shapes around him: tables and chairs. The room looked exactly like the apprentices' library, though the tables were of better quality and covered in less clutter. Wooden pens with metal nibs lay next to inkwells, and on a table in the corner sat a pile of low-quality paper, presumably for anyone to use for taking notes.

Nothing out of the ordinary, though he didn't know what he expected. He held the sorcerous globe high and loosened his grip, allowing more light to illuminate the room. There was only one other door, against a far wall, and it didn't have a handle or a lock. He grinned in the semidarkness. The apprentice he'd asked about the masters' library had said there were rumors of an inner library that had no visible lock and was able to be opened only by masters. It looked like the rumors were true.

Beyond that door should be the texts the masters felt they needed to secure behind not only a physical lock, but a crafted one as well. He just had to open it.

At the door, he brushed a finger against its surface. A faint tingling, humming sensation pervaded the wood. He sniffed, and there was a scent of lemon, but it was very faint.

Closing his eyes, he opened his senses to the patterns of the door. The flowing grain of the wood he discarded, along with the glue surrounding the wooden pins used to join the timbers together; then the metal hinges he felt without seeing. What remained was the crafting on the other side of the door—a metal lock, difficult to open without the proper knowledge.

Drawing from his well, he tried the few techniques he'd experimented with himself for opening sorcerous locks. None worked. He paused to gather himself. Without being able to see the crafting, he was at a disadvantage. But the lock was designed for masters to use, and they had to be sure a lesser sorcerer, such as a journeyman, wouldn't be able to open it. And one of the only things he knew of separating masters from the rest was the ability to split multiple strings from their wells.

He quested his senses at the lock again. There were three, no . . . four, no, five sections of the lock that felt different, like an absence that needed to be filled. Could these be the linking runes? They had the same feel.

Five strings from his well—it was doable, but . . . he'd be stretched.

He split his well into three strings and held them in his mind. Then he separated another string, until he held four. His head ached with the effort, and they squirmed in his grasp, as if eager to get away. Taking a deep breath, he nervously wiped his damp brow. Concentrating, he tried teasing another string out and fumbled with it. Pain burgeoned in his mind as it snapped back, and he winced.

Focusing his will, he drew the fifth string out, and while it wriggled in his mind's grasp, he connected to the linking runes . . . The metal lock released, and he breathed a sigh of relief. He trembled all over, and sweat prickled his skin. His mind felt drained, but he smiled with satisfaction.

He pushed the door open, and musty air washed over him. He was in a room twenty yards square lined with shelves filled with books and scrolls.

A tremor reached him from his watching lion as something disturbed it. Caldan froze in place. The only sound he could hear was himself breathing. Silence hummed in his ears. He felt the lion move as it fluttered to the floor. It fell from the painting as if someone had brushed it off. He swallowed, not daring to breathe. He stood crouched at the open door, waiting.

His tether was still in place, and nothing else happened to the lion; it rested upside down on the floor. He couldn't feel anyone around it or passing by. He waited a minute more. Nothing. Must have been a stray gust of wind that knocked it off.

He turned his attention back to the masters' secret library.

Caldan scanned the shelves for titles, wanting to spend as little time there as possible. The books were ordered, divided into sections on the various crafting disciplines. Hastily, he scanned the spines of the books and shook his head at most authors' attempts to make their writing sound important.

"By the ancestors," he cursed a short time later. There weren't any books on coercive or destructive sorcery that he could see. The only place he hadn't looked was a small chest tucked into a corner under a table. It had a solid iron lock and, as far as he could tell, no crafting to secure it. Taking his chalk, he again scribed some runes and opened the lock.

Inside were a number of leather-bound books, some relatively new compared to a number of brittle ancient tomes. Lifting one, he opened it and flipped through a few pages. *Ah, this is what I'm looking for.* Topic-wise, at least—the principles seemed fairly basic. Since taking one was risky enough, he had to make sure it had the best chance of helping him. He returned the book and began looking at the other titles. *At least I'm on the right track.*

Eventually he found one describing more complex coercive sorcery. It even had a section on what it described as backlash. Caldan recalled Bells had used the word once during one of their conversations about Miranda.

He would have to return the book soon, but perhaps there was a way . . .

Coming to a decision, he took the basic book as well. He wiped off the chalk, careful to remove all traces, and slid the chest back under the table. With both volumes under his arm, he exited the library, relocking both the chest and the door behind him. Splitting his well five ways was a little easier the second time around.

Caldan cracked open the door wide enough to look into the corridor beyond. He heard crickets and the strengthening wind from the storm, but nothing else.

Across the corridor, his paper lion lay on the floor. It twitched and slid along in a gust of wind. Of course. As he'd thought, the wind had blown it off the painting; it was, after all, only paper.

He slipped through the door and scooped the lion into his pocket, then made his way to his room. The books could wait until tomorrow. With all the sneaking around and splitting his well into five strings, he was worn out. Yet he was excited, not only because he might be able to help Miranda, but because he had an idea that would make studying the texts easier.

He couldn't wait to get started.

CALDAN WOKE AS the room brightened in the morning light. He insisted on sleeping in the same room as Miranda, however unseemly it was. With Elpidia gone, he was the only one Miranda had left, and he wanted to make sure he was there in case she needed something. He had left the windows wide open and moved his bed so the light shone on his face. His first thought was for Miranda, and he checked her condition. No change. She was asleep, though, which was a mercy. When she was awake and staring, he almost couldn't bear to look at her.

Caldan kissed her brow. She stirred but didn't wake.

Leaving her to rest, he sat on his bed and examined the books he'd obtained last night. *Borrowed*, he reminded himself.

They looked promising, from what he could determine with his limited knowledge. One clearly covered the basics of coercive sorcery, along with the runes and patterns to create simple craftings. The other dealt with more complex coercive sorcery, from erasing memories to forcing someone to perform basic tasks against their will. This was . . . horrible sorcery. No wonder the Protectors didn't want it known by anyone.

He closed the books and secured them in his satchel, covering them with one of his spare shirts in case someone asked to inspect it. Borrowing two books from the masters' library had left him feeling paranoid and guilty, and though he doubted they'd be missed so soon, he felt the need to be done with them as quickly as he could.

And to ensure that, he had an idea.

He slipped out of the Protectors' headquarters and made his way to the Guild of Scribes and Bookmakers. His ducats were running low, and he'd not thought about how to obtain more. Buying supplies when they were on the run, combined with crafting materials here in Riversedge, had drained his purse drastically, and with the coming expense, he'd be lucky to be left with any gold ducats at all.

At the Guild of Scribes and Bookmakers, he inquired about their charges and grimaced at their steep prices. After being escorted to a side room, he met with a blind copier, a young man who could actually see but couldn't read. He'd be able to copy the books without knowing what they said. Though he didn't have much choice, Caldan handed over the coins and the two books he'd borrowed. A blind copier was expensive, and he was apprehensive about leaving such rare—and dangerous—books with strangers, but the guild staked its reputation on being able to keep secrets, and that was crucial. After ensuring a second blind copier could be found to work on the other book at the same time, Caldan handed the copier all his ducats save a few silvers.

Caldan breathed a sigh of relief. His copies would be ready in a few days, both being relatively thin tomes. If all went according to plan, then in a few nights he'd return the books, with the masters none the wiser. Then he'd be able to study coercive sorcery whenever he wanted, hopefully heal Miranda . . . and maybe eliminate the leverage Joachim held over him.

CHAPTER 31

Felice woke to the sound of Izak snoring and a foul taste in her mouth. She rolled over. The movement caused her to break out into a hacking cough, and she brought up a wad of phlegm. Across the room, Izak remained asleep, and from the empty bottle next to his bed, she guessed he'd remain that way well into the day.

Now she remembered. Her hand ached. Her knuckles were bruised and cut from where she'd punched the wall. After Izak and Rebecci had calmed her down, they'd plied her with drink to dull the pain she felt, both from her hand and mentally.

She threw off a thin blanket and bent over to retrieve her own empty bottle, spitting her phlegm inside before returning it to the floor. She'd been a bit of a mess last night. With Anasoma locked up tight, there was no way she could get a message to the emperor or anyone around him. But what information did she have anyway? A feeling? And not really her own feeling, but that of Rebecci.

She shook her head and winced. Whatever the Indryallans threw at the emperor, she was confident he'd survive, but it was those around him that concerned her. The Indryallans wouldn't go to all this trouble and risk unless they were sure of success. And she was confident their blow against the empire would be measured in the deaths of hundreds, if not thousands.

Next to her bed was a neatly folded pile of clothes, along with a pair of boots—a present from Rebecci and her company. Felice needed to find out what they were up to as well, but that could wait. If she couldn't warn the emperor, at least she could do something to disrupt Kelhak's plans here. And for that, she'd need help from the Five Oceans merchants.

The problem was, her previous attempts to harass the Indryallans now seemed insignificant to her. What were a few minor disruptions in the grand scheme of things? Hardly a wrinkle in their plans, she would wager. She needed to think bigger. Much bigger. Her plan to destroy the ship using the trebuchet had been a start in the right direction, and yet it had failed. Kelhak's sorcery had seen to his and the ship's survival, and therein was her biggest obstacle. She needed to come up with something their powerful sorcery couldn't counter or saw too late to avoid.

She looked at Izak snoring softly, removed her dirty clothes, and dressed in the shirt and skirt Rebecci had provided. She'd prefer pants, but the skirt would have to do. Tugging on the boots, she laced them up and left Izak in the room. She needed to think, to plan.

And to eat some breakfast.

HOURS LATER, FELICE was still sitting in the eatery where she'd wolfed down a breakfast of honeyed eggs and sausages with toasted bread. In front of her was a teapot, half-full, the second she'd gone through as she stared out an open window into the busy street. She was in Dockside, close to the Highroad, but not close enough that she risked being seen by Indryallan soldiers. They mostly kept to the main streets, not daring, or not caring, to patrol the smaller roads and alleys. She was confident she'd be safe from them here, but she knew nowhere was safe from Savine.

She ran fingers through her hair and rubbed at the pockmarks on her cheeks—an old habit she'd once wanted to break, until she'd realized it was a reminder of her beginnings and how far she'd come on guts and merit, along with hard work.

For a moment her thoughts wandered to the day her master had tried to take credit for her work in front of the warlocks and she'd spoken up. To her horror, he'd ended up imprisoned by the end of the day. Not because of her outburst, but that had led them to uncovering crimes her master had committed. All because she'd spoken a few words in anger. From that day, she'd realized words and information were power and had set her course. And the result was . . . here she sat in Anasoma, a city neatly excised from the empire, bladder almost full from too much tea, wondering what she could do to prevent what she feared would cripple the realm.

Kelhak was the key, she was sure of it. But how to get to him . . .

Felice watched the citizens of Anasoma walk past her window, busy with their lives, unconcerned that their city had been invaded. To them, nothing much had changed. Everything had returned to normal.

Normal . . . What made the Indryallans and Kelhak out of the ordinary was their sorcery: the flames on the walls; the shield Kelhak had been able to craft, strong enough to protect a whole ship from the trebuchet shot and their alchemical surprise.

But a sorcerer was only as strong as his craftings and trinkets. Was there a way to destroy them somehow? No, it was impossible. And then she remembered something, something she had thought in her grief and panic when she first met Kelhak. She was looking at the mural, and thinking about Savine, and . . .

She remembered how much she wanted to get her hands on him in the purified land!

If she could somehow lure Kelhak to that circle of ground in the Parkside district that was devoid of sorcery, where his well was useless, then maybe she could actually do something to help the empire.

But . . . she had no way of luring him out. At least now she had Izak, and possibly Rebecci, to help. Rebecci was a conundrum, though. She knew things . . . but was reluctant to reveal too much. Felice had seen the behavior in both those who had plenty to hide and people who were scared. Judging from the sorcerer's display when she'd accosted her and Avigdor, Felice didn't think she was scared.

Her chest clenched at the thought of Avigdor lying motionless on the cold floor of the prison, his blood pooling around his legs. Felice wiped her eyes and drew a breath.

Kelhak was the cause of this mess, but that other sorcerer, Savine, had been the one to murder Avigdor. She had to test her theory, and if that meant Savine paid for his crime, then so much the better.

Felice shook her head. When she was younger and beginning to get caught up in the emperor's court and the politics that went with it, she'd vowed never to use violence as a means to an end. But . . . she'd been young and naive, and it hadn't taken long before a faction of the emperor's court had taken a disliking to her and tried to have her removed, using knives to get the job done. She'd survived that, barely, and took a different vow: to survive by any means necessary and protect those loyal to her.

Savine had killed Avigdor. He had to die. What the sorcerer's relationship was with Kelhak didn't concern her; his motives were dust in the wind. And he'd been able to find her after the trebuchet attack when she'd thought she was safe. That could work to her advantage.

She just had to figure out how to make it happen. And, if that bastard Savine happened to get killed in the process, she wouldn't lose any sleep over that.

For Avigdor, she thought, *and for the emperor, may he live forever— revenge is coming.*

FEATURELESS AND BLACK, the purified land stretched out in front of her. Felice shivered. Whatever sorcery had produced this place, she was glad the knowledge had been lost in the Shattering.

Smooth was how she'd describe it. Except it was covered in dust and dirt, along with dead leaves blown onto the surface from the trees in Parkside. It felt . . . dead. As if some immense force had sucked the life from the ground and left a pool of molten rock, which had cooled and solidified. Under the dirt and dust, she knew there was a glass circle. Nothing had grown on it since it had been formed. Even weeds couldn't survive. And the size of it! Years ago, surveyors had confirmed it was almost a perfect circle hundreds of yards across.

She studied the low stone wall built around the purified land. It stretched out of sight to her left and right. In front of her was an opening, one of only a few in the wall. People still came to see it: mothers and fathers brought their children; foreigners came to see a remnant of the wars that had almost destroyed the world thousands of years ago. There weren't many purified lands in the empire, and Anasoma's was one of the largest, a veritable tourist attraction.

Felice had spent a few hours studying different sections of the circle and decided on this location. She'd even questioned a few people who made their living showing others around the site, offering ill-informed speculations as to what had happened here. Most involved hundreds of sorcerers dying, but she wasn't interested in their fantastical stories. She wanted to know the layout around the edge. She needed to find the location that would best suit her design.

She pulled her gaze from the deadness of the purified land and nodded to Izak. He was waiting nervously in the alley behind her, pacing along the cobbles and furtively glancing around like he expected Savine to appear out of thin air at any time.

Which he could, she admitted to herself. But he was far more likely to appear when she wanted him to. The message she'd sent should be delivered by now, and she was sure the sorcerer wouldn't pass up an opportunity to recapture her and deliver her to Kelhak like a trussed-up pig ready for slaughter.

"Do it now," she said to the burly man leaning against a wall.

He nodded to her, then gestured to his three colleagues. Rebecci had not asked what she was up to but had been willing to loan her four heavies for the day, and Felice had made good use of them.

They moved four wagons to block the street to either side of the gap in the wall surrounding the purified land, far enough away not to be seen by anyone coming down the alley behind her. When the wagons were in place, they lifted a few crates and barrels from them, blocking any access to the area. The street wasn't usually busy, but she wanted no complications, and people wandering past her and through her trap would only be an impediment. Plus she didn't want innocent bystanders getting hurt. Whatever happened here, there would be blood spilled. Hers or Savine's.

Izak approached, leading a horse. The animal was nothing special, but she didn't need it to be. Its role would be short but crucial.

She took the reins from him and led the animal to the gap in the wall, where she'd left a pile of hay. Dropping the reins, she left it to its own devices. The hay was to make sure it didn't stray. She took a rope from one of the wagons and tied it to the saddle. Leaving the remainder looped on the ground, she tied a crude noose in the other end.

Felice looked around. Izak had disappeared, along with two of the heavies. Good. It irritated her when people required constant directions when they'd already been told what to do and what to expect.

She strode into the alley and sat on some steps leading to a deep doorway. She'd always hated waiting, though she'd cultivated the appearance of patience. There was always so much to do. How could people sit still and do nothing?

Felice coughed into her hand and scratched her scab-covered cuts. That'd be a story for her grandchildren, if she ever had time—or the inclination—to marry. *Let me tell you about the time your grandma threw herself through a glass window and fell five stories into a river.* She snorted with amusement.

Alone with her thoughts, she waited. Arguments could be heard as passersby protested about the street blockage, but she left it to the heavies to deal with them. Shadows lengthened as the sun dipped toward the horizon. She shifted her weight to ease numb buttocks. *Patience*, she told herself. *Savine will come; how could he not?*

A scuffling sound down the alley alerted her. There was a flicker of movement.

Dark alleys were the unscrupulous person's friend, and she'd wagered he'd come this way. And here he was.

"Lady Felicienne," Savine said as he approached, stopping a good ten paces from her.

He really was quite good-looking, she acknowledged. Such a shame.

"Someone told me you were here. Normally, I'd be suspicious of such unlooked-for fortune, but I was . . . able to confirm your location."

"Ah," she whispered. "You can't trust anyone these days."

Another cough racked her frame, and Savine gave her a concerned look.

"Kelhak was amused by your escape, which I found . . . irritating. But I'm sure there won't be a repeat this time. I'll make sure you're kept on a short leash."

Savine glanced around, inspecting the alley. "There's no one with you." It wasn't a question.

Felice shook her head. "You've killed everyone I could rely on. There's nothing left for me here. I tried my best and came up short."

"Don't be so hard on yourself. You couldn't have hoped to win against me. Or Kelhak, for that matter."

She found it interesting how he made Kelhak an afterthought. *There's ambition in this one—a lot of ambition.*

Too bad he won't have a chance to realize it.

"Are you going to chop my feet off, too?"

Savine laughed. "Oh goodness, no. That was a demonstration of our intent, and a warning. But I see you didn't heed it, and for that there must be consequences."

Felice thought she detected sadness in his words. Why would talk of consequences disturb him so? She steeled her resolve. No matter.

She stood and rubbed the back of her neck.

Above Savine, atop the building on that side of the alley, Izak and the heavies moved. Shadows plummeted toward the ground.

Felice threw herself backward into the deep doorway, curling into a ball.

A wave of pressure and heat rolled over her. Thunder cracked in the narrow alley, shaking the buildings. As with their trebuchet shots, the alchemical mixture reacted with virulent force.

Felice grinned as the heat dissipated. The stench of her own singed hair filled the air, but that didn't bother her. A gust of cold wind wafted over her, and she uncurled. The alchemical reaction was violent but short-lived, and the immense heat generated dispersed in moments.

Smoke stung her eyes, burning her lungs as she lurched down the steps.

Blackened, soot-stained walls greeted her. Savine lay on the ground against the wall opposite, unmoving. Strangely, his clothes didn't look burned, though he was obviously injured. He'd been standing in the middle of the alley when she ducked into the doorway and was now ten paces away. It looked like he'd been thrown into the wall with great force. Good.

Felice raced for the rope tied to the horse. A smile stretched her face as her heart thudded in her chest. She needed to be quick, before Savine came to; there wasn't even time to remove his craftings. Izak and the heavies would be on their way, but she didn't think it wise to delay. Besides, she hated waiting.

She skidded to a halt and grasped the rope, cursing the necessity that meant the horse had to be so far away in order not to alert Savine.

A dozen heartbeats later, she was beside the unconscious sorcerer, rope noose looped around his feet. She pulled it tight. Savine groaned and stirred.

"Pignuts," Felice cursed. "Izak! Get on that horse."

Savine turned to her. She punched him in the face with all her might.

She coughed, doubling over.

Savine's hand locked onto her arm. His eyes opened, and he grinned at her with bloody teeth. "Oh, you're going to regret this."

"Izak!" she screamed, prying at the fingers fastened on her.

Felice grabbed her knife and struck at Savine. A hazy sorcerous shield surrounded him like a second skin, just in time to turn her blade from his stomach.

Agony exploded inside her head. White-hot needles poked into her mind. She convulsed and fell to the ground. She screamed again, this time in pain. After a few moments, the agony subsided, and she whimpered with relief. Tears leaked from her eyes, and she blinked her sight clear.

Savine sat up and stared at her. "That was just the start. You're going to wish you'd never been born."

Beside her, the rope jerked, and she threw herself at Savine, striking blindly with her knife in an attempt to distract him. If he was dealing with her and didn't realize what was happening, they might still have a chance.

Astride the sorcerer, she thrust at his shield while he laughed. Violet motes erupted from the shield with each of her strikes. The tip of her blade felt like it was sliding across steel. Savine might as well have been wearing full armor, for all the good she was doing.

With a jerk, Savine began moving toward the purified land.

"What . . . ?" he uttered, surprised, the word muffled by his shield.

Felice clamped her legs onto his torso, riding him like a horse. She wrapped an arm around his head in an effort to blind him and struck at his neck. The alley went by in a blur as they sped up, and his shield turned red and violet, so great were the motes discharging from contact with the ground.

They broke from the mouth of the alley.

She screamed, clamping her body against his as he flailed against her. Sparks struck from the cobbles as they were dragged behind the horse. Wind whistled in her ears, and her hair blew around her face, obscuring her sight.

Come on. Please.

Walls flashed past on either side. Cobblestones changed to dirt. Behind them, they left a trail of dust and a line of uncovered, blackened rock.

The purified land.

Savine's shield vanished with a popping sound. He howled with such pain and anguish Felice almost forgot to stab him—then she thrust her blade into his side. A sudden spurt of hot blood covered her hand.

Savine twisted, and she was thrown onto her back. Cloth tore from her, and her skin scraped over the ground. Tiny knives sliced into her flesh as she was dragged along.

Ignoring the pain, she thrust again, only to be blocked by Savine's arm. He grabbed her hair and pounded her head against the ground. She tried to wriggle from under him, but he was too strong.

They skidded to a stop. Izak must have cut the rope, she thought weakly.

Savine was on top of her, with a feral grin and eyes filled with hate and murder such as she'd never seen before. His fist slammed into her face, and her head rocked back. Felice's vision exploded into a white mist. She felt the knife fall from her hand.

No.

She shook her head, and the mist evaporated.

Savine held her knife in his hand and leaned over her.

But there was something wrong. He wasn't looking at her; his gaze was fixed in front of him. Slowly, he raised both arms, staring at the backs of his trembling hands.

"No," he whispered, voice overflowing with dread.

Felice gasped as the hand clutching her knife struck at his own neck. Savine's other hand was barely able to stop the thrust in time.

She scrabbled backward as Savine rolled around on the ground, to all appearances involved in a life-and-death struggle to stop him killing himself.

What was happening?

His face twisted, also at war with itself. His eyes fixed on Felice, filled with horror.

"He has taken me," Savine rasped. "Kill me. Please."

Then—"Nooooooo!" he wailed.

Felice sat still, numb with pain and bewilderment.

Breathing harshly, Savine lumbered to his feet and staggered away from her.

"Please," Savine pleaded, though his pace increased. "You must kill me."

A glow began to surround Savine, though it wasn't a shield. A soft white light emanated from his skin, concentrated around his head.

He lurched away, heading for the gap in the wall surrounding the purified land.

Felice struggled to stand, but her legs wobbled from under her. She managed to get to her knees and began crawling painfully toward Savine. Drops of blood dripped from her tattered back onto the ground.

Izak flashed past her, running toward Savine. He brandished a thin dagger.

Something was very wrong. She could feel it in her bones.

Savine was trying to kill himself. And asking her to kill him. While running away. Almost as if he were two different people. Like Kelhak.

Her hands clawed at the purified land in an effort to push herself to her feet. Her thoughts swirled. Kelhak. Not Kelhak. Savine. Not Savine.

The purified land, dead to sorcery.

"Izak, no!"

Savine faltered, then stopped a few yards from the edge of the purified land. He lurched forward a step, dragging a paralyzed leg behind him. The glow around him had intensified. Individual motes flew free, breaking into smaller particles before dissipating.

With a screech, Izak threw himself at Savine. They both tumbled over . . . and out of the purified land into the street. One of the heavies ran to Izak's aid and grabbed Savine by the arm, twisting it behind his back. He stomped on the arm and bones broke with a loud crack.

Savine howled a wordless cry of agony. And sparkling sorcerous lights formed around his head, swirling, seeming to throb in time with Felice's thundering heart. They buzzed around Izak and the heavy like a swarm of angry bees.

Darkness closed in, and Felice's vision narrowed to a tunnel. Her head drooped and she stared at the ground. Gathering the last dregs of her will, she pushed the blackness aside. She couldn't pass out now.

Felice's heart clenched in her chest. Long moments passed before she had the strength to will herself to action, but before she could, footsteps pounded close to her. She raised her eyes to see one of the heavies.

"My lady, I've got you."

"Izak," she whispered. "Savine . . . the target. What's happening?"

The man wrapped her in his cloak and lifted her in his arms. "The sorcerer's dead. Your friend Izak did for him. Knifed him in the chest, and he bled out onto the street. But . . ."

The heavy hesitated. She could sense there was more.

"What else?"

He strode toward Savine and Izak. She twisted her head to see Savine's body on the cobbles with Izak standing next to it. His hands were covered in scarlet, and his knife lay on the ground, discarded. Looking on was the heavy who'd broken Savine's arm.

The man carrying her grunted. "The sorcerer's body, it . . . changed. You'll see."

They passed out of the purified land and entered the street. She looked down at Savine. His body seemed smaller than before, lesser somehow. And his skin was dry and tight, as if drained of moisture.

"What happened?" she asked.

"I killed him," replied Izak. "And this happened. I think whatever sorcery he was using did this to him when he died."

She met Izak's eyes. He was calm. Far calmer than she thought he should be after what had happened. She nodded. The other three heavies joined them.

"What do you want to do with the body?" one asked, foot tapping the ground.

Felice winced as the man carrying her shifted her weight to a more comfortable position. She could feel her blood soaking his cloak.

"Use one of the wagons and dump it in the river."

"We should keep his craftings," added Izak. "They might be . . . useful."

Felice regarded him evenly. "Yes. Good idea. I'll collect them."

"My lady," said the heavy holding her. "You need a physiker. I know one close by. Then we need to report to Rebecci."

Felice watched one of the heavies closely, then realized what she was doing and dragged her gaze away. He'd been close to Savine when the man had died.

She examined Savine's withered body. It was as if the life force had been drained out of it. "Yes," she said. "We can see her later. Right now, I need help. Just place me down next to the body, and none of you come near. He's a sorcerer, and his craftings might be dangerous." A convenient lie, but the best she could come up with in her condition. "I'll take them all and keep them safe."

Lying on the cold stone street, she rummaged through the corpse's pockets, removing whatever items she found. With a final pat-down, she indicated to the leader of the heavies that she was ready. "Dispose of the body. The river's close. Then meet us back here. You." She pointed to the heavy who'd helped Izak kill Savine. "Stay here; we might need protection."

"Yes, my lady."

Two of the heavies dragged Savine's corpse and flung it into one of the wagons, where it landed with a thump. Felice flinched at the sound and allowed herself the ghost of a smile.

"There are always complications," she muttered to herself.

"Pardon?" said Izak.

"Nothing. We'll get moving as soon as the heavies return."

Izak met her eye. "It's been an interesting day," he said. "But at least we know it works. And now it's just a matter of getting Kelhak out here."

Yes, but we have to be careful. If she was right, then she walked a very thin line indeed. One as sharp as a razor.

CHAPTER 32

Caldan flicked through both books, Bells's coercive sorcery crafting in hand. Too fearful to try anything on Miranda, he nevertheless practiced a few techniques and exercises in his mind that were explained in the basic text. To his disquiet, there was a beauty to coercive sorcery, a complex symmetry he'd been hard-pressed to explain until he likened it to Dominion. While normal crafting required intricate rules and structures, coercive sorcery was *more* complicated. What worked for one person wouldn't necessarily work for another, and a coercive sorcery crafting had to be able to deal with multiple scenarios, almost as if it could make decisions itself, or fall into a predetermined pattern once something triggered a change. In this, it was very much like Dominion: an elaborate game, where the outcome was to overwhelm your opponent. And structures had to be left in place to deal with changes.

He just needed to learn how to play.

HIS THIRD DEFEATED opponent handed over a cloth purse filled with ducats. Caldan took the proffered coins and inclined his head in thanks. She batted her eyelashes at him and made sure her fingers caressed his. A youngish noble from one of the families in Riversedge, she'd approached him at the end of his second Dominion game, when he'd easily defeated the bragging, overconfident son of a merchant.

The woman, Lady Adelfine, said she would be going soon, as the hour was getting late. Caldan clearly heard the improper hint behind her words. He'd come a long way from the young man who'd arrived in Anasoma unprepared and unworldly. Such a short time ago, and yet it felt like years had passed.

Caldan's thoughts turned to Miranda and the *Loretta*, where he'd first met her, and he politely let Lady Adelfine know he'd be staying awhile to continue playing—even though that was a lie.

She smiled, disappointed, but left without another word.

Looking around the smoke-filled air of the inn, he felt disappointment as well, but for a different reason, namely that he'd have to stop playing at all. He'd found the close-by establishment and fallen into a kind of peace playing Dominion again, even if it was to replenish his ducats. The familiar boards and pieces, their feel in his hands, the friendly banter over games, and the mental challenge took him back to his time at the monastery, when everything had seemed so simple. For a while, he'd forgotten about Anasoma, Bells, and—he was ashamed to say—Miranda and Elpidia. And yet, it was helping him to see that the world didn't have to be all bleak. All invasions and death and sneaking and lying. That there could be simple joys, and therefore things worth sacrificing for.

He added his recently acquired ducats to the others in his purse and judged they'd last for quite some time. Side wagers on his first two games had netted him some coin, but after that, no one was interested in betting against him—he'd made the mistake of trouncing his first two opponents ruthlessly, rather than slow-playing the room. In truth, the only reason Adelfine had agreed to play him had been her ulterior motives. Still, he had what he'd come for.

Caldan left and quickly made his way back to the Protectors'. He passed through the gates into the compound deep in thought and was soon back in Miranda's room. She was asleep, for which he was grateful, and he thanked the apprentice for her help, dismissing her for the night. He wasn't comfortable looking after all of Miranda's needs, but the apprentice would be back in the morning to care for her.

He locked the door, opened his satchel, and removed the books he'd taken from the library, along with the copies he'd picked up earlier in the day. He'd been reluctant to leave them in the room, but there wasn't anywhere he could hide them. He figured no one would go through his belongings with Miranda and the apprentice in the room, so he'd taken the chance. Luckily, he planned on returning the originals tonight.

He took out a crafted sorcerous globe and sat in a chair, his copied books in his lap. It was a few hours until early morning, so he might as well make use of the time. Opening a book, he began to read, wishing the originals were already back in the library.

Tonight, he reminded himself.

HOURS LATER, HE once again donned the black clothes he'd made use of the other night. With a final check on Miranda, he slipped outside, two books tucked under one arm.

The hallway was quiet and dark, as it had been when he'd borrowed the books. Rapidly, his eyes adjusted to the lack of light, and the hallway became brighter.

Caldan advanced into the darkness, stepping quietly from one shadow to the next. Light shone around a number of doorways, but it appeared no one was aware of his passing. Soon he found himself outside the masters' library.

Eager to be done, and not wanting to drag out his task any longer, he decided to dispense with the paper lion he'd used last time. Quickly yet purposefully, he unlocked the door with his chalk and entered the library, moving to the other side and accessing his well.

He split it into five strings, and the second lock sprang open. It was much easier this time; the strings still squirmed in his mind's grasp, but he was more practiced at holding and controlling them.

Inside, he again used a chalk crafting to unlock the chest and replaced the books. He wiped away the chalk when he was done, then backed away, fighting the urge to take yet another book on coercive sorcery. He'd risked enough already to get this far. It was best to stop while he was ahead.

He closed the door and used the five strings from his well to snap the lock into place. *Almost done.* Sighing with relief, he turned . . .

And the room exploded into light.

Caldan winced, shielding his eyes from the brightness, blinking until his pupils adjusted. When he raised his head, he saw Master Annelie flanked by two armed and armored Protectors, who both pointed crafted swords at him. Annelie carried a sheathed sword, with one hand on its plain, battered hilt. Caldan frowned, sure it was the sword Simmon had hidden and he'd brought to Riversedge from Anasoma. It occurred to him that she must know what the trinket's function was, and how to use it. Otherwise, why carry it with her to capture him? He doubted she had the strength to wield it as a blade due to its weight, so he guessed that wasn't its primary purpose.

She looked at him, disappointed yet curious. He automatically flicked his gaze around the room, searching for a way out.

"I was expecting Joachim," Annelie said. "Poking his nose in where it wasn't wanted. You . . . I admit to being surprised. A journeyman couldn't have crafted those locks open, let alone an apprentice."

Caldan spread his hands. "I can explain . . ."

"Oh, I'm sure you *have* an explanation. Whether it convinces either me or the other masters is another matter entirely. And to be honest, there isn't any reason I can think of that would persuade me not to deal with you harshly one way or the other. What you've done is unforgivable."

Caldan hung his head in shame and disappointment that he'd failed Miranda. "I did it for her," he whispered. "For Miranda.

Joachim . . . he's hiding something, and claims he can't cure her, but . . . I can't prove it, but I know he can. He's lying."

Annelie sniffed. "We've plenty of time to get to the bottom of this, but for now, you're coming with me."

The two Protectors secured Caldan's arms, and Annelie admonished them to make as little noise as possible. She obviously didn't want everyone knowing what had happened.

Caldan frowned as he realized they'd not searched him for craftings, then reeled in shock. He couldn't access his well. It was as if a smooth barrier had been placed between him and his power.

"That's right," said Annelie, as she saw his expression. "There's more than one way to take down a rogue sorcerer."

"I'm not a rogue."

"That's pretty much what they all say. They all have reasons, justifications, but the Shattering cannot be allowed to happen again. All reasons pale before that fact."

Caldan couldn't refute her words. She was right, he knew. But . . . he wasn't a rogue; he wasn't like Bells and the Indryallans. He just needed to figure out a way to make her understand that.

He remained silent as they marched him along the hallway and down a narrow, out-of-the-way staircase. Then, to his surprise, he was bundled into the back of an uncovered wagon and tied securely with rope. Within short order, they were rolling through the dark streets of Riversedge to a place unknown, one Protector driving the wagon, the other in the back with Caldan and Annelie.

Caldan turned to the master. "Can you make sure Miranda is cared for? She's unsettled if someone she doesn't know is around her, and with Elpidia dead and me . . . well, if the same apprentice could take care of her, I'd appreciate it."

Annelie gazed at him, face hard for a moment, before turning to pity. "We can't look after her forever, but until we find somewhere for her, I'll do what I can. She's an innocent in all this, after all."

"Thank you," said Caldan. "So can I ask where you're taking me? And why is it away from the Protectors' headquarters?"

"To a safe place. One you won't disappear from."

"Joachim. You don't trust him either."

"Keep your musings to yourself. You've no idea what's going on, and it would be best if you stopped talking. I need time to think."

Annelie turned away from him and kept her gaze on the buildings rolling past. She cradled the trinket sword in her arms.

Could the trinket be the reason he was cut off from his well? She'd said she was expecting Joachim and would have been prepared to capture a sorcerer of his caliber. Without access to his well, Caldan couldn't tell if she was linked to the sword in any way, but it stood to reason that it was the cause of his blockage.

And she can control it. I only hope that's enough.

"Joachim will look for me," said Caldan. "He won't rest until I've been found."

Annelie remained quiet, and Caldan decided to do the same. There was no point annoying her, as his fate might very well hinge on her attitude toward him. He didn't doubt his punishment would be severe, but she knew his concern for Miranda was what had driven him to break into the library, and surely that counted for something.

Right?

The wagon trundled along paved streets in a westerly direction. Caldan didn't know his way around the city, but he thought the buildings were becoming less run-down, more maintained, which meant they were entering a prosperous district.

There was a whistling sound and a thud, then another. The Protector driving the wagon keeled over and fell to the cobbles. An arrow stuck out from his chest, having penetrated clean through his crafted armor.

Caldan looked to the other Protector, who'd half stood and was clutching at his side, where another arrow protruded. As Annelie looked at the dead Protectors in horror, Caldan flung himself to the wagon bed.

Annelie uttered a shriek as a shield surrounded her. An instant later, she was hit by arrows from all sides. Her shield exploded with violet motes of light, so many they almost obscured her form inside. Yet every arrow failed to penetrate her shield.

But something was wrong. A high-pitched whine reached Caldan's ears as Annelie's shield crafting strained under the assault. An anomaly, because a few arrows shouldn't have strained a master's shield that much.

Annelie flinched under another barrage of arrows, and Caldan ducked his head as they buzzed around him. A few dropped to the wagon bed, and he was shocked to see they were crafted. Black ink runes were scribed along the shafts, and the steel heads were etched with the same.

Annelie's shield crafting screeched in a fever pitch of protest as it approached overload.

Caldan clawed at the blockage to his well, again in vain, mind slipping over a mirror-smooth surface. "Annelie, free me!" he shouted.

She ignored him. More arrows slammed into her shield, each one hitting with a spark and emitting more motes of light. Annelie uttered a choking sob as her shield popped out of existence. Caldan realized she must have broken the link for fear another strike would push her crafting over the edge and they would all be killed by the sudden release of energy.

She stood still, gasping for breath. Shadows moved atop the buildings around them.

"What do you want?" she screamed. "Who are you?"

An arrow struck her left eye, and her head jerked back from the impact. She slumped to the floor of the wagon, blood trickling down her head onto the wood. Caldan turned his gaze from the gruesome sight. Subdued, elated whispers reached his ears.

He reached for his well, only to find it remained blocked, but he could feel the barrier dissolving. The trinket sword was still in Annelie's grasp. He needed to seize it if he could. He couldn't use it as a trinket, but it was still a sword.

Except his hands were still bound behind his back.

As a rush of footsteps approached, Caldan wriggled toward Annelie. He lashed out at the trinket with a foot, missing. The second time, he connected with the sword, and it tumbled from her dead fingers.

Caldan opened his well as a shadowy figure climbed the side of the wagon and loomed above him. As the barrier to his well finally dissolved, he reached to link with Bells's shield crafting, but wasn't quick enough. There was a blur of movement as something dark crashed down toward his head. He reeled, and as he did a sack covered his head. Rough hands pushed him into the wagon bed and bound his hands and feet.

CALDAN WAS TERRIFIED, but alive. Light streamed over him from an unshuttered window, and he blinked, turning away from the brightness. His head ached, and his mouth was dry. Wherever he was smelled of dust overlaid with an astringent alchemical scent.

He was lying on something hard, but at an angle, not horizontal. He tried to get up, but found he couldn't. A thick leather strap held his chest down. More restrained his arms and legs, all attached to a wooden table that was inclined to the floor.

With rising dread, he looked around. He was in a small room with a dirty window to his left and a door with a metal lock facing him. Whoever had killed Annelie and the Protectors and taken him here would be outside. He doubted they'd leave him alone for very long.

What truly bothered him was that they hadn't killed him as well. Whatever they wanted, and whoever they were, they'd been well prepared. Two armed and armored Protectors, along with a master, were not easy targets, but they'd been killed with an efficiency that implied their attackers were both cunning and resourceful. And ruthless. If he had to guess, they'd done this before. Many times.

The fact that he hadn't been killed—and that he was imprisoned—seemed to imply he was their target all along. He had only two things worth killing for: his trinkets and his blood. And he was sure they couldn't know about the bone trinket; he had kept it well hidden, even from Joachim.

But not my blood . . .

Other than Elpidia—ancestors take her—only Amerdan had any idea he was different, and even if the shopkeeper had been able to understand it was the blood that made him so, Caldan doubted he would have been able to organize this in such a short time. Maybe with Bells's help . . .

He couldn't figure it out. He remembered one of the masters at the monastery once saying *A secret known by two people is known by all,* and since more than a few knew Caldan was Touched, his captors could be anyone.

And it really didn't matter—he was strapped to this table, locked in this room, and whoever had done it meant him no good.

Caldan stretched his neck to peer out the window. He was a few stories above the ground. Outside, there was a drop to stained and cracked roof tiles covered with patches of weeds. At the edge of his hearing was the faint hum of a crowd, too muffled to make anything out, which meant too far for him to shout for help.

Then he saw the bloodstains on the floor around the table, smears and droplets spattered about—too many to count. He had no desire to add to their collection.

Ignoring his pounding head, he strained against his bonds, grunting with effort. Long moments passed as he exerted as much force as he could, to no avail. He stopped, breathing heavily, skin slick with sweat. It was no use; the leather straps were so tight they were almost cutting off his blood flow.

Gruff laughter barked from outside. A man spoke, words muffled by the door, then fading to silence.

Throwing his weight around, Caldan groaned with effort, wrenching himself from side to side. Underneath him, the table creaked and rattled. Yet none of the leather straps moved. There just wasn't enough leverage for him to loosen any of his bonds. Blinking perspiration from his eyes, he lay his head back on the hard surface and licked his lips, tasting the salty tang of his own sweat. He tried to clear his mind. He wasn't getting loose and escaping. He needed to come up with a plan.

The trouble was . . . nothing came to him, and he found himself wondering if this was the end.

Caldan looked at his hand to confirm his trinket ring had been removed. He hadn't been able to feel it but checked out of a vain hope. He wriggled his shoulders and couldn't feel the bone trinket under his shirt, either. Both had been taken.

He opened his well and sensed around his pockets, a futile search for his craftings. *No links.*

At least he could access his well. That was good, he told himself. They couldn't block his well like Annelie had, which meant they weren't able to use the sword, and all he had to do was get his hands on a crafting to make his escape. How he was supposed to do that, though, had him stumped.

Then he heard a sound. A scrape like wood dragging across the floor. Voices came from outside the door. There was another scrape, then a clunk. A bar being removed. Metal clanked on metal, and the lock clicked.

The door swung open, and a man entered. He was short and slim, with a neatly trimmed beard and a smirk. He was well dressed and carried a crafted crossbow, which he kept aimed at Caldan's stomach. He also had a square leather kit much like Elpidia's—so he must have been a physiker. Behind the man, the door closed, and he stood there.

Caldan glared at him, but the physiker remained unmoved. "Who are you?" Caldan said.

The physiker ran his eyes over Caldan's bonds, apparently looking for any sign he'd been able to loosen them. Satisfied Caldan wasn't going anywhere, he placed the crossbow on the floor near the door.

"Who I am is unimportant," the physiker said as he stepped close to Caldan, placing the leather kit on the floor next to the table. He opened it and began removing items, placing each on a cloth he also spread out. Some of them were awfully familiar to Caldan: empty glass vials and hollow steel needles, but there was also a large jug. And the vials were bigger than the ones Elpidia used.

The physiker wet a cloth with something—distilled alcohol, by the smell of it—and wiped the needle. *So he'll steal my blood, but still sterilizes his equipment.* That gave Caldan some hope he might be kept alive—for a little while, at least.

The man continued working. He turned to the jug and poured a colorless liquid into it. He added a sachet of white powder. Using a metal spoon, he stirred the mixture until the powder dissolved.

Before Caldan could react the physiker pinched his nose shut and poured the liquid into his open mouth. He coughed as much of the sweet liquid out as he could but couldn't help swallowing a few gulps.

The physiker stepped back. "That'll thin your blood and keep you alive for a while."

Shaking his head, as if to wake himself from a bad dream, Caldan closed his eyes. Elpidia was dead, and now Miranda would be left without anyone who knew her to look after her. With Annelie gone, who knew what would happen to her?

His heart clenched, and he gritted his teeth against the emotions surging inside him. A sound broke him out of his reverie. Humming. The physiker was humming to himself. Caldan opened his eyes just as a hollow needle jabbed into his arm. He writhed in an effort to dislodge it, but his arm barely moved.

The physiker looked on calmly as he struggled.

Eventually, Caldan ceased struggling, and the man gave a thin smile.

"Good," he murmured. "It's best if you don't resist." He inserted the end of the needle into an empty vial and watched as it slowly began to fill with blood. When it was almost full, he exchanged the vial for an empty one and repeated the procedure.

All the while, Caldan looked on, dismayed and sick to his stomach.

"Shhh, it'll be over soon," the man said, eyes on the vial as it filled.

"You're a physiker," said Caldan.

The man glanced at him then back to the vial. "Yes."

"You're supposed to help people, to heal them." Outrage twisted his words.

The physiker seemed to consider what he'd said, but then shrugged. "I do help people."

"Then help me," pleaded Caldan.

"Oh, I can't do that. A long time ago, I was given a chance to weigh the benefit of a few against the benefit of many. I chose the many."

"And the gold you get paid had nothing to do with it?"

"That the many can pay in hard ducats is only an additional benefit. You aren't in a position to understand why I do this. You couldn't possibly. But if our places were swapped, you'd feel the same way I do."

"You would willingly give up your blood? Not likely."

The man removed the second full vial and replaced it with a third. He said nothing.

"Get this needle out of my arm, and bring whoever's in charge."

"I'm afraid you wouldn't be able to convince them to let you go, but . . . they'll be here soon."

A fourth vial was filled and the physiker sealed them with stoppers. He wrapped a thin strip of cloth around Caldan's arm where the needle had entered his flesh.

"What are you going to do with me?"

"The vials are just the start. There are people waiting for blood, you know. Important people who don't like to be kept waiting."

The physiker packed up his equipment and picked up his kit and crossbow. At the door, he paused. "It'll be like this for a few days. Best you make peace with yourself. It'll make your time here easier to bear."

With that, he exited the room, locking and barring the door, leaving Caldan seething with a combination of fury and hopelessness.

CHAPTER 33

Caldan sensed someone outside the door almost immediately. His skin tingled with the hum of the craftings and trinkets they wore, and his hair stood on end. A sorcerer, surely a rogue. His escape looked less and less likely with every passing hour.

He'd been left to himself for some time. The four vials of blood the physiker had taken had left him light-headed, but he was aware enough to realize they wanted him alive. To milk like a cow.

His mouth was dry, and he had a powerful thirst. How much time had passed, he couldn't be sure, but shadows had begun to creep across the rooftops outside in a sign sunset was approaching. His skin around the puncture had begun to itch.

He tensed his muscles as he heard the bar clunk on the floor and a key enter the lock. The door swung open, and Caldan stared at Joachim in astonishment. He was dressed as usual in black trousers and shirt with silver buttons. Except, this time, he looked pained.

"I'm sorry it had to come to this," Joachim said, voice filled with regret. In one hand he held another jug.

Whether the warlock's remorse was feigned or not, Caldan didn't care. He bared his teeth, snarling. "Is this all I am to the emperor? Someone to be used and then discarded?"

Joachim smiled. "Well, yes, of course. He's the emperor. But he knows nothing about this. If one of you disappears every few years, no one will be the wiser. Even better if they never knew in the first place, which was why finding you was so special. Far less risk of being caught."

Caldan strained against his bonds again, aching to be free so he could wrap his hands around Joachim's throat. For a few moments, it was all he could think of, all he wanted. Eventually, he subsided, ashamed of his murderous thoughts.

"That's better," said Joachim. "Once you accept your fate, everything is easier."

"That's what the physiker said."

"A wise man."

"For a murderer."

Joachim shrugged. "He just wants to help the sick, the diseased."

"And you? What do you get out of it?"

"Besides the split of the profits? Trinkets. Do you have any idea how many I've been able to gather over the years? They're not cheap, let me tell you. They cost, Caldan. A great deal."

"Like your soul?"

"Believe of me what you want, Caldan. I don't care."

"Just like you didn't care when you ordered Master Annelie killed? She didn't deserve to die, and neither did the other Protectors."

"We'll have to disagree. Annelie was sniffing around. It turns out she's been onto us for quite some time. Of course she didn't know I was involved. That's why they were taking you to a safe place. As if any place would be safe from us."

Caldan shook his head. Blood loss and dehydration caused his thoughts to wander. He had to concentrate if he had any chance of leaving the room alive.

"No, I don't regret killing them. You, though . . . You're different from the other Touched we usually capture," Joachim said. "A sorcerer.

So rare . . . Prized by the emperor and his councillors. It seems such a waste, but now that we've started this process, there's no going back. You're too dangerous to drain in the usual way, otherwise we'd keep you for weeks, months even. But it's too risky. Someone might make a mistake, and you'd be able to escape. I'm sorry, I truly am, but you're not long for this world."

He didn't sound sorry to Caldan, more annoyed he wouldn't be able to keep him here and drain him like a waterskin. As scared as he'd been when he left the monastery, Caldan had never thought he'd end up strapped to a table being drained of blood.

The world is a strange place beyond those walls . . .

He licked his parched lips. His head felt heavy. "Perhaps . . ." he managed, surprised at the crack in his voice. "Perhaps I can be of more use to you."

Joachim raised his eyebrows. "It's too late for that. Once, in the beginning, when I first cast eyes on you, I thought it could be possible. But now . . . I know you're a liar."

Caldan blinked, thoughts muddled. He didn't feel guilty about lying to Joachim, but he wished he'd been more honest with Annelie. Now, though, it didn't matter.

"You had a number of interesting craftings on you. But that wasn't the only thing, was it?" Joachim leaned close to his face, and Caldan could feel the warmth of his breath. "Your trinket ring I'll be able to sell, though no one will be able to use it. I can't risk handing it back to the emperor, or there will be questions. And I like to avoid questions. But you also had the bone ring, didn't you? The one I specifically asked about and you denied."

Eyes closed in defeat, Caldan nodded. There was no point continuing his lie. Joachim had everything he valued and was about to take the most precious thing of all: his life.

The warlock reached behind the table and poured water from a flagon into Caldan's mouth.

Caldan gulped at the liquid, but all too soon it stopped. His tongue roamed greedily over his lips.

"I'm going to leave you here for a while," continued Joachim, replacing the flagon. "And I want you to think hard about whether you want to tell me the truth or not. The truth might extend your life for a time; lies might cut it short. Think about the bone ring. What do you know of it? Why would the emperor place such a high importance on finding it? Where did it come from? Answers to some of these questions you will know, and some you may not. But I need all the information I can get from you."

"And what do I get in return? Some extra hours before you kill me? I didn't tell you the truth because I didn't trust you. Seems I was right about that, wasn't I? So why don't you take your need for answers and go straight to hell. The ancestors there will give you what you deserve."

"So brave. So ready to die. But I'm sure you'll see reason. Yes, you'll beg for death—I promise you this is not going to be a pleasant time. And yet, sometimes time is all we have, and it can feel like the most precious thing in the world. . . . And sometimes it's not just your time to think about. What was her name? Miranda . . ."

Without another word, Joachim left the room.

ANASOMA BURNED IN Caldan's dream. Sorcerous blue flames swept down from the walls and incinerated buildings in a heartbeat. Men, women, and children fled screaming in terror, only to be consumed as an immense heat washed over them, crisping their skin to black.

Atop a spire in the city, an unearthly monster anchored itself with clawed feet, wings flapping in the updraft caused by the conflagration. It looked pleased, as if the destruction were its own doing.

What was it? Why did it desire such chaos and devastation?

In the harbor, scores of Indryallan ships, crowded to the rails with soldiers, looked on as the city was cleansed of the taint of the Mahruse Empire.

Cleansed? Why did he think that?

The beast leaped into the air and rode the updraft into the smoke-filled sky. Cheers rose from the Indryallans . . .

Caldan jerked awake, head lolling to the side, heart hammering in his chest. He'd been delirium dreaming. He dismissed his visions as fever wrought, though they cut like a knife.

Tired. He was so tired. He felt older, somehow, as if the last few hours had leached his very life force from his soul.

His breathing was rapid, and when he tried to slow it down, he found he couldn't.

By the ancestors, he needed water, or he wouldn't last much longer. That was clearly Joachim's plan. No need to get your hands dirty when dehydration and blood loss could do it for you. But he wondered if his time was rapidly coming up.

The room was dark. Night had fallen, and they'd not left a lamp for him. It didn't matter. Moonlight spilled across the floor from the window. A cleansing light.

Forgive me, Miranda . . .

Caldan closed his eyes. Just for a moment, he promised himself.

There was a scrape of leather on wood. Someone hissed from his left.

"I smell . . . blood," a voice whispered.

Caldan tried to open his eyes, but his lids were stuck tight. "Help me . . ." he croaked.

Someone moved around him to the door. The wind of the person's passing trailed over him.

"Please . . . water."

For long moments, no one moved. All Caldan could hear was a faint background clamor from outside.

The person moved again; whoever it was stood beside him. Water splashed across his face, shocking him. Hastily, he stuck out his tongue, searching for the precious fluid. A thin stream poured into his mouth, and he gulped. Too soon, it stopped. More splashed into his eyes, and he blinked them open.

Caldan experienced a dumbfounded moment.

"Well, well. Isn't this interesting?" said Amerdan.

Caldan stared at the shopkeeper in astonishment. His thoughts were sluggish, and he couldn't fathom why the man was here. But here he was—the man who'd killed Elpidia. Caldan's eyes flicked to Amerdan's knives. Fear and anger took hold of him, and he wanted to lash out at Amerdan, but couldn't. Both because he was restrained and because Amerdan was his only chance to escape.

"Amerdan, thank the ancestors. Free me. There's probably men outside the door, so keep quiet."

Amerdan gazed at him, moving his head back and forth, searching for . . . what? What did he want? There was a troubled look to him. Caldan remembered the first time he'd met him, the reddish glow to his skin, the stench of rotting meat—and he thought he sensed those things again. Just like before, they were gone before he could really latch on to them.

"Why are you tied up?" Amerdan asked tonelessly.

"I . . . I don't know," Caldan stammered. Though he believed Amerdan to be Touched as well, he couldn't tell him the truth. Not to Elpidia's killer. "I think they want my trinkets. Please . . . you must help me."

"Must I?"

"Yes. We . . . we're the same, you and I. You know it's true."

Amerdan shrugged almost imperceptibly, as if to say *So?* When he finally spoke, he asked, "But *why?* Why do this to *you?*"

"Like I said, my trinkets—"

"But why keep you alive? They could have just killed you and taken them from your body. No, they clearly want your blood. Who is doing this?"

Caldan didn't think he had the strength to sustain his own lies, and so he decided to tell the truth and worry about the consequences later . . . if there was a later. "Joachim," he said.

"Joachim? Who's he?"

"A warlock. Beholden only to the emperor. He killed Protectors, including a master. And he's asked about you. Because of our blood."

Again, Amerdan shrugged, unconcerned.

Caldan glanced at the door. Though they were conversing in whispers, someone could walk in at any moment. His guts twisted at the thought of the warlock finding Amerdan in the room. He hated the prospect, but the shopkeeper was his only hope of escape. And despite his apparent talents—based on what he'd seen, and on the fact that the man had somehow found him *and* slipped into this place undetected—Caldan was sure Amerdan would be no match for Joachim's sorcery. Amerdan would be dead. Killed outright or captured and drained like Caldan. A deserved end for the man, but it wouldn't do Caldan any good for that to happen.

Not yet, anyway.

"You have to free me; there isn't much time."

"There are happenings here I don't understand. Help me understand."

"Joachim could return at any moment." He had to make Amerdan see the danger. "He's a sorcerer. One with a great deal of knowledge and power. He has the use of many craftings and trinkets."

Amerdan's eyes narrowed, and he sniffed. "A powerful sorcerer." He looked thoughtfully at the leather straps restraining Caldan. His hand moved to one of his knives.

"Yes," whispered Caldan fiercely. "That's it. Cut the straps."

Amerdan's other hand reached into his shirt and clutched an object around his neck. He frowned at Caldan, lips moving, as if talking to himself.

"Now?" the shopkeeper whispered, so softly Caldan barely heard the words. "No. It's not the right time. Later, then? What about her?"

Caldan grew increasingly concerned at Amerdan's behavior. Why was the shopkeeper hesitating? He pushed down the fear that rose inside him. Here was an unexpected chance, and it could be wasted if Amerdan took much longer. He glanced nervously at the door once more.

Before he could speak, Amerdan appeared to come to a decision and sawed through the thick leather bonds.

Unable to control himself, Caldan cried out in agony as a sudden surge of blood pumped into his wrists, chest, and feet.

Voices rose outside the door in response to his howl.

"This might get messy," said Amerdan.

Caldan massaged his wrists in an effort to get his circulation going.

"They might not check. They're sure I can't escape." By the ancestors, he felt weak, but he'd do his best to get away. He staggered a few steps away from the table on numb feet, barely able to stand.

There was a clunk as the bar on the door was removed.

Caldan frowned. Then how had Amerdan gotten into the room in the first place? It was then he noticed the window was wide open. Somehow Amerdan had scaled the side of the building.

Amerdan moved to the hinged side of the door. He'd be hidden when it opened. He drew out a pair of knives.

A key scraped into the lock, and it clicked.

Light spilled into the room as the door opened, illuminating the empty table with cut leather straps and scarlet smeared on the floor next to the jug.

A long shadow appeared in the light of the floor. "What the—?"

Amerdan stepped in front of the opening and made a precise thrust. Blood spurted from the physiker's neck, and horrified shock appeared on his face. Amerdan ripped his knife out and thrust again, grabbing him by the hair with his other hand. He wrenched the physiker into the room. The man went limp, collapsing on the floor. His hands clutched at his neck, fingers covered in red. A choking sound bubbled from his lips.

Amerdan rushed through the door and Caldan followed as best as he could. He was amazed at how quickly his strength was returning.

I can see why my blood is so valuable, he thought. *Thank the ancestors they left some in me.*

Two men sat in chairs around a table, cards clutched in their hands, mouths open in surprise.

Amerdan leaped toward them as the cards began falling and they reached for their swords.

Too late.

Snarling with ferocity, Amerdan bowled into one of the men, sending the table crashing. He slammed a blade into the man's chest.

Caldan staggered back a few steps. He moved forward to help, but a wave of weakness overcame him, and he fell to his knees.

Guess I'm not as strong as I thought.

A shout came from in front of him. Caldan raised his arm only to see Amerdan step away from the second man, who collapsed back into his chair. There was a deep gash in his neck, and he coughed, choking on his own blood.

Amerdan was grinning and began searching the men.

Caldan looked around the room and back to the physiker. Of a sudden, he started shaking. He felt sick. Gorge rose into his throat, and he swallowed it down.

A sideboard contained half a loaf of bread and some cheese, along with jugs of ale and water. He rinsed his mouth with water, spitting out the taste of bile, then drank his fill. It wasn't easy. His hands were trembling, and he felt faint. Once he'd slaked his thirst, his stomach rumbled at the smell of bread, and he tore off a chunk, wolfing it down along with a few bites of cheese. He was ravenous, and his stomach gnawed at him from inside, but it would have to do for now. There was no more time to waste.

He could only hope it would see him through the escape.

Stairs led down to the next floor, but he couldn't leave yet.

"Wait," he said to Amerdan.

He checked the two men in case they had his craftings and trinkets but came up empty. A search of the physiker yielded the same results, except the man still had two of the vials of Caldan's blood on him. Where were the other two?

Caldan staggered to the window and dropped the vials. They shattered onto roof tiles below.

Amerdan waited patiently for him, seemingly unperturbed by the scene—or killing three men.

A thought occurred to Caldan. "How did you know I was here?"

The shopkeeper shrugged. "I saw you in the wagon with the Protectors and the other men killing them. Followed them here and waited, watching."

But why? Had Amerdan been looking for Caldan? He knew the shopkeeper was in league with Bells—had he come to kill him but now changed his mind? Again, he had to ask: Why? Amerdan was dangerous, and he dared not trust him anymore. Caldan seethed inside and his head spun. Amerdan had killed Elpidia! A blind man could attribute her death to him. And he'd sided with Bells; he had to have been the one to free her.

Caldan was torn between gratitude for his rescue and a desire for vengeance for Elpidia's murder. He struggled to control himself, hands shaking, and mustered some strength.

The questions could wait. With a glance around the room for any sign of his craftings or trinkets, again unsuccessful, Caldan wiped his hands on his pants and took a breath to calm himself.

"That's two people you've saved me from," he said to Amerdan. "I hope there's not a third."

Amerdan gave him a puzzled look.

"The Bleeder, now Joachim. That's two. I'm in your debt. And I hope there isn't a third time."

"Three. Yes. It's almost there," replied Amerdan cryptically.

"We have to get out of here, but first I have to find my trinkets. They're all I have from my family."

A look of anguish flashed across Amerdan's face, so fleeting Caldan almost thought he'd imagined it.

"Family is important," said Amerdan. "I'm guessing you'd like to find this sorcerer . . . Joachim?"

Caldan swallowed. Yes. He wanted to find Joachim and . . . what? Make him regret his actions? Cause him pain? Yes, he wanted to cut the bastard's head off. He wanted his trinkets back, and to make sure Miranda was safe. Then he could alert the Protectors to what had happened and hope they believed him. Of course, all of that was getting ahead of himself. Joachim was incredibly powerful and—more than likely—had his trinkets.

Which he'd need if he wanted to defeat Joachim.

Ancestors . . .

"For now, let's head downstairs," he said to Amerdan, "and see if he's left my trinkets anywhere."

Next to the stairs down, leaning against the wall, were two bows along with quivers filled with arrows. Taking one of the arrows, Caldan examined the head and shaft. They were just as he'd thought:

crafted. And well done, too. He'd have to study them later to see what he could learn from the runes. In the meantime, he figured he might as well take them. He wasn't really much of an archer, but they'd serve as evidence if the Protectors didn't believe him about Joachim.

Caldan replaced the arrow and slung both quivers over his shoulder by their straps. He grabbed a bow and slung it over his shoulder, too. Returning to the dead men, he took a sword from one of them.

"Let's get out of here," he said to Amerdan, who nodded.

They each took one of the lamps and, as stealthily as they could, descended the wooden stairs, taking care to walk on the edge of the steps to minimize any creaking.

The stairs turned back on themselves, and where Caldan expected the next floor to be, there was no landing; they just continued spiraling down. Whatever this place was, his captors had found an out-of-the-way location to avoid notice. Any noise from the room above was less likely to alert those living close by that something was amiss. With luck, their fight would have gone undetected.

They continued down, and when the stairs eventually stopped at a sturdy door, Caldan judged they'd descended to the ground floor. In this door, a key stood out from the lock. Caldan made sure it was unlocked, then took the key out and peered through the keyhole.

Beyond the door was a wide hallway lit by two sorcerous globes hanging from the ceiling, an extravagance that likely meant this place was probably his captors' headquarters and living area, not just a seldom-used hideout.

There were three doors on the right-hand side, and at the far end was a larger door, secured with two of the biggest locks Caldan had ever seen. That had to be the way out into the street.

Caldan turned to Amerdan. "So you watched the building for a while after you saw me being taken?"

"Yes."

"Did you see Joachim? Pale skin, close-cropped brown hair, black clothes?"

"Ah, yes. He was one of the seven men who ambushed the wagon. They drove it into the yard and dragged the bodies inside. A while later, four of the men left, and the first man I killed upstairs arrived."

Caldan hissed softly. "So apart from the three men upstairs, only Joachim might still be here?"

"It's . . . highly likely. I didn't see him leave."

Which meant he could be behind any of the three doors. What should he do? Escape was so close, and yet he had to try to retrieve his trinkets and craftings. If he left to alert the Protectors and came back, Joachim could have discovered he'd escaped and be long gone. And then Caldan would be forever looking over his shoulder, since there was no doubt the warlock would hunt him down and kill him—he had enough of his blood to make as many compasses as he needed. Caldan would be a loose end that needed to be silenced.

So he had to kill the warlock before Joachim could kill him. He wasn't sure he *could* do it, but it was the only option left to him.

"We have to find him, Amerdan. If we can surprise him . . . maybe . . ."

"I'll help you, for . . . my own reasons. I've survived this far. I can look after myself."

Together, they might stand a chance. A slim one, but it was better than nothing. Caldan explained his scheme. "I'll be able to disrupt the crafted arrows once I'm linked to them. The timing will be tricky, but if Joachim is distracted enough, I'll be able to surprise him. We probably can't get through his shield, but we can try to knock him down and gain an advantage. If we can get Joachim on the floor, and I disrupt his shield and concentration, then we might have a chance. Wait here."

Caldan blew out the two lamps, leaving them in darkness. He opened the door a finger's width, peering through the gap to make sure the hallway beyond was still clear. Taking a few of the crafted arrows, he crouched low and sidled his way along the wall to the first door. Once there, he accessed his well and linked to an arrow. He could feel the crafting vibrate in his hand and hoped Joachim couldn't sense what little he was feeding through his string. Carefully, he placed it beside the door.

Creeping as quietly as he could, he repeated the process for the two other doors, splitting his well into three strings. At the third door, he paused, about to do the same for the entrance, but an idea stopped him.

Stealthily moving back to Amerdan, he shut the door to the hallway and wiped sweat from his forehead. There wasn't much—he was still dehydrated—but it was good to find he was actually sweating. His strings felt stretched, especially the one connecting to the farthest arrow, but the strain was manageable, and he felt he could hold them stable for some time.

"Why did you do that?" asked Amerdan.

Caldan removed another arrow from the quiver and took up the bow. "We don't know which door Joachim is behind, and this way I can cover all three."

"So now we find him, and you shoot him with an arrow? I thought you had another plan?"

"I do. We need to lure him out. Make him think this place is under attack."

"Sounds simple, and simple is usually the best."

Again, Caldan looked through the keyhole and checked that the hallway was clear. Satisfied, he opened the door, nocked the arrow, and drew the bow. Splitting his well into a fourth string, he linked to the arrow and released it.

With a hum and a loud thunk, the arrow hit the entry door just off center. Good enough.

Quickly, he ducked back behind the door and closed it, peering through the keyhole.

Holding his breath, he waited. For long moments, there was no movement. Perhaps Joachim hadn't heard the arrow striking the door. Or maybe he'd left. He could even be asleep, for all they knew.

Caldan calmed himself and took a few deep breaths. He was about to give up and open the door when movement from the middle door caught his eye. It opened, and Joachim stuck his head out. The warlock looked toward their door, frowned when he saw it was closed, then glanced at the entrance door.

Immediately, Caldan pushed as much as he could through the

string from his well and ruptured the anchor. A thunderous roar sounded as the forces from his well destroyed the arrow utterly, taking the door apart along with it. Filaments of lightning arced out as chunks of wood and splinters peppered the hallway. Smoke billowed toward them.

Joachim cursed loudly and ducked back inside. But he was only gone momentarily. Caldan picked up the scent of lemons and sensed Joachim access his well. The warlock reappeared.

This time, he was shielded.

Joachim didn't hesitate. He stood in the middle of the hallway, arms outstretched, ready to do battle with whoever was invading his territory.

Caldan's eyes widened in awe as Joachim drew from his well. Vibrations at the edge of his awareness from craftings and trinkets multiplied tenfold. The warlock's shield turned a dark blue, almost black, and his figure blurred further as the shield became almost too thick to see through.

Hairs rose on Caldan's arms. Once more, his skin felt hot, and his blood boiled in his veins. They were going to die, he could feel it in his bones. But he had to try, for himself, for Miranda, for Annelie and the Protectors.

And he still needed to make Amerdan pay.

Caldan gathered what little strength he had left. He tugged the door open, and side by side, he and Amerdan sprinted toward Joachim.

Caldan drew his sword as Amerdan pulled ahead. Joachim still had his back to them. If he only remained unaware for a moment longer . . .

Their footsteps must have alerted the warlock, as he half jumped and pivoted, turning toward them. A smile lit his face as he recognized Caldan and saw that they were both unshielded.

An instant before Amerdan charged into Joachim, Amerdan was enveloped in a surge of energy as the blue haze of a shield covered him. Violet sparks sprayed as Amerdan slammed into Joachim, sending him flying. The warlock hit the floor, crying out in pain, and rolled toward the next doorway. He was covered in violet motes of strain, but his shield held. He scrambled to one knee, shaking his head—a few yards in front of the third arrow Caldan had placed.

Caldan ruptured the anchor.

Joachim took the full force of the blast from behind and was propelled through the air toward them. He gave a wordless cry of agony, which turned to anger. Scarcely able to believe it, Caldan watched as Joachim's shield, now entirely violet with the strain, quickly faded to the usual blue.

The warlock got to his feet and shot Amerdan and Caldan a look of pure fury. Caldan automatically reached for a shield crafting, but there was nothing . . .

Instead, he broke into a sprint—unnaturally fast. Shock suffused Joachim's face. Caldan came on, aiming his sword for Joachim's chest, and braced himself for the inevitable pain.

At the same time, Amerdan struck Joachim's shield with a fistful of arrows. Sparks flew. The shield turned violet again, then vanished.

Joachim looked on in horror as Caldan's sword entered his chest, stabbing him through the heart. The warlock staggered. His hands clutched at the blade, heedless of the edge cutting his palms.

Calm settled over the hallway as the almost unbearable vibrations ceased. Joachim toppled to the floor, and Caldan let go of the sword. Crimson leaked from the wound, and Joachim opened his mouth, as if to speak . . . then was still, eyes staring at them, unseeing.

"That was easier than I thought," said Amerdan. "Sorcerers aren't so hard to kill, after all."

Caldan's strength left in a rush and he slumped to the floor, shivering. He clenched his teeth in pain as his legs cramped up. Amerdan stood by, silent, as Caldan massaged his spasming muscles.

When the pain subsided somewhat, Caldan turned his gaze from the dead warlock and took in Amerdan's shielded form. Realizing his mouth was open, he shut it. What Amerdan had just done was . . . impossible. "Are you . . . a sorcerer? No, you must have a trinket. You didn't have a well before, so . . ."

Amerdan regarded him for a moment, then blinked. "I found out late, and I've only just received some instruction."

Bells, thought Caldan. Of course, she was teaching Amerdan, though that didn't explain how he now had a well. She must have promised Amerdan training in exchange for setting her free. But had she been able to give him a well? Was that possible?

Extending his senses, Caldan brushed against the telltale feeling of a well. Either he'd missed it, or something else had happened to Amerdan. The more he knew about the shopkeeper, the greater an enigma the man was. Unfortunately, he didn't have time to explore further. "Let's just hope Joachim was the only warlock involved in this. If he has partners in their ranks, we could be in serious trouble."

With a shrug, Amerdan bent over Joachim, searching his pockets. "That's for another day. Now, shall we look for your craftings?"

THE DOWNSTAIRS ROOMS were well-appointed and lavish, and contained more wealth than Caldan had seen in his lifetime. Expensive rugs covered the floors, while the walls were coated in paintings and tapestries. The furniture was the best he'd ever seen—master-crafted beds and lounges, chairs and desks. In each room they found a veritable treasure trove of ducats and gems, along with jewelry and, wonder of wonders, atop a veneered desk, a flat wooden box containing a few trinkets. To Caldan's relief, the box held both his silver and bone ring trinkets.

He slipped the metal ring onto his finger and concealed the bone trinket beneath his shirt. Bells's craftings were also on the desk, and he pocketed them.

Amerdan came into the room behind him, carrying a chest full of gold ducats.

"Take some," Amerdan said. "You've earned it. Take whatever craftings and trinkets you want. The Protectors won't know if anything's missing." He gave Caldan a thin smile and began rummaging through a chest of drawers.

The thought of taking more didn't sit well with Caldan. Most of the coins must have been earned by selling the blood of the Touched, which meant people had died to make Joachim and his cronies wealthy. Likely, the trinkets had been bought with blood money.

But maybe some good could come from what had happened to the Touched. He could sell them and give the ducats to the poor out of respect for Elpidia.

It was only then he realized there was no sign of the trinket sword he'd carried from Anasoma. He frantically ran from room to room looking for it. Nothing.

With rising panic, he rummaged through the paperwork on Joachim's desk, searching for a clue as to the trinket's whereabouts. Luckily, the warlock kept meticulous records, and Caldan found entries in a logbook detailing buildings and businesses purchased all through Riversedge. Joachim mightn't have trusted his men around such a valuable trinket and must have stored it in a safe place.

Or so Caldan hoped. He gathered what he could. But there were questions he needed to ask Amerdan, and he couldn't hold back any longer.

"What happened back at the campsite outside the city? Elpidia was knocked out, and when she regained consciousness, Bells had vanished, and we never saw you again until now. Did you see who freed her, then decide to follow her into the city?"

Amerdan cocked his head, and for a moment didn't speak. "No," he said eventually. "I didn't see who freed her. When I returned, she was gone. I checked Elpidia, and she was fine, and I just . . . wanted to leave everything behind. I was selfish."

A lame explanation. Caldan caught Amerdan's eye, wanting to push the man further, but a threatening gleam stopped him.

He's dangerous, Caldan intuited. *If I push him now, who knows what he'll do.*

The evidence of Amerdan's guilt only grew stronger, but at the moment Caldan had to push aside thoughts of vengeance for expediency. Perhaps he could get Amerdan to accompany him to the Protectors, then unmask him in their presence.

"Come on," he said. "The Protectors need to know about this place. And I want to tell them what happened to Annelie, and the other two as well."

Amerdan stopped what he was doing and stepped close to Caldan. "Fine—go tell them."

"You're not coming with me?"

"No. They can't know I'm a sorcerer. Even if they remain unaware of that fact, if you tell them I was involved and saw forbidden sorcery, they might decide to silence me."

"They wouldn't—"

"They've probably done so in the past, and they wouldn't stop this time. I'm not of the guild, which would make me a rogue. You know what they do to rogues. I'd be forced . . . to take steps at that point."

Caldan couldn't deny the logic of Amerdan's words—or the threat. He hated the idea of lying to the Protectors—*more than I already have,* he thought—but he knew if he protested too much, Amerdan would become suspicious. Eventually, he nodded in assent.

Amerdan looked around at the wealth on display and shrugged. "I'll take some ducats. There are . . . others I need to take care of. But I'll find you again soon. It would be . . . unfortunate if we didn't meet again. I sense a great talent in you."

With those final words, Amerdan left him standing there among the ducats, gems, craftings, and trinkets.

"Wait—" Caldan said, but the shopkeeper ignored him and headed toward the entry doorway. Caldan hurried to catch up.

Outside was a courtyard with iron gates leading onto a street. Between the bars of the gates, people milled around, and one man pointed at Caldan when he emerged. The commotion of their fight must have startled many of the neighbors out of sleep and into the streets to see what the disturbance was.

Amerdan unlatched the gate and pushed his way past them, not responding to any of their questions, and disappeared into the night.

"I'm going to have to stop thinking of him as a shopkeeper," Caldan muttered. He couldn't chase after Amerdan and leave the place open and unattended. By the time he alerted the Protectors, it was likely everything would be looted.

"You," he said, pointing to a teenage boy. Of all the people crowding around, he looked like he'd be the fastest. Caldan handed him a gold ducat, and the boy's eyes widened with shock.

"Run as fast as you can to the Protectors," Caldan commanded.

"Ask for Master Mold. Have them wake him up, if necessary. Tell him Caldan needs him and at least four journeymen, and bring them back here. Tell Master Mold it's about Annelie and . . . the sword. Can you remember that?"

Eyes still on the ducat, the boy nodded.

"Good. If you do this, there will be *another* coin just like this when you get back." *That should ensure he actually does what's asked.* Caldan had him repeat back what he'd said, then, satisfied the boy remembered, sent him on his way.

He turned to the crowd, which had almost doubled in the short space of time he'd been instructing the boy on his message.

"Listen up!" he shouted. "No one is to enter this yard or the building. The Protectors will be here soon, and anyone caught disobeying these orders will be punished."

"Was it the invaders?" shouted a woman from the back of the crowd.

Murmurings rose in response to her question.

"It had to be!" yelled someone.

"They're here!"

"Who are you, anyway? Maybe you're one of them!"

Loud murmurs of agreement followed the last statement, and the crowd took a few steps toward him.

A multicolored haze surrounded Caldan as he accessed his well and linked to Bells's shield crafting. Gasps arose from the crowd, and they backed away, faces filled with fear. Setting his shield stopped their questions.

Caldan paused as he took in their terrified expressions. Using sorcery to intimidate those who didn't understand it . . . they trembled before him, and it felt good. He thought back to Joachim, lying lifeless in a pool of blood. A fitting death for someone such as him.

But he wasn't like Joachim. At times like this, you have to make hard choices, do harsh things; and it's not like he'd need to use his power to intimidate others when all this was over . . .

CHAPTER 34

A gently arching curve of smooth black stone, the bridge stretched over the river. Wide enough for two wagons to pass without touching, it was anchored on each bank to immense blocks of the same stone that penetrated deep into the ground. Aidan had seen a few such bridges, which had survived the Shattering, but never one so impressive. Like almost every other major city, Riversedge was built atop the ruins of a city from before the Shattering. Much of the stone that made up its foundations dated back thousands of years. Deep carved runes covered two pillars at each end of the bridge. Legend had it that only humans and animals could cross, that it was barred to any nonhuman races from the Shattering, like the jukari and vormag.

Well beyond the bridge, a hazy brown pall covered part of the horizon. Riversedge.

Aidan wiped his fevered brow and coughed. It looked like they'd finally find out if the legends were true.

From the village on the other side of the bridge, smoke trailed lazily into the still afternoon air. He shaded his eyes from the sun and could make out people talking in the streets, children playing and laughing. Aidan and his companions had left the shelter of the forest hours ago, making their way across grasslands, which had turned to fields. Farmsteads now dotted the horizon to both sides, but the men feared to stop and warn their occupants. Any delay could mean catastrophe for Riversedge—Aidan didn't really believe there was any power inherent in the bridge to stop the jukari. The legends were just that, legends.

They'd be able to alert the village ahead of them, though, and with any luck the villagers would see sense and wouldn't be reluctant to leave their homes. If they delayed and tried to take all their belongings with them, it could mean their death. But persuading the villagers a horde of creatures created before the Shattering was fast approaching would be a hard task.

"Let's go," Aidan said, and they pushed their exhausted horses toward the bridge.

On the other side, a few curious inhabitants stared at their filthy, bedraggled appearance, while others turned their gaze away, as if trying to avoid being noticed.

Aidan accosted one of the men staring at him, a scraggly-bearded old-timer with a broken-veined nose and cheeks.

"Who's in charge of the village?" he asked. "Is there a mayor or a circle of elders?"

"Mayor," the man replied, scratching at his beard. "Runs the inn, he does."

Aidan looked around until he spotted the town's only inn, a freshly painted three-story building just down the main road.

"You'd better get out of here," he told the broken-veined man. "There's a horde of jukari coming, and they don't take prisoners. Tell everyone. Round up the children, and head to Riversedge as fast as you can."

The man spat into the dirt. "You don't scare me. I don't know your game, but it ain't working. Get out of here."

Aidan scowled. He knew most of the villagers would react the same way. But he had to convince them. And that meant convincing the mayor, whom the villagers would listen to.

Let's hope he has a level head.

Aidan motioned for Chalayan, cel Rau, and Vasile, whose pain was still blunted by the drug Aidan had given him, to follow, and they entered the inn.

It was well maintained, with sturdy benches and tables, presumably to prevent them tipping over or being used as weapons when things got rowdy. Only a few customers were present, and Aidan scanned them out of habit for signs of trouble. There was a pair of what looked like caravan guards carrying a sprinkling of other weapons along with their swords, an old man so far into his cups he was talking to himself, and a middle-aged woman in heavy makeup who lounged in one dark corner. Behind the bar, a serious-looking man in his thirties looked up as they entered, then began to pour four mugs of ale.

"On the house," he said as they approached.

Aidan shook his head. "We don't have time to drink. Where's the mayor?"

"You're talking to him. And what's the hurry?"

Aidan looked him up and down. "You're younger than I expected."

"Old doesn't necessarily mean wise."

"True."

The man held out his hand. "I'm Reidun, mayor of Sour. And before you ask, somebody probably thought it was funny at the time."

Aidan clasped the proffered hand. "Fair enough. I'll get to the point. There's a horde of jukari heading in this direction. If you don't evacuate the village, everyone will die."

Reidun blinked. "You're joking. Aren't you?"

"No. Our injuries came from fighting our way clear of them. They're aimed at Riversedge, so once you get there, you'll have to warn the Quivers and Protectors."

A hazy blue shield surrounded Chalayan, and Reidun gasped.

"We only just survived," Aidan said. "And as you can see, we're much harder to kill than the average person."

"By the ancestors," breathed Reidun. "You're serious."

"Deadly. We'll help round everyone up. There will be homes and farms around here, but we won't be able to warn everyone. Time is wasting. Grab what you can, but make it quick."

Reidun swallowed. "There's a hostler's just outside town. Traders and merchants like to stop here. Tell them Reidun sent you. The owner is smart and dependable. We'll need their horses and wagons for the villagers. I'll go out and round up a few steady people to spread the word. There'll be those who won't believe even me, though. They'll want to stay."

Aidan nodded. "Do what you can. Whoever stays behind . . . grieve for them later, once everyone else is safe."

Reidun hurried outside, leaving them alone with the inn's customers.

"Listen up!" shouted Aidan, and heads turned toward him. "This place will be overrun by a jukari horde. If you stay, you'll die. Get your things and help the other villagers."

"Piss off," muttered the old man.

Aidan strode over and knocked the cup of wine from his hands, then grabbed him by the shirt and hauled him across the room and out the front door. As the old man lay sputtering in the dust of the street, Aidan went back inside. The two guards were on their feet, while the woman was having a laughing fit.

"I don't have time for this, and neither do you. Get out, or die."

A short time later, the village was in an uproar, but it wasn't the chaos of frantically packing belongings and leaving as fast as possible. Some were doing just that, but most of the people Aidan and his men warned sneered at their claims, some with open hostility. Cel Rau had to draw on a few young men who wanted to beat them, fearing they were hustlers of some kind, and they backed away only when he bloodied one across the arm.

Reidun was doing his best, atop a wagon in the middle of the street, shouting over the confused clamor, but he was quickly going hoarse. The only good thing about the commotion was that it was drawing villagers from all corners of the town. Mothers with fearful expressions held children close. Somewhere in the crowd, a child began to cry, spurring a few more to join in. All the men carried makeshift weapons, such as pitchforks, long knives, and even the occasional rusty sword dragged from the bottom of a wardrobe. Though they tried to hide it, they looked almost as fearful as the children.

"This isn't going to be easy," said Chalayan.

Someone clutched Aidan's arm from behind. He turned to find a woman trying to shove a blanket-wrapped baby into his arms.

"Take her! You must save her!" the woman screamed hysterically.

"By the ancestors!" cursed Aidan. "I can't, woman!" He raised his hands above his head.

She thrust the baby into his chest. "Her name's Izobelle. Please. Take her with you to Riversedge."

"Take her yourself! That's what we're saying—leave now!"

The woman didn't seem to grasp what he wanted of her, though. She started to weep and hugged Izobelle to her bosom.

An old man with a rusty sword came over and consoled her. "It's all right, Haylie. Leave these men be. Come with me; there's room in my wagon." He placed an arm around Haylie's shoulders and they moved off.

Aidan mounted his horse. "Come on. We need to round up the stragglers and get them here. As many as you can."

Cel Rau, Chalayan, and Vasile trotted off in different directions.

From his higher vantage, Aidan looked behind him, squinting, searching for signs the jukari were still following; hoping, without really hoping, that he'd find nothing.

A speck of movement caught his eye: a figure, tiny at this distance. Then another. Then more, accumulating, until the green fields turned black. They were moving fast. Far swifter than they had any right to. A cloud of dust rose into the air behind them. He cursed. Vormag sorcery, it had to be. At this rate, the entire village would be slaughtered. They needed more time to get away.

"Cel Rau! Chalayan!" roared Aidan.

Ahead of him, they pulled their mounts to a stop and looked back. Chalayan cursed in his own tongue, and cel Rau spat into the dirt. Vasile stared openmouthed at the impossible-seeming numbers.

People followed Aidan's gaze and saw the jukari horde for the first time. Screams sounded around them, and the crowd erupted into milling confusion. A baby's wail rose over the din. A young woman fell and was ignored, others trampling her in their haste to get away.

Aidan moved his mount closer to Chalayan and cel Rau as Vasile trotted up. "Hurry! Round up as many people as you can. Leave the rest. Tell them to forget about carrying much. If they try to take all their belongings, they'll be too slow. Find me again, then start for Riversedge. If any complain, point out the approaching jukari horde to them. Go now!"

All three raced away, dust trailing behind them.

BY THE TIME he reached the high point of the bridge, midway between the pillars, the village was in total chaos. Aidan saw people already leaving, some on horses and some on foot. Wagons were being loaded and teams hitched. Good. A few lone horsemen were racing toward Riversedge, looking after their own skins.

Maybe they'll remember to warn the city. Aidan didn't put much stock in that hope.

He stopped and dismounted, looping his reins over the saddle horn. With a hard smack on the beast's rump, he sent it toward the village. Someone could use it.

He'd led the jukari to the village, and he'd be damned if he'd let them just roll over it, snatching up those too weak or too slow to escape their clutches. Chalayan knew what to do, and so did cel Rau. But would cel Rau hold his loathing of destructive sorcery in check and allow Chalayan full rein? They had a certain license from the emperor, but each of them had his own reasons for joining Caitlyn, and Aidan knew from what she'd told him cel Rau's was the darkest.

The jukari were no doubt trampling the lush grass with their misbegotten feet and defiling it with their waste. By the ancestors, there were so many . . .

As the horde approached, he pushed all other thoughts to the side. There wasn't time to wonder about such things. In fact, there wasn't much time left at all. Aidan cast a look over his shoulder. Chalayan and cel Rau were cantering toward him. Their horses wouldn't stand for being pushed much more, but Riversedge was close, and all they had to do was delay the jukari on the bridge to allow the villagers to escape. Easy.

Sun burned the back of his neck as he waited for them.

Chalayan and cel Rau dismounted before him.

Chalayan produced a number of his hastily crafted stones and moved to the side of the bridge, where he began placing them along the edge.

"Those are shield craftings," the sorcerer said. "It won't be like the fight the other day, as I'll be too far away to see what's happening. I . . . don't know how we're going to coordinate this."

Aidan took them from Chalayan and tossed the craftings along the bridge toward the jukari, where they rolled, then tumbled to a stop. "We can't. Just do what you can, and when you see I'm about to be overwhelmed . . . Well, you know what to do."

Chalayan and cel Rau exchanged grim looks.

Aidan ignored them and drained the last drops from his green vial. If the opening had been wider, he'd have licked the inside clean. Oh well, probably for the best. He needed to keep his thoughts clear.

As Chalayan crossed to the other side and placed more craftings, Aidan unbuckled his sword belt and, fumbling with his one good hand, drew his blade and tossed the belt aside. It would only get in the way, and with one arm out of action, the fewer distractions the better.

"That's them all," said Chalayan. "A few nasty surprises for our jukari friends. With any luck, some vormag will go down as well. Don't stand between the craftings; stay back toward the village. I'll do my best from the other side, but with my threads stretched thin and being so far away—"

"Just do what I told you. We can't stop the jukari, only delay them, give them pause."

"Are you sure—?"

"Yes. There's no other way." He needed to do this, if not to save the villagers, then perhaps to justify killing Caitlyn. *This is what we were meant to do, Cait. Remember?*

Chalayan kept his eyes on the bridge, not meeting his eye. "Good luck, then."

The sorcerer turned and mounted his horse, heading back to the village at a trot.

"He's never forgiven you for Caitlyn," said cel Rau.

Funny that. Aidan watched Chalayan's departing back. "I know. And this new sorcery he's learned . . . Now that he has a taste for it, I fear the worst. It's in his nature. Caitlyn understood that . . . until she forgot it. Do you, my friend?"

Cel Rau sniffed and gave a single curt nod.

Aidan clasped his shoulder. "Good. Remain watchful. Never forget our true purpose. You know what to do, if it comes to that."

Cel Rau mounted his horse and turned to survey the bridge, gaze lifting to the approaching jukari horde. His hands grasped the pommels of his swords so hard the knuckles were white. After a moment, he relaxed and turned to Aidan.

"Die well," he said, and urged his horse toward the village without a backward glance.

A calmness settled over Aidan, unlooked for yet welcome. It wasn't the painkilling liquid, for his thoughts were still clear. Clearer than they had been for some time.

It's because, finally, my conscience is clear. Here I can delay the jukari and vormag as much as I can in order to save the villagers and— hopefully—atone for my sins.

He stood in the middle of the ancient bridge and watched the jukari advance. A cool wind whipped across the river and over him, ruffling his clothes. He made sure the sling cradling his shattered arm was tied tight and wouldn't hamper his movements.

Their tiny figures grew larger and larger. A loose, spread-out formation became narrow and tightly packed as they funneled toward the bridge.

A quick check behind him confirmed both Chalayan and cel Rau were well away but had taken up a position in the main street of the village, where they could keep their eyes on the bridge. He could have used both of them here with him, but he'd had to consider the greater good: Riversedge. The empire. Gazija's message. All those things were more important than him.

A man had to stand for something in his life.

Guttural barks and howls reached his ears as the jukari loped closer. As they approached the bridge, they slowed, puzzled by the single man standing in the center. They weren't stupid, these creations from the Shattering. That was why they were so dangerous—unlike wild beasts, they could reason.

If only they'd been created with empathy.

At the beginning of the bridge, the jukari stumbled to a halt, milling around in confusion. Perhaps the bridge itself awakened some memory of times past and baffled them. No matter. Abominations. As he kept his eyes on the jukari, a few vormag pushed their way to the front. Worse abominations. They must have been scared of whatever power remained in the bridge; otherwise he was sure they would try to obliterate him with sorcery where he stood.

Aidan felt their black eyes on him, considering, weighing. Harsh commands were uttered, and a smaller jukari moved toward him. It hesitated, then took a timid step forward between the pillars.

Nothing happened.

The jukari took another step. Then another. With a howl, it broke into a run and headed straight at him, a few of its fellow horrors following behind, baying for his flesh.

Good thing we didn't rely on the power of legends.

Aidan tried to swallow, but his mouth and throat were too dry. A quick nervous glance behind told him Chalayan and cel Rau were still watching. He'd known they would be, but he couldn't help himself.

He waited as the first jukari lumbered up the bridge toward him. A runt, it carried only a dagger, but that was almost as long as a sword to him. It came at him, growling, a feral snarl plastered across its inhuman face. Behind the creature, more jukari flooded between the pillars, urged on by the vormag.

Aidan felt a chill deep in his bones, a hollowness in his stomach, and a tightness in his chest. He was deathly afraid. But he'd made his choice, and he wouldn't let the terror overwhelm him.

"For you, Caitlyn . . ." he breathed.

Black, murderous eyes rushed at him; steel from the jukari's unholy forges was raised high. Aidan stepped to the side as the jukari stabbed down—a terrible novice strike that almost made him laugh. He evaded with ease and punched his blade deep into his opponent's neck. Blood sprayed as he wrenched his sword out, and the jukari stumbled a few steps to a stop.

Aidan spun around, ignoring the fatally wounded jukari. It was the rest of the horde he'd have to worry about.

A score of the monsters pressed toward him. Gray skinned, with black, yellow, or orange eyes; semi-intelligent horrors. Shrieks and howls of glee preceded them. Aidan breathed deeply and readied his sword, preparing to fight. And yet, that wasn't actually the plan.

What was the holdup? What was Chalayan waiting for?

The leading jukari were almost upon him when shields from two of the sorcerer's craftings finally hummed into existence, one to his left, another to his right. They blocked passage on the edges of the bridge, so the jukari couldn't flank him. Unfortunately, the domes weren't large enough to cover the width of the ancient structure and left a small pathway between them, wide enough for two jukari.

As the jukari near the shields milled in confusion, one leaped through the gap—a big one, swinging a massive greatsword.

Aidan ducked under the flashing blade and cursed as his own slash skidded off the creature's crafted breastplate. It hacked at him again, with far more finesse than the first jukari. Aidan twisted, narrowly avoiding the blade, which struck the stone of the bridge beside him, sending shards flying and setting the sword to ringing.

For the first time, he noticed the brute's armor was made to fit it perfectly. Breastplate and armbands, even the mail underneath, all made to size. A worrisome detail.

He cut wildly at the jukari in an attempt to keep it at bay. Sharp hums filled the air, like bees passing close to his ear. Guttural, anguished cries came from the bridge. He risked a fleeting glance to see silver threads of . . . something . . . some sorcerous force . . .

emanating from a number of the craftings Chalayan had left on the bridge. They floated on the breeze, then whipped back and forth.

Just like Aidan had seen Chalayan use in the clearing.

A web of pulsing, glittering filaments sliced through flesh and bone as if they offered no resistance. Jukari fell as limbs were severed from bodies. Dark blood splashed across the stone. Howls of pain and dismay erupted. Feet slipped on the slick surface.

Aidan's opponent snarled and stepped back, eyes wide as it took in the fate of its comrades. Farther past the whipping threads, the jukari charge stopped in its tracks. Two vormag pushed their way through the throng.

The brute of a jukari turned toward Aidan, and they locked gazes.

A wild slash, a feint that turned to a thrust, almost knocking his sword from his hand as he parried the blade. By the ancestors, the beast was fast. It moved the greatsword as if it weighed nothing.

Aidan shouted, hoping to distract it. He didn't know if the vormag could counter Chalayan's sorcery, but he wasn't about to wait around to find out.

Gritting his teeth against the agony from his shattered arm, he dodged more slashes from the jukari. One arced past his sword as he desperately tried to deflect it—and struck his thigh. Pain blossomed, and warm, sticky blood soaked his pants. His leg buckled underneath him.

For a few heartbeats, he staved off death as the jukari rained blows down on him. Stroke after stroke he deflected or dodged, using his smaller size to his advantage, until his sword dropped from numb fingers. In despair, he gazed up at the jukari.

VASILE LOOKED AT the bridge in horror as the tiny figure of Aidan struggled against a jukari almost twice his size. He barely breathed, almost in a trance. He couldn't look away. Something dark flashed among the other jukari behind the blue shields, too small to see at this distance. Moments later, howls of agony reached them. Next to him, Chalayan jumped up and down and yelled unintelligible words in his tribal tongue. He was grinning like a child, yet his eyes were feverish and strained. From what Vasile knew, sorcery at this distance was taxing to the extreme, but Chalayan seemed to be reveling in it, the exertion a perverse kind of challenge and reward.

He could understand why the sorcerer was so excited: he'd stopped the jukari horde in the middle of the bridge as surely as if they'd found a wall in their way. The front lines of the jukari swelled, then subsided, even backing off a few steps. Whatever Chalayan had done, his deciphering of the ways of destructive sorcery had certainly come along in leaps and bounds.

And yet . . . Aidan was on that bridge, fighting for his life.

Not exactly a moment of triumph.

Cel Rau turned his gaze from the bridge and regarded Chalayan without expression. Vasile caught his eye, but the swordsman's face revealed nothing of what he was thinking. Cel Rau went back to watching Aidan's violent struggle.

Vasile sucked in a breath as Aidan went down on one knee. Blows from the jukari pounded at the man, but somehow he parried them all—except one. Aidan's sword fell to the ground. The jukari took a step forward and loomed over him.

As Aidan was about to die, cel Rau spoke. "Now, sorcerer."

"What's happening?" Vasile hissed.

Chalayan laughed with glee. "I'm doing what needs to be done. The jukari horde can be stopped at the bridge—if it isn't there. Watch."

The jukari raised its massive sword high over Aidan just as bright silver threads twisted around the bridge. A filament of sorcery sliced open its shoulder, and its downward swing went wide of Aidan.

"Do it now, Chalayan," cel Rau said. "I'd rather it was done by us, not the jukari."

Chalayan nodded, intense concentration on his face. He raised his arms and made a twisting motion with his hands.

The threads spun in the air, crackling like lightning. Jukari began dying. Halves of the creatures fell to the ground. Some threw themselves down to avoid the sorcery, some turned and ran. One thread passed through the neck of a vormag, and its head separated from its body. Red shields enveloped its fellows, and Chalayan cursed vehemently as his sorcery was deflected. Aidan had thrown himself to the side and lay immobile, hands covering his head.

Vasile's heart clenched in his chest.

Blue shields sprang up behind the jukari on the bridge, blocking their escape.

"Quickly, sorcerer," growled cel Rau.

Vasile realized Chalayan was having too much fun. In a situation where Aidan was about to die and countless jukari were being slaughtered, the sorcerer was enjoying himself.

Rolling thunder echoed across the bridge. In an instant, the space between the threads turned black. Something about it made Vasile sick; just looking at the power twisted something inside his mind. It was . . . wrong.

"Yes!" gloated Chalayan.

Smoke billowed from jukari as their bodies burst into flames, obscuring the bridge.

"And . . . now," said Chalayan.

Vasile staggered as a great weight descended on him. He felt as if he weighed double or triple what was normal. The smoke from the jukari spun in a circle, forming a whirlwind above the bridge. Multicolored lightning arced out, striking the bridge, leaving yard-wide blackened scores in the stone.

Another clap of thunder. The air distorted as a wave of pressure rushed from the bridge. It slammed into Vasile, Chalayan, and cel Rau, sending them tumbling.

They scrambled to their feet.

"There," said Chalayan. "They won't be crossing the bridge now. It was a shame to destroy it, but—"

"But you didn't," said cel Rau.

"*What?*" The shock in his voice reflected the disbelief on Chalayan's face.

For cel Rau was right. Despite the powerful sorcery unleashed against it, the bridge remained standing, spanning the river as it had since the Shattering. Jukari corpses littered the structure, sprinkled with vormag. Of Aidan, there was no sign.

A group of vormag walked slowly onto the bridge. Shields covered them, and they each had one arm raised in the air. Tendrils of sorcery flowed from their hands and along the bridge. Something had stopped Chalayan's sorcery from destroying the structure, and Vasile wagered it was the vormag. A group of five of them were holding hands, mouths moving in unison. Because whatever they'd done to stop Chalayan, they obviously weren't finished.

As Vasile had the thought, a dark violet globe appeared above the vormag and shot into the air. Then another, and a third. Two veered toward the village, while the other . . . came straight at them.

"Chalayan!" said Vasile.

The sorcerer created a shield around himself, then expanded it into a dome to cover all three of them. Vasile's skin tingled and crawled as the sorcery passed over him.

The vormag's globe slammed against the shield, splattering as if it were made from liquid. The violet sorcery dribbled down the side, and Chalayan laughed. Clearly he was over having his bridge-destroying sorcery thwarted.

Vasile looked to the village just as the other two globes hit. Wooden buildings erupted into flame instantly, and splashes of virulent sorcery left trails of fire on the ground.

On the other side of the bridge, the bulk of the jukari horde remained alive. They weren't crossing, but it was only a matter of time before the vormag forced them across.

Vasile shivered with dread at the forces he'd seen unleashed. "If the Shattering wasn't enough to destroy the bridge," he said to Chalayan, "then I don't see how you thought you'd be able to."

Chalayan gave him a dark look filled with . . . hatred? "And yet you were the one to lead me to this sorcery, Magistrate. Look! Look at what I've done! And that's hardly scratching the surface."

"You *did* hardly scratch the surface," Vasile reminded him.

Chalayan waved his hand as if that was a minor irritation. "Bah—the power is *mine* now. With a few months of experimentation, I'll be ten times stronger! Imagine what I could do then!"

Vasile swallowed and stepped back from the sorcerer. Drunk on his own power, reveling in the destruction, Chalayan had a wild look in his eyes.

"That's what I'm worried about. This," observed Vasile, "was how the Shattering began."

Chalayan merely laughed at him.

"Aidan and I agreed," cel Rau said solemnly. His blade flashed. One moment it was in its sheath, and the next, cel Rau stood still, his sword and arm extended in a straight line. It was as if the sword had simply appeared there without traveling through the intervening space. A scarlet stain coated the first two inches of the steel.

Chalayan clutched at his throat in a vain attempt to stem the spurting blood. He uttered a bubbling gasp. His eyes rolled into his head, and he collapsed.

Vasile looked on in horror as Chalayan twitched on the ground, blood leaking into the dirt.

"Don't be afraid, Magistrate. Aidan gave the order. The sorcerer was useful for a time, but his desires got the better of him. He was weak. We could both see it."

Yes, but he also maintained our shield! But Vasile said nothing—what possible protest would make a bit of difference now? *Mad. These people are all mad.*

Numb, all he could do was nod, even as he watched cel Rau methodically taking the craftings and trinket from Chalayan's corpse.

"Come," cel Rau said. "We've bought some time, but we should hurry."

Vasile followed the swordsman's lead and mounted his horse. They turned and aimed for the dust trail left by the fleeing villagers heading for Riversedge.

As they rode, Vasile thought about these three strange men. His companion rode next to him, a savage wrapped in silence. Chalayan had been powerful, but also mad for power. And then there was Aidan . . .

As far as Vasile was aware, Aidan hadn't told a lie. He was a rare breed. A good man, killed to defend those who would never even think to thank him.

"Good-bye, Aidan," whispered Vasile. "May the ancestors shelter you. You'll be sorely missed."

CHAPTER 35

Caldan stood to the side as Master Mold directed the Protectors to secure the building. The master disappeared inside, and soon after, a Protector came out with a bunch of keys and locked the iron gate, making sure the curious bystanders were denied access. Two armored journeymen were positioned inside the gate, as well as two Quivers. Along with the Protectors, Master Mold had arrived with a squad of soldiers he'd dragooned on the way.

Caldan rubbed tired eyes and yawned, running a hand over his head. He still felt weak, probably an aftereffect of the blood loss, and a hollow pit in his stomach told him he needed to eat to regain his strength. But Mold had asked him to wait, so wait he did. For a few minutes, until he couldn't stand it anymore and went inside to look for food. Amerdan and he had found a small kitchen at the back during their search, so Caldan made his way there.

Drinking his fill of water, Caldan grabbed a bottle of cider and uncorked it. He was about to look for a glass but then shrugged. After what he'd been through and seen, maybe he needed the whole bottle.

The kitchen was well stocked, but with so many expensive foods he didn't feel like eating. Honeyed crickets? Jars of pickled baby eels with onions? A brown paper package containing a brick of . . . was it cured and pressed jellyfish?

His stomach roiled at the thought.

After poking around, he managed to put together a decent meal of dried fruit, more bread, and cheese, along with thin slices from an aged leg of ham.

Halfway through his meal, a bleak-faced Mold poked his head in and, seeing him, pulled up a chair and sat beside Caldan. Two Protectors followed him, senior journeymen, and took up position on either side of the door. Without asking for permission, Mold took a swig from the bottle of cider and followed it up with a longer pull. His eyes were red-rimmed, and there was a hard set to his jaw.

"Is there anything stronger?"

Caldan nodded. "I saw a few bottles in . . . I think the first room. Looked like expensive wine and spirits. They spared no ducats making themselves comfortable."

"We found Master Annelie and the other two Protectors covered with canvas in a cart out the back. I don't know what they were going to do with the bodies. Probably dump them in the river, or bury them in the countryside."

Caldan nodded, keeping quiet. He could tell Mold was struggling to come to terms with what had happened. It seemed he'd been close to Annelie.

"When Annelie didn't return, I sent someone to check on her. They found the safe house empty, and I feared the worst." Mold eyed Caldan. "I thought you'd done for them. Gotten yourself loose and somehow overpowered a master and two journeymen. When we received your message, I'd hoped . . . well, I'd hoped Annelie was still alive."

"I'm sorry. I had my hands tied when we were attacked. I might have been able to do something, but . . ."

"No need to apologize. You're still in a great deal of trouble, but I need to hear your side of the story. What happened?"

Careful with his words, Caldan said, "We were waylaid in the street. Both journeymen were killed with arrows before we knew what was happening. Master Annelie managed to access her well and put a shield up, but . . . they used crafted arrows that somehow drained her shield. They worked efficiently, like they'd done this before."

Mold nodded. "A few Protectors and sorcerers have gone missing the last couple of years. No one could work out what happened to them. But go on."

Caldan hesitated. Why would Joachim have killed sorcerers if they weren't Touched? He must have coveted their trinkets, and perhaps that was the lead Annelie had followed.

He wrestled with the idea of telling Mold the truth, but he felt it was important to keep his promise to Amerdan, if only because the justice was Caldan's—and his alone—to claim. "I was knocked unconscious, and when I woke, I was locked in the room upstairs. I managed to free myself and killed the guard who opened the door, then his two colleagues. They were unprepared, and I surprised them. I think they were drunk. I found a quiver with their crafted arrows in it and took a handful. When I ran into Joachim downstairs, he activated his shield, but I disabled it using the arrows. And then . . ."

"Then you killed him."

"Yes."

Mold let out a long sigh. "If I hadn't seen this mess myself, I wouldn't have believed it."

"I scarcely believe it, either. Judging from the luxuries they've gathered, Joachim and his men must have been killing people for their trinkets for years."

"And what about the room you were locked up in? The table with straps, the bloodstains on the floor. Any idea why you were left alive?"

Caldan forced his breathing to remain even and met Mold's eyes, holding his gaze steady. "I've no idea."

"No? Joachim hadn't taken an unnatural interest in you? Nothing you talked about at our headquarters, perhaps?"

"Nothing I can think of."

Mold grunted, took another swallow of cider, and handed the bottle back to Caldan. "Think harder. I know what you've been up to, and why Annelie had you taken prisoner. Ah—" Mold held up a hand as Caldan was about to protest and lay out his excuses. "I know you think it was for a good cause, to try to heal your friend Miranda, but certain inflexible rules have been handed down to the masters over the centuries. What you've uncovered here, and the fact you decided to stay and report it to us, are strong marks in your favor. But . . . I've very little leeway."

"I understand." And he did, especially because Caldan was sure no one realized he'd had the books copied. And if his only crime was stealing from the masters' library, then there'd be a fair chance breaking Joachim's murderous trinket-stealing ring would go a long way toward ameliorating his punishment. Or so he hoped . . .

"Just remember," Caldan continued, "that if it weren't for me, Joachim would still be free to murder and steal. He'd have killed Annelie and the journeymen and escaped punishment. You'd have no idea he was behind it, and they'd be floating in the river. By the ancestors, I could have kept the whole thing quiet and taken the building for myself. With the ducats here, the trinkets . . ." Caldan shook his head in wonder. "I could have lived until the end of my days in luxury, and no one would have ever known. But that's not who I am. Miranda needs my help, the Protectors can make use of me, and Bells has to be stopped. So . . . here I am."

Mold glared at him, and Caldan made sure he didn't flinch. Eventually, the master's expression softened. "You've exposed a great evil, but . . . the cost was high. Someone will have to pay for that."

Caldan nodded solemnly.

"There will be a trial for your indiscretion," Mold continued.

"We both know it's more than an indiscretion. There's no need to sugarcoat it. But you know I was doing it for Miranda."

"Caldan, let me say this as clearly as I can: there is no justification for what you did. You knew it was wrong, and you went ahead and did it anyway. And because you did, Annelie and the other Protectors died." Mold raised a hand to forestall Caldan's objection. "Maybe they would have been targeted anyway; we don't know. But this is where your desire for forbidden knowledge has led us."

Caldan looked at the man, neither cowed nor defiant. "So what now?"

Mold gestured for the journeymen to approach. "It's out of my hands. Quite simply, you know too much. There are rules we have to follow in certain circumstances. Even the Protectors have to answer to someone. We aren't free to do whatever we want."

"Who do the Protectors answer to?" asked Caldan, knowing and dreading the answer.

"The emperor's warlocks, of course. You'll have to give evidence to them of Joachim's crimes. I'm detaining you until there can be a trial, most likely when the warlocks arrive with the emperor's forces."

Would he be able to submit himself to whatever punishment was decided, or could he be powerful enough now to defend himself from them? With trepidation, Caldan couldn't help but recall Avigdor's words when they'd first met: *No one leaves the Protectors.*

Little did Mold know, he might be handing Caldan over to be killed. Not because he'd tried to find out more about coercive sorcery, but for what he was.

His bone trinket pressed against his chest; it felt as if it were burning, and he resisted the urge to touch it. His family had died for this secret. He couldn't let the warlocks take him.

Mold's voice brought him out of his reverie. " . . . and you'll be kept a close watch on. Joachim might not have been acting alone, and if the only witness was eliminated, there'd be no proof of his wrongdoing."

He means they want no more trouble from me until I can be safely handed over to the warlocks.

Heavy of heart, Caldan could only nod, indicating to Mold he'd heard and understood.

He still wasn't sure he agreed, though.

MOLD HAD PLACED Caldan in the custody of the two journeyman Protectors, as the master wanted to stay and supervise their investigation of Joachim's hideout—which would likely take a long time. Caldan had been marched into the streets, and during the last few minutes he must have formulated and discarded a dozen escape plans. Each one had been risky, and involved him unleashing torrents of sorcery, which meant the possibility of injuries and putting the Protectors against him forever. And he'd prove to them they'd been right in their suspicions, that he couldn't be trusted with the knowledge of destructive and coercive sorcery. If he went down that path, there'd be no going back. And most likely, he'd be hunted down and killed. If they were able to overcome him . . . After all, his abilities were growing, and quickly. At what point would he be able to not worry about the Protectors and what they could do to him? As Joachim had told him: being both Touched and a sorcerer was rare indeed. What would he be capable of if his skill continued to grow? He'd show the Protectors, and they'd have no choice but to leave him alone if he bloodied their noses, or even worse.

No, what he needed was a shrewd plan. For the truth was that he had to escape and give himself at least an hour's head start. With enough time, he'd be able to get far enough away and . . . what? What would he be doing? He'd be a wanted man, with every Protector and possibly warlock hunting him down. He didn't have many options, as he saw it. Flee to save himself and eventually be captured and dragged off to be imprisoned for the rest of his life, or be drained by the emperor and his warlocks. A life spent in hiding was no life at all. The thought of constantly looking over his shoulder, wondering if today would be the day he'd be found, was distinctly unappealing. Was this the life his parents had led before they'd died?

Then there was Miranda. She was in this appalling condition because of him, and he owed it to her to do everything he could to bring her back to normal.

The Protectors' headquarters was only a few minutes away now, so he had to do something, and soon.

"I really need to go back and talk to Master Mold," Caldan said. He stopped and looked back the way they'd come.

His escort pushed him, and he stumbled, then glared at them.

"Keep moving," the eldest one said.

He'd rarely spoken so far, and when he did, he used few words. Caldan's eyes strayed to the pouch at the Protector's belt before he could stop himself. His craftings were in there, and his trinkets. They knew he couldn't do anything without them and thought they'd be able to handle him as he was—cowed by Mold, no craftings or weapons, and nowhere to run to.

A coach drawn by four horses was coming up the street toward them, and the kernel of a plan sprouted in Caldan's mind.

"Mold is making a big mistake," he said. "There are things I didn't tell him. You need to take me back there so I can speak with him."

Caldan felt the older Protector access his well, so he held his hands up in submission. He needed to push them, to make them think he was focused on going back to see Mold, but if they lost their patience and restrained him, his plan would fail.

"I'm sorry," Caldan said. "I'll keep quiet."

"You'd better. There's a coach coming. Move to the left."

Caldan did as he was told, keeping his eyes on the lathered horses approaching.

Wait, he told himself. *Soon.*

Taking a breath, he pivoted and slammed a fist into the elder Protector's jaw, making a grab for the pouch at his belt an instant later. The Protector's eyes glazed over, and he dropped, just as Caldan's tug broke the ties of the pouch holding it tight.

"Hey!" exclaimed the other Protector.

Caldan dashed in front of the coach. Horses shied and whinnied in fright, but Caldan was past them and hurtling down a side alley.

"Stop right there!"

He leaped a pile of garbage and careened across the next intersection, barely missing a woman with two children. A well surged with power—the Protector activating his shield. There was another shout behind him, and he swerved down a street to the right, as if heading back toward Mold.

Then he took the next left, and left again—which pointed him back to the Protectors' headquarters. At the next crossroads, he paused, panting, and peeked around the corner. There was no sign of the Protectors, and with any luck they'd think he was moving in Mold's direction. Good.

Caldan took off as if his life depended on it.

Which indeed it might.

It didn't take long before he made it back to the Protectors'. Outside the walls, he stopped to catch his breath. It wouldn't do to enter the compound flustered and panting. He needed to act like he belonged there, although he knew now he never would.

Caldan stood up straight and tried to keep his expression calm. He was through the front entrance and inside within moments, only having to nod to a couple of Protectors he passed.

First, he went to his room and gathered up his satchel, making sure the copied texts and his crafting pieces were still hidden, which they were. As he'd guessed, none of the Protectors here knew what had happened overnight, and they had no reason to stop him. Strapping on his sword, he went to Miranda's room and packed her belongings, slinging her pack over his shoulder.

Caldan wrapped her in a blanket and picked her up. By the ancestors, she was light. Then he left and descended the stairs.

In the courtyard, a Protector gave him an inquiring look.

"I'm taking her to a physiker," Caldan said. Which wasn't a lie, really.

The woman nodded and let him be.

Sighing with relief, Caldan exited through the gate and was soon trying to lose himself in the streets of Riversedge.

BY THE TIME Caldan found a room to stay in, it was almost dawn, and the horizon had a gray cast to it. He'd had to carry Miranda all the way to one of the city's gates, where the inns and lodgings were used to travelers arriving at all hours. The room he'd chosen wasn't cheap, being one of the better presented establishments, but he'd thought it a better place to leave Miranda unattended while he could sort out something for her. She deserved far more than he could provide, and the Protectors—and Joachim—had proven themselves all but useless in their efforts to cure her.

He was exhausted. Barely able to keep his eyes open, he stumbled up the stairs and inside their room, locking the door behind him. As gently as he could, he laid Miranda on one of the beds. He pulled up her blanket, in case she wriggled and it shifted down in her sleep. Her eyes moved under her closed lids, and she moaned weakly, whether from a dream or a nightmare or because she was hot, he couldn't tell. The air in the room was stale, and he left the window slightly ajar.

Caldan bit back an angry curse. Miranda's skin was still pale. All the inactivity couldn't be good for her, and she definitely looked thinner than when they'd first met. He needed to entrust her care to someone more qualified than an apprentice Protector. Although he could safely assume he wasn't one anymore—especially after escaping from them.

He squinted tired eyes, then rubbed them in case it helped. It didn't. Never mind; he could snatch a few hours' rest before going out again. Without stopping to wash, he changed out of his soiled clothes and slipped into his bed. There was so much to do, a short break was all he could afford. He needed to make sure Miranda was being cared for and then begin crafting.

Relaxing was difficult, as his thoughts kept returning to the unsanctioned books on coercive sorcery. Somehow he'd have to make time to study them as well. Tomorrow—today, he corrected himself— was going to be another busy day.

CALDAN IGNORED THE brightening room for another hour before dragging himself out of bed. He readied himself, touching his trinket ring to make sure it was still there, and the bone ring. Strapping on his sword—he couldn't take any chances now—he checked Miranda. She had to be his first order of business this morning; he had an idea to ensure she received the best of care.

Caldan paused in the process of pouring a cup of water for Miranda to drink. It struck him that even in her almost comatose state, she'd been the one directing his actions. Everything he'd done had been for her—and now here he was, hiding from the Protectors, hoping he'd have time to learn and craft as much as he could before he faced them again. For it surely would come to that.

And it surprised him that he didn't care. The Protectors had shown they were ineffective—restricting knowledge because it was what they'd been ordered to do. Then, when something happened that they should have been able to help with, they wouldn't.

Not wouldn't . . . couldn't.

He sighed and made sure Miranda drank all the water. She slowly drained the cup with small sips. When she tightened her lips and refused more, he made sure she was comfortable and left the room, crafting the door locked with a rune pattern chalked on the inside.

After asking around, he paid a visit to a nearby physiker's. When he had explained Miranda's situation, leaving out any mention of coercive sorcery, the woman was only too glad to take on the task of Miranda's care throughout the day. He gave her the address, handed her enough ducats to pay for the first two days, and promised more to come. Thanking her profusely, he then went about sourcing raw materials for his crafting.

With a successful trip to the clockmaker out of the way, Caldan found a silversmith's and was able to come away with almost everything he needed, including a few rare earths. After a moment's thought, he also paid the woman in order to use the small forge she had set up in her backyard. She couldn't spare it until tomorrow, which was fine by him; he'd need the time before then to go over his designs and work on the schematics of his links, anchors, buffers, and activation runes. A check of the equipment in the forge assured him all was in good order and he wouldn't be scrambling for tools and bits and pieces when he needed them.

By the time midday came around, he was back in their shared room. The physiker was due to arrive soon, and he settled down next to Miranda. He wished she were conscious, that he wasn't in so much trouble, and that he could pay her back for that meal at the House of

Eels. Another lock of hair had fallen to cover her face and he brushed it over her ear.

Caldan settled back and started making sketches of possible craftings, calculating alloy percentages, and configuring rune patterns.

When the physiker appeared, he left her to tend to Miranda, descending the stairs and finding an out-of-the-way bench in the building's internal courtyard. He sat there, massaging a ball of wax in his hands. He still hadn't decided what to actually smith-craft tomorrow, but he needed to make up his mind soon—he was desperate to prepare himself for a potential showdown with the Protectors. Making sure no one was around, Caldan removed a metal arrowhead from his pocket—the only thing, apart from his own possessions, he'd taken from Joachim's hideout. It was covered in tiny runes seemingly scribed onto the metal, but he could see, and feel, that they were slightly raised. How they'd been drawn on the metal was a mystery to him, but they certainly hadn't been inked.

The arrows were a complex crafting, and he didn't even recognize half the runes. Each had a standard single link, and an anchor along with a buffer, but after that, he couldn't fathom what they were designed to do. Or rather, he knew what they did, not how they did it.

He thought back to the night raid with Simmon and Jazintha, when he'd killed the rogue sorcerer . . . His sword had pierced the shield somehow. At the time, he'd thought he'd been able to penetrate the sorcerer's shield because of his sudden burst of speed and strength.

Touching the surface of his trinket ring, he traced the knot-work pattern and the stylized lion. Joachim might have told him, eventually. Maybe. But everything the warlock had said was now suspect. Caldan was left to rely on his own intuition and perceptions.

The physiker emerged from the stairwell, and seeing Caldan, she came over and reassured him Miranda was comfortable, and that she'd return in the evening.

When he entered their room, Miranda stirred, interrupting his thoughts. She squirmed, breath coming fast. Caldan stroked her brow and hair until she calmed. He couldn't stand much more of seeing her like this. He glanced at the satchel containing his copied books; could feel them beckoning him. His crafting could wait until tomorrow. If all else failed, he could just make another shielding wristband similar to the one he'd made before. At the moment, there were more important things to worry about.

Removing the books, he took out a sorcerous globe and positioned it to provide light to read by when the sun set. With a tingling sense of trepidation, he opened one of the texts on coercive sorcery. Since the Protectors couldn't help Miranda, he had to learn as much as he could himself. And if what he learned gave him an edge against the Protectors, then so much the better.

A few hours later, there was a knock on the door. Caldan rubbed his eyes. By the ancestors, he was tired. He groaned as he shifted his weight and ran his tongue around his parched lips. Time had flown, and he'd forgotten to drink or eat. A glance at the window confirmed the sky was darkening to night, and he stood up, staggering, as one of his legs had fallen asleep.

He quickly hid the coercive sorcery books in his satchel and opened the door.

Of course: the physiker again. He smiled and exchanged pleasantries with her as she entered and busied herself with Miranda's care. She stopped and raised an eyebrow at him as he looked on, and he stammered apologies. He checked she'd be able to stay with Miranda for a few hours, then gathered his satchel and left the room.

Caldan's stomach rumbled, reminding him he'd gone too long without eating. And he felt slightly dizzy, which wasn't surprising after such a loss of blood. He required nourishment to replenish himself.

Close by the inn where he'd played Dominion, there was a night market with plenty of restaurants. A short walk, and he decided on a quiet-looking place where he wouldn't be disturbed. Not long after that, he was presented with a platter of roast beef and potatoes, along with a large bowl of greens. Setting to, he turned his thoughts to crafting and coercive sorcery.

Both books had been enlightening, to say the least. As he'd thought, Bells had been sparing in her explanations, claiming the sorcery was too complex to be learned in a short span of time. But from the descriptions and diagrams in the books, it made a certain sense to him how coercive sorcery worked. It was intricate, there was no doubt about that, but no more complicated than a game of Dominion against an expert opponent. He was starting to realize the most complex sorcery was not only about practice; it was also dependent upon how many strings from your well you could split off and control. There were exceptions, such as the Bleeder, but in the end, it came down to talent.

The very first shield-crafting lesson he'd received back in Anasoma had been designed to separate out who could split their wells into multiple strings. Only two at that stage, but it gave the masters an idea of who had potential. And as he'd seen with the crafted locks they used in their library here, he'd hazard a guess that most journeymen never progressed past three or four strings.

Caldan thought back to what Bells had told him about multiple strings: *Coercive sorcery requires at least seven threads split from a well, and a deft handling of each.*

It meshed with what he'd reasoned. He almost cursed when he realized he'd revealed to the masters he could maintain five strings. Whom he could trust was still in question, and for the time being, he had to keep his abilities to himself until he knew more.

What he needed to do was use his knowledge to create craftings more effective than any he had before. He'd almost finished designing two new automatons, and they were certainly original—but he doubted they would be enough to help him with what must be coming.

A reckoning with the Protectors.

Sorcerous mechanical hybrids were not unknown in history, but they were rare. Few sorcerers could fashion them, and as yet no one had come up with a use for them. It seemed a sound choice for another crafting.

With his mind made up, Caldan returned to Miranda's room, finding the physiker gone. Well, he wasn't paying the woman to stay in the room and do nothing. She must have finished her tasks and left, having other business to attend to.

Though it was late and he had a lot of work to get through tomorrow, Caldan took some time to review his crafting designs. Making minute changes to some of the schematics based on his decisions in the restaurant, he smiled.

Bells's craftings and his own theories had brought his sorcery along in leaps and bounds.

THE PHYSIKER HAD arrived early, to make Miranda comfortable before leaving to tend to her own clients. He watched the woman lay out her equipment, small vials and instruments from a leather kit similar to Elpidia's. He blinked rapidly. Elpidia. He clenched his hands into fists until his knuckles ached. Amerdan would pay for killing her.

As the physiker unpacked, Caldan realized if worse came to worst, Miranda would be left here on her own—without him to care for her. Worryingly, she was awake less and less during the day, a sign that whatever Joachim had done to her hadn't done much to arrest her decay. Maybe that had been the warlock's plan all along: to make Caldan think he'd stopped her decline, and that she would be healed eventually, while in reality she was no better off.

If the warlocks took him, she'd likely be left to die or live out her life in this altered state of degradation. A horrible thought.

Turning to the physiker, he reached for his coin purse. "Excuse me. I was wondering if you'd be able to find better accommodation for Miranda. I fear this isn't the best environment for her to recover in. Perhaps there's a reputable hospice you know of in the city? Or maybe you have a spare room yourself?"

"Yes, of course. There are several hospices in Riversedge, some better than others. The quality of care depends on how much coin you have, unfortunately."

Caldan held out a handful of gold and silver ducats and looked the physiker in the eye. "Excellent. As soon as possible, please."

They made arrangements, and he left the physiker to her ministrations, planning on starting his crafting work early.

CALDAN PLACED THE fine wax carving tool down on the bench and massaged his hand. Through the walls of the forge came the sounds of people and traffic going past, but it wasn't at all distracting. It was a pleasant backdrop to the familiar sounds and smells of the forge, which he realized he'd missed.

He wiped sweat from his brow, taking care to avoid dripping it on his paper schematics, and drank from a cup of water. Replacing the carving tools in their leather folder, he brushed the bench clear of wax scrapings. He stared at the wax medallion for a few moments, then nodded. It was good work.

Time to take stock of his equipment for the next stage: two wax rods for flues, and a mold to encase the medallion with alchemical plaster. During one of the breaks he'd taken to rest his fingers and hand, he'd carefully weighed the metals and rare earths for his alloy and set them to melt in a crucible in the furnace. A quick check, and he confirmed they were ready. Taking a thin metal rod, he gave the alloy another stir, careful to ensure he didn't spill any of the metal.

In an identical procedure to when he'd made his shield wristband, he prepared the wax medallion casting with flues and encased it within a layer of alchemical plaster. As the mixture began giving off heat, he relaxed and waited for the reaction to harden the casting.

When that was done, he used tongs to place the mold close to the heat of the forge. When he was satisfied the alchemical plaster had hardened and the wax had melted, he tipped the molten wax onto the furnace, where it hissed and bubbled as it was consumed.

His thoughts drifted back to when he'd created his shield crafting, not so long ago. He shook his head. It felt like a lifetime. Again, he accessed his well and used the tongs to pour his violently shimmering alloy into the mold. As the stream of brightly glowing metal flowed into the hollow space, filling the runes and patterns he'd carved, he quested his sorcerous senses into his creation, testing the anchors, buffers, and control glyphs. Licking salty sweat from his lips, he connected to the first link, and the second, sending power coursing through the liquid medallion. Then he split a third and fourth string, also connecting these to the spare linking runes.

He'd modeled his design on Bells's shield crafting, which was far more complex than his first effort. His wristband was a crafting most journeymen couldn't hope to match, and this medallion would be a magnitude more intricate.

Now all he had to do was wait, maintaining the four strings and his power flowing through the patterns until the medallion solidified. He removed the mold from the furnace and took it to his bench, placing it on a metal holder so as not to burn the wooden surface.

Minutes passed, and he frowned with the effort as his head began to ache. He'd been able to split his well into five strings before, but only for a very short time. Holding four strings was supposed to be easier than five, but maintaining the linkage for long periods could be a problem; he was already tiring. Clenching his teeth, he let out a soft moan before steeling his will. He would not fail in this smith-crafting. It was essential he had the means to protect himself.

Only then could he concentrate on healing Miranda. And try to find Bells and Amerdan—to avenge Simmon's and Elpidia's deaths.

As he focused on maintaining his well and the four strings, he lost track of time. The noise of the outside world faded into the background until he was scarcely aware of it.

Then his strings twitched and began slipping from his mental grasp. He hissed, clutching at them desperately. But he was too tired, and there was no strength left in him. One slipped free, then another. As each was sucked back into his well, it became easier to hold the others, but there was no point now. He closed his well. Had he been able to maintain the flow long enough for the imbuement to take?

Draining his cup dry, he waited a few minutes to gather his strength. He carried the casting with the tongs to a barrel of water and plunged it in. After a few moments, Caldan cracked the cast and retrieved the medallion. He couldn't wait any longer. Despite his exhaustion, he split his well into four strings and linked to the newly made crafting.

His skin tightened as the shield enveloped him. The scent of lemons and hot metal pervaded the space around him. He held out a hand and saw a multicolored haze covering it like light reflecting from fish scales. A second skin, similar to Bells's shield crafting.

He'd incorporated Bells's design into his, with a few minor adjustments. Her artistry had become clearer as he'd sketched. Runes and linkings he never would have thought of puzzled him at first. And then it had all clicked into place, like a confusing Dominion strategy that he'd seen for the first time. By contrast, his original shield crafting seemed crude to him now.

Reaching his senses toward it, he felt the enhanced density of the shield. It drew a torrent from his well. Not only would it need a sorcerer who could manage four strings, that sorcerer's well would have to be able to cope with the flow.

But he could use it. Closing his well, he cut off the four strings, and the multicolored haze enveloping him winked out.

It was fine work. Very fine work . . .

Already, his knowledge of sorcery far outstripped what he'd learned at the monastery, and he possibly knew more than many masters did, in theory, anyway. If the Protectors found him, or more of Joachim's kind, they'd find a very different reception from what they expected.

He needed to be able to look after himself, because if he was going to accomplish anything for Miranda, it was going to be because of his own ability, and no one else's.

CHAPTER 36

"Why the change of plan?" asked Izak.

Felice considered a number of different ways to answer the question. In truth, she wasn't sure herself this was the best option, but it had to be better than returning straight to Rebecci. Softly, carefully she must step. The path before her was narrow, and on either side loomed a bottomless pit. If she couldn't manage to walk it . . . any misstep, no matter how small, could be the death of her.

"You," she said to the heavy who had broken Savine's arm, allowing Izak time to finish him off. "What's your name?"

The man paused for a moment, glancing at his comrades, who were out of earshot. "Rebecci told us no names. It's safer that way."

Felice tapped her cheek. "Then nameless you shall remain. I want you to stay close to Izak. You've shown initiative, and I respect that. I don't think this is over yet."

"What?" whispered Izak. "What are you up to?"

"Me? Nothing. We've just killed one of their top sorcerers, who,

I might add, is linked to Rebecci and that company of hers in some way. When they find out, I've no doubt Kelhak and his Indryallans will retaliate. We'll need to prepare for that eventuality . . . and how to replicate what we've done here."

"But—"

"Enough, Izak," she snapped. "Give me room to breathe, and to think."

Catching the other heavies' attention, she waved them over. "I have need of your services for a while longer. I know you were meant to disappear once the job was done, but I'm sure Rebecci will see you well compensated."

Their leader shrugged. "Sure. What do you need us to do?"

"Protect us, for now. We need to find a safe place and send a message to Rebecci to organize a meeting. There are some things I need to discuss with her."

"Why don't we just go meet her now?" asked the man who'd helped Izak.

"Because it might not be safe. We could be followed, or the sorcerer's friends might already know he's dead and be coming after us."

Izak frowned. "How would they know he's dead?"

"Because they're sorcerers." Felice waggled her fingers at him. "Who knows what they're capable of?"

"You would. That's your job: information on everything."

"True, but there are always surprises. It takes a smart person to realize they mightn't know everything about a subject, especially when they think they *do* know everything. And I'm a smart person."

Izak shook his head. "That doesn't even make sense. If you know everything about something, then you should think you don't?"

"Exactly. Now, if you don't mind, I need time to think."

She left the men standing there and strolled across the street, sitting on someone's doorstep. They were exposed here, too close to the purified land and the scene of her successful murder, but she'd been reluctant to head off in any direction before she formulated a plan.

Think, she urged herself. *What's your best option? You pride yourself on your Dominion game, and here you are paralyzed, unsure of yourself and what the best move is.*

As Izak paced back and forth in front of the heavies, she discarded a number of scenarios as being too risky, and another two as being incredibly stupid. Really, she only had one choice, which was no choice at all.

She stood. "Right. Time to send a message to Rebecci."

"I'll take it," said a heavy, tapping one foot. "Just tell me what to say and where to go."

"No. A written message is safer. Besides, I've no idea where she'll be. It's best if we arrange a meeting. So . . . I'll need a pen and paper." She looked at the heavies for a moment. "Never mind. We'll have to find some. It's just as well we're in Parkside, then. I'm sure one of these nice nobles will be able to help us. Or one of their servants."

A short time later, Felice exited a noble's mansion through the servants' door. A few well-placed ducats and she'd been able to persuade one of the servants her master wouldn't miss a few sheets of paper, along with a pen and ink.

She squinted up at the moon and went to join Izak and the men, who'd waited outside across the street.

"Izak, bend over."

"What?"

"Just bend over. I need a surface to write on."

"Oh, as you wish."

Felice directed him to a position where the light of the moon was sufficient to see by and hastily scrawled on a page. It wasn't long before she found a street urchin to deliver it to the offices of Empirical Commerce, where Rebecci was now based. She frowned at the girl's back as she ran down the street toward Dockside. Even in such a wealthy district as Parkside, children were homeless. She'd never realized how bad it was for some families. Delivering Felice's message was probably the most savory thing the girl had done for a ducat for a long time.

Felice shook her head. The Mahruse Empire wasn't perfect, but . . . she'd no idea what some girls had to do to avoid starvation. And she hadn't wanted to know. Once the Indryallans had been dealt with, she vowed, she'd make some changes.

With Izak and the heavies in tow, she led them in the same direction the girl had gone: Dockside. It wasn't long before the wide, tree-lined streets of Parkside gave way to the narrower streets of Five Flowers. Owing to the inhabitants' luxurious lifestyles, a few of the streets they passed through were teeming with activity, even at this late hour. Various food stalls stretched down side streets and alleys off the main road, mostly congregating close to intersections with clusters of taverns and inns. The scent of roasted spices and herbs overlaid the ever-present stench of the city, though in Five Flowers the perpetual stink wasn't nearly as bad as in Dockside or Slag Hill.

At one such street, Felice made them stop at a restaurant and eat, buying the men a few jugs of ale to share between them. They drank happily while consuming vast quantities of bread and meat of unknown origin heavily loaded with garlic and a spicy red paste. Maybe goat? No reputable restaurant was open at this time, and this place was the best she could do. Also, it got them off the street and made them less visible, and she needed to waste some time.

Hardly a word was spoken between them as the massive platter of meat rapidly diminished before her eyes. The heavies poured cups of ale for everyone, and Felice and Izak joined them in a toast.

Felice's eyes narrowed as Izak drank along with the heavies. She did her best to hide her expression. "Izak, I thought you didn't like ale. Always drinking whatever abominable spirit was the latest fashion."

"Nothing wrong with joining the men here in a toast, is there?"

Felice made herself smile in return. "I guess not. Just don't drink too much; we've still some work to do."

"As you wish."

She left them to their low-key celebrations, scanning the crowd in the restaurant for anyone suspicious. Had that man in the red coat and hat been staring at them? She deliberately looked away while trying to observe him in her peripheral vision. A blond woman approached the man and sat in his lap, and they laughed like good friends. No, he didn't look like he was spying on them. Perhaps the group of women . . . Felice cursed at herself under her breath. She was becoming paranoid. Not that she didn't have reason.

Or that she was about to stop.

What if Rebecci couldn't meet them? What if she didn't even receive the message? Would Savine's followers be able to track them as the sorcerer had? She needed contingency plans.

Felice signaled to a waiter for another jug of ale and poured Izak and the heavies a round. "Last one," she said. "After this, we'll head to a safe place and wait for Rebecci to arrive."

Izak wiped foam from his goatee and leaned forward. "Where are we going?"

"Back to the Cemetery."

Izak frowned. "Is Rebecci going to be able to find us there?"

"Oh, I'm sure she will. She's been there before."

"You didn't mention this earlier."

Felice studied his face, then glanced at the heavies. Her thoughts were still buzzing with actions and consequences. She had to be careful. "You didn't need to know. Now, finish your drink so we can go." She coughed, covering her mouth with a hand. Her infection lingered, but she guessed she should be thankful she was still alive. Avigdor couldn't say the same. *They'll pay for everything they've done,* she vowed, *even if I have to cut Kelhak's throat myself.*

She led them out of the restaurant and pushed her way down the crowded street, hardly seeing the food stalls and the people they passed. Five Flowers gave way to Cabbage Town, and the streets narrowed. Buildings loomed over them on either side. Well-lit roads turned to shadows and darkness; the only light to see by came from the moon and whatever spilled from between door cracks and windows.

Felice hurried Izak and the heavies as much as she could, claiming the risk was greatest when they were on the move, that they were exposed when traveling from place to place. But she knew this wasn't so. You were most at risk when you were one step behind and had no idea what was about to happen. With luck, she'd be the one a step ahead this time.

She turned north until they reached the river Stock, which, when joined by the river Modder at the beginning of Dockside, turned into the river Sop before emptying into the harbor. Even at night, the stench of the contaminated water was overwhelming. Following the river, they crossed it using a ramshackle wooden bridge, one she knew hadn't been approved by the city's officials.

Once, not so long ago, the bridge would have worried her. It was a sign of disorder in an otherwise orderly society. And the polluted river was just another sign of civilization, a necessary evil. Now, though . . . she couldn't help but think of the Indryallans' mantra when they'd invaded. The Mahruse Empire was corrupt, they'd announced. The wealthy profited at the expense of the weak. For that was what they'd called the poor: weak and less fortunate. In her heart, she couldn't help but agree with them. But fixing what was wrong with the empire would have to wait. Invasion and murder wasn't the way to initiate change for the better.

As they entered Dockside, she brushed away Izak's attempt at conversation. She needed all her wits about her. He gave her an annoyed look but thankfully held his tongue.

They emerged onto the docks without incident and made their way north toward the Cemetery. "Come on," she said to the heavies. "It's not far now."

She led them along the waterfront until they passed the beginning of the Cemetery. From the dilapidated and rotting ships, makeshift bridges and gangplanks crossed to the street. They had been put together from whatever spare wood could be found, usually parts of the ships themselves, and lashed together with old rope spliced into usable lengths.

Felice laughed, breathing in the air as they crossed one of the creaky bridges onto the deck of what looked to be an old trading vessel, shallow drafted and wide beamed. It always delighted her that one of the worst places in Anasoma to live, the Cemetery, a floating slum, had the freshest air in the whole city.

The ships hardly moved sideways in the swell, tied as they all were to at least three or four other abandoned vessels. They rose and fell gently, far easier to traverse than lone ships in the harbor or out at sea. It wasn't long before they reached the one Felice had taken for her own hideout not so long ago.

She hissed at the rats on the deck, but they didn't move and uncaringly watched her pass. Down into the hulk they went, and she cursed at her locked door. She didn't have the key.

"Break it down," she ordered the men, pushing her way through them to give enough room. It took seven hard kicks from one of the heavies before they were through.

As they entered, she lit one of the lamps, then directed Izak to light another. Her heart almost lifted as the illumination chased away the darkness and her familiar room materialized.

She found a piece of paper, ink and pen, and sat in her armchair, one leg over an armrest.

"What do we do now?" asked Izak, and the heavies looked at her expectantly.

"You make yourselves comfortable and wait. I've a note to write."

She left them to their devices and dipped her pen in the ink. After a moment's thought, she scratched her suspicions on the paper and was done. It had to be the heavy . . . but she was fearful she had it wrong and it was Izak after all. Blowing the ink until it dried, she sat back and sighed, bone weary. It had been a hard few days and an eventful night. And unless she missed her guess, it might not be over. She could count on one hand the times she'd been wrong.

Felice started at the knock on the door. Chairs scraped on wood as all three of the heavies stood abruptly. Izak hadn't moved from another chair on her right, and she noted the heavies had long knives drawn.

She rubbed her eyes and coughed. Her hand felt for the note she'd folded in half, then half again. Still there. Good.

"Come in," she said, then to the heavies, "Don't try anything; you'll likely regret it."

Hinges squeaked as the door opened to admit Rebecci, rail thin, with her white hair a tangled mess. She looked straight at Felice and nodded. "Lady Felicienne." She turned to Izak. "And Sir Izak."

Izak rose and bowed from the waist.

Felice noted his gesture and pursed her lips, nodding. She hoped her guess was right, or likely she'd be dead soon. "Lady Rebecci, it's—"

"Please, I'm no lady."

"Ah . . . Rebecci, then."

"I see you've kept my men alive. And I take it from the looks of you, you've a story to tell."

The sorcerer looked nervous, Felice noted. Rebecci's eyes flicked left and right, lingering on Izak, where she licked her lips and dropped her gaze to the floor. *A terrible actress,* thought Felice. *She's had time to prepare, and this is the best she can do?*

Rebecci's hands were clamped together behind her back, clutching an object. A crafting, surmised Felice. She'd better know what she was doing. Then again, she wouldn't be here unless she was confident in her abilities.

Felice approached her and held out the note she'd written earlier. When Rebecci took the paper, Felice stepped back. "Read that. And while you do, I'll pour myself a drink."

She left Rebecci unfolding the paper in front of a puzzled-looking Izak and moved behind the three heavies, locating a glass and using her shirt to wipe the inside. She uncorked a bottle and sniffed the opening, wrinkling her nose. Shrugging, she poured herself half a glass of red wine. When she turned, glass and bottle in hand, Rebecci was staring at her.

"Do you understand?" she asked the sorcerer.

Returning a curt nod, Rebecci swallowed.

"Good," said Felice, praying her deductions were correct. She smashed the bottle into the head of the heavy in front of her—the man who'd come to Izak's aid in the fight with Savine. The one who'd been keen to take her message to Rebecci. The one who kept tapping his foot.

Fragments of glass and red wine sprayed over her, and she flinched. That was for Avigdor.

The heavy crumpled like an empty shirt, and his companions shouted in surprise. Izak jumped back, mouth agape.

A multicolored layer covered Rebecci, and she stepped forward, boots crunching on broken glass, muttering to herself. She was pale and trembling.

As long as she has a solution and gets the job done, thought Felice.

As the heavy groaned amid shattered glass and wine, the sorcerer revealed what she'd been clutching. A diamond the size of a chicken's egg, encased in a thin silver cage covered with runes. Rebecci placed the crafting on the back of the prostrate heavy's neck. The heavy stiffened and ceased moving. He uttered a strangled moan.

"By the ancestors!" exclaimed the leader of the heavies. "What's going on?"

Izak closed his mouth and stuttered. "Wh— . . . yes, Felice, what's happening?"

"Quiet, all of you! Rebecci here is about to save our lives."

Rebecci gave her a hasty look of gratitude, though tension filled her face. "Does he have any of the craftings?"

"No," replied Felice. "I made sure I took them all. No one's touched them since."

"Good." Rebecci turned back to the heavy and pressed the diamond into his neck.

Flesh sizzled, and smoke drifted up from burning hair, its stench filling the cabin. Around the diamond, glowing lines appeared under the man's skin, penetrating into his flesh. Felice watched as two extended toward the back of his head.

"I'll ask again: What's going on?" The leader of the heavies had drawn his knife and was pointing it at Felice.

"Hush," she said. "This man isn't what he seems."

The heavy frowned. "What do you mean?"

Rebecci flashed her a warning look before returning to her task.

"I believe the sorcerer we . . . disposed of may have done something to him. Rebecci here will confirm whether that's the case, and whether we are safe or not."

The heavy looked puzzled but held his tongue. After a glance at the man on the floor with the shielded Rebecci leaning over him, he sheathed his blade.

"You've some explaining to do."

Felice smiled, eyes hard. "Not likely. You'll be paid for your services, then go on your way, making no mention of what's happened today. You didn't hear anything, you didn't see anything. Is that clear?"

The heavies hesitated, and then the leader nodded. Seeing him agree, the others did the same.

"In fact," added Felice, "you may as well leave now." She went to her desk, and from the back of a drawer she withdrew a coin purse. Not the best hiding place, but the majority of her fighting funds were in a locked box sunk in the bilge. She poured the ducats into her palm, hesitated, then divided them evenly. Handing the portions to the heavies, she cautioned them. "Not a word. If we find out you've been talking, it'll go hard for you."

"As you wish, my lady. This is far more than we're usually paid, so feel free to call us any time you need our services."

"I'll keep that in mind. Now, out."

They looked to Rebecci for permission. She nodded and they filed out.

Once they left, Felice breathed a sigh of relief. "Izak, stop looking like you saw one of the ancestors' spirits and find another bottle of wine. I think we'll all need a drink after this."

Izak skirted a wide berth around the heavy on the floor and went looking for another bottle. She left him and bent down close to Rebecci, whispering in her ear.

"What are you doing? I assume I was right?"

Rebecci wiped her sweaty brow, not taking her eyes off the diamond crafting, which was now glowing with a sickly green diffuse light. "Yes. Though, how you were able to guess is—"

"Savine tapped his foot when I first saw him. It was an unconscious, or nervous, habit. After we'd killed Savine, or thought we had, I noticed one of the heavies now had the same mannerism—when before he hadn't. It was then I suspected there was a chance he could be . . . compromised. Now, what are you doing?"

"Containing him. For the moment."

"Savine?"

Rebecci nodded. "I . . . I'm reluctant to do this but . . ." She shook her head. "It's for the best. I hope I'm forgiven. Usually, the First Deliverer would be the one making this decision."

"I'm sure it's fine," Felice said, wondering if the First Deliverer was the same as the man Rebecci had spoken of at the bank, Gazija. "So you're only able to contain Savine. Not remove him?"

"Later, perhaps."

Rebecci's voice held a great deal of strain, and Felice grew concerned. She had no idea what the sorcerer was doing or how much it drained her. If something went wrong . . . "Your people are on their way?"

"Yes," said Rebecci with a nod. "We decided it would alert Savine if too many of us came at once. If it was just me, and he thought you had no idea what had happened, he'd be off his guard. You said it was Izak, though."

"I thought so at first but changed my mind."

"What gave him away?"

Felice shrugged. "It had to be him once I'd eliminated Izak from consideration. There were no other options." His annoying quirks were too hard to mimic, and she knew him too well.

She looked up as Izak approached, another bottle in hand.

"I'm afraid there's only spirits left."

"Perfect. Pour a measure for the three of us. I suspect we'll be needing a strong drink, and I for one want something for my nerves." She gave Izak a smile, not because she was nervous, but because he was.

"Ah . . . yes. Good idea." Izak found a few small glasses and poured them a drink. Felice took the offered glass, as did Rebecci.

Boots thudded toward them from the corridor outside—Rebecci's people.

Felice raised her glass. "Here's to secrets," she toasted, and drained her spirits in one gulp.

CHAPTER 37

Sitting cross-legged on Miranda's bed, Caldan could feel the warmth where she'd lain, and he missed her already. The physiker and her helpers had just left, having come with a stretcher to collect Miranda and take her to the hospice. He regretted not spending more time with her in Anasoma. He had been slow to realize she was more to him than just a friend.

The hospice was on Southgate Avenue, and he vowed to see Miranda as soon as he had time. Perhaps he could read to her again, as that seemed to calm her when she was restless.

Lines of sunlight streamed in through gaps in the window's shutters. From outside somewhere, a rooster crowed, and below his window, two men were arguing. Caldan stood, yawned, and opened the shutters, breathing in the air of Riversedge, redolent with unwashed bodies, smoke, and effluent. Curiously similar to Anasoma's, and yet subtly different.

Moving back to the bed, he removed the components for his craftings. For these, he wouldn't be casting any pieces himself. They were too small and fiddly to fit any cast runes, and the silversmith's forge didn't have the proper equipment anyway. For these, he'd had to rely on the clockmaker. And that meant he'd have to scribe his craftings on the surface, either by scratching with a sharp implement, or with a pen and ink. Etching was not fine enough for the control he required, and come to think of it, there would be problems scratching the runes into the metal as well. That left a pen and ink.

Taking all the metal components out, he laid them on his bed and separated them into two piles. When he'd made his first working automaton, he'd thought his knowledge of crafting was extensive. It was only after his encounters with the Indryallans, and examining Bells's craftings, that he realized he'd barely scratched the surface of what sorcery was capable of. And destructive and coercive sorcery were only part of it. With the expanded knowledge and skills he'd gained, he could see such potential in his craftings that he wouldn't have thought possible a few months ago.

Caldan took in the intricate pieces of metal in front of him and ran a finger down a few of the complex parts. The clockmaker's workmanship was exceptional, as he'd expected. But the pieces needed a sorcerer's touch to make them come alive.

He paused, turning the thought around in his mind. Was it really possible? The most complex automatons were still under a sorcerer's control and required almost constant concentration. Coercive sorcery manipulated the mind, so . . . could it be used to mimic a mind? The idea intrigued him, but he filed it away. He already had too much on his plate for the time being. All his effort had to go into doing whatever he could to heal Miranda.

Returning to his mechanical pieces, he prepared his pen and ink, making sure the viscosity was just right. It was a difficult ink to use and had to be made in small batches. An alchemical reagent caused the ink to harden rather than dry, which enabled it to adhere to the metal with a strong bond. Once applied, it wouldn't rub off or flake loose. But that meant going through a lot of pens, which had to be discarded once the ink set; and it required a sure hand to scribe the crafting runes quickly and without error.

Caldan was exhausted after such a long day, but at the same time invigorated. The sense of accomplishment he'd felt with his successful smith-crafting gave him impetus to ignore his weariness and push ahead with this second project.

Stifling a yawn, he poured a small amount of ink into a wooden spoon and added a few drops of alchemical reagent. Dipping his first pen in the liquid, he gave the ink a stir, opened his well, and set to work.

Hours later, he sat back and frowned. He'd almost run out of pens, but the job was done. His mind ached from holding on to his well and the strings for such a long time. But it had been necessary to imbue the pieces, the same as it had been with the medallion. Each segment acted as a separate crafting, and they all had to work together as a whole, in synchrony. And that was where most sorcerers failed with automatons.

Caldan almost laughed out loud comparing the simplicity of his doglike automaton to the ones in front of him. The two he'd been working on were still in pieces, but they were orders of magnitude more complex than what he'd even thought possible.

If the last few months had taught him anything, they'd shown him he needed to be prepared.

He pushed one pile to the side and began piecing the other together, clicking and locking parts into place, sometimes using pliers as the pieces were so delicate and fiddly. But after an hour, he was done.

A metal beetle fit into his palm.

It looked delicate, so thin was the brass that composed its body and wings. It was made in the same way as one of the songbirds the clockmaker in Anasoma had shown him. But this beetle was different, covered in minuscule crafting runes, the smallest Caldan could manage with the magnifying glass and slender pen the clockmaker had provided him.

Caldan had taken what he'd learned from both clockmakers, Bells's craftings, and his own knowledge and combined it all into this creation. Two round moonstones made up its eyes—the best gems he could afford, and inferior to what he wanted, but he had to make do the best he could.

It was an overcomplicated design, but one that meant very few sorcerers would be able to wrest control of his smith-crafted automaton from him, and he'd likely be able to retaliate against them before they did. While he was fine-tuning his schematic, he'd remembered the scratching and scrabbling at his linkage when they were escaping from Anasoma. Bells or Keys, he wasn't sure which, had tried to push him out and assume control of his creature. At five strings, he'd be stretched thin, but he was sure the complication would go a fair way to preventing appropriation of his control, at least by anyone less than an extremely skilled master sorcerer. And if he was facing someone that skilled, then he had bigger problems than just command over his creation.

He was on the run from the Protectors, Bells was still on the loose, and Amerdan was out there, somewhere—a man who likely had some answers to Caldan's questions about being Touched, and who had to be brought to justice for what he'd done to Elpidia. All Caldan had to do was find them.

Slipping the beetle to the bottom of his satchel, he returned to work on the other crafting. His eyes and fingers ached, but he was so close to completing it, he couldn't stop now.

CALDAN PAUSED AS the last piece clicked into place. Fine work. He'd have to thank the clockmaker again. With a start, he realized the darkness outside the window had turned to gray as dawn approached. He yawned. His limbs felt heavy, but he was strangely happy. Or perhaps satisfied. He didn't think he'd be truly happy until Miranda was herself again.

His newest crafting lay there like one of the clockmaker's windup toys. Except this was no toy, and it bore no similarity to the doglike automaton. It was shaped like a man, with tiny garnet eyes. Only two handspans in length, it was entirely covered in crafting runes. Whereas the doglike automaton had space left over, Caldan had crammed as much as he could onto this crafting's surface. Not to make it more powerful—in fact, he'd decided not to include a shield as part of its design—but to make its movements smoother, as effort-less as any natural animal's. Each piece was as integrated into the whole as he could make it. He'd stretched himself as much as he was able. Sorcery integrated with clockwork mechanisms and movement.

He wondered what the warlocks would say about that.

CHAPTER 38

Aidan dragged himself out of the river and through the mud using his good arm. The sticky sludge sucked at his clothes, at his limbs, and stank like a long-dead thing. Pushing with his feet on the slippery bank, he was able to leave the water behind and hide himself in some reeds. Scratches covered his arms and face, and mosquitoes buzzed in his ears.

Far in the distance came the sounds of the jukari, hooting and howling as they crossed the bridge and plundered the settlement on the other side. Whoever was left there was likely being killed and eaten. He hoped no one was stupid enough to have remained, but he knew there were always people exactly that stupid.

He snorted, spat out phlegm tinged brown with muck, and coughed. He was shivering, soaking wet, and his shattered arm ached like it was rotting from the inside. The bridge was downriver from the city, and the water was disgusting. You'd have to be a fool to willingly throw yourself into such polluted water, but he'd had no choice.

Aidan rolled onto his back and stared at the sky. *Rest a little while longer*, he told himself. *Get your strength back.*

His sword lay at the bottom of the river somewhere, and all he had left was a slender dagger. Against hundreds of jukari, it wasn't much at all.

When Chalayan's craftings had started buzzing, Aidan knew something was coming. As the volume had increased until it hurt his ears, and the jukari milled around howling, he'd decided the bridge wasn't the best place to die. So he'd thrown himself off, and just in time, too. His ears still rang from the sorcerous detonations, and an arc of lightning had struck the water next to him, just as he was about to break the surface.

Smoke still coiled into the air from the bridge. He didn't know what Chalayan had done. Didn't want to know. Such dangerous knowledge was a curse on mankind. Cel Rau would act. They'd spoken about Chalayan and a situation like this. Some secrets had to remain buried, and if corpses went into the grave alongside them, then so be it.

Aidan crawled through the mud and reeds until he gained firmer ground. He staggered to his feet, covered in sludge, but it would dry and flake off. Shielding his eyes from the sun, he examined the bridge. It was a fair distance away, as he'd let the current take him downstream, but he could still make out jukari and a few vormag. The majority of their force had already crossed. The settlement was burning.

Filthy abominations.

The haze of Riversedge was on the horizon to the west, but he couldn't go in that direction. Today wasn't the day he'd end up in a jukari cook pot. So north it was, until he could be certain he wouldn't run into jukari patrols. Then he would turn toward Riversedge.

Aidan sighed, cradling his broken arm, and trudged off, placing one foot in front of the other. That was the key. One step at a time.

"IT'S NOT UP for discussion," said cel Rau flatly.

Vasile sighed and looked skyward. *By the ancestors, this man is immovable.* "Why not? We can't protect all these people. Why don't they move faster?"

"They think the Quivers will arrive and save them. They can't think of any other outcome."

"But we haven't seen a Quiver for days."

"No."

"So . . . they have faith in the emperor's protection, which won't be coming, will it?"

"No. If the Quivers are smart, they'll stay behind the walls of Riversedge."

Vasile tugged on his reins as his horse tried to slow. It was exhausted. They all were. "And leave all these people to die? They'll be slaughtered by the jukari. There's no way they'll reach the protection of the city walls in time."

"No."

Vasile glanced at the villagers and farmers around them. They'd caught up with the bulk of the refugees quickly after leaving the settlement, where cel Rau had . . . slaughtered Chalayan, his friend, like a butcher kills a cow. Swiftly and mercilessly.

Vasile stumbled as a sickening thought intruded. He waved away cel Rau's concerned look and managed a stiff smile. It was his idea that had led Chalayan to discover the secret of destructive sorcery. Maybe he was next . . . Would cel Rau decide he was a liability? That what he knew had to be expunged from the world?

Had Aidan been the only force restraining cel Rau?

"We need to protect these people," said cel Rau.

Vasile stared at him. "From the jukari? From the hundreds, if not thousands, of the creatures behind us? What . . . how are we going to do that?"

"Kill jukari. And vormag. Stay ahead of them."

"Are you mad?" hissed Vasile, regretting his outburst immediately.

"No." Cel Rau frowned. "I don't think so. They're traveling slowly now, but when they see the horde coming and no Quivers to save them, most will go faster. Then, the stragglers we can't save. Those too slow or too weak."

"So we'll try to keep the jukari from taking as many as possible, all the while staying ahead of the horde so we don't get overwhelmed by numbers. And we'll do this all the way from here to Riversedge." Vasile gazed to the smudge on the horizon that denoted the city. "Which is what, a day away?"

Cel Rau shrugged. "A day. Maybe less, maybe more."

"Doesn't it matter?"

"No. We get there when we get there."

Vasile nodded. "I'll help, then. I'm not as good as you with a sword, but I'll do my best."

"That's all I'll ever ask. Any help is better than none."

"Do you think this is the wisest move?"

Cel Rau spat to the side of the road from atop his horse. "The Quivers will do the smart thing. Most of these villagers will do the smart thing, once they feel the jukari's breath on the back of their necks. I didn't say I was wise."

And if I die while we attempt this, thought Vasile, *then cel Rau's problem vanishes, leaving him with clean hands.*

VASILE FOUND HIMSELF gripping the reins of his horse painfully tight with his good hand. Behind him, cel Rau had dispatched another jukari with his usual efficiency. He then remounted his horse and caught up to Vasile, ignoring the heartfelt thanks from the family he'd saved: a couple and their two children, both girls, dressed in rough, homespun clothes.

Cel Rau motioned Vasile to stop, and they waited for the tear-streaked family to hurry past. Looking toward the bridge where Aidan had made his last stand, they saw the jukari milled like ants. Only a few had raced ahead to try and catch the refugees from the settlement, but more and more left the main group, heading in all directions. A hundred yards away, two more gray-skinned jukari loped toward them, both wielding swords that looked like daggers in their huge hands.

"They won't make it," said cel Rau.

"Who? The family?"

Cel Rau nodded. "Too slow. The children slow them down."

Vasile swallowed bile that rose in his throat. Hot sun beat down on him, and he needed a drink. He sipped from a waterskin; it would have to do.

"Then we'll have to do all we can to delay the jukari."

Cel Rau flashed him a grin. "That's the spirit. They'll be like waves breaking against sea cliffs."

More like ants swarming over helpless insects, thought Vasile. But he returned cel Rau's smile as best he could. "There are two more coming for us."

"Always, Magistrate. Evil never rests."

As the creatures came closer, Vasile urged his horse nearer to cel Rau's. The swordsman dismounted again.

"I fight better on foot," he said in response to Vasile's questioning look.

Not me. He'd rather face the jukari from horseback. Cel Rau was his only chance, and if the swordsman went down . . . he'd rather be mounted than trying to run. He was willing to fight, to do what he could, but he didn't have illusions about his abilities as a warrior.

As the jukari approached, he could see the larger one's skin was shinier, more snakelike than its companion's. And rather than the mottled gray of the jukari he'd seen so far, darker, thin, black stripes threaded across its arms and legs, neck and face.

"I'll take the big one," said cel Rau, drawing his two swords.

"As opposed to the less big one," Vasile noted.

Cel Rau grinned. "That's the spirit. All you need to do is hold it off until I get there. Wrap the reins around the saddle horn and use your legs to guide your horse. You've had enough practice on this journey." He walked casually toward the jukari along the road.

Vasile urged his horse to catch up with cel Rau and drew level. His hand ached from squeezing the reins, and it was slippery with sweat. The air smelled of dust, horse, metal, and the rancid stench of jukari. His horse tried to back away, but he held it steady and did as cel Rau suggested, quickly binding his reins so they wouldn't get in the way. He then drew his sword.

Cel Rau sprang at the jukari, swords weaving in a complex pattern. The smaller monster jumped back and to the side to avoid being gutted, leaving it clear for Vasile. Exactly as cel Rau probably planned.

He urged his mount toward it and swung his blade down . . . only to miss the jukari entirely as it dodged. It snarled through a mouthful of pointy teeth, claws from its free hand gouging his thigh. Pain and blood erupted from his leg. It raised its sword high over its head. Vasile drove his mount into the beast, knocking it off balance. As the blade sliced down, Vasile parried it to the side. His horse reared, frightened by the blood and the stench of the jukari. Vasile clung to the animal, sword slipping from his grasp as he clutched the saddle with his only good hand. The horse crashed down on the jukari, hooves striking its head and chest with a thud. A crack of breaking bones sounded. The monster crumpled to the ground, yowling in agony. The horse reared again and slammed down onto the jukari, silencing its cries of pain, then shied away.

Vasile slid from the saddle and groped in the dirt for his sword. Risking a glance, he saw cel Rau had his jukari well in hand. It bled from multiple cuts to its legs, arms, and face.

He stumbled to his prone jukari and plunged his blade into its chest. It coughed up blood and spit and stared at him with hatred, yellow eyes wide. The dark liquid dripped from its mouth, and it hissed at him through stained teeth. Vasile withdrew his blade and plunged it deep again, and again, until it was still.

Gasping for breath, he turned to cel Rau. The swordsman noticed Vasile's fight was over and stepped inside the reach of his jukari's long arms. He sprang from the ground, using the jukari's own knee to boost him up. With one swift thrust, he buried a sword into the creature's heart through its armpit.

As the jukari moaned and scrabbled on the ground, lifeblood leaking out, cel Rau turned and left it lying there.

"So far, that's four to me and one to you, Magistrate. You've some catching up to do."

Despite himself, Vasile couldn't help but smile.

CHAPTER 39

Caldan watched the fair-skinned, slender blond woman who was taking bets, keeping a keen eye on the Dominion games in progress. She was trailed by a young boy and girl, who barely reached her shoulder. Each of the youngsters carried a wooden board onto which were clipped stacks of small squares of paper and a thin-necked ink bottle, and it was on those slips that the bets were written out. They were then taken to one of the two cashiers close to the entrance, and each of these was guarded by two huge, angry-looking men bristling with knives. It wasn't a perfect system, and Caldan could see a number of ways of not paying up if you lost, but he guessed it worked well enough.

So far, he'd kept to the edges of the room, where the shadows were darker and he was less likely to be noticed. Groups of people, from pairs to five or six, also gathered close to the walls, mostly nobles and merchants engaged in hushed conversations with whispers and furtive looks. Some stared daggers at each other, but despite the obvious hatred, that was as far as it went. Caldan decided this Dominion house was also a meeting place for those who wanted to conduct business deals and size up their opposition, a neutral venue with an informal truce in place. A number of nobles and well-dressed merchants passed by him, eyeing his clothes and bearing before continuing on, which was well and good; he was unremarkable enough to avoid their interest.

His ducats were running low, which was why he was here, but so far he'd made a single wager on one of the smaller games—placing all his remaining ducats on a certain victory by a noblewoman. It hadn't netted him much in return, a few silver ducats from the low odds, but he had to start somewhere. At this rate, he'd have to come back every night for a few weeks to win enough ducats to cover all his needs. It was irritating, and his thoughts kept returning to playing a few games himself, but it was too risky, and he didn't have many ducats to wager yet, anyway. It just wasn't worth it. But he couldn't be conservative, either—he'd never make enough.

He needed to find a game and take a risk.

One of the Dominion matches in progress caught his eye. Entering the second half, the boards were a tangled mess, and it looked to be anyone's game. But he could see that one player, a sallow-faced man, was positioning himself well, making every move count, while his opponent's moves were less effective. Oh, they'd look well thought out to the average Dominion player, aggregating and consolidating his positions, but ultimately they'd prove his downfall. Caldan recognized some of the sallow-faced man's defense and attack groups from a number of famous games from the past he'd studied, so the man must know what he was about. And indeed, his next few moves proved the result was beyond doubt, though those around the board hardly seemed to recognize it.

The fair-skinned blond woman and her assistants paused close to the game to exchange pleasantries with an older man, who he assumed was one of the regulars. Caldan took the opportunity to approach them.

"Excuse me," he said, interrupting the woman. "My apologies, but I'd like to make a wager on this match here."

The woman glanced at him before turning to the man she'd been talking to. "Will you excuse me for a moment?"

"Of course." The man stepped away and returned to watching the game in progress.

She smiled, then turned to study the board for a few moments before speaking. "Three to two for either player," she stated, then pursed her lips, waiting from him.

Caldan fingered his meager supply of ducats in his pouch, then rubbed his thumb over his trinket ring.

Dare he risk it? He trusted his judgment of the game, but still . . . it was a lot to lose. No, his ring was too valuable for him to risk in any wager.

"I'd like to wager something of value rather than ducats." He produced his smith-crafted beetle from his pocket and placed it on one of her assistants' wooden tablets. Even in the low light away from the Dominion sets, its metallic carapace shone, causing the minuscule crafting runes to stand out in contrast. "It's a sorcerous crafted beetle."

"Really?" drawled the woman. "It looks pretty, but I've seen mechanical contraptions just like it. I'd put its worth at say . . . one gold ducat."

Caldan snorted. One gold ducat was a third of its worth, even if it had only been a windup mechanical novelty. "I think you know it's worth far more than that."

He opened his well and linked multiple strings to the beetle, making it crawl around the wooden board. The girl holding it gasped in surprise, while the woman's eyes widened. He activated the beetle's shield, at a low level, enough to have the multicolored haze cover the carapace for a brief moment.

"What was that?" exclaimed the woman.

"Sorcery. As I said, it's a sorcerous crafted beetle."

"Very well, two gold ducats, then." She licked her lips and eyed the beetle.

Caldan clenched his mouth shut to prevent himself from laughing, then realized she was serious. And why wouldn't she be? He'd come begging to her without enough ducats to make a decent wager. To her, he was desperate, and desperate people did stupid things, just like he had to.

"Agreed," he said reluctantly. "On the sallow-faced man there to win."

"That's Lord Loubster to you." She nodded to the girl, and the youngster began scribbling on a square of paper.

"Ah, excuse me, that's mine," exclaimed Caldan as the woman picked up his beetle.

"In situations like these, the house retains the collateral until the wager is decided."

It figured. "And if I lose?" It seemed like a good question to ask.

"You have a day to come up with the two gold ducats you lost in return for the collateral; otherwise the house gets to retain whatever was offered as assurance, no matter its value."

Caldan nodded. His options were limited.

The girl handed him a piece of paper, and he took it.

The woman gave him a wide smile. "I'll be seeing you later, then."

All three moved off to another gentleman, who had been waiting impatiently to the side.

Caldan watched the game with renewed interest, and with a fair amount of trepidation. A short while later, he saw the girl assistant who'd handed him his wagering slip approach Lord Loubster, exchanging a few words with him before wandering away.

Loubster looked around nervously before returning his attention to the match, arousing Caldan's suspicions. From then on, the noble's moves weren't quite at the same level of competence as they'd been previously. He made a number of glaring errors, looking chagrined at the derogatory remarks directed his way from the onlookers, but waved away their concerns with an offhand comment.

Caldan's stomach churned when Loubster made two moves that were brilliant in their stupidity. He doubted anyone else realized, but he'd just lost the match, since his moves were cunningly disguised as defensive, but that's exactly what the lord had done: deliberately lost the match. When Loubster stood and, red-faced, admitted defeat, everyone around his table was none the wiser.

Except Caldan. He clenched his fists, and his nails dug into the palms of his hands. He'd been had. The woman who'd taken his wager had conspired with the house and Loubster to throw the game. His crafted beetle must have been more valuable than he thought, for all the good it would do them.

Caldan approached the woman, fixing his mouth into a weak smile.

"Bad luck," she said, tone dripping commiseration.

"Yes." Caldan found he had to pause and take a deep breath before continuing. He could sense the beetle in her belt pouch. Even if he linked to it, it wouldn't be able to get free. And making a scene in the packed room would get him noticed, which was the last thing he wanted. "So I have a day to return with two gold ducats?"

"That you do. I'll be here tomorrow night. You can see me when you have the coin."

She knew very well he didn't have any ducats and most likely had no way to obtain two golds before tomorrow night.

"I'll see you then," Caldan said through clenched teeth.

He left the woman standing there and exited the building, blood boiling in his veins, face hot. It was late at night, and he couldn't think of any way out of his situation other than one unpalatable, risky venture.

But there was no helping it. He wasn't going to let the woman get away with stealing his crafting, and his hopes of using Dominion to replenish his ducats wasn't working as well as he'd wished.

Like I said—I'll have to go all-in . . . no matter what the game turns out to be.

He made his way through back alleys and narrow streets to the building where Joachim had imprisoned him. A Protector was guarding the iron gate, but there were no lights on inside. It was too valuable a building to give up, and as he'd guessed, the Protectors would keep it to sell later or use as another of their outposts scattered around the city. And if that was their plan, they might have left quite a few valuable items inside, possibly even all the ducats. With luck, that is. And he hadn't been lucky tonight so far.

SKIRTING A WALL darkened in shadow, Caldan ducked into a side alley and looked up. The top of the wall was a yard higher than his extended reach, but with a running jump . . .

His hands grasped the brickwork, and he pulled himself up and over the other side, dangling by his fingers and then dropping to the ground. Crouching low, he scanned the courtyard for signs he'd been seen. There was no hue and cry, and the Protector near the gate was now sitting on a stool and covering a yawn with one hand.

Caldan crept to a side door and crafted the lock open, using his chalk to scribe the runes. Inside, it was pitch-black, dark enough that he feared bumping into furniture. Patiently, he waited until his eyes adjusted and he could discern vague outlines. As stealthily as he could, he made his way to Joachim's room.

"By the ancestors," he cursed.

The room had been ransacked. All the valuables had been stripped, leaving only the furniture, rugs, a few chairs, the desk, bookcases, and a cabinet. They looked empty, a fact he soon confirmed. No doubt these would be next to go, once transportation was arranged. It seemed the Protectors wouldn't be using the residence; they'd be selling it off.

Maybe the other rooms aren't stripped yet, thought Caldan. But he knew he'd likely find the same scene. He was about to leave when something tugged at his awareness. It was so faint, he wouldn't have noticed if it weren't dark and he weren't focusing on using all his senses. A crafting, almost imperceptibly vibrating at the edge of his consciousness.

Where was it? He closed his eyes to help himself concentrate. He took two steps forward, then one to the left. It was . . . under his feet?

Under the rug.

Quickly, he rolled the rug up to reveal a hatch in the floor, a couple of handspans across each side. It surely wasn't big enough to hide much, but someone had obviously gone to the trouble of making and concealing it under the rug, along with locking it with a crafting.

After all his practice, Caldan felt confident he'd be able to get past the crafted lock, and accessed his well, extending his senses. He sucked in a breath. A simple lock had one or two links for strings. The lock in the masters' library had five. This lock had seven. It had to be Joachim's. Possibly his most valuable possessions.

But seven strings . . . Caldan had never stretched himself beyond five before. The very thought made him dizzy as his mind recoiled. It was possible, though, with enough practice. But to extend himself to seven strings now . . .

He'd never know until he tried.

Caldan sat cross-legged on the floor with the locked hatch in front of him. He unlinked from his sorcerous globe, leaving him in total blackness. He breathed deeply, in and out, focusing on his breaths, as the monks had taught him.

One sense at a time, he distanced himself from outside sensations. Underneath him, the hard floor fell away until he felt suspended in the air. He closed his ears to noise, leaving only the sounds of the reverberation of his own breathing and the pumping of his heart.

Barely thinking, letting the process occur naturally, he accessed his well and split off three strings. Another breath, and he split off one more. Another breath, another string.

Holding five felt almost effortless now. He anchored them to the linking runes on the underside of the hatch. Though they were hidden, he could still feel the space they occupied.

Without conscious thought, he split off a sixth string. His breathing stopped as pressure bored into his mind from all sides. Caldan forced himself to start breathing again, but his breaths came short and fast. The sixth string squirmed in his grasp, and he struggled to hold on to it.

Calm, he chided himself. *The pain will lessen. Focus on your well.*

For long moments, he sat, forcing himself to regain composure, ignoring the pain in his head. Eventually, his chest loosened and he breathed easier.

A drop of sweat hung from his nose, tickling it, and he wiped it away. Despite the distraction, the six strings didn't snap back, and he remained in control. Caldan spent the next few moments holding on to the strings, reinforcing his control. It wouldn't do to linger now; he could already feel his strength draining rapidly.

He braced himself and, with utmost care, split a seventh string from his well. He gasped as spikes of pain penetrated his mind. He let out a low moan, struggling to maintain his grip on even the original six strings, which had all of a sudden become as slippery as wet eels.

The agony was too much . . . He couldn't . . .

He clamped onto all seven wriggling strings, refusing to let them slip out of his grasp. Gasping for breath, he forced a linkage with the sixth string. Straining himself to his limits, it was all he could do to push the seventh string to link. But link it did, and the scent of lemons filled the air as the compartment clicked open.

Caldan immediately let the strings absorb back into his well, and as the pressure in his mind eased, he slumped to the floor exhausted.

But he'd done it. Seven strings. His head felt like he'd taken a beating. A warm wetness dribbled from his nose. He sat up and wiped it away. Blood, for certain.

In front of him, the hatch was ajar enough to slide fingers underneath and pry it fully open. Inside was a wooden box small enough to fit in his palm. There was also a coin pouch. Caldan hefted the coins and looked inside. All gold, at least thirty. Probably Joachim's getaway stash, in case things went wrong. A different-colored gleam caught his eye at the bottom of the pouch. Feeling around, Caldan could discern a few other round objects. He tipped the coins onto the floor, and toward the end, out spilled four deep-green gemstones. Emeralds. An unexpected treasure, and enough to keep Miranda well looked after for a long time, should it come to that.

Returning the ducats and gems to the pouch, he turned his attention to the box. It looked like a jewelry box, the kind jewelers used to display their rings and brooches.

Caldan opened it and froze. As he'd hoped, it contained a trinket. A ring, still attached to a finger that had been sawn off at the third knuckle. And recently, too, judging from the early stages of decomposition. Gingerly, he slid the ring from the finger. Blackened skin came away from flesh, and a rotten stench filled his nostrils. He left the finger inside and closed the box, returning it to the hideaway hole and closing the hatch. He covered it with the rug, not bothering to craft the lock closed. His head still ached from unlocking it, and he wasn't about to attempt seven strings again so soon.

Caldan secured the trinket in his pocket. It belonged to the Protectors, could actually have been owned by one that Joachim had killed, for all he knew. And even though he had left them—just as they had all but rejected him—he felt a twinge of guilt. But there was nothing for it. It made no sense to leave it behind, and he knew he could find a use for it. True, unknown trinkets were dangerous things, best to be wary of. Yet it could be of great help to him if he could figure out its function. Or he could always sell it. Either way, there was time to worry about that later.

Blood from Caldan's nosebleed covered his hands. He wiped them on his pants—he could afford to wash his clothes now—and left the room. A few moments later, he scaled the outside wall and disappeared into the night.

CHAPTER 40

Amerdan stepped out of his dirty clothes and handed the bathhouse woman the chit he'd paid for earlier. She averted her eyes but cast fleeting, appraising glances at him. His absorbed talents meant he'd developed layers of hard muscle he usually kept hidden under his clothes, a side effect he'd found disturbing at first, then accepted as his due.

"These will be laundered for you and ready tomorrow, sir."

He sniffed. "There's no need. I've new clothes to change into, and these are a bit ragged. Do with them what you will."

The young woman stared at his filthy clothes with surprise. "The cuffs are a little frayed, and they're only a little mussed. Perhaps—"

"I said take them. They're of no use to me."

She kept silent and nodded.

Stupid people. She and the other creatures inhabiting this place weighed on him, as did the dust and grime. He found he missed his shop in Anasoma, which he could keep clean and tidy. An oasis of calm, while the animals dirtied themselves outside his door. Here, though, he couldn't get clean enough. And he stank of Bells.

Not long now, he told himself.

Leaving the bathhouse woman, he entered the hot baths, making sure he placed his basket of new clothes where he could see them, careful not to touch them with his dirty hands. A young girl left a towel on a stool for him, along with soap and a comb.

"Bring a few more buckets of hot water."

Amerdan waited until she left, then used a ladle to rinse himself with hot water before lathering with the soap. Once he was clean, he wouldn't soak in the hot baths. The thought of immersing himself in water that dozens of other people had bathed in almost made him retch. It was enough that he could wash away the rancid grime of the city and feel like himself again for a few hours. It would have to do.

The girl appeared carrying two more steaming buckets. She placed them next to the other bucket and stood there, waiting.

"Bring two more."

The girl left again, and he continued to cleanse himself.

Bells would expect him back soon, and he smiled. She had proved useful. He still hadn't been able to discern what she was working on, though. This morning, she'd seemed unusually distracted. She'd slotted a few of her craftings together so they clicked into place. With his new-found sorcerous abilities, he'd been able to determine that whatever she was making had seven linking runes. Far more than he'd been able to master so far. With Bells's guidance, he'd managed two strings, but only for a few moments. It annoyed him that this was an ability he had to work on, but . . . the rewards were great. Far greater than he'd imagined.

Again, the girl returned with two buckets.

"That's all; five is enough."

She smiled shyly at him and nodded, standing to the side. Waiting.

Amerdan jerked his head, indicating she should leave, and she scurried away. He had paid for one of the best baths in the city, and he knew exactly the services they provided. But he was having none of that. The nobles and merchants who visited here were hardly better than animals rutting in the dirt.

Finally clean to his satisfaction, he dried himself off with the towel. After dressing, he took his friend from the bottom of the basket. Dotty winked at him, and he nodded, placing her inside his clean shirt.

"Come—let's see what Bells has been up to."

FROM A DISTANCE, Caldan watched as the Quivers at the gate scanned the people coming into the city for anything untoward. They took a few travelers to one side for questioning and searched one of them. He suspected it was more to relieve the boredom than anything else.

The sky had lightened and was getting brighter. During the time he'd remained leaning against a wall, the queue to enter the city had grown, until there were too many people to count. As the sun finally peeked over the hills to the east, and a second squad of Quivers reinforced the first, they opened the other half of the gate to allow more people to enter, and they and their livestock and wagons flooded in.

A line formed to exit the city, but it was mostly ignored, and Caldan surreptitiously joined the rear of a group of eight men and women. It wasn't long before he passed through the gate without incident.

Outside the city walls, makeshift huts and dilapidated dwellings dotted the countryside, occasionally clumping together to form ramshackle communities. Caldan left the group he'd used as cover and hurried down the paved road as fast as he dared.

Keep calm, and don't look back.

One hand fingered his shield crafting in his pocket, in case he needed it. But he would shield himself only as a last resort.

Caldan traveled down the road, peeling off onto the first well-traveled track he found. It was wide and rutted from wagon wheels, which meant it should lead to a modest village or a substantial farm. Now that he was out of sight of the road, he took his beetle from his pocket and sent it flying ahead, its senses alert for people and— most especially—other wells besides his own. The fair-skinned blond woman who'd taken his bet hadn't been pleased to see him and his ducats. She'd smiled at him through gritted teeth while marking his debt as discharged and handing over his automaton. He'd been stupid to make a wager in an unfamiliar establishment, and lucky to come away with his crafting. He'd bid the woman good day and left her steaming.

Occasionally, Caldan stopped and sat beside the track, sending his senses into the beetle and seeing through its crafted eyes. He couldn't be too careful this time. As far as he could determine, the bone trinket was his only leverage, and if he were found with it in his possession, it meant any advantage he had was lost.

A short time later, he saw what he was looking for: a group of houses clumped together around a communal well made from gray stone blocks and protected with a wooden cover to keep dust and leaves out.

He pulled a fist-sized rock from his satchel. His bone trinket was tied to the stone with a leather thong wrapped multiple times around and through the ring. Caldan hesitated, then took two kerchiefs from his satchel. *Best to be sure it isn't damaged,* he thought. He wrapped the stone with one kerchief, using the other bunched up as a cushion protecting the trinket.

Glancing around to see if anyone had noticed, he replaced his satchel strap on his shoulder and continued on toward the houses, which were remarkably quiet. Better for him, he supposed, if no one was around.

He'd come up with the idea when he'd realized that one day soon he'd have to face the emperor's warlocks, based on how Simmon had hidden the trinket sword. It was an ingenious hiding place, but one he'd have a little trouble with in Riversedge: The flow through the aqueducts that brought water to the city was sometimes quite strong. A heavy object, like the trinket sword, was no problem. But smaller, lighter objects could be washed away with the current. He needed a normal well.

Caldan used the well's crank to wind up a full bucket of water, ostensibly to wash his face and hands and drink his fill. At the same time, he sent his automaton in a circle around the village, then a wider one around the outside. There were no signs of life, not even a dog or chickens. Strange.

He took his time, making sure no one was watching, but the village was still and silent, as if everyone had packed up and left yesterday.

He shrugged and dropped his river stone over the edge, as close to the center of the well as possible. A few moments later, he heard a splash, and satisfied he'd know where his bone trinket was when he needed to retrieve it, he turned and left the village. At his back, it was as quiet as it had been when he'd found it.

CALDAN SLOWED HIS pace as he neared the gate into Riversedge. Only an hour or so ago, the queue to enter the city had been orderly and controlled. Now, though, a mass of people was pushing to get inside. A few were arguing with the Quivers on guard and gesticulating toward the east, where Caldan noticed for the first time trails of smoke on the horizon, winding their way into the clear sky.

Outside the gate, farmers, merchants, teamsters, and traders were pushing one another in their eagerness to get inside. Among them were many dirty and raggedy dressed men, women, and children. Caldan guessed they were the residents of the makeshift dwellings outside the city walls. Everyone was fairly civilized at this point, but it wouldn't take much for chaos to break out. Whatever they were concerned about, it didn't look like the Quivers had much of an idea what to do.

And more were coming.

All along the road, groups of people approached Riversedge, laden with possessions. Carts were filled with furniture, wagons with produce and crates and chests. Off in the distance, clouds of dust thrown up from different locations in the countryside indicated many more people were moving toward the city.

Caldan took in the wild eyes of the scared citizens pushing to enter Riversedge, along with the Quivers' harried, frantic looks at one another.

"By the ancestors," he cursed. Something was very wrong, and he could reach only one conclusion: the Indryallans were coming. Why they'd waited so long was a mystery, as was what they hoped to achieve.

He tapped a heavyset man on the shoulder. An irritated face turned to appraise him.

"What do you want?" asked the man gruffly through a mouth of yellowish teeth.

"What's going on? Is it the Indryallans?"

"Huh. We might wish it were. It's worse than that. A horde of jukari have been spotted to the east. Entire towns and villages have been burned to the ground! And you know what they do with the people they capture?" The man shuddered and then leaned in close. "They eat them."

Jukari? In a large group? Caldan remembered reading about the creatures a few times in books on the Shattering and the centuries after. If he recalled correctly, they were rarely seen outside two or three at a time, and never near civilization. Certainly never much farther than the empire's borders.

"Have the reports been confirmed?"

The yellow-toothed man gave him a sharp look. "I don't know, but I wasn't staying around to find out."

A quiet voice came from behind them. "I saw them."

Caldan turned to see a woman holding hands with a tall man. Both were lean and hard-looking and wearing workmanlike leather clothes. Judging from the horses behind them, laden with furs, they were trappers.

"Where?" asked Caldan. "How many?"

The woman looked at her partner, who nodded. She glanced down, scuffing at the dirt on the road with the toe of a boot. "It was only two days ago. In the morning. We were heading into town with our pelts to sell after a few weeks trapping. It's a nice little town . . . was," she corrected herself. "It was nestled in a valley, and we came at it over a ridge only to see the buildings burned to the ground. It must have happened at night, else we would have seen the smoke. There were at least a hundred jukari that we could see. Filthy gray creatures. They were gathered in groups, eating . . . I don't know what, but . . ." Tears welled in her eyes.

Her man put his arms around her. "Shh. The Quivers will take care of them."

She nodded, a short jerky movement. "We ran. As much as we could, warning anyone we found on the way. We can only travel so fast, but since then we've been passed by others who've seen things, terrible things. They've come from everywhere." She gestured around them. "As you can see, I don't think there's only one group of the monsters."

Caldan thought she was right. It looked like the whole countryside was on its way to Riversedge for protection. "Why haven't the Quivers alerted everyone in the city? They need to prepare."

Yellow-tooth scoffed. "What, and panic everyone? I doubt they know what to do."

The line moved ahead of them, and they shuffled toward the gate. Surprisingly, it didn't stop, and they kept moving. It looked like the Quivers at the gate had decided to dispense with their usual inspections and questions in order to prevent the gates becoming a bottleneck and the crowd descending into chaos. A wise move.

Caldan nodded his thanks to the trappers and the other man as they passed through the gate. To the side, the Quivers on duty stood and watched the influx of people into the city. They looked . . . worried. Not a good sign. They hadn't been much use when Anasoma was invaded. How could they face a horde of nightmarish creatures from the Shattering? With luck, the city's walls would stop them dead, but if they were breached . . .

Caldan sighed wearily. He couldn't escape Riversedge, and it was likely the Protectors were on their way to the walls now. And he'd only just escaped from them.

CALDAN MINGLED WITH the crowd at the top of the wall, looking out at the approaching flood of refugees, which had increased tenfold.

In the distance behind them, smoke plumes rose into the sky. The people who now hurried toward the gate cast anxious glances over their shoulders and looked far more harried and frightened than those he'd spoken to earlier. The jukari must have been right on their tails.

Keeping his head low, Caldan elbowed through the throng to the back and leaned on a merlon. Speculation was rife among the Riversedge residents, and there was an edge of panic in their voices and bearing.

Just then, to Caldan's right, a squad of Quivers barged their way up a wide stone ramp leading to the battlements, passing a massive catapult set atop the tower near the gate. Protests followed in their wake, which were ignored. Then Caldan saw Master Mold, and behind him two armed and armored Protectors.

Finally, Caldan thought, making sure there was a mass of people between him and Mold. It looked like he needn't have worried, as Mold and the Protectors only had eyes for the refugees pouring in, and the tiny dark specks chasing them. Caldan noticed the plain hilt of the sword Mold wore—the trinket sword.

Mold and the Protectors engaged in a heated conversation, heads close together, hands gesturing to punctuate their words. Eventually, Mold shook his head and turned to stare over the wall again. He wrung his hands; then, as if aware of what he'd been doing, he hunched his shoulders, dropping a hand to grip the sword hilt tightly.

Caldan looked around for another way off the wall, but he was too close to the gate. The ramp Mold was at the top of was the only way down from here. Never mind, Mold wouldn't stay long. It also looked as if he'd decided not to do anything to help—and Caldan couldn't help but wonder why. The jukari had gathered in larger numbers than he'd ever heard of before and penetrated this far into the empire. Something was very wrong . . .

Shouldn't Mold be gathering the Protectors to assist?

The Quivers should be out there guarding the people coming in, and so should the Protectors. If they rode out, they could scout the jukari for themselves, then safeguard the refugees on their way here. Otherwise, people were going to die. A lot of people.

Instead, both the Protectors and Quivers were hiding behind the city walls.

With growing frustration, Caldan shook his head and peered out between two merlons at the fleeing people. What good was sorcery if it couldn't be used to protect ordinary citizens?

The Protectors' edict to deal only with outlawed forbidden sorcery was a mockery. Caldan could only think such conservatism would just get a lot of people killed, and once more he felt he'd made the right decision to leave them.

I won't be ruled by them . . . but there's nothing stopping me from helping, is there?

For now, though, he had to wait, both for Mold to leave, and to see developments outside the walls.

DOZENS OF PROTECTORS had trickled in over the course of a few hours as the sun continued its journey toward the western hills. In truth, they were a fearsome sight, clad in crafted plate armor and carrying shields and swords. The accumulation of craftings, along with the occasional trinket, set Caldan's bones to vibrating. Some of the armor looked newly smith-crafted, while other pieces were ancient. One set of plate was even jet black, forged by a process he could only begin to guess at. The crafting runes covering its surface were old, far more stylized than those he'd seen in use.

Mold had segregated the Protectors into smaller groups and directed them to guard positions around the wall once the jukari arrived. And now he was speaking to each of the groups separately.

Let them talk, thought Caldan. What use was sorcery if it had to be rationed for fear of . . . what? Would some farmer seeing a Protector rescue him from jukari suddenly be able to use destructive sorcery and go on a rampage, bringing another Shattering on the world?

No, this was policy shaped not by fear of the power getting out of control, but the fear of someone losing control of power. So who stood to gain if destructive and coercive sorcery were suppressed? Who had the Protectors doing their bidding, concealing any sorcery other than what they wanted the population to know about, but used forbidden sorcery themselves? The warlocks, like Joachim.

And, ultimately, the emperor himself.

What better way to keep such sorcerous power to himself and those around him than to suppress its practice?

Caldan began to wonder just what use the Protectors were. What Mold and the Protectors were doing now, not *protecting* the people fleeing the jukari, just seemed so . . . horribly wrong.

The thought was treasonous, clearly, but Caldan was beginning to wonder what loyalty he owed to a man who would allow his own people to perish just to keep a secret.

The dark smoke from the fires was getting closer, as were the plumes of dust in the distance. A shadow had begun to darken the land to the east at the very edge of his vision. Caldan frowned, squinting up at the cloudless sky. That was no shadow.

He raised a hand to shield his eyes from the sun. His other hand inched down to clasp the hilt of his sword. Slowly, the shadow crept closer, until he could make out individual figures: jukari. They had to be. And not just a few groups banded together—the trappers had mentioned a hundred or so. Here, there must be thousands of the creatures.

In front of the horde raced other tiny figures—humans, trying to outrun the jukari. Caldan watched, horrified and sickened, as the shadow swallowed the slower-moving people before it.

Caldan glanced at Mold. The master's face was grim, but he turned back to talk with some Protectors.

A few groups in front of the horde broke off and headed east and west toward side roads converging on the main thoroughfare, while the remaining force continued toward Riversedge, devouring more victims as it advanced. Farmers, traders, trappers, merchants, fathers, mothers, children . . . the jukari didn't discriminate. And all the while, the Protectors did nothing.

He could almost hear the Protectors' justifications. *If forbidden sorcery is known, weak-willed sorcerers will use it only for their own gain. We cannot risk another Shattering. We do what we can in secret. It's always been that way. It's necessary.*

"No," Caldan whispered under his breath. "It's not."

He released his grip on the wall and rubbed his hands. He'd been grasping the stone so hard they ached. Once, in Anasoma, he'd thought he'd found a place among the Protectors . . . but no more. If the warlocks were anything like Joachim, hiding sorcerous knowledge for their own gain, then he didn't think they'd have his best interests at heart either, let alone those of the citizens of the empire. Which meant *they* were exactly what the Protectors were supposed to guard against. And the Protectors had been corrupted to serve them.

"Master Mold," exclaimed a Protector twenty yards away on the wall. He was pointing out at the jukari horde. "Look! There's someone fighting the jukari."

Caldan turned his attention to the mass of tiny figures, as did Mold. He squinted, trying to make out what the Protector had seen.

"On the road," the Protector added. "Two men are killing jukari, the ones that get too far ahead of the mass."

There . . . yes. Caldan sucked in a breath. At this distance, they were tiny, but two men definitely were killing jukari out there. One on horseback, leading another mount, while his companion was on foot. And it looked like they were trying to give fleeing refugees enough time to escape. As he watched, a jukari came at one. Caldan could see that it towered over him, even at this distance. Somehow the man remained standing, and the jukari fell to the ground. They ran from the fallen beast toward Riversedge, staying between the last of the refugees and the advancing monsters.

Two men against the flood of jukari, doing their best in the face of overwhelming odds. He glanced at Mold, who remained unmoved. And the Protectors watched, their inaction a blight they didn't even comprehend.

"By the ancestors," he cursed, turning his back on the jukari. "I can't watch this."

Caldan glared at Mold. He couldn't stand here and do nothing.

He made for the ramp, passing three Quivers who were readying the catapult with head-sized stones. He jumped atop the battlements, breaking into a run and leaping from merlon to merlon, to avoid the crowd and bypass Mold. A reckless anger drove him. He was beyond caring if he was seen; he needed to do something to stop the slaughter.

Mentally, Caldan checked his gear. Trinket ring, craftings, and a plain but well-made sword. It would have to be enough.

"Caldan!"

Caldan flinched at Mold's shout, but he kept going. He looked up, meeting Mold's eyes. The master's face was red, and he pointed at Caldan. But it was too late. He was past and racing down the ramp, shouldering and elbowing people aside. A quick glance behind him confirmed Protectors were following, hampered by the crowd.

At the bottom, he turned toward the gate, which was still open, searching the incoming crowd for what he needed. There: a Protector sat astride a sturdy brown horse.

Caldan grabbed his arm.

"Hey!"

"Sorry," Caldan said, and pulled with all his might, jerking the armored Protector from his saddle. The man landed on the cobbles with a crash.

In moments, Caldan was on horseback, pushing his way past the people surging through the open gate.

"Make way!" he yelled. "Let me through."

Annoyed shouts followed him as people were shoved out of the way by the bulk of the horse. They flowed around him and closed in behind him, again blocking any attempt to stop him. Protectors tried to reach him, but against the surge of the crowd, they had no chance. People wanted to get into the city, not out, and the Protectors couldn't fight through to catch him.

Caldan itched between his shoulder blades, and he hunched down over his newly acquired horse. If Mold was going to try something sorcerous, now was the time . . .

He opened his well and linked to his new shield crafting, feeling the familiar tightening of his skin as the multicolored shield surrounded him. Sucking in air, Caldan steeled himself and drew as much as he could from his well to reinforce his shield. Such a torrent, he'd never felt before. His hair stood on end, and the air felt as if it were vibrating. A harsh buzzing sound filled his ears, and the scent of hot metal and lemons was almost overpowering.

Abruptly, his well slammed shut. Caldan's mind recoiled from the whiplash as the raging torrent ceased in an instant. He felt like he'd been doused in ice-cold water and shivered violently, head aching. He fell forward, pressing onto the horse's neck, almost throwing up as his stomach twisted. His breath came in short, doglike pants.

Caldan glanced over his shoulder to see Mold pointing the trinket sword directly at him.

By the ancestors, did the sword do that?

So this was its function. And he had no way to defend against it.

Then he was clear of the gate, and he guided the horse to the side, out of the way of the train of people shoving their way into Rivers-edge. He gave the horse its head, cantering down the side of the road toward the oncoming jukari horde.

Men, women, and children all gave him startled looks as he rode past, some shouting their concern he was riding the wrong way, others cheering him on, as if one man could do anything much against the jukari.

But without access to his well, what could he do?

Reaching his senses out, he tentatively tested his well. It was still blocked, but the barrier felt somehow less dense, as if whatever obstruction the trinket had placed was itself eroding.

Distance. The barrier was weakening with distance.

Caldan kept riding. He could make a small difference, and that was what he craved. Inside Caldan, something had broken: his flight from Anasoma, when the Protectors had all been killed, only to have Bells escape and be betrayed by Joachim; the unveiling of the distortion of the Protectors; Miranda's damaged mind he couldn't heal. He needed to do something. All his hardship and decisions so far had left him with nothing.

The refugees thinned considerably after the first few hundred yards. Those he passed now had an air of desperation about them, wild eyes and sorrowful expressions, as if they expected to be run down and slaughtered within sight of the city walls.

Suddenly, the power of his well came flooding back, and Caldan laughed. Now he could do something.

He urged his horse on. Ahead, somewhere, were the two men doing what the Protectors should have been doing, and he meant to join them, and ensure they and as many refugees as possible reached Riversedge alive.

There. The man on the horse wielding a bloodstained sword. For a moment, he blocked Caldan's view of his companion, but the man guided his sweat-lathered mount toward a group of terrified men and women, urging them to keep fleeing, and the other man was revealed. Covered from head to toe with splashes of black jukari blood and dust, he looked like a tribesman from the Steppes, dual-wielding curved swords with short blades.

Caldan tore his gaze away from the men and looked toward a group of baying jukari. One or two, the men could face, but it looked as if some had held back and joined with others that had caught up. Six were coming toward them now at a loping run. Impossible odds, and yet the tribesman was walking calmly toward the creatures, while his companion followed close behind.

It was Caldan's first sighting of a jukari. They were exactly like he'd read about, resembling the pictures he remembered sketched in a book at the monastery. Gray skinned and tall, head and shoulders above a grown man, with savage grins and jagged, sharp teeth.

With a shout, the swordsman leaped at the lead jukari, swords swirling in a lethal pattern. Blood sprayed from sliced flesh, and jukari howled with inhuman pain. On his horse, the other man stood in his stirrups and attempted to batter a jukari edging around his companion. Not a fighter, this one. Then Caldan noticed he had one arm wrapped in a sling and was still doing what he could.

Caldan flashed past the fleeing men and woman, scarcely sparing them a glance.

"Go!" he shouted to them, as if they needed to be told. It was all he could think to say.

Out of the corner of his eye, he saw three more jukari loping toward the men only a few dozen yards away and closing fast. Nine.

They would be overwhelmed. Caldan's blood burned in his veins like molten metal, and sweat dripped from his face.

Thrusting a hand in his pocket, Caldan withdrew his smith-crafted automaton and threw it into the air. With barely a thought, five strings separated from his well and linked to the beetle. Shiny bronze wings opened, and he sent it buzzing toward the three jukari coming at them from the left.

He turned his attention to the tribesman holding off five jukari, as incredible as that seemed. Guttural cries filled his ears, along with shouts from the two men, and a rancid animal stench pervaded the air, combined with the scent of blood.

A horse screamed as a jukari's massive sword buried into its shoulder. The man riding had only just swayed out of the way of the flashing blade at the last instant. His mount stumbled, and he was thrown clear, uttering a hoarse shout of agony as he landed on his injured arm. His companion buckled under the assault of heavy jukari swords.

Caldan glanced desperately to his left and gave his beetle a sequence of commands, then drew his sword, urging his horse straight at the five jukari ahead. Agonizing pain filled his mind as he forced more strings from his well. A multicolored shield enveloped him, and with a thought, he extended it around his mount.

An instant later, they crashed into the first jukari, knocking it flying. His horse screamed with terror, but the shield absorbed much of the impact, sparkling purple motes spreading over them. Momentum barely checked, Caldan slashed his blade into a stunned jukari's face, splitting it in two. The creature's head jolted back with the impact as it dropped lifeless to the ground. He raised his blade again, a ribbon of black blood flying, and slammed it down at another jukari. Steel rang on steel as the creature raised its own sword and blocked his blade. Caldan screamed, blood boiling, and struck again. The jukari's sword broke in two. His blade sliced deep into its shoulder, and it howled like a thing of nightmare. Caldan easily turned its broken sword as it attempted a thrust with the splintered end. Another slash, and he opened its throat. Then he was through the group and out the other side.

The three jukari that remained alive hesitated, giving him time to deal with the other group.

On the ground now, his beetle opened its carapace, and out rolled a tiny sorcerous globe. Caldan had learned his lesson beneath Anasoma with his first metal automaton. There was no gain in destroying that which took so much effort, and expensive materials, to create, when a smaller crafting would do. His beetle buzzed back toward him. A quick glance, and he confirmed the tribesman was backing away toward his friend, who still lay prone on the ground.

The new group of three jukari snarled as they approached, jaws gaping, and stepped toward his globe. Caldan's head was about to explode, he was holding so many strings. It was too many. He had to decide which ones to cling on to, else all would slip from his grasp. His shield vanished, and he linked to the sorcerous globe, pushing as much power into it from his well as he could. Brightness erupted from the ground. Jukari staggered and shielded their eyes.

Caldan ruptured the anchor.

The globe was annihilated by the forces from his well. A clap of thunder reverberated from the site as an invisible force knocked the jukari flying. Strands of lightning surged over their bodies, blackening their skin and sending out billows of steam. Caldan relinked to his shield, almost too late, as the forces washed over him and his mount. He gritted his teeth as his shield sparkled a deep purple, but he managed to keep the strings in his mind's grasp. Tendrils of lightning flooded over him, crackling with intensity. His shield withstood the forces assailing it with ease. Caldan wiped his brow, his only concern now that he was holding too many strings—they might slip from him at a critical moment. The tribesman and his friend were too far away for him to protect.

Caldan rushed the remaining three jukari, only to see the swordsman take one down with graceful slashes to its thighs and stomach. It squealed, flailing on the ground, clutching at its innards.

The two remaining jukari darted away, turning tail to flee. The swordsman looked about to chase but stopped after a few steps. Caldan glared at their retreating backs as they raced away, but the swordsman was right: no point chasing them when they could be moving closer to Riversedge. There was no time to waste.

He urged his horse toward the swordsman, who was rushing to his friend's aid. He slipped out of the saddle. The man on the ground groaned, face white and mouth clenched in pain. A short distance away, his horse lay in a pool of blood, still alive, trembling. The second horse he'd been trailing was a few dozen yards away, staring at them.

"I'll fetch a horse," Caldan said. "If we can get him up on it, he'll stand a chance."

The swordsman nodded curtly, not saying anything. He sat his friend up, who let out a shriek and clutched at his bandaged arm. A score of heartbeats later, Caldan had the spare horse's reins and led it back. Together, they hauled the injured man onto the horse, where he sat uncomfortably, head lolling back and forth. They wrapped the reins around his good hand.

The swordsman sniffed. "It'll have to do. Get on your horse."

Caldan met his gaze. "And what about you? You need to recover, after what you've been through. I'm fresh enough. You ride, and I'll run alongside. I have a feeling we'll both need our strength before we're safe in Riversedge."

The swordsman grunted. He eyed the jukari Caldan had killed with revulsion, and his hands gripped the hilts of his now-sheathed swords like he expected to use them at any moment. "Thank you for saving us. I'm Anshul cel Rau, and that's Vasile." His companion didn't look like he'd heard them. He was almost done in and barely clinging to the horse.

"Caldan. I wish we'd met under better circumstances."

Anshul let out a laugh. "Killing jukari's a good circumstance. You're a sorcerer." He gave Caldan a narrow-eyed look before turning away.

"Something like that. Someone had to do something to help."

Anshul seemed to weigh Caldan's words, then nodded thoughtfully. "There are vormag among the jukari. They're sorcerers as well, but cowardly and not as skilled as you. They'll hang back for the time being, until they gather some courage. Enough talk. We have to keep moving."

Vormag . . . Caldan dredged the name from deep in his memory. He'd read about them years ago, in an ancient text on the Shattering. Sorcerous creations like the jukari—except they hadn't been remarked upon as anything special. *Abominations*, the text had called them.

Caldan followed Anshul's gaze toward the jukari horde. The two running from them had stopped and were waiting for more of their kind to bolster their numbers. He needed no further encouragement.

"Let's go, then." Caldan indicated for the swordsman to take his horse, and he led Vasile's mount toward Riversedge.

He felt . . . good. For the first time in a long time, he'd used sorcery in a good way. No ambiguity, no sneaking. He had saved lives and killed monsters—surely there was a place for that kind of sorcery in the world? That was a question for another day. All he had to do now was concentrate on getting back to Riversedge alive. As he jogged toward the road, leading the injured man's horse, he saw the swordsman eyeing the blackened circle of grass littered with three charred and smoldering jukari with interest.

He's likely never seen such sorcery before.

The swordsman flicked him a blank look Caldan couldn't decipher before turning his horse to ride alongside, holding Vasile's shoulder to keep him in the saddle.

AMERDAN WONDERED IF Bells had any idea what he really was. Probably not, he decided. To the sorcerer, the wonder of someone having more than one well was enough to make her giddy. He was someone to be protected . . . nurtured. And given to her God-Emperor as some kind of gift.

But the only gifts exchanged would be their talents to him.

Amerdan watched her as she assembled her crafting: metallic shapes covered with acid-etched runes and symbols, only a few of which he recognized. To be fair, everything he knew, he'd learned from her; knowledge she deigned to hand out to him when she wasn't busy with her crafting. He'd pushed for more once or twice, too eager to have it all and be done with the sorcerous slit. But she'd told him it could be harmful to his progress, or his mind, or some such drivel. Still, until he knew better, it was best to be cautious.

But the need . . . Sometimes, when her back was toward him, he imagined his knife inside her. He'd had to close his eyes and restrain himself. Even now he warred within himself, between the need and whether he really required her to develop his sorcerous talent.

Soon, he promised himself once more.

"What does it do?" he asked for the fourth time.

"I told you, it's far too complicated to explain."

Amerdan's fingers twitched toward his knife. Inside his shirt, his rag doll brushed against his skin. "So you said. But I didn't ask how it works. I asked what it *does*."

Bells paused at her work. In her hands, she held a flat metal disc with a hole bored through the center, one of a dozen she'd begun threading onto a steel rod attached to a thin stone base. Once they were all placed onto the rod, it would look like a layered cake made of various different crafted metals.

"It's a focus, of sorts. It will allow a sorcerer a long distance away to home in on my location and transfer his power here."

Amerdan studied Bells. Her hands caressed the metal disc almost lovingly. Not accustomed to being disturbed, he was nevertheless . . . unsettled. Why would she need someone else to know her location and give her power? Perhaps she wasn't strong enough to face the emperor on her own. Except . . . from what he knew, her sorcery should far surpass anything the emperor could manage in his defense. He fingered the coin now linked to him that would give him safe passage to the emperor.

"But you need me to take it close to the emperor now. Where will you be?"

Bells smiled at him. "That won't be necessary anymore. I've been given new orders. We only have to get as close to the emperor as we can, among his forces. Then it'll all be taken from our hands when he arrives."

"He? Aren't we going to kill the emperor?"

Still smiling, Bells's eyes took on a faraway look. "No, that's not our task anymore. The God-Emperor himself will be here soon. He's able to come here thanks to our work. All this senseless warring will be over when he does. I can't wait for you to meet him."

CHAPTER 41

They were sitting in the pouring rain.

By the ancestors, cursed Felice to herself. *What's wrong with these people?*

It hadn't been raining when Rebecci had sent the remaining heavies to take Savine's new body back to the Five Oceans Mercantile Concern's offices. When the sorcerer had gestured for Felice to follow her to a wharf that jutted out into the harbor, she had in turn told Izak to go with the other men. He'd said nothing, but the look of relief on his face was thanks enough.

She'd caught up with Rebecci at the end of the pier, where the strange woman ignored her repeated questions. Frustrated, Felice had sat down next to the sorcerer, legs dangling over the side, and stared out at the ocean. Soon after, the dark clouds above started drenching them with cold water. It did nothing to alleviate her frustration.

Felice shivered and stuck her hands in her pockets. She hadn't fully recovered yet, and she worried the chill rain might trigger a relapse of her sickness. *Bloody sorcerers.*

Once more she prodded Rebecci with the toe of her boot. "What are you doing?"

Finally, Rebecci turned her head to face her. She looked even thinner now that the rain had soaked her clothes and they clung to her body. Even her wild hair hung lank against her head and face. Felice suppressed a laugh. She looked like a wet cat. One that hadn't eaten for weeks. She was as thin as a stick. It was a wonder the wind didn't blow her into the sea.

Maybe the water weighs her down.

"Thinking. Communicating with the First Deliverer."

Rebecci turned away from Felice and continued staring out over the swell. From this angle, Felice could see the sorcerer's lips moving, as if she were speaking without making a sound. Both hands were in her lap, wrapped around something: the metal-encased diamond crafting, Felice assumed. Rebecci's hands had a greenish cast, as the light from the gem penetrated through her pale hands.

But Felice was done sitting in a downpour for no apparent reason. She'd managed to get Rebecci talking, so she continued. "Is Gazija the First Deliverer?"

Rebecci hesitated, but eventually nodded. Felice felt like she'd won something, even with just that little confirmation. Of course, it left other questions, specifically about the rather ominous title. Deliverer from what?

"Deliverer from our annihilation," said Rebecci in response to her unvoiced question.

Uncanny. The woman made her decidedly uncomfortable.

"What's he saying, then?"

Rebecci remained silent.

Felice hunched her shoulders and bent her neck, trying in vain to avoid the fat drops of rain. Atop a pier next to her, a seagull squawked and peered at her with beady yellow eyes. She'd had just about enough of these people and their obfuscations.

"Let's get out of the rain, Rebecci. What's the point in staying out here?"

Rebecci stood, and green light flashed as she placed the crafted diamond in her pocket. "It helps obfuscate my sorcery."

Felice blinked, then swallowed. Decidedly uncanny. "From who?"

With just a hint of a smile, Rebecci pointed behind her along the wharf toward the city. "Them."

Approaching them came two small figures, both rail thin, like Rebecci. A small boy and girl. They strode along the wharf with an assurance beyond their years. And their clothes—Felice had never seen children wearing such finely woven cloth. Or the craftings she spied around their necks and fingers.

A dozen yards away, they stopped and stood there, not saying a word.

For long moments, the only sound was that of the rain drumming into the wooden wharf. Beside her, the seagull squawked again.

"Will you tell me what's going on? Please," Felice asked Rebecci.

The skinny girl made a noise that sounded suspiciously like a titter. "Rebecci," she called out in a high voice. "Release Savine to us."

"I will not. The First Deliverer has made his judgment."

"A frail old man, stuck in the past."

"A hero who saved us all, you included."

The child sneered. "Ancient history."

"Still relevant." Rebecci took a step forward, slightly in front of Felice. "Turn back from your path," Rebecci told the boy and girl, voice raised, "or you will suffer the same fate."

The boy and girl looked at each other, exchanging words in hushed whispers. Shrugging, the boy turned on his heel, striding back down the wharf. The girl stood there, glaring at Rebecci, as if her look could melt stone.

"Ward yourself," the girl said. "We'll be coming for you."

"I always do. Now go, before I scourge you here and now."

The girl uttered a hiss before turning to follow the boy, both retreating far more casually than Felice liked. They watched them until they disappeared down a street in Anasoma proper.

"Child sorcerers?" she asked Rebecci. "They weren't children, were they?"

The thin woman shook her head. She looked even paler than normal. "Far from it." She hesitated. "The First Deliverer thanks you for your assistance, and I'm to explain a few things to you."

Felice looked up into the gray clouds, water sprinkling her face. "Oh, I think I've pretty much worked everything out."

GAZIJA HAD BEEN one of the councillors to the high king for two generations before his world was shattered. Even in the beginning, when everything went wrong, he'd been confident he'd be able to save his people. For years they'd fought with hardened steel and virulent sorcery, until they'd been backed into a corner. Their choice was to serve or die. Yet he'd found a third option, confident in his sorcerous ability to rescue his people. And they'd trusted him. Placed their fragile lives in his hands.

And he'd failed them.

The forces assaulting him from his well had been too strong for him to master. In the end, his flesh had burned from his bones, before they too were consumed.

Before this happened, desperate, dying, he'd fashioned a crafting unlike any he'd attempted before. Holding the binding symbols in his mind, he'd combined both controlled destructive sorcery and coercive sorcery into a vessel, of sorts—a crafting compromised purely of organized energy, held together by strength of will, able to contain his essence, his awareness.

And he'd survived. After a fashion.

He'd found himself in a strange, newfound world, almost insane with the agony he'd endured. Yet he *had* survived. Trusting him, his people followed his directions. One-third of them didn't make it.

And those who did . . .

He saved them, yet condemned them all to an eternity of suffering and torment. A bodiless existence that required them to feed on innocents to survive. They'd become parasites.

In a century of searching, he hadn't yet found a way out of their repulsive subsistence. And with time, another third of his people succumbed to despair, letting themselves just . . . evaporate, or be willingly imprisoned in inanimate craftings.

His greatest shame. And they worshipped him, still.

"Gazija? Can you hear me?"

He turned at the sound of the voice, leaning on his walking sticks for support. This body was almost done, but he wouldn't take the easy path and replace it yet. He had to set an example.

"Yes, Luphildern, what is it?"

"The mercenary captains are nervous. We're lucky the river splits before Anasoma and we could come up the branch from the ocean to the south. But they haven't been up this river before and want to know what to expect. And what's going to happen when we arrive."

"So what did you tell them?"

"The usual. But they're not satisfied. The weeks they've spent cramped in their ships are starting to wear on them, I fear."

"Bah! For what we're paying them, they should keep quiet and enjoy the scenery."

"I think that's one of the problems. We're paying them a great deal, and so far they haven't had to do much. Some of them are becoming suspicious."

"You'd think getting paid and not having to fight yet would be cause for celebration. Apparently not."

"Some of the captains are agitating for more information about what they'll be facing. They know they're heading deeper into the Mahruse Empire and think they'll be fighting the Quivers. And they're worried about getting trapped inside the empire with no way out."

Gazija grimaced. "I'll talk to them. Get the captains together. I suppose it's about time I told them what to expect. It might be their first time fighting jukari and vormag, and it would be best if they knew. And it might also be their first time as heroes, if the emperor forgives their trespass into his empire."

Luphildern shook his head. "What possessed their sorcerers to go down that path? To create such monsters?"

"Desperation," replied Gazija, something he knew about all too well. "But then again, maybe they were just insane."

Which, he feared, might be something close to home, too.

AIDAN TRUDGED WEARILY away from the bridge. He'd been walking for hours and still thought of himself as heading away from the bridge rather than toward Riversedge, because the truth was, he hadn't walked very far.

To say he was exhausted was a gross understatement. His arm ached like it had needles embedded in his flesh, and he couldn't think for the pain. Twice he'd found himself standing still, not moving, as he withstood another barrage of searing agony. He didn't even know how long he'd been there, in those moments. When he gathered the strength to move again, mosquitoes hummed around him, disturbed from their drinking of his exposed flesh, and he realized how thirsty he was. How long had it been since he'd tasted water?

He found a trail of flattened grass leading northeast, not exactly the direction he needed to go in, but it would do. The long grasses were tiring to wade through, and anything that saved his energy had to be taken advantage of. Stumbling along, feet dragging across the green and yellow path, Aidan thought for the first time that he might need help, or he might not manage to reach the city. Just when the thought crossed his mind, he spotted figures ahead in the distance, some walking, others on horses or with carts. He blinked dry eyes and swallowed as best he could with his parched throat. He managed a halfhearted wave before letting his arm drop, realizing he'd stopped again. They wouldn't likely wait for him; he'd better keep moving. Aidan sighed deeply, grimacing as his injured arm shifted.

A paved road appeared in his vision. He stopped, both feet now on firm stone. He looked up, shaking his head. He'd been so focused on moving one foot in front of the other, he hadn't even seen the road ahead.

Someone hurried past, leading a laden packhorse.

"Ex-excuse me," he croaked.

The man didn't look back and kept moving. He was in a rush, as he would be, if he'd heard of the jukari.

Aidan looked down both sections of road. To the west, a line of people and animals traveled away from him, toward Riversedge. Not a soul was traveling in the opposite direction, from what he could see. To the east, more people approached, and a few hundred yards away came a squad of Quivers, looking polished and soft, as if they'd never seen real action in their time as soldiers. Even their horses' coats shone, freshly brushed, like there hadn't been better uses of their time.

Aidan suppressed another sigh. Riversedge was in for a bloody fight if its only defense was composed of Quivers such as these.

As the Quivers approached, he drew out a small pouch from his pants. It held his most valued possessions, and after a moment of searching, he pulled out an engraved metal disc the size of his palm. Their . . . Caitlyn's . . . writ. From the emperor himself. Their mandate, which had protected Caitlyn from so many atrocities and enabled them to draw supplies from any outpost of the emperor's forces they wanted to. It tingled in his hand, like something alive. He'd always disliked the object, imbued as it was with sorcery, but it was valuable, and he wasn't about to throw it away. Caitlyn had bade him hold on to it as she couldn't stand the way it felt, either.

When the Quivers were within ten yards, Aidan coughed, clearing his throat. He held up the shining disc, one of the symbols of the emperor's power that no one would dare fake or lay false claim to.

"In the name of the emperor, I ask you to halt."

Shocked looks greeted his outburst, and their gazes were drawn to the writ. One of the Quivers nudged his mount closer. He looked annoyed. The man took his time examining the metal disc through narrowed eyes. Eventually, he sniffed and tipped his head.

"What's this about, then? We've had a rough time getting here, and we're in a hurry. There's been an invasion in Anasoma and rumors of sorcerous creatures from the Shattering in the surrounding countryside."

Aidan took in their soft hands and immaculate uniforms and gear. He almost laughed, then stopped. These men were what stood between the jukari and the people of Riversedge.

CHAPTER 42

N ow!" yelled Caldan, and he threw himself into the drainage ditch beside the road, covering his ears.

Cel Rau landed a few yards away, and Caldan ruptured the crafting he'd left on the ground before the jukari attacked.

A wave of force washed over them, pressing them hard into the damp earth and weeds. Crackles of lightning played around the edge of the ditch, but he'd calculated the safe distance effectively. Though he still held on to the shield surrounding them, he didn't want to stress it unduly, knowing they might need it later.

This was the fourth one he'd destroyed, and he'd become proficient in determining the radius of destruction based on the strength of the crafting. As he only had paper craftings left, the area wasn't large, but it was enough to kill any jukari close to the source.

He scrambled to his feet, glancing toward Vasile on the horse to ensure he was still mounted. Vasile's mount seemed quite happy to keep wandering down the road away from the commotion behind it, trailing Caldan's commandeered horse, which left Caldan and cel Rau to deal with the groups of jukari coming for them.

More blackened, smoking jukari corpses littered the road. Outside the charred circle, a lone jukari snarled at them, glancing at its dead fellows and edging around the ring toward them.

Caldan shouted and sprang at the monster. In the blink of an eye, he crossed the distance between them, and his blade hacked deep between its head and shoulder. Blood spurted, black and almost glutinous. The thing whimpered and crumpled to the ground. Caldan blinked sweat from his eyes and gasped for breath. Unlike the previous times he'd had sudden bursts of strength and speed, this time the feeling stayed with him. Though it seemed to ebb and flow, it didn't fully dissipate, as if it knew it would be needed soon and stayed in a state of readiness. On his finger, his trinket felt heavy and warm, like its weight had increased, and it burned from within.

Rupturing the craftings was the crudest, and only, form of destructive sorcery he knew. It gave them an edge when facing big groups of jukari, as long as they could get out of the blast. Once again Caldan wished he knew more about the sorcery, forbidden or not. In situations like this, he'd find it very useful to be able to control the forces like he'd seen Bells do. More than useful; almost essential.

Cel Rau came to his side as Caldan wiped his sword on the jukari's coarse clothes.

"That's eleven to you," said the swordsman. "You've passed Vasile, but you've still a ways to catch up."

Caldan nodded grimly. "Let's hope I don't. If I do, it means we'll likely be overrun, and then you won't care about the count."

Back along the road, ever-shrinking black circles marked where he'd had to revert to using destructive sorcery. In the closest spots, jukari corpses still smoldered. As good a swordsman as cel Rau was—and Caldan gauged the tribesman was one of the best he'd ever seen—they wouldn't have survived so long without Caldan resorting to destroying his craftings and shielding them from both the explosions and the jukari weapons. Overloading craftings and shattering their stability was unrefined and wasteful, but he really had no choice if they were to make it through this alive.

"Come on," said cel Rau. "There's more coming."

Caldan raised his head. Already, another two groups of jukari were rushing toward them. He glanced quickly past Vasile to where a family of five hastened to the protective walls of Riversedge. Close. They were so close now. He fancied he could make out the figure of Master Mold atop the wall next to the gate.

He ran a hand over his hair and massaged the back of his neck. Wearily, he blew out a breath.

The swordsman slapped him on the back. "We'll do our best. That's all we can do."

Caldan pulled his gaze from Mold and took off after cel Rau. In between fights, they made the most of the time to cover as much distance to Riversedge as they could. There were no refugees between them and the jukari; all that were left were ahead of Vasile.

At least we've given them time.

Except, of course, Caldan had never been that lucky. Because as they reached Vasile, cel Rau uttered a few harsh words in a language Caldan didn't recognize and pointed to their left and right.

"By the ancestors," muttered Caldan.

Two separate groups of jukari had skirted the road and passed them by, likely while they were fighting other jukari. For them to be so far ahead and not seen until now, they must have made a wide detour around them. Either they were part of other jukari groups approaching Riversedge, or they'd deliberately bypassed Caldan and cel Rau as too difficult and headed straight for easier prey. And behind them came three vormag. The sorcery-wielding creatures were enveloped in shields. They stopped and joined hands. An eerie wailing came from their mouths, and around them the grass began to wither and blacken, then it burst into flames. As they chanted, the blaze extended in a line to their left and right.

A sorcerous barrier, realized Caldan. Similar to what the Indryallans used on the walls of Anasoma. The vormag were leaving the jukari to sate their desire for blood, while using their sorcery to pre-vent whoever remained outside Riversedge from reaching the city.

Caldan probed at the barrier and recoiled at the writhing fury of the vormag's wells. They felt like jagged rents in reality, far removed from the wells he was used to sensing. As he was about to pull away something latched onto his senses and he screamed in pain as spiked hooks dug deep. He felt his mind, and his well, wrenched toward the vormag. He could feel their hunger and hate. Frantically he slammed his well shut, leaving himself defenseless. But at least the vormag's grip dissolved when there was nothing to hold on to.

Whatever else the vormag had planned, Caldan didn't want to wait around to find out, and if he didn't act swiftly, the family running for Riversedge would be slaughtered.

Caldan's blood boiled in his veins. His trinket pricked his finger, as if it had grown barbs. He waved cel Rau ahead, toward the spare horse.

"Use the mount. Make sure Vasile's all right. I'll take care of these. You just make sure you stay in front of the jukari behind us."

"But then you take the horse."

"I'm faster without it."

Without waiting for a reply, Caldan surged forward, legs pumping as fast as he could move them. The road and trees flashed past in a blur. Ahead, the father of the family was watching behind them down the road, relief on his face. He obviously hadn't seen the jukari com-ing at them from both sides. Or the vormag's fiery barrier blocking their path. They were a hundred yards from the gates of Riversedge and didn't seem to realize they wouldn't make it to safety.

They would if Caldan had something to say about it.

Caldan desperately urged himself to greater speed, boots slamming down on the stone-paved road.

High-pitched screams sounded from the family as their three daughters saw the barrier. They stopped, the father gathering his daughters to him, wife clutching at his arm.

"Don't stop," Caldan whispered to himself, knowing they'd made a potentially fatal mistake. He flung his smith-crafted beetle into the air, sending it toward the vormag. He had one more sorcerous globe, but he could always destroy the automaton if it came to that. He leaped the drainage ditch to the east and raced toward a group of jukari, aiming to place himself between them and the family.

"Keep going!" he shouted at them.

They looked at him with fear-filled faces. After a moment, the parents half carried, half dragged their crying children with them. Seeing them start moving again, Caldan adjusted his direction slightly to intercept the jukari, and for the briefest instant transferred his awareness to his beetle, seeing through its eyes. Now eight vormag, with six jukari he was heading toward. He didn't have a choice.

Gritting his teeth, he was preparing to destroy his beetle when arrows rained down on the jukari. Both groups crumpled under the onslaught of heavy arrowheads slicing through flesh and bone. Moments later, all that was left of the jukari were corpses sporting arrow shafts like pincushions. Finally, they were close enough to Riversedge for the Quivers to take some action, but that still left the vormag. With their barrier up Caldan and the family would be trapped, but he knew the vormag were too strong for him to face alone. Perhaps they could be forced to abandon the wall they'd created.

Caldan dove his beetle into the midst of the vormag. He dropped his last globe, linked to it, and ruptured the anchor.

Smoke and dust surrounded the vormag. Caldan looked behind him and their fiery barrier crackled and died, leaving a charred line on the ground. He yelled in triumph. Then a breeze blew and revealed the vormag were still standing. They'd covered themselves with shields, though one was bent over, clutching at a gash in its leg.

He could feel their gazes on him.

Caldan screamed as razor-sharp teeth ravaged his well. He fell to his knees, hands clutching his head. They were almost inside him. Choking back a howl, Caldan drew as much as he could from his well, trying to use its erosive force to prevent them latching onto him. A thrust from one of the vormag tore into his well only to jerk out when it encountered his roiling power. The tearing stopped.

Caldan found himself on his hands and knees, head bowed, panting heavily. Sweat dripped down his nose and onto the dirt. He dragged himself to his feet.

Arrows from the Quivers inside Riversedge hailed into the vormag's shields, which were almost entirely covered with sparkles. The ground around them bristled with arrows, so many had the Quivers loosed on them. With eerie cries and howls the vormag turned and retreated, shafts from the Quivers following them.

If they were unhindered, they would have torn me apart, realized Caldan.

He raised his sword in a salute to the Quivers on the wall as cheers reached his ears. On the road, the family continued toward the gate. Safe. They would make it. Now to see to cel Rau and Vasile.

He broke into a sprint. A few dozen yards behind cel Rau and Vasile came a bunch of baying, slavering jukari. The men were only just keeping ahead of the creatures.

Caldan flashed past the mounted men. As before, he didn't know how long his enhancement would last, but while it did he exulted in his speed and was in awe of his own power. He activated his shield and crashed into the closest beast, blade darting. His sword moved as if of its own free will, becoming a blur of violence. Caldan cut one creature from shoulder to hip. He stepped toward the jukari on the left. A slice upward. Black blood sprayed. He pivoted. His sword moved with blinding speed. The jukari barely reacted, as if they moved through water, movements delayed and sluggish. A slash down through a thigh, and a jukari howled. Caldan spun and cut. Stones slippery with blood. A final stroke, another jukari falling.

Caldan stood still, his sword covered with black blood raised above his head in the upper guard position. Around him lay jukari, dead and dying, their foul ichor pooling on the road. A bead of sweat ran from his right temple down his cheek. Chills swept over him as his body cooled. His trinket ring felt normal, as if whatever sorcery it wrought had faded to nothing.

He looked at the jukari, bemused. Was this to be his path? To understand his trinket and be able to release these surges at will?

The thought made him giddy. The power he felt . . . it was intoxicating.

Caldan's strength left his legs, and he tottered unsteadily. Who was he to wield so much power? And would it really be his, or would he be chained to the emperor with no choice but to obey or be killed? Caldan felt he knew the difference between right and wrong, and he should use his skills only to help people. But he might not end up with any choice in the matter.

Along the road, and spread for hundreds of yards either side, uncounted jukari poured toward him. Far too many for one man, no matter his talents. Caldan watched as they approached, clamoring for . . . what? Howls and inhuman cries filled the air. They wanted to kill, but why? What drove them? And after centuries of remaining hidden, apart from the occasional sighting or encounter, what had banded them together and made them penetrate this deep inside the empire?

A buzzing hail of arrows streaked over him and thudded into the jukari. Squeals and harsh barks of pain came from the wounded and dying. The creatures still able to move loped away, fleeing out of arrow range, and dragged their fallen comrades with them.

Caldan pulled himself from his reverie, turned his back on the death he'd caused, and headed toward the city. Ahead of him, Vasile and cel Rau were almost there, and Caldan was gladdened the two of them had made it. His own progress was slow going, but eventually he found himself before the gates. As he approached, a commotion penetrated his awareness. On the wall, the Quivers were shouting, bows and swords raised in the air in salutation. They weren't cheering for their own kills of jukari.

They were cheering for him, and cel Rau, and Vasile.

On the wall to the left of the gate, Caldan saw Master Mold looking down impassively. Caldan called his beetle to him and secreted it in his pocket. As he walked toward the gate, the cheers grew louder.

The gates were shut and barred, securing the city from the jukari horde, at least for the time being. The Quivers lowered ropes, not willing to risk opening the gates in case the jukari charged. Caldan helped cel Rau secure Vasile, who was lifted clear of the ground and to the safety of the top of the wall. Sadly, the horses were left to fend for themselves. Before he was pulled up, Caldan watched as they fled along the outside of the walls. He hoped they'd be safe.

Cel Rau grabbed his arm in a fierce grip. "Your secret's safe with us," he said quietly.

Caldan peered into the swordsman's dark eyes. He couldn't discern what was going on behind them. "What are you—?"

"Don't be a fool. We know more about sorcery than you think. After this, we need to talk."

Caldan swallowed and gave a curt nod.

Cel Rau stepped to the wall and grasped one of the ropes, letting himself be hauled up.

Caldan made one final survey of the scene behind him. Dead and dying jukari littered the road, staining it black with their blood. He still gripped his plain sword, the blade covered with congealed jukari blood. He thought of how much he hated the sight. Hated the thought of all this death and destruction he'd caused, and the exultation he'd felt at the time. He didn't want to kill, and he knew necessity had driven him today. But tomorrow? And the day after? He wasn't sure. His future was murky. Miranda was still sick. Amerdan was still free. Bells and the Indryallans were still invading, and the jukari still needed to be dealt with. Worst of all, he was once again without a home—not that it meant the Protectors or warlocks would just leave him be. And he had no plans to simply give himself over to them, not if it meant lies and servitude and, ultimately, the loss of his soul.

Death. Blood. He had thought his future murky, but the more he thought on it, the more it seemed etched in stone.

There has to be another way.

He let the blade slip from his fingers, and it fell to the ground with a dull clank. Grabbing one of the ropes, he allowed himself to be hauled up to the top of the wall, where he was crowded by a group of cheering Quivers yelling and clapping him on the back and shoulders.

He couldn't think of a reason to celebrate.

CHAPTER 43

Rebecci wasn't happy, Felice decided. Though the pale woman was hard to read, Felice thought she'd been able to discern a number of warring emotions on the sorcerer's face, and none of them were positive. The problem was, she couldn't understand any of the emotions, like despair. Why Rebecci would feel such a thing after successfully capturing Savine, Felice didn't know. And fear, that was there as well. But fear of what? Or for what?

Or both?

Felice snuggled further into a padded armchair and took another sip of plum wine from her bulbous goblet. She looked around the room, noting the plush rug and finely crafted furniture. On the windowsill sat a number of glass figurines, each a stylized animal holding various objects. A lion clutched a book, and a bird held a scepter in its beak. Though unlike any she'd ever seen, they reminded her of Dominion pieces. They were dust free, which showed someone cared for them.

"Are those figurines yours?" Felice asked Rebecci.

Rebecci nodded distractedly. She was staring at the silver-caged diamond, as she had been for the last half hour, since they'd entered the room. It lay on the desk between them. The sickly green glow had faded to a tiny flickering light.

"There's a time for secrets," Felice said. "And a time for answers."

Her statement hung in the air.

Rebecci tore her eyes from the crafting for an instant before returning. Long enough to lock gazes with Felice.

"I should kill you," the sorcerer said. "You know too much."

Felice stiffened, then relaxed and shook her head. "If you were going to do it, I'd be dead already. No . . . you want me for something. You need me for something."

"The rat is out of its hole, as they say. Or used to say, where I'm from."

"And where is that?"

"Nowhere you've heard of."

"I've heard of a lot of places. But I figure you're right. I wouldn't have heard of where you're from, because it's not in this world, is it?"

Rebecci leaned back in her chair and closed her eyes. She looked exhausted—the bone-weary tiredness of someone who'd been living under a heavy burden for a long time.

"I can help you," Felice said.

Rebecci took her eyes off the greenish diamond. She stood, trembling, and leaned her weight on the desk. "The First Deliverer warned us this time would come, and so it has. We are a remnant of a remnant. And I fear we are not up to the task. But I suppose that's why the First Deliverer is going to try to convince your emperor of the threat, and to trust us. Whether he succeeds or not, we will be sacrificed."

Felice narrowed her eyes at the mention of sacrifice. Rebecci plainly believed she was doomed whatever happened. But Felice was never one to think there was only one outcome. If Dominion had taught her anything, it was that no cause was hopeless.

"Whatever happens, we need to keep trying. And if I'm to help you, I'll need some answers. You never know, I might see a way through this for you. For your people."

A look of sadness tinged with grief came over Rebecci's face. "I hope that you do," she said, clearly not believing it.

"Then I want to know about Kelhak. He's not really Kelhak, but he's not one of you."

"It's Kelhak's body. That much is true."

"Then who's controlling it? Or is it a . . . what? Something dangerous. That's what this is all about, isn't it?"

"Trust me, you don't want to know what it is."

"That's where you're wrong. I *have* to know. If the empire, the world, is in peril, I have to do something about it."

"The First Deliverer has a plan, but none of us know the whole of it, only bits and pieces."

Felice nodded. Gazija, the sorcerer Rebecci and her fellows revered. The man she was supposed to have met outside the city. But if he was trying to stop Kelhak and wasn't here in Anasoma . . . that's why Rebecci was still here, and why she needed Felice. They had a plan, one Rebecci thought she'd die trying to accomplish.

A whimpering from the sorcerer brought Felice out of her thoughts. Rebecci looked even paler, and she was trembling.

"Rebecci," Felice said, a cold knot of fear spreading from her stomach. "What is it?"

Rebecci moaned softly, then brushed away a tear forming in her eye. "It's evil. It destroyed our world in a desolation. And it followed us here."

"Then I need to speak with Gazija. I take it that's possible?"

"Maybe. If I trust you enough."

Felice spread her hands. "Who else is left?"

Rebecci didn't look happy, but she nodded.

"I need to tell you something," the sorcerer said. "Gazija has a task for me. It's . . . risky. But it could end the war early."

It didn't take a genius to figure out what would spell the end of the Indryallan invasion.

"Assassination," Felice said, the word leaving a bad taste in her mouth.

"I've contacted a . . . someone. They'll be able to help. I've outlined everything in my notes. They're in a hidden compartment in a drawer of my desk."

"And why are you telling me this?"

Her bottom lip quivered, and Rebecci wrapped her arms around herself. She gave a slight smile, which quickly vanished. "Because I'm scared."

Felice nodded. *Of course.* "You think they could get to you first."

CHAPTER 44

Caldan allowed himself to be bundled into the back of a wagon beside a prostrate Vasile. The swordsman, cel Rau, glanced at him, expressionless, before returning to ministering to the injured man. As soon as he sat, suddenly exhausted, four Quivers joined them, and the wagon started rolling.

When he'd made it to the top of the wall, the Quivers had treated Caldan like a hero. But he knew Mold would try to restrain him again, and he couldn't allow that. Luckily, he was on the other side of the gate now, far from Mold and his Protectors. And after what had happened, the crowd in the streets was thicker than ever before. Caldan had urged the Quivers to bundle him, Vasile, and cel Rau down the ramp, on the pretext they had urgent information for the Quivers' commander. And the Quivers were only too happy to oblige. Caldan didn't want to think about what the Protectors would do to him if they caught him. His display was against everything they believed in. They might even declare him a rogue sorcerer.

The wagon jerked and wobbled as the Quiver driving it urged the horses to greater speed. Ahead of them, Quivers on horseback cleared the road.

Caldan rubbed the bridge of his nose with his thumb and fingers. A massive ache emanated from inside his head, a legacy of holding so many strings for so long. In truth, he didn't know how many he'd held at times. Nine at most; surely it couldn't have been more than that. Five strings for his automaton and four for his shield crafting. In the confusion and panic, he couldn't be certain, but that seemed about right. Plus another when he linked to his sorcerous globes.

Ten? How was such a thing possible?

He turned to the closest Quiver. "Quickly! Go as fast as you can." They seemed to regard him with awe, or at least a healthy respect.

The oldest one cleared his throat. "Our commander will want to hear what you've done. All of you. And likely want to thank you personally."

Beside him, cel Rau grunted. "Why isn't he on the wall?"

The Quiver gave them a puzzled look. "On the wall? He's coordinating the defense of the whole city. He needs to be in a central location."

"So he hasn't even seen the jukari?"

"No, I don't think so."

Cel Rau chuckled to himself and used a waterskin to trickle water into Vasile's mouth. Caldan couldn't be sure, but it looked like most of it spilled out onto the wagon bed. He frowned, also puzzled. The swordsman made sense. Why wouldn't the man commanding the Quivers be on the wall coordinating his men?

"What are you doing about the jukari?" Caldan asked.

"Holding the walls. Protecting the citizens."

Again, cel Rau chuckled.

"And that's all?" Caldan said.

"Our job is to guard the city. The emperor is on his way, and his forces will crush the jukari once they arrive."

"And when will that be?"

"Er . . . soon. A day or two, I think."

"And what would have happened if the emperor's forces hadn't been so close?"

The Quiver stiffened, and Caldan realized he'd gone too far. These soldiers were only following orders. It was their leaders who deserved to be rebuked. The fact they hadn't sent any Quivers out to protect the refugees fleeing the jukari stirred a hot anger inside him. And the Protectors had remained on the wall and done nothing. Besides himself, only cel Rau and Vasile had thought about shielding those most in need. Only they'd thought of doing what they could to ensure as many people as possible reached Riversedge alive.

Vasile let out a moan as the wagon lurched.

Caldan met cel Rau's eyes.

"He'll be fine," the swordsman said, "once we get him to a physiker. He's been through much the last few weeks."

Caldan nodded, glad the man would survive. After what he'd seen, he didn't think he could handle another death. Out there, outside the walls of Riversedge, there'd been too many people cut down by the jukari. Senseless slaughter.

Behind the creaking wagon, they were trailed by two Protectors on horseback, who must have managed to push through the crowded streets. They hadn't said anything, just positioned themselves behind the wagon and followed along. A warning, and probably guards to make sure he didn't do anything against their rules again. They were following at a discreet distance, but Caldan knew why they were there. Maybe that was the point. Unless he died, he'd never be free of the Protectors.

A hum at the edge of his awareness, and the faint scent of lemons, indicated at least one of the Protectors was using a crafting. Caldan opened his own well and kept himself ready. Mold had probably decided he was now a liability; Caldan had to be on his guard. He was pretty sure that with the Quivers around him, all treating him like a hero, the Protectors wouldn't be able to act. But he also had little doubt it wouldn't take them long to convince the commander of the Quivers he should be released into their "care."

He extended his senses and judged their wells. Both were narrow and constricted, with rough edges. Whatever their talents, they would barely be able to hold on to a crafted shield at full strength. But he'd learned from Bells and the Bleeder, everyone had different talents, and a narrow well didn't mean a sorcerer wasn't dangerous. He kept holding his well open, ready to link to his shield crafting at the first sign of anything suspicious.

One of the Quivers broke into his thoughts, addressing them all. "Excuse me. We, the men and I, want to thank you all for what you did out there. I've never seen anything like it. You faced down the jukari, allowing a great many people to reach Riversedge alive."

Cel Rau looked grim. "A great many more died."

To Caldan, the implication was obvious: they died because no Quivers were sent to help. But the soldier continued, oblivious to the underlying meaning of the swordsman's comment.

"We recognized you were a sorcerer when we saw your shield. That must be how you avoided getting injured by the monsters. But . . . we saw flashes of light out there, and heard explosions. Are you . . . are you really able to control sorcery from before the Shattering?"

All the soldiers were staring at Caldan intently, with a mixture of awe and fear. Cel Rau was also staring at him.

"No," Caldan said glibly, shaking his head. "I'm nothing special. The explosions were an alchemical mixture that burns with a fierce intensity. There's nothing sorcerous about it."

Cel Rau gave Caldan a blank look before returning to minister to Vasile, while the Quivers looked disappointed.

They trundled down the streets in silence for a time. Word must have spread of their escapades, as a number of people came up to thank them. Some young women handed cel Rau flowers woven into a circle, and a smile broke through his usually impassive face. Quivers stationed on corners saluted as they went past, fists against their chests. Small children trailed behind the wagon, getting in the way of the Protectors following.

A wave of pungent lemons wafted over Caldan, and he froze, blood cold. Half standing, he stretched his senses, testing the air. It came from the northwest. A pulsing sorcery, strong and potent. If he unleashed everything his well had to offer, he'd be hard-pressed to match such power. Abruptly, it vanished, leaving him thinking for a moment he might have imagined it. But no, a great sorcery had been crafted close by, within the city.

"What is it?" hissed cel Rau.

Caldan realized his hand was groping for a sword that wasn't there. Forcing himself to relax, he ignored the curious looks from the Quivers and leaned in close to cel Rau.

"Sorcery. And powerful sorcery, at that."

"Where?"

"I don't know exactly. To the northwest."

Cel Rau glanced at the Protectors trailing them. "They don't appear concerned."

"I don't think they're sensitive enough to have felt it."

"There are sorcerers everywhere in any big city. Why are you worried?"

Caldan bit his thumbnail. How much did cel Rau really know about sorcery? Would revealing certain knowledge put cel Rau in danger? He didn't have many options at the moment, and he did know the man was prepared to put his own life on the line to protect others who needed it. That had to be good enough for now.

"Most of the Protectors are on the walls, watching the jukari. As far as I'm aware, the emperor's forces haven't arrived yet, so his sorcerers aren't near. And judging from the flare of sorcery, it was far more powerful than most of the sorcerers I've ever met could manage . . ."

Bells. It has to be her.

"Spit it out," said cel Rau when he saw Caldan hesitate.

"A sorcerer we've been tracking, one of the invaders from Indryalla. She's in the city. It has to be her doing. And whatever she's up to . . . she means the empire harm."

"And why are the two Protectors following you?"

Caldan's mouth opened in shock, and he closed it. The swordsman didn't miss much. Before he could reply, cel Rau continued.

"I know who the Protectors are and what they do. Which means I know why they're keeping an eye on you after your . . . antics. As far as I'm concerned, your actions speak to me more than theirs. So . . . I'm with you. Vasile will be all right; the Quivers will look after him."

There was more implied in cel Rau's words than simply a pledge of support. And Caldan couldn't help but agree with him. After a few moments, he came up with a plan.

"We have to find the origin of the sorcery. Whatever Bells is planning—"

"Bells?"

"Ah, yes. Bells is her name. She has to be stopped. The Protectors haven't been able to find her."

"And you think you can?"

"Maybe. If we are lucky enough to get close to her. The crafting she used is powerful, and I've a talent for discerning sorcery."

"So I've seen. If you're right about this Bells—"

"I'm right. What are the chances it's another powerful sorcerer?"

Cel Rau grunted. "You'd be surprised." He looked back at the Protectors trailing them. "We'll ditch these two?"

The Protectors would only get in the way, and Caldan certainly didn't want them involved if he could avoid it. Besides, they'd proven themselves all but useless. Better to shed them like old skin.

"Let's make a break for it."

Cel Rau stood and bent close to the Quiver driving the wagon. "We're going to get off here," he told the surprised soldier. "Give my friend the best care. We'll be back for him soon." He met Caldan's eyes. "Now?"

The crowd was thicker here and likely to hinder the Protectors. "Now," agreed Caldan, and they both leaped over the side of the wagon.

AMERDAN FLOATED IN the radiant power of his well. It bathed him in its violet light. For long moments, it was all he could think of; it saturated his awareness. The blistering forces beckoned to him. It was a sweetness he'd never known he longed for. Closing the well off was almost painful to him, but he knew he had to, lest the chance passing of a sorcerer or Protector reveal his abilities.

Soon, though, I will be powerful enough that I won't have to worry about that. Bells had begun chipping away at the barrier blocking his second well, and breaking through couldn't come soon enough for Amerdan.

Standing next to their table, Bells frowned at him. He smiled at her, as a lover might. It was what any woman would want from him in her situation . . . he assumed.

"Stop playing around and help me," she commanded. "It's done, and I'll need your help after I test it. It's too heavy to lift on my own. It'll take the two of us to get it down the stairs and into the cart."

"Of course, Bells," he purred sweetly. "So we're about to take it close to the emperor's forces?" *About time. If he didn't need her, she'd . . .* The need rose inside him, threatening to overwhelm his control. It had been too long. Steeling his mind, he forced it back down.

Amerdan moved close to Bells and stroked her hair. *He'd need to keep some to make a stick figure for next year's Ghost Festival.*

Bells brushed away his hand, returning his smile. "Keep an eye on me, my love. Testing my crafting will require handling a lot of power from my well. It'll only be for a few moments, but there's a chance I could lose consciousness."

"Then how will you use it when the time comes?"

"I have you now. Before, I was going to have to risk it and hope for the best. You're not quite ready to help with sorcery yet; there's a few things I need to teach you first."

"And in the meantime?"

"Well, you won't be doing much on your own. I'll be controlling all the forces and the different threads. I'll just be borrowing power from your wells. With your help, it'll be easy."

She reached out and squeezed his hand. Amerdan forced himself to abide her touch. Usually, he was able to brace himself beforehand and the sensation wasn't altogether unpleasant, but lately she'd taken to touching him without warning. It was disconcerting.

"This won't take long. And don't look so worried; I'll be fine."

Bells turned to her crafting, and he sensed her open her well. Finally assembled, the metallic artifact looked unassuming: a stack of round metal plates, each inscribed with crafting runes and symbols. He'd studied each plate as Bells had finished it, committing the runes to memory. He'd have to learn what most of them meant, but he figured that was only a matter of time.

His skin tingled as Bells drew power from her well. He looked on enviously as she broke it into multiple strings: four, then six, then eight, and finally, nine. A clever trick he'd yet to master. Whenever he tried to create more than two strings from one of his wells, his head felt like it was splitting apart, and he almost threw up.

As he watched, the bottom plate of the crafting began to glow with a violet-tinged light. Faintly at first, then with increasing intensity. As it shone like a candle, the second plate joined the first. Then the third and fourth. Amerdan's ears ached and the room seemed to feel smaller, as if it were being compressed, and them along with it.

Soon, all the discs of the crafting shone, giving off a radiance as bright as a hundred candles. Amerdan blinked against the glare. Then abruptly, they winked out. He sensed Bells close her well, and she slumped into a chair.

She sat for a moment, breathing heavily. "Good," she said. "Give me some time to recover, then we'll move it to the cart. Once we're on our way, I'll have regained strength enough to teach you what's required later."

"For when you borrow my power and activate the crafting?"

Bells nodded wearily, but he could tell she was pleased. "Then the God-Emperor will join us."

CHAPTER 45

"This part of the city," said cel Rau, "is not a place I'd like to be at night. And it would be a worse place to live."

Caldan looked around at the dilapidated buildings on either side of the street and the piles of rubbish clogging a side alley, and couldn't help but agree. Roaches crawled over the garbage, apparently immune to the light of day and the people moving past them. A small child picked through one of the piles. He was filthy, clad in dirty rags, and snot trailed from his nose to his upper lip.

"Anasoma had similar sections. I . . . didn't think the empire would be like this. It's supposed to be . . . I don't know, grand?" He pitied the people inhabiting such districts. Their lot in life was bleak, and they had little chance to escape it. For all its glory and advancement, the empire had many flaws. Not least the way the poor were treated.

Cel Rau spat onto the street. "All cities have slums. And the bigger the city, the more deprived people there are."

Caldan thought the man was going to say more, but he didn't. Apart from a few instances, he hadn't strung more than a few sentences together at one time. A man who valued his words. Caldan could respect that.

He closed his eyes and accessed his well. For show, he fed a trickle of power into his shield crafting, only for an instant, which caused him to appear hazy, and the air around him wavered. He could feel cel Rau step close.

"Can you sense it still? Which direction is it coming from?"

"Yes," hedged Caldan. The source of the original outpouring of power had been around here, that much was true. But it had stopped, and he had no way of determining where it had come from unless it began again. Knowing Bells, she wouldn't be that stupid.

"This way," he told cel Rau and started toward the wall to the north.

The narrow streets were a maze, quite often ending with no warning, causing them to backtrack. Caldan had all but given up on finding Bells here, but he had to spend some time lingering in the area in case there was another power surge. As he'd suspected, she was too smart for that.

He turned into a wider street, this one lined with one boarding-house after another. Then they hit a crowded main thoroughfare. A few hundred yards to the north were the city gates.

Caldan pushed his way through a group of people congregating around a squad of Quivers, haranguing them with questions about the jukari. From their expressions, they weren't pleased with the soldiers' responses to their questions. Ahead, the traffic came to a halt, with laden horses, wagons, and carts all funneling toward the gates. In stark contrast to the east gate, where the direction of the traffic was into the city, at this gate, everyone wanted to leave.

As they made their way through the throng to the wall, he saw most of the people trying to get out of the city were merchants and traders, along with some very frightened-looking families. Those he could understand, wanting to leave in case the city fell, not trusting the Quivers after their initial response. The merchants must have wanted to reach the emperor's forces, he realized. An army on the move needed many things to keep them going, and there was profit to be made.

"Fools," remarked cel Rau.

Caldan followed his gaze to see the gates wide open. With a jukari horde to the east, the likes of which hadn't been seen in hundreds of years, if ever before, the city should be locked up tight—it wasn't like they couldn't flank the walls. Instead, the Quivers were letting the traffic through. He couldn't help but agree with the swordsman.

He stiffened as someone's well tugged at his awareness. It was a strange pulsing sensation, as if whoever was accessing their well was experimenting. It was a feeling he knew well from when he'd first begun his sorcerous training at the monastery, a stretching of new-found muscles. It came from the northwest . . . beyond the gate.

Caldan let the barest trickle of power seep from his own well, extending his senses past the line at the gate and out over the wall. There wasn't just the new sorcerer testing a well, there was a crafting. It resonated with spent power. It had to be the one he'd sensed earlier.

And that meant Bells had left the city and was heading directly toward the emperor's forces. "By the ancestors," he said under his breath.

"What is it?" cel Rau asked.

"The crafting I sensed earlier is outside the city and heading toward the emperor's forces. I have to believe Bells is with it, and she has another sorcerer with her now. Whoever it is isn't that strong, but either way, the two of them and a powerful crafting getting closer to the emperor can't be a good thing."

"No, I would think not."

"We need to go after it."

Cel Rau studied him, taking his time. Then he nodded.

"Let's go."

"STOP TESTING YOURSELF. There will be plenty of time soon."

"As you've said before." Amerdan struggled to keep accusation from his voice.

The sorcerous bitch smiled at him and rested a hand on his knee. He closed the well he had open and urged the horse to greater speed.

Soon they were bumping along the hard road at a decent pace, passing the slower, lumbering wagons laden to almost overflowing with food, ale, and spirits, and merchandise of any kind people thought the emperor's forces would want to spend their hard coin on. There was a dullard naiveté to the townsfolk . . . no one could defeat the mighty emperor. In their minds, the jukari horde was beaten purely by virtue of the emperor being there.

He looked away and out along the road. Far in the distance, he could discern a great many people moving this way. It had to be the emperor's army. *So close.* Amerdan shifted his weight on the seat of their cart and squeezed the reins tighter, imagining Bells's throat in their place.

THOUSANDS OF SOLDIERS had begun digging in and making camp. Everywhere Caldan looked he saw hard-faced veterans clad in well-worn functional armor. No gaudy display pieces for these men. No, they were the emperor's finest, tempered by constant skirmishing with the tribes of the Steppes, the Sotharle Union of Cities, and jukari at the edge of civilization. Mounted soldiers carrying emblazoned bucklers and wide-bladed scimitars patrolled the perimeter. Their hostile stares put Caldan ill at ease as he and cel Rau made their way from the ragtag makeshift town the merchants and traders from Riversedge had set up a short distance from the army. Stalls were erected along the road, with people hawking their wares to the soldiers. An area composed of small tents already had a line of soldiers queuing up. Scantily clad women with faces obscured by headscarves emerged from the tents to disappear inside with a new soldier as another left, often buckling his britches or tucking his shirt in.

Outside the main congregations of soldiers, laborers were digging a long line of holes in the ground, and as Caldan watched, a Quiver squatted and used one as if there were no one around to see. He looked away.

"An army has certain needs," remarked cel Rau, as if he'd seen Caldan noticing both the prostitutes and the privies.

Ahead was a checkpoint where Quivers were stopping everyone attempting to enter the encampment proper. A number of officious-looking soldiers carried sheaves of paper and were recording the contents of all wagons entering; they carried mostly foodstuffs and barrels of water and weak ale, and the soldiers directed them to various parts of the military camp. Caldan was certain the crafting and the person experimenting with a well were inside the camp somewhere.

As they approached the checkpoint, horns blasted from the walls of Riversedge, hooting proclamations reverberating across the plains surrounding the city. Both Caldan and cel Rau turned to look back, wondering what the commotion was about, to see ranks of Quivers from Riversedge marching through the northern gate. Leading them out were horsemen carrying banners flapping in the breeze. At this distance, Caldan couldn't see if there were Protectors among them, but it was highly likely. The Quivers continued at a slow pace along the road toward them.

"Fools," remarked cel Rau again.

"Why?"

The swordsman spat in the dirt. "The emperor's brought more than enough soldiers to deal with the jukari before they continue to Anasoma."

Caldan thought he saw why cel Rau thought the Quivers were fools. "So the Quivers in the city are joining them for the . . . experience . . . and the glory, leaving a bare minimum to defend the city."

Cel Rau nodded. "With the emperor here, there's no danger to the city, but it's still bad strategy. They're effectively abandoning their post." The swordsman shrugged. "Not our concern, though."

"Right. Let's keep going."

The line to the checkpoint was long and getting longer, and with each wagon and cart being checked thoroughly, there'd likely be a delay before they could enter the camp. Cel Rau pointed to the west, where a trail of people came from the traders' settlement. Soldiers and citizens traveled both ways along a path beaten between the settlement and the camp, and there were no soldiers checking who entered the army's encampment.

Caldan nodded his agreement to cel Rau, and they made their way to the unguarded access point. Underfoot, the grass had been trampled into oblivion from the tread of so many boots. A short distance inside the camp, three different paths diverged to separate sections. Far in the distance, they could see the tops of tents flying colored flags and banners. Around them, the soldiers were erecting tents of their own. Made from ragged and patched material, they were nevertheless functional and evenly spaced in straight lines. In the middle of every ten or so tents was a clear space where soldiers gathered, cleaning gear and equipment and eating cold rations. They were rough-looking men with unshaven faces and loud voices. Somewhere to their left, a fight broke out, the combatants goaded on by raucous cheers.

They stepped to the side to let other people pass.

"Which way?" asked cel Rau.

Caldan pointed to the trail that led more or less toward the larger tents. "This one should get us closer to the emperor, and that's where Bells is probably going. I fear we need to hurry."

He realized the only other person he'd told about his guess of Bells's intentions had been Annelie. Now she was dead. Was he just clutching at straws? Nothing else he could think of made sense, and with the power of the crafting he'd sensed, his suspicions only grew stronger.

He strode down the trail, motioning cel Rau to follow. Even safe amid the emperor's army, the swordsman looked ready for anything. His right hand rested just next to the hilt of the blade on his left hip, thumb hooked into his leather sword belt as if he expected to draw at any moment. Caldan licked his lips, remembering he'd dropped his sword outside the city gates and now had no effective weapon of his own. His only blade was a small knife he carried for utility and used when eating. If it came down to it, he doubted a sword would be effective against Bells, but he still felt uneasy without one.

As they made their way toward what he assumed were the tents of the commanding officers and their retinues, the rough soldiers on the outskirts of the camp gave way to more respectable-looking men. Stained, patched tents were replaced by new versions, and the soldiers' gear also looked newer and in better repair. On their right, four long trains of tethered horses were roped in straight lines with plenty of room for the beasts. Young boys and girls were scooping up the horses' leavings with shovels and using barrows to wheel away the waste. Ahead was the largest tent they'd seen yet, surrounded by a plethora of slightly smaller versions. That had to be the emperor's lodging, Caldan reasoned. They were now the only nonsoldiers on the well-trod path and were receiving curious looks. A number of times, lean, fit men carrying bundles of leather-bound folders rushed past, presumably messengers on their way to other parts of the army.

A squad of soldiers blocked the way in front of them. Clean-shaven and wearing polished armor, they carried spears held upright. Their leader, the only one wearing a sword and not carrying a spear, kept his eyes on them as a man with a harried expression waved them over. The man sat on a rickety chair behind a table, on which numerous papers were held down with rocks to stop them blowing away. To his left was a pot of ink and a number of pens.

"Excuse me," the man said loudly. "Over here."

Caldan exchanged a glance with cel Rau, and they made their way over to the table.

"State your names and ranks, and your business. I assume you want to see the commanders, but . . . you don't look like the representatives from Riversedge we were expecting. Far from it." The man narrowed his eyes. "Just who are you?"

"My name is Caldan, and I'm a Protector. We have urgent information for the emperor."

Cel Rau raised his eyebrows, and Caldan saw him suppress a smirk.

"Really," drawled the man. "Let me just go and interrupt his lunch. I'm sure he'd be delighted to see you."

Behind them, the soldiers chuckled.

The man sighed, shaking his head. He picked up a pen and dipped it in the ink. "What information do you have? I'll make sure someone gets it."

"We need to talk to someone in charge right away. This is important."

"I'm in charge *here*, so you talk to me. Now, out with it, or I'll have these nice men here run you off."

"I don't know what you expected," said cel Rau.

"Joachim sent us," ventured Caldan. "He's a warlock. He's given us information they need, now." He hoped his gambit would work. He had no idea if the warlocks were known by name or what their status was, but as powerful sorcerers, mentioning them had to hold some sway.

"Then I'm sure you'll have no problems handing over the mark he would have given you."

Caldan frowned, stomach sinking. "Mark? He didn't—"

"Of course he didn't. Because he didn't send you, did he? You're the most incompetent spies I've ever seen."

"What? We're not spies!"

A few of the soldiers blocking the way to the large tents lowered their spears and pointed them at Caldan and cel Rau.

"That's exactly what spies would say."

As the soldiers advanced, Caldan accessed his well and prepared for the worst.

But cel Rau dropped an engraved silver disc the size of a thumbnail on the table.

"Well, well, well," said the man. He picked up the disc and closed it in his fist.

To Caldan's normal senses, the disc tingled, and as his well was open, he could see it was a crafting. But . . . was it? He frowned. Power flowed through it, a trickle, but it was there nonetheless. He extended his senses, checking cel Rau for a well. Nothing. And around them there was no sign anyone close was a sorcerer either. Then who was linked to it to feed it power? He probed the crafting and sucked in a breath. There were no linking runes he could find on the surface of the disc. And the only sorcerous objects that didn't need linking runes were trinkets, but . . . could it be? It wasn't made of the same unknown alloy all other trinkets were—except for his bone ring—but it was a trinket nevertheless. A tiny thread of sorcery led from the disc and into cel Rau's head.

Coercive sorcery, it had to be.

The man held the trinket out for cel Rau, who secured it in a belt pouch. "It's attuned to you, all right. A sub-writ, but it's genuine. Where's the full writ?"

"Either on its way, at the bottom of a river, or among the jukari," cel Rau replied.

"Huh. Well, this'll get you as far as the warlocks, but no further. You'll have to convince them if you want to go higher up."

"That's sufficient."

Caldan swallowed and looked at cel Rau. The swordsman appeared relaxed, as if nothing had happened. Caldan realized, for him, nothing had. But it meant cel Rau worked for the warlocks, and Caldan suddenly wondered if he could trust the swordsman.

The soldiers raised their spears and parted, leaving a gap for them to enter and head toward the command tents.

"One of these soldiers will escort you to the warlocks' compound to make sure you don't get lost," said the man behind the table. "It's to the west."

To Caldan, the gap between the armored soldiers was a line he didn't want to cross. Cel Rau noticed him hesitate. "What is it?"

"I . . ."

At that moment, a surge of sorcery pulsed from the command tents. It felt the same as the crafting he'd sensed in the city. Bells *was* here. A sudden gust of wind set banners and flags flapping, whipping up clouds of dust, causing soldiers to shield their eyes.

A resonating thrum filled the air as a dome of sorcery the height of four men appeared in the middle of the command tents. It was barely fifty paces from their position. Another pulse of power rippled over them, emanating from the shield. It turned as black as the darkest night, and to Caldan's senses felt as dense as tempered steel. Whoever was inside was both obscured and protected by the strongest sorcerous shield he'd seen.

Caldan could feel the crafting inside the dome. It set his mind on edge, twisting the air around him. His teeth rattled in their sockets as the crafting sucked up more power.

Around them, soldiers shouted, and dozens of them rushed toward the dome, hacking at the surface with their swords. A few arrows also struck the shield, all to no avail.

"I take it we're too late?" shouted cel Rau over the din.

"Maybe. I certainly have nothing that can deal with this. Maybe the warlocks—"

Before he'd even finished speaking, glowing yellow globes arced through the sky from the west. The warlocks must have judged the situation to be desperate, else they wouldn't use destructive sorcery so brazenly. With crackling thumps, six globes pounded into the black shield, which erupted in bright white sparkles. Virulent sorcery covered and splashed off the dome, spattering the soldiers around it. They screamed in pain and terror, falling to the ground as their skin melted and smoked. A few with minor splashes of the warlocks' sorcery staggered away clutching arms, legs, and faces. After stumbling a short distance, they too fell to the ground, momentarily writhing before they were still. The screaming and shouting survivors backed away.

"By the ancestors," breathed Caldan. It was a bloody, chaotic mess. No one was in charge, and no one had any idea what to do. Bells had shrugged off the warlocks' first response as if their sorcery were an annoying insect, and no options were coming to him. He had told cel Rau there was nothing he could do, and he certainly meant that. But he needed to try something. Joachim's arrows sprang to mind, but he doubted they would be strong enough to make a dent.

Frantically, he cast around. There must be something he could use. His eyes alighted on the paper and pens the man at the table had been using.

"What are you doing?" exclaimed cel Rau as he rushed for the table.

"Something. Anything," he replied. There was no time to waste. Bells's potent crafting was gathering power to itself, far more than he'd even thought possible. He glanced up as more globes descended on the dome, these ones red and green. Thunderclaps filled the air when they struck, and Caldan winced as his ears erupted in pain. Around the dome, soldiers were flung back, struck by an invisible force. They landed in lifeless jumbles among their smoldering comrades. Was this what Bells expected? All part of her plan? To let the warlocks' retaliation kill off the soldiers for her?

There was no time to think about that now. He slid four pieces of paper across the now-deserted table and dipped a pen in the ink. He was sure he couldn't destroy Bells's shield like Joachim had Annelie's, and Amerdan had Joachim's, but maybe he could force it to split and create a gap. A variation of Joachim's crafted arrows, then, linked to divert the forces creating the shield.

He scribbled furiously.

FOR AMERDAN, THE black dome covering them held a singular interest. Bells had explained no one could see inside, but it wasn't until he saw the soldiers' reactions that he came to be convinced. He sensed the forces she was drawing from her well to maintain the shield and felt he could match her, if only just. But the sorcery used in its creation was beyond him, for now. He'd have to take the crafting from Bells when all this was over. Curiously, no sound penetrated the shield, either. Around them, blood and parts of soldiers splattered the ground. The mouths of the survivors opened wide in soundless howls. Amerdan could imagine their gibbering cries. It was as if he were looking at a painting in which the subjects moved.

Bells kept the shield crafting in one hand, while her other rested upon the metal discs, which remained on top of their cart.

"Yes," Bells murmured, with a depth of emotion he thought was . . . longing?

Under his hand, her bare neck trembled. He had to maintain contact for her to draw from his wells to bolster her craftings. He crowed inwardly as another ragged chip of one barrier damming his well broke free and dissipated. Since Bells had drawn more and more from his wells, the virulent forces had begun eroding the barriers further, an unexpected yet welcome side effect. Already one well was completely clear, while the other had widened considerably. Soon both would be free and unfettered. He'd have the wells of two sorcerers. And if all went according to plan, he'd subsume Bells and Caldan. Four wells, combined with the knowledge Bells had imparted to him, and her craftings. He would be . . . a god. With the God-Emperor of Indryalla about to arrive, he'd have to be careful, but he was confident he'd soon have him under his knife and absorbed as well. Then he could—

What? What did he want? What was his purpose? The thought struck him to his core. He was no longer content to wander from place to place and kill whatever vessel caught his eye.

A groan from Bells brought him back to the present.

"What is it?" he asked calmly.

"Maybe nothing . . . I'm not sure. This crafting is beyond me, so—"

"You don't know what it does?"

"I was told what it does, but . . . something's wrong."

Worry tinged her voice. More than worry—a rising panic.

"So should your God-Emperor be here now?"

"I'm not sure. The crafting's building more power than it should need. It just keeps drawing more and more. I—" Bells broke off with a gasp of surprise, and he felt a tremor run through her body. Violet threads twisting like snakes began seeping from the crafting. Undulating in the small space, they grew, lengthening and moving ever upward, as if seeking something.

"No!" wailed Bells, and she sank to the ground as her legs went limp.

Amerdan knelt beside her, hand still resting on her neck. "Tell me what's happening."

As he spoke, the threads touched the roof of the dome and slipped straight through the barrier. When they did, he felt the crafting pulse with energy, and his skin crawled like it was covered with ants. Outside the shield, the threads grew. One yard. Two. Then three. They waved and contorted as if blown by the wind. Except they issued in all directions.

CALDAN DROPPED TO his knees as his mind felt like it was being turned inside out. He scrabbled to hold on to sanity, clutching at whatever threads of consciousness he could grasp. He still held the four paper craftings he'd finished penning. Cel Rau lay in the dirt beside him, eyes open wide with pupils contracted to pinpricks. Blood trickled from one of cel Rau's ears, though he'd managed to draw both swords before he'd collapsed.

The world took on a jagged edge. The shapes of soldiers twisted as ripples from Bells's shield pulsed through them. More emanated and seemed to search him out. Each one lanced into his head as it passed through him. Around him, men began screaming. Reality was being warped, molded. Violet threads drifted from the crafting, accompanied by a high-pitched keening. They traveled in lazy arcs, slicing through flesh and bone like a hot knife through wax.

Caldan bent over, his free hand clawing at clumps of grass in front of him. A spasm ripped through his muscles, and he convulsed in agony. Terror overcame the emperor's soldiers closest to Bells's shield dome. Hardened veterans and green soldiers alike fled, screaming and clawing at their heads. But Caldan's pain lessened quickly, and looking up he saw cel Rau also struggling to his feet.

Caldan seemed less affected by whatever overwhelmed the soldiers, as did cel Rau. Whether it was because Caldan was a sorcerer, he didn't know, and why cel Rau wasn't incapacitated would be a puzzle for another day. If they survived.

Lethal sorcerous threads twisted toward them, as if drawn to their life-filled bodies. Caldan was finally able to activate his shield and clamped a hand on to one of cel Rau's arms, spreading the shield to cover him. Multicolored sparkles erupted as the threads slithered over them. Caldan's shield held, but only just. It whined and grew warm and sucked enormous amounts from his well. Only four strings to maintain the shield, but already his head ached from the strain.

The threads passed over them and moved on, as if they were seeking easier prey to latch on to. Caldan couldn't be sure, but those extending to the west looked thicker and livelier, lengthening at a much faster pace than the others. West was where the warlocks were supposed to be, and where the destructive sorcerous globes came from.

To their right, one hapless soldier found himself cornered by two violet strands. He was about to duck under one when they whipped forward and passed through him. He didn't make a sound as he dropped to the dirt, body carved into pieces. One of hundreds lying motionless around them.

As the deadly threads moved farther from the black dome, they split apart. Like roots from a living plant, tendrils broke off and began seeking their own paths, extending farther into the army's encampment.

The flow from Caldan's well subsided once the threads passed them over. He took a few moments to recover. Sweat poured from his skin, and his shield felt stifling. He staggered to his feet and stood among the dead and dying soldiers of the emperor. By his side, cel Rau also dragged himself upright.

He looked at Caldan with an expression of pure fury. "This abomination must be stopped."

Caldan kept his grip on the swordsman's arm. "Come, then. We have to get inside that shield."

They staggered toward the dome, trying to avoid pools of rapidly cooling blood and body parts, but by the time it loomed close, their boots were covered in scarlet, and their steps left bloody imprints in their wake.

Caldan uncrumpled the four paper craftings he'd hastily scrawled and placed a hand on the shield. It felt hard and dense, like a huge, polished chunk of onyx. He attempted to fix one of the paper craftings against the shield, high and to his right. It wouldn't stick.

"By the ancestors!" he cursed.

"What's wrong?"

"I need all four to be in place before I can link and join them. But they won't stick to the shield. Stupid. I should have thought of that."

"Give me one. I'll try something."

Caldan handed cel Rau one of the sheets of paper, and the swordsman stepped toward a dead soldier. As Caldan watched in horror, cel Rau wiped the back of the paper in a congealing pool of blood. He slapped the paper against the shield, and when he removed his hand, it stayed in place.

"Will that do?" asked cel Rau.

A trickle of blood oozed out from under the paper and began to make its way slowly down the shield.

Caldan swallowed. "Yes. Let's do the other three. I need them to make the corners of a square big enough for us to get through, so I'll place two near the ground."

Stomach churning, Caldan followed cel Rau's lead and smeared the other three papers with blood and stuck them to the dome. Over their heads, violet threads continued to propagate from the top of the dome, and even finer tendrils of lightning crackled between them.

"Look to your shield!" shouted cel Rau.

Caldan glanced up to see more globes descending toward the dome, and them. Cursing, he pushed as much from his well and into his shield as he could, extending the barrier to cover his craftings on the side of the dome so they weren't destroyed.

Globes plummeted toward them. Both Caldan and cel Rau cowered as they struck. Corrosive power splashed across his shield, and again the crafting grew warm, then hot, as it struggled to dissipate the forces assailing them. The whine from the crafting rose to a shriek, but it quickly subsided as the sorcery from the globes died down. To Caldan, this group of globes didn't feel as potent as the last few. Perhaps the thicker sorcerous threads that had gone west were assailing the warlocks, and they were spending resources defending themselves.

Caldan pushed his weariness aside and prepared to link to his paper craftings. With luck, they'd work, because if they didn't, he had no ideas left.

"DON'T YOU SEE?" Bells wailed. "The God-Emperor has decided the empire's forces are to be destroyed. I'm to be sacrificed. There's no escape for us now. We must accept our fate."

Amerdan hissed in anger. *We?* The sorcerous bitch had killed him. "They're not through yet. We can still flee. They'll have to try and disable your crafting, and it'll be the perfect diversion."

Bells lowered her head, long dark hair falling to cover her face. She shook with emotion. "No. If the God-Emperor has decided I'm to die, then so be it. He needs me to maintain the link to the crafting. And I'll do it until I draw my last breath."

"You can maintain the link from afar by drawing from my wells."

"I . . . I don't know."

Bells looked him in the eye. Amerdan could see she was resigned to her death here. Which meant he couldn't absorb her talents. He uttered a low growl and glanced outside. He was surprised—and yet, not that surprised—to see that Caldan and another man were near the shield. He watched as they started to slap blood-covered pieces of paper to the barrier, where they stuck fast.

What are you doing, Caldan?

"I'm sorry," Bells was saying.

Sorry? What good is sorry? It usually just gets you killed. "Give me your shield crafting. The one making the dome. You can use your normal one now that the soldiers around us are dead. They'll not be troubling you."

"You're going to leave me?" Bells looked at him with sadness in her eyes, then nodded slowly. "You're right to go. This wasn't what I thought would happen."

Amerdan sensed her separate strings from her well and link to a new shield crafting she'd made along with the others. He glanced at Caldan and the man with him and saw they'd stuck two more sheets of paper to the dome. He couldn't be sure, but he assumed they were attempting to breach the barrier—what else could they be doing?

Dotty writhed under his shirt.

Flee, she screamed at him.

But then both Bells's and Caldan's talents would be lost, along with the God-Emperor's, who had declined to join them. The thought of losing such opportunities when they were so close filled him with anger. But there would be other vessels. And other sorcerers.

Amerdan drew out his trinket from under his shirt. As his hand brushed Dolly, she squirmed rubbing against his chest. He squeezed the trinket hard, unsure of what to do.

I should flee.

But . . . he couldn't. He couldn't lose this chance at more power.

There's time for Bells, there must be . . .

"I'll take over the shield. Then you can rest for a few moments, regain your strength before they make it through."

Bells nodded. "I'll delay them as much as possible, but I fear it won't be long."

Amerdan placed the warm metal trinket against the back of her neck, fingers maintaining contact with her skin. Reaching down with his right hand, making sure she wouldn't be able to see, he drew out his knife.

The black dome shield barely flickered as his multiple wells took the strain from Bells, and with an audible sigh, her shoulders slumped.

"Promise me you'll present yourself to the God-Emperor after you escape. He needs to know about your wells. Tell him . . . I forgive him. My real name is Sorche. Use that information to get past the functionaries and sorcerers that surround him." Her hand reached up to stroke his, which was resting on the back of her neck. "Promise me."

Amerdan breathed in the scent of her hair and the air around them, fragrant with dirt and sweat and the blood of dead, useless soldiers. He soaked it in, savoring it. A shiver ran down his back as the need filled him.

"I promise."

He plunged the knife into the vessel's throat, and it made a gurgling sound. It clutched at him, nails scraping the skin on his arms as they wrapped tight around it. It struggled, as they all did. To no avail. In his hand, the trinket glowed bright and hot. A cord of pulsating light grew from it and into the wound in the vessel's neck.

The vessel uttered a wordless cry tinged with loss.

"Shhh," he whispered into its ear. "It's all over now. It's over."

He felt Caldan's sorcery attempt to breach the shield and barely held on to his strings linked to the crafting. The man was strong, but nowhere near as powerful as Amerdan was with his two—soon to be three—wells. The shield held.

Amerdan convulsed with agony as color leached from the vessel's skin, turning it a brittle gray. He clamped his mouth shut to avoid crying out as the luminescent cord vanished. He collapsed to the ground, panting hoarsely, still clutching the desiccated vessel.

There was another assault on the shield he barely fended off. Whatever Caldan was doing, he had more skill with shields and how they functioned than Amerdan had and was trying different ways of breaking it. He'd be through soon.

SUPPRESSING THE URGE to punch the shield, Caldan groaned with frustration and wiped sweat from his face. He'd been so close then, the shield had almost buckled. Its structure was new to him; somehow it was cycling through layers, continually renewing and swapping them.

Cel Rau studied him for a moment before speaking. "Whatever you're doing, you'd better do it faster. The sorcery is still moving through the soldiers. Hundreds more have died since we reached the dome."

Caldan glanced at the top of the shield dome and felt a weight bear down on him. He drew as much as he could from his well for one last attempt to break through. "This is it," he croaked. "If I can't do it this time, I won't have anything left."

Cel Rau only nodded. "Then you'd better do it."

With a thought, Caldan relinked to his paper craftings, and instead of trying to breach the shield, he attempted to align them with its forces. Bells's power needed to bypass the space inside his craftings rather than struggle against the absence he wanted to create. And he could feel it working. Inside the square space he'd created, the blackness lightened to a swirling gray. The hard barrier twisted as it was sucked into his craftings, leaving a transparent square in the darkness of the dome.

Beside him, cel Rau lifted his swords, but before they could enter, the dome winked out of existence. Red-hot needles of pain exploded inside Caldan's mind as he absorbed the backlash from his broken sorcery. As he collapsed to the ground, he felt and heard cel Rau rush forward. He pried his eyes open to see a cart in which rested a strange crafting generating the violet threads. On its back with its top half hanging over the side of the cart was a desiccated corpse. It had long black hair, adorned with a number of crafted bells. Fresh blood surrounded a puncture wound in its neck.

Cel Rau was rushing a man on the other side of the cart. Caldan's mouth opened as he recognized Amerdan. Just as cel Rau's blades flashed at him, the shopkeeper turned black as a shield enveloped his skin. Cel Rau's blades skittered across the shield, causing white sparkles to materialize before they were absorbed. Amerdan slammed into cel Rau, sending him flying into the side of the cart. Swords slipped from unconscious fingers.

The onyx figure stepped toward Caldan, and he linked to his own shield crafting.

Amerdan's head jerked to the side as his attention was drawn to the west. Caldan heard him hiss in frustration before glancing back toward him. In a flash, Amerdan was gone, sprinting across the dead soldiers to the east.

He was getting away . . . but the crafting generating the threads was still active. It needed to be stopped.

Ancestors!—Amerdan would have to wait. The longer Caldan delayed, the more innocent soldiers would die. He looked to the west to see around two dozen people approaching—men and women of all ages. They were surrounded by multicolored shields flashing in the sun like fish scales. The air around them thrummed with sorcerous power, and the hairs on Caldan's arms stood on end. Through his senses, he knew they wore potent craftings and trinkets. They had to be warlocks. Surely they'd know how to disable the crafting.

He winced as a number of them joined hands, and again globes of destructive sorcery arced toward him. They weren't going to disable it—they were going to destroy it now that the shield was down and it was unprotected. He was almost spent. So very tired. But cel Rau wouldn't survive the onslaught, and neither would he, unless he pulled himself together. Even with that thought, though, he could see the swordsman was too far away. *If only . . .*

With a groan of effort, he *reached* for cel Rau and somehow extended his shield to cover the swordsman. He marveled at what he thought was impossible—shielding someone without touching them—but he had no time to dwell on it.

Bells—her body needed to be preserved so they could examine her, to see what had been done to her. Whatever it was, it wasn't natural.

But Caldan felt a rush of weakness as he tried to push his shield toward Bells's withered corpse. She was too far away. As the globes descended on them, he gave up, focusing on protecting himself and cel Rau.

Power washed over him like a wave on the beach. Hard. Concentrated. Not just an unleashing of pure force from someone's well, like his raw attempts had been. There was something . . . containing it, amplifying and directing it.

As the ground shook, and corrosive elements set the cart aflame, he sensed the warlocks pouring their wells across the distance and into the crafting. It reminded him of the way a breeze blew a candle flame this way and that, or a strong gust of wind both fanned and directed the flames of a campfire. Amid the annihilation of the emperor's army, by both Bells's crafting and the warlocks' sorcery, enlightenment dawned on Caldan: he knew how to focus destructive sorcery!

Paper, wood, clay, stone, and metal were too weak to contain such amplified, potent forces. Something else was used as a substitute: a sorcerous barrier much like a shield that could itself contain the destructive sorcery, immune to erosion, to the corrosive forces issuing from a well.

His shield absorbed the punishment the warlocks dished out, and the crafting in the cart began to melt. The cart collapsed as its structure burned from underneath the crafting. Metal discs slumped to the ground and spilled, molten, across the dirt. Whatever runes she'd used, and how it functioned, he'd never know.

The warlocks' combined might faded, leaving his eyes smarting from the flashes of light, and his mind aching from the exertion. But both he and cel Rau were alive. Of Bells, there was no sign, her body and craftings consumed by the warlocks' sorcery. The threads had fragmented from it when it was destroyed. They'd broken from its surface, ends still trailing in the air. And although they were no longer being renewed, they were still spreading in a circle around the army.

Caldan levered himself to his feet and checked on cel Rau. The swordsman was still breathing. Around him, screams echoed, and he forced himself to gaze upon what Bells had wrought.

In all directions, violet sorcerous threads were still pursuing fleeing soldiers, cutting them down midstep. Some scrabbled on the ground, attempting to cover themselves with their dead comrades in the vain hope the sorcery would pass them by. Impossibly, the deadly threads swayed back and forth, even though the crafting was destroyed. Surrounding them was a sea of death: lifeless bodies covered with congealing scarlet splashes; limbs separated from torsos; soldiers, servants, tradesmen, cooks, women. The sorcery did not discriminate. Metal armor was instantly melted through, no match for the potent forces. Swords that hacked at the threads had their blades cleaved in two. In the end, all that was left was to turn and flee, to trample over those who fell or couldn't keep up.

The emperor's forces were decimated. Without a single opponent to face them, they'd been slaughtered. With all he knew of Bells, Caldan couldn't imagine she'd been the instigator of such an atrocity. She'd done terrible things in Anasoma, but under orders, and on the assumption that killing a few people would allow thousands more to live. This . . . She couldn't have known what she was doing. Had Amerdan manipulated her? Or was he also a tool?

Footsteps approached. He was surrounded, and the warlocks looked at him with barely disguised fury.

"We broke through," Caldan gasped. "But one of them got away. He ran to the east."

"Silence!" barked a woman with a wrinkled, suntanned face.

Caldan bristled at her tone. "Can't you stop them? The threads?"

The woman glared at him, declining to answer.

A young man with a beardless face answered.

"No. They have to be left to dissipate."

Like the other warlocks, he was dressed impeccably in fine black pants and shirt, and a black woolen coat. All the men were dressed similarly, while the women substituted black shawls for the coat. Their buttons were silver, shaped like many-petaled flowers, the same as Joachim had worn. The only sign they were in the middle of an annihilated army was their bloodstained boots.

"They'll kill hundreds more by the time that happens."

The young man merely shrugged. "Thousands. We have survived, though, as has the emperor."

Caldan's blood went cold at the man's insensitivity. He shook his head in disbelief, but . . .

He had no illusions about what the warlocks would do to him. They knew coercive sorcery and needed to get to the bottom of this disastrous attack in a hurry. They'd try to tear whatever information he had from his mind without regard for the consequences.

A scratching at his consciousness alerted him, and just in time, he linked to Bells's coercive sorcery crafting and erected a seamless barrier to their probing. He'd learned a few things from the masters' text he'd had copied. Enough to protect himself, but that was all. Scratching became clawing, which in turn became a pounding. He held firm until their attempts subsided.

The young man in front of him snorted in amusement. "It seems you're more than we thought."

"Joachim asked me to seek you out."

"That pignut—" blurted the wrinkled woman.

"Calm yourself, Thenna," snapped the young man, and she subsided. It looked like he outranked her, young though he was.

"I was with the Protectors until Joachim found me. He's . . . dead, though."

"Good riddance."

"Now, now, Thenna. He was one of us." The young man turned his attention back to Caldan. "What's your name, and why did our brother Joachim tell you to seek us?"

"I'm Caldan, and he didn't. Not really."

"Out with it, or I'll smash through your little barrier and scoop your mind clean. Believe me when I say I can do it, if I'm so inclined."

Caldan tried to swallow, mouth suddenly dry. He considered all the angles before finally saying, "I'm Touched. And a sorcerer, as you can see. Joachim tried to kill me for some reason, but I managed to overcome him. The Protectors think he and some associates were killing people for their trinkets." He held out his hand, showing them his own trinket ring. "This was passed to me by my parents, who died when I was young." That should give them enough to chew on.

The young man exchanged glances with a number of warlocks around him. He pursed his lips as he thought.

"We knew he was up to something, Devenish. Don't tell me you—"

"Hush, Thenna. I don't want to tell you again. Very well," Devenish said eventually. "We'll find the truth in the end, anyway. Stay close to us for the time being, until we work out what to do with you. There's a jukari horde still to deal with, and a city to defend. You'll have plenty of chances to prove your worth in the coming days."

Caldan realized the warlocks were worried, and not about him. With the army decimated, the jukari might have the advantage. And the city had sent Quivers to reinforce them, leaving Riversedge defended by a relative few.

"It's no coincidence, the jukari?"

"Curious, is it not?" replied Devenish. "If I were a betting man, I'd wager they're part of a complex plan."

"Yes. But why didn't the jukari attack the emperor's army straightaway? They had plenty of time to come at them, but they didn't. It's almost as if they pulled back. The vormag must have ordered them to."

"So? This sorcery would have killed them, too, if they'd still been fighting the emperor's forces. They were lucky to have escaped."

"You don't understand. How did they know?"

"What do you mean?" asked Devenish.

"They shouldn't have known the sorcery was coming, and yet it's as if they did. They broke from the city and retreated so they weren't caught in the discharge. Which means they knew the sorcery would strike, both the timing and how powerful it would be."

Devenish gave Caldan a calculating look, then nodded. "Of course, you're right. You've a smart head on your shoulders. The jukari and vormag are in league with the Indryallans. And we're in for a harrowing time. They must have found a way to manipulate the creatures and unite them into a fighting force instead of their usual squabbling bands. I fear this God-Emperor. He means to destroy the empire, and for no reason we can fathom."

"Hai, Devenish," shouted another warlock. "There's ships coming up the river. A lot of them."

Caldan looked south to the river, and sure enough, more than a score of ships had appeared. They were all seafaring vessels, mostly wide, twin-masted cargo ships, along with four carracks, each with three masts.

The thunder of war drums reached them, echoing around the battlefield. It seemed to come from all directions. A host of inhuman figures raced across the ground from the east, toward the tatters of the emperor's army, darkening grasses and fields already scorched by sorcery.

The jukari were coming.

Howls sounded from the beasts. Flashes erupted among the horde, ribbons of light arcing from one emanation to the other.

Caldan almost cried out in relief . . . but then realized the flashes hadn't been caused by warlock sorcery. Vormag shields had popped into existence.

Thenna gave the oncoming tide a fearful look. She clasped her hands over her head and rocked back and forth. "Vormag as well," she breathed. "Dozens of them. Where did they come from?"

"It doesn't matter," Devenish said. "Compose yourself, Thenna. What would the emperor think?"

As Devenish chastised her, Thenna swallowed and lowered her gaze.

"The ships will have to wait," Devenish continued. He raised his voice to carry above the roar of the battlefield. "Open your wells, my warlocks. We won't go down without a fight." He raised an arm and waved a signal to the Quivers. Those that remained were forming orderly ranks, behind which sat commanders on horseback, issuing orders relayed by trumpet blasts. One of the generals raised his arm in response, and Devenish stretched his in the direction of the jukari horde.

Thenna's resignation and Devenish's brave front unnerved Caldan. Was there nothing else they could do but die fighting? Around him, he sensed wells open, and power flowed through craftings as warlocks prepared themselves for the onslaught.

An initial wave of charging jukari met shields held by a line of Quivers with a thunderous crash. Sorcery in tendrils of violet floated above the vormag and jukari, distorting the air as it writhed into the sky. It swept out, straightening, then plummeted into the ranks of the nearest Quivers, flashing with coruscating brilliance. Men and women fell into pieces, as if carved by giant knives. Fire burst from their insides, splashing in all directions.

Soldiers collapsed. Some that remained standing fled, their horrified wails shrieking into the air, but others stood firm. The flames eating at the dead Quivers quickly dissipated as the vormag tendrils retreated, snakes gathering themselves for another strike.

"By the ancestors," breathed Thenna.

"To me, warlocks!" Devenish cried. "All gather to me!"

Out of thin air, a staccato burst sounded, like shattering steel. An overpowering smell of lemons and hot metal assailed Caldan, even as he felt reality twist and fold around him. His stomach recoiled at the sensation, and he staggered to one knee.

Blinding light erupted, and he shielded his eyes with a hand. All sound ceased. The very air *cracked* as if it were breaking. The earth beneath his feet lurched.

Then, he sensed a lot more wells close by. A dozen at least—some wider than others, a few jagged and narrow—but all were drawing power. Caldan gasped with disbelief. They were coming from the same location—from the same person.

Caldan groped for his craftings. Somehow he was on the ground, having fallen onto blackened grass. He raised his head.

Standing in a still-smoking circle of charred earth was a man.

He was dressed in the finest armor Caldan had ever seen— exquisitely smith-crafted pieces inlaid with reddish alloys, eye-bewildering patterns punctuated by gemstones. His platinum hair hung past his shoulders, and he was pale-skinned. He looked to be middle-aged, until Caldan caught a glimpse of his eyes. They were a burnished violet that shone with an inner light, as if the power of his wells lit him from the inside. The hum of activated craftings and trinkets filled the air, so thick it seemed to crawl across Caldan's skin and ruffle the hair on his arms.

And he had more than a score of wells. It was impossible.

The warlocks fell to their knees, confused faces alternating between their emperor and the nameless horde that was fast approaching.

There was no one else it could be: Zerach-Sangur—the Mahruse Emperor—had come to battle the jukari.

"Rise, my people," the emperor said, voice steady despite the situation. His words resonated, deep and clear, like a chorus speaking in unison.

Caldan glanced frantically at the jukari racing toward them. They were close enough now he could see mottled gray skin and yellow eyes. Shouts in their own indecipherable language rose to a clamor, and their fetid stench washed over him. He looked back to the emperor and warlocks. Why didn't they do something?

The warlocks pressed themselves flat onto the ground, prostrating themselves. Apart from Devenish. He rose to his feet, envy and pride warring in his expression. Caldan levered himself to his knees.

"My emperor," Devenish said. "There are vormag—"

"I know what they are. And today, they will weep for their creators."

Devenish's jaw worked, as if he wanted to say something, but he only nodded, then cast a frenetic glance at the oncoming creatures.

A night-dark sphere surrounded the emperor, then rippled and dissipated, leaving behind a barely visible surface. Caldan's sorcerous sense was dulled by it, a feeling he'd never had before. Whatever shield the emperor could generate, it eclipsed even Bells's obsidian one.

Nevertheless, Caldan could still sense a power buildup. His bones shook, and his skin crawled.

The emperor replied to the vormag's sorcerous attack with filaments of his own. But no violet threads; these were wires of sorcery woven into cables. Caldan sensed a concentration of power he never would have thought one man able to contain.

As straight as a rule, the cables tore upward. A hundred yards into the air, they split. Blinding lights flashed, and balls as searing as the sun shot toward the jukari and vormag.

A conflagration cascaded over the advancing creatures. There was a sizzling, popping sound of water hitting red-hot metal. Jukari flesh was flayed from bones to reveal glistening viscera.

Vormag shields winked out under the barrage. Limbs erupted in multicolored flames. Flailing bodies fell writhing to the ground. Excoriating torrents flowed over them, taking jukari and vormag alike. The front wave of what had seemed an unstoppable horde was now a blistering, smoking ruin.

The sky darkened with arrows launched by the remaining Quivers. Many had recovered from their terror, the appearance of the emperor and the potency of his sorcery giving them heart.

Jukari and vormag were slaughtered.

The emperor laughed, a sound that chilled Caldan to his core.

Devenish looked on with unabashed envy.

The enormity of the power the emperor had unleashed staggered Caldan. He trembled. An oppressive weight drove his knees into the dirt. He wanted to run, to get as far away from these people as he could, but his legs wouldn't move. This was beyond him. He had no business among these sorcerers.

Scattered survivors of the first waves of jukari retreated as fast as they were able. They careened across the ground, stumbling and yammering, returning to the bulk of the multitude, which had grown as more joined from the rear.

Of the retreating waves, hands pressed against mortal wounds. Clawed feet stumbled. What had appeared as a dark mass of atrocity streaming toward them now retreated like the tide going out. Fallen jukari and vormag were left to themselves. Most were minced, others mewling with pain. Arrows followed them, some finding flesh, most falling harmless as the creatures fled out of range.

As impressive as the emperor's onslaught was, the majority of the jukari and vormag had escaped unscathed. And in the distance, more of the creatures were pouring in, swelling their ranks into a seething, predatory horde . . .

The emperor raised his arms, metal-covered limbs burnished with sorcerous light. More cables swept out, their radiance illuminating the underside of storm clouds above.

Clouds? wondered Caldan. *Where did they come from? Moments ago, the sky was clear.*

Without any apparent signal, the jukari retreat turned into a rout—their animal howls lessened, becoming fearful and subdued. Only, it wasn't anything the Quivers were doing. Nor did it appear to be the emperor's sorcery. Caldan saw the way they glanced at the darkening skies, yowling in panic.

The black-churning clouds spiraled into circles with protruding spouts, like draining water.

A fleeting look of dread passed across the emperor's face, quickly quelled to a masklike calm. He'd noticed it, too. Seen what it was that had frightened the horde. And for an instant, even the emperor had looked panicked.

His sorcerous cables retracted, power flowing back into him. Gouts of raw sorcery erupted from the clouds, raining down upon the broken ground. Unearthly violence ripped through the earth. Dirt and vegetation flew, sprinkling back down in clouds of steaming dust. The bones of the earth shivered with sorcerous reverberations.

The cloud spirals paused, then wavered, probing the air like leeches. Shining tongues of sorcery wrapped around them, slowly at first, then quickening.

The emperor growled, a primal animal sound ripped from the depths of his throat.

A bolt plummeted down from one of the spirals, hammering the ground a hundred paces away. All shadows were banished by boiling light. The earth glowed orange, then smoked, then radiated heat as it melted.

For heartbeats, all Caldan could do was stare as the ground turned to liquid and ran down channels and troughs in the earth.

"Warlocks, scatter!" roared the emperor. "Keep your shields raised and spread out. I will draw this sorcery to me!"

Warlocks ran in all directions, stumbling across the uneven ground.

Inside his barrier, the emperor stood tall, as if he were unconcerned. But Caldan couldn't forget the flash of panic on his face before. Caldan opened his own well and linked to his shield crafting, backing away from the emperor in case he was wrong.

A surge of power hummed, and to Caldan, the emperor's multiple wells vanished, as if they never existed. The instant they did, the wheeling clouds slowed. The spirals drifted like charmed snakes again, eager to identify what they were after.

One of the funnels descended from the swirling clouds, striking the earth where a warlock stood. There was a detonation, like the pop of burning wood amplified a thousand times. And the warlock's well disappeared, snuffed out like a candle. The cloud spiral retreated, leaving behind a smoking, charred corpse.

Seconds later, another spiral plunged down. And another warlock lost her life.

Above Caldan, clouds circled, and a funnel formed. Pressure built as the atmosphere churned.

Wells, Caldan realized. *They're targeting wells. And that's why the emperor closed his.*

Fear gripped him, but he clenched his jaw and sealed his well. His shield winked out, leaving him defenseless. Caldan held his breath and waited. The spiral above him didn't move. It still quested, searching.

His eyes were drawn to the emperor, who remained motionless, as if any hint of movement would attract a sorcerous volley he had no hope of countering. To the warlocks, who thought his sorcery was paramount, he must have looked like a bastion against evil.

Caldan's heart hammered in his chest. Some warlocks quailed as the power in the clouds increased, to a point where Caldan thought he felt an answering resonance from his own well, even though it was closed to him.

As if a power of unimaginable proportions called to it.

Around him, warlocks cried out in despair. Others fell to their knees and wept.

Caldan felt a hopelessness come over him. How could he combat this?

He ground his teeth and steeled himself. He wasn't going to cower like the warlocks. And somewhere there were answers to what was going on. This war . . . the Indryallans . . . Kelhak . . . It was much bigger than any of them realized.

But the emperor clearly knew what was going on.

Suddenly, the spirals retracted, curling upward and into the roiling clouds. Within moments, the clouds themselves dissipated, and the miasma of sorcery diminished. Sunlight broke out over the battlefield, and the last wisps of darkness were blown away by the wind.

There was no trace of the sorcery that had made the emperor tremble.

"Enough!" the emperor shouted. "I have saved you and beaten back the jukari. Close your wells and look to the wounded. Have the Quivers harass the jukari until they're pushed away from Riversedge." He turned to Devenish, who remained close by, and lowered his voice. "And Devenish, bring me five Descendants. Tonight."

The emperor turned his back on the jukari and strode across the rent earth, peering into the smoke-filled sky. Whatever sorcery he'd used to appear, he wasn't using it to leave.

A quick glance confirmed the ships were still approaching up the river. Who they were and why they had appeared preyed on Caldan's mind. It couldn't be a coincidence.

The horde simmered in the distance, a menace, but not attacking. A primal, animal stench filled his nostrils, and their baying and clashing of weapons rose to a roar. Their numbers were overwhelming, and if they attacked and there was no sorcery to repel them . . . it wouldn't go well for the Quivers and the warlocks.

Maybe they were scared of the emperor's sorcery—but then Caldan recalled the look of panic, and the closing of the emperor's wells. The emperor hadn't dispelled the vortices. They'd lost his scent when he closed his wells . . . and the bastard used the warlocks to . . . They were decoys. Nothing more than a diversion to save his own skin.

The emperor wanted to appear the savior, but in reality he'd drawn the sorcery away from himself, to the warlocks.

Caldan looked over the massed horde. Even at this distance he could feel their primal savagery, could see their eager, predatory stares. If the vormag reached the same conclusion—that the emperor was outmatched, and that he didn't dare use his sorcery for fear of what it might attract . . .

They weren't stupid. They'd figure it out, sooner or later.

And when they did, there'd be no stopping the horde this time.

AFTERMATH

Vasile woke to a haze of pain and shielded his too-sensitive eyes from the light of a lamp. He blinked as they watered, and there was a scuff of footsteps at his side.

"Magistrate," Aidan said. "I'm glad you made it through."

"I thought . . . you were dead," Vasile croaked.

"Not yet. Where are cel Rau and Chalayan?"

"I don't know where cel Rau is. We met up with a sorcerer outside the city, though, and I'd expect them to be together. As for Chalayan . . . Cel Rau killed him after the sorcery on the bridge. He made it sound like you'd both agreed Chalayan was too powerful."

Aidan merely nodded.

ON THE DECK of one of the ships pulling into the docks of Riversedge, Gazija looked out over the city and the surrounding countryside. Smoke rose from great swaths of blackened grass and churned earth marring the fields. Crows circled and landed on the scars, cawing and squawking, feasting until they were almost too full to fly.

"It is as you said it would be," said Quiss from behind him.

Gazija turned slowly to face him. "It was necessary." He whacked Luphildern on the leg with a cane. "We must make the best of the situation and ingratiate ourselves with the emperor and his warlocks. Come.

"It has begun."

This ends

BLOOD OF INNOCENTS.

What happens next is recounted in

The Sorcery Ascendant Sequence,

Book Three

To the Reader,

Having readers eager for the next installment of a series, or anticipating a new series, is the best motivation for a writer to create new stories.

New release sign-up. If you enjoy reading my novels as much as I enjoy writing them, then sign up to my mailing list at http://eepurl.com/BTefL. I promise to notify you only when a new novel is released, so no spam e-mails!

Share your opinion. If you would like to leave a review, it would be much appreciated! Reviews help new readers find my work and accurately decide if the book is for them as well as provide valuable feedback for my future writing.

You can return to where you purchased the novel or simply visit my website at http://www.mitchellhogan.com and follow the links.

There are also a number of websites like Goodreads where members discuss the books they've read, want to read, or want others to read.

Send me feedback. I love to hear from readers and try to answer every e-mail. If you would like to point out errors and typos or provide feedback on my novels, I urge you to send me an e-mail at mitchhoganauthor@gmail.com.

Thank you for your support, and be sure to check out my other novels!

Kind regards,
Mitchell Hogan

ACKNOWLEDGMENTS

With love, to Angela and Isabelle.

I would also like to thank:

Derek Prior, without whose editing and advice I doubt I'd be where I am today.

Michael J. Sullivan and his wife, Robin, who provided much-needed guidance and selflessly spent a great deal of time answering my endless questions.

Ray Nicholson, for his excellent feedback and insight. And for picking up the small (and possibly major) errors that almost slipped through.

But most of all I need to thank the readers, those people who took a chance on an unknown author and purchased *A Crucible of Souls*. Without you this book would have taken a great deal of time longer to write. Now I'm able to write full-time and I'm living the dream. For that I will be forever thankful.

ABOUT THE AUTHOR

When he was eleven, Mitchell Hogan was given *The Hobbit* and the Lord of the Rings trilogy to read, and a love of fantasy novels was born. He spent the next ten years reading, rolling dice, and playing computer games, with some school and university thrown in. Along the way he accumulated numerous bookcases' worth of fantasy and sci-fi novels and doesn't look to stop anytime soon. For ten years he put off his dream of writing, then he quit his job and wrote *A Crucible of Souls*, Book One of the Sorcery Ascendant Sequence. He now writes full-time and is eternally grateful to the readers who took a chance on an unknown self-published author. He lives in Sydney, Australia, with his wife, Angela, and daughter, Isabelle.